<u>Book II</u>:

Brooklyn's Lilac Brew

978-0-9725548-3-1

Published by Twin Griffin Books

www.TwinGriffinBooks.com

To the dark heroes of the world

Twin Griffin Books
PRESENTS

Also by Justin Thomas

The Ghost of Gabriel's Horn: Book I of the Fable Avenue Saga (2012)

A Company of Moors (2010)

Code-47: Memoirs of a Hip Hop Heist (2008)

12 Stories High: The Imaginative Trip Thru a Black Mind (2006)

Epic Poems

In Thirteen Pieces (2016)

The Son Dial Tone (2012)

The Ronin Poetz (2000)

This was thirteen years ago, but time meant nothing to the celestial onlookers in the sky as they gazed at the story below, peering down at a borough in New York City called Brooklyn. Their sight bore into the ground, underneath the earth, where two A-Trains came to a stop inside Brooklyn's Utica Avenue station. The trains' grinding halt roused the metals of track and train to scream and holler like a choir of banshees. One was on its way uptown, 207th Street its last stop. The other was making its way to Queens on the Lefferts Boulevard track. The sounds of their massive, screeching squeal swam the air currents. The resonance rattled the tracks, up through the ceiling, and rumbled the ground above with a low murmur. The noise caused a few waiting passengers to pin their ears shut.

The invisible volley of noise waved up and down. It writhed above the tiled floors of the station and around the load-baring, red, steel pillars that extended from floor to ceiling. The banshee cries continued to scurry. Their echoes scuttled up the stairs, through the turnstiles, and out into the crisp, autumn air. Simultaneous pings issued a communiqué, a high-pitched ripple coming from the trains, sounding off moments before the multiple doors opened all at once. Doors like wombs birthed passengers who called Utica Avenue their final destination. With them came clouds of conversation that strengthened the air with sounds of chatter from exiting subway riders who swapped places with the riders-in-wait on the platform. The new sounds hurried above ground to follow the quieting waves of noise that had exited moments earlier. A C-Train heading to Manhattan burrowed into the station on the local track, hollering to a halt. Its metallic cry weakened to a braking sigh that joined the channel of chatter topside.

The Fulton Park entrance to the Utica Avenue station exhaled the sound of trains stopping and starting. A slow crawl of tired footsteps inched up the stairs, people just finishing their workday attached to them. Excited youths wriggled past the slow movers while bellowing loud conversations. Murmurs and chatter echoed up the stairs and out of the station. The spirits fabricated from the sound, using any hint of noise to stay more than muffled, spread through the park, swirling like free radicals, escaping onto Chauncey Street and then up Stuyvesant Avenue, using the thoroughfare as a tunnel. The escaped spirits crossed Bainbridge, Decatur, and MacDonough Streets.

The invisible undulation of sound never strayed from its path up Stuyvesant. The noise prolonged its life by attaching to sounds found at each cross street. It picked up the glowing noise of loud conversations vibrating from gathered friends and neighbors outside brownstones, from thumping music blaring from parked cars, and from traffic moving through the Bedford-Stuyvesant area.

But three hundred and forty miles per second came to a quieting standstill on the street located between Macon and Halsey.

Fable Avenue.

The sound hushed not out of loss of strength, but as a form of courtesy to the area. Here, it moved onto the street, as any curious spirit would do, splintering in either direction, tiptoeing up and down the road. The quieted sound passed brownstone after brownstone and spied stores and other businesses at the corner of each block. Houses on either side of the street varied in sizes and hues, standing close and tight like an impenetrable line of defense. The street was spotless. There was no speck of dust or loose dirt for the fresh gust of air to sweep around. All the leaves that had fallen because of autumn's effect had been raked, bagged, and left on the sidewalk for pickup. The air coasted around the bare trees. It spiraled around the peculiar, blossomed flowers, spreading their natural perfume like bees with pollen. The muted spirit admired the flowers' brilliance, their glow an otherworldly iridescence radiating from petals defying the autumn crisp air by refusing to yet wither.

Fable Avenue stretched from Bedford Avenue to Broadway. At the street named Sumner, which was also called Marcus Garvey Boulevard, there was a subway line on which ran the 8-Train. This train line, dubbed the *Black Line* or the *8-Ball Ride*, was an express to Harlem, its final stop on 163rd Street and Amsterdam Avenue.

On these Brooklyn streets, neighbors, friends, and families engaged in conversation outside residences. The talk wasn't quite as loud, but nevertheless, laughter, gossip, and jokes were shared among the street's residents just the same. The air mixed with a relaxing melody of jazz playing somewhere on the street. The music was light and calm to all who heard it, but it could have just as well adorned a melancholy scene with its melody. The fusion of air from the Utica Avenue station made a sudden stop and peeked inside the parlor-floor window of a brownstone located two houses from the corner of Fable and Patchen Avenues.

Emma Forrester was seated at a hexagonal, wooden dining table positioned close to the window. Emma was thirty-one years old, dark-skinned with wild, curly hair. Her almond-brown eyes were often bright, illuminated with life to sparkle as amber and gold. At present, her eyes were dull, drained of light and vitality. Her chin lay in the cup of her left hand. Her right hand caressed the rim of a half-empty glass of brandy with a single finger. The bottle, also half empty, rested in front of her. Her body was warm from the spirit, belly half full, but she was far from optimistic as the drink's effect seeped up into her head. Smoke swirled in front of her like an acrid apparition, attached to the rolled herb burning in the ashtray.

Emma's head jerked up as she resisted the drink and smoke's pull into sleep. She sniffed and wiped her nose then returned to her stable position of head rested in hand. Emma's vision blurred as her eyes looked at the sketchbook lying on the other side of the table, flipped opened to a single page. Her drawing came into focus while everything else remained blurry. The opened page hosted Emma's detailed, penciled illustration of a folkloric eidolon called a *yumbo*. The Senegalese faerie was female, naked, and with tight twists of hair, shimmering wings, and wide eyes absent of irises and pupils. The yumbo was perched on a tree branch.

Emma rolled her eyes, grabbed her glass and downed the rest of her drink. She poured herself another, fumbling with the bottle. Drops of brandy splashed onto the table and dripped down the glass. Emma put the bottle down and grumbled. She didn't reach for the glass. Instead, she reached for the reefer stick burning away in the ashtray. She lifted the rolled herb to her lips and took a long drag. Emma exhaled a stream of smoke. Her eyes narrowed and focused on the little girl seated across the table from her, and she pushed her cheek out with her tongue. She took another drag and blew through a part in the side of her lips. The smoke streamed straight up and filled the room. Emma looked at the little girl thinking she was a figment of her imagination, but she was real. Emma kept forgetting she was there watching her.

The little girl was named Fey. She was six years old, and she was Emma's daughter. Emma looked at her, the curiosity in her eyes swelling with a foggy, drunken haze. The little girl was her own six-year-old image staring back at her with the same almond-brown eyes widened with curiosity, fear, and sadness. Her daughter had been trying to ignore her, keeping her eyes on the sketched creature in front of her. But, Fey kept looking up at her mother every time she moved. Fey had never seen her mother like this, dulled and drained. "Ain't shit to be done, so let me tell you somethin', child," Emma said with a voice sounding as if she'd just come from sleep. "Don't. Ever. Marry no damn codebreaker. You hear me? Don't marry no codebreaker." Emma took another drag. She exhaled and then placed the reefer stick back into the ashtray. The ashes broke away, speckling her platinum wedding band and engagement ring that also lay in the ashtray.

Fey looked up at her mother. "Mamma…?" she said, hesitant.

Emma reached for her drink. "A man who's a codebreaker knows your every move," she continued. Her speech was slow and slurred. "I mean, your father always had a guess on me." Emma flapped her lips. She leaned across the table. Her eyes narrowed, trying to fight the blurred vision and stay focused. She said to her daughter, "His perception always had him paranoid. Shit." She leaned back and took a sip of her drink. Fey's sad eyes dropped away from her mother and back to the yumbo drawn in detail on the open page of her mother's sketchbook. "His paranoia had him codebreaking things all wrong, even when he was right," Emma continued after another sip. She put her glass down on the table, but didn't let go of it. "He was constantly asking me if I was laying up with another man." Emma's voice trembled away. Her gaze, watered with tears, wandered to the window. "How dare your father leave," she looked back at her daughter and concluded with force in her voice, "*days on end.* No word. No nothing." Emma's enraged words made Fey jump with each syllable. The young girl's eyes locked onto her mother.

Emma looked as if she was relaxing, but her voice said otherwise. She growled at her daughter in a low, angry voice, "The nerve of your father. That damned man. He'd disappear for weeks at a time, and then he'd just stumble back up in this house with no word as to where he'd been. Scratches on his back from some other woman." She drank. "Sometimes he'd be crying, looking for sympathy," Emma said with disgust. "He'd ask me to hold him. He'd beg me to love him, to lay with him, and nurse him back to health." She took another sip, hand possessed with mild tremors. "No goddamned answer on where he'd been." She looked at her daughter and scolded, "Your father!" Emma's eyes watered. She shook her head, eyes pregnant with tears. "He'd be so fucked out of his mind he couldn't remember anything about where he'd been or what he'd done." She sniffed and said like a revelation, "Or maybe he just didn't want to tell me what he was guilty of." She bit her lip. Her emotions pushed a heavy tear under her left eye. It trembled as if channeling Emma's anger, moving closer to the edge. And then it dripped down her cheek. Emma wiped the stream away, and then wiped her eyes clear of all welling. She sniffed again and took another sip of her drink. She aimed her glass at her daughter and groaned indignantly, "But he started *demanding* answers from me, that bastard. He'd always want to know where I would be if I was late, you better believe. Yes, you better." A sip. "But hey, if he wasn't gon' tell me a damn thing, then I wasn't gon' tell him a damn thing. Hell, no I wasn't."

Six-year-old Fey's big, brown eyes couldn't look away from her mother. She barely blinked, too scared to do so, fearful something dire would befall her mother should she not keep her eyes on her.

She did not move.

Emma leaned back, glass against her lips, and said in a proud voice, "I'd tell that no-good bastard father of yours that I was on my period when he wanted to lay with me." She looked at her daughter and snickered, "You'll understand that tactic when you're older." She snickered again, looking away from her daughter. "Went so far as to let him see me dress myself up, even when I wasn't bleedin'." Emma reminisced, drank, and chuckled to herself. She swallowed and said as she finished her gulp, "Then he started suspectin' somethin'. That's when he started demandin' answers." Emma exhaled and almost looked as if she sobered up. She smiled and lifted her shoulders as if she was receiving a hug. Fey almost believed her mother had returned to normal, but she watched instead of smile along with her. The little girl waited, and Emma expressed through a proud grin, "I became a mystery to your father." She tightened as if the invisible hug around her tightened as well. "He thought he knew everything, your father did, or thought he could figure everything out." Emma loosened and she exclaimed in the same proud voice, "But not me." She lifted her glass and took a sip. "Not when I became a *real* woman, liberated and free. I was the great mystery that no man can figure out." She volleyed laughter. It was uncontrollable. Emma tried to cover her mouth, but her body shook and doubled over as she laughed. Fey watched, wide eyed. Emma's glass hit the table, causing the little girl to jump. Emma laughed and laughed. She sat up straight, glass in hand. She composed herself, keeping her smile. "And your father would seethe with anger, and I'd smile because there was nothing he could do." Then Emma's smile faded. She cocked an eye on her daughter. "I had the law on my side, best believe, girl. That was *my* trick. A conjuror. The phone was my magic source. Nine-one-one was my chant." Her head shook. "And your father knew that, and that no-good bastard would get *hea-ted.*"

Fey saw her mother's eyes swell again with tears.

"I wish he would lift a hand to me," Emma said through a buckling voice. "I'd have that nigger locked up where he belongs. I'd at least know where he is without having to follow him." She finished her drink in a big gulp, gently placing the glass down and reaching for the stick of reefer. Fey watched her mother. The little girl's body was stiff, but her eyes moved, following her mother's hand to table, astray, and mouth. Emma puffed and exhaled a stream of smoke like a dragon. She pointed to her daughter with the reefer stick. "I followed your father once." She nodded her head and said, "Yes, I did. And I saw…" Emma's voice trailed away. "I saw…" She turned away from her daughter. "I saw…something…"

Emma did see something. Flashes. A memory played over and over, coming at her like strikes of lightning. Angry, clenched teeth.

Hollering and cursing. There were sounds of a cracking whip. Then the flares of memory ceased, and Emma got up from her seat and walked to the window, moving as if a thousand pounds was strapped to her body.

Fey's eyes followed her mother, and the little girl waited. She wanted her mother to say something. The silence was scary to her, but she also appreciated it. Her mother was thinking, and it frightened her.

Emma took a drag and said as she exhaled, "Your father ain't comin' back, little girl." She smoked the last of her herb and crushed the remainder against the windowsill. Fey blinked, and her eyes finally fell away from her mother, dropping back to the sketched yumbo on the page.

Emma stepped away from the window, almost tripping. She focused as best she could. She put her hand on the back of the chair to keep from stumbling and made her way to her daughter. She reached out with her hand and grabbed the next chair, moving closer to where her daughter sat. Emma inched forward, her body heavy, her head and vision bubbling with drink and smoke. She grabbed the back of Fey's chair and positioned herself behind her daughter, dragging her feet instead of taking proper steps. She bent down close to her daughter's pressed and curled hair and asked, "You like mamma's drawings, little girl?"

Fey gave a slow, affirmative nod. Her mother's breath sprayed against the top of her head like mist. The little girl could smell the mixture of smoke and drink on her mother's breath and clothes. She didn't like it, and the smoke was now making her dizzy. Emma kissed the top of her daughter's head. "Then keep them," she told the little girl.

Emma stood up straight and sighed. She walked away without stumbling. Her intoxicated demeanor expressed itself through tears. Emma cupped her mouth as she moaned. She left the room to go upstairs.

Fey looked up at her mother. *"Mamma!"* the little girl yelled. *"Mamma!"*

Tears appeared in Fey's large, brown eyes. One escaped, dropped, and splashed onto the face of the sketched yumbo and spread, blurring the penciled creature's features. Fey hopped off her seat and called again as she left the room, *"Mamma!"*

The room was empty. The table was unoccupied, and the chairs were pivoted away from it, desperate for company. Fey continued to call for her mother at the base of the stairs. The page supporting the penciled, perched yumbo remained saturated with Fey's single tear that masked the mythical creature's face. Then, Fey's mercurial teardrop dissolved, withering the paper and the yumbo's already blurred countenance. The wet paper and the clouded penciled features then fixed as if time moved backwards, and the yumbo's face was revived. Fey called up to her mother again, and at the sound of the little girl's cry, the yumbo's large eyes, absent of irises and pupils, blinked.

The penciled creature turned its head, and in the same motion, animated its face to mold a concerned expression. *"Mamma!"* the little girl cried out again. The yumbo responded, its neck bending to the left, and its left arm reaching out. A silvery luminescence appeared as the yumbo's twisted locs emerged up and off the page, becoming solid with volume and mass into the physical, three-dimensional world. Fey cried out again to her mother, and the yumbo's three-fingered hand poked through the page as slender, cylindrical digits. The yumbo's left arm extended up into the world. It bent, and the creature palmed the page, pushing down to force her silvery, radiating body out of the sheet of paper. The yumbo turned its body, its head still inside the page, her backside facing up. The creature's glimmering, lilac wings sprouted and expanded. The irradiated fore and hind wings fluttered for a few moments, and then settled. The wings' glow dissipated. An intricate, black, spidery design ran throughout the lilac wings.

The yumbo then slid her right arm out of the paper, planted her hand down, and palmed the page. She pushed against the sketchbook using both hands, lifting her head and standing up straight. The winged sprite took a deep breath. She was still up to her knees in paper. The yumbo put her weight on the freed leg, lifted the other out of the paper, and stood atop the page she'd been sketched into. The yumbo was now solid and sturdy, birthed into the world. She breathed rapidly, as if she had just come from being held under water. She put a three-fingered hand on her chest and looked around, surveying her surroundings with large, curious eyes.

An indigo glow appeared at the center of the yumbo's forehead. Anxiety devoured the curiosity in her eyes as the room disappeared, shifting and molding into another environment. She was upstairs in the master bedroom, standing on the bed. The sketchbook was still underneath her, acting as her stage. Emma was standing there, back to the bed and the silvery, glimmering sprite. The yumbo looked at her. Emma was standing at her dresser, staring inside the opened top drawer. She didn't move for a while, still as a statue. Then she removed her sweater, revealing a web of irregular, fibrous tissue stretched across her back, remnants of flogging scars and injuries. Emma dropped her sweater, and the garment piled atop itself next to her. She took a breath, tears in her eyes. She reached into the drawer with both hands and parted the clothes.

Emma drew her hands back. With her right hand she covered her mouth, resuming her uncontrollable sobs. "I…saw…something…" the yumbo heard Emma whimper while hiccupping on her tears. Emma wiped her face, hand flopping about her cheeks and lips. She sniffed and stood up straight. She took a deep breath and repeated in a slow, craggily voice, "I saw something." Emma slumped. She bent over, resting her upper body on the dresser drawer. She continued crying.

The yumbo watched Emma flinch three times before standing up straight again. Emma reached inside the drawer and pulled out a loaded .38 caliber handgun. She trembled as she wiped her nose again. Emma closed her eyes, cocked the gun, and put it to her head.

"Mamma!" came Fey's voice up from the base of the stairs.

Emma trembled. Her eyes opened and her head turned to the door. "Baby…" she said in a low voice. Then she faced forward again and closed her eyes. "Mamma's a mystery…" she said in a soft whisper.

The yumbo gasped, and as the little, silvery sylph blinked her large eyes, the scenery deliquesced, dripping away and dwindling back into the dining area. The yumbo looked around erratically, eyes widened by desperation. The indigo glow resonating on her forehead disappeared. The yumbo flinched, reacting to a gunshot's loud, thunderous holler echoing through the house. The indigo glow appeared again, and the yumbo could see Fey's similar reaction as the little girl stood at the bottom of the stairs. The glow dispersed. The creature's wings illuminated and spread. The yumbo's distraught expression relented to a newfound determination. She jumped into the air, flapping her wings to maintain flight. She soared out of the room and into the hallway, becoming a silvery stream of light.

The yumbo paused in her flight at the base of the stairs, forming out of the silver streak. She looked up and saw little, six-year-old Fey Forrester struggling to climb the stairs. She fluttered her wings and raced passed Fey. The little girl jumped as the yumbo shot by her as a gleaming strip of silver and lilac.

Fey stopped climbing to better observe the yumbo. The silvery, winged illumination, floating at the top of the stairs, formed solid again, and she and Fey stared at one another with sad expressions. Fey's stubbornness was more determined, and the little girl proceeded up the stairs. The yumbo drifted to the master bedroom and peeked inside. The flap of her wings slowed, and the expression on her face turned doleful. She moved her head and saw Fey climb over the final steps and enter the upstairs hallway. The yumbo blurred into its silvery flight, a glimmering, hoary line of light rushing toward Fey. She stopped inches away from the little girl's face, causing her to jump and almost fall back and plummet down the long flight of stairs. But Fey maintained her balance.

Fey stared transfixed at the hovering pixie. The yumbo looked back at her. The little girl wanted to ask the spirit why she looked so sad. She wanted to ask the spirit what she saw in her mother's bedroom. The curious little girl paced forward to find out for herself. She took one, careful step. The yumbo hovered backward. Fey took another step, and the yumbo again floated rearward. But before Fey could take another step, the yumbo raised both her hands, signaling the little girl to stop her forward motion. Fey stuttered, "B-b-but Mamma…" Her eyes looked past the floating diminutive spirit to the master bedroom's entrance.

A bright light emanated from the yumbo's palms. It splashed into Fey's eyes and masked her sight. The little girl didn't move, too scared, as she was now blind. Her eyes glowed with the bright silver light that masked them. The yumbo turned her head and looked over her shoulder at the entrance to the master bedroom. She then faced forward, looking at the six-year-old girl. Fey looked around the hall, panning her head up and down, left and right, trying to see through the light that blinded her.

The yumbo took a deep breath then hurried past the distracted six-year-old. Her silvery stream buzzed down the stairs, passed through the front doors of the brownstone as if they were made of cloud and fog, and out onto Fable Avenue. The yumbo formed solid, hovering in the middle of the street. She looked left and right, face still caked with desperation. She closed her large eyes and concentrated. The indigo glow appeared on her forehead. She opened her eyes and made another attempt to look in both directions. When she looked left, her vision became like a spyglass as it zoomed in on a brownstone that lay far down the road, across Stuyvesant Avenue.

Her sight peered through the brownstone's façade and saw, in his study on the parlor floor, a bald and clean-shaven dark-skinned man in his early forties seated in a plush, Victorian-style chair. He conversed with his wife, a caramel-colored woman who was around the same age as he. She too was seated in a chair of the same style, and both had concerned expressions as they talked about two men. One man they spoke of was named Lewis. The other man's name was Stanley. Then the yumbo's vision detracted. She looked up at the Forrester residence and used her sight to peek through and observe the little girl at the top of the stairs. Fey was still blind, but she had her hand against the left wall, making her way to the master bedroom.

The yumbo sped down the street, retaining the indigo glow on her forehead and using its extrasensory perception to keep an eye on Fey's blind journey through the hall. The little girl was inching closer to the master bedroom, just as the yumbo was speeding closer to its destination.

Residents gathered on Fable Avenue for idle chat noticed the silver and lilac streak race by them, but they paid the yumbo's flight no mind, being accustomed to Fable Avenue's preternatural charm. Older residents did give a curious eye to the phenomenon, however, as it had been ordered in recent days by the street's sole patriarch and three matriarchs not to showcase such wherewithal. The older residents looked in the opposite direction of the yumbo's flight path trying to gauge a point-of-origin. Those trying to figure it out could deduce nothing. But they saw the yumbo's gray and lilac glimmer disappear as the creature formed solid at the front door of 347 Fable Avenue. This was the home of Vencil Peters, called Papa Solomon, and his wife, Thelema Heathwicke-Peters, called Madame Jeliya.

The yumbo knocked on the front door, pounding hard. She was courteous enough not to ghost through the solid barrier and disturb Papa Solomon and Madame Jeliya. But the sprite knocked hard, considering the urgency and in an attempt to convey the same. Her vision peered through the front entrance, indigo light on her forehead glowing brighter and providing sight beyond the door. The yumbo saw the response to her actions as the sudden banging alerted both Papa Solomon and Madame Jeliya. Papa Solomon got to his feet, and the yumbo witnessed him tell his wife to stay seated. He left the room and walked to the front door and opened it. The yumbo's natural and extrasensory sight became one. There was Vencil Peters, Papa Solomon. The yumbo looked up and up and up, and in awe at the human, onyx tower. She fluttered up to Papa Solomon's face and he asked in a deep, commanding voice, "Why so sad, little yumbo? Emma know you off your page?"

The yumbo answered by turning her head and pointing up the street toward the Forrester residence. Papa Solomon poked his head out and looked in the direction the sprite pointed to. He saw nothing, but the yumbo did. Her indigo sight displayed for her the vision of Fey Forrester standing in the doorway of her mother's bedroom. The little girl was too scared to move. She trembled in place and dared not step inside where her mother's body lay. Fey was still blind by the light left in her eyes. From where she stood, had she been able to see, the bed would've obscured the gruesome scene of her mother's lifeless body.

The yumbo's extended sight drew back to the scene in front of her. The indigo light on her forehead continued to glow. She turned her head to Papa Solomon and she pointed to the indigo glow swirling at her forehead's center. Papa Solomon fixed his eyes on the swirling sphere of light, instantly yanked inside the creature's memory. The events that had earlier transpired at the Forrester residence played in front of him. He blinked as the events led back to the present moment. The vision was gone, and the yumbo was glowing and hovering in front of him. He gasped and took a step back. His face contorted into an irritated articulation. He clenched his teeth and balled his fist as he cursed, "Damnit!" He turned and called to his wife, "Thelema! Thelema-baby, we have an emergency."

The yumbo followed Papa Solomon inside. The two sets of doors leading into the brownstone closed behind her by the polite yumbo's will. She hovered over Papa Solomon's shoulder as he entered his study. Thelema was already on her feet when they entered, showing concern on her face. Papa Solomon hurried toward his wife, putting his hands on her shoulders. "Thelema-baby, I need you to prepare your workspace. Something terrible has happened to Emma Forrester. Little Fey's going to need a blessing."

"Did Lewis return? Did he hurt Emma?" Thelema asked.

Papa Solomon shook his head. "No, Thelema-baby. It's much worse."

"Is it Stanley?" Thelema inquired further.

"Thelema-baby, just prepare your workspace," he pressed.

Thelema shook her head and assured, "I will, Papa. I will." She hurried past her husband and headed to the basement.

Papa Solomon made a quick pivot and rushed from the brownstone. The yumbo glided close behind him. As Papa Solomon left the house, and Thelema scurried to the basement, the phone started ringing. No one picked up. The phone rang and rang and rang, and then it stopped. No message was left when prompted.

In the Forrester brownstone, Fey continued trembling outside her mother's bedroom. She inhaled and caught the acrid scent of iron and smoke in the air. The odor pinched her nose, and sadness overwhelmed her. She exhaled and started crying. Each tear that streamed down her face took with it a glow of the light that masked her eyes. Down, down, and down poured away the light as Fey cried more and more. The grim scene of her mother's lifeless and bloodied body revealed itself. A picture developed, and the little girl saw something. Her vision was still blurry. She strained to focus through the tears and the remaining light barring her perception. But through the haze and blaze, the little girl could make out the image of her mother's body lying on the floor between the dresser and the bed.

Fey's eyes widened as the final glimmers of light slipped away and the blur of the fog from her tears faded. The little girl's mouth dropped, reacting to the scene materializing in front of her. Her eyes almost ingested a clear picture when a pair of arms scooped her up.

Papa Solomon whispered a tranquil incantation into the six-year-old girl's ear, and Fey Forrester fell fast into a gentle sleep. Papa Solomon passed the cradled girl to a man named Wilson Barnes. He was just as tall as Papa Solomon, in his mid-thirties, with brown-skin and cornrows. Papa Solomon said to Wilson, "Take her to Madame Jeliya. She's preparing a blessing." The yumbo hovered above his shoulder.

"Absolutely, Papa Solomon," replied Wilson. "Your son and Martin are on their way."

Papa Solomon shook his head, a solemn expression on his face. "Thank you, Wilson," he said. "I'll wait here. I'll catch up with you later. Tell Madame Jeliya that I'll call Savannah. I'll take the responsibility to inform the girl's grandmother." He turned his head toward the master bedroom. "My God. Savannah…" Papa Solomon dismissed Wilson with a head nod. Wilson backed away. He turned and walked down the hall. At the stairs, his steps were careful as he descended with Fey Forrester cradled in his arms. He left the house, leaving the door open.

Papa Solomon stared inside the master bedroom. He leaned against the entrance and slid down against the door's molding until seated on the floor. He reached out a focused thought to Emma Forrester, hoping to feel a faint sign of spirit left in her. There was nothing, and Papa Solomon grieved for Emma Forrester's passing. He mouthed a sacred chant, a blessing for her. The yumbo landed next to him. She walked farther into the room until she was standing at the feet of Emma's body. The yumbo's eyes expanded with sadness, and the creature dropped its head.

Papa Solomon saw a vision of the gun used in the deed. Fingerprints appeared on the handle, and an otherworldly instinct popped into Papa Solomon's head suggesting the pattern didn't belong to Emma Forrester. Before he could discern to whom the impression marks belonged, the gun's image disappeared from his mind. But Papa Solomon realized the significance his second sight had offered him.

"I understand," he said, eyes closed and in a low voice.

It was minutes before anything stirred. Papa Solomon didn't even move when he heard his son Oliver calling him from downstairs. "Dad," shouted Oliver Peters as he led a team of paramedics, which he was a part of, into the house. He directed his team to stay at the foot of the stairs. "Wait here," he told the three-person team, his suggestion laced with sorcery. Oliver called again, "Pop!" Papa Solomon didn't move until his son was over him, shaking his shoulder. He got up and put his arms around his son.

Oliver was in his early twenties. He was of average height, possessing reddish-brown skin, a wide head that sported a bush of natural hair and a pair of glasses. A well-groomed line of hair went from one side of his face, down under his chin, and up the other side. There was also a mustache, just as well groomed but unconnected to his beard, running across Oliver's upper lip.

Oliver spotted the yumbo in the room. He pulled away from his father's embrace and instructed, "Make sure the yumbo's gone, Pop. There're civilians downstairs."

"Of course, son. Of course," said Papa Solomon, his voice sounding as if he'd just woke up. "Is Martin downstairs? Wilson said he put in a call to both you and him."

Lieutenant Martin Kimball scaled the stairs before Oliver could answer. The officers under his command waited downstairs. Papa Solomon moved past his son and met the lieutenant with an extended hand.

"Papa Solomon," Martin greeted as he removed his police cap and tucked it under his armpit. He shook Papa Solomon's reaching hand. The thirty-two-year-old cop was equally as dark, broad, and towering as Papa Solomon, with a scraggily beard and low-cropped hair atop his rectangular-shaped head.

Papa Solomon waved Oliver to him, and when he was close he said to both men, "The two of you handle this situation. I'll be at my house if questions need answering. I'll make a statement there." He said to his son, "Tell me where you'll take the body. I'm going home to call Emma's mother. She'll want to know where her daughter's been taken." He then said to the lieutenant, "There's still no word from Lewis or Stanley. I want you to investigate this to your full extent. What happened in there looks self-inflicted, but I got good instinct Stanley and his wife have a trick playing."

"Yes, Papa Solomon," the young cop stated. "Any possibility Lewis was here?"

Papa Solomon shook his head, no. Martin asked more questions, and Papa Solomon answered them, barely paying attention. He was concentrated more on the fact that Martin wasn't built to be a simple officer. His mind was always on the puzzle, looking to put the unseen picture together. A private investigator would suit Fable Avenue's interest far better. They'd had enough cops inside.

Papa Solomon took a deep breath. He patted both Martin and Oliver on the back as he walked back to the room and instructed the yumbo to disappear. The Senegalese faerie jumped up and dived through the floor. Papa Solomon looked down the hall at Martin and his son and signaled them to lift the sorcery influencing their respective squads, and allow them upstairs. He, himself, walked downstairs, the rush of paramedics and police officers hurrying past him as Oliver and Martin lifted their enchantments. Papa Solomon made his way to the dining area and stood over the table. He stared at the open sketchbook and sighed again. He looked over his shoulder and then up at the ceiling. "It's clear," he declared.

The yumbo poked its head through first, and then it crawled the rest of its body through the ceiling. She clung to the ceiling for a moment, inspecting the open page now absent of her sketched presence. She jumped down and landed on the open spot above the tree branch where she was drawn to be perched. She looked up at Papa Solomon, and the two of them gave a nod to one another. Then the yumbo crawled back into the picture. When she was tucked inside, perched, still, and once again a detailed, two-dimensional drawing, Papa Solomon closed the book, picked it up from the table, and exited the brownstone.

Lights atop parked police cars and parked ambulance vans flashed without sound. Papa Solomon turned away from them and headed up the street, informing a female cop stationed outside that Lieutenant Kimball was going to take his statement at his own house. Papa Solomon walked the blocks back to his home. On his way, he instructed gathered Fable Avenue residents to go inside, only revealing that a terrible incident occurred at the Forrester home. He met Wilson Barnes waiting outside his house, standing inside the gated area, near the stairs. Papa Solomon opened the gate and walked through.

"Fey is in Madame Jeliya's care," Wilson informed.

Papa Solomon patted the young man's shoulder. "Thank you, Wilson." He leaned close and told him, "You heard a gunshot come from the house and you ran and got me." Wilson agreed. Papa Solomon further explained, "We went back, pounded on the door, the little girl let us in, I found her mother, and I had you bring her here, away from the scene. You made the call to Lieutenant Kimball." Wilson again nodded in agreement. "Head back down there now and oversee everything. Give the story I gave you. Martin and Oliver know better, we just need something official."

"Yes, Papa Solomon," said Wilson before leaving through the gate and heading up the street to the Forrester home.

Papa Solomon trudged up the stairs and through the front doors. He made his way to the kitchen, being met by his wife as she ascended from the basement. She walked over to Papa Solomon and informed him, "Little Fey is fine, and Wilson told me everything." Thelema put a gentle hand on Papa Solomon's shoulder. She continued with a cautious expression on her face and tone in her voice, "Now, Papa, I know you wanted to bear the burden of calling Savannah and telling her about her daughter and grandchild, but I've already made that call. She's on her way from Mount Vernon."

Papa Solomon understood. He closed his eyes and asked, "How was she?"

"Very distraught," Thelema answered. She admitted, "I didn't know exactly how to phrase it. I said Emma hurt herself. I couldn't use the word 'killed', but she pulled it out of me." Thelema started weeping. Her words tripped as she spoke them. "I told her. I told her what happened." Papa Solomon pulled his wife close and embraced her.

"It's okay, Thelema-baby," he comforted her. "It's okay. It's alright now."

Thelema cleared her throat to keep her words audible. "She asked if Lewis might've been involved," she continued, head against her husband's shoulder. "I said I didn't think so, but we wouldn't rule that out as a possibility." She looked up at Papa Solomon. "She didn't ask about

Stanley, but I could sense she had her questions and theories." She stepped out of Papa Solomon's embrace and fixed herself. "As do we all, I guess, Papa." The kitchen phone rang and startled Thelema. Both she and Papa Solomon stared at the device. It rang several more times before Thelema said to her husband, "It's been ringing off an on. No I.D. But I don't need some gadget to tell me who's on the other side of that call."

Papa Solomon approached the phone. It rang twice more before he scooped it up and answered, "Hello…?"

"Papa Solomon," a voice answered back.

Papa Solomon looked at his wife. He replied, "Stanley…?"

There was no immediate answer. Papa Solomon was patient. Thelema was not. Her desperate expression pleaded for Papa Solomon to identify the caller, at least some validation to what she already knew. Papa Solomon waved down her anxiousness. Thelema tried to remain still, but she paced. Papa Solomon, through hand gestures, sent Thelema to check on Fey below. Thelema agreed, not minding the order, as she welcomed the distraction. Papa Solomon placed the sketchbook on the table and walked to his study. He could hear the other person on the line fiddling. Then after clearing his throat the person asked, "How's Emma?"

Papa Solomon boiled, but he didn't allow his emotions to surface. He asked in a calm tone that required all of his concentration, "Where's Lewis, Stanley?"

"He's right here, Papa Solomon," the other answered with a slight tone of regret. "He's right here."

"Put him on," ordered Papa Solomon, his voice still calm.

"Forgive me, Papa Solomon, but you can't see me," said the voice on the other end. "I'm gesturing," the man clarified. "I'm tapping against my heart. Understand? Lewis is right here. Right. Here." Anger was rising in the voice. Nothing was said for some time, but the voice on the other end of the call broke the silence after the long pause. "Papa Solomon, I want to know if I have your attention."

"You do, Stanley," the Fable Avenue patriarch responded. "You always have."

Papa Solomon could hear shifting, as if the person on the other end was adjusting positions in a seat. He knew the man on the other end was nursing a glass of wine. Not to get drunk, but to breathe and relax. Then he heard a sip taken, and the man continued, "Lewis' last gift, accorded to me, is an acute vision. I know the moves you can make. I get it now, all of it. I understand your extensive research and the outcome to all your ceremonial rituals. Take one step in the right direction, and more people will get hurt. I won't need to keep an eye on you. I'll know, thanks to Lewis and his gift." There was light chuckling, and the voice stated, "Do you know that Lewis brought me close to my mother? It was just as I wanted. I haven't had that feeling in so long, Papa Solomon. I felt what my mother felt. I could actually feel. That's something I haven't been able to do in such a long time if ever at all." There was more chuckling. Papa Solomon listened without interruption. The voice continued, "My mother felt that. You know? That thing she and I are missing. That feeling of being alive. My mother felt close to that feeling when she stole your great-grandmother's voice and sang with it. I sort of perceived that growing up. I never truly understood it until I was much older, though. I'm talking much older, long after my mother passed." The voice paused again, but this time the pause was short. "She never abused your great-grandmother's voice, despite how you all tell the story. I never liked your revisionist history. My mother was mean, but she honored that voice. Trust me. She did." There was a reflective hum, and then the person confessed, "I never thought I would feel that kind of spirit, personally. I thought I had it when I was young. I was happy too, just smiling and dumb. Innocent as can be. When my mother passed, I understood I never had it. Lewis helped me see that, he and my wife." There was another pause, and then the voice clarified, "My wife really. She always told me." Then the voice joked, "Always listen to your wife." He sighed. "But I needed confirmation. Lewis confirmed what my wife already told me. Now I feel alive. I feel soulful, Papa Solomon. Vencil." There was chuckling again. Then in an eerily calm voice, the other on the line said to Papa Solomon, "I feel alive and soulful because I know I've hurt you—all of you on Fable Avenue. This is just the new me saying hello, Papa Solomon. My actions have disturbed your tight-knit community, and I'm finally breathing. I'm inhaling and exhaling, and I have my best friend Lewis to thank for that, his contribution and the potency of his trick. I thank the good people of Fable Avenue too. Pass that on to everybody there once all the mourning is done. You tell them that Stanley Fallows says 'thank-you.' Thank you, Papa Solomon. Hurting you all made me taste the air. It made me feel everything."

Papa Solomon shut his eyes tight and rubbed them with his forefinger and thumb. Then he spoke, "Stanley…"

But he was interrupted. "You don't have to tell me how Emma's doing. I know. I know precisely how she is. I know down to a mathematical precision of understanding. I see the world now, its code, and I can break it. Just tell that little orphan Annie named Fey that her father is in my thoughts, and he is in her Uncle Stanley's heart. Close."

The conversation was over. There was a click and a dial tone. Papa Solomon turned the phone off. He got up and walked back to the kitchen, placing the phone back onto the receiver. Thelema returned from the basement. "Papa, is everything okay?"

Papa Solomon didn't answer. He picked up the sketchbook and opened to the page with the sketched yumbo. "We need to call my sister in Queens," he said after a while of gazing at the drawing. "She don't need to come here, but she should know what's taken place. Tell her I'll be there in the morning. It's too dangerous to travel tonight."

"I figured," said Thelema. "I made a call to Top Hat. He's going to send out a blessing to Savannah as she makes her way here from Mount Vernon. She might be able to bless herself, but her thoughts are everywhere right now. Stanley might put a trick on her." Thelema paused and then asked, "What about Lena?"

"We'll go to her place now. Together," he emphasized. Thelema embraced him as his voice trailed away. Papa Solomon composed himself and asked, "That little girl still doing okay?" Asking the question brought to mind the cruel statement he'd heard expressed about the six-year-old girl in the last moments of his phone conversation.

"She's fine," assured Thelema.

"Good," said Papa Solomon, his voice barely audible. "Let me take this to her. I'll be right back, Thelema-baby."

Thelema remarked on the whereabouts of their daughter, "I'll make a call to Leah. She's up the street at her friend's house. I'll tell her to stay put. She don't need to be in all this. I'll bring her home later. Maybe I'll ask Loretta if she can stay the night."

Papa Solomon agreed. He walked downstairs into the basement, his wife's workspace. The red and gold lights were dimmed to a serene hum. Lush flora was spread around the room, some of which were bright, golden sprouts of wheat. Star charts encased in glass frames hung on the wall alongside West African masks and Moorish tapestries. Paintings of black women in various time periods mixing herbs, gazing at the stars, or handling vials bubbling with exotic liquids rounded out the gallery. Water flowed from out of the wall, the area around it built to look like a waterfall on the side of a mountain situated in a tropical paradise. There was a large bookshelf filled with shamanistic tomes. On the far side of the room was a large altar that held an Egyptian crook and flail. In front of the altar was a chaise lounge where Fey Forrester rested in a peaceful sleep. An African blanket, stitched from brownish-reds and golden-colored wool, lay over her, the veve symbol for the goddess Erzulie emblazoned on it. Next to the chaise was a side table with an unlit lamp.

Papa Solomon walked over to the table, moved the lamp to the carpeted floor, and put the sketchbook in its place. He looked at the drawing and said to it, "I need you to watch over her, little yumbo." The drawing stirred at the sound of Papa Solomon's voice. The yumbo emerged from the page, climbing up into a solid, glowing form. She sat down, facing forward with her legs folded. "Good," said Papa Solomon. "Things probably gon' get a little messy, loud perhaps, when this young girl's grandmother shows up." The yumbo looked up at Papa Solomon. "In haste, she'll probably snatch her girl up and not take this sketchbook. If that happens, can you follow them back to Mount Vernon?"

The yumbo nodded, yes.

"Good," spoke Papa Solomon. He turned and stated, "My wife and I will be back."

Then Papa Solomon ascended the stairs and joined Thelema in the kitchen. The two of them walked outside, across the street, and up several houses to the residence of the third matriarch of Fable Avenue. Her name was Lena Franklin. The community called her Lady Arachne. She was already on her porch, dressed in a night robe, her locks up in a blue head wrap. She was looking down the street at the flashing lights. She turned and saw Papa Solomon and Thelema walking up to her. Lena stepped down to greet them. "Papa Solomon, Madame Jeliya," she spoke their titles. Before either of them said a word, Lena announced, "I already know." She opened the gate to her house and turned around as Papa Solomon and Thelema walked through. "Come on," she said walking up the stairs to her front door. "Let's make that call to Carolyn. Top Hat is in my workspace, concentrating his blessing on Savannah for her to get here safely."

Thelema followed Lena into her home.

Papa Solomon stopped, taking a moment before he entered. He pivoted and attempted a glance at the goings-on down the road. His sight paused, however, and his gaze instead observed the street's pristine cleanliness, its calm and quiet, and the charm that blossomed from its chill-defying, iridescent flowers. The flashing lights outside the Forrester residence reflected off the polished, sanitary urban setting. Even at a distance, the red and blue lights' wild flicker muted the radiance bubbling from the unique flora. Papa Solomon guessed that intrigued residents were at their windows, curiosity in full bloom on their wide gazes.

He sighed, shook his head, and walked inside Lena's house. He locked the doors behind him.

Today was the first day of a new age.

Nineteen.

Gordon Goodspeed sat on the edge of his bed looking at a wall that had been blank for seven months. He was dressed in black slacks, black dress shoes, and a black suit jacket that covered a white dress shirt buttoned up to his neck. Gordon sat hunched over, elbows on his knees, and hands locked together. Gordon observed the wall as if something was there. Between him and his imagination, there was. Gordon saw a clock's face with one thin hand ticking backwards as a countdown. The metronomic tick was real, supplied by the actual clock resting on Gordon's nightstand.

He did not move to address the ticking, but after a minute or two Gordon turned his head and checked the real clock for the time. It was fifteen minutes to nine. Gordon noted in his head that on this day, October the eighth, his time of birth was precisely at ten-seventeen in the morning. He also made note that if he had the ability to travel back nineteen years ago at this very moment he wouldn't have been born yet. He even voiced it aloud as he turned his head to the curtains and said, while looking at the stream of sunlight coming through the drapery, "I haven't been born yet." The statement was made in a sarcastic, matter-of-fact tone.

Gordon took a breath and rubbed his knees. He looked back at the clock. Not even a minute had passed since his last glance. Gordon stood up, cleared his throat, and walked to the window. He moved the curtain aside with one hand, put the other in his pocket, and looked down onto the street. The pulse of Harlem pumped vibrantly, though pedestrian traffic was winding down from the early morning. There were still two, spotted lanes of people rushing to the subway or returning from having dropped their children off at the school up the street. Cars coursed up to the Bronx or down into Midtown Manhattan.

Gordon observed the day, bright and blue with the sun shining proud on Harlem. Gordon wasn't fooled by the bright burst of sunlight. He removed his hand from his pocket and felt the window. There was a chill spread over the glass. Gordon groaned. With his nineteenth birthday came a private, hallowed ceremony. And for reasons Gordon was not aware of,

Papa Solomon and his sister, Miss Carolyn-Theresa Dumas, felt it necessary for it to take place outside on this chilly, early autumn morning.

Gordon looked up and down the road from his vantage point at the window. He spotted no signs of Papa Solomon's car, a well-kept, black, nineteen-seventies Cadillac. Gordon felt he had time. He stepped away from the window and walked to his desk. He opened the drawer and searched frantically through it. He wanted to find something that belonged to his mother, something that he could hold of hers while he went through the ceremony, something that could at least keep his thoughts warm. He found nothing but miscellaneous items he'd tossed inside over the years. He looked through the other drawers on his desk and found much the same thing.

Gordon looked at the tall dresser next to the desk. He already knew that there was nothing in it but clothes. His closet would yield the same. He looked around the room. All manner of trinkets, pictures, and electronics had been confiscated from his room for the past seven months in preparation for this day. Gone was Gordon's thirty-two-inch, flat screen television that rested on top of his desk. Gone too was the gaming console and his laptop. Gordon's smartphone and other handheld devices also had no place in his room. Gordon didn't miss these items, as they were in other areas of the house. And it wasn't as if he was forbidden from using them. He could swipe his phone to make calls, but he had to leave his room to pick it up from the kitchen counter downstairs, or he pocketed the item before he left the house. He still played his video games and used his laptop to hook into social media or rummage through online sites for research or other means, but this was all regulated to the basement of his family's brownstone.

And of course, the walls were bare. None of his collected paintings, old photographs, movie, Yankees, or superhero posters accented his room. Even the Fable Avenue community's cultural symbols were absent, removed. This was how it was supposed to be. For seven months. The confiscation of Gordon's personal items wasn't all at once. Month by month he was dispossessed of his things until nothing remained. Nothing electrical was allowed in the room, especially when Gordon took rest for the night. The lamp and clock on the nightstand operated through other means. Gordon loved the lamp. It was a thick, solid globe of glass perched on a copper stand with a crystal at its center. Three taps and the crystal hummed a radiant, hypnotic brilliance.

It was the lamp that allowed Gordon to continue respecting the traditions he was born into as he was stripped of his belongings day-by-day. Right now, the otherworldly lamp couldn't stop Gordon from wishing he had something familiar. He looked at the top of the dresser, it was bare of his models of mythic creatures and favorite action figures, some of which he received as presents from his mother before she passed. One of his favorites was a mighty, nine-inch figure of an African warrior with onyx-colored skin and intricate gold lines drawn around his body like a circuit. It was sculpted at his mother's request by a community toymaker living in New Jersey. Gordon wished he had the toy figure now, something to take before going to this ceremony in honor of his nineteenth birthday.

He looked at the closed door and waited, wanting for it to open and his father to come through. Gordon's brown eyes focused intently for a moment, but the door's handle never stirred, nor did a knock echo from the other side accompanied by his father's voice requesting permission to enter. Gordon considered the possibility of his older brother Cedron coming through and greeting him with a birthday salute, but that would've been too great an effort for Cedron. Gordon stepped away from his desk and to the door, opening it and walking into the hallway. In front of him was a railing leading down the hall and to the stairs descending to the parlor floor.

Gordon put his hand on the railing and took a few paces down the hall. He peeked over the railing and listened. He could hear the deep bass of his brother's voice, but he couldn't make out much of what was being said. But Gordon knew his brother Cedron was probably addressing two common friends whose routine it was to show up at this early time of day. Cedron helped coordinate some of the drivers in their family cab business. Two close friends. Gordon suspected that Raymundo "Raymond" Ma Chao Shaw was one of the two people being addressed by Cedron. Raymond was a young Filipino man with a boyish charm that was a wonderful cover for a devious streak. His older brother, Edmundo, was no different in demeanor. This caused Gordon to refer to the two as the "Haskell" brothers, rather than the Shaw brothers, an allusion to the 1950s, sycophantic character of Eddie Haskell on the popular show *Leave It to Beaver.* The Shaw brothers knew how to smile and patronize authority with *"Yes ma'ams," "No sirs,"* and *vice versa.* However, once the authority figure disappeared, their sneaky, deviant nature came through. Raymond and Cedron were best friends, old schoolmates.

Gordon inferred that the second person Cedron addressed was a young Jamaican man named Benjamin "Benny Jah" Brickhouse. Benny was Gordon's best friend, born in Queens, but lived between New York and Jamaica for the first ten years of his life. Both of his parents were a part of the Fable Avenue community. His mother was a middle school teacher and his father co-owned the cab service with Gordon's father. Benny's family moved across the street when Benny turned twelve, strengthening their friendship.

Gordon considered that the address Raymond and Benny were receiving from Cedron had little to do with the cab company. Gordon reversed his steps until he was once again directly outside his room. He looked up the stairs, keeping his eyes there for several moments before walking up. Once on the third floor, Gordon aimed his gaze at his father's room. The door was closed. He walked toward the room and stopped just outside the door. He stood there. Close. The tip of his nose a hair's breath away from the door. He placed his fingers gently against the door, turned his head, and put his ear to it.

Gordon heard nothing.

He stepped back and knocked on the door several times.

"Dad," Gordon called. He heard his father's slow, shuffling movement in the bed. He knocked another time and called again, "Pop…" His father stirred, rising from bed. Gordon heard his father address someone, *"It's my son. It's an important day for him."* Maximilian's voice was rising from sleep just like he was. Gordon was aware that his father was speaking to another nondescript woman he'd picked up. One different every night, or every other night, with no one long term since his mother's death. Gordon made a low sigh as he heard his father's voice. He rolled his eyes and waited as his father threw on gray pajama bottoms and a t-shirt. The door opened, and Gordon stepped back as his father, Maximilian Goodspeed, emerged from the master bedroom. All seemed well for the moment. It's what Gordon was hoping for, a look at his father. He and Maximilian smiled sincerely at one another.

Father and son weren't exactly mirror images. Maximilian was tall with a brawny frame and a triangular-shaped head on which rested a bushy and wavy taper-styled haircut. Outlining Maximilian's face was a thin stream of hair. Gordon, on the other hand, was a little less than average height, standing at five-seven and with no more to grow. His head was ovate, a perfect egg shape from the small, ovoid curve of his chin to the wider ovoid curve at the top of his head. His hair was a stormy array of tight twists, which he was made to grow over the last seven months for this specific day. Gordon was clean-shaven, another principal for today's birthday ritual. But father and son shared the same golden-brown eye color and the same burnished brown color in their skin.

Gordon took a furtive, quick glance to the bed behind his father. The bed's billowing comforter covered the woman laying in it, and Gordon ascertained nothing of her identity, save her long, bone-straight, black hair that spilled out from underneath the covers. Gordon put his eyes back on his father, trying to remain inconspicuous about his inspection, but it didn't work. Gordon saw his father's guilt beam through a sly grin. But there came a shift in his smile as pride appeared. Maximilian moved into the hall, backing his son away from the room and closing the door.

"Papa Solomon should be here soon," Gordon informed.

"Yeah," Maximilian replied, guilt cleaned from his smile but still residing in his one-word answer. He continued to stand in the doorway, hands in his pockets, beaming at his son with a proud smile. He motioned for Gordon to follow him to the stairs. "You nervous?" Maximilian asked his son.

Gordon laughed off the question. "What I got to be worried about, Pop?" he asked rhetorically. "Have my hair washed, get a blessing, spend the night at the house over in Brooklyn. Ain't nothin' but a thang."

Maximilian stopped at the stairs and turned around. "You think this is nothing but a 'thang,' but this a big 'thang,' now. We ain't had a Goodspeed go through this rite for a while." Gordon raised an eyebrow at his father whose excitement appeared unsuited to him. Maximilian clarified, "I got reservations. I do. Considering all the…" his voice trailed away. He shook his head and waved his hand. "I don't even want to get into it." He paused and then concluded, "But my father and his father before him really believed in these traditions. It's not about Fable Avenue's patriarchs and matriarchs." And then Maximilian's voice spilled with sentiment as he admitted, "Your mother was fond of all this too." He put his hand on Gordon's shoulder. "I've become cautious, but you'll do fine, Gordon."

Gordon confessed, "I was feeling…isolated. Was waitin' for you or Cedron to come and greet me for the day. I was lookin' for somethin' in my drawers. Somethin' from mom."

Maximilian shook his head. "You know that can't be, Gordon," he told his son. "Not for today. You've been stripped of your possessions for a reason. You supposed to be new. No charms or trinkets from myself or your mom." Maximilian watched his son give a silent, affirmative nod of the head. "Cedron and I will put all your belongings back. Maman Anansi will come through and give them a proper blessing." He stressed, "*Everything* will be new, even your old possessions." Gordon continued nodding. Maximilian moved to the side, back against the wall. "Go on downstairs, son. I'll be there shortly. I got some things to speak to Papa Solomon about when he arrives." Gordon nodded his head and then started down the stairs, walking past his father. Maximilian said to Gordon, "You forgot about the tattoo you gon' get. You ain't nervous about that?"

Gordon turned, walking backwards down the stairs carefully but coolly while holding onto the rail. He said up to his father, "Been lookin' forward to it. I want that Ka Mauri spirit on my shoulder."

Maximilian's face expressed surprise. "Oh," he said to Gordon. "You don't want that Dii Mauri sign like your brother and me?"

"Aw, Pop," drawled Gordon. He double-tapped a clenched fist

against his chest and pointed up to his father. "I got nothin' but love for you and Cedron. I just want a warrior brand over a scholar and keeper's brand."

Maximilian rolled his eyes. He pointed a stern finger at his son and reminded Gordon, "You know they don't mean a thing? It's just a tradition."

"Yes, Pop," acknowledged Gordon, an apology in his tone, but with smile still intact. "I just want what I want."

Maximilian rolled his eyes again. "Aight. Okay," he said, turning and heading back to his room. "Call up when Papa Solomon arrives." He said back to his son, "And there ain't gonna be an incant to numb the tattoo. You gon' feel that."

Despite his father's notification, Gordon felt better. He hurried to the second floor, down the hall, and with excited strides descended the stairs to the parlor floor. The stairs led into a wide hallway that stretched more than half of the brownstone's length. The front entrance was located opposite the stairs, a little to the right of the bottom-stair landing. Sunlight beamed through the front windows and brightened the off-white walls. The room was accented with Victorian-style woodwork, inlaid with intricate, African symbols. A spherical, Moroccan chandelier hung from the ceiling. In the center of the wooden floor lay a long and wide African rug stitched with red, black, and gold fabrics, shamanistic icons woven into the design. Centered atop the rug was a round, wooden table with a potted, lilac flower resting on it. On the other side of the room, was a wide ceiling-height mirror hanging on the wall. A longcase clock was in the corner of the room, a sconce next to it. A Moorish arch shaped the entrance to an elegant kitchen and dining area. At the right of this entrance, going down underneath the staircase, was a wheelchair-accessible ramp descending into the brownstone's garden level where a study, a family room, and Cedron Goodspeed's bedroom and bathroom were located.

Gordon stepped into the wide hall and made a sharp turn toward the dining area. Cedron Goodspeed was crammed in the entrance, his back to Gordon. He was surrounded not by two of their close friends, but three. Jamie Ryan was the third. He was a tall, light-skinned young man who was a year younger than Cedron and Raymond, but graduated in the same class. Jamie was an impressive dancer who studied dance in college, concentrating in the art of tap. Gordon was surprised to see him, which showed on his face. He managed to hide the irritation he felt for his brother to drag Jamie into whatever misdeed he plotted with Benny and Raymond. Jamie was, at the moment, holding a round and wooden, cigar ashtray that was inset with a brass cup for the ashes.

Cedron rested his cigar inside the ashtray after taking a quick glance over his shoulder and seeing Gordon enter into the wide hallway. He ordered Jamie, "Take that into the kitchen. I don't want its smoke on my brother. This his day." Gordon watched as Jamie did as he was told, scrambling into the kitchen and setting the ashtray next to the sink with the cigar still smoking inside it. He returned, in haste, to the party gathered around Cedron. Gordon saw his brother's head turn, eye cocked to him. Cedron grinned and announced in a deep voice over his shoulder, "Here comes the prince." Gordon approached, stepping cautiously toward his brother. Cedron was a massive and strong six-foot-ten-inch hulking figure that, even though bound to a wheelchair ever since a bullet struck his spine at the age of nineteen, was still a colossal presence. Cedron coolly maneuvered his wheelchair to spin around and face Gordon. The others stepped back as Cedron pivoted.

Cedron was dressed in blue jeans and a white turtleneck that was covered by his old high school varsity basketball jersey, number thirty-six. He waved Gordon closer, "Come on, man. Come closer. Let's see the prince on his day."

Gordon finished his approach, his friends applauding. He beamed a modest grin and jokingly gave audible *"thank yous"* while shaking hands and giving hugs and fist bumps to his friends. Even Raymond knew today was special for Gordon Goodspeed. Though his family wasn't officially a part of the Fable Avenue community, his father received a blessing from Matriarch Heathwicke-Peters to keep their family's medical practice afloat. The blessing was successful, and in exchange, Raymond and his older brother Edmond were asked to give service to the Goodspeed-Brickhouse cab company when drivers were needed. Raymond's father also co-owned a small blues and jazz lounge with Papa Solomon and other adult members of the Fable Avenue community. The club was called Hours, and it was based in Harlem. It was restored from an older club known as On The Hour that was open during Harlem's golden age of jazz. It was located several blocks up from the historic Harlem Dixie, which was now the city-run Harlem Area Museum of Jazz and New York Sound.

Gordon came to his brother. Cedron's titan build was a taller, bulkier image of their father, save for Cedron's dark skin and low-cut hair. From his wheelchair, which looked too small for his enormous musculature, Cedron gazed at his brother, smiling. "Come here, little brother. Come here." The two brothers gave one another a shake and hug. "You got your second gateway rites today." Cedron looked at Benny and Jamie and teased, "You boys don't know nothin' about that." He was commenting on the fact that the second gateway rites were a set of rituals reserved for Goodspeed boys and girls that reached the age of nineteen. Cedron continued his commentary. "It's a little early for the ceremony, but

I guess that's the caution Papa Solomon and Maman Anansi are taking, right?" He was referring to the fact that it was customary for the second gateway rites to be performed precisely nineteen days after the nineteenth birthday of a Goodspeed child, but for reasons unknown, Gordon's ceremony was coming directly on the day of his nineteenth birthday. "Hope your eyes get fermented, kid. Get your brew stirred. This here throne is all I got for my rites." Everyone groaned at Cedron's comment. Raymond and Jamie remarked that Cedron was still whole. Benny remained silent, an uncomfortable look on his face.

"Bruh…" spoke Gordon.

"What? What? You girls relax," Cedron said hushing everyone's concerns. "Whatchy'all think, you gazin' on tragedy here? Please! I'm a king in this chair. This *my* throne."

Jamie patted Cedron on the shoulder and assured, "W-w-w-we kn-kn-know, K-K-King. Whu-whu-we kn-kn-kn-know."

Cedron looked over at Raymond and Benny. They gave assurances through head nods. "Alright, then. We got order." He looked at Gordon and said, "And you got a ceremony. Keep a blessing over you. I know they'll have you protected." Cedron paused, and then he asserted, "Of course, if this was you here, it wouldn't be much of a tragedy." His eyes panned Gordon up and down. "You ain't shit," he sneered.

"Whoa!" Gordon barked.

Benny yelled in Gordon's defense, "Cedron!"

"Relax, relax," Cedron said waving down the commotion. "It was a poor attempt at a joke. Relax. Goddamn. Y'all catch soft like it's the flu. Thicken up." Cedron opened his arms and said to Gordon, "I swear. No harm. And you best thicken up, bruh. You gettin' tatted," he changed the subject and beamed a smile. "You gonna have that Dii Mauri seal of approval."

A smile shined through on Gordon's face, dispersing the anger conjured in him by his brother. His smile grew wider when he said to Cedron, "I'm gettin' that Ka Mauri, sun."

Cedron sat back, his face spattered with surprise. He flapped his lips and shook his head. "Hold up, hold up. Goodspeed college boys like us are supposed to be scholars and council members. Dude right here wants to be a warrior?" Cedron relaxed and expressed, "Aight. Okay. I wanna see this. Let's see how your tat' rite goes."

Cedron wasn't in college anymore, however. His scholarship had been taken from him after the calamitous incident of being hit by a bullet meant for a friend he was trying to keep out of trouble. There were incants that calmed his anger over the incident, but Gordon felt his brother's despair and hostility was only buried. And there were no incants strong enough to heal him, though they did help mitigate the damage. There were trembling movements in his legs but no feeling.

Benny flapped his lips. He opened his arms wide, making a face as he commented, "Come on, sun. Everybody know the Dii Mauri of the house and the Ka Mauri of the field." There was an ever so subtle hint of a Caribbean cadence accenting the pronunciation of Benny's words. He looked at Jamie and asked, "Am I right, my Ka Mauri-marked brother? Am I right?" Jamie smiled, shaking his head and pointing at Benny to give assenting confirmation. Both Gordon and Raymond chuckled at Benny's description.

"Okay, okay," said Cedron rolling his eyes and again waving down the hysteria filling the room. "That's a good one. I'll give you that. But it's a damn shame we gotta take some sacred, ancestral beliefs back to some slave shit." He looked at Gordon and lifted his shoulders. "But whaddya gonna do, huh? Niggas. Well trained."

Gordon stated, "Hey, Pops just reminded me that the tat' is all for tradition. They don't mean anything. Besides, a lot of them brothers and sisters kept these traditions alive while enslaved."

Cedron made a face. "You right. But, well, Pops got a Puerto Rican chick on his arm right now and everywhere else, I assume. He ain't thinkin' about the ink on his shoulder or any traditions. He rockin' that chick out. Probably had an incant goin' to make sure we ain't hear no noise. As usual." Cedron noticed a slight change in Gordon's mood. He remarked, "Hey, it's good at least somebody gettin' ass up in here. You been under orders to be an angel for seven months now."

Gordon exhaled and rolled his eyes. "I know. And I've had to be cool through spring and summer, when these girls is lookin' they finest."

Cedron held a sly grin. "That's okay, kid. Whether the brew is stirred in you or not, you goin' through your rites. You finally gettin' your hoodoo ink. Us Goodspeeds gotta wait a moment. You gon' be a new nigga. You gon' be straight."

Someone knocked on the front door, halting Gordon's response. He turned around, walked to the door and opened it. The day's chill scampered inside, but Gordon paid the breeze no mind. He was expecting to see Papa Solomon standing in front of him, but instead it was Papa Solomon's son, Oliver. "Ollie!" Gordon greeted. "Ollie Raz!"

Gordon was embraced by Oliver and given a hard slap on the back. "There's the man of the day!" Oliver addressed. He stepped out of the embrace, and with a smile held out a balled fist. Gordon made a fist and bumped it against Oliver's. "It's your rite, Negro," Oliver stated. He tossed his thumb over his shoulder, pointing at the black, vintage Cadillac behind him. "You suited up?" asked Oliver, as he looked Gordon up and down.

"Good. Papa Solomon is waiting. Come on. We're heading to Woodlawn in the Bronx. My aunt is waiting there." Oliver noticed Cedron and the others behind Gordon. Oliver teased loud enough for Cedron and the others to hear him, "Tell these crooks and their mastermind goodbye," he said. Everyone threw up their arms and huffed, mocking Oliver's statement. "Yeah, your boy here is getting cultured while you knuckleheads are gettin' into trouble. I know how you riff-raffs are. Whatchu idiots plottin'?"

There was a playful response from Cedron, and Oliver retorted. Gordon didn't hear any of the exchange. He was too busy looking behind Oliver and noticing that Papa Solomon wasn't in the car. The Fable Avenue patriarch was across the street speaking with Benny's mother on the porch. Benny's younger brother, Dajon, was in the doorway, not in school. The conversation appeared serious. Gordon turned around and penetrated the banter between Cedron and Oliver as he asked, "Hey, Benny. What's going on with your little brother? Why he ain't in school? Papa Solomon's talkin' to your moms."

Benny let out an irritated sigh as he walked over to Gordon. "Dajon was suspended from school," he answered Gordon. And before Gordon could ask why, Benny gave him the following answer: "He got into a fight with some kid. My mom wants Papa Solomon to put him on street duty. Clean up." He then requested, "Keep a good eye on him, will you Gordon."

"An eye…?" questioned Gordon.

Oliver added as he stepped further into the house, "Yeah, we're gonna swing by and pick him up once your rites are finished."

Gordon huffed as he contorted his face. Before he could comment, Maximilian Goodspeed rushed down the stairs. "Ollie," Maximilian called as he came into the hall. "Papa Solomon outside?"

"Yessir," Oliver responded. "He's across the street now, talking to Missus Brickhouse."

Maximilian continued past Oliver, patting him on the shoulder. "Thanks." And then he was gone through the door. Papa Solomon was on his way back to his car, and Gordon watched his father run and catch up to him before he was able to slip into the backseat.

"Raymond," Gordon heard Oliver call. "You still at that art school?"

"Not this semester, Ollie," Raymond answered.

"I'm tellin' you, kid," Oliver continued. "We need to get up on a project. Our skills together, we can get somethin' fired up."

"Soon, soon, Ollie," Raymond said smiling but in a dismissive voice.

"Okay," Oliver yielded. He turned around to leave. "I'll be in the car, Gordon. Savor your goodbyes. You ain't seein' these hooligans for the next three days." Oliver left the house, closing the door.

Gordon presented his friend Benny a parting shake and a hug. With Benny in tow, Gordon walked back to Cedron and the others and did the same. Everyone wished him well. He made his way back to the door and called for Jamie to follow him. He whispered to his friend, "Ain't you got class today? Whatchu doin' here gettin' involved with these knuckleheads?"

Jamie stuttered, "I g-g-got the-the-the day uh, uh, off." He took a breath, focusing on his speech before it was spoken. He made soft snaps with his fingers, making no noise. This was a technique that he used to keep the rhythm in his voice from stammering too much. In front of strangers, Jamie would often hide his hand in his pocket or behind his leg to keep this action from being conspicuous. "K-King ne-needs my ride. I'm. On. Shift at the company." A guilty expression ran across his face. His snapping ceased and his voice stammered again. "G-G-Gordon, l-l-l-look. Eh-eh-eh…" He paused and made the soft snaps again. "It's aaaa-an…" He stopped and started over, snapping his fingers as he spoke slow and steady, "It's. An. Easy. Score. Three-hundred dollars. Simple. Ed-mond and Cedron… They. G-g-got. This. On lock."

Gordon sighed. "Okay. Fine. But let this be it. Don't let these dudes drag you into another scheme. And be careful."

"I-I-I know, G-Gordon."

"And keep an eye on Benny, please," Gordon instructed. He made a face and said, "I gotta make sure his brother ain't becomin' some knucklehead too." Jamie assured he would, and then he again wished Gordon well on his rites. He walked back to Cedron and the rest just as Maximilian walked back inside. "Okay, Pop," said Gordon to his father. "I'm ready." Then he joked, "I think…" Maximilian said nothing, but he hugged his son, and then he walked him through the open door.

Diving into the day's chill was far different from having a simple stream run through the house. Gordon pushed his hands in his pockets and hurried to Papa Solomon's ride. Maximilian stayed on the porch. Oliver lowered the passenger window and hollered, "Get in the back." Gordon did as he was told, entering the car from the passenger's side. Oliver started the car just as Gordon slipped in. Papa Solomon sat behind Oliver. He was dressed in blue jeans, brown loafers, and a flannel shirt covered by a dark brown leather jacket that was overlaid with patches honoring the Tuskegee Airmen and various Negro League baseball teams. A black fedora was propped atop Papa Solomon's bald head.

"How you doing, Gordon?" he greeted with a smile. "You ready for this?"

There was a beat before Gordon replied, "Doing fine, Papa Solomon. I'm okay."

Papa Solomon instructed Oliver, "Five-Seventeen, East Two Hundred and Thirty-Third Street."

"Will do, Pop," Oliver said. He checked his mirrors, and when all was clear, he pulled away from the curb and onto the road.

Gordon looked back at his house. His father and the others gathered on the porch. Cedron was at the door. Papa Solomon's voice brought his attention back to the car's interior. "You seemed hesitant to answer me, so I'll repeat. You ready for this?"

"I was just thinking about my dad," was Gordon's response. "He was my first thought. My brother was the other. I just have questions, Papa Solomon."

Papa Solomon chuckled. "Well, go ahead and ask," he said to Gordon. "Don't be afraid." Before Gordon could say anything, Papa Solomon lifted a hand. "No need. I'm sure you got reservations. I promised to keep you safe through all this. Your father made me, so I assured him."

Gordon took a moment before inquiring, "Why we goin' to Woodlawn for the ceremony instead of your family's business here in Harlem?" He didn't want to appear as if he didn't trust Papa Solomon's authority, or believe his choices were witless, if indeed there was risk involved with carrying out his second gateway rites.

Papa Solomon informed, "Our community has eyes on it, and those eyes have been watching us for the past thirteen years." Gordon listened closely to the elder. "That incident at the Forrester residence," Papa Solomon continued. "That was a rattle snake of a bite to our community." Papa Solomon felt the need to emphasize, "We was hit by an outside presence that was once an insider." Gordon then watched the fifty-four-year-old man go silent, and Gordon guessed Papa Solomon was reflecting on that evening that occurred thirteen years ago.

Gordon remembered that night, the commotion mostly. He'd just turned six several days earlier. Gordon's family was visiting the community, having dinner at the Goodspeed brownstone where his great-grandfather once lived. The brownstone was now open to the entire Goodspeed clan. His father went outside to investigate the commotion. Savannah Forrester had arrived in Brooklyn from Mount Vernon. Gordon remembered her screaming, furious at Papa Solomon. His father, along with other community members, got between the two elders. Some made an attempt to calm Savannah Forrester. Gordon called to mind his mother scurrying he and Cedron upstairs. She later explained that little Fey Forrester's mother was "hurt." Over the years, Gordon's parents would give Cedron and him more and more detailed pieces to the truth of what happened that night.

Fey Forrester's mother killed herself. There was talk of her being depressed. Her husband and she had been going through hard times. At that moment, Lewis Banneker and Emma Forrester had been separated. But here was Papa Solomon declaring her suicide an attack on Fable Avenue, the influence of a wicked trick.

"I received a warning that night," said Papa Solomon in a sad tone. "It came through a phone call. It was after the police and paramedics showed up, Martin and Oliver leading both units." Gordon glanced at Oliver who continued concentrating on driving. Papa Solomon revealed, "The warning stressed that we were not to engage in certain ceremonies that would move us closer in the right direction. Even now, as it was then, we're still taking baby steps with all this. Trying to understand our reality in this world. We pressed on, though, and then it hit." Papa Solomon looked directly at Gordon and told him, "The Goodspeed's second gateway rites have been under attack." Then he sat back as he stated, "At least that's our conspiracy theory, mostly my wife's. She's deduced that you all's ceremony must be a step in the right direction for our community. Your great-grandfather set it up, said little as to why. He was always worried about outside forces. Madison came off as paranoid to many people, but he was respected in his old age. Your grandfather, Cameron, he upheld tradition."

Gordon just nodded his head, his thoughts centered on his great-grandfather, Madison Goodspeed.

Papa Solomon told Gordon, "But they must be of some importance, to garner such attacks. Old Stanley Fallows, he can see our moves before we make 'em."

"Stanley Fallows?" Gordon interrupted with his inquiry. "Is he related to Sarinda Fallows?" Gordon then said in a mock spooky voice, *"Sarinda Unhallowed. Oooh! Sarinda the Everwalker. Oooh!"* He and Papa Solomon exchanged smiles as Gordon ceased his antics. "That woman you elders try to scare us little Fable Avenue boys and girls with if we don't eat our vegetables."

Papa Solomon chuckled. "Yep. That woman. Miss Sarinda Fallows. Stanley is indeed related. He's her son." Then his voice became stern. "And his threat, like his mother before him, is very real. We elders might play, but this is very serious. Stanley is a subtle man. Dangerous. You little boys and girls get to play and make light, but we elders keep worried."

Gordon nodded, respecting Papa Solomon's words.

Papa Solomon sat back. He said, "And his trick to know our moves, well, I can guess as to why he's capable of such a feat." But he waved his comment aside. "Sometimes your enemy can guide you better than your own senses. My wife, Madame Jeliya, she noticed and relayed to me her observations. She's concluded, and I quote, *'Our enemy's bastard eyes keep close watch on our culture.'* What's recently occurred is an attempt to stop the rites from being performed. Your brother was an attack, your two cousins before him too. Zachariah died in that car accident just two days before his rites. Your cousin Khamila was also in a car accident that put her in a coma for two weeks. We skipped the twins altogether, Isaiah and Cheryl, even before your brother's time. That was under great precautions, and neither of them, nor your aunt, seemed to mind."

Gordon asked, "So what makes me the sacrificial lamb?"

"Your father knew your mother wouldn't want you or your brother skipped," Papa Solomon answered. "And he don't want to upset the spirit of your grandfather and great grandfather." Papa Solomon raised an eyebrow and looked over at Gordon. "Does that Forrester girl go to your college? Fey?"

Gordon shrugged his shoulders. "Yeah," he said in a low voice, eyes away from Papa Solomon. To not seem rude he looked up at the elder when he relayed, "I think going to school in Brooklyn is a way for her to try and ease back into the community. She's had her questions the few times we've talked."

The revelation excited Papa Solomon. "Oh," he said. "Well that's good to know. You friendly with her?" asked Papa Solomon, his inquisitive voice hopeful.

"We've talked," Gordon replied, lifting his shoulders, a signal that helped iterate his relationship with Fey wasn't much more than a few conversations. His eyes looked away from Papa Solomon. He expressed his sentiments about Fey Forrester the only way a nineteen-year-old young man could. "She's cute," he remarked. "She's *very* pretty," he annunciated. "But she's weird." Even in his peripheral, Gordon could see Papa Solomon's face develop a perplexed expression.

Oliver stopped the car at a red light. His eyes went up to the rearview mirror and watched Gordon. He took the moment while the car was at a stop to turn around and say to him, "You come from the Fable Avenue community and have the nerve to call someone weird? That's a homegirl, sun."

Papa Solomon and Gordon chuckled at Oliver's comment. "He does make a point," said Papa Solomon. Oliver faced forward and waited for the light.

Gordon cocked his head to the side and covered his nervous smile with his hand. He wiped his smile away and cleared his throat. He noticed Papa Solomon hadn't lost his grin, and the elder's gaze upon him never faltered. Gordon knew Papa Solomon wanted an answer, despite the smile on his face, which was clearly a shit-eating grin inspired by Oliver's commentary.

"It's just weird," was all Gordon said. "She's weird." Then Gordon explained, "She has her MP3 player's headphones in her ears while sitting under a tree, and she's sitting there and drawing in her sketchbook—which I do think is cool." Gordon's nervous smile reappeared. His eyes looked down in front of him, seeing the scene he described more than anything else. "Her lips are moving, like she's singing along to what she's listening to." Gordon's face became contemplative, his smile faltering. "But I can tell, she's not singing. She's not mouthing lyrics. It's like she's having a conversation." He looked at Papa Solomon. "Maybe she's talking to her mother's spirit. I know it sounds weird." He said as if it was a confession, "Hey, I'm lookin' weird now, but…" Gordon paused to collect his thoughts. He said, "It looks odd because she's not part of the community anymore. I mean she could be communing with something. Like I said, her moms." Gordon inquired to Papa Solomon, "It's possible her grandmother kept her grounded in our culture, isn't it?"

Papa Solomon nodded. "It's possible," he answered, considering the thought. "In fact, I'm hopeful of it. I always am when these rites take place."

Gordon didn't ask why. Instead, he continued talking. "I just remember the time when Cedron was fifteen and he found Kepler when Kepler was living on the streets and talking to that spirit," said Gordon, his voice defensive. "Cedron could see who Kepler was talking to, though no one else could." Gordon concluded, "I can't see the other side of her conversation, if she's havin' one." Thinking about it made Gordon nervous about his rites. Perhaps he didn't have what Cedron had. Maybe there was no brewing spirit to be stirred inside him. Maybe the more deserving brother was at home, paralyzed from the waist down. Maybe Stanley Fallows got it right, if the conspiracy was indeed true.

"Okay," Papa Solomon acknowledged. "But she might be blocking you with an incant." He sat back and said as a sigh, "That little girl's grandmother was mighty angry at us, and I can't blame her. We failed her daughter, all of us did. Hell, I did. I can see Savannah teaching her granddaughter to keep secrets even from us."

This was something Gordon hadn't considered. However, even with the incensed commotion of that night, he knew little of the politics. He sat back and reflected on Papa Solomon's point as Oliver moved the car forward, the light now green.

There was silence for a moment, a long pause before Papa Solomon spoke. "I do hope Savannah has kept her granddaughter cultured," he voiced. "Take her out of the community but don't take the community out of her." He leaned close to Gordon and said in a more stern voice, "Stay close to Miss Forrester. If your rites go correctly, we'll need her grandmother's blessings and directions for creating a proper altar for you. We need an in to connect back with her."

"Will do, sir."

Papa Solomon divulged, "Little Fey Forrester's got an uncle that keeps in touch with her. He's over in Jersey. He's more like his father who was an outsider. He keeps his eye on his mother, but he don't bother with us Fable Avenue folk. Savannah's oldest child is worse than him. She don't want much to do with her mother."

"Oh," was all Gordon could say.

"It was like that before Savannah left the community," Papa Solomon explained. "I reckon ain't much changed since then."

"Oh," Gordon repeated.

They continued to Woodlawn Cemetery in the Bronx. Oliver turned on the radio and tuned it to a channel that played jazz and old school hits. "So, Gordon Goodspeed," began Papa Solomon as the music filled the car. "How *have* you been?" It was an attempt to lighten the conversation's tone. Gordon looked over at the beaming elder and smiled back. He answered that he was doing fine, and light conversation occupied the car for the rest of the ride.

Gordon looked up as Oliver pulled into the Jerome Avenue entrance to the Woodlawn Cemetery. They passed through the iron gates, up the winding road, and into a parking lot. Gordon took a deep breath and fixed himself as Oliver parked between two cars. He looked at Papa Solomon for a cue, his eyes momentarily glancing at the rearview mirror and noticing Oliver was also waiting for his father's word.

Papa Solomon looked at Gordon and said to him, "Come on, young man. Let's go."

Gordon nodded. He opened the car door and stepped out. Papa Solomon and Oliver emerged from the car seconds after him. Gordon shook his arms in an attempt to relieve anxiety, and he took another deep breath to do the same. He invited the air's chill more so than when he'd walked out of his house and into the day. Now, the brisk air cooled Gordon and slowed the tension swelling inside him. Papa Solomon made his way around the car and passed him. Gordon took that as a cue and followed close in tow. Papa Solomon said to him, "I know the atmosphere is a little cooler than normal. This is usually done indoors at my sister's house in Queens, or our place of business in Harlem." He slowed his walk and Gordon was next to him within two steps. Papa Solomon patted Gordon on the shoulder. "Under customary circumstances, you'd have family and community members around you. There'd be a small celebration back at Fable Avenue before you were isolated for a couple days. I'm sorry we have to deprive you of that, Gordon."

"I know, Papa Solomon," said Gordon, his understanding tone sincere. "Change is for caution." He noticed Papa Solomon give an affirmative nod, and then Gordon glanced back at the car where Oliver was still fiddling with the interior. He noticed Oliver reach for and grab an item he'd missed out of the glove compartment. Papa Solomon's son swiped his jacket off the passenger seat and stood up. He made a swift motion, tucking what Gordon believed was his shirt into his pants. Oliver then put his coat on around him, closed the door, locked it, and caught up to him and Papa Solomon. He walked past them instead of keeping pace. He hustled to the front entrance of the Woodlawn lobby and opened the door. That's when Gordon noticed the Model 29 .44 caliber revolver tucked into Oliver's pants. Gordon looked up at Papa Solomon, a peculiar expression on his face. Papa Solomon returned the look, eyebrow arched high. He waited for Gordon to inquire, and Gordon did. "Caution, Papa Solomon?" he questioned.

"Madame Jeliya is back in Brooklyn," Papa Solomon began his answer. "She's working real hard to keep us outside of time. It's not like we got permission to be doing what we gotta do here. Oliver carries the piece in case something gets extreme. It's real and loaded, but it's only for show. I'll work an incant from there if we come across someone who think they an all-American cowboy." Papa Solomon waved Gordon forward. "Just keep on, movin' on, now."

Gordon took a peek over his shoulder. The day was still. There was no movement in the street, neither pedestrian nor motor vehicle. Gordon could barely see past the iron gate and down the winding driveway. But he could tell that nothing was moving. He thought he caught a glimpse of a car blurred by time's pause. As well, there was the halted movement of someone mid-step, walking past the grounds. Gordon moved forward. He strolled through the door first, held open by Oliver. Papa Solomon followed, and then Oliver followed him in, closing the door behind them.

The lobby was a revival of gothic architecture. The room was structured like a long archway, at one end of which was a reception desk. A young woman with a pixie cut to her brunette hair was seated behind the desk. She was in mid-conversation with an elderly gentleman, a boisterous expression frozen on her face. A wide smile colored the elderly gentleman's visage, his mouth open and at a standstill from his chat with the cheerful employee. Gordon noticed a man and woman, who looked to be in their mid-thirties, seated on a wooden bench. The woman was stalled in her action of removing an e-reader from her purse, and the man was in mid-scratch of his hair. Gordon wondered if the two were together, brother and sister, husband and wife, or of any relation to the elderly man standing at the front desk. Of course, he also speculated they could've just been strangers. Gordon didn't wonder long. Papa Solomon and Oliver guided him out of the lobby, through a pair of stained-glass doors, and onto the hallowed grounds of the cemetery.

The day turned hazy as Gordon stepped back outside. Clouds encroached on the shimmering, blue welkin, and the sun ducked behind them as if it was a chief manservant excusing himself from his master's workroom to allow privacy. Nature's movement was preternatural, and Gordon guessed that other means communed with Her to enable an instantaneous amendment. Fog crept onto the burial grounds. The change was as beautiful as it was haunting.

Gordon continued to follow Papa Solomon and Oliver. They

trekked past mausoleums and an assortment of erected memorials. They moved into the large graveyard, passing through the rows of headstones and grand memorial statues. Gordon spotted Papa Solomon's older sister, Carolyn-Theresa Dumas, sitting atop one of the gravestones. She wore a long, sleeveless white dress with frills at the hem. The ruffled, shoulder-wide straps of her dress hid the black, circular, Dii Mauri tattoo inked on her left shoulder. A ceremonial, lilac colored apron was worn over her dress. A headscarf covered her thick, ash-colored Afro and she wore white slippers on her feet. She moved against the stillness of time, unaffected by the transcendental pause in the atmosphere.

Carolyn-Theresa Dumas, called Maman Anansi, chief matriarch of Fable Avenue, was fifty-six years of age with a round face and silky, oak-brown skin. She held a cigar in her right hand, and in her left, a polished, wooden African goblet half filled with rum. Her head was cocked back in laughter, cigar smoke escaping through her guffaws. She was laughing at the anecdotes recited by the man who stood near her. He was a tall, handsome black man dressed in a black tuxedo with tails on the jacket. Approaching closer, Gordon noticed sewing pins sticking out of the man's arms.

Papa Solomon chuckled as they drew nearer to his sister and the tall man. "Old Black," Papa Solomon called the man to attention. The man he called 'Old Black' turned and stepped into Papa Solomon's handshake that transitioned into a gentleman's embrace. He greeted Papa Solomon with his title and then stepped away from the brotherly hug.

Papa Solomon moved aside and walked up to his sister who, upon his approach, hopped off the gravestone after taking one last puff from her cigar. It was this action that caused Gordon to notice the items placed in front of the gravestone. Carolyn had been careful not to disturb them when her feet hit the ground. Laid in front of the gravestone of a man named Benjamin "Black Herman" Rucker, dated as being born on June 6, 1892 and passing April 15, 1934, were a bottle of rum and two ritual bowls. One was filled with water. The other was filled with a mix of water, oils, juices from various fruits, and a sprinkle of herbs. There was also a quill made from a large feather, a white face-towel, an old eight-by-five, leather bound book, and a card that was four-by-two in dimension. Drawn on the card was a detailed, colored picture of an African woman wearing a blue dress with a wide, frilly bell. On her head she wore a beaded veil attached to an elaborate headdress. She swept the earth floor with a broom, a small campfire burning near her.

Carolyn hugged her brother and said with cigar smoke seeping from between her lips, "Vencil! There you are, boy! Rucker's been entertaining me with some of his old exploits, most of them about the behind-the-stage antics and politics of his grand shows. Miss Trinidad was here too, prepping her voice to give a concert in the ethers later on. I'm gon' have to tune my radio to hear that. Oh, Mister Dumas and I will dance to that tonight!" Her eyes fell on Gordon and she moved away from Papa Solomon. She took two strides to stand in front of him. She passed her cigar to Papa Solomon and said, "Here, Vencil. You puff on that." Papa Solomon took the cigar from his sister. Carolyn took a moment to set down her goblet of rum, and then she stood up and cupped Gordon's chin in the palm of her hands. "Ah, Mister Goodspeed," she said to him. "You are so handsome. Today is your day, child."

Papa Solomon puffed on the cigar and exhaled. He said to his sister, "Carolyn, that boy is no child."

Gordon's eyebrow rose in reaction to Papa Solomon's statement. Carolyn continued to beam and replied to Papa Solomon, "I know that, Vencil. He's a young man. Nineteen years old today. Are you ready for the day, Gordon?"

"Yes, Maman Anansi," Gordon replied, addressing the chief matriarch with her proper title.

Maman Anansi removed her hands from Gordon's face. She ordered him to take off his coat and shirt, and when Gordon looked hesitant she said to him, "Gordon, don't you worry. I'll have an incant warming you. You pay this chill no mind. You think I'd be out here with no sleeves if I wasn't cozied up to a warm incant? Now go on and strip up top until you're bare."

At the same moment, Papa Solomon requested Oliver and Rucker to make a sweep of the grounds. "I know nothing should be moving, but that doesn't mean nothing can be moving. You know?" Oliver and Rucker nodded their heads. Papa Solomon said to Rucker, "I also want you to give my wife some assistance. She's working real hard to keep us outside of time."

"Thelema's doing this by herself?" asked Rucker.

Maman Anansi moved her eyes to Rucker. "You've had me entertained, Rucker, but not distracted. I've been helping my sister-in-law this whole time." Rucker's eyes widened amazed at Maman Anansi's revelation. "I'll have to let go so I can perform this boy's rites. Madame Jeliya will need every ounce of her concentration when I do so."

"Of course, Maman Anansi," Rucker said still impressed. He assured both Maman Anansi and Papa Solomon, "The transition will be even. Madame Jeliya won't feel any burden."

"Thank you, Rucker," said Papa Solomon.

"We'll keep an eye out too," Oliver vowed.

"And if we do see something?" asked Rucker. "Or sense something?"

Maman Anansi took Gordon's shirt and suit jacket, folding them neatly and placing them over the gravestone. "You won't," she answered Rucker. "We are well guarded. We are well outside of time. Stanley and his wicked wife will be none-the-wiser, even with their strongest trick. They ain't lookin' for this." She turned around and ordered, "Now go on, you two."

Rucker bowed, and then he and Oliver left to attend to their sweep of the grounds.

Maman Anansi turned to Gordon. He was shivering, the cold pricking his bare skin. Maman Anansi closed her eyes and communed with Rucker, giving him the reins to assist Madame Jeliya miles away in Brooklyn. Free of that burden, Maman Anansi refocused her thoughts, calling upon the voices of her late mother, grandmother, and great grandmother to guide her own. She sang in a slow, sultry blues note that resonated like a spiritual, *"Oh, burden, burden. Lift away now and go on."*

Maman Anansi's voice was like an anesthetic needle prick. There was a sharp puncture from her voice, and then came soothing warmth that annulled the cold. Gordon relaxed. Maman Anansi's soulful incanted notes shrouded him. He waited patiently as Fable Avenue's chief matriarch next instructed Papa Solomon. She requested her brother to pass the card and to return her cigar. He did as his older sister ordered, and she took the two items passed to her. Then Maman Anansi directed Gordon to kneel and close his eyes. "Keep your head up straight, Gordon," she told him.

On his knees, head up straight, and upper body bare, Gordon waited with his eyes closed. Papa Solomon began clapping in a slow, steady rhythm. Then Gordon felt the blow of cigar smoke cloak his face. He didn't inhale, and therefore didn't cough. He could hear Maman Anansi waving the smoke away, using the card with the colorfully, detailed picture drawn on it. More smoke was blown against Gordon's chest and shoulders, and Maman Anansi waved it away as she had done before. Gordon could hear Maman Anansi walking behind him. *"Cleansing smoke,"* he heard Maman Anansi sing in a deep, soulful harmony as she fanned the card above Gordon's head. She puffed on her cigar, blew more smoke around the back of his neck, shoulders, and down his back. *"Wash the ghosts away,"* she recited in song, sweeping the card around Gordon, clearing the smoke away from his naked, upper body. Papa Solomon backed his sister's singing with soulful howls and ongoing, rhythmic claps.

Maman Anansi puffed and exhaled smoke around Gordon's hair, and then she moved it away with the card. She repeated the words she sang earlier, and Papa Solomon clapped and wailed behind her voice. Gordon felt a vibration running through his body, and it seemed his knees left the ground. Though he wasn't floating, Gordon wouldn't have been surprised if he opened his eyes and saw himself hovering above the ground. But a higher sense touched everything around him. He was very aware of the gravestones, the grass, the entire grounds, and the bodies buried within the earth. The burial ground was filled with experience. Time stacked upon time. Stories stacked upon stories. Emotion came like a tidal wave, but Gordon was able to ride it as Maman Anansi blew smoke around him and waved it away. Gordon's awareness of time at a standstill was heightened; giving him an understanding that any movement made against the stillness was divine. The puff of smoke was divine. The wave of the card was divine. Maman Anansi's voice and Papa Solomon's backing vocals and clapping were divine. The surrounding stillness, the movement, and the buried experiences all connected to Gordon.

Papa Solomon ceased clapping.

Maman Anansi guided Gordon to bend his neck forward and then he felt the mixed solution of water, juices, oil, and herbs saturate his hair. The tincture was still cool, but it wasn't biting against Gordon's scalp, coursing through his tight twists at the root. Maman Anansi hummed a spiritual as she rubbed the solution deep into Gordon's scalp, and though she made sure that none of the mixture dripped past Gordon's brow, he could taste the sweet solution on his lips and tongue. The more Maman Anansi worked the concoction into his scalp, the more Gordon tasted it, and it started to satiate him. Gordon hadn't realized how hungry he'd been, but the concoction made him very aware of his appetite as it was massaged through his scalp and somehow fed his hunger and quenched his thirst.

Gordon kept his eyes closed, but he could sense Maman Anansi dipping her hands in the bowl that was filled with solution. She finished washing Gordon's hair, but had not yet completed the cleansing ritual. The next thing Gordon felt was the second bowl, filled with only water, being poured gently onto his scalp. Maman Anansi dried Gordon's head and hair with the face towel, and then told him to open his eyes and stand.

The day was still possessed by gray and fog, but it was brighter to Gordon. Maman Anansi instructed him to dry his scalp and hair as she turned and picked up the African goblet half filled with rum and the bottle of rum as well. She filled the cup back to the top. Papa Solomon took the bottle from his sister and placed it down as he took up the large feathered quill and the bowl filled with water. He took a stance in front of Gordon and began dipping the feathered end of the quill into the clear water. He ordered Gordon to stand up straight, and Gordon did. Papa Solomon bent his knees a little and then brushed the wet feather against Gordon's chest in a pattern of various ancient African, theurgic symbols. Gordon chuckled for the first few strokes, as they tickled. He tightened his chest and stomach muscles until Papa Solomon's feathered brush strokes couldn't be felt.

Gordon was quiet for the rest of the ritual. After nine distinct water tattoos were brushed onto him from chest to back, the exercise was complete.

Maman Anansi stood in front of Gordon as Papa Solomon moved aside. She presented the wooden goblet to Gordon. "Take and drink. Cover the six outer directions before you do so."

Gordon took the ornate, wooden cup. Maman Anansi moved away from him as he took a big sip of rum from the goblet. Gordon tilted his head back and spat a hazy spray of rum into the sky. He spat a hazy burst toward the ground, and then to his left, right, in front and in back of him. Then he swallowed the remaining rum. Maman Anansi stepped forward and took the cup. She said to Gordon, "We are descended from a conscious people of incantors and conjurors." She smiled and added, "This be true." Gordon smiled back and nodded his head in respect. Maman Anansi continued, "We also come from a people displaced. Broken and enslaved. That understanding must *never* be ignored." Gordon nodded again, a stern expression fixed on his face. "So be our duty, Gordon Goodspeed, as conscious incantors and conjurors to redraft a proper composition of the entirety of our history. We will make our story whole, wide, and expansive like the cosmos that it reflects. We will make rain, pulled from Iemanja's water, and her waters will be respected. Cleanse. Drink. Swim. No one will be an enemy to her water." Maman Anansi then concluded, "But if there be burning crosses and white hoods at the gates of our community for pumping cleansing water and churning Yeye's cosmos, then we shall call upon the lilac flame to strike them down."

Papa Solomon called out, "Bones, brains, and clouds covered in the cosmos' ink. You walk as the cosmos. The cosmic fabric a ghost as your shadow, then solid it be your flesh." He stepped up beside his sister. The two made room for one another as they stood in front of Gordon. "Your ancestors' spirits danced around you at nine," said Papa Solomon, speaking of the first gateway rites given to all nine-year-old boys and girls of the Fable Avenue community.

"You were then dipped in Ayizan's blessed water," Maman Anansi recounted with a smile. And then Papa Solomon joined his sister to speak as one, "And your pieces came together at the age of fourteen."

"Now, your hair has been washed," said Maman Anansi.

"And your body has been brushed with favors in a language used by the great old ones before you, before us all," Papa Solomon continued the benediction.

And Maman Anansi concluded, "Gordon Goodspeed, through your second gateway rites, you have received on this day, a blessing." The two of them smiled. Papa Solomon reached out a hand, which Gordon received and shook with a firm, hard shake. He then turned to Maman

Anansi and walked into her embrace.

Gordon stepped back, a wide smile on his face. The two elders continued to praise him as they each indulged in the rum and cigar. Maman Anansi turned around and took Gordon's clothes off the gravestone to return to him. He received his shirt and put it back on. Buttoned up, Maman Anansi handed him his suit jacket, and Gordon too placed it back around him. As he smoothed out his jacket, Papa Solomon presented to Gordon the dingy, leatherbound book. He instructed, "Don't open it. Not yet."

"Yessir," said Gordon, fingers in a position ready to do just that. But he stayed his movement as Papa Solomon placed his hand over the front cover of the book and kept it closed.

Papa Solomon emphasized, "There's an incant holding it together. It's old."

"Understood," assured Gordon.

Then a pair of arms wrapped around Gordon and lifted him up, taking him by surprise. Oliver hollered, "And he's received his family blessing!" He set Gordon down. "My dude. How you feel?"

"Feel okay," Gordon said, regaining composure from Oliver's actions.

"You ain't finished yet, kid," Oliver reminded. "You get your tat' in a couple of days. I got a nightshift tonight with a day on call tomorrow, but I'll be helping Wilson run the curio shop. I can get to you Friday."

"Okay. Cool," Gordon accepted.

Rucker reported to Papa Solomon and Maman Anansi, "There was nothing on the grounds. Nothing manifested, nothing sensed."

"Thank you, Rucker," Maman Anansi expressed. "Any commune with Madame Jeliya?"

Rucker nodded. "She's doing fine," he revealed. "She didn't feel a thing when I took over for you. I was a little worried about myself, though. Having that bottle of rum on my grounds got me a little loopy." Everyone chuckled. "But Madame Jeliya's on her own now, and she's stated she won't be able to keep us cloaked for too long. You all better get moving."

"Well," Maman Anansi stated, "let's hurry on as the spirit suggests. Will you gentlemen gather these things here? Thank you." She told Rucker, "Don't you worry about none of this, Rucker. Your job is done here. This is going off the grounds to my car."

"Understood, ma'am," he said as he bowed.

Maman Anansi hugged Rucker. "Thank you so much."

"My pleasure, Maman Anansi. My pleasure," he assured.

Rucker and Papa Solomon shook hands and exchanged farewells. Then the well-dressed man turned to Oliver and said, "Good scoping the grounds with you, Oliver." And Oliver replied by saying, *"Absolutely, Old Black."* Rucker faced Gordon and shook his hand. "Congratulations, Gordon Goodspeed. I do hope something comes from this blessing."

Gordon replied, "If nothing else, Mister Rucker, we've at least brought back a family tradition."

"Yes, indeed, Gordon. Yes indeed."

Rucker stood to the side as Papa Solomon and Oliver gathered the items around the gravestone. Papa Solomon instructed Gordon not to participate. "Oliver and I got this. Just relax y'self for a moment," the elder ordered.

Gordon didn't mind. He did need to relax. The tingle of a heightened awareness still stirred inside him. But it wasn't long before Oliver and Papa Solomon collected all the items. Maman Anansi kept the goblet of rum in her hand, nursing the few sips that were left. With everything together, the group said their final goodbyes to Rucker, and left the grounds. Rucker watched them all disappear through the cemetery. Once they were out of sight, having returned to the lobby's entrance, Rucker's image faded, and so did the fog.

Gordon stepped through the stained-glass doors back into the lobby. He followed the others passed the room's still occupants and into the parking lot. Gordon noticed the clouds pull back and reveal the morning's bright, blue sky and dazzling sun. Sound and motion were restored to the day. The incant breathing warmth through Gordon's body started receding, but enough remained for him to withstand the air's chill. He stood back and watched as Maman Anansi opened her car's trunk and Oliver and Papa Solomon set inside the items used in his ceremony.

Maman Anansi closed the trunk, stepped to Gordon and cupped his chin with her hands together. "I am so happy, Gordon," she said to him with a sincere expression. "I'm so happy we've been able to accomplish this second gateway ritual for you. Like you said, at the very least, we've restored a tradition."

"Yes, Maman Anansi," Gordon replied with half a smile, feeling the chief matriarch was coddling him too much like a child.

"Now," she began, letting go of Gordon's chin. "I'm heading to Harlem to bless your things. You'll have your room back. I'll tell your father and brother you did well. I'm so sorry this rite couldn't be performed within its usual setting, but this has been for the sake of precaution."

"I know, Maman Anansi," Gordon assured her.

"Follow us," Papa Solomon instructed his sister. "We're heading back to grab the youngest Brickhouse boy. He was suspended from school for a fight. His mother wants him on community duty."

Maman Anansi scowled, furrowing her brow. "And let it be duty too, *hard* duty, not just a longer practice of his violin. That boy loves that instrument too much. There's no way an extended practice would be punishment. Real duty, hear?"

"Of course, Carolyn," Papa Solomon retorted arms up.

Maman Anansi rolled her eyes, but fixed her face when she returned her attention to Gordon. "You listen to Papa Solomon's guidance with that book, Gordon."

"I will," he told her.

Maman Anansi kissed his cheek and bid Gordon and the others farewell. Oliver hugged and kissed his aunt and walked to his father's car to assume his position in the driver's seat. Papa Solomon hugged his sister before she slid into her car, then he and Gordon trekked across the lot where his Cadillac was parked. Oliver already had the car running. Gordon and Papa Solomon returned to their respective seats. When the two were strapped in, Oliver backed up and pulled out of the parking space. He maneuvered the vehicle through the gates and onto Jerome Avenue. Maman Anansi was close behind.

Gordon looked out of the back window and asked Papa Solomon, "Will she be okay? She drank a good amount of rum."

Papa Solomon replied in a relaxed tone, "She'll be fine. She didn't have too much. Besides, she's been savin' her strength for today. That rum had no real effect." He blinked his eyes, trying to focus. "I'm a different story, on the other hand." He chuckled and then slapped Gordon on the shoulder. "I'm just playing, young man." He asked, "But what about you? Those good gulps of rum, and the herbs rubbed into you got you swimmin' in the head?"

"I feel fine, sir," Gordon answered. He looked through each window and then returned his gaze to Papa Solomon. "I do feel a heightened sense of awareness." Gordon chuckled as he further explained, "It's like I'm conscious that everything exists." He chuckled harder. His eyes happened to look up to spot Oliver. He was smiling, as was Papa Solomon.

The elder notified, "The tincture in your wash might have you seeing things. Don't worry. Awake or in a deep dream, you might experience some things." Gordon's light mood cut. Papa Solomon read the concern spelled on Gordon's face. "Like I said, don't worry. It's natural," he reassured. Gordon tried to relax. Papa Solomon had more news. "You might experience a discoloration in your eyes. Again, that's normal." His eyes went to the book in Gordon's lap. Gordon looked down at the book too. "Now, let's talk the purpose of that old book. What you got there is the *Nigrum Nigrius Nigro*." Papa Solomon translated, "*Black, blacker than black itself.* It's the philosophical night, the palpable shadow. Your great grandfather, Madison Goodspeed, secured that book a long time back, in London. People say it's not the real thing." Papa Solomon made a face and exclaimed, "We'll see. Regardless, it has our rites and customs written inside." He leaned toward Gordon and said, "Listen closely, this next set of instructions are the most important for the rites to continue." Gordon became attentive. Papa Solomon relayed to him, "Nineteen seconds, after the nineteenth minute, of the nineteenth hour, you will turn to the nineteenth page of this book and stare into it."

"That's quite specific, Papa Solomon," Gordon jibbed.

Papa Solomon beamed. "It is indeed, young man," he replied with a kind nod. He lifted a stern finger and reminded, "Follow to a tee."

"Yessir," said Gordon. He asked to be sure, "The nineteenth hour is seven o'clock this evening, correct?

"It is indeed," Papa Solomon repeated. "But we're leaving out the nineteenth day after the nineteenth birthday part of all this. I hope the spirit understands how desperate we are. Hope we can connect to it even if we're not word-for-word aligned with the instructions. Hope it can adjust with us." Papa Solomon sat back and looked out the window. Gordon did the same as Papa Solomon remarked, "That's a lot of hopin' goin' on." Oliver turned the radio on, and the music was the only sound inside the car the entire ride back to Harlem.

Gordon had more questions, but he kept them to himself. He wanted to know what gazing into the nineteenth page of the *Nigrum Nigrius Nigro* under the prescribed circumstances would bring. What was the book's origin? If gazing into its pages were a success, what then? Gordon hypothesized nothing occurred with any of his cousins that had gone through the second gateway rites. The rites wouldn't have been repeated if any of their outcomes were favorable. Cedron never went through the rites. He was too busy healing from his injuries, and when he awoke, there was too much concern to carry out the ceremony.

In Harlem, parked outside the Brickhouse residence, Papa Solomon exited the car. Oliver turned the radio down, but started no conversation. Gordon watched as Papa Solomon came around the front of the car, stepped onto the sidewalk and then up to the Brickhouse's front door. Gordon turned his head and observed in the opposite direction, across the street, Maman Anansi spring from her car and walk up to the front door of his house with a proud, regal sway in her step.

"Your aunt retired yet?" Gordon asked Oliver. "This year or next year?"

"Next year," Oliver answered looking in Maman Anansi's direction. He turned his head to respond to Gordon. "Her firm is hurt," he said with a smile. "She brought her blessings to them. They don't even know it. But they saw the results. It made them the hottest law firm in New York. Maman Anansi represented all her clients proper." They both eyed Maman Anansi knocking on the front door and wait for an answer. "But, they still got Maman Anansi Two-Point-O there. Won't be the same, though. No offense to my cousin. Mother and daughter ain't gonna be the dynamic duo after next year."

"How is Stephanie?" Gordon asked.

"She's okay," Oliver updated. "She continues to express her hurt even though Maman Anansi and Uncle Andre were able to conjure Enock's spirit." Then Oliver added, "He's doin' okay, his spirit's cool. Stephanie and him talk, but she's still hurt by his passing. But that was her little brother, y'know."

Gordon nodded and then asked, "How's your sister?"

Oliver turned around, grin on his face. "Who's askin'?"

"Me. Only me."

Oliver made a face. He answered, "Tell *Cedron* she's still doin' fine out there in Chicago."

"Man, it's only me askin'," Gordon reiterated. "Only me."

"That's cool," Oliver addressed, unconvinced. "She always askin' about Cedron, catchin' up on him, even when she with another dude. You want to give your brother a heads up, she'll be in town at the end of October for the Spirit Festival."

"I'm sure they'll be on opposite ends of any room we gather in," Gordon expressed.

"Not something she'd like to do, but I suspect that too," Oliver commented. "She still likes your brother, but he…doin' his thing…"

"Yeah…" Gordon responded. He saw his father answer the door and greet Maman Anansi, bursting with excitement to see her. Gordon saw the chief matriarch return a smile to his father and then shoo him into the house so Maximilian couldn't get a peek at him. The front door closed once Maman Anansi entered, and Gordon once again shifted his attention to Papa Solomon's task. He was already returning to the car, twelve-year-old Dajon Brickhouse walking next to him. He pointed to the backseat and Dajon entered. Gordon moved over, making room. Papa Solomon hopped into the passenger's seat. He turned and dropped house keys into Gordon's hand. Gordon accepted and pocketed the keys. "For the house in Brooklyn," Papa Solomon said to him. "From your father. Thought I'd wait 'til after the ceremony to give you 'em." He closed the door and Oliver pulled the car onto the street, making a way to Brooklyn. Gordon glanced at his house as they drove off, hoping to get a glimpse of his father or Cedron. But all he saw was the front room through the windows, and no one stood near them.

Gordon scoped Dajon. The brown-skinned boy was silent and sulking, his nimble build scrunched up against the door, head on the window. He wore jeans, sneakers, and a black and purple hooded sweatshirt. Atop his head, covering his low-trimmed hair was a navy-blue skully.

A soft tone rang in Gordon's right ear, appearing to come from a tingling sensation running from the back of his neck to the crown of his head. The tone buzzed, its timbre shifting as if someone was tuning a radio. Gordon concentrated and then realized the soft resonance was echoing as Dajon's young voice. *Let me explain,* it said in a warbled buzz reflecting the voice of the twelve-year-old boy sitting next to him. Instead of being intrigued, Gordon contorted his face into a grimace. Dajon looked up, having felt Gordon's eyes on him. Gordon said to him, "You want to explain why you're breakin' my heart, kid?" He jabbed a finger in Dajon's direction, eyebrows raised. "Your stupidness is messin' with *my* day." Gordon's exasperation was mimicked in his tone.

"I'm sorry, Gordon," Dajon expressed with sincerity.

"My day!" Gordon stressed. "The day I receive my blessing, and a day that's sacred to my family and our community." Gordon breathed. "I oughtta rope you up, kid. What the hell sorta trouble you gettin' into? You ain't one of them wannabe thug idiots. You understand that you come from something."

Dajon already heard much of the same angry and disappointed speech from his mother and father, and a little from Papa Solomon before getting into the car. But with Gordon, as mad as he was, Dajon felt he had a chance to divulge his side of the story, considering his brother Benny hadn't been around as of late.

"It was my friend!" exclaimed Dajon, confidence and volume increasing in his voice.

Papa Solomon asked from the front seat, "You got into it with your friend, li'l man?" Papa Solomon sounded suspicious, though his voice continued to resonate with disappointment when he asked, "Or are you coverin' for him?"

The tingling and resonance again came to Gordon. The sound tuned, shifting into a soft echo of Dajon's protesting voice. *No,* it said. *But now I can give my side.* Gordon, looking attentive, waited for the sentiment to present itself through Dajon's lips. The boy shouted in defense, "No, no! It ain't like that, Papa Solomon. Not at all, I swear!" Dajon was relieved to have the attention his side of the story deserved. "This kid I got to know recently, his name's Noah. His family just moved here a couple of weeks ago from the Bronx. He was gettin' hassled by these two big kids, high school kids. Bullies," Dajon clarified. "They always doin' somethin' to somebody at some time. They've tried to jump on me, especially when they see me carryin' my violin. I just make fun of 'em. I start embarrassin' 'em. They back off. Ain't ever got violent with me. Maybe I got a conjure, some good light shinin' on me or somethin'." He looked at Gordon and expressed, "I make them fools look dumb. Other kids are scared of 'em. I mean, so am I, but, if I'm gonna get a beatin', I might as well get some verbal licks in. But it's luckily never come to that with me." Dajon spoke quickly, but was articulate. "I saw them jump Noah. Violent. They punched him and threw him down. They kicked him while he was on the ground." He paused, and though he wasn't ashamed at defending his friend, his voice sounded otherwise. "I jumped in. I was stickin' up for him. I was defendin' him."

Gordon redefined his expression from a scowl to a proud grin. "Is that right? You laid these big kids out?"

"Gordon!" Papa Solomon hollered from the front. "Don't encourage this boy's antics, no matter how noble." Papa Solomon's deep, authoritative voice ushered in complete silence. But it didn't stop Gordon from tossing a congratulatory wink of his eye at Dajon who, feeling better, returned a smile. Then Papa Solomon asked, "So, li'l man, you laid them boys out?"

Gordon winked again at Dajon.

The twelve-year-old boy answered in a dignified voice, "On the floor, but not out cold." Gordon applauded Dajon. Oliver blurted praises. It was reluctant, but Papa Solomon beamed a subtle smile and nodded his head in approval. "I surprised 'em," Dajon recounted. "People think I ain't about nuthin' cuz I look like I ain't got nuthin'. And two seventeen-year-old idiots was not expectin' what I gave 'em. And I wasn't using any incants to aid me." But Dajon pushed the envelope of everyone's approval when he expressed, "I beat they asses!"

"Whoa!" Gordon and Oliver barked together.

Gordon smacked the back of Dajon's head. "An elder's present. What's wrong with you, sun? The mouth."

Dajon apologized.

Papa Solomon ignored the language Dajon used. He told the boy, "Don't be too proud goin' all Batman on them boys. You find another way to handle things, hear? And you're still on block detail. Cleaning."

Dajon wanted to tell Papa Solomon that he was more partial to Spider-Man or The Flash, or anybody from the X-Men. Instead he uttered in a deflated voice, "Yes, Papa Solomon."

The Fable Avenue patriarch asked, "These two boys affiliated with people you should be wary of?"

"No, sir," Dajon answered.

Papa Solomon still advised Dajon to be cautious of retaliation and suggested the young boy receive a blessing to protect him. "We'll have it extend to those around you. We don't want someone else hurt in an effort to come back at you."

"Yes, Papa Solomon."

"I'll explain the ordeal to your mother," Papa Solomon assured Dajon. "She's furious, and I know she didn't let you get a word in edgewise. The truth should calm her down some. I can only guess what your father's like, but I'll explain to him too."

"Thank you, sir."

Then Papa Solomon requested Dajon recount the brave narrative on how he defeated two oppressive tyrants in the area who skipped their own school to terrorize his. Dajon relayed his tale with grand excitement. He was descriptive, and his story needed no embellishment. Dajon gave a backstory to the ordeal, bringing in other characters as victims, including a girl named Melinda, which everyone guessed was Dajon's crush, considering how his voice elevated and eyes widened a little more when he spoke about her. Dajon said she was smiling when he and the two boys were carted away. He was taken to the principal's office, while the two bullies were escorted from the premise by police officers. Papa Solomon repeated for Dajon not to take undue pride in the altercation.

Soon the car was passing into Brooklyn, and not too long after, was on Fable Avenue. Oliver slowed the car close to the curb, making a stop at 421 Fable Avenue, the Goodspeed's Brooklyn residence. Gordon tapped Dajon on the shoulder with a balled fist. "Stay out of trouble," he advised Dajon in a joking tone. The young boy responded with a chuckle that he would. Gordon said to Oliver, "I'll see you in a day or two, right? For the tat'."

Oliver replied, "You definitely will, kid. I get to perform *my* ritual on you. We'll see what you're made of. Dii Mauri or Ka Mauri. Oh, and don't worry. There's no incant, but you won't feel anything."

Gordon opened the door. He and Papa Solomon jumped out at the same time. With the *Nigrum Nigrius Nigro* under his arm, Gordon walked around the back of the car and up onto the sidewalk. Papa Solomon allowed Gordon to take lead through the waist-high iron gates and over to the garden entrance. Gordon removed his keys from his pocket. He unlocked the entry gate, opened it, and then unlocked the heavy, wooden door beyond it. Gordon stepped inside a small hall area that opened to a semi-open-floor design. A large family room was the first area to step into. The kitchen was on the right. Closer to the back of the family room, located also on the right, was the dining area. Load-bearing walls in a T-formation separated the rooms. Mounted on the wall facing the front room, were family photos surrounding an entertainment center. All electronics had been removed for the purpose of Gordon's rites.

Gordon walked farther into the family room. Papa Solomon followed after locking the gate and door behind him. Gordon set the medieval tome on the round coffee table and took a seat on the couch. Papa Solomon sat next to him and asked, "You'll be okay?"

Gordon nodded. "Yes, Papa Solomon," he replied. "There's clothes upstairs in the bedroom I usually sleep in. The heat's been turned on for the season. I know how to adjust it. And either my father or uncle stocked the fridge." Gordon made a face. His eyes went to the ceiling, and then he inspected the rest of the room. He put his eyes back on Papa Solomon and stated, "But all forms of entertainment are gone. I feel like I'll get cabin fever."

Papa Solomon chuckled. "Well, go out to the courtyard to get fresh air." Then Papa Solomon added sternly, "Only the courtyard. But that's just for tonight, up until you gaze into that book." He pointed at the tome. "Call me only in case of an emergency. Like I said, the herbs in the concoction worked into you might have you seeing things. You don't worry. Again, you might have a discoloration in your eyes. But you'll be fine." Papa Solomon stood. He said to Gordon, "And don't be sad if nothing happens. That's okay too."

Gordon nodded his head. He was caught between the emotions of wanting something to happen, just to see what that 'something' would be, and then there was a side of him that would be relieved if nothing happened at all. And though Papa Solomon expressed an assured sentiment that all would be fine should nothing come of today's ritual, Gordon's ear picked up a subtle tone of disillusion peppering the elder's words.

Papa Solomon continued, "I'll bring somebody by with a proper meal." He moved around the coffee table. "No need to stand," he told Gordon. "I can see my way out. You just relax from here on out."

Gordon wanted to tell Papa Solomon about his heightened senses connecting with Dajon and empathizing with the young boy, but he figured Papa Solomon would explain it away as just being a side effect of the solution rubbed into his scalp. So, Gordon just sat there, watching Papa Solomon leave the house. He heard the car door open and shut, and then he heard the car ease away. Gordon stood up and walked to the garden entrance and locked the doors. He started unbuttoning his shirt as he walked to the stairs. He made his way up to the parlor entrance and then to the next level to find sweatpants and a hooded sweatshirt to change into.

Raymond Shaw stood attentive at the rear passenger-side door of a black town car parked curbside at the luxurious Wolverhampton hotel in Manhattan. He waited patiently for his pickup next to the Goodspeed-Brickhouse livery vehicle. His were a trio of executives ending their three-day stay in the city. The men were returning to their base of operation in Chicago after attending a business conference. Upon pulling up to the curb, Raymond placed a call informing the front desk that he was outside and waiting to transport the men to LaGuardia Airport. His brother, Edmundo "Edmond" Yiao-tian Shaw, answered the phone at the front desk and relayed Raymond's message to the room of Janek Coleman, one of the businesses executives.

Jamie Ryan sat in the car's passenger seat. This was his shift, but for the purpose of a well-calculated artful dodge, Jamie's presence called for him to play the role of an orientating new hire. His nervous jitters only added to the role. He looked outside the car window and watched the hotel's revolving doors breathe a herd of people in and out, the exiting patrons looking for a place to go and for transportation to get them there. Jamie looked up at Raymond who remained still while other cabdrivers honked or hollered for attention. Then he witnessed Raymond place a single finger against his Bluetooth earpiece, and Jamie assumed it was Edmond notifying Raymond that the businessmen were on their way out. Raymond nodded. Both he and Jamie put their attention on the hotel's revolving doors. One-by-one, the three well-dressed businessmen emerged from the hotel. Each had a suitcase in hand and a duffle bag thrown on a shoulder, smiles on their faces.

Raymond stepped up to Janek Coleman, having seen the gentleman a day earlier during surveillance with Edmond. Janek was the oldest of the three, approaching his late forties. He was white, bald, with a thick, graying mustache and an average frame. There was no mistaking Janek as anything other than the alpha male of the crew, the seasoned veteran of whatever business dealings these men had. The other two gentlemen were much younger, late twenties to early thirties. They were cut from the same mold as Janek, alpha males in training. All that separated them from Janek were their full heads of flowing hair, one brunette and the other blonde, and their clean-shaven faces.

"Hello, Mister Coleman, sir," Raymond addressed the alpha businessman. Raymond reached for Janek's suitcase and bag. Janek thanked him. Raymond turned to the other gentlemen and reached for their bags. The men politely declined Raymond's offer, believing all of the bags would be too much for him. Raymond insisted, "Oh, no. It'll be okay. It's cool, guys." His tone was soft and courteous, as non-threatening as one could be. Janek ordered his protégés to give up their travel grips, and Raymond proved he could handle the bags with ease. He turned and led the men back to the livery car. Jamie followed Raymond's walk, head turning as the troupe moved around to the back of the car.

The trunk was already popped open. Raymond lifted the lid and organized the businessmen's travel bags inside. He positioned the bags all the way on the left side of the interior. At the back of the trunk was a long, empty duffle bag. Raymond made sure not to lay the businessmen's suitcases and bags atop the wide, deep spare tire compartment. The spare, however, was missing. Lying inside, curled in a tight, fetal position was Benjamin Brickhouse. The compartment, like the trunk, had been unlocked and was open just a crack. Even with the businessmen standing behind Raymond, they were none-the-wiser of Benjamin "Benny Jah" stowed away inside.

Raymond closed the trunk and walked to the passenger-side, rear door. He opened it and waved a hand to usher the men inside, smile on his face. The businessmen slipped into the car, the brunette protégé first, the blonde protégé second, and Janek Coleman last. The back was spacious enough for all three men. Raymond kept his smile until he closed the door. He turned and his well-mannered smile shifted into a sly grin. He removed his phone and dialed as he slipped into the front seat. He pressed a button on his Bluetooth earpiece and asked, "Settled in?"

"Settled," replied both Benny over the Bluetooth earpiece and Janek from the backseat.

Raymond beamed a smile up at the rearview mirror while eyeing the three men in the backseat. He looked at Jamie, smile still on his face. He said, "Always check your rearview before moving into traffic. The last thing you want is an accident with passengers in the car. It's not only bad for business, but you best believe there won't be a tip." The businessmen laughed. Janek agreed aloud. Raymond winked in the rearview mirror, checked his directions, and then steered the car onto the road. "LaGuardia, gentlemen?"

"Yes, good driver," Janek replied.

Raymond complied, and then continued to instruct Jamie on the proper etiquette for being a transport, service provider. Janek, with his men, went over the three-day stay, the conference, and what they would take back to Chicago. Inside the trunk, Benny Jah slid the spare tire compartment top off of him. The town car's trunk was spacious, but Benny maneuvered cautiously inside. He reached a gloved hand into his pocket and fished out a small flashlight. He flipped it on and crawled toward the duffle bags and suitcases. He opened one after the other, flashlight in his mouth, and rummaged through the luggage. He swiped MP3 players, watches, rings, two computer tablets, and a bundle of reserve cash. He stuffed his findings into the spare-tire compartment, covered the opening, and locked it closed. Then Benny made sure to prop the luggage, bags and cases, as he found them.

Benny snaked his body around, wiggling toward the large duffle bag at the back. He unzipped the bag, crawled inside, and zipped himself in. He lay flat to keep the bag's empty, wrinkled appearance. He cut the flashlight's power and dug into his pocket again. He removed his smartphone, turned it on, and grimaced as it buzzed. The noise wasn't too loud, and Benny dismissed the caller and dialed Raymond. "We've hit our marks."

"Okay," Raymond responded. "I have a drop at LaGuardia. Should be fifteen, twenty minutes. That okay?" His reply made it appear as if he was conversing with a dispatcher.

"I can breathe well, but hurry," Benny said to him.

"Is the pickup ready? All packed?" Raymond asked.

"I'm in the bag," stated Benny. "The grab is in the bag."

"Okay. Won't be long," assured Raymond.

Benny hung up and turned off his phone. He lay still, slowing his breathing and keeping it under control. He didn't worry. He thought about Gordon and the rites he was undertaking. He wished his friend well, and then his thoughts shifted to his brother. He hoped Papa Solomon wasn't too harsh on him, but he knew that Dajon would be cleaning various streets in Brooklyn, not just Fable Avenue. Benny understood the consequences, but he wondered how his brother had gotten into a violent tussle at school that even involved the appearance of cops. Benny promised if Cedron didn't keep him too busy with schemes, or their father didn't keep him too busy with actual work, he'd sit down with his brother and have an earnest talk with him.

The car turned, slowed down, stopped for lights, and continued on. Benny felt every turn. He remained relaxed as he waited for the final step that came with a grab such as this. The car stopped. He heard the pop of the trunk and went still. He believed even his heart slowed to a stop. He could feel Raymond lifting the businessmen's bags, and he listened as

Raymond played his courteous act. The trunk closed. Benny remained still. Through the trunk he could still hear Raymond giving his synthetic, polite goodbyes, wishing the businessmen a safe flight. *"Where you returning to?"* Raymond asked. Janek answered, *"Chicago."* Raymond responded, *"A wonderful city. I have an uncle there,"* he lied. *"I hope New York treated you well."* Janek assured Raymond it had once again, as this wasn't their first visit. Benny waited through all of this. He heard the official goodbyes and then the car door opened and closed. Raymond pulled away. Benny waited a moment, and then he unzipped the large duffle bag and emerged from it. It was easier now to negotiate inside the spacious trunk. He turned his flashlight on and moved the duffle bag behind him. He unhinged three clips at the back of the trunk and began pushing. He pushed hard once, harder twice, harder a third time. The back wall fell forward, and Benny crawled through to the backseat.

Raymond chuckled. He moved his eyes to the rearview mirror and asked, "What's our take, Jah?"

Benny flipped the backseat up, the hinges snapping into place. He sat back and took a breath, turning off his flashlight and pocketing it. "We got cash. Probably close to twenty-eight, twenty-nine hundred. Maybe a clean three thousand." He saw Raymond and Jamie grin. "We got a couple computer tablets. We got jewelry. Some MP3 players."

Raymond nodded. He stopped at a red light and said, "Let me call this in." He dialed Cedron first, putting him on hold as he dialed his brother Edmond to complete the conference call. Raymond spoke in code, "Hey, guys, the Giants scored well in today's game. But you guys did lose the bet we had from last night. Benny did the research and found out Moses held two tablets, and there's a description of him wearing jewelry in some translations. He definitely had something for him to tell the time with, and some music boxes."

"Yeah, but did he have any gold?" his brother Edmond asked, boyish, excited smile in his words.

"Yes he did," answered Raymond, passing through the light as it changed to green. "Almost three thousand pounds worth. Roughly twenty-eight hundred pounds."

"Ah," Edmond expressed delighted. "Well, we lost the bet, but King will have his tribute. That said, Raymond, we'll meet up after I get out of work here. I have to get to the store and return some items at the palisades. You and Benny come along."

"Okay. Will see the two of you later. Peace." Raymond hung up. He informed Benny and Jamie, "King and my brother are pleased." He told Jamie, "Take your next fare when it's called in. I'll give you the money our marks gave me, plus the tip. And it was a good tip. A hundred. Business cats always tryin' to showoff." Jamie thanked Raymond. "Benny and I will jump out and take the Seven into the city, and then we'll head back to Cedron." Raymond then told Benny, "We'll get these items to Edmond. He has a fence waiting. We'll get the stuff to him after he gets off work. Can you get a car?"

"Yeah, I can get the minivan," Benny responded. "Cedron can come with us." Benny didn't believe at all that Edmond and Raymond were the type to skim money. But having Cedron there would keep the transaction one hundred percent honest. Everyone would get their proper cut, and King would have his proper tribute.

"Pull out the backpack underneath my seat," Raymond ordered. "We'll stuff our grab in there. That's what I brought it for."

Benny pulled out the flattened, empty backpack that would carry the day's contraband. He set it aside and reminded Raymond and Jamie, "Most important, we're protected. This one is in the books."

"Thanks for that," said Raymond.

"Not a problem," Benny responded smoothly. "All these guys will believe is that some bag checkers at LaGuardia, or even O'Hare, snagged their shit. They'll be reimbursed. At the end of the day, it's money for us." Benny sat back, head against the window, thinking about Gordon, his younger brother, and the blessing surrounding this heist. Most importantly, he thought about the young woman who gave him the protective blessing, despite its cost coming from his cut.

"So how've you been passing the time?" asked Neyeli Kimball to Gordon Goodspeed. It was 6:40 in the evening. The sun's light clung to the day with a loose grip. The darkening, reddish-purple sky was too wide and threatening. Each passing minute noted the slip of the light's grasp. Gordon Goodspeed and Neyeli Kimball, a nineteen-year-old woman with orange-brown skin, hazel colored eyes, and a bright smile sat in the dining room of the Goodspeed's Brooklyn residence.

Gordon answered his friend, "I haven't." He dug into the plate of food Neyeli brought him from her family's restaurant. The plate was a fresh, hot mix of well-seasoned fish, kale, and red beans and rice.

This wasn't the first meal brought to Gordon. The first was a brunch, prepared by Neyeli's father, and brought to him by Papa Solomon. Neyeli prepared this meal after returning from her day on campus at Timothy Drew University. Neyeli leaned back in her chair, jean-covered legs crossed. "You been bored?"

"Not as much as I thought I'd be," Gordon admitted as he took a sizable mouthful. He chewed as he complimented, "This is good, Ney." He chewed more and swallowed. "I know you're studyin' business and marketing to keep the restaurant goin', but you better be preparing stuff in the back as well as running things up front."

Neyeli shook her head and smiled. "Thank you, Gordon," she said, leaning forward. She grabbed the Hima-style jug on the table and pulled an empty cup toward her. She poured the contents of the jug into the cup and handed it back to Gordon. He took a big gulp and Neyeli instructed in a soft voice, "Easy, lion. There's a kick in that drink. Rum. A little spirit for your spirit," Neyeli chuckled.

The drink was a mix of fruit plus the rum. It was a special drink served at Neyeli's family restaurant, with both an alcoholic version and a non-alcoholic version. It was called *dragon spit*, and no one quite knew where the name came from, but little Fable Avenue boys and girls loved to say the drink's name with giggles and drink it with delight. And the rum variant, often coupled with spices, always enlivened adult parties held on Fable Avenue. The amount of rum flavoring the contents of Gordon's jug was very mild, adding flavor but far too little alcohol to put him in a relaxed, dreamy state. But even though Neyeli had prepared the drink on Papa Solomon's orders, she felt the need to warn Gordon of the rum content, considering his heightened state after his gateway ritual.

Gordon heeded Neyeli's advice and slowed both his drinking and eating. He swallowed and said as he scooped another forkful of food, "Your boyfriend's scheming today."

"My boyfriend?" Neyeli retorted making a face.

Gordon smiled, fork hanging near his mouth. He looked up at Neyeli and clarified, "Benny." He saw Neyeli roll her eyes at the name. "Don't know what he's doing with my brother and that small crew, but he's gonna get himself into trouble."

Neyeli sucked her teeth and rolled her eyes again. "He'll be fine, like he has been for the last couple years he's been doing this. No need to worry about Benny."

Gordon paused. There again came the tingling sensation he'd felt in the car. Once more it ran from the back of his neck to the crown of his head, buzzing like a soft tone. As Gordon concentrated on the murmur, just as he'd done before, its timbre shifted like a tuning radio. The vibration increased as Gordon focused on the manifestation of a single thought, and that same single thought became more and more clear. Then he spoke his revelation aloud to Neyeli. "You've been giving him protection incants." He smiled and waited for Neyeli's confession.

"Not for free," she said folding her arms.

Gordon's expression dropped. He said in a disappointed tone, "*Neyeli…*"

Neyeli waved away Gordon's tone and crossed her arms. "Please, Gordon, don't go all Papa Solomon on me, or any of these other elders." Her grin returned and she looked away, wide eyes devouring everything around the room except Gordon. Then, with a flirtatious laugh not meant for Gordon, she returned her eyes to him. She fixed herself and said with a bit of concern, "I tried talking him out of it years ago. Trust me." She shook her head disappointed. "He became very loyal to Cedron after he was shot."

Gordon grimaced. "I know," he said in a low voice. He bit into the food gathered on his fork.

Neyeli questioned, "What's the matter?"

Gordon chewed and swallowed before he answered. He placed his fork down on his plate and sat back. "Benny was protecting himself. The closer I got to nineteen and my second gateway rites, the more danger I was in. He sided up with my brother because, hey, the danger haunting my brother already got him."

"I don't know about that, Gordon," Neyeli said, cautious to not start an argument. Gordon believed what he believed, but she didn't.

Gordon went back to eating. He said without looking up, "Well I do. Everyone whispered that there was a hex, a curse against performing the rites. Papa Solomon pretty much confirmed it this morning before my ceremony. Hell, it was the reason it was done in such an undercover way—and days early. Something—or someone—has been keeping an eye on us, unhallowed and ironically fallowed, I suppose. A good reason to stay away as my nineteen and time came up to bat." He collected more food from his plate with his fork, placed it near his mouth, and before he was about to take another bite, he dropped the fork and said, "Do you know Benny asked me to keep an eye on Dajon? And I'm thinkin', like, can't *you* do it, sun?" He went back to his food, now taking a bite and chewing through his anger. The food's taste dulled, and Gordon huffed.

"How is little-man Dajon?" Neyeli asked. "I heard he was on duty. What he do?"

"Got into a fight at school," Gordon answered as he finished his bite. "Nothin' much to worry about. He's suspended for a week." Gordon saw Neyeli's expression widen with alarm. "He was defending a kid from bullies," he explained. "A noble cause, right? We all would've done the same. Papa Solomon relaxed after he'd heard what the fuss was about, said he'd tell Dajon's parents and calm them down too. I know Mister Brickhouse is pissed." Gordon exhaled hard. "Then I wonder what he'd be like if he knew Benny was gettin' into dumb shit."

Neyeli shooed Gordon's comments away. "Like I said, you don't worry about Benny. He'll be fine."

"Your protective incant that strong?"

Neyeli cut Gordon a look.

"Okay…" Gordon said half-joking.

Neyeli spoke defensively, "Considering some of the activities that go on in our community—"

"You mean niggas?" Gordon conjectured.

"No," Neyeli responded. "I mean right here. On Fable Avenue. *Our* community." She then named, "My uncle's practice. The things he investigates for Lady Arachne. Wilson and Top Hat, and the things they're tasked with, also by Lady Arachne. The misfit crews around the country."

"All on orders for the better of community and culture," Gordon retorted. "Your boyfriend and my brother are doin' knuckleheaded shit. They've had some small, righteous grabs, but that ain't their intentions no more."

Neyeli disagreed, and protested, "Benny is *not* my boyfriend!"

Gordon chuckled. He took a bite. "All of what I said, and that's what you concentrated on? Okay. But you like him," he said as he chewed. "He like you too. He's just stupid, and you're enabling stupid." Then Gordon asked, "What time is it?"

Neyeli checked the watch on her arm, rattling the various bangles and chains decorating her appendage. "Six-fifty-five," she answered. "Have we killed enough time?"

Gordon chuckled harder. He nodded his head and said, "Absolutely. Let's come up with another argument." Neyeli laughed at Gordon's comment. "What's your uncle been investigating for Lady Arachne?"

Neyeli's voice turned sincere when she answered, "I believe everybody is on standby, holding their breath and waiting on what happens to you." Gordon nodded his head. Neyeli asked, "So have you felt anything?"

"Tingles," said Gordon continuing to eat. "Like an otherworldly sense." He looked around the room, pointing with his fork. "And I'm very aware of everything around me. I feel like I'm connected to everything by an invisible string." He assured Neyeli, "It's not overwhelming. I have to concentrate to really get the feel, at least for it to be strong. That's how I've been passing the time." He laughed. "It's like I'm high. I've been touching everything. Every object has this new feel."

"That's why I told you about the dragon spit having a bit of flavor in it," Neyeli said.

"We got the best type of elders," Gordon chuckled. Neyeli, intrigued, raised an eyebrow. Gordon continued, "They tryin' to get me high and drunk just to look inside some book. I had to drink rum today. Good rum."

Neyeli giggled. Gordon asked for the time again, and Neyeli answered that it just turned seven o'clock. "I'll leave these last few minutes to you, Mister Goodspeed," Neyeli told him as she stood from her chair.

Gordon put his fork down and got up with her. He led Neyeli to the door, opened it for her, and let her pass through. She leaned back over the threshold and kissed Gordon on the cheek. "Have a good reading in that book, Gordon."

Gordon accepted Neyeli's kiss with a smile. He remarked in jest, "I might not be Benny, but I'll do, right?"

Neyeli smiled. "*Happy Birthday*, Gordon."

"Thanks for the meal, Neyeli," Gordon said in a sincere voice.

Neyeli looked at her watch and told Gordon, "Seven-oh-three, Gordon. Tick, tick."

Before Neyeli walked away, Gordon said to her, "Hey, sista. You watch after Benny and I'll watch after Dajon."

She retorted, "I thought I already was." Again she leaned toward Gordon and gave him another kiss on the cheek. "Happy reading," said Neyeli while walking away.

Gordon closed and locked the doors. Too anxious to finish his meal, he cleaned his space at the table. Afterwards, he took a seat on the sofa and put the *Nigrum Nigrius Nigro* in his lap. His eyes went to the clock. 7:05. Fidgety, Gordon returned the aged book to the coffee table. He peeked at the clock again. 7:05, still. Gordon sat back, crossed his legs with ankle on knee, and he spread his arms across the back of the sofa. His foot tapped to a beat he heard in his head, a particular song. The song played on. Gordon closed his eyes and listened, and time passed. The songs final notes faded, and Gordon looked at the clock again. 7:08. "I could've sworn that song was longer," he remarked a little frustrated.

His foot continued to shake, this time not to a beat but nerves. He uncrossed his legs, leaned forward, and interlocked his hands. He started to hum a song from start to finish. He looked at the clock. *Seven-thirteen, good enough,* he thought. Gordon grinned as he considered another approach. He closed his eyes and concentrated on the clock. At first the ticking was low, but with Gordon's concentration, it became a thunderous and funky bassline. Each second thumped away as a beat Gordon bopped his head to. Time quickened until the last five seconds of 7:18. Gordon's eyes opened. He picked up the *Nigrum Nigrius Nigro* and opened the tattered tome to the first page just as 7:19 ticked into attendance.

The beginning pages described the first and second gateway rites, and the rites for adolescent boys and girls, ages fourteen and thirteen respectively—the numbers designated to Ausar and Auset, also called Osiris and Isis. The descriptions, written in Afro-Arabic, Greek, and Latin, were accompanied by vivid etchings. Gordon counted each page aloud, one a second. The book's pages became blank after page fourteen. Gordon continued to flip until page nineteen. He focused on the blank page, staring into it.

Gordon was still. He braced himself like a passenger on an amusement park's ride before its first, steep dip down. He continued looking deep into the page, head now cautiously cocking back. Nothing happened. He counted to nineteen again and blinked. A bright, violet light flickered like the flash from a camera. It burst off the page and slapped Gordon in the eyes, startling him. He flinched, looking up from the book. The violet light flooded his vision, and a mild burning sensation welled in his eyes. There came a hiss and cackle like that of a growing fire. The burning became heavier, scratching and biting the nerves in and behind his eyes.

Gordon dropped the *Nigrum Nigrius Nigro*, and the book landed closed on the floor. Gordon's mouth hung open as he attempted to scream, but he choked on his holler instead. His inability to express the pain chewing at his eyes only increased the sting, which in turn affected Gordon's balance as he tried to stand. He waved his arms with abandon, eyes wide open, trying to catch himself. He fell face first against the couch, staggering to recover. The pain continued swelling, building at the back of his eyes and shooting to Gordon's irises. Gordon struggled with the air in his throat. He pushed and managed to communicate a short, stifled squeal. Small as the noise may have been, it was at this moment when Gordon found his full voice. The simple noise rose from Gordon's opened mouth, squeaking like a hawk's distant cry. And then, much like the pain in his eyes, it built into something heavier.

Gordon gushed a geyser of heavy sound and loud air.

Shutting his eyes provided no relief from the pain. On his knees, and wondering which god or goddess to pray to, Gordon buried his face deep inside the couch's soft upholstery, muffling the scream he'd worked so hard to release. Tears burrowed through the sides of his tightly closed lids, adding to the throbbing, stinging agony electrocuting his eyes. Gordon shifted, pain choking him. His feet dug into the area rug as if he was trying to push the couch through the wall. His feet started to slide, slipping under the coffee table. Gordon curled his body. He turned over, back against the couch, head back and face aimed to the ceiling. He panted and grumbled grunts to express the pain.

The *Nigrum Nigrius Nigro*, lying next to Gordon's bended knee, opened of its own will. Its pages flipped and flipped and flipped and flipped until page nineteen was open to the world. A silky hum shivered harmoniously from the page, accompanied by a pulsing, lilac-colored aura.

Gordon caught his breath. The pain in his eyes eased as the book's lilac murmur silenced his gasps and grunts. Gordon relaxed. His breathing eased, and he dared himself to open his eyes. "Okay…" Gordon wheezed. "On three, eyes open." He realized how close the number three was from one, and wasn't quite sure if that was enough time. But if he didn't open his eyes now, Gordon felt he would forever keep them shut. He thought, *Maybe I should count to nineteen.* The decision wasn't inspired by anything cultural concerning his rites, only to prolong the action of opening his eyes. But he kept to his three count.

One. – This…

Two. – Is…

Three. – Insane!

It wasn't instant. It was a very hesitant action. But Gordon did open his eyes, the lids trembling as if with fever. Gordon's sight was blurry. Tears wet his irises, but the room came into focus. He heard the hum from the book coming from his left. His head turned cautiously toward it, and Gordon peered down into the throbbing, soft glow. The violet flash appeared again. Gordon jumped back by reflex, but it was too late. Again his eyes burned and stung. His running tears only swelled the scathing sensation.

Gordon braced himself against the pain. Instead of indulging in it, or even putting up more of a fight, Gordon tried another approach. He concentrated, using his heightened senses to focus on the pulsing, lilac aura humming from page nineteen as if through a speaker. But as his eyes remained closed, the book's light intensified. Its physical make became like liquid, scrawling across the nineteenth page as separate images. Musical notes. The images fluttered like butterfly wings and lifted from the page in a spiral pattern. The animated notes coiled around the room, corkscrewing back toward the book. But instead of diving onto page nineteen, the glimmering notations rushed into Gordon's ear. The musical notes became a single, feminine voice that sang to Gordon, *"Go outside."*

Gordon jumped up, eyes remaining shut tight. He staggered toward the dining room, hands searching for something to balance on. The couch was first. When that support gave way, Gordon stumbled across the room and smacked his shoulder hard against the T-shaped wall. His body twisted from the impact, but Gordon remained upright. He shuffled his feet forward and collapsed against the table, between two chairs. Gordon took a moment, his body pinched with pain from collisions. However, Gordon was happy to receive the straight-edged impacts, his body's nerves compensated to feel the collision by taking away some of the sting from his eyes. After a few breaths, Gordon turned his head to the left and opened his eyes for a split second to gain a proper trajectory to the back door. Pain pushed against his eyes, but the pain didn't hinder Gordon's advance. He used the chairs for support, moving forward. He reached for the doorknob, turned it, and opened the door.

He passed through. It was night, the day now faded. It was dark all the same to Gordon as he kept his eyes fastened shut. The pain wasn't as heavy, but there remained a burn with weight enough to still affect his balance. He stumbled to the middle of the outside area, knocking into lawn chairs and stools. Gordon again welcomed any impact that mitigated the sting in his eyes. He rested on bended knees and elbows, eyes splotched with wetness around them, nose running. He waited while bearing the pain. October's chill whisked around him, but Gordon didn't mind. He waited.

Inside the house, the *Nigrum Nigrius Nigro's* nineteenth page continued humming with a pulsing, lilac brilliance. Again the brilliance became like liquid and spread into musical notes across the face of the nineteenth page. The glyphs were different in shape, but just the same, they fluttered up and off the page. The notations flew, their pattern a corkscrew, following Gordon's path to the brownstone's courtyard. Gordon received the glimmering notations in his ear. He heard the feminine voice sing to him, *"Look up! Watch the sky!"*

Gordon exhaled a hard, tired sigh. He rose, still on his knees. He aimed his face to the dark sky. His three count came in three breaths, and then he opened his eyes. He braced for pain but felt none, though the heavy feeling remained in his pupils. His eyes continued pulsating, throbbing like a beating heart. But there was no burning sting, and Gordon was grateful for that.

Eyes wide open. Gordon watched a thin cloud stream across the starry sky. It twisted and corkscrewed like the musical notations, and it became thicker and thicker, darker and darker. The celestial exhaust funneled, dipping to Earth like the terrestrial end of a tornado. Its target was Gordon Goodspeed, and all he could do was watch. He couldn't move, and he found the pain in his eyes returning. Burning. Burning. Burning. The only movement Gordon had was a trembling in his body and throbbing in his eyes. Something preternatural kept him fixed in position. So he watched the cosmic rush spiral down to him. The supernal liquid doused his eyes, cooling the burn. The cosmic funnel pushed Gordon onto his back. His body sprawled out, damp eyes cooled and free of pain.

He stared for a moment, and then he blinked. Then he stared again. Gordon watched the sky. The nighttime was bare of clouds, calm of everything except the glimmering stars. The millions of glowing, celestial gleams came with a harmonic resonance that made Gordon smile. After the pain and intensity of the moment passed, Gordon's smile bubbled into fits of coughing laughter. He rolled to his side and got to his feet after taking one last glance at the starry sky. The night's cold cloaked him, but Gordon still didn't seem to mind. He welcomed any feeling as long as it wasn't the burn that earlier possessed his eyes. The prominent sensation coursing through Gordon's body now made him feel as if he'd taken a much-needed bath after a long wrestle in the mud.

Gordon straightened up the courtyard, setting right stools and chairs he'd knocked over. He found it peculiar that a lilac shimmer resonated off any object he aimed his gaze toward. He also noticed a hazy lilac ambiance coruscating at the edge of his vision. He looked around in contemplation. He looked at his hands and saw the lilac radiance gleaming off his palms. He looked up again, thought for a moment, and then rushed inside. The door to the backyard remained open, Gordon paying it no mind. He hurried up the stairs to the front hall, darted into the guestroom on his left, and into the bathroom connected to it.

The bright, lilac light illuminated the bathroom wherever Gordon aimed his eyes. He turned on the light and looked at his reflection in the mirror. His eyes were aglow, sprouting a wondrous, lilac-colored brilliance. Gordon was immediately entranced, a smile just as bright as the color in his eyes. He stepped toward the mirror, reaching for his image. He wiped the light's reflection with the tip of his fingers. Then he ran his free hand over his eyes. The light was warm to the touch, and it had a thick, liquid-like feel. He continued looking in the mirror. Lilac-hued strands streamed from the edges of his eyes like wild, lighted lashes.

Gordon observed the phenomenon until ticking interrupted his fixation. The ticking was slow and rhythmic, sounding like a longcase grandfather clock. He was quite certain that no corner of the house was decorated with such an object, but there ticked its rhythm. He stepped out of the bathroom, shutting off the lights. He followed the noise, caution in his steps. He made his way down to the garden floor and walked into the kitchen where he believed the noise was coming from. Gordon's glowing eyes had a new fixation as he saw atop the counter several unexpected items.

There was a Maasai Seme short sword. Next to the sword was a goblet similar to the one used in his second gateway rites. A fancy pen was propped inside it. A coin engraved with the phrase *The Word* rested next to the polished, wooden chalice. All of these objects lay over an aged piece of papyrus. Scribed there on the Egyptian sheet were seven hieroglyphs representing seven magical words. There also were the twenty-six letters of the English alphabet, each written alongside a corresponding mystical music notation. There was also written the words *Thirteen more to come. Her thirteen walk tall and fearsome across the land.* Gordon's bright, lilac eyes could read the paper even from the far distance where he stood.

Gordon approached the objects, and the objects dissolved from reality one-by-one. Their fade from the counter paused Gordon's approach. He weighed the possibility of whether he was under the influence of the alcoholic beverages he consumed in his ritual, or the herbs washed into his hair. He concluded that he was neither high nor drunk. This was reality, and Gordon judged that he'd rather have been under the influence.

Tick-tock continued the unseen clock. Gordon resumed his search. He went into the dining room. Nothing. He stepped out into the backyard to see if a longcase clock had appeared there, a phenomenon that, considering the night's events, wouldn't have been the strangest of occurrences. Nothing. He shut the door and locked it and moved to the front room. Nothing. Gordon walked to the basement, and halfway down the creaking stairs, the ticking ceased.

Standing still, Gordon waited for the ticking to resume. There was only silence. Gordon considered, *If the ticking has any meaning, it'll return.* After his thought passed, Gordon realized the edges of his eyes were no longer brimming with a lilac aura. He made his way back to the parlor-floor bathroom. He flipped on the lights and looked in the mirror. The radiant glow was gone, but his irises and pupils remained lilac in color.

"I wonder if I'll be mistaken for Elizabeth Taylor," Gordon joked in a deadpan manner. "Or Remy LeBeau." He grinned at the second alternative, marveling at the color swirling in his eyes. He posed in the mirror, stance like a comic book superhero. Then Gordon made gestures as if he was tossing objects from his hands. His actions were accompanied by swishing noises he provided as sound effects. "Take that, *mon ami!*" he uttered loud in his best Cajun accent.

After playing out his superhero fantasy, Gordon turned off the light and left the bathroom. He made his way down to the garden floor and swiped the *Nigrum Nigrius Nigro* off the floor. The book was still open to page nineteen. Gordon flipped to the beginning and discovered that he understood the Afro-Arabic, Greek, and Latin instructions. He tried to speak the languages aloud but his pronunciation and accent were garbled. He commented, "Maybe I'll be able to speak the languages tomorrow. For now, I read."

Gordon glanced over the written words. The languages only repeated one another, describing the ancient rites of the Fable Avenue culture. Some entries touched on the rites' origins, stretching back to ancient Africa, originating in Central Africa, and applied with modifications through time and the continents regions. The African Moors tempered the rites, omitting large, elaborate dramatics employed by earlier, African cultures. The Moors edited from the rites a staged retelling of a mythology that explained the purpose of the rites. This description was written in a very ancient African script and not translated in any other language. It was also noted that the rites were edited for secrecy, but the spiritual blessings and prayers were kept. It was written of the second gateway rites: *To raise the lilac flame and reveal the spirit's name.* A second line read: *The black of the cosmic sky will bless the eyes. Age ten added by nine. Rites will not bless initiate, only the right time. The spirit arrives not through rite but on its own time. The extinguished cobalt-blue flame will reignite and open the sky. The grand wish the prize.* Gordon thought that was a touching sentiment, and it did add some insight.

Gordon was excited to find more writings beyond the fourteenth page. His excitement, however, deflated when he realized there was not much. All he saw was an interesting sketch of schematics for a sarcophagus. There were elements of an Egyptian bed attached to it. *The Alchemical Chamber,* the page read.

Gordon shut the book and placed it on the coffee table. He stood, walked to the dining room, unlocked the back door, and stepped through.

The cool air greeted Gordon as he stepped into the backyard, circulating around, under and over him but never penetrating for him to feel it. Gordon didn't bother to pull the hood of his gray, Yankees sweatshirt over his head. White gym socks covered his feet, and he was otherwise dressed in black sweatpants. In truth, it was the celestial blessing that accorded his relief from the cold.

Gordon sat down and watched the sky. The stars burned brighter to him. He heard their harmonic resonance, low and subtle, like background music. A cosmic jazz band played just for him, and he enjoyed the symphony. He observed tendrils of energy, visible only to him, extending from star to star, connecting the eradiated, heavenly bodies. Out of this connecting of starry hosts, Gordon saw hieroglyphs illuminating the sky. None of the more popular zodiacal constellations appeared. All of the cosmic etchings were ancient symbols. Gordon understood what the stars were saying to him. *Dooley,* the stars sang and read in one section of etchings, *the lilac flame. Dooley,* they read and sang in another set, *the dark hero.*

"Anxious as I might be," Gordon replied to the heavens. "If that applies to me, I say to fate: challenge accepted. Throw out the first pitch."

Stars entertained Gordon Goodspeed as they conducted music and revealed hidden configurations. There was no need for television. There was no need for video games. There was no need for terrestrial radio or music. A cosmic concert played good, old *conjure 'n' soul*, passing the time for Gordon Goodspeed. It wasn't the outlined glyphs in the sky or even the harmonics the stars echoed that impressed him. It was the simple fact that this was a phenomenon ongoing in existence, right there for all to see, but no one saw it except him.

Gordon watched and listened while reclined in a lawn chair and sipping straight from the jug containing the last of the rum-mixed dragon spit. Any song he thought of, the stars played as an instrumental, and Gordon loved ranging his celestial requests through all genres and hear the stars' instrumental interpretations. It was midnight when Gordon stood up and walked back into the house. He took one last, smiling glance at the stars before shutting the door. With no one to play for, the sentient, cosmic concert ceased in Gordon's absence. The starry glow of the night sky returned ordinary as Gordon moved to the brownstone's interior. After swiping the *Nigrum Nigrius Nigro* from the coffee table, he ascended past the parlor floor, up to the second level and into the bedroom he used when his family visited Fable Avenue. Gordon didn't bother turning on the room's lights. The muted glimmer in his lilac eyes provided a faint view of the dark room. Gordon put the *Nigrum Nigrius Nigro* on a nightstand next to the bed. He removed his sweatshirt, exposing the black tank top worn underneath. He dropped the hooded garment on the floor and slipped into bed. Gordon shut his eyes. Strangely enough, his stamina drained like water squeezed from a sponge, and he was quickly pulled into a deep sleep.

One hour passed. Ticking from a longcase clock roused Gordon from sleep. The noise tapped at his ear like a wryneck bird pecking wood for insects. Still befuddled by sleep, Gordon's eyelids trembled as he opened them. He exhaled a low groan, reacting to the disturbance of his calm, deep rest. His eyes opened. Gordon rolled them with great effort, annoyed. His vision adjusted to the room's near-darkness as if equipped with a *tapetum lucidum*, the shiny layer of cells that assisted cats and woodland creatures to see in the same conditions. But his aptness to peer into near shadow came from the cosmic-gifted lilac shimmer resonating in his eyes. Sleep still fogged Gordon's view, and the faint, shadowy outline of the room waved in a blur. There was one shadow, distinct and unmoving, that Gordon noticed in peripheral. His eyes moved rightward, placing in view the shade standing at the entrance. Trepidation was an adhesive keeping Gordon's body fixed in place.

There was a woman cloaked in shadow standing in the doorway. Gordon's blessed eyes comprehended only minor details from the darkness shrouding the figure. He inspected the feminine shade's contours and thus determined the woman's attire. A long, floral skirt with a waist sash, and a ruffled, off the shoulder top covered a dancer's frame. Her feet were bare. Her hair was an Afro puff-styled ponytail. Gordon stared into her visage, but only blackness was there.

The ticking ceased, or so Gordon believed. His concentration on the woman in front of him stifled the tick-tock of the ever-truant longcase clock. The tick-tock was still there, however, but the noise that hauled Gordon from sleep was muted, not only by the shaded woman's presence, but also by her movement. She took a step toward Gordon. Her approach was slow, as if cautious. Trepidation continued to fasten Gordon in place. A heavy, oppressive feeling perched atop his chest, and weighed heavier as the feminine shadow crept closer. *Tick-tock,* Gordon did not hear. He was too busy breathing in short, hiccup-like gasps. Unable to sit up or move away, Gordon slumped further underneath the covers. His lilac eyes, wide open and brimming with anxiety as well as light, looked on as the woman bent down over him. Her image waved like a reflection in water, adapting to the physical surrounding. She became solid, and Gordon remained fixed in place as a chill inside him spread like a spill. He felt as if something was swallowing him whole. He was drowning, but there was no water.

Then a light flickered into existence underneath the shaded woman's neck, illuminating her face and revealing her countenance to Gordon. The woman was dark-skinned with bewitching, exotic eyes and full lips. Gordon recognized her from fading childhood memories. He better recalled her from old family photographs. Seeing the contours of this woman's face, being face-to-face, broke Gordon's unease like an impairing fever. Gordon's eyes welled with tears that shimmered lilac. His wide gaze, once possessed with anxiety, melted into sad curiosity. This woman was his mother. Her face preserved at that age of her passing years ago.

Althea Miriam Goodspeed.

Gordon and Althea looked at one another curiously. Gordon never once questioned his faculties, but he did inquire why the spirit of his mother presented herself to him. Did she have something for him? Althea inspected her son like an intrigued lioness. Gordon postulated that she must have been wondering if he was truly her youngest child. He rose up a little. Althea was silent, but still with a curious gaze. She moved away. This allowed Gordon to rise completely in the bed. They continued to stare at one another for a long, silent moment, and then Gordon, sounding like both a question and an answer, uttered, "Mom…"

Althea didn't respond to Gordon, distracted instead by the sudden occurrence of the master bedroom's light turning on upstairs. Both Gordon and Althea turned their heads to the door. Light beamed from the hallway upstairs. Gordon glanced at his mother and noticed her outfit was made up of the colors red and gold. Althea stood up straight, an irritated expression on her face. Every movement committed by his mother's apparition startled him. Althea's spectral form flapped like a curtain in the breeze. Gordon focused his eyes on his mother. A sensation tickled his neck, and he surmised his mother's spirit strained to stay tangible in the corporeal world. Gordon blinked. His mother's figure moved to the door. She peeked her head into the hall and looked up at the next floor where the light from the master bedroom beamed. She was veiled in a vexed expression. Gordon remained put, observing his mother.

Althea stepped into the hall, inspired by the immediate, feminine giggling coming from the top floor. Althea's image blurred, and then she disappeared. Gordon heard traipsing in the hallway, and then the distinct sound of footsteps ascending the stairs. The footsteps' clamor faded with each step upward. Then the house was calm of noise and movement. The giggling ceased, but the light upstairs remained aglow. Gordon didn't move. He waited. He listened and he watched but nothing happened, minute after passing minute. He was alert now, sleep dissolved from him. Gordon tossed the covers off his body and hopped out of bed in a single move. In two strides he was at the door, imitating the gestures earlier executed by his mother. He peeked into the hall and looked up at the next floor where the light from the master bedroom beamed. Gordon waited again, believing he would either see his mother's image come into existence descending the stairs, or hear the giggling female.

When nothing occurred, Gordon stepped into the hallway and ascended the stairs. The light emitting from the master bedroom burned Gordon's vision. It was bright and fluorescent, flooding the upstairs hallway. Memories of the burning sting from earlier in the night came to mind. Gordon proceeded cautiously, shielding his eyes and trudging closer to the master bedroom. He moved as if against a heavy wind in a sandstorm. Instead of walking into the room, Gordon put his back to the bright light and reached inside to feel for the light switch near the door. His hand skimmed across the wall, feeling and feeling. His arm extended, and his hand felt. He came across the rigid light panel and flipped the switch off.

Gordon heard the disturbing cry of a woman hollering in agony from a birthing pang. The sound receded before he could comprehend it. The brilliant spill of light from the master bedroom extinguished. The house was once again dark and calm. There was no ticking, no music, and no hum. Gordon, anticipating his mother's return, remained still. She did not appear. Gordon made his way back to his bedroom after a short time. He checked the clock before crawling into bed. It was 1:18 in the morning. Gordon lay flat in the bed, staring up at the ceiling. He pondered a question in his head, asking of his mother why her spirit had not presented itself to his father so they may enjoy one another's company once a year, as was customary for the departed spirits of beloved ones in the Fable Avenue community. And just as he thought of the question, again out of his peripheral, he caught the specter of his mother sitting in the chair positioned near the window.

Gordon looked at his mother. He could see her face through the darkness. She was smiling at him, warm and motherly. Sadness accented the expression in her eyes. Gordon rose up in the bed, cautious and acting as if any sudden movement would frighten his mother's spirit away. But her presence remained. Gordon's mouth quivered a moment, struggling to bend upward. Eventually, he managed to smile at his mother.

The upstairs light returned, bright and overwhelming.

Gordon and Althea turned their attention to the invading light. Both were annoyed, their faces ruffled in a grimace with brows furrowed. Althea waved her fingers in the direction of the doorway, and the bright light retreated. There was a faint, muttered giggle, a woman's flirtatious chortle that faded with the light.

Gordon looked at his mother. She remained upset, turned away from him, and peered out the window overlooking the backyard. Then Gordon understood. He told his mother, "He does it to forget you." He explained further, tone apologetic, "There's a different woman every other week, or there're long periods of nobody and heavily indulging in work." His mother continued to stare out the window. Gordon said in the same apologetic tone, "It ain't right. It ain't wrong. It's just human."

Althea glanced at her son with a scornful expression that wasn't meant for him. Then she appeared contemplative, and she relaxed her manner. She nodded at her son and went back to looking down at the backyard. After some time, Althea stood up, gaze still on the area below. She put her hand and forehead against the window, closed her eyes and smiled. Althea disappeared. Gordon flinched as she faded, and then he reacted to a sound. Music. It was a piano playing a soft melody. Gordon hopped out of the bed again, covers thrown off him. He paced to the hallway and looked around. Nothing was there.

The nape of his neck tingled. The quiver climbed, buzzing from the back of his neck to the crown of his head. Then there came the shift, the feel of a tuning radio frequency. Gordon turned his head and spied the window. He crossed the room and looked down into the backyard where he saw his mother's apparition dancing a free-form contemporary sequence. Her gracious rhythms followed the melodious play of the piano, and there was no worry of the objects around her as she ghosted through them.

Gordon smiled as he watched his mother. Althea danced all around. Gordon snatched the comforter from the bed and curled into the chair beside the window. He marveled at the routines his mother danced. After the completion of three routines, Gordon drifted back into sleep. He dreamed of a memory from when he was six years old. His mother danced in the large front hall of their Harlem brownstone. His father, Maximilian Goodspeed, held her up with the music he played on the piano.

The piano was sold three days after Althea Miriam Goodspeed died.

Morning. Gordon awoke in bed, not the chair. He was tucked underneath the comforter as his mother used to have him when he was younger. He opened his eyes and realized he had a boyish grin on his face. The sun's light gently stroked his cheek, and Gordon didn't want to move. Of course, he didn't have to. He didn't know what time it was, and he didn't care. Gordon had nowhere to go and nowhere to be. He thought of contacting Papa Solomon, but he considered the old man would eventually make an appearance. So, Gordon determined, that until he heard the doorbell ring or the elder's knock against it, he was staying put. There was only one thing that inspired Gordon to stir. The bathroom. He didn't have to use it. He only wanted to know if the lilac color remained swirling in his irises and pupils.

Gordon looked at the chair in the corner. It was empty. He turned to the clock. It was 7:19. He chuckled and said, "Seriously?" He looked at the ceiling and asked, "Not even seven-twenty one? Seven-nineteen. On the dot." His grin widened. "Aight. Okay," he said closing his eyes. He rested for a short while longer, indulging in the comfortable tuck-in. Then he maneuvered from the bed with a sly ease, slipping from underneath the covers like a snake shedding its skin. He reached down, grabbed his sweatshirt, and slipped it over him. The sun might've been beaming, the day free of clouds, but the house was chilly and nothing mystical warmed him. Gordon's Yankees sweatshirt would have to do.

He left the room and traveled to the bathroom at the end of the hall and looked into the mirror. His eyes were radiant with a lilac shimmer. He took a moment to admire the hypnotic, swirling lilac color. His admiration was interrupted when he heard a man's voice come from downstairs. He couldn't make much of the words, but his heightened instinct tugged at him, informing Gordon the voice was coming from the kitchen on the garden level. The sound caught Gordon off guard, but he concentrated and listened for it again. He heard it clearly this time, his concentration drawing the voice closer. The man said, speaking to another, "We play every song in this book. *Every* song. In order. Dig?"

Gordon turned his head in the direction of the voice. He stepped into the hall, and he listened with his head over the banister. His heightened sense of hearing picked up other voices in conversation. Downstairs. Nervous, he paused. There were noises as if others shuffled about. He called, "Papa Solomon…?"

There was no response and the talking continued as Gordon's voice went unheard. His whole body tightened, and the sensation never faded or concentrated in his neck or went up to his crown. Instead, it tightened into anxiety. The same heavy feeling descended on him when his mother's shaded specter stood over him. He took a quivering step toward the stairs. Two steps, then three steps. He was at the top of the stairs. He listened and still heard conversation. He walked down to the parlor entrance over to the stairs descending to the garden level. He paused at the top of the stairs. He tried to relax his breath by clenching his teeth.

"I'm just hoping the sound keeps its groove when the album is pressed," the same voice spoke.

Gordon put his right foot on the next step down. The heavy feeling and buzz simmered. Gordon took another step, and more of the sensation lifted. Taking his time, he made his way down the remaining steps. He descended into a room that was unlike his front room. It was covered in beige wallpaper with a gold *fleur de lis* pattern running up and down its face. There was a bookshelf against a solid wall where the entrance to the dining area was supposed to be. There was a fireplace substituted for the entertainment center. A couch was situated in the same place as Gordon was used to. A coffee table too. But there were, on the other side of the coffee table, chairs far more plush and fancy than the ones that were there last night.

Gordon stepped into the room, observing its differences as he traipsed toward the kitchen and the voices in conversation. He only saw, extending from the kitchen, people's shadows on the floor. He inched closer.

"Boy," said an old man. "Do you think old age makin' us weak with our tricks?"

Gordon stepped in the kitchen's entranceway. The kitchen was different, not just the spacing and design, but also the appliances. They looked new, though from a past time period. There was a table and chairs. At the table sat four people Gordon heard of but never met. The first two men were old, in their mid-sixties. Gordon knew the men were brothers. Both had stocky builds and only a few shades of brown separated their skin tones. The biggest difference was in their build. One of the brothers, the oldest, was round in his frame. The younger of the two was squarer in his. The rounder man was named Jackson Henrik Fable. The square fellow, wearing glasses with thick lenses, was Gaston Fable.

These were the Fable brothers, but Gordon didn't speculate that he'd somehow appeared in their home. The Fable brothers' brownstones had been locked for decades with no manner of incant able to unlatch either window or door. It was a Fable Avenue legend, a story real and palpable. Children and adults within the community respected the fastened houses. The two houses locked when the Fable brothers' passed, their music having faded, as it was called. Jackson Fable faded in 1969. His brother Gaston faded in 1972.

The maternal side of their family debated over who would receive the real estate and control the Mississippi crossroads the brothers guarded. Their brownstones on Fable Avenue magically led to the crossroads through another exit in the home. Votes were made, and a very old man named Satchel Eledas, called The Old Goon, won out. But with the doors locked on one end, and the house invisible on the other, without even Papa Solomon's mystical horn able to call the property into existence, Satchel was still left out of the family real estate. But he was old, and he was very patient. Talk put Old Goon well over a hundred years old. Gordon met him on occasion when he was younger, and he didn't believe the man was older than sixty or so. But who knows what a good incant could do.

For the moment, as time was now rewound to back-in-the-day, Gordon listened as Jackson Fable insisted, "That groove gon' have them otherworldly notes booming from one copy of this album to the next. Folk that hear the music, understand them notes, they gon' come flockin' to this here street, just like Madison say. The *right* folk, now."

Jackson and Gaston Fable addressed two young men. One man had average brown skin, and he was also of average height, which Gordon could see when he stood up from the table. What came as a surprise to Gordon was the young man's hair. They were in tight, twisted one-inch curls that Gordon didn't consider was of the time period he was observing. But here was this young man flaunting them. A quick vibration crawling up the back of Gordon's neck produced a name, and he then knew he was looking at the legendary Horatio Peters, called Son of the Trumpet King, or Prince of the Trumpet. Grand titles aside, Gordon knew that Papa Solomon, born Vencil Peters, and his older sister Maman Anansi, born Carolyn-Theresa Peters, called Horatio Peters "father." Oliver Peters, his younger sister, Leah, and all of their cousins called him "granddad."

Gordon stepped into the kitchen. None of the room's occupants took notice of him. He didn't need the shuddering twinge in his neck to help him with the other young man's identity, but it came regardless and produced the tall, dark and fancy attired man's name. Jonathan Richard Concheroot. He was father to Wilson Barnes, and many other Fable Avenue residents, by way of many Fable Avenue women. It was said that

Johnny Concheroot's sexual exploits doubled the Fable Avenue population. This was not something to be said in the company of Dorothy Barnes, Wilson's mother. She was Johnny's first Fable Avenue courtship, and the woman he had the most children with. The two never married, always off and on again. But despite his *tour de force*, as it were, many said she was the only woman he ever really loved.

Gordon viewed Fable Avenue through the window. The day was partly cloudy, gray and sun mixed together. There was a dusting of snow on the ground. Cars were parked along the sidewalk, their make and model was the late 1950s. Gordon turned his head, scanning the kitchen. He spotted, mounted on the wall on the opposite side of the room, a calendar next to a telephone. The month was November. The year was 1958. Gordon again viewed the faces of the men in the room, and then once more reviewed the room before looking back outside. *Perhaps,* Gordon wondered, *this was the Peters' residence before the renovation, or maybe Mister Concheroot's Fable Avenue home.*

The conversation between the men continued as Gordon inspected his surroundings. "It's been a year since this street done popped up out the blue," continued Jackson. "Our tricks can't keep suspicion away on why this street so empty of residents." Jackson abridged, "Madison's had this place under shadow. Now it's out in the open all empty."

Johnny interjected, "Empty houses in this area are nothing new."

Jackson retorted, "Well, boy, we still don't want someone coming in and snatching up the real estate, legally or otherwise. This place has to look legit, and not through a trick. We need to alleviate the burden Gaston and I are under keepin' folks' noses out our business."

"Especially since a lot of our spirit is taken out of us helpin' y'all record," Gaston's scratchy voice concluded his brother's sentiment.

A baby started crying, the sound coming from upstairs. Everyone looked in the direction of the stairs. Horatio walked out of the kitchen to attend to his wife, Delia-LaRue Amat, Maman Anansi and Papa Solomon's mother. The newborn baby crying was the older of the two, Maman Anansi, Carolyn-Theresa. The thought put a grin on Gordon's face. He snapped back to the reality of yesteryear when Horatio commented while walking away to attend to his wife and newborn daughter, "If my wife can sing through nine months of pregnancy, then the two of you can keep your work up with your tricks while we record. And you can also keep suspicion from our street."

Gaston joked, "*Our* street? Who you, boy? That street sign got *our* family name on it," he said pointing to him and Jackson. Jackson chuckled at his brother's playfulness, and he agreed with a nod of his head to add to the joke. "And as for your wife, Horatio, she still young and pretty. We ain't."

Jackson's chuckle ceased, and he grimaced at his brother's comment. "Speak for yourself, old boy!" he barked at Gaston, voice and facial expression appearing sincere. "I still got *my* prowess," Jackson spoke in a mock rigid manner.

Gaston responded to his brother as he rolled his eyes, "Negro, please! You only pretty once a year when you dance with your wife, tryin' to match her restored youth, you old fool. And even then, you being pretty is debatable."

Johnny jumped into the Fable brothers' banter, keeping the conversation on topic. "The real *trick* is this album's distribution. That old man, Madison, couldn't score that?" He looked at either Fable brother. "We lucky he got us a recordin' space. I thought the legendary Madison Goodspeed was supposed to be some great trickster." Johnny then hollered, "Horatio, you think we can compose somethin' that could help that along? I know we tryin' to avoid the suits, but…" Johnny's voice trailed away as he felt the absence of Horatio's presence. He called again, "Horatio? Horatio?" He cursed, "Damn! The minute he slipped a ring on that woman's finger he slipped a bun in her oven."

Jackson assured, "You ain't got to worry, 'bout that. Madison said he'd handle it all. If not him, his son or daughter. They tricks—or *incants* or *conjures* as they say are better words to use—know how to get things. Trick folk minds like a confidence man."

The scene froze. Gordon froze too, affected by his own sense of anticipation. One-by-one Johnny and the Fable brothers faded from existence. Nothing changed; neither the front room nor the kitchen returned to the areas resembling the Goodspeed family house. Gordon waited cautiously for something else to happen. He turned his head to the window to see what was happening outside.

Loud jazz music thundered through the house!

Gordon jumped back! It took a moment for his heart to settle, and for the rest of his nerves to make peace with the music's volume. It was a full band booming their sound, and Gordon believed the music's origin was the basement. He walked to the stairs and descended into a recording studio that was likely never a part of the house. He'd stepped into somewhere else, and he was observing Horatio and Delia's jazz band in session, recording the only album they would ever chronicle. Gordon took a seat in the middle of the staircase. He'd heard the recording before, but this was live. Musical sounds that he'd only heard the stars play, thunder-clapped from the band. Jackson and Gaston Fable were there to provide mystical chants to insure the music's mysticism was picked up in the recording. Delia-LaRue Amat sang and scatted charmed notations, calling cosmic spirits with her voice. The average ear would hear only earthly sounds and lyrics. But ears attuned to the higher, mystical harmonics would pick up the true nature of the songs and behold their story and spirit.

Conjure and soul.

The song had an affect on Gordon as he concentrated on the music. The environment bubbled. Through its ripples, Gordon saw the flash flicker of past images. The images were of the distant past. Moorish Spain. Africa. A plantation. Slavery. Rebellions. These were glimpses of a story Gordon understood was part of Fable Avenue's cultural history, but seeing them one after the other, attacking his senses, charging Gordon all at once like a maddened mob, rattled him. He tried to close his eyes or look away, but the images followed him behind his eyelids. He jumped to his feet and turned to leave the basement. The door shut! Gordon turned back to the recording session. Images rushed him. There was a bayou village. A beautiful, voluptuous, red-haired white woman cackled. She danced on a muddy road, a veil around her face. The bayou village burned around her. A flash of bright light ended the scene as the fire grew and grew.

The music stopped.

Gordon looked around. The recording studio dissolved back into a semi-finished basement. Gordon's eyes went to and fro, viewing the change in environment. He was still, hand gripped hard on the railing.

The doorbell rang once, and then it rang twice more.

Gordon let go of the railing. He turned around and walked upstairs. He expected to return to his residence's front room, hoping a visiting Papa Solomon was the cause behind the doorbell's ring. Gordon had so much to tell him, and he desired to do so now. Instead, he re-entered the room with the bright-patterned wallpaper. He turned his head to the door. Horatio Peters stood there, door open. Surprise was painted on his face with a hint of concern. Horatio did not move, stunned at the sight of the man standing at his door. He fixed his features and greeted, "Stanley. This wasn't expected. Come in."

Gordon stepped closer before the invited man entered the room, wanting to get a better look. Then the man made an appearance. Stanley Fallows, a handsome, strawberry-blonde-haired white man was well dressed, sporting a gray three-piece suit. His matching gray fedora was in his hand, politely removed as he entered the house. An uneasy smile was on his face, and a beautiful woman was on his arm. She was dusky hued with raven-colored hair that draped in lengthy, bouncing curls. Her long, orange and yellow dress and high heels gave the appearance that she was much taller than she was, though she was taller than average for a female. She had dark eyes and a round face. Around her neck was a silver choker decorated with smooth and round emeralds.

Stanley introduced her to Horatio. "This is my wife," he said. "Lucretia Tolvaj-Fallows," he presented the woman and her name.

Horatio gave Lucretia a warm hug and a kiss on the cheek. She smiled, leaning into Horatio's kind gestures. Horatio stepped back and said, "It is a pleasure to meet you, Lucretia, a pleasure and a surprise." Horatio looked at Stanley and reached out his hand. Stanley removed his arm from around his wife and accepted Horatio's gesture. They shook, and Horatio said, "Congratulations, Stanley. Congratulations. When did this happen?"

"When I departed for Europe with the band I manage," explained Stanley. "Well, not right then. I took my mother's advice and visited her mother's people. I traveled to Eastern Europe. Saw sights. I got to know my mother's side of the family. I met Lucretia there. Her family is part of the same community as my mother's family."

"That's nice," said Horatio, trying to maintain the surprise in his voice. Gordon concentrated on Horatio's behavior. The buzzing sense on his neck revealed that Horatio was nervous. He informed Stanley, "Delia and I are married." Stanley congratulated Horatio on the news, also commenting to Horatio that the marriage figuratively made the two of them family. "I guess it does," Horatio replied. He continued his news, "We have a two-year-old daughter, Carolyn-Theresa, and there's another on the way."

"Well, damn Horatio!" Stanley said with a wide smile. "You two didn't waste any time." Light laughter filled the room, and then the conversation came to an abrupt, awkward pause. Smiles just as awkward remained. Stanley finally said, "Horatio Peters. That is your name, is it not? Your real name?"

Horatio exhaled through a guilty smile. He confessed, "Yes, Stanley. That's my name. My real name."

Stanley reached behind him and closed the door. He aimed his hat at the couch and said, "Can we have a seat, Horatio? We need to talk."

"Absolutely," Horatio complied.

Their images faded, but their voices remained. "I heard the record, Horatio. I saw everything. I know what my mother is guilty of. All her crimes."

"I'm sorry, Stanley," Gordon heard Horatio's voice say.

Then their images appeared again. Stanley and his wife were sitting on the couch. Horatio Peters sat on one of the upholstered chairs. He'd brought the chair closer to the couch. In the other upholstered chair sat Delia-LaRue Peters. Delia was seven months pregnant and holding a cute, two-year old Carolyn-Theresa Peters in her arms. Delia beamed a smile at Stanley, glad to see him.

Lucretia, though well-mannered in her silence, was more distant in her demeanor. Then she looked distracted, her eyes darting around as if sensing something. Her gaze looked in Gordon's direction, and Lucretia's look became curious. Gordon didn't believe the woman could see him, but she might've felt his presence. He moved behind Horatio's seat and watched as Lucretia put her attention back on the conversation.

"I would understand if you didn't trust me, Horatio," said Stanley in a forgiving tone.

"It's not that, Stanley," Horatio assured. "I'm just not the person to make a decision on the matter," he explained. "And you'd have to understand the caution other people on this street might have when it comes to letting you into our culture's rebirth."

"I would indeed," Stanley yielded. "But I am here to make peace. I want to find peace for my mother's spirit. Like I've said, Horatio, I know your hand was forced." Stanley held back emotion. He took time to concentrate before speaking his next words. "It's taken some time for me to come to terms with my mother and my own…birth." Stanley described, "My unnatural conception. My mother. Her deeds. Horatio, I know you had to end my mother's long, unholy life. Her tricks had to come to an end." Lucretia embraced her husband. "With a new start, I believe we can achieve great things, Horatio. These are trying times right now in America. There's a lot of tension, but I believe we can do twice as much good. There's a destiny for Fable Avenue, and we all play a part."

Horatio nodded. Delia adjusted the fidgety two-year-old that barely fit on her lap because of her expanding, pregnant belly. "We're figuring that out now, Stanley," said Delia. "There's so much to research. There are still stories to uncover that hold pieces of the puzzle, bringing us closer to understanding what we're all here to do for the world, or maybe, just ourselves."

"And I can help," Stanley pleaded. He didn't sound desperate, but his voice was elevating toward it. He took a moment to relax, looking away and smiling as he remembered something. He said, with his eyes back on Delia, "There was something I saw. Something I remember, to be correct. It was something your grandmother said just as she gave birth to your mother. Right before she passed away." Then he quoted, *"Dooley is a lilac flame, fluttering and flickering and shooting up into the sky where I see three moons reside. Red. Black. Green. There are golden halos surrounding them and they beam a kiss. Ah, procure this grand conjure and wish."* Stanley's boyish grin widened. "It's that part, that, '*Ah, procure this grand conjure and wish*' that has me."

Delia, holding a polite smile, told Stanley, "We've been inquiring about that line too." There was something apologetic about her tone, and Gordon sensed that Delia now shifted with unease behind her polite smile.

"I can help," repeated Stanley, desperation a little louder in his tone. He adjusted, sitting up, hunched forward. "There are places that won't permit you entrance, whether the Negro abolishes segregation or not. There are libraries with untapped information, tales and legends to ponder and decipher. Casting your tricks to gain entrance would only garner suspicion on your community."

"We say *incants* or *conjures*, now, Stanley," informed Delia as she again adjusted her daughter. "Not tricks. We even use the word *blessing*."

Stanley nodded his head and apologized. "Pardon me if I misspeak again. I don't mean to offend." Stanley took a moment for his apology to be accepted. Then he said, "There are places I can get into without the use of incants. There are places Lucretia is privy to. Her culture is much like Fable Avenue, and they don't represent my mother's interests. She's also studying anthropology." Lucretia shied away as Horatio and Delia spoke aloud their admiration. "I ask, in a desperate plea, that in return for my services, you help me put my mother's presence to rest."

Horatio and Delia stared at Stanley.

Stanley, seeing perplexity on Horatio and Delia's faces, clarified, "I have nightmares. My mother. I don't see her, I hear her. She's screaming. It's distant, but disturbing. Its volume fades in and out. It's her spirit. She's yelling. Her words are garbled. I believe she's crying for help, begging to be extinguished. I need your help."

The scene paused. Stanley and Lucretia faded from the couch. Jackson and Gaston Fable, holding glower expressions, faded in place of the husband and wife. The lights in the room turned on as if a dimmer was dialed up. Horatio and Delia remained seated in their chairs, but their clothing changed. Two-year-old Carolyn-Theresa disappeared. Gordon glanced over his shoulder at the kitchen window to see that night had bloomed. He returned his attention to the conversation at hand.

"He heard our music for what it is," Horatio said as if making a point in a debate. "I believe he's sincere."

Jackson and Gaston's eyes moved to Delia. "I hummed an incant over him as he rested," she told the two of them. "I heard Sarinda screaming. It was no trick." Her voice possessed a hint of defeat. Gordon concentrated on the pregnant woman. His tingling awareness appeared, and he perceived Delia having a difficult time talking about the woman named Sarinda. Gordon knew she spoke about the sly, python that little Fable Avenue boys and girls knew as Sarinda Unhallow. Her proper name was Sarinda Fallows. Her myth coupled her with a man named Curly, a vile associate waiting for Sarinda Unhallow's command to snatch bad little boys and girls. Curly would bring the naughty boy or girl to Sarinda, and the woman would feast on the boy or girl's soul. Sarinda Unhallow thrived on misdeeds, and she could hypnotize a child to act in devilish ways. Then the child was ripe for plucking, and Curly would come and take the child for

Sarinda to feast on. So said the parents and elders of Fable Avenue to the little boys and girls of the community.

"Playing the horn didn't soothe him, either," Horatio noted.

The Fable brothers remained silent, scowls frozen on their faces.

"We wondered what should be done with Stanley, how he should be treated," Delia spoke. "We pondered his outcome even before we put his mother down." She looked at Horatio, and his eyes met hers. Delia smiled when she said, "There were some pretty heated arguments between Horatio and I, to say the least."

Horatio apologized to his wife, "I'm sorry, Delia-baby."

"Oh, please, Horatio," Delia responded. "I was just as stubborn, if not more. You were being cautious." She turned to Jackson and Gaston. "I tried, Mister Jackson, Mister Gaston. I tried to drape Sarinda's persona over Stanley. I tried to see him as an unnatural creation because of how he was conceived. But I couldn't. He was still like family. I still regarded him as a cousin, despite his unholy mother and her attack on my family."

Jackson and Gaston looked at one another. Jackson sighed and said, "Sarinda conceived Stanley to be as his father."

"We know," Horatio assured. "We saw everything etched into motion through Delia's father's artwork. He's supposed to be of his father, but she didn't give him his name. That could mean all the difference."

"Sarinda is saying something to Stanley in these nightmares of his," Delia announced, tone like a warning. "Her message comes through as the disturbing screams he hears. I recommend we decipher this message and mute it before it can influence Stanley. We can finally be free of this harpy and all her tricks."

"At best we keep an eye on him," Horatio added. "Stanley and his wife Lucretia, their culture. And if he can provide us any information, get into places we can't—as he promises—we'll be closer to knowing what this is all about, incants and our story."

"Can't argue with that," grumbled Gaston. "Madison will probably warm up to that idea."

Motion paused. Everyone but Gordon faded from the room. Gordon saw the wallpaper run like a gossamer liquid from the walls, exposing the garden-floor front room he was accustomed to. The upholstered chairs blanched from existence, replaced with modern seating. The way to the dining area opened, and the kitchen shifted into the Goodspeed's cooking area. The darkness in the window gave way to the morning of October the ninth, present day. Gordon remained still as all the changes took place, and he was delivered into the familiar setting of his family's Fable Avenue brownstone.

Someone knocked on the door, but Gordon didn't move to answer it. Silence haunted the scene for a moment, and then the knocking continued. Gordon turned toward the door. He focused his senses, and just as he expected, the tingling reverberation buzzed up his neck and to the crown of his head. The solid walls dissolved away for a moment, and Gordon eyed Papa Solomon standing at the garden entrance, knocking. The house's solid barriers covered the image as Gordon broke his concentration. He walked to the entrance, unlocked and opened the door.

"Good morning, Papa Solomon," Gordon addressed.

"You okay?" asked the elder.

"I'm fine, sir," Gordon answered.

The day was bright and beautiful with the sun and its rays, but autumn's crisp air held the larger influence.

"I've been calling the house for an hour or so," Papa Solomon stated. "I figured you were still at rest."

Gordon leaned back to get a glimpse at the clock above the mantle. It was half-past ten o'clock. He said looking at Papa Solomon, "I've been up since seven-thirty."

"Oh," stated Papa Solomon in a contemplative tone. He waved his hand forward. "Let me on through, young man. Let me get out this chill."

"Yes, Papa Solomon," said Gordon moving aside. He walked back into the front room. Papa Solomon closed and locked the doors behind him.

The elder asked Gordon, "You didn't hear the phone?"

"No, sir," Gordon answered. He faced Papa Solomon. "I've been seeing things, experiencin' things." He took a step closer to Papa Solomon and pointed to his eyes. "I have a discoloration in my eyes, Papa Solomon," Gordon revealed.

Papa Solomon inspected Gordon's eyes, tilting the young man's head back, and peering closer into the lilac-colored pupils. Gordon observed the old man's reaction to the lilac aura brightening his irises and pupils. Relief blossomed on Papa Solomon's face, and there appeared a smile just as bright as Gordon's new eyes. The community's patriarch chuckled as his eyes watered. Then he put his arms around Gordon and pulled him close into an embrace, taking Gordon by surprise. Papa Solomon aimed his head back and hollered elated, squeezing Gordon tighter as he yelled.

Gordon choked as he was squeezed between Papa Solomon's chest and tightened grip. He inhaled deep when Papa Solomon let him go. But Papa Solomon's exhilarated assault didn't end there as he shook Gordon excitedly.

"You got the stir in you, boy," Papa Solomon said as his enlivened spirit simmered to a calm tone. "Goddamn! You got the brew in you." He took a deep breath, put his hands on Gordon's shoulders, and looked up at the ceiling. *"Madison! Mom! Pop!* This boy is stirred." He smiled at Gordon, palmed the young man's hair and rubbed wildly. His smile broke into a chorus of happy laughter, and then Papa Solomon took another breath. "Let me relax. Goddamn!"

Gordon guessed nothing like this had happened before in all of the second gateway rituals. "I've had some night," he commented. "And a bit of a morning."

Calm, and with his hands resting again on Gordon's shoulders, Papa Solomon said, "No one has received a discoloration in their eyes." He closed his eyes and said grace. "Thank the spirit for presenting itself at this time." He opened his eyes. "The spirit understood our desperation. Hell, maybe it was just as desperate to make an appearance." Gordon nodded. "How you feel?" asked Papa Solomon.

Gordon fidgeted. "You use the word 'stirred.' Appropriate. It's like there's a lightning storm inside me. I've been keeping calm, focusing."

Papa Solomon shook his head. He uttered, "Yep. Yep. That sounds right, young man. Your brew been stirred. Madame Jeliya will remedy that excited storm in you. It'll only be temporary, so watch your emotions." Papa Solomon and Gordon nodded at one another. Papa Solomon waved his hand and ordered Gordon, "Go and wash up for the day. Let's get you to Madame Jeliya. You can tell me about your night and morning on the way."

"Yes, Papa Solomon," uttered Gordon. He darted to the stairs, and started to rush his ascent when he heard Papa Solomon shout for him to watch his excitement. Gordon slowed his steps, and finished his ascent with a casual walk. He removed his sweatshirt, tanktop, and sweatpants as he walked into his room. Despite Papa Solomon's warning to ease his excitement, Gordon undressed in a hurry. While naked, he rummaged through the drawers and closet. He swiped a pair of light-blue jeans, boxer briefs, another tanktop, and a brown sweatshirt embroidered with the Negro Leagues' New York Black Yankees logo on the front. He pitched each item of clothing atop the bed and went to the bathroom down the hall to wash up.

Ghetto washing is how Gordon referred to bathing at the sink with a rag and bar of soap. Others called it *bird bathing.* Regardless, it was to save time and not keep Papa Solomon waiting too long with a shower, which he desperately wanted to take, warm and soothing. *Perhaps a relaxing bath later, considered Gordon.* For now, Gordon hastily scrubbed and washed the required areas of his naked body using a washcloth, the running water in the sink, and a bar of soap. He dried with a face towel, rubbed on deodorant, and brushed his teeth. He gargled with mouthwash, spat and commented,

"All this mysticism and no conjure to just be clean." He chuckled at his joke, tidied the area around the sink, and then left the bathroom. He returned to his bedroom and put on the clothes he'd picked out. He said, "Even with an incant to clean me, I'd still bathe. You just never know. Just because I got mouthwash, it doesn't stop me from brushing my teeth." He went to a drawer, opened it, and removed a pair of white socks. "And who the hell am I talking to?" His eyes looked up and spotted the *Nigrum Nigrius Nigro*. "Maybe I'm talking to you, spooky thing." He slipped on his socks and then walked over to the aged tome. He picked it up and left the room, returning to the garden-floor.

Papa Solomon sat on the couch. He was relaxed; smile still beaming. He looked at Gordon and stood. Gordon handed Papa Solomon the *Nigrum Nigrius Nigro.* "Some new pages appeared," he told the Fable Avenue patriarch. "Or maybe I can see them with the way my eyes are."

Papa Solomon flipped to the new pages. He saw the schematics for what was termed the *Alchemical Chamber* and said, "I seem to have found it." His eyebrow lifted as he flipped the newly filled pages. "Okay…" he said, voice and demeanor shifting back to the ever-pensive Papa Solomon. His head went up and down the page, turned to the next several pages, and did the same, perusing the sketches down to their finest detail. "Now we have more to research." He shut the book and motioned for Gordon to lead the way. "I'll keep this book while Madame Jeliya performs a conjure on you. Steady that storm inside you."

Gordon reached down and gathered his keys and wallet in a single, swift motion as he passed the coffee table. He pocketed the items and continued to the door, opening it and allowing Papa Solomon to walk through. Gordon followed, locking the doors as he exited the brownstone. Then he walked alongside Papa Solomon as the elder led him onto the sidewalk and down the street to his Fable Avenue residence.

The street was quiet. The morning rush to work or school had passed. A few cars traveled along the street, and several residents walked by and greeted Papa Solomon and Gordon. No one noticed Gordon's eyes, their new color muted by the bright, autumn sun. Gordon asked, "How's Dajon?"

"He's fine," Papa Solomon answered. "He's over there with some other knuckleheaded kids. Top Hat and Wilson are on 'em. They got them boys working on a block on MacDonough. They'll get around to the other streets by day's end. Good, hard work."

Gordon didn't mention his night, and Papa Solomon didn't inquire. Gordon didn't focus an attempt to extract and decipher Papa Solomon's reasoning. He only continued to follow the elder, arriving shortly at 347 Fable Avenue, walking through the waist-high iron gate, and into the house by way of the garden entrance. The space was large, and furnished with an entertainment center decorated with ritualistic objects as well as a widescreen television and a sound system. Several Moroccan lamps hung low in the corners. Also in the room, along with a couch and chairs, was a wide, rectangular, load-bearing, decorative sculpture. The piece was sculpted from onyx and marble, painted with gold, brick-like patterns at the bottom, and a white stripe painted above that. The black area above these painted patterns was decorated in silver and gold African symbols. At the front of the large, functional sculpture, facing the stairs leading up to the parlor floor was a faux fireplace.

Gordon viewed the space that was often used for ceremonies or in-house gatherings for block parties. He could see the ghostly images of the old-style kitchen and front room where he'd witnessed the conversations between Papa Solomon's mother and father, Johnny Concheroot, Stanley Fallows, and the Fable Brothers. The faint images faded away, but left a grin on Gordon's face. Papa Solomon led Gordon upstairs into the parlor floor hall, and then straight into the kitchen. Papa Solomon first laid the *Nigrum Nigrius Nigro* on the table, and then he took several steps to his left and opened the basement door. A staircase descended into the basement. Gordon walked close behind Papa Solomon as they made their way down into Madame Jeliya's *sanctum sanctorum.*

Papa Solomon called, "Thelema-baby, you down there? We're here."

"Yes, I am, Papa," a sweet, feminine voice answered back.

Gordon always considered Madame Jeliya's laboratory another world. It was equipped with its own ecosystem of running water from a waterfall, wild flora and caged, winged and chirping fauna, and the soothing resonance of bright reds and golds humming throughout the room. At the center of this universe, was a lovely, fifty-two-year-old woman with skin kissed and blessed with the color of rich caramel. Her body was plump with age, yet her full-figure was alluring in its shape, elegantly displayed through her flowing dress that was patterned with drawings of pomegranates. Long, coiled, but not locked, hair draped past her shoulders. Atop her head was a blue headscarf pattered with stars. At the moment, she was feeding two of her caged birds. She was dropping feed through a small, open space at the top of the cage. Placing a covering over the small hole, finished, and wiping her hands, Thelema Heathwicke-Peters, called Madame Jeliya, turned and greeted her company.

"How are you, Mister Gordon Goodspeed?" she asked with a courteous smile.

"I'm doing well, Madame Jeliya," Gordon answered. "And thank you for your protection yesterday when—"

Madame Jeliya's gasp cut short Gordon's words. Her calm and peaceful aura erupted into an excited manner. She marched over to Gordon, passing her husband. She inspected the young man's eyes. "Oh. My. Goodness," she exhaled. "My goodness!" she repeated. Like Papa Solomon before her, Madame Jeliya cupped Gordon's head and tilted his face to get a better look at the lilac glow of his eyes. "Like precious gems. My, my, my," she said as a whispered gasp. "What spirits have you seen with these new, blessed eyes of yours, young man?" Gordon was set to answer, but Madame Jeliya insisted, "Come, Gordon. Come take a seat here." She turned around and moved the luxurious array of pillows resting on the lengthy chaise lounge. "Sit, sit," she insisted in a kind manner.

Gordon sat down. He looked up and saw Papa Solomon and Madame Jeliya staring down at him. Gordon had to chuckle at the anxious smiles on the elders' faces. Papa Solomon put his hands in his pockets and said to Madame Jeliya, "He's having some fun with us."

"Hard not to," said Gordon. "You guys lookin' at me like that."

"Gordon, you do understand the step forward we've made?" inquired Madame Jeliya.

"I do, Madame Jeliya."

"So," she began, "how was your night?"

Gordon said to Papa Solomon, "I followed your instructions to a tee." He recounted, "I turned to the nineteenth page, nineteen minutes after the nineteenth hour and counted to nineteen. It took a while, but something happened. There was a flash, a violet flash, like a camera. It jumped off the page. My eyes started to burn, and I dropped the book." Gordon noted, "I was sitting on the couch at the time." He breathed deep as he recalled the pain in his eyes. "My eyes were on fire. The pain was somethin' awful. There was a hum, and the pain in my eyes calmed. I thought I could open them, but when I did, more pain just came at me." Gordon then backtracked, "Well, I saw this purplish glow coming from the nineteenth page—the book was on the floor, opened. The hum was coming from there. I looked back into the light, and BAM! Mad pain. And I couldn't scream. I kept choking when I tried. I forced it, but couldn't yell like I wanted to. Then, I heard a woman's voice. She sang for me to go outside. As hard as it was with my eyes closed, I made it. My eyes were burning still. I was out of it. I was crawling on the ground, knocking over the chairs and stools in the backyard."

Madame Jeliya made a sorrowful expression with her face. Her hand covered her mouth. She sympathized, "Oh, no, you poor child."

"It hurt," Gordon emphasized, though he didn't need to. His audience understood. "Then the same voice sang into my ear again. She sang for me to look up, and I did. I opened my eyes and looked at the sky."

A pensive smile appeared over Gordon's face. "I saw a cosmic cloud funnel down toward me. It struck my eyes and extinguished the burn, and the next thing I know," he lifted his hands, pointing to his eyes "I got these Betty-*purples*."

"Lilac," Madame Jeliya corrected.

Gordon proclaimed, "Purple sounds more masculine." Madame Jeliya chuckled at Gordon's sentiment. "C'mon, Madame Jeliya, you want me to tell people I got flowers in my eyes? Light purple, maybe. Pale violet, that sounds cool."

"You have *lilac eyes*, Gordon," Madame Jeliya insisted with a stern, yet polite tone. "And they are beautiful."

Gordon bowed at the neck. "Yes, Madame Jeliya." He then said to both she and Papa Solomon, "But that's not all. While I was admiring my lilac eyes—that were far brighter than they are now—I heard ticking from a grandfather clock. It kept coming. It wasn't loud, but it was annoying. I searched all downstairs, but it stopped when I went to the basement. Objects started to appear, swords and scrolls and goblets and coins. They faded as I approached them. Then I watched the stars for a while. I saw patterns spring out of them, ancient hieroglyphs, not like Egyptian hieroglyphs. I heard music coming from the stars. They played whatever I thought of. I stayed outside for a long time and listened, not bothered by the cold. Didn't have much more on than what I have now. Something inside me was keeping me warm."

"That's sweet," Madame Jeliya said, beaming a tender smile at Gordon.

"After that, I went to bed," Gordon continued. "About an hour into sleep, the grandfather clock started ticking again, woke me up. It was making me restless, and just as I started to stir, I saw a woman in the doorway. She walked up to me, and I got nervous. Didn't move. A light glowed, and I saw her face. She was my mother." Gordon's eyes started to tear. "We had a moment, to say the least. A while of a moment. We talked. *I* talked," he corrected. "Private things." Gordon didn't feel the need to make his conversation with his mother public. Papa Solomon and Madame Jeliya saw and respected that. "I watched my mother's spirit dance in the courtyard. A piano from…somewhere…played for her, holding her up." He wiped his eyes and sniffed. "But this morning, I stepped into the past. I saw your father and mother, Papa Solomon. I saw old man Jackson and old man Gaston. I saw Stanley Fallows. That was something. It was all about the beginning of our street, our community. The first year or two. Maman Anansi was there. She was two, all jittery and cute. Your mother was pregnant with you."

Papa Solomon reflected. "I've heard so much of those times," he said. "So much so that I feel like I was there. Them early days. Well, I was a little baby." Madame Jeliya embraced Papa Solomon's arm. "Stanley and his wife coming into our community. He didn't live on the block. He stayed between Manhattan and Long Island."

Gordon explained, "When you knocked on the door, I was just coming out of watching your mother and father talking to Jackson and Gaston Fable about the whole Stanley Fallows situation."

Madame Jeliya's eyes widened as concern splashed on her face. "Gordon…" she said, tone matching her eyes. She was looking at his hands. They were shaking wildly, and his knees were bouncing erratically. Gordon noticed this and focused so as to ease the shakes in his body. Madame Jeliya had another solution. "Gordon, lay across the lounge. The brew has you anxious, but we're going to take care of that. Lay flat."

Gordon didn't hesitate. He more dropped against the lounge than relaxed himself across it. He tried to be as still as possible, his body still shaking. Madame Jeliya assured him everything would be fine, but it didn't ease Gordon's worry. She asked for him to close his eyes, and Gordon did as told. He trembled as if cold.

"Vencil-baby, set the record," Madame Jeliya ordered. Papa Solomon was frozen in place, fear growing behind his pensive, widening stare that watched Gordon convulse. His wife's voice pulled him from his entranced state as she called again, "Papa, the record!"

Papa Solomon shook his head over and over. "Yes, Thelema-baby," he stammered. He turned around and walked to one of the room's corners. He rolled out an old-time record player sitting atop a marble and wooden stand with wheels on the legs.

Gordon's body continued shaking. He remained conscious, trying to concentrate and soothe the wild tremors. But his body's quiver kept him from focusing. His breathing and heart rate increased. Anxiety showered him, perspiring from his forehead. Gordon believed he'd rather have had the pain burning his eyes than the loss of control over his faculties, if he indeed had a decision. He looked up. Madame Jeliya stood over him, bending down and putting the palms of her hands at the temple of his head. She spoke an incant, soft and comforting. The words eased Gordon's trembling, and then he heard the jazz music begin to play. Gordon no longer gave his convulsions any attention. He focused on the music. He heard a voice that was not attached to the record, but spoke in rhythm with the music.

"If Adam existed literally – in the flesh physically – Instead of meta-euphoric, allegoric-scientifically – I would be his flesh flickering, candle sunlight quivering, perfect molecular molded rendering, second manifestation – For on the Eve of my birth I fed on information – And this is how I knew I was a male child."

Gordon went to sleep, and dreamed vivid dreams. He was entertained with a tale set in Moorish Spain and narrated by the same voice that spoke in the same rhythm of the jazz album playing to soothe his tremors. The music also followed Gordon into the dream. Its notes, much like the rhyming voice, narrated the concrete images that danced in his slumber. The backdrop of Moorish Spain, and the story of two lovers, evaporated in a lilac haze. The pale-purple fog lifted, and there again were the two lovers. It was Africa, a new lifetime. The lovers fled kingdom after kingdom that was overrun with menacing slave traders whose lustful appetites were sated by the trade of human flesh and an overwhelming need to see African streets run red with the blood from any who resisted. The lovers were captured, and the man tossed overboard a slave vessel to drown or be devoured by sharks. But his voice would live through the beat of his unborn son's heart. It would speak in Morse code, tapping and drumming messages of rebellion. The sound would ripen into the son's voice as he matured into a young man. His mother's spirit would baptize his father's voice with harmony. The vicious imagery of American slavery didn't break the young African man born into its climate. He would speak to angels, and little African girls hiding in shadow. The land tilled while tensions filled, and rebellion tempered the atmosphere. Angels, African bewitchments, and fellow slaves helped the young African man burn a plantation to the ground at the sound of a horn enchanted with all the mystical notations of the cosmos, all of Tehuti's hidden sounds.

Gordon's dream moved from burned plantation to a battle consisting of free black men and women defending an island's coastline against an onslaught of piratical slave ships. The son, with his father's voice and mother's harmony blessing him, helped lead the defense. Horn in hand, and pressed against his lips, the magic reverberated. When the lilac dust settled, Gordon heard three gunshots accompanied by the flashing images of three shadowy figures, smoking guns in their hands, overlooking the bleeding body of a jazz musician. Another lilac haze took the dream's narrative to a long, dusty, Mississippi road. It was August 25, 1957. A 1955 Chrysler Imperial rumbled down the road, leaving a trail of dust in its wake. Inside the car, sitting in the passenger seat, was Papa Solomon and Maman Anansi's father, Horatio Peters. The musical dream continued this new story with only music and images, the poetic narration ceased.

Madame Jeliya continued to hover over Gordon, face to his, palms on either side of his head. "Stay relaxed, Gordon Goodspeed," she told Gordon's sleeping body. "We've been waiting for that spirit inside you to present itself. Breathe easy, young man." Papa Solomon watched his wife work her incant. Gordon's violent tremors subsided, and Madame Jeliya stood up straight, standing next to her husband and observing Gordon as he rested. "Papa," Madame Jeliya addressed her husband. "We can't keep doing this."

"I know, Thelema-Baby," Papa Solomon responded. "I know. We need Savannah to help this young man. He needs a reading for a proper altar." He pointed to the stairs and said to Madame Jeliya, "I got the *Nigrum Nigrius Nigro* upstairs on the table. There're some new writings, blueprints actually. A resting chamber. Probably for him. Have no idea how we'll build it."

Madame Jeliya embraced Papa Solomon. "We'll find a way, Papa. We always do." She kissed his cheek. Papa Solomon returned the gesture, kissing Madame Jeliya's forehead.

"It is exciting, Papa," remarked Madame Jeliya. "We're at a new stage." Both turned and walked toward the stairs, still embraced. They left Gordon to rest, walking up into the kitchen and taking a seat at the table. Madame Jeliya rested on Papa Solomon's lap, arms around his neck, and her nose nestled in his cheek. Jazz crooned from the basement. "We need to celebrate. All this calls for a parade, Papa, outside of time."

Papa Solomon smiled at his wife's wish. "That'll take a lot out of us, Thelema-baby. But we do have the Four Days of the Spirit Festival at the end of this month. We could make it something special. The entire street. Invite everybody in the community that can get here." Papa Solomon kissed Madame Jeliya on the mouth. "We're stronger at October's end, and all throughout November. We ain't young, but who knows the possibilities with the spirit inside that boy. Might give us all a little kick." He chuckled.

"What's got you laughin', Papa?" Thelema asked her husband, eyes pregnant with adorable curiosity.

"I'm a little excited about all this," Papa Solomon admitted.

Thelema commented, "According to what I'm sitting on, Papa, you more than a *little* excited." She chuckled too, once again nestling her nose in Papa Solomon's cheek. She whispered a sensual sentiment into his ear, "You got a spirit of your own, don't you now, Papa. You got a stir inside you."

Papa Solomon grinned. "Oh, I got a conjure for you tonight, Miss Lady."

Madame Jeliya kissed her husband deep. She moved her head away, and her mouth turned to a sensuous smile. She tapped his nose and said to him, "You keep thought on that conjure, Papa. We got some work to do." Her voice turned serious. "What about Savannah? That boy needs a proper reading and an altar. You said Gordon goes to school with her granddaughter, Fey?"

Papa Solomon nodded in the affirmative. "Yep. That's a start," he told his wife.

"Or maybe you could give her a phone call or visit," Madame Jeliya suggested. But before Papa Solomon could protest she added, "But I'm sure Stanley has an eye up there in Mount Vernon. Hell, us celebratin' might rouse that demon-crazy warlock from whatever shadow he's hidin' under. We'll have to disguise that as our regular end of October street festival." She turned her head toward the basement entrance. "Though, this young man with the lilac eyes might hold a key to challenge Stanley's offense." Madame Jeliya thought about her last word, and then she corrected, "*Defense.* Everything about Stanley has been defensive." She turned to Papa Solomon and tapped his nose again as she said, "Regardless, that young man needs an altar aligned to him. Keep him focused and calmed."

Papa Solomon breathed deep. He pondered another solution to the dilemma at hand, a third option. "My father's horn could relax him. I know a few incants that ought to, uh, assist me in playing it."

"You sure, Papa?" Madame Jeliya asked.

Papa Solomon nodded. He said, "If I can lift it, then that means I'm supposed to be able to play it. I'm fifty-some-odd-couple-two-three-four years old. I can't stay intimidated by a legacy I haven't properly indulged in. I'll learn."

"Well, you'll get started soon enough," said Madame Jeliya, bouncing off Papa Solomon's lap and to her feet. "Right now, you need to make a phone call to Gordon's father. Tell him his son's brew has been stirred. Talk in code," she reminded. Papa Solomon grimaced as his wife turned her back, making a fuss at having to be careful over an open line. He knew. In fact, Maximilian and him had already worked out a code. Madame Jeliya relayed, "I'm going to Lena's to tell her she's due for a reading."

"You gonna be alright?" Papa Solomon asked his wife.

"I'll be fine. Lena won't bite. At least not now," Madame Jeliya chuckled and walked out of the kitchen to retrieve a few items before leaving the house. She said from another room, "Once you finish with your phone call, you get some proper rest, Papa. Hear? You were up all last night with worry."

"I will, woman. Damn!" Papa Solomon pouted at his wife, grimacing at her again for treating him like a child. Madame Jeliya yelled back to her husband that she was just trying to help him, and to stop acting like a baby. Papa Solomon burst into a low chortle, face now possessed with a smile. He said to his wife, "I know, Thelema-baby." He did so appreciate his wife. Papa Solomon got up from his chair. He picked up the phone and dialed Maximilian's cell phone number. Gordon's father picked up immediately. "How's everything, Papa Solomon?" he asked anxiously.

Papa Solomon answered back with a rhetorical question. "How you doing, Max?" he greeted. "Where are you?"

"At the station, directing traffic," Maximilian answered. "To be honest, I can't keep still," he felt the need to add. "How's the renovation going?" he coded his question.

"Well, uh, as you know there's water in the basement and the pilot light is out," Papa Solomon responded.

"Yes…"

"But Gordon's been a great help," Papa Solomon assured.

"That's great. Good," Maximilian replied, trying not to sound too excited. He wanted to hold his proud reaction until he heard precise confirmation about his son's rites.

That's when Papa Solomon said in code, "He'll be able to clean up the water, and he'll get the pilot light going again."

Maximilian didn't shout. He said his son's name asking for clarification. "Gordon…?" Then there again came a set of small gasps of excitement from Maximilian. "Can I come through?"

Papa Solomon pressed, "Gordon's had a busy night, but he made progress. Good progress," Papa Solomon stressed. "Gordon's resting now. He's a bit overwhelmed, the work and all, but we're further along than we've ever been with getting this house in order. We'll get to the water and pilot light. There're still some things to figure out before we jump into that. But come through once work's done."

"I will, Papa Solomon," Maximilian said, doing his best to mute his excited state.

"I'll see you then, Max. Bye."

The conversation ended. Papa Solomon smiled and put the phone back on its charger. He walked to his study, leaning in the entranceway. His eyes spotted a bright golden trumpet situated on the desk at the far end. He stepped inside the room, making his way to the desk. He stood over the horn, hands in pockets, examining the bright, golden instrument, marveling at its polished frame.

"Look," he stated, reaching out to lift the horn off its stand. He stayed his hand and said, "We've got to be more than friends with our relationship. I'm going to kiss you, and you gon' kiss back. Dig? You gon' be my second wife, and you gon' make the proper sounds a wife makes when a good man kisses her." He lifted the trumpet from its stand. "I know your story. You are a Peters' instrument, shaped long ago. I have my father and grandfather's blood in me. I can make you sing." He placed the horn back, returned his hand to his pocket, and exited his study. He walked up the stairs to the master bedroom on the top floor and treated himself to a well-deserved nap.

Horatio Peters led a procession down Fable Avenue filled with music and jubilee. The parade was a celebration announcing to the world Fable Avenue's emergence out of the blue. Brooklyn had a new street, and New York City had a new subway line. The 8-Train, dubbed the *Black Line* or the *8-Ball Ride*. The Great Spirit and the grand gods lent assistance, burrowing into the world's population the acceptance of Fable Avenue as if it resided in New York City's history the whole time.

A lilac haze flooded the scene as Horatio and his band concluded their final notes. Delia-LaRue Amat hollered a melodious send off, one last scat to accompany the band's music. The song faded behind the lilac cloud, and Gordon Goodspeed awoke from slumber well rested. His vision focused, surfacing through the sleep in his eyes. Madame Jeliya came into view. She was sitting in a wooden chair, removed of her headscarf, reading a book. Her eyes met Gordon's. He sat up feeling restored and without anxiety of the stir inside him.

"Rested?" Madame Jeliya asked.

Gordon nodded and responded, "Yes, Madame Jeliya. I feel relaxed. What do my eyes look like?" he asked.

"They still have their lilac aura, Gordon," Madame Jeliya assured.

Gordon was relieved. "I saw it all," he notified Madame Jeliya. "I saw Papa Solomon and Maman Anansi's mother and father bring Fable Avenue out of the blue. I saw their past lives. I saw the past lives of Elder Horatio's parents too."

"That was the music, Gordon," Madame Jeliya told him.

Gordon looked at the record player. It was off, and the album from Horatio Peters and his band had been stored away. "We hear about all that growing up," said Gordon. "It's recited to us at every festival. But it's something else when you see it." Madame Jeliya agreed, and Gordon suggested, "Maybe we should play the music at the next festival. Have everyone experience the story."

"I don't know if all those images would be appropriate for the younger ones in our community," Madame Jeliya objected in a polite tone. "Everyone learns our story at his or her own pace. Maybe we can edit it a bit."

Gordon understood.

Madame Jeliya stood. She put her book on the chaise lounge next to Gordon and instructed Gordon to rise. Gordon rose to his feet and followed Madame Jeliya upstairs. Gordon walked close behind, and once upstairs, in the kitchen, he spied the clock on the stove. It was 1:30 in the afternoon. Madame Jeliya stopped at one of the cupboards, opened it, and pulled out a jar of mint leaves. She opened the container and plucked several leaves free. She handed the leaves to Gordon and said, "For your breath, Gordon."

Gordon took the leaves and started chewing. The mint was strong, flavored with an incant, having been grown in the Peters' backyard garden. Madame Jeliya sealed the jar with its lid and returned it to the cupboard. Again, she instructed for Gordon to follow her, and Gordon traipsed in tow. They moved to the hallway. Madame Jeliya removed one of her coats off the coatrack and slipped it on. She opened the doors and ushered Gordon through, shutting and locking each door as Gordon and she exited.

"Come on, Gordon, we're going to Lady Arachne's house," Madame Jeliya said as she made her way down the stairs. Gordon offered his hand as balance, and Madame Jeliya accepted. "Thank you, young man," she expressed. "There's more to be done with you, Gordon. You're still going through your rites. They're not over. Lady Arachne has to do a little scrying with you."

Gordon returned to the chilly October day. Down the stairs and through the gate, Madame Jeliya led the way to the house of Lena Franklin, called Lady Arachne. On the way, the pair came across Wilson Barnes and his girlfriend, Phylicia Abdala, an Afro-Brazilian girl with rich brown skin and long dreadlocks. Wilson greeted Madame Jeliya with a respectful hug and kiss on the cheek. She leaned into Wilson's greeting, and then exchanged the same salutation with Phylicia.

"How are you Madame Jeliya?" Wilson asked.

"I am fine," Madame Jeliya answered standing straight. "I'm taking Gordon here to see Lady Arachne."

Wilson turned to Gordon and tossed air punches at the young man. Gordon played along, dodging and countering. Then Wilson noticed the glow in Gordon's eyes. He covered his mouth with a balled fist and expressed, "Get out, sun!" He looked at Madame Jeliya and asked, "This for real?" He turned to Phylicia, pointing at Gordon. "You see this?"

Madame Jeliya beamed. "It's for real, Wilson."

Phylicia smiled too, looking at Gordon. "That's great, Gordon."

"Now, the two of you keep this hushed," ordered Madame Jeliya with authority. "This puts us on greater alert than ever." Wilson remained in awe at the lilac color in Gordon's eyes. Madame Jeliya snapped her fingers, making Wilson turn his attention to her. "Say nothing, hear? Keep this low. Wilson, the matriarchs and Papa Solomon will hold counsel, and most likely we'll be calling on you and Top Hat for your skills. Lady Arachne has Martin investigating the whereabouts of an item she needs procured—by any means. And you know what that means."

"Okay," Wilson said, hinting he'd already known what item Lady Arachne was seeking. "I'll stay alert. I'm just walking Phylicia to the shop to help run it while I deal with these kids cleanin' the streets. But I'm ready when the order is."

Madame Jeliya nodded and said, "Thank you, Wilson. Until then, you keep them children in line. Let's be on our way, Gordon." She and Gordon moved to the other side of the street. Wilson yelled to Gordon, *"I'ma get up with you later, man!"* And he and Phylicia continued on. Madame Jeliya and Gordon walked up to the house of Lady Arachne. The front door opened just as Madame Jeliya and Gordon ascended the stairs. Lady Arachne appeared wearing a dress with blue, black, and white patterns. Other patterns on the dress were gold-colored solar crosses and silver moons. Lady Arachne was tall and slender with dreadlocks flowing far past her shoulders. She was as dark and beautiful as the richest and most fertile soil the Earth had to offer. She aimed a bright, inviting smile at Gordon, her eyes, as slender as her frame, watching him come closer.

Gordon felt drawn to Lady Arachne, pulled in by the gravity of her stare. He remained collected, but his breath left him. It was always like this in the presence of the third matriarch named Lady Arachne. There was not a man on Fable Avenue that did not escape adolescence without having a strong, short-lived liking to her. And this attraction appeared to intensify as she aged. Lady Arachne, Lena Franklin, was fifty-one years old. And she was as enticing as any woman half her age. And then she spoke, "Mister Goodspeed." Her voice sounded like a slow, creaking door, but it was soothing. Gordon found it sexy, breathy and sensual. Lady Arachne turned to Madame Jeliya and greeted hastily, "Thelema."

"Lena," Madame Jeliya retorted. It was polite, but Gordon could hear a cold snap residing under Madame Jeliya's tone.

Lady Arachne focused on Gordon's eyes. "Splendid," she said through her smile. She turned. Her movement was like a curtain in the wind. Then she walked into her house, a silent suggestion for Madame Jeliya and Gordon to follow.

Gordon took a step forward, watching Lady Arachne's long, irregular waving movement. But Gordon stopped, shook himself from his entranced state and made a courteous gesture allowing Madame Jeliya to move ahead of him. Lady Arachne waited for her guests to come into the hallway. She shut and locked her front doors with the use of a soft-spoken incant, and then asked of Madame Jeliya, "Please, have a seat in the library, Madame Jeliya. I'll give this blessed young man his reading downstairs."

"Why thank you," Madame Jeliya replied with a mechanical, courteous nod.

Lady Arachne opened the sliding doors, exposing a large reading and study area. "There is fresh wine and cookies for you to indulge in, Madame Jeliya. I prepared the cookies myself."

"Thank you," Madame Jeliya repeated. She stepped into the room as Gordon and Lady Arachne continued through the hall and into the kitchen.

Lady Arachne's parlor floor was similar in layout to Papa Solomon and Madame Jeliya's. There was no entrance to the basement from the kitchen, however. Gordon followed Lady Arachne down to the garden level. The first room was an elaborate dining area. An intricate, brass chandelier adorned with hanging, crystal shards hung above a long, rectangular, wooden table that was decorated with a purple runner. Eight chairs surrounded the table. There was a chair at both ends, and three on either side. There was, in place of a couch as in Gordon's family residence, a wooden-framed glass cabinet displaying all manner of fine plates, vials, and even a section for herbs and spices. The door to Lady Arachne's courtyard was positioned next to the case.

Gordon was led across the dining area and into a small room. Lady Arachne turned on the lights, not by the flip of a switch, but with the twiddle of her fingers. A glow with no readily seen source lit the purple room. Black and white lotus flowers were painted on the walls. Two, thin, yellow pillars, extending from floor to ceiling, were at the far left and far right of the room, opposite the entrance. Centered in the room was a rectangular, wooden table. Its edges were carved with intricate designs composing the faces of various Orisha and Lwa, veve symbols, Kemetic hieroglyphs, and the zodiac. The work surface functioned as a large Opon-Ifa divination table, a map of consciousness derived from the Yoruba of Africa. There was a seat on one side and a wooden bench on the other. A small, black and gold silk cloth with a set of tarot cards situated on top rested on the table.

"Have a seat, Gordon," said Lady Arachne, motioning toward the bench.

Gordon sat down on the bench. Lady Arachne shut the door and sat down opposite him. Her skin appeared to hum with a faint glow of the room. Gordon felt as if he'd stepped into a dream. His head lightened, and his senses heightened. But the storm inside him did not stir. Lady Arachne stared at Gordon with a smile. "I have waited to see those eyes glimmering in this room for a long time. Many accidents have kept this spirit from finding a home. You are blessed, Gordon. Stirring inside you is a finely brewed ink that will help us pen the rest of our tale." Lady Arachne nodded, and Gordon returned a nod. "Let's get started, shall we." There was a fading, Southern accent clinging to her words, a hint of her South Carolina upbringing.

Gordon relaxed his posture. He watched Lady Arachne close her eyes and put her fingers to her temple. She started to hum. Gordon grinned at the matriarch. She ceased her humming, opened one eye and chuckled through pursed lips.

"Just kidding," she said.

"You always do that, Lady Arachne," Gordon commented, his grin opening to a polite laugh.

"It's just to break the tension. Feel better? Then let's continue." Lady Arachne fixed herself. She motioned to the deck of tarot cards and said to Gordon, "You know how things are done."

"Yes, Lady Arachne."

Gordon picked up the tarot cards.

Lady Arachne removed the black and gold cloth from the table, folded it neatly, and set it at the corner of the table. She said to Gordon, "You go ahead and close your spirit-filled eyes, chil'. Focus on a question. Your hands will find the answer in the cards, and I'll help you interpret your path."

Gordon shut his eyes. He focused. His hands began shuffling the cards. He heard Lady Arachne instruct him to count to nineteen, and he did. He counted to himself, but as if he was counting aloud, when he reached nineteen, Lady Arachne expressed for him to stop. Gordon paused. He opened his eyes.

"Now cut the deck," Lady Arachne directed. "Three times," she specified.

Gordon put the shuffled deck of tarot cards on the desk and split the deck into three. He pushed the three separate decks together, and the cards slipped in between one another making the deck whole again. Gordon waited, and Lady Arachne had another set of instructions for him. She repeated for Gordon to shuffle the cards and to count to nineteen. Gordon followed the matriarch's orders. He shuffled the cards and counted in his head, and again Lady Arachne asked him to stop just as he reached the end of his count. She pointed to the folded black and gold cloth. Gordon set the deck atop it. His eyes followed Lady Arachne as she stood up tall. She took the deck of cards in hand and announced, *"The Chariot."* She flipped the first card and placed it on her desk inside a gold rectangular frame painted into the wood. *"The Fool,"* Lady Arachne announced before flipping the very card into position inside another gold rectangle painted next to the first. Five more spaces waited to be filled. Lady Arachne called out each card before flipping them into their respective slots, and she never looked down to check if her announcements were ever incorrect, which they were not. *"The Ten of Wands. The Two of Wands. The World,"* she called and flipped before pausing. There were two more gold frames waiting to be filled.

Gordon ran his eyes along each card, attempting to decipher their meaning and relevance ahead of Lady Arachne's reveal. But he saw nothing, not even with his new eyes. He looked at Lady Arachne for an answer. But Lady Arachne didn't fill the last two spaces. Instead, she laid a second set of cards adjacent to the empty spaces, aligned vertically. Again she announced the cards before turning them over as she drew them from the deck. One by one she trumpeted, *"Three of Cups, reversed. Ten of Cups, reversed. Five of Wands. Nine of Swords."*

Gordon hated hearing the word "reverse" when dealing with Tarot. He wondered what calamity was hovering over him, waiting to fall like a piano in an old-style, loony cartoon. Lady Arachne called out the *Page of Cups, the Page of Wands, the Page of Swords,* and *The Page of Pentacles.* She pulled each card and placed them close to the corner of Gordon's right-hand side. She placed over the Page cards all the cards of the Knight, calling them out before turning them over. She did the same for the Kings.

"These are you, Gordon," Lady Arachne explained. "Your stages," she elaborated. "Initiate. Warrior and defender. King. Your blessed spirit is made up of all the elements of the cosmos, and all the elements of the Earth. You wear all suits." Gordon remained still, anxious for the final cards and the translation to those previously drawn. Lady Arachne read Gordon's emotions with a hidden eye. "Be still, Gordon. Don't let that brew get stirred again. I heard about your episode."

Gordon took a breath and a moment.

Lady Arachne waited for Gordon to ease, and then she said, "Good. Now let me continue." She spoke, *"The Lovers."* Gordon liked to hear that, but something peculiar took place. Lady Arachne made the motion of flipping a card over, placing it down into the next-to-last rectangular slot. But no card was in her hand. He thought his eyes played a trick on him, but before he could process the moment, Lady Arachne was calling, *"The Six of Cups."*

The final slot was filled.

Lady Arachne returned the remaining cards to the folded, silk cloth. Gordon saw her face turn apologetic. Her tone was just the same when she explained, "I don't possess The Lover's card, Gordon. My deck is not authentic. I blessed this deck with a strong incant. Its charge is powerful. Took me days, honey. I slept just as long when it was all over." She chuckled and said, "And that was when I was as young as you—maybe a little older." She moved her hand over the stacked cards sitting on the silk cloth. "I also sketched and colored these cards. I used all my blessing and talents to copy every stroke of a very ancient deck of cards that have been lost to time. I have Detective Kimball and Professor Khepri investigating, following every clue I discover. We're close to finding the deck."

Gordon observed Lady Arachne's sadness. There came the vibrating, tingling sensation on the back of his neck. It stretched this time to the tail of his spine and then sprang to the crown of his head. Melancholy poured over him like a strong wave. The back of his neck started burning and it became just as intense as the sting in his eyes. Gordon worried about the "brew" that stirred inside him. He clenched his teeth as his body shook with a subtle tremble, enough to worry him. Gordon breathed easy. He focused on the calm sleep, the rest he experienced hours earlier. It washed the vibrating tension electrocuting, flashing, stirring and conjuring the storm inside him. It scoured and scrubbed the tension away, and before long, Gordon was calm again. Once at ease, and mostly to distract himself from the trembling sense he wrestled with, Gordon asked Lady Arachne, "Why could you not draw The Lover's card, if you don't mind me asking."

Lady Arachne exhaled. When her breath drained, Gordon's tension ceased. Gordon breathed easier. Lady Arachne answered, "I can't see it, as far back as my eye can gaze through time. I cannot see The Lovers card." Gordon believed the smile that crawled across Lady Arachne's visage was haunting. The sadness in her eyes appeared to brighten her beauty. "How appropriate," she articulated, eyes turning reminiscent. She fixed her countenance and pointed to the first card, *The Chariot.* She returned to business and proclaimed, "An arrival. Here we see our present state, Gordon, the spirit inside you, born through your rites." She pointed to *The Fool.* "The start of your journey, Gordon. This is you."

Gordon lifted an eyebrow and inspected the card with the whimsical scene of an African youth dressed in ancient robes trotting toward a cliff's edge, one foot dangling over. His life's possessions slung over his shoulder, sack at the end of a long wooden pole. A black hyena barked up to him, and a black and gold sun, with the face of a cat, shined down on him. "I'm a fool," Gordon pondered aloud. He thought to himself, and then he looked up at Lady Arachne and declared, "Agreed."

Lady Arachne cocked her head and made a face, crooked smile beaming. *"Gordon!"* she hissed playfully. "You know better. This is signifying the beginning. You are innocent, pure and open, as you receive the blessing of this lilac spirit. It's empowered you with its sting, not poisoned you."

"Got me right in the eyes," Gordon commented under his breath.

Lady Arachne heard Gordon's sentiment, to which she remarked, "Oh, no, Mister Goodspeed. I told you I heard of your night's ordeal. Madame Jeliya told me everything while you rested. The funnel that stretched down from the cosmos, and relieved the burn in your eyes, *that* was the spirit's sting." With the conversation resolved, Lady Arachne moved on. She pointed to the *Ten of Wands*. An African man carried a load of ten heavy staves. "You will carry a great burden, Gordon. But you will endure." Then came the *Two of Wands*. "You will oversee the affairs in your kingdom. You will keep it safe." Her finger moved to *The World*. "And thus there will be a new world."

It all sounded grand, but Gordon didn't believe he was anymore wiser for hearing Lady Arachne's prophetic proposition. He wanted to know how he would get from one step to the next. Then, Lady Arachne aimed her finger at the reversed *Three of Cups*. The picture was of three African women raising goblets and rejoicing. But the image was reversed, upside down to Gordon. "This one concerns us matriarchs. We must be cautious when dealing with all this," Lady Arachne commented. "We must stay aligned in thought. We must work out our disagreements. Of course, you know that ain't the easiest thing to do with us womenfolk."

Gordon drawled, "Miss Arachne…"

"Oh, Gordon, I tease," she replied waving her hand down. The *Ten of Cups* was next. An African family lifted their hands to the heavens. Ten goblets appeared high in the sky against the backdrop of a rainbow. "Fable Avenue will prosper, but something will taint the prosperity. It might be built on false pretense." Lady Arachne pondered this possibility, but gave no revelation of her thoughts. Then there was the *Five of Wands*. Five boys scuffled, using staves as weapons. Lady Arachne divined, "The youth stirred, armed against one another."

Gordon reflected on his interaction with his brother, Cedron and their friends. He also thought about his conversation with Neyeli. He stayed silent. Lady Arachne defined the final offset card, the *Nine of Swords*. Etched onto the card was an image of a woman sitting up in bed after a nightmare, her face covered, trying to smother the foul dream's torment. Nine swords hung on the wall. "You have to relax your anxiety, Gordon. With the spirit in you, you're as much a danger as you are a blessing."

"Yes, Lady Arachne."

The matriarch pointed to the *Six of Cups*. An older boy planted gifts into six cups and handed them to younger children. "This is you, Gordon. You are the gift giver. You can bring a wish into existence, and you can magnify a blessing."

"What is the Grand Wish, Lady Arachne?" Gordon asked in an innocent voice.

"Ah, an utterance by Maman Anansi and Papa Solomon's great-grandmother long ago," Lady Arachne confessed. "We are still trying to decipher it. But with your spirit blessed, you will play a role in procuring whatever it is, Gordon." Lady Arachne swiped two more cards from the deck. She announced before flipping them over, covering the spot where *The Lovers* card should have been placed. *"The Ace of Wands! The High Priestess!"* She flipped the cards into place, one atop the other, offset. "You will have a secret art with a woman you behold. Isn't that romantic." Then she ordered, "Come. Up. Your reading will stay with you, Gordon. Ponder it, but don't overwhelm yourself with it."

Gordon remarked, "There's a lot of dysfunction in those cards."

"Oh, Gordon," Lady Arachne said, shooing away his worry. "Don't you pay all that too much mind. This is not set in stone. And if so, there are ways to crumble stone." She came from around the table and took a seat next to Gordon on the bench. She slid close to him, her arm at first brushing gently against his, and then it pressed a little harder. Her touch was like a battery. Gordon's neck jittered and buzzed. The feelings reverberated, up and down, from the root of his spine and up to the top of his crown. Again and again. But the electric storm inside him remained calm, never stirring.

Lady Arachne leaned her head close to Gordon, almost as if nuzzling her nose to his ear. She said, sensuous voice creaking, "The cards were always tools for a person to gain a clear understanding of their life. Think of it as an early form of psychology. Yes, there's great meaning and lessons locked into them, and my conjure pulls from the cards the greatest of truths. The theurgic symbols are most powerful. But too strong a mind can make the bad of the cards manifest just as much as the good." Lady Arachne hopped up from the bench. "Let's not keep Madame Jeliya waiting any longer than she has. Come on."

Lady Arachne's frame, no longer up against Gordon, was like the release of two magnets pulled apart. Gordon's neck cooled, and the sensation riding his spine eased. Gordon obeyed his elder. He stood and followed Lady Arachne out of the room, across the dining area, up the stairs and into the kitchen.

"Thelema," Lady Arachne called. There was no answer back. Lady Arachne called again, "Thelema." There was still no answer. "Madame Jeliya," Lady Arachne yelled.

"I'm here," Madame Jeliya responded. "I'm still in the library."

Gordon found the exchange odd. He glanced at Lady Arachne's face to see a reaction, but the reticent woman showed no distress. He and Lady Arachne walked through the hall and to the library. Madame Jeliya sat patiently with a glass of wine in her hand and a half-eaten cookie in the other. She was chewing. She swallowed and complimented, "These are delicious, Lady Arachne."

"Thank you," Lady Arachne replied with an odd smile. Madame Jeliya finished her glass of wine and her cookie and stood. Lady Arachne trotted to her and took the empty wine glass from her. "Let me take that from you, Madame Jeliya," she said.

"Thank you," Madame Jeliya expressed in a surprised tone.

"Gordon is finished here," Lady Arachne reported. "An interesting read. He has his path to ponder."

Madame Jeliya thanked Lady Arachne once again. "Gordon," Madame Jeliya summoned, "Let's get you home, up the street. We can all rest for a moment and think about the possibilities of our new path."

Lady Arachne stepped into the hall and unlocked and opened her front doors. Gordon and Madame Jeliya walked through, but not before the pair of them presented Lady Arachne with a friendly hug and kiss.

"I'm sure Maman Anansi will be arriving soon," Madame Jeliya said to Lady Arachne as she stepped out of the house. "We'll counsel with Papa Solomon and some of the street's servicemen."

"Indeed," Lady Arachne responded.

"Good day, Lady Arachne."

"Good day, Madame Jeliya."

The doors closed. Gordon walked across the street with Madame Jeliya, and up a few houses, to the Goodspeed Fable Avenue residence. Gordon unlocked and entered through the garden entrance. Madame Jeliya remained outside. "Papa Solomon will be through later, Gordon. I'm heading back to the house."

Gordon faced her. He stepped up to Madame Jeliya and gave her a departing embrace. "Thank you, Madame Jeliya."

"You're most welcome, Gordon," she told him and then kissed his cheek.

Madame Jeliya turned around, wished Gordon a good day, and then walked away. Gordon closed and locked the doors. He rushed to the kitchen to prepare a sandwich. He was well rested, but he hadn't eaten all day. He opened the refrigerator and pulled free bread, Provolone, mayonnaise, mustard, and spicy Cajun turkey slices from *Frenchie's* deli located on the corner of Fable and Stuyvesant. His stomach bubbled as he gathered the ingredients from the refrigerator, tomatoes and lettuce included. Gordon constructed his sandwich, and then he returned the ingredients to the refrigerator, poured a tall glass of cranberry juice, and then took a seat in the dining room. The back of Gordon's neck flickered with vibration. He ignored it and decided to indulge in his meal. The sandwich hung inches from Gordon's mouth when someone knocked on the door. He put the sandwich down and groaned.

Gordon hopped up from his seat and answered the door. Oliver Peters and Wilson Barnes stood outside. Their wide, proud grins shined on Gordon like a spotlight, eventually erupting into loud, congratulatory shouts. Gordon opened the door wider, allowing the two men inside, and both Oliver and Wilson charged and grabbed Gordon, lifting him.

"My boy got them eyes!" Wilson hollered. "The spirit is back in town, baby!"

Oliver opened his grip on Gordon to turn around and close the garden-entrance doors. Wilson tossed Gordon into the front room. Gordon landed, keeping his balance by hopping around until both feet were planted firmly. He noticed the *Nigrum Nigrius Nigro* in Oliver's hand. Oliver turned and handed the book to Gordon. "My father said you might need this back," he informed Gordon. "He had me jot down some things he wanted to study once he's done resting. I made quick copies of those new sketches too."

Oliver was dressed in his paramedic uniform, ready for his shift.

Gordon took the book and invited Wilson and Oliver to join him in the dining room. He made his path through the front room, tossing the aged, blessed tome onto the couch. He moved to the dining area and sat down in front of his sandwich. "You guys want one?" he asked being polite. Wilson and Oliver both declined as they sat down. Wilson asked if he could grab a drink from the refrigerator and Gordon gave him permission.

Wilson called from the kitchen, "This place looks like it was robbed. They dragged everything out of here."

"Everything's coming back Saturday," Gordon shouted. He took a long, overdue bite, chewed and savored every moment of the taste. He swallowed and sipped his drink. "I needed that. Ain't had a meal since last night." As Wilson returned to the room with a glass of cranberry juice, Gordon remarked, "It's been somethin', my rites. I've had lights flash out of books, burning up my eyes. I've had the cosmos wash 'em out and give 'em a lilac glow and color. I've seen spirits. I've seen past events. What next?"

Oliver pointed and reminded, "You got a tattoo to get tomorrow, sun."

"I can handle it," Gordon said, reflecting on the events of his rites. He took another bite, chewed and swallowed. "That Lady Arachne," he commented, again reflecting. He witnessed Oliver and Wilson's sly grins appear. "You know how she just draws you in? And you gotta understand, all my senses are heightened. It's weird. She's in her fifties."

Oliver nodded, an uncomfortable smile on his face. "Every young kid had a crush on her. I couldn't. She was so much of an aunt to me."

Wilson nudged Oliver and teased, "You did, and you couldn't *help it*," he completed Oliver's phrasing. He sipped his drink and then concluded, "Some of you boys had crushes, and some of us became men through Lady Arachne."

Gordon beamed. "Yeah, I've heard." He bit into his sandwich again. "But there's a sadness to her. She knows how to channel it into something else. Something powerful. Not just sexual, even though that's there."

"She a bad chick," Wilson added. "She powerful. That's why she a matriarch. They all bad with there's."

Oliver asked Wilson, "You on call for a smash and grab?"

"Yeah," Wilson responded. "Martin and Macario on the hunt for them cards she wants. Her research got them close to somethin'. After that, Top Hat and I are up to bat. I retrieve, and Top Hat work his spookism to keep me in the shadows."

"I'm not tryin' to be the center of attention, but do these cards have anything to do with my rites?" Gordon asked as he chomped again at his sandwich.

Wilson answered, "They do." Then he thought about it for a moment and said, "But they don't." Elucidating on the matter didn't help much when he concluded, "But then again they do. You know what I'm sayin', sun? Like they do, but they don't. You know?"

"No," said Gordon raising his eyebrows. "You gon' have to clarify that for a brother." He and Oliver eyed one another and started giggling like teasing children

Wilson explained, "She'll be able to get a clearer picture as to what you're supposed to do with them eyes and that spirit. Her readings will be on point. Nothing vague. She'll be able to tell you how many times you'll go to the bathroom tomorrow. She'll be able to tell you which sistas are really diggin' your stuff. The exact day and time you die. She'll be nice, more so than she already is." He gulped his drink. "I might need a crew. I'll holler at your brother and Benny and them Shaw dudes."

"It'll cost you," Gordon remarked, feeling awkward about the subject.

"King gon' get his tribute. Bet," Wilson assured.

"Sure," Gordon said sitting back, the same awkwardness echoed in his movement. He again considered his conversation with Neyeli. Perhaps Cedron and his pack were not just protected, but the elders of Fable Avenue looked the other way because it was a form of practice for other purse-snatching mischief. Gordon straightened his demeanor so as not to make his discomfort obvious. "How's Dajon?" he asked.

"He fine," Wilson answered. "He cool. He had him a run-in, now he here." Wilson opined, "I personally think he did right by knockin' them bullies out. And they was so much older than him," he remarked.

"I know, right?" Gordon jumped in.

"But Dajon gotta be careful," Wilson pointed out. "He ain't like them other knuckleheads we got out there on that chain gang." Gordon and Oliver started laughing at Wilson's description of the punishment delegated to the young boys and girls. Wilson turned to Oliver and emphasized, "No, seriously. Sun, y'pops is a Warden. He runnin' a good program. I mean, it's always been here. But y'pops *and* y'aunt really run these kids straight. I know. *Personally.* I was stupid once." He lifted one single finger and stressed, *"Once."* Then he thought about it. "Okay, maybe twice." He thought about it again. "Maybe three times." Then he confessed, "Okay, maybe I had a bad year. Or two. Or a while. But I got corrected, shit. Our peoples here made sure of that. We've all had our moments. We can't talk." He said to Gordon, "You too. You've been roped up and cleanin' blocks from here to Harlem." Wilson raised his shoulders excitedly as he declared, "But we from Fable Av'. We got a foundation. These stupid-knuckleheaded-dummy kids runnin' around doin' dumbness tryin' to prove somethin'? Unfortunately, they ain't got what we got. But they get straightened out here. Even them ones whose parents is reluctant to send they kids this way."

"Right," Oliver interjected.

Wilson shook his head, annoyed look on his face. "They first talkin' all that *'Stay away from them Fable Avenue folk. They weird. They ain't Christian. They talk all that hoodoo and Voodoo.'"* Oliver and Gordon laughed at Wilson's antics as he imitated the voices and gestures of outsiders suspicious of the Fable Avenue community. "But what happens when they son or daughter start actin' dumb? They run straight past the church and to your pops," he pointed to Oliver, "or to the matriarchs, and them Negro-dummies start *begging* to get they kid in a Fable Av' program. They want the gateway and the assembly rites and everything else."

Oliver added, "And of course, they want a blessing, especially when they need somethin'. A job, promotion, an apartment," he listed.

Wilson agreed, head bobbing up and down. "Yep, yep," he said after a few nods. "These Negroes can call us spooky all they want, but they just don't know. This street's culture kept this neighborhood alive. We talkin' strong, black spiritualism. Through the good times, and definitely through them rough times, we held it down. Imagine if our conjures ain't been at work. Even when our blessings was low 'cause of the ebbing seasons, we was still holdin' it down. That's black culture at work, sun. That's hard. That's tough. That's us. That's Fable Avenue. We ain't stop everybody from gettin' shot or locked up—and we got our own knuckleheaded politics. But with our power, we've done what we can to keep this area above water. *Everybody* has come to us for a blessing. We've had Church goin' Negroes, Nation of Islam brothers and sisters, my Five Percent dudes; Zulu Nation cats." He emphasized the next two names while jabbing his finger, "Malcolm *and* Martin been through here. I repeat: strong, black spiritualism. Some cats is lazy. They don't wanna put they time in, do some spiritual work. And what happens when you don't do the work? You fuckin' with the spirit, sun. You gonna get hurt."

"Yeah," Oliver agreed, his words expressed in a sad tone as he reflected. "Dudes go out, they don't follow the patriarch or matriarch's specific instructions, they blessin' don't pop off right, and suddenly they talkin' about how *we* hucksters."

"Oh, man!" Wilson blurted. "Top Hat *hate* them type of folk." He took a beat and then continued, "But, they the same dudes that give that one more try, goin' line for line on the instructions, and then what happen? *Boom!* They got what they want. They blessin' is in abundance." Wilson pounded his chest. "You gotta make that promise, sun. Like Professor Khepri always says. You gotta say that and mean it." He said as an example, and with heart, "*I promise.* Then you make your confession. But, you know, these hardheaded Negroes don't get it. Let them do them. I got artifacts to look for at gunpoint." Wilson started chuckling as Oliver and Gordon erupted in laughter. "For real, you know. I got the real enemy to rob. These knuckleheads is robbin' each other while we fight the good fight and get shitted on. And half these cats waste the opportunity they blessin' gives them, 'cause that's what happens when you ain't got structure. You don't know how to handle success."

Gordon and Oliver nodded their approval.

Wilson reached into his pocket. He asked Gordon, "Yo, sun, can I smoke a cigar?"

"Do you, man," Gordon permitted.

Wilson made a face and flapped his lips. "Look who I'm askin'. This a Goodspeed. Your grandpops and your great-grandpops—I knew them before they faded, before they crossed—them dudes love their cigars. I won't even mention your pops." Wilson pulled out a ready to smoke cigar and a book of matches. He lit up and puffed. Gordon didn't mind the smoke. He continued to eat his sandwich.

Oliver pulled out a small notepad and pencil. He opened to a blank page and sketched an ashtray in no time. He ripped the page out and placed it at the center of the table. Wilson puffed on his cigar and then blew the smoke over the drawing. The paper folded and shifted into a small glass ashtray.

"Thanks, sun," said Wilson to Oliver.

"Not a problem," Oliver replied pocketing his art materials.

"Ollie Bootleg Raz," Gordon winked.

"It's somethin' else, ain't it? Christmas is always good with this dude around," Wilson remarked, nudging Oliver again. He turned and told Gordon, "Y'pops and I were smokin' it up a couple weeks ago. I was uptown at the cab depot. I was puttin' time in. He needed drivers for the day. I was done with my shift and helpin' around the office. We was chillin' hard. We started a game of Majestic Tarot. Y'pops is nice, sun. There were some other Fable Av' cats there. He cleaned everybody out. I looked at him like, *'Yo, I thought we was friends, sun.'"* All three started laughing. Wilson said as he chortled, "I was like, *'What did I do in a past life or this one to be treated like trash?'"* More laughter. "He treated all of us like we had on high heels and he was wearin' the wide hat. And apparently we owed him money."

"Yeah, my pops is good like that," said Gordon. "And he taught me and Cedron a few tricks."

"Then I'll just play you and your brother for fun and not money," Wilson remarked. He then continued his story. "We had to switch to poker. Some civilians showed up, regular folk. Then we formed up like *Voltron* to straight rob these dudes. We was exchangin' looks like, *'You wanna win this hand? Okay, okay. I got 'em.'"* Wilson concluded his story. "We went to the Hours club after. Y'pops got up and played piano. Fuck whatever goes on here on Fable Avenue, *that* shit—your father playing the piano—sun, that was magical. Straight hard with it." Wilson puffed and exhaled. "But y'pops was taught by the best when it comes to the piano. *My* pops," he smiled. "My pops really dug how your father played. He admired it. I used to be mad jealous over that. But, you know, I learned my father didn't love me any less, or your pops any more."

Gordon acknowledged, "I saw him this morning. I came downstairs and stepped into the past. Saw y'dad," he told Wilson. He looked at Oliver, "Saw y'granddad and the Fable brothers putting this all together. They were planning the album, the music that brought Fable Avenue together."

"That must've been some shit," Wilson said contemplating. "Those were some heavy days." He tapped ashes into the ashtray. "You know he still try and get into my mom's spot, my pops? His spirit knocks once a year. My moms tells him to go dance with them hussies he was runnin' around with. She serious too. She don't let his spirit come in when he comes to dance." He scowled his face in an absurd manner and said, "My moms is like, *'Yo father came here last night on his yearly visit.'"* Gordon and Oliver were thrown back into laughter. "She still angry. Straight furious. But she got every right to be. But hey, I got many a half-brothers and half-sisters. My pops was stupid. Damn-near every single chick on two legs that moved into Fable Avenue, he was on."

"The rejection goes both ways," Gordon inserted. "I saw my mother's spirit last night. She's sad. You know, my father shackin' up with any chick he sees."

Wilson shifted in his seat. He leaned toward Gordon and said in a sincere voice, "Y'pops loved y'mom. Her death shook him up. Trust. Some dudes go to the bottle. Y'pops goes to one woman after the next. But, he a good dude. He got heart and spirit. He's hurt. It ain't like he's some gigolo like my pops."

"Of which you're cast from the same mold," Gordon commented tending to his sandwich again.

Wilson sat back. He looked down with a guilty grin. "Hey. I. Don't. Know. What. You speak of. All my kids are from one chick. We ain't together, but I take care of mine. And my girl I'm with now has tamed me. Of course, havin' my pop's picture up in my altar don't help. I'm callin' his spirit up to walk with that same swagger. My pops was my superhero. He wasn't perfect, but he was that nigga. Like Lady Arachne, she that chick. I don't care what kind of culture we got here. We always gon' have that nigga and that chick. Shit, people think *I'm* that nigga."

"With good reason," Oliver joked. Wilson blew his cigar smoke into Oliver's face and cursed at him playfully. Oliver laughed and wiped the smoke aside. Then he checked his watch. "I got my shift," he said rising from the table.

Wilson followed. "I gotta get back to these knuckleheaded kids."

Gordon rose with them after taking a bite from his sandwich. He led the men to the door and opened it for them. "See you tomorrow, Gordon," said Oliver. He and Gordon exchanged a handshake and a brotherly hug. Oliver played around, pushing Gordon and taking air strikes at him. Then he pushed him into Wilson's handshake and embrace.

"Okay, young man!" Wilson expressed. "You ain't got to worry, we got you covered." He let go of Gordon and walked toward the door.

"I'll see you two later," Gordon said to them. He told Oliver, "Tat' tomorrow. This'll be interesting."

"You'll do fine, man," Oliver promised.

There was another exchange of goodbyes, and then Gordon closed and locked the door. He returned to the dining room just as the glass ashtray dissolved into the air. The ashes disappeared with it. Gordon sat down and finished his meal. On the final bite and swallow, the back of his neck buzzed. A moment later, a soft, harmonious hum came from the front room. Gordon turned his head as he finished his drink. He spied a light, purple glow coming from the couch. It was in sync with the humming. The arm of the couch hid Gordon's view, but he understood the *Nigrum Nigrius*

Nigro emitted the glow and hum. The vibrating light was like a purple sunrise coming from the horizon.

Gordon was hesitant to respond, but he eventually stood up from his chair, putting down the empty glass. His steps were cautious, as usual. He walked into the family room and approached the couch. He looked down at the book. The glow billowed from between the early pages. Gordon reached down and took up the tome. He paused for a moment, hand hovering over the book's cover. He took the time to brace his eyes from the potential of any flashing burn he might receive. Then Gordon opened the book, flipping to the glowing page. It was the very page with the odd schematics marked *Alchemical Chamber.* The outline of the sketches emitted the hum and soft, purple aura.

A longcase clock started ticking.

Gordon's eyes bubbled with an enchanted, lilac blaze. The door leading to the basement creaked open, and Gordon turned his head and watched with an irradiated, curious gaze.

Gordon stood at the top of the stairs. His bright eyes peered down into the gray, dark basement. His expression was stoic. The *Nigrum Nigrius Nigro* was in his hands. The longcase clock's loud tick-tock attempted to rival thunder. The sound was coming from the basement; there was no mistaking. Gordon proceeded down, his movements not of his will. When his feet touched the cellar floor, he pivoted and walked into the middle of the room. Facing the far wall, Gordon dropped to his knees. His eyes widened, stretching with vast amounts of pain to the size of eggs. Unlike the burn that scratched his eyes the previous night, Gordon's reactive scream was not suppressed. It filled the basement with as much intensity as the glow in his eyes, which were at the moment, streaming bright and thick strands of lilac light at the wall in front of him.

Gordon's body dropped forward. He caught himself from falling, the palms of his hands pressed hard against the floor. The *Nigrum Nigrius Nigro* landed on the floor next to him, no longer in his grip. Gordon continued facing the wall. His eyes expanded like the features on an animated character, and his screams grew louder.

The thick, lilac strands of light spilling onto the wall's surface created an outline of a *vesica piscis*. The almond-shaped area was the height of a door, and the light pouring from Gordon's blazing eyes filled the empty framework. When the entirety of the sacred, geometric space was radiating with lilac energy, his eyes ceased their bright glow and returned to normal size. He dropped onto his side, curled into a fetal position, and panted. His eyes were tightly closed, and his brow poured perspiration. Gordon moaned away the remaining pain in his eyes, but he kept them closed, missing the moment when two figures, male and female, stepped through the lighted, almond-shaped doorway. Their flesh was made of light. The male was dark purple, and the female's flesh was the same color as Gordon's new eyes.

The woman walked over to Gordon's curled body, her foot planted inches away from his face. Her brilliant glow brightened the darkness swirling behind Gordon's tightly closed eyes. He took a breath and opened his eyes at the end of a three-count. Gordon flinched at the sight of the woman's candescent flesh that writhed with small, coiled strands of light. His eyes moved up her naked, glowing frame. Gordon crawled away from the woman, cautious as he moved. His eyes remained fixed on her. The glow of her flesh was so intense that Gordon could barely make out facial features behind the light of her face. Her hair was like a wild, coiled lightning storm. The woman bent down. Gordon could see she was smiling. Her smile was as warm as her glow, and he noticed African features on her face: full lips and broad nose.

Gordon looked in the direction of the naked, glowing man. He too had African features behind the light of his face. They were easier to see, considering his glow was a dark purple. Gordon noticed his hair was a wooly dome. His stance was authoritative, legs apart, and his arms behind his back. He was stocky, but muscular. His nature was part king and part ward or soldier.

The glowing woman spoke, causing Gordon to look back at her. "Easy," she said, but not through her lips. Her voice resonated from the glow of her flesh, and it sang, "Up, young man. Up. Rise."

Gordon stood up, assisted by the glowing woman. Her lighted touch felt as warm and liquid-like as the lilac strands that burst from his eyes. But she was solid, no different than Gordon's flesh, save the glow. He rubbed his eyes as he straightened. The throbbing pain had subsided. He watched the bright woman bend down again and retrieve the *Nigrum Nigrius Nigro*. She passed the book to the glowing man. He took the book from her and stepped back, returning to his military-like stance. Then the woman guided Gordon to an old recliner.

"Sit," her glow crooned. "Sit."

Gordon sat down in the chair, movement still slow and cautious, eyes still fixated on the glowing woman. He looked at both luminescent figures, from the man to the woman. The woman bent down. She inspected Gordon's lilac eyes, but never did she reach for them.

She addressed Gordon, her lighted flesh singing, "Let us do our jobs, young man. We handle this and we glow. We handle this and we glow." Gordon nodded his head. The woman stood up. Her body continued to repeat, *"We handle this and we glow,"* as she walked toward the glowing man. Both he and she inspected the book, opening it and studying its text. After running through the pages with script and sketch, the female looked at Gordon and sang, "We shall return. Do not worry." Gordon nodded again. The fluorescent specters turned and walked back through the glowing door. Their bodies sang in harmony as they departed, *"We handle this and we glow! We handle this and we glow!"*

Gordon kept his eyes on the glowing portal. Minutes passed before the two entities returned, the *Nigrum Nigrius Nigro* still in their possession. The woman was holding the book and other items when she re-entered the basement through the glowing portal. The man dragged physical materials through. He placed the materials down near the wall opposite where Gordon was seated. The woman placed the *Nigrum Nigrius Nigro* on a workbench near the portal. She also placed the other objects in her hand on the workbench. There was a bag and a flat, rectangular and reflective, black object. Gordon believed it was a mirror made of onyx. He looked closer, but became distracted when the woman stepped away from the objects and made her way to him. He looked up at the radiant woman as she stood over him. Gordon peered into the brilliance emitting from her visage. He could see the contours of her face expressing a sad expression, but she managed a smile.

It took effort for Gordon to speak, but he inquired in a careful whisper, "Mom…?"

The woman shook her head, no. With melancholy still in her eyes, the woman turned to the wall where her male companion was placing down materials. She raised her hand and pointed. Strands of light flowed from her fingers. The light intertwined and shaped into small, glowing hieroglyphs that fluttered against the wall. Gordon read the first line of the lit engraving. "Here. We. See. Sand," Gordon translated aloud the ancient, brightly lit language. His eyes moved to the glowing woman, looking for an answer and a reason to continue reading. But she had already returned to the workbench. The glowing man was now at her side and fiddling with the *Nigrum Nigrius Nigro.*

Gordon saw the man open the book, forty pages. He placed the rectangular, flat onyx object atop the pages on the left. It fit perfectly. The woman waved a hand over the onyx object, and her body sang an unintelligible blessing. The onyx object fastened to the pages, and the pages turned black. The glowing man opened and closed the book, making sure the black mirror was fastened in place. He let go, and instead of the pages and cover flopping open, it remained upright like an opened laptop computer. It was as if the book had hinges now rather than a flexible spine.

The woman pointed a glowing finger to the exposed pages. Her flesh sang, and small holes formed wherever she pointed. The man opened the sack and pulled out gems, slipping each finely cut piece into a hole. The woman's body glowed brighter, as did the man's. Both chanted, and the gems became fastened inside the holes. The remaining pages also turned black. It was like a computer's keyboard made of twenty-four precious stones and gems for the keys. Although he was drenched with anticipation, Gordon couldn't help but smile.

The woman turned back to him. She pointed to the far wall where the script lay. Her expression was like a teacher guiding a child's attention to a blackboard. "Read," her singing flesh insisted.

Gordon turned his attention to the wall. His eyes read the script, and as he finished the first line, the world dissolved away in a bright, lilac flash. There was an image of a sandy sea, a heat-blistering desert. Distant images blurred and waved as heat breathed up through the golden sea. A voice narrated.

Here. We. See. Sand.
Pregnant belly dunes
The horizon, our Caesarean
Cut
We up, over
A thousand clamors
Shuffle, shuffle and ruffle the calm
The heat sighs. A low wind sings and a swirl tumbles
Billowing down these rolling, sandy hills
Here are we. An army of horses, fish, and rams.
We walk the lion's land, surveying golden, crushed waste

Alkebulan is not the same. Not even in name.
She has become finely divided rock – nature mirrors us
Sun scorched instead of kissing us
This land is now Osiris in the Ament, a furnace
Without cold – Af-Ra – Heat, reeks our motherland
Basilisk licked into granular particle, sunny quartz bits
An abandoned place, once glorious face, a desert
This is how home looks now
Forestation receded – by angry war and nature's wound, retreated
Only sand ripples where we step and breathe
This golden sea bleeds proof of nature's gentle creativity
Even as motherland weeps wounded
Her tears turned to waterless, sandy reefs
There is so much beauty in this endless
Golden, natural scrap heap

Our cavalry wears the desert – browned, tanned robes
Rain-bows in our hands. Air-rows on their breaths
And quiver
In rows of ten, our thousands trot

The fishers, ferocious, wear the sea as their color

Waving in waves. Their feet drip footprints on dry motherland.
A moving oasis, an army of aquatic life breathing words
For weapons or blessings

And the rams wear green. Left wing, their armies flank.
Emerald horns adorn helmets
In hand, weapons gleam, glimmering
Flushed,
The faces of blades blush with the stains of sacrifice
And strife

But war is behind us, faded
Peace, loosely woven and braided
War will come again, as consequences intend
Tock-tick, the cosmic clock, flipped backwards
The ages are confused. Twelve in our Father's house
Are doomed to be disguised from our eyes
The war we walk away from, over foresight interpretation
Has more to say
War pauses only to prep – practice its speech, until the need
For War to speak again. Scream.
Louder

For now, an emancipation from war – we have come home
Both she, motherland, and we
Her children
Desolate
Seared
We return to her,
The last of a failed generation

We come bearing uncertain alchemy in our speech
Prayers laced with pleas
Our frames may extend to the heavens
But our spirits crawl the Earth. We are gods, humbled.
Motherland. She. There. A lone, sable maiden sitting on ebony chair
A high priestess
We bow to her, come to ask for forgiveness
"State your business," she says
Disappointment possesses her tone

'We are a reaction. This faction. The world population.

Kings and queens. Warriors. Scholars. Artisans. All class of citizens.
We. Observed. The Wall.
Every scratch, every etch that was sketched
We saw its mouth
Opened
Screaming our future
And we. Will. Be. Broken.
Our crowns will crumble
The wall speaks, of bumbling, broken speech,
Created sentiments, harmful prayers
    From the caves of our mouths, learned upright
On two syllables, walking. We will serve the cursed words' dictation.
So has it, in stone, been writ

Mother, we of your matter, made war against this
Our future. Carved on a wall.
We could not figure its all in all this
Was this just a warning? Can we fight the storm?
Embrace it? Civilize it. Turn it. Or, treat it kindly like family.
We had no answer. No one agreed.
So…we made war with one another.
Scared, we scarred the land, weaponized egos in hand.
You, motherland, spirit once whole
    Divorced, broken into seven. We know you suffered the most.

Peace only stalls our disagreement
Egos are dressed in different sects and factions
Philosophies, made mockery in council
The dissatisfied will rise,
And war will reign again among our people
The storm will be made physical, literal
Three thousand miles across the sandy paved way
Barren mountains will roar
We will fall to sword. Broken more and more.
Little-by-little until shipped away as slaves.
So sayeth The Wall. Its hands, that we into, played.

Every kingdom we now create
Will only serve as a grave
    Reminder
    Faintly lit
To echo once brighter days."

Motherland, our high priestess
Speaks silence
Louder than my pleas
Her Medusa gaze
Reversed to self
Her visage is stone
Her face. Becomes. The Wall.
If only her anger was a façade

We wish she stayed this way
Silent. Stone.
But her tone makes desert heat turn tundra
Dictating our dejection, our judgment

'Fate's scripted-sketched wall is built only of stone
If made of air, script unseen, there would be an issue
But stone is grown. Sketched. Crafted. Shaped.
With great force, can pressure crumble – break
Nothing set in stone is set in stone for you
Never did you wear fate's woven cloth
The cosmos your skin: proud, heavenly black body – live freely
Naked, you've pranced playfully through life picking profitable prophecies
Fate to you is a suggestion. You are a spirit separate of its lattice.
You, first-born children, are risen – The Wall was only heeded warning
But now from this conduct, wars erupt
        Stirs virgin lands to wake for lust
The sacred text of the Earth, no longer scripted
In the cosmos' free-willed ink
This world? Its spirit sinks. Its three moons: red, black, green
        Look! As now, like eyes they blink
        But from existence. Faded into one, ashen, blanched body. Neglect.
And this one sickly moon, Earth shall she reflect

But even while barren, there in Her are treasures still
Made claim by warring, whorish Barons, who wanton in their want
Will want to chain you
Subdued for duty – from here to the world,
You will build kingdoms for Tantalus, and never satiate him
Over and over
He will attempt to drink, to eat
Just a carrot waved in front of an empty sole purpose

Tantalus will make you work for wages absinth of your reflection
He will paint images of you and call them mirrors
Muddled, mocked, misshapen silhouettes
Epileptic shadows stretched to represent you roped up
Dangled, puppet, Marinette
For your ill comport: You. Will. Hang.
By the fingers of Tantalus; or so help me gods,
    In a Northern wilderness, your shade will decorate my trees
And when my clouds rain down on you, swinging ornaments
Do not mistake that for you, I as your Mother Nature weep
My disappointment in you, my natural children, is too deep

Jealousy taints your vain
Proudly pumped pride through all four chambers of your heart
Day-by-day, chains upon chains you will pray
If then you beg to be a slave
    Let your kings and queens forget their crowns
    Let your warriors lay down their swords
    Let your farmers inhale the smoke of poisoned land
    Let your scholars and priests sing corrupted, foreign mythology
        In perfect harmony – if indeed you believe your pitch cursed
Fall down! Lift sword only to one another! The ripe bounty of the Earth be damned!
Double, double—meaning—your coiled hair be trouble, spin, spun – ruse!
I will have you confused!
You think you've seen war? My script is heavy with it. Just wait.
Hordes of a horrible plague carried on two legs from the mouths
    Of lateral mountain graves
    Will come
And you will serve the sound of Tantalus' command
So forget, forget, and forget. Your black fleece made golden.
Coveted by interest piqued men; piqued women.
Love of self, experienced vicariously through cursed vocabulary
So, go! Love those words, and know thyself.
Then you will remember
    Your covenant to me. Motherland.

So, let the hanged man haunt you
Anger sever you
Only through this alchemical fission, properly applied
    Mathematical equation
I pronounce
Your vision will be new, clear

For all the generations you rebirth blind
You will see, on your final return, with lilac eyes
Open and bright. Clean. – By the womb of the Cobalt Flame
Three moons returned. Red. Black. Green.
Surrounded, shimmering halos gleam, circled, cipher stream

And as you will not mistake my rain for tears
Do not mistake my punishment for lack of such
My first children, born out of the black
And into the blue
I bestow this fate out of love for you

For twenty-five thousand years you will birth
A versed lineage
And in each of those years construct you will a fraction
Of a new language to speak a grand wish
Here are your pens. Get started. Good speed. God speed. Leave me be.
I have my own script to draft." motherland drinks a parting glass.

Then, her hand and head lift
Fingers twirl, making the cosmos swirl
And writ upon the cosmic fold's brilliant assemblage,
Bright cosmic script, there do the stars shift
Heavy, heavenly planet bodies drift, weightless – then still, remain, fixed
This new celestial rotation makes black cosmic waves ricochet
And we weigh heavy with burden

A heavenly menagerie holds back our dark energy
The embrace of our dark matter
Our cosmic cloth torn
Fate now our vestments
We seek sacrifice as a birthright
Under these new stars
Born
Ritual now our guide to the fabric of the heavenly sky
Anansi spins our tale as Milky Way silk. Star connected to star.
His widowed mother wears an hourglass on her back
She mourns while poisoned stardust pours through her
Empty one glass. Fill the other. This, our time.

Tock-tick. So shall it be writ. Under foreign, celestial penmanship,
Our story is told. This is not stone. In the stars, fate is set.

And we stand here ill, littered and 'ret to go. Our judgment come.
"Let your story unfold and be done," says motherland

The horizon swallows the sun,
Thus adjourned are we

End act one

A lilac brilliance folded the desert scene back into Gordon's basement. Gordon's breathing was heavy. His teeth were clenched. His hands gripped hard the chair's arms, and his body trembled in anger. His brow furrowed and his eyes bent in ire. He moved his vision to the left, spotlighting the glowing figures standing at his side. Both held apologetic expressions. Their glow sang a sorrowful dirge, and Gordon's anger eased, causing his body to relax. His grip loosened, and his clenched teeth parted. In unison, the glowing figures said in harmony, "We shall return." And then they disappeared through the glowing door as it faded. The wall in front of Gordon was blank of script and image.

Gordon remained fixed in the chair. He pondered the images he'd seen and how they'd impacted him. It was the ancient world that he'd glimpsed. It was a very ancient world, and it had been, according to the narration, in a state that religions referred to as a garden or paradise. But there came a fall. War was fabricated, and nothing was the same after. For their disobedience to Mother Nature, and for their reckless behavior against one another, the original people of the world were fated to plunge into despair.

Gordon's neck shuddered with a buzz.

"Gordon!" he heard someone call. *"Gordon!"* It was Papa Solomon. He was outside, banging on the door. He had company. Gordon blinked his eyes rapidly. He jumped up and dashed upstairs to answer the door. "Gor—Oh!" said Papa Solomon as the door opened and his fist was stayed, in mid-swing to pound the door again. "You step into the past again, young man?"

The sun was setting. It was close to five o'clock.

"Papa Solomon," greeted Gordon. "Come in."

Papa Solomon stepped inside followed by another man. His name was Makali Khepri, a professor of mathematics at Timothy Drew University. Professor Khepri was forty-seven years old. His family was a part of the Fable Avenue community, though not settled on Fable Avenue proper. Instead, they lived in New Jersey. Though he was born and raised in the Garden State, Professor Khepri's mother and father weren't American born. His parents hailed from Mali, but his father's roots extended back to Tanzania.

Professor Khepri wore a brown suede jacket, and underneath, a suit and tie to match. He had dark brown skin, a well-groomed mustache, and a pair of round glasses on his face. Under his arm was a wooden case, the contents inside for Gordon. But Gordon never took notice of Professor Khepri's possession. He continued formality by shaking the professor's hand, welcoming him inside. Papa Solomon shut and locked the door.

"Yes, Papa Solomon," Gordon answered his elder. "I saw history again. It was far back. Ancient." He walked toward the basement. "There's materials down here you should see. Spirits appeared; a man and a woman." Gordon galloped down the steps. He turned on the lights for his two guests as they entered the basement.

Papa Solomon and Professor Khepri inspected the items brought to Gordon. There placed in the corner of the room were thick vines cut from a forest. There was a very large, ovate stone. It's presence left Gordon confused as to when it was carted into the basement, but he figured it might've been when he was observing the animated scenes of the ancient past. There also were palm boughs, down feathers, tanned goatskin and other hides.

"The light in my eyes opened a doorway on that wall," Gordon explained pointing to where the almond-shaped glow had been. "A man and a woman stepped through. Their skin was made of light. I could barely make out the features on their faces. The woman did most of the…talking. It's like their voices came out of their glow, not their mouths. And they sang. They brought all this." He walked over to the newly configured *Nigrum Nigrius Nigro.* "And look," he continued. "They used some type of incant to do this to the *Nigrum Nigrius Nigro.*"

All three of them inspected the re-forged tome. But Professor Khepri was just as interested in observing Gordon's lilac eyes. Gordon noticed, and Professor Khepri apologized, "Sorry, Gordon. I didn't mean to stare. We've read about these eyes for so long, signifying the spirit coming through. It's so different to actually view the brew stirred in someone's eyes."

Gordon replied with a grin, "Quite used to it by now, sir." Gordon asked about the reconfigured book, "Any idea as to what this is now?"

Both men were silent as they inspected and contemplated. The professor set the wooden case in his grip next to the *Nigrum Nigrius Nigro.* He removed his glasses and leaned in for a closer inspection. He ventured a guess when he said, "Looks like a fancy black mirror for scrying." He turned to Papa Solomon who nodded in agreement.

"Well," said Gordon, "I'm sure my brightly lit visitors will explain its use."

"We'll settle for Makali's answer for now," Papa Solomon stated. "He has something for you, Gordon. It's the next step in your rites. It's in that case."

Gordon put his hand on the case, but he hesitated to open it. "Can I open it now?" he asked to be sure.

"Yes, Gordon," assured Makali, an anxious tone lying underneath his excitement.

Gordon unlatched the box and lifted its lid. He expected to see inside some type of cultural trinket or bauble. Perhaps he'd find feathers strung together and sprouting from African burlap, or an incanted, miniature Zebra mask, or something of the sort. Instead, Gordon discovered a pair of welding goggles, the lenses of which appearing to have been carved from black onyx gemstones.

"For many generations my family carried the Eyes of the Angel," Professor Khepri stated. Gordon looked up at him. The professor's eyes watered. "It is said of them, that they are to be looked through by lilac eyes. Eyes with the brew stirred in them." Makali held back the tears gathering at the edge of his eyes. "My family has spoken of this moment for so long. Our duty. My father passed last year. My aunt, his sister, just last month. My uncle before that. I wish they were here to see this. Hell, I was beginning to think it would be my son or my daughter that finished this journey. But it's me."

Gordon didn't mean to interrupt Professor Khepri's moment, but he needed to ask, "What will it do for me? Will I see something grand?"

Professor Khepri bubbled with laughter. He wiped the tears from his eyes and commented, "Look at me getting all emotional, and when it boils down to it, I really couldn't tell you what's supposed to happen." He fixed himself before telling Gordon, "Our family has kept that item since the late eighteen hundreds. Those gems weren't always fastened inside welding goggles. That was done to disguise them. Stare into them, I guess. Supposedly they are an angel's eyes. They were given to my many-great-grandfather." The professor turned his attention to the black mirror and the keyboard of gems. "Maybe scrying into this crude mechanism can give you some insight."

"I'll see what I can make of all this tonight," Gordon said to the professor and Papa Solomon.

The doorbell rang!

The back of Gordon's neck buzzed. He concentrated for only a moment, and then he said aloud, "It's my dad!" He looked to Papa Solomon, and then his eyes went to Professor Khepri. "It's my dad!" he repeated. He closed the wooden box, shut the newly fashioned *Nigrum Nigrius Nigro*, snatched up both items, and rushed upstairs to the parlor level. Papa Solomon and Professor Khepri were close behind.

Gordon lay the two items down on the stairs that led up to the second level. He unlocked the brownstone entrance doors and stepped out to greet his father with a hug. Maximilian accepted his son's embrace. He stepped away and gazed at his eyes. *"That's my man!"* Maximilian hollered as he slapped Gordon hard on the chest with a quick whip using the back of his hand. Gordon took the hit and lifted his arms to shadow box his father. Goodspeed father and Goodspeed son traded air jabs, ducking and dodging in play.

Then Gordon's eye caught the woman at the bottom of the steps, standing outside the waist-high iron gate. She was not the young, Puerto Rican woman his father had been with the morning of his birthday. It was another woman. She was a young, pretty Haitian woman, and as Gordon's neck tingled with an electrifying quiver, he sensed she was not of the Fable Avenue community, hence her distance. Gordon thought about his mother as he stared at the woman. His memory took over his view. He saw the scene of his mother sitting in the corner of the room, her face wrapped in choler. Gordon's eyes returned to his father as the memory vanished. He fixed his face from open-mouth hurt and surprise to a forced smile and laughter, trying to regain the moment he'd had with his father.

But then Gordon wondered why Cedron hadn't shown up. He wondered where his friend Benny was. But he considered that, for safety reasons, they might not have been informed about his rites' progress.

"Papa Solomon didn't give me all the details," Gordon's father said to him. "He just told me there's progress. So, how did all this come about?"

Gordon opened his mouth to explain, but his eyes went back to the woman waiting for his father. His mother's memory came to him again, the scene of the previous night. He stuttered on unintelligible words, eyes going between his father and the woman he arrived with. The woman was dressed conservatively and looked very lovely. But she wasn't his mother. Gordon looked away from both the woman and his father, but it was too late. A brewing, electrical storm stirred inside him. He continued to stammer, losing concentration. He tried to focus on the blessing he'd received from Madame Jeliya and the words he was trying to express. "There was a light," he finally got out. "It came from, uh, the, uh, the book. The *Nigrum Nigrius Nigro.*" He pointed to his face and said, "The eyes…" he tried to smile at his father. "And then, uh, and then…let's see… There was…"

Papa Solomon and Professor Khepri stepped out of the house, breaking through Gordon's awkwardness like a ray of light through a set of clouds. Gordon moved out of their way, taking a stance two steps from the top. He was thankful for their presence. He watched Papa Solomon and Professor Khepri greet his father and hoped that the formality would take time, but it wasn't long before all the attention again shined on Gordon.

"Papa Solomon, Professor Khepri," Maximilian finished his polite greeting with the two of them. "Gordon was just telling me about his night, but," he looked up and spotted the woman he'd arrived with waiting for him. "Hold on," he said in a low voice. "This is rude all around. This should be a private conversation, plus I got her just standin' there. Where is my head? These are sacred rites." Maximilian trotted down the stairs and to the woman.

Gordon climbed up one step and turned to see his father whisper into the woman's ear. She beamed a polite smile, relaying that she understood. He heard his father say he would introduce her later. The woman turned and got into his father's car to wait.

"Pop, it's okay," said Gordon. He looked up at Papa Solomon and Professor Khepri, and then back to his father. "I've gone through a lot. I'm feeling exhausted."

Maximilian hopped back up the steps. "Okay, okay," he acknowledged his son. "I understand. Well, my rites didn't make it this far. But I can imagine." He stared at his son. He patted Gordon on the shoulder and said, "And your…grandfather and great-grandfather would've enjoyed this. Both of them," he said as he patted Gordon again.

And mom! Gordon thought the words so hard he believed he'd pierced and injured his father's mind. *Mom!* He screamed at his father in his head. But he uttered not a word. *I saw mom,* Gordon wanted to say, but didn't. *You've hurt her…*

Gordon backed away from his father, up the brownstone's stairs. He passed between Papa Solomon and Professor Khepri, and he entered the house. "Gordon," his father called, and Gordon turned to face him. "I'm proud of you, son. I am. We…all are. Cedron don't know yet, but he'll be proud, young man."

And mom… Gordon thought again. But instead, he said through the door, "Love you, Pop." He turned around and gathered the items he'd left on the stairs. His father, Papa Solomon, and Professor Khepri continued their conversation as Gordon climbed the stairs. Papa Solomon closed the first door so as not to let the house's heat escape. Papa Solomon informed Maximilian of Gordon's eventful night, though he skipped the detail of Althea Goodspeed's spectral appearance to keep the moment upbeat.

Gordon walked into his room and set the *Nigrum Nigrius Nigro* and the small wooden box with the goggles down on top of the dresser. The house was quiet enough for him to hear the conversing voices of his father, Papa Solomon, and Professor Khepri. Gordon stepped outside his room and proceeded down the hall to another bedroom. He walked inside and looked outside the window. He didn't move the curtain aside, as he wanted to be unseen. He listened. There wasn't much to the conversation. His eye peeked through a sliver of a view between the curtains. He focused as something odd appeared. Gordon saw a web of light entangle Papa Solomon, his father, and Professor Khepri. The light then retracted into a ball, hovering between his father and the other two men. Stems of light unfolded from the bright sphere, and a new configuration appeared. It was a *merkaba,* a symbol composed of two star tetrahedrons. A voice echoed a sentiment he'd heard in the mystical narrative, *"The last of a failed generation."*

The configured body of light disappeared from between the three, conversing men.

Thunder bubbled inside Gordon. He balled his fist and felt the first strike of lightning from the waking storm inside him. He clenched his teeth and closed his eyes. He took a breath and focused on the memory of the calm sleep Madame Jeliya had earlier placed him under. He thought about his blessing as in and out he breathed. The storm rumbled away. Gordon opened his eyes, calm again. He returned to the hallway, making his way back to his room. He heard the doors close and lock downstairs. He stopped in the hallway, waiting. He could hear Papa Solomon and Professor Khepri walking away. He heard his father's car start and drive off. He was alone.

Gordon entered his room and stood over the remodeled *Nigrum Nigrius Nigro.* He opened the wooden case and looked at the onyx-lensed goggles. He rested his hands at the edge of the dresser drawer and leaned down. He looked at the tome, and then he looked at the goggles. Tome. Goggles. Then his head, free of will, turned to the chair situated in the corner. He thought of his mother and said, "I'm sorry." Gordon stood up straight and punched the palm of one hand with a fist made by the other. "I understand both sides," he said to the chair. "I wish I could trade him," he continued, "His concrete memories of you for my faint memories, faint feelings, and the emptiness of what's forgotten." Gordon waited. He pushed his balled fist harder against his open palm, teeth grinding together.

Nothing responded.

He dropped his arms and head, and questioned, "Who am I talking to?"

The *Nigrum Nigrius Nigro* crept open. The face of the black mirror lifted up to greet Gordon's question as if to answer it.

Gordon remarked, "You listening to me, you spooky thing?"

The *Nigrum Nigrius Nigro* closed.

"Oh, come on," Gordon drawled. "*Nigro* please! Where my *Nigrum* at?" Gordon joked, feeling better. "Oh, come on, *Spook*," he branded the item.

The ancient tome opened. Gordon knelt down at eye-level with the ancient device, smile on his face. His reflection shined clear in the black mirror. His eyes blazed lilac. "So, you cool with that moniker, huh, Spook?"

The mirror emitted a low hum followed by a shimmering lilac-colored aura glowing on its face. The aura shifted into tiny-font glyphs. They floated off the mirror's face and flooded Gordon's eyes. The assembly of glittering, gliding words birthed pictures for Gordon to see. He saw the image of two white men conversing at a table, outside at a cafe. Then, there was an auction house in London. Two black men, one with light skin, the other with dark skin, used the shadows to maneuver around the grounds of the estate. This image played long enough in Gordon's eyes for him to recognize both men. The light-skinned man, older than the other, was named Joseph Pepper IV. He was dressed in a bowler hat, white shirt, brown slacks and brown suit jacket covered by a formal Inverness coat. In his hands was a cane inset with seven sapphires.

Tagging behind Joseph Pepper, close to the shadows, was Gordon's great-grandfather, a young Madison Goodspeed. He wore gray slacks, a dark shirt with suspenders, and a jacket and gloves. On his oval-shaped head was a navy-blue driver's cap.

Gordon, transfixed, reached for the *Nigrum Nigrius Nigro.* He lifted it off the drawer and walked to the bed, eyes aglow. He lay down in the bed, tome on his chest. His eyes closed in synch with the fold of the *Nigrum Nigrius Nigro.* Gordon, free of will, wrapped his arms around the closed tome as if it was a prayer book. He went to sleep and dreamed a vivid dream of the past.

A Deadbeat Auction, or Sister Nani's Silent Bid

"He calls his cane the Wand of Blue Light."

A lilac haze dissolved, and the interior of a New Orleans café appeared in its absence. Several fans rotated above patrons who were enjoying their brunch. A calendar near the kitchen's entrance read *AUGUST* accompanied by a photograph of the New Orleans Saint Lewis Cathedral. Thursday 23 was circled in red ink. Days previous to Thursday 23 were both circled and had a large, red X marked through them. The year was 1917.

At the end of the hall situated left of the kitchen entrance, and past two doors marked as the men and women's bathrooms, was a door leading to the courtyard. More patrons were seated outside. Most of the occupied tables were filled with customers. A lone man sat at a table engaged in the day's newspaper. A tall glass of lemonade with ice was sweating in front of him on the table. Two hot beignets brimming with the aroma of fried dough and powdered sugar were paired with the drink. The man's name was Ethan Steel Cassidy, a former Confederate solider with a pinch of trick running through his veins that assisted in keeping intact his youth. That youth was a boyish charm, with dirty-blonde hair, soft blue eyes, and a squared jaw. A tailor-made, light brown suit covered a chiseled frame.

"Ethan!" a man greeted in a delighted voice.

Ethan folded the newspaper in his hands and slapped it on the table. He stood up and reached out a hand to the broad-shouldered, older-looking gentlemen in front of him. "Curly Burneside," Ethan returned the greeting.

"And how are you?" Curly asked through a smile.

Ethan didn't answer immediately. Instead he waved his hand to the empty chair next to him and requested, "Please, have a seat, Curly."

Curly removed his white, wide brim fedora and planted himself in the chair. He put his hat on the table. A black waiter hurried up to take his order. Curly asked for scrambled eggs, toasted wheat bread, a side of two slices of bacon, and a glass of orange juice. A polite tone in his voice strained to smother the sadistic timbre in his command. Curly then added before the waiter scurried away, "Let me have some pancakes and syrup with that too, boy. Now go on." The waiter bowed at the hip, smiled at Curly, and remarked that the order would be on the table soon. "Not too soon," Curly snapped through a grin, his eyes looking at Ethan and not at the black waiter. "Don't have my food undercooked, boy," he continued with a subtle threat in his tone, his eyes now turned to the black waiter. "And don't take too long either, having my food overcooked or cold by the time it gets to me. You understand, boy?"

The waiter strained to keep his bright smile. "Yessir, I do. I'll have it perfect."

Curly's grin widened. "Then there's no reason to congregate around here, is there, boy. Go on and put my order in. Thank you."

"Thank *you*, sir." The black waiter bowed again, and then he was gone.

Curly looked at Ethan who was smiling at him. Curly lifted a single finger and tapped the air, his face pensive. "I like this place," he said observing the eatery's outside patio and lowering his hand. "You have these other places trying to change the service around. I think it's an attempt to reclaim something Old World, a European atmosphere." He looked up at the mixed, European gothic and Moorish-revival architecture of the adjacent buildings. "New Orleans owes its taste to the French. That's this city's excuse. But nowadays you see this Old World revival going on a lot down South. Not in the architecture, but in the people and the way they're carrying themselves." Facing Ethan, Curly exclaimed, "I don't mind change too much. I've seen so many things change in my lifetime, whether that be over time or in a matter of seconds before my eyes. So, I don't mind change," he reiterated. "But there's just some things I'm used to." He tapped his finger on the table and declared, "And I like when niggers serve me." Then he digressed and asked Ethan again, "How are you, Ethan?"

Ethan answered coolly, "I'm doing right fine, sir."

Curly narrowed his eyes and added to Ethan's words, "But you need help. Am I right, son?" He grinned, already knowing the answer.

Ethan's expression became stoic. "Yessir, I do," he addressed, a stern but polite tone in his voice. He asked Curly, "What is the binding factor, Curly, that's had us cross paths in New York and now here in New Orleans?"

"That nigger Joe Pepper," Curly answered without hesitation.

Ethan's boyish innocence dissolved away, exposing the hardened, trained soldier underneath. He put his hands together, forearms on the table, and leaned forward. "Governments have backed away from *our* interests. Tricks and charms and trinkets are but a hobby. This last war has proved too costly, and I see a shift toward economics as their main concern—par for the course, indeed, but the pursuit of our interests will take a back seat. But I'm still focused on our interests, Curly."

"So are the politicians," Curly said with a grin and a snicker.

Ethan grimaced, "We'll be like the Negro, a slave pimped out for governments' financial gains and power retention." He paused, face still stoic. "Now I've done some figurin', and I figure we'll have to look to one another for help in this New World Order." Now Ethan was smiling, All-American charm beaming through. He said to Curly, "Let's have a small reunion, you and I. The *Ordo Mystica*."

Curly scoffed playfully, "Such a loose organization."

"But effective," Ethan stressed. "We took care of Mister Randolph, did we not?" Curly agreed with a nod. "I have a proposition, Curly. I need your help taking care of that nigger Joe Pepper, student of Mister Randolph's. His end should be the same."

Curly again chuckled. "Miss Fallows is ahead of you, Ethan," he told the well-dressed soldier. "She's closing in on Pepper right now. He's twenty minutes away, in a town called Water Bug Hollow."

"I know where Pepper is," Ethan said, eyebrow raised. "Sarinda will not be catching him, if that is her pursuit. Pepper is, as you would say, a slippery nigger," Ethan stated as a matter-of-fact. He pulled out a silver cigarette case from the inside pocket of his suit jacket, opened it, and picked out a cigarette. He put the cigarette in his mouth. "Oh, he'll whisk away, steps ahead of Sarinda," Ethan surmised. He offered, "Cigarette?"

Curly declined with a shake of his head. But he did yield to Ethan's statements about Sarinda's chase for Joseph Pepper, though he said as a kind of rebuttal, "Miss Fallows is not pursuing Pepper. She knows he's heading to London after his visit to Water Bug Hollow. She's already guessed you'll pursue him there. But, Miss Fallows is more interested in an item our slippery nigger possesses. A veil. She believes he's going to hide it there in Water Bug Hollow because it's hallowed ground. Miss Fallows believes she can break the area's consecrated ambience and snatch the garment."

Ethan struck a match from a small book of matches that he removed from the same pocket as his silver case. He lit his cigarette, puffed and exhaled, and leaned back, legs crossed. "Joe will realize the story behind you and Sarinda. He's smart. He's very smart. And on top of that, he's lucky." Ethan stretched his arm to the ashtray and tapped several ashes into the receptacle.

Curly's authoritative weight dropped into his voice as he told Ethan, "That's why, with Miss Fallows' keen insight, she's asked for you to take care of Pepper in London."

Ethan perked up. He replied, "Oh, I am returning to London to kill him Curly, but I need your help. Yes, Miss Fallows is correct. Pepper *is* going to London, and I am *indeed* going after him." He puffed his cigarette and then said to Curly, "The item he possesses, this veil that Sarinda covets, it's nothing compared to what's over in London."

Curly, intrigued, raised an eyebrow.

Ethan addressed Curly's curiosity with answers. "He's being hired to pursue the same books that myself and my benefactor desire, though we will obtain the books legally."

"How is Brice?" Curly asked.

"Mister Cadogan is quite fine," Ethan answered, tapping more ashes into the ashtray. "He pays well, Curly."

Curly smiled, appreciating the subtle offer. The waiter placed Curly's meal and drink in front of him. Curly, grabbing his knife and fork, blared like a drill Sergeant, "Up straight and attentive, boy." The young black waiter became upright at the command. Curly sliced into each portion of his meal and took sample bites. He hummed, delighted. "Excellent, boy. Excellent service. The cooks were not rushed or delayed. You are dismissed."

"Thank you, sir. I'll check in to see if things are alright."

Curly said with a smile, "I know a waitperson's duty, boy. You don't need to announce your job."

"Yessir. I apologize."

The waiter hurried away.

Curly said chewing on a bite, "So, Brice wants me to be his nigger, is that it? For a hefty price?" He shook his head. "I cannot comply, Ethan. I'm sorry, but I must decline. I cannot leave Sarinda's side, not even for a moment. She's like a niece to me."

Ethan countered, "A niece you've been trying to take to bed since she was thirteen, so you've told me. A woman early, you described her."

Curly laughed the sentiment away. "Her father was like my brother," he remarked, diving back into his meal. "I was almost killed at his side. Hell, I was almost killed at the side of Miss Fallows' husband. Her private war includes me. It's *our* war. Pepper intrigues her. Always is when it comes to people like him. A nigger her father owned deflowered her. That was on her mother's orders. It's given her an odd attachment to the nigger—cruel as she can be to them. But that's her people's way, on her mother's side." Curly chewed, swallowed, and then wiped his mouth with a table napkin. "But she was scared when the South lost the War. She thought the Negro everywhere would rekindle their culture and rain down a hellfire of tricks on us. They've had their hoodoo, small outfits of traveling tricksters, but we took care of that." He thought for a moment. "That was exciting, Ethan. I'll admit. You should've stayed, but you started jaunting over there to London."

Curly resumed eating. Ethan smoked his cigarette. There was silence between the two men. Ethan admitted, "I don't like Sarinda. She's a beautiful woman, and I'm honored by her trick upon me. Her trick made me a better soldier. Hell, it made me a soldier. I was, after all, forced by my father to enter a war I didn't much care for. You heard correctly," he said when he noticed Curly look up from his meal. "Believe it: A proud Southerner that did not care for the war. And that is because, fellow Southern gentleman, I believe in the hierarchy of authority." Ethan further explained, "You see, I respected my older siblings, but over them are my mother and father. I respected my parents, but over them was the law of the land, the pride of the South, which my parents too so much respected. But over the South was the Union, the all of the United States. The President. And if he so chose to inch toward the Negro's freedom, so be it. *That* is how deeply I respect authority."

Curly gave Ethan a curious eye. "You sired a nigger child," he teased with a grin.

Ethan answered with no shame, but defense in his voice, "I did. And the first thing my daddy did when it was revealed I'd fathered a child with one of our Negro girls was have me put the girl down with a bullet. She was fourteen. I was twenty. She took advantage of me. I was still naïve about women, even at that age. I was a farm boy, nothing more. I was very passionate with her. I think she started to love me, because she always allowed me to express great passion with her. Great passion. I was free with her." Ethan smoked. He exhaled and reflected before continuing. "I was supposed to drown the child, but I convinced my father to sell him, and so my child was sold." He smoked more, exhaled, and then he crushed his cigarette out in the ashtray. "That wasn't the first time my father had to handle such an incident. My older sister went through the same ordeal. Our older brother cut the Negro boy's penis off as punishment for the offense of soiling my sister's womanhood. The slave, who was seventeen years old, he bled out. My sister, on my father's orders, drowned the baby girl. My daddy wanted the same thing with me. But I said, *'Let me sell it, sir.'* You see I had to refer to my son as 'it' because it wasn't a 'him,' or even had a name. And my father wanted no acknowledgement of him as anything other than chattel. My son was chattel. So, I told my father that I'd sell it like I did the calves with the cows he let me keep. And he looked at me and said, *'That's mighty appropriate, boy, considering it's from a heifer's belly.'*" Ethan chuckled at the memory. "I'm glad you mentioned my father. He was a hypocrite like Sarinda. But I still respected my father, the Lord bless his resting soul. He is, after all, the man whose seed I'm from and the man who raised me, tough love as it often was. I don't have to respect Sarinda, and I don't."

"She is the authority, however, Ethan," Curly reminded.

Ethan drew another cigarette from his case, and placed it in his mouth. He took out a match and lit his second cigarette. "Sarinda lost my respect when I had questions and she refused to answer them." He pointed his cigarette at Curly and told him, "And it wasn't because she didn't have the answers, so don't pull that excuse." Curly simply smiled and continued indulging in his meal. "Sarinda believed her position of authority over me—and you—depended on my lack of knowledge. She believes the same with you."

Curly continued smiling and eating, hiding his judgment of Ethan behind his cordial demeanor. He wanted to tell the young-looking soldier that he didn't require answers from his benefactor, Miss Sarinda Fallows. He'd known enough from her tricks, and though he hadn't retained his youth in the same way Ethan had, he was alive and healthy. And he had been alive and healthy for a long, long time. For that, and that alone, Curly was grateful to Miss Sarinda Fallows.

"I had more questions," barked Ethan as he smoked. "And Sarinda feigned ignorance. I would only have respected her more had she given me those answers, my humble knee bent in total service."

Curly didn't look up from his meal when he addressed Ethan, "It's the culture she comes from, on her mother's side. You can understand their secrecy. Besides, it's not like you're so forthcoming. Pepper still believes a Negro slave woman blessed you with your power."

Ethan couldn't argue, but no excuse would sway his sentiments on Sarinda Fallows. "She and Brice would be great together." He tapped ashes into the ashtray and said as a sigh, "He's head-over-heels with Sarinda." He brought the cigarette back and added, "But he understands my disdain for her. That's because of Pepper. Joe kept secrets too. He used to be partnered with us, for all his paranoia of the white man. But he used us as we used him."

"Where did you meet Pepper?" Curly asked pushing pancakes into his mouth.

"New York. Far after the war," Ethan answered. "I had to get away. Sarinda's trick made me stronger on the battlefield; it kept me young. I moved and fought in ways no enlisted man could. But even with me, the war could not be won. When it ended, Sarinda continued to use her tricks to calm my mind from the horrors of the war. And all three of us had fun with our *Ordo Mystica.* But, something was missing."

"Your child," Curly interjected.

"That's the second reason I left you two," Ethan confessed to Curly's assumption. "I was curious. I had a son. The people I'd sold him to no longer owned him. They gave him to a Negro family that they freed. The family settled in Massachusetts, and then I heard they left America altogether, went to London. On my search, while in New York, is where I met Joe Pepper. Good, knowledgeable young boy. His family didn't trust me. They knew better, I guess. Joe was in his early twenties. He wanted to go to London to study. I wanted to find my son. We had common ground, wanting to travel. In Massachusetts, we met Brice—who you have to thank."

Curly paused from eating. "For what?" he asked as he swallowed and wiped his mouth.

Ethan answered, "I constantly returned to America, to you and Miss Fallows, because of him. He was so enamored with what I had to say about Miss Fallows, her tricks, her charms, and her culture's history. Everything he'd studied had come to life. Pepper had charms and trinkets, but Brice didn't trust him because he was a Negro. He appreciated Pepper's ability to translate text. Not necessarily the language, but what it meant once we had the English translation. Pepper understood the spirit of the text." Ethan looked at the beignets and wondered if he was hungry enough to take one. He didn't, but he continued to wonder even as he spoke, "Pepper's grandmother was something else. She could've stopped Sarinda dead in her tracks. I liked Pepper and his family, suspicious as they were about me. Brice only kept Pepper in our circle for his knowledge of ancient symbols, and the ability to understand translated text. Everyone was conscious of using the other. No one cared. No one said anything. We all benefited."

"Understood."

"Joseph kept disappearing, and Brice became suspicious of that," Ethan stated. "Brice had me follow Pepper, all throughout Europe, Africa and back to the states. I discovered that Joe Pepper had a new benefactor, an old, Jamaican, black hag that runs a Negro orphanage in London. They call her Sister Nani."

"I've heard of her, through Miss Fallows, of course," Curly noted.

"Brice and her play games," said Ethan. "It's all about who can swipe an item before the other. Sister Nani knows where my child is. He could be dead now, for all I know. My boy would be fifty-four years old now, I believe. I'm sure he'd be shocked to not only see his white father, but to see me looking so young. There's no need to see him now, if, of course, he's still alive."

"You ever meet this Sister Nani?" Curly asked. He reached for a beignet. "Do you mind?"

Ethan shook his head, no, pushing the plate of beignets toward Curly. "I did speak to Sister Nani on occasion, acting as a spy for Brice," Ethan admitted. "She wouldn't give me answers either. Told me to move on, which I see now was correct, considering. My child was gone from her care—she cared for the family with my son when they got to London. She helped them, long, long ago. She admitted to me she knew who I was because of her incant—as she calls her tricks. But she wouldn't tell me anything about him. Nothing. The trail to find my son went cold, but the heat was always there with her, and she kept that from me. I wanted to kill her, but even with my strength, my speed, she can still best me. So, I dedicated my life to Brice's game with her. I would follow Joseph, and then I would snatch the items he was seeking before he'd get there. I'd be awake while he slept. I always waited for him to sleep."

"Joseph is good at what he does, so I hear. That nigger is the best," Curly laughed. Ethan scoffed at the notion. "Consider the laws in effect, my friend," Curly told Ethan. "Negroes can't go everywhere they want, but that nigger Joe seems to whittle his way in. He does have some fine items in his possession."

Ethan kept his scowl and said, "I've seen Joe operate with as much impunity, if not more, than most whites. Trick, incant, a conjure or bauble or trinket might influence his steps, but I've seen him move freely. Thus that puts us on equal grounds, good sir." Ethan took a drag of his cigarette. He held the smoke for a long time, in contemplation, and then he exhaled. Ethan said, as smoke filtered through his lips, "He has a partner, though. A man named Madison Goodspeed. He's young—by *our* standards—from Jamaica, and a thief. Sister Nani raised his parents. The trick in my skin has to work hard to get at both of them. Madison has wonderful tricks. His disadvantage, however, is that his tricks come through rituals. You can catch him off guard. He's not like the old ones. Few are. But his tricks give him an edge in darkness." He grinned. "I do admire that. His tricks keep him well hidden. He's good. Never really gone head-to-head with him, so this outing will be fun. To take both him and Pepper, and possibly that old Negress hag." He leaned forward and asked Curly, "You sure your answer's 'no'?"

Curly reiterated his answer, sounding like an apology, "I'm afraid it is, Ethan. I'm on an important assignment with Miss Fallows. But have your fun."

Ethan sighed. "Well, tell Miss Fallows I will take care of Pepper." He put his chin against a planted, balled fist holding his cigarette. He said with a reminiscent smile and voice, "I do this in honor of the glory days, my friend. In honor of our government-funded, loose, and dare I say, half-assed organization."

"Should we toast?" asked Curly with a smirk.

Ethan shook his head, mind still reminiscent. "No," he answered. He took another drag, hard and long. He exhaled and said, "I'll have to come with a good strategy with Pepper. He's my mark. He and that hag."

His eyes moved to Curly. "He doesn't have strength, but he has an item, a peculiar bauble. Not a small trinket either, it's his cane. It's said to be blessed with an alchemical anointment that contains crushed sapphires. It's also encrusted with seven sapphires." Ethan further explained, "He called the item Wanda. I thought it was in honor of his mother or grandparent, perhaps a favorite aunt. But I learned soon enough that Wanda was a feminine play on the word 'wand.' In truth, he calls his cane the Wand of Blue Light. He says the power of Shango and Indra is carried in his cane. It's fascinating when you think about it."

"Oh?"

"He fashioned it in India years and years ago," Ethan told Curly. "A Dravidian man gave him the formula to anoint the cane. It's not an ancient item, that's what I find fascinating. Pepper created it. He is now a part of legend and mythology." Ethan smiled. "It's too bad that I have to end his story." He took a drag of his cigarette. "Hell, I thought I saw the last of Pepper when we clashed out west. Like a good, Southern plantation boy, I even put Pepper up against another nigger. But Pepper had that Thunder John bandit and his Brother Dogs."

"Are the myths true about the Brother Dog savages?" asked Curly.

Ethan nodded his head. "Every bit. Wild and reckless, they are." He reached out his hand to Curly, who accepted and shook. "I wish you would join me, old friend. I was pleasantly surprised when my jaunt back to New York had me cross paths with both you and Pepper. I did believe you would come with me. But you are a man of loyalty. Money cannot sway you." He leaned back, letting go of the firm handshake.

"Yes. And I will tell Miss Fallows that you'll handle Pepper. She's come to realize many trinkets have slipped from her grasp because of him," Curly said. "She will be most thankful."

Ethan professed, "I'm a better soldier and man because of Sarinda. I won't forget that, but there are some things I can't respect about her. Regardless, give her my best."

Lilac fog invaded Ethan and Curly's reunion. It was not part of the atmosphere, however, but the pale-purple smog monster devoured the environment. Then the fog rose like a stage curtain, and there revealed was a steamship storage room packed tight with wooden crates, both new and tattered leather luggage cases, strapped sacks, and caged animals. Plugged into the small area was a motley assortment of cramped stowaways trying to make space where they could among the stored items. Every ethnicity and creed of person colored the storage space. Alone or in a small pack, some were clean, and some were dirty. Some were family, and some were friends. Others had blankets around them while some were burdened heavy with clothing, which was all they possessed. All were, pun notwithstanding, in the same boat. Regardless of prejudices, hand gestures were devised as signs and signals to alert one another of a legal crewman's patrol as they nosed through every room on random searches. This area was but one of many, as there were stowaways throughout the large steam vessel.

Madison Goodspeed and Joseph Pepper IV were nestled among this particular farrago of illegal passengers. In a corner, cloaked in shadow, no one saw them. The two of them boarded early, covered by shadows in ways the greatest of thieves would've envied. They each carried a bag with two changes of clothes and toiletries inside. Bread, fruit, sliced turkey meat, cheese, nuts, and water were also stored with them. Joseph packed a bottle of cognac given to him by his Louisiana sweetheart, Theresa Amat. Each item of food had been properly prepped with an incant to keep them fresh for the trip. Joseph's older sister, Adrian, performed the blessing.

Madison and Joseph were comfortable in their small space, though there was barely enough area for the two of them to lie out on the separate blankets they'd brought along. They used their bags as pillows. At the moment, they were up, backs against a set of wooden crates, and engaging in conversation. Joseph's sapphire-encrusted cane was propped up next to him. A guard had made his final sweep of the area for the night. The others were asleep. Madison and Joseph kept their voices to a whisper, though it was not necessary. The same shadow they hid within also masked the sound of their voices.

Madison removed his cap and rubbed his bald, dark-skin head. "I know I keep harpin' on it, Pepper," Madison whispered in a thick, English accent, eyes on Joseph, just able to see the older gentleman's features in the dark. "But seein' your happy face keeps bringing up the subject. I can see your bright smile through the dark." He heard Joseph chuckle, and though Madison couldn't see his friend, he knew he was probably blushing like a schoolboy. And he was. "So she said, yes, Pepper? Your sweetheart, Theresa."

Joseph nodded his head, beaming wide. "My man, Madison, it wasn't an official proposal," Joseph clarified, removing his glasses and wiping them with a cloth, despite the darkness around him. He just needed something for his hands to do. Joseph's body had been tense since he'd left Water Bug Hollow, Louisiana. "I announced to her that when I return, I would bring to her a grand treasure and a proposal. But she was accepting of the simplicity and the preview I offered her."

Madison slapped his friend on the knee. He joked, "A glimpse at the rest of her life with you, eh? You looking to settle down from the adventure, eh, Pepper?"

"A bit more lecturing and less jaunting, I suppose," Joseph said peering into the darkness. "If Theresa asks of it," he added.

"Ah, Pepper, the right woman will ask nothing of you, knowhadamean, eh." Madison thought of his words and then decided to say, "Of course, most people are usually afraid to ask something of the people they love, right."

"True, good Madison, true," Joseph agreed, but he was too happy to worry about the absence of adventure from his life. For the moment, he was pleased with the task ahead and the life he was to have with the woman he loved thereafter. "Theresa and I will discuss it later, I suppose." He nudged Madison with his elbow. "And I can always task a more youthful man such as you to take an adventure."

Madison rolled his eyes and plopped his cap back on his head. "I'll be all knackered between your tasks and Sister Nani's. Conjures and adventures are fine, Pepper, but I just want to settle somewhere, and it's about time I did, thirty-six as I am. I should be lookin' to settle some." He said a little louder than a whisper, "I want me a pub and café, all as one. Not too fancy, like a lot of them places in Harlem. Somewhere everyone could come to. I'd be the gaffer of it. Cook a little somethin' for the people, knowhadamean. I'd have a fine meal or drink for my customers, I would. All the meals of the world presented to them, mostly black inspired, even the European ones. On the menus, I'd have a history of the meal talkin' about how Africans introduced the meal into a particular region, and how the people put their own spin on it." He was louder, but had little to worry about as the other stowaways weren't disturbed. Madison looked down, contemplative. He heard Joseph agree and then said in a softer voice that still retained his excitement, "Harlem was a spell, Pepper, was it not? Ah, you're used to it, but I don't often see that kind of sight. You got a pretty woman singin' up a conjure, or you got an incant of music lightin' up every spot, every night, blessin' the city, whether the people are aware of their power or not."

Joseph interjected his commentary, saying as a subtle sigh, "Most of these Negroes know not, I'm afraid."

Madison ignored the comment and continued, "A black bloke such as m'self could do right." Madison adjusted himself in his spot. "I was waitin' for you there, I was, in Harlem. I saw a black man walk in. He was new to the city, from another part of the States. He was all mired in rags, looked tired from his long journey from wherever the start might've been. People took him in, bathed him, and gave him new clothes. Other black people, workin' together, had this man lookin' like the Mayor of Harlem in less than a minute's time. The man was all toffed up like he was the King of Diamonds, I tell you. I've never seen anything like that. And as my own personal tale, I had every girl lookin' at me. Their eyes all wide, ears all open listenin' to me talk. I'd settle down for them, Pepper. I'd toss my casual rags off and walk about the streets in a fine suit, I would."

"Would you?" Joseph laughed.

"I would. It's Harlem for me." Then Madison asked Joseph, "Hungry, Pepper?"

Forgetting the darkness muted them, Joseph answered in a hushed voice, "No. Too excited to eat, Madison," he exclaimed. "I'm not even worried about Cadogan or Ethan. I'm sort of anticipating seeing them, we as Sister Nani's soldiers against Cadogan and his ruffians, old Ethan being one of them." Joseph turned his head and spotted his cane. He reached out for the object and gripped it tightly, bringing it to him and laying it on his lap. The sapphires hummed with a faint, blue glow. Joseph tapped the cane and said, "Easy Wanda. Easy, now." The glow faded. "This will be a tricky affair, my man Madison. Getting both on and off the grounds of wherever the auction is held will prove dangerous."

"Sister Nani has it covered, Pepper," Madison comforted. "If not she, then my shadows conjured, knowhadamean. I'll have you home and to your sweetheart in no time."

Joseph's eyes remained fixed on his cane. He announced as a low hiss, "I'll have to kill Brice and Ethan both, Madison. Theresa will be in danger, should they live."

Madison didn't argue, but he did have to say, "Been waitin' to snuff out their tricks." Then he remarked, "Sister Nani's old. She's taking too long to do something. No offense to her as a wise woman, but a move has to be made. Someone's got to go, eh. It'll make jauntin' over this world easier, but I'm sure there will be others after Ethan and Brice." Madison paused to think about the subject at hand. After a passed moment he said, "Of course, Pepper, we use them as much as they use us. A black bloke can't get into every place on his good looks. There's laws about the world."

"There's always a way around them," Joseph chortled.

"Sure is, Pepper. How's about a drink? Some of that fine brandy you got stored away, sir. Let's share the bottle again."

Joseph reached for his bag, propping his cane back into place. He pulled his bag to him, opened it, rummaged through, and removed the bottle of cognac. Joseph opened the bottle and took a swig. Madison watched Joseph's faint silhouette, waiting for the bottle to be handed to him. "What should we toast to?" Joseph asked finishing his swig and handing the bottle to Madison.

Madison lifted the bottle and said, "To Joseph Pepper the Fourth, continuing a line of three Peppers before him."

"Two," Joseph corrected.

The mouth of the bottle stayed inches away from Madison's lips. A few drops of cognac spilled onto his shirt. He ignored the small droplets and asked, "Two? Aren't you the fourth, Pepper?"

"Yes," answered Joseph. There was a beat and he presented another answer, "…and no." Madison couldn't see Joseph's face, but if he had, he would've observed an odd, guilty grin on the scholar's visage. Joseph knew what type of confusion his answer might've caused.

"You're going to have to explain that one, Pepper."

"My grandfather," Joseph replied. "He was Joseph Pepper the Second. But he was the first."

Madison half-joked, "Not helping, there, Pepper."

"He was a slave in the state of Georgia," Joseph further explained. "He was called Pepper by the other slaves because he had a mighty temper, fiery like—"

"Pepper," Madison concluded with no disrespect.

Joseph nodded. "Indeed." Then he returned to his grandfather's story. "My grandfather's master used my grandfather's temper to his advantage, keeping the other slaves in line. That was one of his tasks. But one night, it backfired. It was the night of my father's birth. The slave master, drunk, taunted my grandfather that the child might've been his. The slave master had raped my grandmother on several occasions. It could've been true, however, it was not. As it's understood, the slave master had not mistreated my grandmother in some time. But proper math and timing of incidents in conjunction with my father's birth was not on my grandfather's mind. He was enraged. He'd lost it. He beat his slave master bloody and unconscious, and he did so in front of the other slaves. My grandfather would later tell me that he understood the center of his anger that night. You see, good Madison, my grandfather never knew his father. He was absent, taken away to some slave system within the South. His mother was hardly there for him or his half-siblings, some of who were of the slave master's father and his brothers' seeds. My grandfather grew up angry at his circumstances, but he could only express that anger physically toward the other black slaves, and he got away with it. His master gave him a promotion, of sorts—as I've said—keeping the other black slaves in line. He was a brutal man, my grandfather. Not very big, but very strong. He was hurtful to my grandmother too until he found out she was pregnant. But he was still angry, and he did his job well hurting the other black slaves of the plantation." Joseph reflected on the story, and then he continued, "When my father was born, my grandfather was so happy. He wanted a family. He wanted a *whole* family. His master's taunts took that away from him. His anger was stirred, but after he'd beaten his master to a pulp, the anger was gone. As the story goes, my grandfather apologized to the other slaves for the way he'd treated them. Then, he took my grandmother, and their newborn child, and they fled into the night." Joseph pointed up with a single finger and said, "North was the obvious place to go. My grandmother said a blessing that kept them safe." Joseph pondered and then stated, "I'm not quite sure if it was an actual incant. But my grandparents were not found and recaptured. No, instead they reached the state of Delaware after days of travel. My grandmother only says that a blessing kept them safe, and I say again that I'm unaware if she meant an incant of sorts. I assume both yes and no. I don't believe it was something my grandmother was truly in control of, or even fully aware of beyond superstition. But with a newborn child, and all three hungry and barely hydrated, they crossed into Northern territory and were taken in by a woman of mixed-race. Her name was Clair Stephens, a remarkably wealthy woman living in Delaware."

"Wealthy?" Madison said surprised. "And black?" his astonishment continued. "I mean she was of mixed ancestry as you state, but still, huh. In those days? I guess that shows my own ignorance. I apologize."

Joseph nodded. "No need to extend such an apology, fellow traveler," he assured. "History has a lot of surprises concerning the Negro, and it strikes many with such emotion. As long as you don't doubt it, good man, because of some form of indoctrination, I am otherwise not offended." Then Joseph returned to the tale of his family's history. "Miss Stephens' husband, long since passed, was unmistakably black. Miss Stephens was able to pass. I've been told that she said her husband often played as her servant," he elucidated. "Miss Stephens was sixty years of age, or so. She was widowed and without children. She educated my grandparents on proper, societal etiquette. She also blessed my grandfather with a first name. Joseph." Joseph beamed, recalling his father talk about these tales with such pride. Joseph continued, telling an intrigued Madison, "Happy to have two names, my grandfather jokingly referred to himself as *'Joseph Pepper with Two names.'*" He turned to Madison and lifted his brow as he said, "This eventually became Joseph Pepper the Second when he entered society as an educated and free man. I also note that my grandmother, named Rose Sept, or Rose the Seventh, inspired my grandfather. He saw her anew, and she him. He'd directed his anger properly at his oppressor, and no longer at her. He learned her story. She was the seventh child born to a slave out of New Orleans. Ultimately, sold as *'Child number seven.'* Their slave master's wife gave my grandmother the name Rose because of her reddish complexion. But now, refined, educated, and able to blend into society as free blacks, Joseph Pepper the Second, my grandfather, and Rose Pepper, my grandmother, found work in Buffalo, New York through an associate of Miss Stephens. My father, months old and only referred to as 'boy,' was named Joseph Pepper the Third. So, there you have it. I am the fourth and the third."

Madison air clapped, as if noise would disturb the sleeping stowaways. Joseph beamed, though it could not be seen in the dark. He continued his family's history as the two men retired for the night. He spoke of his grandmother believing so much of the blessing that protected them that she began studying spiritualism, and that was how his father and aunt and uncle were raised. Their family would travel often to New York City and mingle with the black spiritualists of the day, including Mister Paschal Beverly Randolph. Joseph revealed that when his father was eighteen he made a permanent move to New York City's Five Points area, taking a job as a mailroom boy in a black law office.

"Around that same time, my mother, who was seventeen years, was settling in the Five Points district. My mother and my maternal grandmother were runaway slaves. In Five Points, they were living under new names. My mother was now calling herself Clover Trudeau. Her slave master named her Sadie. Can you believe that? My grandmother was not allowed to name her own child. The same slave master gave my grandmother her name. She was called Anna, but she took the name Grace once they escaped to New York. Trudeau, their new surname, was taken because it was the first name spied in some logbook when they reached the city. Under these new personas, my mother and grandmother worked as assistants at an all-black grade school, literate as they were—unbeknownst to their slave masters, of course. Many perceived the two as sisters, considering my grandmother was only fifteen years older than my mother. My father and mother met one night at a black social gathering and fell in love on sight of one another. My mother confessed everything about herself to my father over the course of their courtship, even the news that her uncle had joined them on the escape but was killed, and that she and her mother were possibly still pursued by her uncle's killer who also was their former slave master's overseer. His name was Dayton Ingleton, and my mother was sad to admit that he was her father."

"Oh, no," Madison remarked, drawn in by Joseph's family story.

"It goes further, Madison," Joseph replied, getting sleepy as he was now resting on his side. Despite the uncomfortable makeshift bed of blanket against the steel floor, and the makeshift pillow of his traveling sack, Joseph was still drawn to sleep. But Joseph asked, "You know of the Draft Riots, my man?"

"Heard of 'em, I have," answered Madison.

Joseph said, "Well, this man—my grandfather, I must admit—Dayton Ingleton, he participated in the Draft Riots, taking advantage of the chaos to find my mother and grandmother. Following information that they might've escaped the city, Dayton tracked my grandmother and mother a few miles outside Five Points. The confrontation was loud, with threats of violence. But the confrontation was also isolated." Joseph paused, his mind conjuring up the scene of events that next took place. Then, slow and dramatic, he described them, "My father gunned down Dayton as the angry brute made a move to assault my grandmother. His body was buried in an undisclosed location. After that, my father didn't want to return to Five Points after the riots. He wanted to live in a place called Weeksville like so many blacks had done. But my grandmother assured they would be protected." A little excitement in his voice, but still only in a hush, Joseph iterated, "Now, my maternal grandmother, she was a little more aware of conjures. She had a spirit inside her."

"Yes," said Madison. "You've told me. She could draw out an old bauble's power. Did so with Kalifia's veil, right Pepper?"

"Right indeed, Madison," Joseph articulated, his thoughts on his grandmother and her ability. He also thought about the veil Madison had spoken of. He had presented it to his sweetheart, Theresa Amat when he visited her in Water Bug Hollow. He hoped it would keep her safe, as it was intended. He wanted to introduce Theresa to his mother and father, mostly so he could tell his mother, *"You see, mother, I will be married."* Joseph chuckled to himself. He then concluded his story, "Well, a very small, black collective remained in the area after the violent Draft Riots. My mother and father made it work. I was born ten years later, two older sisters before me."

Lilac fog inched its way into the storage room and smothered the scene. Through the haze could be heard voices, angry and loud. *"Nigger Stowaways!"* a voice shouted. *"String 'em up!"* another yelled. There were more voices calling for the dismemberment of the illegal boat hoppers.

The lilac fog dissipated like leaves in the wind. It was daybreak in London, at the docks. A single copper dragged a chained Madison Goodspeed and chained Joseph Pepper to a police carriage. The copper's name was Latham Armstrong, an ex-soldier with more heart than brawn, but effective at his job. Latham was tall, around six feet. His face was lined and aged by the hardships of war and the life of a soldier. Being a copper on the brutal London streets didn't help much either. His eyes looked tired, though he was often very alert, the trained soldier always at the ready. A thin beard and mustache outlined his face, and despite his age, had a youthful color to them. His hair battled between golden brown and white, but at the moment was covered by a copper's cap. His face was a scowl as he battled the mob of sailors around him. However, his countenance often looked the same when he was calm.

He swung Madison and Joseph about, using their bodies to keep the people away from him. "I've to do my duty, understand. Now back off!" he hollered at the angry and groping people trying to get a hold of Joseph and Madison.

Latham tossed the men into the open police carriage. He shut and locked the doors, and then he turned to face the mob. "Back off, the lot of you!" he warned again. Latham parted the sea of people and came to the steamship's captain who was holding Joseph and Madison's bags, and Joseph's cane. Latham snatched all three items from the captain. "Ease your men, Captain," Latham told the ranking seaman, the handle of Joseph's cane pressed firmly against the captain's chest. The captain believed he felt a shock like a static charge for a brief moment, and he reacted with a jump. "Ease your crew, hear?" Latham declared, "You're not pirates. Your boys are gettin' all ruffled over a couple nigger stowaways. You know you got more in there, some of the lot Germans and Russians. A couple of harmless boys lookin' for a lift is nothing to get excited about. No threat to Crown, they are."

The captain huffed, "My men been at sea, copper. They're restless. A little action won't do no harm. Let 'em make these niggers a little more black and some blue, eh."

Latham backed away. "These boys will be booked proper." He looked at the crowd and yelled, "And I'll book anyone else that seems to believe they're above my enforcement." He gave a final snarl to the captain and walked back to the police carriage. "Go about your business!" Latham hollered. *"You shall all forget the ugliness that has occurred here,"* he yelled to the mob. Latham paused and exhaled. Shouting his final words to the crowd alleviated him of the stress of the moment, and more. He blinked and then went about his duty, moving to the front of the carriage. He tossed the bags and cane on the wide seat, and then jumped aboard to take the reins of the horses. "Come, come!" he commanded. "Go now."

The sailors parted, making room for the carriage. A few knocked their fists against it or pushed the cage as Latham passed them by. The copper shouted, "*Back off!* Or you'll have the lot of coppers like me down here to take *you* in as well." Latham slapped the reins and sped off. No one gave chase, and the mob's anger subsided. One-by-one, the people blinked away the memory of the incident and returned to their duties at the dock.

Latham moved the carriage down the street, stuck behind automotive traffic. After cursing the precinct's budget, Latham turned off the street, and then he turned again. This street was empty, as the day was just starting and residents were still in their homes. Latham stopped the carriage, turned and knocked against the cage. He whispered, "Mister

Madison, Mister Pepper, the two of you okay? Didn't rough you fellows up too much, did I?"

"No," Madison replied. "But the theater is probably your next calling, knowhadamean, copper."

Latham was relieved. He joked, "Always wanted to give the stage a try." Then he said to Joseph, "You okay, Mister Pepper? You've had better trips to London, I suppose."

"Indeed, good man, I have. But necessity is necessity," Joseph replied.

Latham faced forward. "Alright, you two sit tight. We'll be at The Library soon enough. Sister Nani's been anxious. Enjoy the ride as best you can, sirs." The horses trotted forward, winding through London's backstreets that became muddier and muddier. The houses in the neighborhoods they traveled through went from proud-standing to dilapidated and moth-eaten until Latham steered into a section of London that brimmed proud with life despite being racked with ruin and poverty. Blacks young and old scurried about with smiles on their faces that worked just enough to dull the pain in their hearts. A job was a job to them, and they were thankful to have one. A place to live was appreciated; there were more that had less. Government coin didn't extend to this area. The streets and houses were grungy, but the people made due even among the desolation and inevitable crime.

Latham parked the police carriage in front of a large, rundown, blue and white storage house. Its paint was peeling and its siding was beginning to crack and loosen. There was a large sign slapped on the front of the building that read: *The Rose Hill, On the Boulevard.* This was Sister Nani's orphanage. It was often referred to by its proper name, as the sign proposed, but many dubbed the building *The Library* because of the grand amount of books Sister Nani accumulated over the years. If a room wasn't packed with books, it was a playroom or sleeping area for the children she took in. The only rooms where play and books were not permitted were the kitchen, bathing and toilet areas. However, many of the more energetic children made those rooms an area of play, for which they would receive a severe scolding from Sister Nani or one of the other adults of the house.

Latham hopped off his seat just as two black men emerged from the warehouse. Both jumped up onto the carriage's seat and kept the horses steady as Latham traveled around back and unlocked the cage. "All right, then, out with you," he said to Joseph and Madison. "Come on." He flipped through his keys and found the master for the iron handcuffs shackling Madison and Joseph. He unlocked the two men.

"Thankful," said Madison, removed of his shackles. He tossed the iron handcuffs into the cage, as did Joseph once Latham unlocked his bindings. Madison looked up at the storage house-turned-orphanage. This was home, though he could call Jamaica that too. But this was where his family began. His mother and father were raised here, and they fell in love here too.

The front doors opened again, and from them came Sister Nani hunched over with a cane. Her wrinkled brown skin was aged by wisdom and heartache, but there was joy in her ninety-two-year-old face. She waved Madison to her, and he stepped up on command. He bent down and gave her a gentle hug and a kiss on the cheek. "Sister Nani. Everything been okay?" he asked her.

Three children spilled out into the street, coming from The Rose Hill front doors. Sister Nani barked at them, "What? You boys get inside, now! You got class! No time to start deh day like dis," she huffed, her pronunciation of words battling between a thick Jamaican accent and a British twang. "Dis cane don't just hold me up, it'll beat your butts. Come now. You all are smarter than that! *Reginald! Don't you dare!*" The boys turned and ran back inside, the boy Reginald ceasing to dive further into whatever activity Sister Nani had anticipated from him. She looked up at Madison and commented, "T'ings deh same, you know. T'ings deh same." She looked over Madison's shoulder and spotted Joseph. "Dhere's deh spice. Dhere's deh Pepper." She tapped the back of her hand against Madison's arm. "You brought him back, Madison, ah!"

"Hello, Sister Nani," Joseph greeted with a smile as he rubbed his wrists where he'd been shackled.

"Barely recognize you all duhtied up, Joe Pepper," Sister Nani teased, giving an old woman's joyous cackle. Joseph was always forced to listen closely to her, trying to distinguish her words as they traveled between thick accents. "You boys got bags?" she asked.

"Here they are," said Latham handing Joseph and Madison their respective travel sacks, blankets and coats tied around them. He tossed Joseph his cane, and Joseph thanked him. Latham then said to the elderly woman, "How are you, Sister Nani?"

"Old and crazy," Sister Nani commented. "How'd everything go at the docks?"

"A bit of a party, it was," Latham admitted. "But the incant you blessed me with worked like a charm—though I suppose it was a charm, eh. No mind, though. No one there will remember a thing."

"Good, Latham. Good work," Sister Nani congratulated. "How's Merwin?"

"Still keeping track of The Line, Miss," Latham said as a matter-of-fact. "His contacts said Burton, Bradley and Pierce will be hosting The Line's auction in April. The location is still unknown, but there have been two suggestions. One is on the grounds of the Bell-Sherwin Foundation. The other is the Avon Crest estates. I can secure a map of both areas. It'll be easier than casing either of the two grounds. Give us a closer eye without a bother of suspicion." Latham believed he'd said too much aloud and in public. He looked around, and felt secure when he saw no one but the district's black residents milling about the street. But for caution, he spoke in a hushed voice. He bent down to say to Sister Nani, "Merwin's contacts continuously assure him that the *Nigrum Nigrius Nigro* and a recently bound and blessed *Seshat Songbook* will be on display."

Joseph inquired, "How recently bound is recently bound?"

Latham peered up at Joseph. He straightened and answered the scholar, "Middle Ages, Merwin tells me. Supposedly put together in Ethiopia and then carried over to West Africa. Members of The Line recovered it—or to speak more properly, *took* the book from Senegal. The people there referred to it as *The Book of Asm-Ism.*" Latham added, "I do wish we could find the whereabouts of the objects' holding. But from the rumors I've heard, there's a hidden rifle aimed on every man standing guard should they even think of trying anything. Guards for guards, eh? That's how The Line operates, I guess. Rumor or not, it'll be easier to swipe the books when they're being auctioned off."

The gathered party traded looks that all turned to Sister Nani.

"Get to your day's patrol, Latham," Sister Nani told him after quick contemplation. "I'll call for you and Merwin when ready. I t'ank deh bot' of you for your duties."

"Yes, Sister Nani," said Latham. He walked back to his carriage and politely dismissed the two gentlemen keeping the reins. He climbed aboard, shouted a final farewell over his shoulder, and trotted away. The day was getting brighter, and the environment was developing out of the darkness like a photograph.

"I don't mean to present myself as rude, Sister Nani," Joseph exclaimed, "but I could use a bath and more comfortable attire." He slapped the underside of his bag.

Sister Nani turned around and walked back inside. She waved her hand, motioning for Joseph and Madison to follow. The men holding Latham's police carriage followed as well. Inside the spacious area, broken up by rooms cluttered with toys or books, Joseph and Madison walked close behind Sister Nani into one of the rooms stuffed with volumes upon volumes of literature covering all topics and genres. Also in the room were a few chairs where they could take rest.

"Jeremiah!" hollered Sister Nani, calling one of the men that helped keep Latham's carriage. Jeremiah stepped inside, standing at attention.

"Prepare deh bath and deh showah." She looked at Joseph and Madison. "Which one of you wants what? Bath or shower?"

"I'll take the bath, Sister Nani," said Joseph.

"Okay," acknowledged Sister Nani. "Bath got to be filled first. It'll be warm. Jeremiah will make sure deh showah stay that way too. Children been up and washed. Dhey're in class now, out deh way."

"Thank you, Sister Nani," Joseph expressed.

Jeremiah exited the room to handle his duties.

Madison inquired, "Any read on Ethan and Brice? Authenticity can be declared, judging by their eagerness to get a hold on these items."

Sister Nani agreed. She slapped her cane down, both hands planted firmly on the handle.

"Good insight," Joseph complimented. "Merwin is close to Brice. We'll have Merwin talk to him. Have Merwin drink a soothing round of Sister Nani's tea to keep him trustworthy." He turned to the aged woman. He shook his head with a smile, "Merwin and Latham still under your charm, Sister Nani?"

Sister Nani replied with a chuckle, "My charm don't expire. I keep dem boys sippin' my tea. Dhey listen. Don't have to do much with Latham. He's seen things in his travels as a soldier. He understands deh world's hidden politics. Don't like what he saw and continues to see."

"The two of them have proven useful," Joseph commented. "A good check on our villains' behavior would do well, though I believe we're on the right track to recovering these items for you, Sister Nani." In his erudite manner, Joseph said, "The *Nigrum Nigrius Nigro* will prove authentic. It should, supposedly, tell us itself whether it is or is not. From what I've studied, holding the book will give a person vivid dreams. It can reveal the authenticity of any item, its pages suddenly filled with description of the history of an item placed upon its open pages. As for Sheshat's Songbook, I believe we will find it blessed, blank, and waiting for musical invocations to be scripted inside. We will compose wonderful hymns and see our history. No one will be able to deny where we come from!"

"Dhere should be rituals written inside the *Nigrum Nigrius Nirgo*." Sister Nani noted. "Don't forget that. I'm lookin' for something that can ground my boys and girls here. Somet'ing dhey can partake in and call a culture. Somet'ing definite and not so fractured. I'm lookin' for real rites of passage for boys to become men, and rites of passage for girls to become women. Fix dis whole district. Can't have dhem sippin' incanted tea and milk an' t'ink everyt'ing okay when it's not. We need more. Bring deh greatest of our magic back."

"I agree, Sister Nani," said Joseph. "I agree."

Jeremiah returned and announced, "Mister Pepper, your bath is waiting."

Joseph jumped up. He picked up his bag and cane. "Right now I seek a warm bath. A great treasure to me," he joked. He walked past Jeremiah, items in hand.

Jeremiah said to Madison, "I'll fix the shower in the other bathroom. Make sure the plumbing is running hot water for you. I'll be back."

The room filled with lilac fog that wiped away the scenery only to bring it back once it lifted away. It was later that day. Sister Nani sipped tea and rested on the couch in the same room. Joseph entered, bathed, primped and perfumed. He was clothed in a fancy suit, cane in hand. He removed his bowler hat as he entered and placed it on the arm of an unoccupied chair. He leaned his cane against the same piece of furniture. The children were on break from learning, and they ran about the large living area of the storage place, up and down the stairs, inside and out. But male and female caregivers kept watch over them, assisted by older boys and girls of the orphanage.

Joseph closed the door to keep both his conversation private, and to keep the noise from entering. He sat down on the same tattered, upholstered chair where he laid his hat and cane. Sister Nani, now wearing a high-waist skirt with sash and white blouse, bedecked in many bangles and necklaces, turned to Joseph, leaning on her cane and asked, "You've something to tell me, Joe Pepper?"

"Yes, Sister Nani," he answered. "It's about the tomes we wish to acquire. We desire them for simple means, Sister Nani, but there must be something greater about them if men are willing to kill to keep our hands from them."

"Absolutely," Sister Nani agreed. "Once we possess dhem, Joe Pepper, we'll see exactly what script our black eyes are meant to see. We'll translate its meanin', like you did for Ettin and Brice."

Joseph chuckled, not so much hiding an offense taken at Sister Nani's reference to assisting Ethan Cassidy and Brice Cadogan in earlier times, but at her pronunciation of Ethan's name. It was fitting, he judged. It was even more amusing as he considered the fitting pronunciation through her accent was not altogether purposeful. He believed a spirit worked through Sister Nani appropriately designating Ethan Steel Cassidy as the monster he truly was.

"Sister Nani," Joseph said ending his chuckle, and changing the subject a bit. "It's my pleasure to reveal to you that I am engaged, putting it simply."

"Ah," Sister Nani said, face aglow, "To dhat singer in America's south. Theresa."

"Yes, Sister Nani. Theresa Amat," Joseph extended. "And I gave to her Kalifia's Veil, not a ring, for proposal."

Sister Nani slapped her cane against the floor and shook her head as she smiled wide. "Great Iyansan!" she exclaimed. "Great Iyansan!" Sister Nani looked up at Joseph and said, smile still wide, "Now I know you've said dhat gu'l has a skeptic's heart, but she believe in you, Joe Pepper." Sister Nani slapped her cane against the floor a second time. Again she shook her head and smiled. "By Kalifia! Deh t'ings dhat gu'l gon' see wit' dhat veil. I envy her, I do."

Joseph informed, "I met a woman, a distant cousin to a white family that sends aide to Water Bug Hollow. Miss Sarinda Fallows was her name. She was so intrigued by the area's story. Her side of the family looked down on the Negroes of that area. They also look scornfully at the MacRitchies, the descendants of the white man that befriended and assisted Curtis 'The Water Bug' Hollow with emancipating the property. Miss Fallows was determined to know those roots." Joseph leaned forward. "I thought I would've seen Miss Fallows when I arrived, or before I left. And in my excitement of spending time with my beautiful songbird, Theresa, I forgot to ask if this Miss Fallows woman had already come and gone, or even inform Theresa of her coming."

"Seem like white folk all over have more interest in our history dhan we do," Sister Nani commented. "Deh world is weird, Joe Pepper. All dhat old spirit and magic from Africa carried around deh world and so little of it in use by deh ones dhat own it. History of deh Negro has gotten complicated. British whites separate us different here dhan dhem American whites do over deh watah. We colonized from here to Africa an' to deh Caribbean. I keep my head about me. I teach dhese children. Dhere will be a bunch of Joe Peppers and Madison Goodspeed boys running around. Dhere will be many Sister Nani's waving magic around as if it's nothing." Sister Nani snapped her fingers. "You think we're dangerous now, Joe Pepper. Just wait."

Joseph nodded his head, somber demeanor on his face. "Yes," he said. "Dangerous." He leaned back in his chair. "Sister Nani, it's always been a game between you and Brice, Ethan and me. But I believe this game must come to a close. As I plan to settle, I wish not for either of the two to invade my personal space, having my wife-to-be involved."

"I understand, Joe Pepper," Sister Nani agreed. "But wit' deh veil of skepticism lifted from your Theresa, an' by Kalifia's veil, she just might be able to put Ettin and Brice down for good. She's going to be powerful, Joe Pepper. But I understand your concern. If on dhis smash and grab you have a moment to kill dhese two men, don't hesitate to snuff your proper villains. You don't need my permission for dhat, Joe Pepper."

"I do," Joseph insisted. "I do, Sister Nani, if for the simple fact of not allowing that to be my sole mission, clouding my perception of the task at hand. It might interfere with our chances of obtaining these sacred African tomes."

Sister Nani lifted her shoulders and in a nonchalant voice stated, "Dhen make dhat part of dhis task. Brice doesn't usually peek his head out like we're told he will. Dhis will be an excellent moment." Sister Nani tapped her cane twice on the floor and said as an order, "Kill our enemies, Joe Pepper. I demand it!"

"It will be done, Sister Nani," Joseph assured.

Sister Nani gave a nod. She reached for a piece of paper resting on the table behind her. She picked up the paper and walked it to Joseph. He stood up, protesting the old woman's approach. "Sister Nani, no, no, let me come to you," he said stretching his arm for the piece of paper. He took it from her while she was several strides into her approach. Then he insisted, "Here, Sister Nani. Have my seat."

"Oh, Joe Pepper, dhere are plenty of seats around here, boy," she scolded playfully. "If I want a seat, I'll take one. Now, you sit back down. I have another task to fill you and Madison's time."

Joseph did as told. He looked at the piece of paper Sister Nani handed him, and then his eyes went to her.

"Dhat's an ingredient I need for a new brew," she expounded. "It's in Spain. I need you and Madison to get me dhat spice and bring it back 'ere. If dhem books don't tell us not'ing, dhen that brew will. It will *show* us something." Sister Nani raised a finger and twirled it. "Vivid dreams, Joe Pepper. Vivid dreams." She relaxed her arm and said, "*Destiny Swallow* is what this drink called."

"It shall be retrieved, Sister Nani," Joseph complied.

"Good," Sister Nani retorted. "In deh meantime, you want to keep your sweetheart safe, you don't write. No communication. Don't even try to relax and enter her dreams."

Joseph nodded as he folded the paper and tucked it inside his pocket. "I told her to keep the veil close," Joseph informed. "I gave her rituals for her to abide by. I warned her to give no one permission to hold the veil. She'll do well."

Again the lilac brume swept away scene and time. Many images mingled behind the fog. Voices penetrated the pale-purple mist. There first appeared a scene of Joseph Pepper IV and Madison Goodspeed returning from Spain with *Destiny Swallow*'s remaining ingredient as a prize. It was a rare plant called *Ibn Bassal*, not to be confused with basil, as Madison joked, and its foliage only bloomed on the site of a former Moorish temple turned church turned library. Sister Nani was delighted. A thick lilac haze, though, impeded the celebration. Then it was gone, blown away by an invisible force. There in one of two kitchen areas of The Rose Hill orphanage, Joseph Pepper IV, Madison Goodspeed, and Sister Nani sipped from small cups of tea brewed with the rare plant. That night, when they slept, each of them dreamed vividly.

Joseph dreamed of his sweetheart, jazz singer Theresa Amat. She sang with all the power of her beautiful voice. She was on a stage in front of a white audience, veiled with the garment he'd presented to her. The audience disappeared behind a foreboding, black cloud, and the same darkness swallowed Theresa's band. The music ceased, but not Theresa's voice. She sang loud and powerful, the absence of the music only increasing the strength of her voice. But there came a click-clack loud enough to invade Theresa's sweet, melodious bellows. However, she ended her song undisturbed by the click-clack chatter of high heels tapping against the stage. Coming up behind Theresa, walking with a seductive sway, was the voluptuous figure of Sarinda Fallows.

Theresa lifted her veil and turned around to see the red-haired, green-eyed woman. She smiled kindly and nodded at Sarinda as if saying, *"Hello, and who are you?"* Sarinda grabbed Theresa's arm with one hand and lifted the other to reveal a syringe in her grip.

"I want that veil," Sarinda declared.

A blue, spherical ball of light radiated from Theresa's forehead. The intention of Theresa's smile changed. Her eyes looked apologetic. And then she expressed, *"No. My Pepper would not have it so."*

Sarinda Fallows proceeded to stab the jazz singer in the forearm with the syringe. The needle cut straight through Theresa's arm with every jab Sarinda made. Blood, smoke, and a frothy liquid poured from Theresa's wounds. The jazz singer never screamed or looked worried. Instead, keeping her smile, she looked down at her belly and watched it grow pregnant. She rubbed her belly and said, *"It's a girl."* Theresa bubbled with sweet, light laughter. She told Sarinda, *"If I don't put you down, Miss Fallows, my daughter will. And if she don't,* her *daughter will. And if you have heirs, my children's children's children will put them down too."*

This is what Joseph Pepper dreamed.

Madison Goodspeed had dreams too. It was a bright day in Brooklyn, and he walked down a street empty of people. A row of mighty brownstones stood on either side of him. But despite the street's emptiness, he heard a bustle of activity. There were happy greetings and friendly conversations. Madison felt a great pressure against his whole body, squeezing him. It wasn't oppressive, but it was heavy, like a shadow conjured in ritual. He was outside of time. The feeling was all around him, but didn't affect his steps.

Then a voice spoke, *"It's a fine place, isn't it?"* The voice was coming from behind Madison. He turned around and saw a black man in an old-fashioned, expensive business suit approach him. *"Pardon me,"* he said to Madison as he finished his approach. He reached out a hand and introduced himself, *"My name's James Weeks."*

Madison accepted the man's hand and shook. *"Hello, sir. My name's Madison Goodspeed."*

"I know who you are, Mister Goodspeed," the man calling himself James answered to Madison's surprise. *"I've been waiting for you, and it's a pleasure to meet you, Mister Madison Goodspeed. Yes, indeed it is."* James extended and waved a hand around at the empty street. *"All you see here is part of a purchase I made back in eighteen-thirty-eight."*

"Is that right, Mister Weeks? That's a mighty long time ago."

"From where you are, it is a long time ago," James agreed. *"That was eleven years after New York State abolished slavery. I'd come up here from Virginia. Down there I was a stevedore. That's a dockworker, in case you were wondering."*

Madison laughed, not offended. *"I know that there, friend,"* Madison informed as he continued to chuckle. *"Might not have much knowledge, but I got that, knowhadamean."*

James held a smile when he next addressed Madison, but he wasn't joking when he told him, *"You have a* great *deal of knowledge, Mister Goodspeed. More than most.*" Then he digressed as he said, *"But anyway, I got myself some land with the help of a man named Henry C. Thompson, another freed Negro. With my purchase, I did what I could to create an Eden for the Negro. Y'see, I purchased from one fellow Negro, and then fellow Negroes flocking from all around the East Coast, and running from slavery, purchased from me. And the dollar stayed in our pockets."*

"That's a proud tale to tell, Mister Weeks," Madison commented.

James nodded and continued, *"We worked hard, us Negro landowners. Freed Negro men and freed Negro women. Like Rome, this wasn't built in a day. It took Weeks."* He winked at Madison, and Madison smiled back. *"I myself had a handsome dwelling over on Schenectady and Atlantic Avenue,"* James announced. *"But this street, it represents the heart of this community. The spirit. It's yours if you want it."*

Madison quipped, *"Let me guess, 'All these things I will give you if you fall down and do an act of worship to me.' Is that your game?"*

Again, the smile remained, but James expressed in a sincere voice, *"I understand your trepidation, Mister Goodspeed, but no. This street is yours if you want it."* Madison thought about the offer. He never considered what lay before him a dream. James said to him, "*Conjure me and we'll partake in some wine and cigars. We'll discuss the deal. But, there won't be much to discuss. This real estate is yours for free. Keep it safe and tucked underneath a shadow. Don't let just anyone walk its hallowed sidewalk. Let only those who hear the music and see their history walk these streets. I warn, caring for this hallowed street will get dangerous."*

Madison's hand connected to James' as if their flesh was made of magnets. They shook. *"We'll have the wine and just talk nonsense, knowhadamean,"* Madison quipped. *"But we'll make the deal now. I'll take it."*

"A fine sale, Mister Goodspeed!" James said. *"This street extends from Broadway to Bedford," he noted. "But there's more to this deal than our words and a handshake. There needs to be some construction, y'know. Some spiritual elbow grease has to make this all real, Mister Goodspeed."* James retracted from the handshake. He tapped Madison on the shoulder and then casually turned around and walked away. Over his shoulder he said, *"Look me up when you get to Brooklyn."* Then he corrected, *"Or, more appropriately, look up for me. It's not too hard."* He turned around and instructed Madison, *"Just drip some sage and cedar oil on some cinnamon chips. Crush some abre camino over it, and set a rose's thorny stem ablaze with camphor. There's usually more, but that's all it takes for me. You know the drill after that, though. Spit some liquor in the seven directions. I'll definitely come. I'll see you then, Mister Goodspeed. There's still more real estate to build on."*

James Weeks took four steps forward, and then his image faded.

Madison continued his journey down the street. But the New York scene gave way to a dusty, Southern intersection surrounded by wild, tall, golden grass. Madison stepped off the paved road and onto the dusty path, into the center of the crossroads. The sound of conversations and greetings dropped away. A simple breeze remained. Madison turned to address the issue. He was taken aback by the absence of the Brooklyn scenery. Only the long stretch of country road remained in front of him. In the distance, a young black man approached him.

"Well, now, who's this?" asked Madison as he inspected the young man approaching him. He wore a fedora atop his head, brown slacks and suspenders over a white, buttoned collar shirt. A trumpet, attached to a strap, was slung over his arm like a traveling sack. One hand was in his pocket and a smile was on his face. He couldn't have been older than seventeen, but there was something mature about him. Madison stood still as he approached. He stopped in front of Madison, smile wide and knowing. Madison leaned back, body braced. He asked, *"Are we acquainted?"*

The young man pulled his hand free from his pocket. He reached out an inviting hand and answered, *"The name's Pete Peters. That book for me?"*

Madison hesitated from asking what book in particular the young man was referring to, but he followed the man's eyes and looked down. He was surprised to find in his hands an old, leather book. Madison held the book out and asked the young man, *"This yours?"*

Pete Peters, as this man said his name was, didn't answer. He took the book from Madison's hands, appreciating the gift. He opened it and saw nothing but blank pages. Pete tossed off his trumpet and set it on its bell, down on the dusty road. He dug into his pocket again and removed a pen. He showed the pen off with a proud smile, and then sat cross-legged on the ground. He started writing.

Madison watched as the young gentleman composed musical notes onto the first page. Another breeze blew by. Madison looked up and down each of the intersecting four roads. He asked the man, *"Is this a crossroads?"* Pete Peters looked up, smile on his face. *"Heard about them, I have. Never came across one."*

Pete dived back into scripting his musical composition. *"Lot of legends about these places."* Pete made a face as he scripted. *"But, there is one that ain't true,"* he commented. He looked up and told Madison, *"Ain't no devil at the crossroads. No souls get sold here."*

Madison retorted, *"That's good to know, that is. Never believed in that one myself."*

"This crossroads belongs to an old, old, old family," Pete reported. *"Old family,"* he reiterated. *"Been guarding over this crossroads since the early eighteen-hundreds. Just got new management, though, two young brothers. Music teachers. Their father, he married the right woman. Her family, they're part of the Eledas people who're in charge of this intersection. Her sons guard it now. I know all this because we're dreaming."* Pete finished his composition. He laid the book flat and, much to the surprise of Madison, it stayed open. Pete stood up, taking his horn with him. He pressed the horn to his lips. Madison's face lit up with a smile on the first note. Pete rallied together a set of humble harmonies that requested permission to enter. Madison didn't only hear Pete play his horn, but he heard a voice form out of the music. He looked around and wondered who it could be talking to, and where was it asking permission to enter. That's when he noticed the ripple in reality.

Heat waves wriggled from the rightmost corner lot off the intersection. The same phenomenon appeared out of the blue on the lot directly across the street. Two quaint cottages with Moorish facades molded into existence. Pete's music ceased, and the ripple and heat waves dissipated.

Madison stared, eyes slanted in observance, mouth ajar in amazement. Then he sobered as he saw the trumpet player snatch up the book from the dusty road and toss it to him. Madison caught the book close to his chest, and Pete said to him, *"Keep it. I think they got one inside."* Pete threw his thumb over his shoulder. Madison's eyes moved toward the front door of the cottage facing him. It opened, but no one stepped out.

The front door on the identical house across the street opened just the same. Pete stepped up to him and asked, *"Can you be of help?"*

"As best I can, considering the circumstance."

Pete ignored Madison's sentiment and stated, *"Look, I don't know if you're dreaming or I'm dreaming. Perhaps we've stumbled into each other's dream. Dreams work just like life. But I need you to remember all this."* He patted Madison on the shoulder and smiled. *"I'll see you in Harlem, brother, years from now, I guess. Name's Pete Peters. Remember that. Tell me I gotta get to the crossroads."*

Pete turned around, smile still on his face. He walked up to the house at the rightmost corner of the intersection and stepped inside. The door closed, and both houses disappeared.

This is what Madison Goodspeed dreamed.

Sister Nani, in her dream, peeked in on both Joseph and Madison's dreams. In the morning, she presented her interpretation. "Joseph, your Theresa gonna be all right. By Iyansan, she will." To Madison she expressed, "Harlem callin' your name. *Exu Enu Barijo.* Messenger of our Tale."

It was vague just the same, but there were other issues at hand. There were ancient tomes to steal and a need to plan their thefts. Over the counsel between Madison, Joseph, and Sister Nani sneaked in the lilac fog. Time sped off behind the pale-purple haze, the months tick-tocking away as mere seconds. When the scrub of the lilac fog washed time away, Madison Goodspeed, Joseph Pepper, Latham Armstrong, and a heavyset white man named Merwin West stood at attention, being addressed by Sister Nani. Merwin, like Latham, was a copper. He was a little under six-feet tall, bald, with a thick mustache curled across his upper lip. Both he and Latham were assigned to guard The Line, an auction delivery system filled with items, trinkets and tomes from yesteryears and past millennia. Merwin, a self-proclaimed folklorist, was a lieutenant in the guard. He had been providing Sister Nani with information for months, and now the hushed location of the auction was known: The Bell-Sherwin Foundation.

The troupe occupied a typical book-clustered room within the Rose Hill orphanage. Books were stacked every-which-way along the walls. In the center was a table. Sister Nani sat facing the four standing men, table behind her. She palmed the handle of her cane with both hands, hunched over in contemplation, chin resting atop her hand. On the table behind her, partially unfolded, was a map of the interior layout of the Bell-Sherwin Foundation house in the city of London. There also rested, in much the same state, a map of the Avon Crest estate grounds and the schematics of the elaborate manor's interior. Next to the maps were four small teacups. Two cups were empty, recently drank by Latham and Merwin. The other two were filled, and as ordered by Sister Nani, for Madison and Joseph to renew their strength upon return.

On Merwin West's information, as far as the public was concerned, nothing but a private ceremony for wealthy businessmen was occurring at the Bell-Sherwin Foundation. Despite this, there would be coppers on guard, stationed around the estate grounds only to present the look of warding, but the security was to be very minimal. The Line never wanted to draw attention to itself or the items it auctioned, rare and priceless as they could be, by showcasing a plethora of paid guards and coppers.

Sister Nani dismissed Merwin and Latham to have a private word with Joseph Pepper and Madison Goodspeed. Merwin picked up the maps and rolled them up before leaving. Sister Nani stood up as the door closed. She pointed to the teacups. "I'm old. I can sacrifice myself. I've had good years," she said to the two gentlemen. "Dhis new brew, you can't keep drinkin' and drinkin'. You'll hurt yourself. Hurt your head. Your mind will have you see t'ings when you're not supposed to. But I've kept drinkin'. Not too much," she assured. "My eye sees clearer, though." She tapped the center of her forehead and said, "Dhis eye, you know, eh." She relaxed her weight on her cane. "But I can't do dhis alone. You will drink too. Dhis brew here isn't for your strength. I just said dhat for Merwin and Latham to hear. When deh two of you return wit' our prizes, we must immediately get to work. I've seen some t'ings." Sister Nani pointed to herself and then to Joseph and Madison. She said to them, "I know each part of our story. Deh role we play. I see it, and we have work to do." She tapped her cane twice against the ground. "Hurry on back, Joe Pepper and Madison."

Joseph and Madison bowed toward Sister Nani.

"On our return," said Joseph. He stood up straight and tapped his cane twice against the ground as well. Joseph, who was dressed in an Inverness coat covering a lavish suit, coolly pivoted toward the door. Madison, dressed in a jacket, gloves, cap, gray pants, and black shoes, followed Joseph out of the room.

Sister Nani sighed. Her face dropped into a sorrowful expression as she made her way to the table, her old bones balanced against her cane as she walked. She stared at the two cups of incanted tea for a long while, and then she knocked one over, its contents spilling across the table. "Good speed, Joe Pepper," she said. "Goodspeed."

And then again the lilac fog came, erasing the scenery and substituting it with Merwin West and Latham Armstrong standing at attention with a mighty squad of policemen summoned from various districts. Tucked inside an alley's shadows, Madison Goodspeed and Joseph Pepper kept a close eye on the police assembly. Madison commented in a hushed voice, "Quite a large party, considering the description. The sight of that army would make more noise than we've heard The Line is trying to make. A little whisper appears to be a loud conversation with that lot of coppers, I'll say."

"It appears so, Madison," Joseph Pepper replied.

"You considering a ruse, Pepper?" asked Madison as he shifted the empty satchel strapped around him.

"I do," Joseph answered. "But I also believe The Line's sleight of hand where they present a bank of information while committing at the last minute to something else entirely. None of what we've been told about this auction will hold true, I presume. The Bell-Sherwin Foundation will not host the auction. It might be at a place altogether different from the Bell-Sherwin Foundation headquarters and the Avon Crest estate." Joseph looked up. He grinned and commanded, "To the rooftops, Madison. This is where the adventure truly begins."

Still covered in shadow, the two men stole farther into the alley. They ascended a building's fire escape and climbed until on the roof. With the moon covered by gray clouds, and they cloaked in shadow, Madison and Joseph hopped rooftop to rooftop until they viewed from above the assemblage of London's police force. Joseph and Madison knelt down, eyes peering over the edge of the rooftop. Capped policemen listened attentively to their orders issued by district captains who were handing out assignment paths. The policemen were not marching to the auction's location all at once. They would first walk or ride their shifts, and then few-by-few they would be relieved of duty, but not for the night, but for guard at the auction's location. At the auction's site, the coppers would receive firearms to go along with their truncheons.

Joseph adjusted his glasses, looking for Merwin and Latham in the crowd. Madison pointed them out, and both men kept them in view. The crowd of policemen separated, each going about their assigned shifts and tasks. Joseph and Madison moved to the next building with a quick run and leap. Madison's shadowy incant, conjured earlier through a ritual, shaded them from sight. Their silhouettes, unnoticed in the night, blurred and waved as they hopped from rooftop to rooftop, landing soft as if against a cushion. Their feet were assisted by an incant Sister Nani blessed into their step to keep them quiet.

Madison took the lead, as he was able to keep a better eye on Merwin and Latham. The two coppers never separated. The lieutenant put a good word in for Latham, asking his captain to permit the hardboiled and well-trusted soldier into his unit to help protect The Line's auction. It was just the two coppers for the moment. They walked their shift, sifting through a small crowd on the London streets. Joseph and Madison rested behind a chimney. Madison checked his pistol, a Webley & Scott Mark VI revolver. All bullets were accounted for, loaded into their respective chambers.

Joseph situated the cane in his gloved hand against the chimney and checked his nine-cylinder LeMat revolver. Madison looked at the antique pistol. "You do love that old thing, don't you, Pepper," he whispered.

Joseph replied, "A friend's gift. It's old, but it works, my good man. Scares the hell out of people when it roars, but I mostly carry it as a good luck charm." He holstered the weapon and picked up his cane again. "You know it's always been Wanda here that keeps my enemies at bay in a tussle. How's the street look?"

Madison peeked from behind the chimney. Pedestrian traffic was thinning, and he saw no sign of Merwin or Latham. He turned to Joseph and said, "They must've turned up a street for their shift. Hope they don't get pulled away while we're here."

"The night would be lost," remarked Joseph.

Madison took another peek. "Ah, wait! There's our boy, Merwin." He reached into his pocket and pulled free a coin. "He's lookin' up and around, probably lookin' for us. He came out of an alley. Hold up. Stay here." He stepped from behind the chimney and walked close to the edge of the building, crouching low. He flipped the coin onto the street, and it bounced in front of Merwin. The copper noticed the coin's impact and tumble onto the street. He looked up and saw nothing.

"Pepper," Madison called. "Merwin can't see me behind the shadow. You think you can go to the street and meet him?"

"Too risky," said Joseph as he crawled up behind Madison. "But, let's shine some light on the situation. Back up, just a bit. Don't want to expose us with this." He and Madison crawled back several steps. Joseph then lifted his seven-sapphire-encrusted cane, closed his eyes, and concentrated while tightening his grip on the mystical walking stick. The handle glowed golden, its light humming in and out of existence with purpose to its rhythm.

Merwin didn't only notice the light; he read its vibrating glow, in and out. It was Morse code. *It is Joseph and Madison. We are up here. We will be waiting here,* it read. The glow ceased. Merwin nodded. He put his attention back on his shift and continued walking. Pedestrians that noticed the light made remarks that it was an odd place for a house to have a shining bulb. Joseph and Madison returned behind the chimney.

"The spirit that wants to settle is in conflict with the spirit that wants the adventure," Joseph remarked. "The duel continues, Madison."

Madison peeked behind the chimney every-once-in-a-while. All traffic appeared to cease. Only the glow of London's electric street lamps remained flickering about the road. Footsteps aroused Madison's interests. He leaned his head around the chimney and took a glance, but often it was a citizen on their way to some destination. When Merwin and Latham did appear, they were only walking their shift.

An hour passed. Madison checked the street, alerted by Merwin charging from an alley. Latham stood at attention just below the building Madison and Joseph were atop. "We've been relieved of tonight's shift, Latham," Madison heard Merwin inform. Joseph walked, crouched with Madison, to the building's edge. They looked down and noticed Merwin was not alone. Two other coppers surrounded him. "These gentlemen will handle our shifts. Let us retire." Merwin glanced up. Joseph sent a simple signal alerting Merwin that he and Madison were at the ready. The clip-clop of horse hooves signaled the arrival of a police carriage. "We've been given a ride, Latham. Tell me, does your sister still dream of a lavish wedding at a manor like the Avon Crest estates? Small, but elegant, I agree."

Joseph and Madison looked at one another and nodded. They turned their heads to witness Latham and Merwin head inside the police carriage. They could hear Merwin joking that being inside the carriage's cage reminded him of his fiery youth. Latham remarked with a laugh, *"Mine too, sir."* The pair stood up and continued their spirited flight across the rooftops, following the carriage hosting Merwin and Latham. When the carriage turned onto another road, Joseph and Madison hurried down a ladder, slipping into an alley. They rushed into the streets and were almost run over by several cars. They backed away, drivers cursing at them.

"What I wouldn't give for an autocarriage right now," Joseph exclaimed as he and Madison jumped out of the car's way. He kept an eye on the police carriage as it continued up the street. Madison grabbed Joseph by the arm and pulled him into another alley.

"This way, Pepper," he said in a determined whisper. "We know where they're heading. We can snatch us a couple of horses and be off. We have the shadows at our advantage and command. C'mon."

Joseph followed Madison as the black Englishman led him through a twist of alleys and backstreets. They emerged from one alley and stopped suddenly. Madison and Joseph's eyes went wide as they witnessed, from across the street, a driver park and jump from a hackney-horse-drawn cab and enter a pub. Joseph knocked the handle of his cane against Madison's chest and pointed toward the parked vehicle. He had a plan, and he smiled.

"The whites back home in the States call me a 'fancy nigger,' Madison!" Joseph exclaimed with a grin.

Madison retorted, "Don't sell yourself short, Pepper. I'm sure the whites here in England say the same, probably without use of the word *'fancy.'*"

Joseph didn't lose his grin. He asked Madison, "Care to be a fancy nigger's driver?"

Madison scoped the area. "I can drive that cab, no problem. Be the best driver you've ever had. But, we got too much light, and not enough shadow to grab the taxi. We'll be put under the jail, as they say. Knowhadamean?"

Joseph didn't answer. He gripped his cane's handle and concentrated, eyes opened. There was a faint buzz coming from where the end of his cane touched the street. Joseph eyed the closest of the surrounding street lamps. One-by-one, the continuous electric sparks that produced the flicker of lights inside the carbon arc street lamps surrendered to an unknown force. The lights dimmed and then were suffocated. Shadows fell over the streets. Pedestrians were startled by the phenomenon and observed the now quiet lights. Cars slowed and stopped.

Joseph tapped his cane twice and signaled for Madison to lead the way. The two men walked the shadows like a path, their physical frames invisible inside the umbra. Joseph unlatched the carriage and slipped inside, taking one last glance around at his surroundings. The groups of London citizens were huddled under the extinguished street lamps. Madison hopped onto the driver's bench. He slapped the reins of the horse and moved the cab forward. He wasn't worried about the mingling crowds observing any noise made. Both the sound of the reins and the clip-cop of the horses' hooves against the London streets were now muted by his control over the shadows. Madison turned down several streets, keeping his best to ride down areas with an abundance of shadow to stay hidden within the incant he'd conjured in ritual.

"Sit back, you fancy nigger," Madison hollered over his shoulder. "I'll take it from here. Next stop: the Avon Crest estates."

Joseph relaxed for the moment. He said a prayer to his beloved jazz songbird, Theresa Amat. He hoped the prayer carried fast over the wide water separating him from Theresa. And when it reached her in Water Bug Hollow, Louisiana, he wished for the prayer to activate the magic anointing the veil he'd gifted her. "Be wary, my lady," Joseph said as if Theresa occupied the carriage with him. "There are devious forces about." But as the carriage bounced and bumbled over the London streets, Joseph, with his hands out in either direction to brace against the wobbly ride, concentrated his thoughts on the present situation. "In the name of…"

"Relax, Pepper," Madison shouted back to him. "It's bumpy, but we're on track."

Madison maneuvered the ride forward, keeping both the horses and the carriage as steady as possible. He knew at one point he'd have to slow the beasts carrying them, and he and Joseph would have to make their way up to the grounds of the Avon Crest estates on foot.

The tremulous ride became smoother outside London's city limits. Madison steered onto a path winding in the direction of Avon Crest manor. It was dark now, save for the swinging lamps attached to either side of the carriage. Madison tugged the reins to slow the mighty steeds. He was being cautious, considering the possibility that other riders heading in the direction of the auction's location might appear, autocarriage or horse-drawn. Madison wasn't too worried about being discovered. Under shadow and incant, he and the rest of the carriage could not be seen. However, a collision with an unaware traveler traversing the same route was a probable scenario.

But the road was steady and without interference. Madison and Joseph abandoned the carriage off the path, and then made their way through the wooded area on foot. Soon the two of them came to the edge of the forested path they traveled. The trees dropped away to reveal the wide-open, quaint grounds of the Avon Crest manor. There, at the center of the four-acre area, was the grand Tudor-style boutique manor house. Coppers as sentries canvassed the area. Lights flickered and sprawled out across the lawn, limiting the stretch of shadow Madison and Joseph could use as cover.

"My goodness, Madison," whispered Joseph as the two of them lay stomach to ground at the wooded area's edge. "Residing in that manor is the world's richest, most powerful, and deadliest of influential people. There lays the unseen hands that move world events like chess pieces on the board."

Madison was more interested in the shining light posts stationed around the estate. "Think Wanda there could blow out these lights like candles?" asked Madison.

"Indeed, Madison," Joseph replied. He propped the end of his cane against the ground and tapped its end. Then Joseph concentrated. Two lights vanished, and the shadows grew. Joseph and Madison jumped to their feet. They heard a copper curse and shout orders to get the lamps working. The two of them slipped into a shadow and were unseen to even the coppers that walked alongside them. They were still careful as to not bump any guard, which would cause their physical frames to unwrap from the incant's shadowy fold for a brief moment. They found it easier to maneuver through the grounds keeping close to the sides of the manor. Joseph and Madison kept an eye out for Merwin and Latham. "You believe they could be stationed inside?" asked Madison.

"It's altogether possible," Joseph answered. "We need to find an alternative to the front entrance. There's a lack of shadows in that brightly lit hall. Then we have the grand luxury of finding where The Line is keeping the tomes we seek. Hopefully they haven't been auctioned off yet." Joseph and Madison both peeked around the corner. The coppers restored the two lights, but Joseph and Madison were out of view, tucked around the side of the manor.

Madison peered hard, looking for Merwin and Latham. None of the coppers looked familiar. He suggested, "Let's continue around. We might bump into our friends or find a way in."

The pair moved further along the manor's perimeter. Latham Armstrong and several other policemen were covering the area. Madison and Joseph swerved into a maze of low hedges, keeping low and in the shadow. Only a few lights shined, and the shadows were wide and in abundance. Madison said to Joseph, "Stay here. I'll reveal myself to Latham. Hopefully his friends won't notice, or he won't be too startled."

Joseph stayed low and behind a wall of short hedges. Madison moved away, taking the safety of his conjure with him. The shadows followed him. He neared Latham, walking up alongside of him and the other policemen without notice. He tapped Latham on the arm, and his image appeared in the moment he made physical contact with the copper. Latham was startled, but not enough to alert his fellow policemen. The other coppers in the troupe hadn't noticed Madison's sudden appearance and disappearance, but Latham signaled them that he was going off to check another section.

"We'll meet back here in a moment's time," he said to the group. They nodded their heads in return and continued on their walk. Latham hurried away. His fellow coppers had their back to him, and Madison grabbed his arm and came out of the shadows, or rather Latham was dragged into his invisibility. "So, you're here, you and Pepper."

Madison pointed to the hedges and said, "Pepper's over there. Know a good way in?"

"Kitchen entrance," Latham answered putting an eye on the patrol he'd left. Their backs were still to him.

"Don't worry about them," Madison said. "You're gone from view as long as I got your arm."

Latham looked at Madison. "Fine then. As I was saying, there's the kitchen's staff," he continued. "Negroes aren't permitted on the grounds. A disguise won't do. But, if you're lucky enough to get around them, you'll have to find your way to the top floor. Eight guards are outside the room where the auctioned items are held. One item is auctioned off at a time. There are twenty-one items. Your items are numbers fifteen and eighteen. They're on item nine, last time I heard. That wasn't too long ago. They're probably on eleven by now, maybe even still bidding on nine."

"I'll tell Pepper," Madison informed. "Don't worry about us. We'll be covered right."

Madison went to let go of Latham's arm, but the copper grabbed his hand.

"Wait, Mister Goodspeed," he said. His face became sincere. "Sister Nani has some things planned, in case this all goes wrong. She has in order a plan to keep the children at the orphanage safe, and I will slip away to assist her with that. Don't you worry. Merwin is inside to help. And I want you to know, this outfit is only a disguise now. I'm amongst your order. Anything happens, and I'll draw on these coppers, I will. Don't need a sip of incanted brew to walk with you all. I drink the tea simply because it tastes good." Latham smiled, and Madison smiled back.

"Very well, old friend," he said patting Latham's shoulder. "Watch for our signal, loud or otherwise."

"I'll keep my eyes and wits about me," Latham assured. Then he warned, "Be careful. Brice and Ethan are amongst the guests."

Madison thanked Latham for the information. He let go, dissolved into shadow, and returned to Joseph. He relayed everything Latham told him, and the two journeyed through the shadows to the rear entrance leading into a small pantry and hallway attached to the kitchen. Joseph tapped his cane, concentrated, and extinguished the lights in the large cooking area. The staff groaned and cursed the phenomenon while Joseph and Madison took advantage of the dark and sneaked through the shadows in the room.

In every room the pair journeyed into, Joseph tapped his cane. He extinguished or made the lights flicker long enough to allow the duo to maneuver through the shadows woven in the absence of the light. Twice a guard or two spotted them. And twice Joseph and Madison engaged, knocking the policemen unconscious and tossing their bodies into empty rooms. Up one, two, three, and then four levels of the grand manor, Joseph and Madison sneaked. They hid against wall and shadow. Joseph's mystical cane proved useful, draining the manor's lights. No one was the wiser to the magic. *"Even the wealthiest can't throw money at the spontaneous and inconvenient hiccups in the latest technology,"* opined a copper on guard.

Pressed up against a shadowed corner at the top of the final set of stairs, Joseph and Madison waited. The small shadow cast over them was just large enough to keep both men covered. They peered down the hall. There was the door leading to their prize. Eight guards swarmed around it.

"I suggest this plot, Madison," Joseph said, whispering on instinct. "When the next object is up for auction, and it's retrieved, that is when we strike. The door will be opened. I will siphon the power from the lights, and in the confusion, we will make our way through the shadows and inside the room."

"It's a plan, Pepper," Madison agreed.

The pair remained pressed against the wall and without movement, save their eyes as a well-dressed gentleman with white gloves ascended the stairs, passed them without notice, and moved into the swarm of coppers on guard. The police parted, and the well-dressed man removed a key from his pockets. He unlocked the door to the room holding the items waiting to be auctioned. Joseph tapped his cane twice as the man turned the knob on the door. Joseph concentrated, eyes on the man as he pressed the door open. The lights flickered and a policeman cursed, "Damn! Not again!"

The lights' glimmer continued to dance in and out for a few more moments, and then the top floor hallway lights cut. The guards scrambled. Joseph and Madison raced to the door, concealed in shadow. The well-dressed gentleman coolly entered the artifact room. Joseph and Madison swerved through the policemen and slipped inside, Madison grappling the well-dressed gentleman, covering his mouth. Joseph shut the door and tapped his cane to restore the manor's top-level electrical flow. The room's lights turned on. Four seated coppers stood up and drew weapons. Joseph planted his cane against the ground and focused for only a moment. Electrical tendrils jumped up from the floor and whipped the coppers unconscious. Their bodies crumpled on the floor. Joseph lifted the end of his cane and pressed it against the well-dressed gentleman's neck.

From outside, a guarding policeman yelled, "Everything okay in there?"

There was silence for a moment. The well-dressed gentleman aimed a wide, nervous gaze at Joseph. Madison, hand still clasped over the man's mouth, answered in place of him. "We're fine," he said quickly.

"Speak tonight's safe and clear signal," the copper yelled from the other side of the door.

Madison answered with a phrase Merwin supplied him and Joseph, "The king dines with his knights."

"Good. Now, carrier," a copper called from the other side, "Speak *your* signal."

The carrier's eyes went to both Joseph and Madison. He nodded his head quickly, Madison's hand gripped tight against his mouth. But Madison didn't let go. Instead, Joseph spoke in his proper, erudite tone, "I still carry down to greater society, good gentlemen."

"Well, then," said the copper, "hurry. Let's keep these items moving. Come on."

Madison kept the item carrier in a tight grip. Joseph looked behind him and saw a long table holding the auctioned items. There were only two tomes among the remaining items. Both aged books were cased inside glass. A piece of paper labeled 'Item 15' was placed in front of the glass case holding the *Nigrum Nigrius Nigro*. *Seshat's Songbook* was labeled 'Item 18.' Both cases were locked. Joseph turned to the item carrier and demanded in a whisper, "The key."

The man, eyes still wide, shook his head in protest.

"It would not be in your best interest to hold it on you," Madison warned in a hushed voice. "Give it up!"

The man continued to shake his head. He put his hands in his pockets and turned his pockets out. He dug into his jacket pockets, turned them inside and out, pulling no key from them. Then he put his hands together as if in prayer and moaned a plea. He shook his hands, and Joseph understood he was begging. Joseph backed away and again pressed the end of his cane against the item carrier's neck. "Let him go, Madison. I believe he has something to tell us."

Madison opened his grip on the item carrier's mouth, but kept the man grappled close to him. The item carrier whispered, "I do not have the key. I have been assigned to retrieve and carry items eight to twelve. The carrier after me has the key to item fifteen, but that will be his last item. The carrier after him will have the key to item eighteen. The bidding does not go in order."

"Damnit!" Joseph cursed.

But Madison suggested, "Give us cover in shadow, Pepper. We can break the cases and the sound will be muted. Turn off all the manor's lights and we can move even if there's chaos. As long as we have the items, the hysteria won't matter."

Before Joseph could agree or modify Madison's idea, the item carrier screamed, *"There are two niggers in here! Help! Two niggers are robbing us!"* A pinch of electricity crawled into the gentleman's neck, traveled up to his brain and struck him unconscious. He dropped to the floor, sprawled out. Joseph aimed the handle of his cane to the glass case holding the *Nigrum Nigrius Nigro*. A noise like thunder rattled from the cane's handle. Joseph's arm bucked as an invisible force leapt from the cane and crashed against the glass casing, shattering it. He turned to the glass case holding *Seshat's Songbook*, aimed the handle of his cane, and the same phenomenon occurred. Madison jumped to the table, and with gloved hands, slipped each book into his satchel.

A policeman kicked the door open, his fellow coppers behind him, guns raised at Joseph and Madison. "Go ahead, boys! Have an itchy finger," yelled the first policeman through the door. "If these sneaky niggers try a trick or two, they'll have our bullets to deal with."

Joseph stayed his hand and any idea of making a movement to use the power in his cane.

"Hold on," a familiar voice ordered from the hall. "Hold fire! We don't want to alert the good party downstairs that there are things about," the voice came again. The copper pushed through the mass of policeman clogging the doorway. It was Merwin West. He held a paper with a printed sketch of Madison and Joseph. "We were warned about these two," he said. "An American black and a Jamaican black. Here!" He slapped the paper into the chest of one of the coppers on guard.

The copper examined the wanted poster. "I've heard no such thing."

"There's many things on this night that we're all not privy to," Merwin responded in a stern tone. "Now, there are two gentlemen guests downstairs familiar with these two outlaws. I will retrieve the pair. Confiscate their weapons in the meantime."

"No need," said Joseph, carefully drawing his LeMat revolver and bending down to the floor, keeping his eyes on the police the entire time. He opened his hand and let his firearm go. Joseph raised his body and hands and kicked the weapon over to the police. Then he ordered, "Madison, the same."

Madison removed his firearm, bent down, and dropped it. He did the same with his satchel strapped around his shoulder. He stood and kicked his revolver over to the police. One copper retrieved both weapons. Madison and Joseph kept their hands high.

A policeman cocked his firearm and asked, "How did you two slip in here and knock everybody out?"

Joseph lied through a grin, "There are some among your numbers, copper, that would accept a good bribe."

Before the policeman could process the information, there came voices from the hall. "They've surrendered their weapons, kind sirs," reported a voice.

"All of them?" a voice asked, Joseph recognizing it as belonging to Ethan Cassidy. Then Merwin entered the room with Ethan Cassidy, Brice Cadogan, and Thomas Burton of Burton, Bradley and Pierce in tow. The horde of policemen parted to make way for the gentlemen following Merwin.

Ethan Cassidy was dressed in a gray suit, and he wore glasses. A grin popped on his face for a moment as he spotted Joseph Pepper with his hands high. Next to Ethan was Brice Cadogan, a man in his early forties, of athletic build, and well-groomed, raven-colored hair atop his head and across his lip. Thomas Burton, also near Ethan, was a middle-aged man of average height with thin, receding gray hair and a pudgy, square head and face. Ethan's moment of grinning at Joseph was brief as he noticed the cane in Joseph's hand.

"This man is still armed," Ethan warned, keeping his eye on Joseph's cane. "Be careful, all of you." Ethan put his arms out wide in an attempt to hinder the coppers behind him from making a charge. Then Ethan's grin appeared again. "Joseph, Joseph, Joseph. Brice and I were going to make bids to hold, for the allotted time allowed by The Line, the items you're trying to rob. You could've taken them from us after this auction."

"The adventure wouldn't be the same, Ethan," Joseph retorted. "You know that. A sneak into a highly guarded, secret location? We're striking while the iron is hot. Who knows in which secret location you'd store the items."

"Coppers, lower your weapons," commanded Ethan. "I will strike first. This man is dangerous. As I've said, he's still armed."

Joseph ordered, "Madison, your satchel."

Madison bent down to retrieve his leather bag. A cop fired his weapon at Madison, but the bullet deflected back and tore through the hand holding that copper's gun. The policeman dropped his gun and clutched his bleeding appendage.

"I said lower your weapons!" Ethan hissed.

Madison retrieved his satchel from the floor, strapped it across his body, and stood. Now visible was a faint, electrical dome surrounding him and Joseph who held his cane like a torch. His will conjured through his cane the soft, electric dome that surrounded Madison and himself.

"Back away," warned Joseph as he took a step forward. "Unless any of you would like to be in a week-long coma, I suggest you back away and let us go. You're dealing with forces you know nothing of."

Brice ordered, "Everyone into the hall. Now!"

The coppers, Ethan, and Brice backed away into the hall as Joseph and Madison inched closer to the door. "Our weapons, please," Joseph ordered in a polite but threatening tone. "We wish you no harm, but our weapons if you please."

The copper who had earlier picked up Joseph and Madison's firearms laid the requested weapons on the ground. Madison scooped both revolvers up from the floor just as Ethan commented, "You won't get too far, Joseph. I know where you'll run, from here to the States. I know all your haunts, and for each one, I will haunt you there. I will find the prizes I desire at the cost of the people you care for. I have governments at my side. Even with all your tricks—you, Sister Nani, and Madison there—my ambition outweighs all that."

Joseph didn't listen. He continued stepping forward, out into the hall, and toward the stairs. His conjured shield domed around him, Madison at his side. The police guards, Ethan, Brice, and Thomas Burton kept their eyes on the pair of black men sneaking closer to the stairs. Ethan dared to inch toward Joseph and Madison. "I know where you're going," he again expressed to Joseph.

"Then I'll see you there," Joseph winked back. He and Madison made it to the stairs. They traveled backward, keeping an eye on the coppers, the auction's host, and Ethan and Brice. Madison took a peek over the railing. More coppers were ascending the winding staircase. "No need to worry about them, Madison. A good sleep is all they'll receive if they come near us."

Ethan stopped his approach toward Joseph and Madison. He turned, grabbed the banister, and looked over the side. He watched the ascending policemen advance, slow and cautious on Joseph and Madison. Drawing nearer to the pair, the police backed away once they noticed the faint, mystical dome writhing with electrical strands surrounding them. Ethan turned around and pointed at several coppers, including Merwin West and said, "You, you, you, you, and you. With me. We will follow these two. Mister Cadogan, this is my affair. I will return your tomes. Mister Burton, our bid is the safe return of the books. Convince the gentlemen of The Line that Mister Cadogan shall have full possession of these books. They will not be out on loan." Everyone nodded at Ethan's proposal. Then, with coppers in tow, Ethan hurried down the stairs after Joseph and Madison.

Joseph, cane held high like a torch, descended with Madison into the manor's main hall. The squad of policemen in front of them continued backing away. Madison spied the front entrance, and with Joseph, moved toward the door. The doorknob passed through the mystical dome and Madison turned the knob and opened the door. He and Joseph scurried into the night, the two of them fading into the shadows. Behind them, inside the manor, the incident was not reported to the bidding guests. The unconscious item carrier and coppers came to, and the auction continued with news that items fifteen and eighteen, the *Nigrum Nigrius Nigro* and *Seshat's Songbook*, were forgeries. This was noted by the expertise of Brice Cadogan and Ethan Cassidy.

Outside, on the Avon Crest Estate grounds, Joseph and Madison dashed into the woods, returning to their stolen, hackney horse-drawn cab. Madison again took the reins and Joseph slid into the carriage. "To The Library, Madison!" Joseph ordered. "There's no doubt that Ethan is on his way there."

Madison slapped the reins against the horses and pulled forward, racing through the woods and back into London. When they arrived at The Rose Hill orphanage, Jeremiah was outside, patiently waiting for Madison and Joseph's arrival. The shade blanketing the carriage lifted, and Madison rolled up to the front entrance. Joseph jumped from the carriage and said, "This place will be crawling with villains soon enough, Jeremiah. We must alert Sister Nani!"

Jeremiah answered, "Sister Nani is gathering the last of the children and taking them to the docks, Mister Pepper. There's a boat waiting there. We're leaving for Jamaica." Jeremiah looked up at Madison and informed, "Your father is there with an old friend. A Chinaman, the man you call Uncle Bohai."

Sister Nani stepped out of the house, amazement splashed on her face. She approached Joseph, arms out, and looking as if she was going to cry. "Oh, Joe Pepper, you've returned. You've come back." Joseph bent down and allowed Sister Nani to plant multiple, enthusiastic kisses on his face. Sister Nani then said to Madison, "Oh, Madison, my boy, I knew you would be here," she looked at Joseph with a wide smile, "but you, Joe Pepper have defied the fates, you have."

"We're in great danger, Sister Nani," Joseph reported in a stern voice. "Ethan pursues us. We have the books."

Sister Nani confirmed with a nod of her head. "I know, Joe Pepper. I know. Right now, we're getting the remaining children to the docks."

"Madison," Joseph called, facing his partner-in-adventure. "How much longer do you believe your blessing will last?"

Madison answered, "It's weak, but I'll manage. Exhausted a little, I am. I got sleep cookin' in my eyes, knowhadamean."

"Hold strength, good man," Joseph said with pep. "Protect Sister Nani and the children. I'll hold Ethan here. I'll catch up."

"He'll have coppers with him," Madison said as a protest.

"Won't take much for Wanda to put them down," Joseph countered. "And Merwin should be with his troupe. I'll have an ally. Just keep Sister Nani and the children covered in shadow."

Sister Nani commanded Madison, "Take your carriage into the alley. It's sturdier than the one we've been using. It'll be a tighter fit. There're six children and three adults."

Madison nodded and guided the carriage through the alley adjacent to the orphanage. Joseph said to Sister Nani, "Stay here until Ethan arrives with the police. He needs to see us go into the orphanage. You'll escape out the back, Madison will cover you in shadow, and you'll be off. I'll hold off the coppers and stop Ethan here. If I don't, he'll keep pursuing us no matter where we escape to."

Sister Nani leaned to the right and saw two police carriages and two police automobiles making their way up the street. "Wait won't be long, Joe Pepper. Here they come."

Joseph heard the putter of the autocarriages. He turned around and tapped his cane against the street. The autocarriages sparked, and their engines burst into flames. The coppers jumped from the vehicles, tumbling against the street. Getting to their feet, the coppers ran up the street, guns drawn and shouting for surrender.

"I recognize Merwin's voice," Joseph said to Sister Nani. "Inside. Now."

The horse-drawn police carriages, and the policeman now regulated to sprinting, neared the orphanage. Merwin, on foot, took lead. He ended his run and screamed, "Joseph Pepper! Madison Goodspeed! You are ordered by the authority of the London police to surrender your persons and the items you have, on this night, stolen."

Ethan Cassidy opened the carriage door and hopped out of the horse-drawn vehicle. He fixed his suit and yelled, "And on charges of conspiracy, Sister Nani, Head of this Negro orphanage shall too surrender her person."

Merwin pivoted and faced Ethan. "Mister Cassidy, I won't tell you again, no arrests will be made tonight on this elderly woman."

"Unless there's a lucky turn of the spade, right Officer," Ethan grinned. He removed his silver cigarette case and then a cigarette from it. He tucked the case into the inside pocket of his jacket with one hand, and put the cigarette between his lips with the other. An electric spark whipped against the end of the cigarette, lighting it. Ethan took a drag. He smiled, removed the cigarette from his lips and yelled, "Thank you, Pepper! That's a fine play, old friend." Ethan said to Merwin, "Be careful. He'll put your men to sleep and on their asses." He moved away, smoking and carrying on with a charming, Southern grin. He said as he looked up at the orphanage, "You know, Pepper, you are hurting the children—" Ethan saw something in the alley. He adjusted his glasses, the lenses of which were endowed with a trick. He peered into the darkness. Though Madison's escape was cloaked in shadow and shaded from sight, Ethan's heightened vision spotted the carriage with the orphanage residents inside.

"They're making an escape!" Ethan yelled. "Get that son-of-a-bitch!" He tossed his cigarette away.

Joseph emerged through the orphanage's front doors. "You can let them go, Ethan. It's me and the books you want."

Ethan took only three strides forward. But they were long strides, and they were quick. Joseph slipped back inside the orphanage. He moved aside as Ethan's body crashed through the door with the power of his otherworldly might. Joseph ducked the splinters and large stakes of wood whirling about from the crippled doorway. He looked up and saw Ethan. The Southern soldier was quick, his movements almost unseen, appearing as a blur. He leapt at Joseph, tackling the black scholar to the ground. The impact loosened Joseph's grip on his cane, but he held the item firm enough not to lose it.

In the same motion of his attack, and too fast for the naked eye to catch, Ethan was on his feet with Joseph's collar in his grip and Joseph lifted high off the ground. It was to the scholar's advantage, however. Upright, Joseph stabbed Ethan with the end of his cane. The force of the hit, coupled with the electric charge emitted, caused Ethan to let Joseph go. Ethan backed away and braced himself. Joseph flipped his cane, gripping the handle with both hands as if it was a broadsword's hilt. Joseph swung his cane like a sword. Ethan, though off balance, managed to block Joseph's relentless attacks by using his forearms as guards. The trick coursing through Ethan gave him the ability to withstand the blows from the cane and the electric charges that spat at him on contact. When Ethan saw his opening, he kicked Joseph in the stomach, knocking him back. Joseph maneuvered the hold on his cane to catch himself.

Three policemen entered, guns raised and ready to fire on the American scholar, but from above came gunfire! The three policemen scattered, giving a quick peek to see who was raining bullets on them. They ducked away, into rooms and behind furniture, but none were able to see their former copper-in-arms, Latham Armstrong, holding the pistol used against them.

The display distracted Ethan for a brief moment, but Joseph remained focused. A pulse of electricity rippled through the floor and lashed the coppers in hiding, knocking them unconscious. The same electric attack wrestled with Ethan who gyrated with the intense shock.

"Latham, stand your ground!" Joseph hollered. "There are more coming!"

Ethan, strength sapping, swung a fist at Joseph, connecting in the abdomen. The strike shattered three of Joseph's ribs and cracked two. The ex-Confederate still had power, and Joseph felt it, bracing against the pain with gritted teeth. He swallowed the pain, pounded the end of his cane against the floor, and a sound like thunder echoed through the orphanage. Ethan's body, lashed with charge, lifted high into the air and then dropped against the ground. Joseph again slapped the end of his cane with force. Another electrical wave writhed through the floor, all of it jumping on

Ethan's body. Joseph balanced his weight on his cane and stood. He opened his arms, letting the cane go. The item twirled in the air of its own accord, became perpendicular, and then slammed end first into the floor.

Another electrical wave surged into Ethan's sprawled body, jerking him every which way in agony. Joseph snatched his cane, tapped against the floor, and turned around just as the entire orphanage went dark. Ethan, suit seared and brimming with smoke, rose to his knees. He caught his breath and adjusted his glasses. Joseph gripped the end of his cane with both hands and slammed the handle into Ethan's jaw. Ethan fell on his back, weak but conscious. His feet scrapped against the ground as his body rocked back and forth. Latham traveled down the stairs, moved in with his gun cocked, and fired three shots into Ethan's chest. Ethan bucked. The bullets barely broke his skin, but they hurt him.

"C'mon, Mister Pepper," said Latham. "To the carriage left behind. We can still make the docks."

"Yes," Joseph acknowledged. "Yes, indeed, Latham. Let's go."

The two men traveled through the orphanage and exited out a side door leading to the alley. A horse-drawn carriage was there waiting. Latham jumped up to steer as Joseph slipped into the passenger's compartment. Joseph now found himself using his cane for assistance. He held the side of his abdomen, nursing battered ribs.

In the orphanage, Ethan coughed and stirred. He planted a hand on the ground and stood up straight, taking a great deal of strength to do so. Merwin and several coppers rushed inside. "Need assistance, Mister Cassidy?"

"I thought I told you to follow that carriage, goddamnit!" Ethan growled.

"I apologize, sir. What you saw was gone before we had a chance to pursue," Merwin explained. "We await your next order, sir."

"Take me to the docks," Ethan said, panting his command. "And we arrest that Negro hag when we get there! Agreed?"

"Yessir," Merwin acknowledged.

Lilac haze wiped the scene away as Ethan and the police exited the orphanage that was now abandoned of life and all its books. When the fog lifted, there were the docks. Over the horizon, the faint glimmer of a new day touched the sky. Sister Nani and other orphanage workhands finished boarding. Madison waited at the docks, his father, Grant Goodspeed standing next to him as they both gazed with anxiety through the London night.

"If it's at all possible, dad, he'll be here," said the younger Goodspeed.

Grant put an eye on his son. "Just relax."

Madison nodded with an anxious tremor in his quickened head movement. He turned around and eyed the cargo ship behind him. He said to his father, as he looked forward, "Sister Nani has to keep us inside time to wait for Pepper, dad. If he comes, and Ethan is behind him in pursuit—"

Grant interrupted his son and assured, "Then I'll meet this Ethan Cassidy fellow strength to strength, my son. Strength to strength." He pushed his chest out, hands in his pockets and wore determination across his countenance.

The thunderous sound of horse hooves pounded in the distance. The rickety carriage steered by Latham Armstrong and carrying Joseph Pepper rounded the corner. Latham tugged back hard on the reins, and the horses slowed their speed and planted their hooves. The carriage barely held together as it came to a shaky halt. Latham recovered from the bumpy brake in movement, jumped off the driver's bench, and reloaded his firearms. Joseph opened the carriage, planted his cane against the ground, and stepped out, almost falling to the ground.

Madison and his father rushed to Joseph's side.

Latham finished loading his sidearm and raised it in the direction from which they had come. "You okay, Mister Pepper?" he asked.

"Ribs bruised and broken, good man," Joseph winced.

A pop like a champagne bottle rang out in the air!

Latham's knees gave way, and he dropped to the street with a bullet in his shoulder.

"Hold your fire, I said!" a voice yelled, recognized as Merwin.

Joseph held his cane up like a torch. Madison and Grant helped Joseph stay on his feet, his body curled and knees bent in pain from his broken ribs. Joseph concentrated and produced a faint, mystical dome shielding him, Madison, and Grant Goodspeed. Joseph asked Latham, "Are you okay?"

"Hit," the copper groaned. "Bullet didn't go all the way in, but I'm hurt."

"You're outside my protection," Joseph told Latham. "If I drop this aegis your former coppers will take their chance and kill us all," Joseph continued. "They're listening to Merwin less and less. He's doing what he can, but the police are at Ethan's command." Then Joseph proposed, "Get up. I'll stay behind you. They won't be able to get you. Get up and run to the boat." He turned to Madison and inquired, "Your shadow?"

"Gone," Madison answered.

The well-concealed policemen fired more shots. The bullets ricocheted off Joseph's conjured aegis, but noise made the occupants under the dome flinch. Joseph stumbled, but kept going the dome shielding him, Madison, and Grant. Latham struggled, but managed to get up. He stayed low, and with Joseph behind him, moved forward, toward the ramp leading to the cargo boat. Gunfire continued popping through the air, penetrating the darkness like the sun's light on the horizon. The bullets deflected off the mystical dome like insects too close to light.

Joseph stumbled again. The dome faded for a brief moment, but the adventuring scholar regained concentration. He stopped moving forward. Madison and Grant stopped with him. Latham turned around and screamed, "Pepper, are you all right?"

"I'm fine," he answered groaning. He slipped again, but caught himself. He took a breath. "Damnit all! One hit and he had me," Joseph cursed. "The ambition I possess." He inhaled again, and then he said, "Madison, do you have our guns on you still?"

"Locked and loaded," Madison informed.

Joseph ordered, wincing, "Give your father the LeMat. I'm going to drop this electric buckler, and your fire, along with your father and Latham, will keep me in cover. Understood?"

Madison handed his father the heavy nine-round revolver. He said to Joseph, "Understood."

"Good. I will catch my breath first, and on my count, we will run. Understood?" Joseph asked again.

"Understood," both Madison and his fathered replied.

Joseph inhaled, but not too deep, as taking a breath caused him pain. He expressed there would be a three count, and then he counted off. On one, Madison, Grant, and Latham turned in the direction of the gunfire aimed at them. On two, they cocked their pistols. Then came three. Joseph's mystical shield dropped away and the three, armed men pulled their triggers over and over while running backward up the ramp.

The concealed coppers didn't return fire, not wanting to give away their positions until the bullets ceased buzzing in their direction.

Joseph moved quickly, using his cane to limp up onto the cargo ship. It was then that the policemen's true motive for ceasing to pursue or fire was exposed. Ethan Cassidy, with a crash, landed in front of Joseph in a fighting stance. Joseph attacked him with newfound vigor, but Ethan again blocked with his forearms, absorbing the strikes of the cane and its electrical surge.

The other's turned around, their weapons aimed.

Joseph, handle of his cane gripped like a broadsword, tossed a mighty swing at Ethan. The soldier caught the cane with both hands, a current of lightning coursing through him. Sparks jumped from the cane and whipped Ethan on his chest, scratched his fingers, and slapped his cheeks. But he kept a tight grip with all the power he could muster.

"Here, Ethan, is the solution to our very own, personal final problem," Joseph shouted to his nemesis. He positioned his grip between Ethan's grips and then, with valiant, rallied strength, he forced both himself and Ethan over the edge of the ramp leading up to the cargo ship. Their bodies plunged into the dark water. Neither man loosened their grip on impact. Under water, Joseph focused one last conjure through his cane. He exhaled a gargled, bubbling scream, and then delivered a ferocious, electrical force that cut Ethan unconscious.

Ethan Cassidy's insentient body exhaled one last breath, and then it inhaled as much water as its lungs could hold until he drowned. Ethan's body sank deeper. Joseph Pepper IV's final, focused blow with his cane had done what no war or other violent situation could accomplish.

Ethan Cassidy was dead.

For Joseph Pepper IV, his focused blow snatched from him the remnants of his own vitality, and he too passed out under the water, sentenced to drown.

On the ramp, Madison, his father, and Latham looked on in horror. A wave rippled the water, accompanied by a low sound. Merwin West and the other coppers ran to the docks and looked down in the water.

Nothing stirred.

Grant Goodspeed and Latham Armstrong dragged a reluctant Madison up onto the cargo ship as he screamed down to the waters for his good partner-in-adventure, Joseph Pepper IV, to rise. Grant whispered an incant into his son's ear, and Madison went unconscious. Grant and Latham cradled Madison's body and jumped aboard the cargo ship as it moved away from the docks.

"Should we pursue?" a policeman asked.

Merwin holstered his unfired pistol. "Why? They've only stolen forgeries," Merwin lied.

"Forgeries?" another copper questioned. "Then what was this all for? This chase?"

"To kill Joseph Pepper the Fourth," Merwin lied again. "I will let Mister Cadogan know. Joseph Pepper the Fourth is dead." Merwin gave one last eye to the departing cargo boat, saying a prayer for his escaping friends, and then he stepped away from the water.

Like Latham, he too did not require a sip of incanted tea to make him assist Sister Nani in retrieving the items belonging to her culture. He too drank the tea simply because it tasted good.

The sun lifted behind him.

Lilac fog covered the scene.

"*I had me some of that new brew,*" an old woman's voice said through the shimmering, lilac haze. "*I can see bettah now. More clear. And I'm not talkin' 'bout wit' my two eyes, understand, Madison, boy.*"

"*Yes, Sister Nani,*" Madison's sulky voice replied. It seemed his mind was somewhere else, focused on a departed friend.

"*You will see clearer too when you take a sip,*" Sister Nani continued. "*I didn't t'ink Joe Pepper was coming back. I was prepared for it. I got my hopes up dhat he'd defied fate when he returned wit' you. I thought he would be takin' this boat to Jamaica wit' us. But he played out his story as the fates decided. You let his sweetheart's story play out too. Don't go lookin' for her and tellin' her Joe Pepper's fate. You hear?*"

"*Yes, Sister Nani,*" Madison repeated.

"*Good,*" said Sister Nani. Then she warned, "*Don't drink too much of dhis brew. It'll make your mind see too much. You'll see t'ings at deh wrong time. Your mind might not be able to handle it.*"

"*Yes, Sister Nani,*" Madison said again, his voice still sullen.

"*We're not organized like dhem white societies dhat got dhem secrets,*" Sister Nani commented. "*Our secrets,*" she emphasized. "*But our people are like deh cosmos. We expand and contract. We look all confused. We look misplaced, an' it's going to get worse for us. But dhere's a picture dhere dat we make. From star to star, our story will shine, read right, and tell itself.*" Sister Nani's face came forth from the lilac fog. "*I know my part. I know your part too, Mistah Goodspeed,*" she chuckled.

Gordon Goodspeed's eyes opened as he was pulled from his vivid dream. His eyes, opened wide, shined with their lilac brilliance. Their glow brightened the now dark bedroom. It was night, a little after midnight. Gordon moved the *Nigrum Nigrius Nigro* off his chest, and placed it next to him on the bed. Then, he rose up in an eerie manner, like a vampire from its coffin. His movement was robotic, stiff, and not of his own accord. While sitting up, he turned his body to the left, knees bending over the bed. His feet touched the floor. Gordon stood, walked around the bed, and out of the bedroom. Gordon moved down the hall, bright, glowing eyes providing light in the unlit corridor.

Down the stairs. Parlor entrance. Down the stairs. Garden floor. Down the stairs.

Basement.

Gordon stepped to the center of the dank room and turned to the wall opposite the stairs. His face trembled as his eyes widened and their glow intensified. The wrenching pain Gordon felt from his expanding and swelling eyes dropped him to his knees. He was now fully awake. Just in time to feel the circumference of his eye sockets dilate.

Gordon opened his mouth to scream, but at the same moment he stiffened his lower jaw, trying to ease the pain stinging every nerve in his body. His mouth trembled, and only a muted, gurgled groan expressed his agony. He wrapped his arms around himself as if cold. His body shivered just the same, and all the while his head faced the wall, and he never looked away. But he couldn't if he tried. He was locked into position.

Gordon's glowing, enlarged, cartoonish eyes birthed thick, lilac-colored tendrils. The snake-like strands writhed from Gordon's eyes and connected to the wall in front of him. The tendrils of light gathered and expanded to create the glowing, almond-shaped doorway. And as before, the glowing male and female figures stepped through.

Gordon's eyes returned to normal. Their intense lilac glow disappeared, and he dropped to the floor. A euphoric feeling covered Gordon as the pain caused by his ordeal lifted. Gordon took a deep breath, and beamed a drunken smile. He rubbed the basement's cement floor as if it was silk. And though his body was pressed firmly against the floor, Gordon was convinced he was floating. His eyes were closed tight, and he reveled in the rapturous and intoxicating relief from the pain he'd experienced. Gordon coughed hard, choking a bit. Then he inhaled, coughed, and exhaled rapidly, but he still felt exuberant.

Gordon opened his watering eyes, and his blurred vision focused. The basement light turned on by itself. He saw the glowing female pass her male companion an object. It was a repoussed bronze jar that had occult symbols engraved all around its body. With her hands free, the glowing woman came to Gordon's assistance. She bent down and cradled her illuminated arm around Gordon's back, put a glowing hand on his chest, and helped him to his feet.

"Stand," her glowing flesh sang. *"Stand."*

Gordon stood straight. He assured the glowing woman that he no longer needed assistance, but she continued to hold him, guiding Gordon to the old, ragged chair stored in the basement. Gordon sat down. Ragged as the chair was, it was still comfortable. The glowing woman returned to her glowing, male partner.

"The *Nigrum Nigrius Nigro* works, uh, the black mirror you attached to it," Gordon announced. "It's like my own little ancient laptop," he chuckled. "There's a spirit inside it. It comes through. It must be ancient. Knows a lot. I call it Spook. It seems not to mind."

The glowing woman faced Gordon. He observed her face, and behind its radiant blaze he believed he perceived her smiling at him. "Kam-Ptah," the glow of her flesh sang. "Kam-Ptah," it repeated in harmony.

Gordon figured the woman was telling him what the ancient device was known as. *Kam-Ptah.* It sounded much the same as the modern device, *'computer'*.

"I'm aware of the book's origin," Gordon continued. "How it got into my great-grandfather's hands, that is," he clarified. "I had planned to tap into another object I was given. A pair of goggles—do you know what goggles are?" Now the male faced him. Gordon waved his hand, brushing aside his question by saying, "Not important. But it's the lenses. They're called the *Eyes of the Angel.* Does that mean anything to you?"

The glowing woman and the glowing man turned their heads and looked at one another. Then they returned their attention to Gordon. The woman approached him. She took his arm and her glowing flesh commanded in song, *"Stand, stand."* Gordon rose from the chair. Another set of words merrily harmonized from the woman's glow, *"Show me. Show me."* She let go of Gordon, allowing him to lead her up to his bedroom.

Gordon hopped up the stairs with the glowing woman floating up behind him. The glowing man didn't follow. He set the large, copper jar on the workbench and then walked to the materials brought earlier. Gordon, at that time, led the way up to the garden floor, then the parlor entrance, and then to the bedroom. He turned on the bedroom lights and stepped inside. The glowing woman followed him as he moved to the other side of the room.

Gordon picked up the wooden case holding the goggles with the onyx lenses. He opened it and presented the case to the glowing woman. She accepted, and then she examined the object, running her fingers along the goggles' lenses. She put her hand against her chest, and made the motion of gasping, though no air or noise came from her. Gordon watched the woman turn, remove the goggles from the case and walk to the side of the bed where the reconfigured, black-mirrored *Nigrum Nigrius Nigro* lay on the mattress. She opened the tome and placed the goggles against the jeweled keyboard. She closed the book, laying the black mirror over the goggles. Standing straight, the light of her body ordered Gordon, *"Sleep. Sleep. Dream. I will help my husband build for you."* The woman's bright image faded, returning to the basement.

Gordon looked down at the *Nigrum Nigrius Nigro* and the goggles sandwiched between its black mirror and the jeweled keyboard. He slid onto the bed, sitting legs crossed in front of the reconfigured tome. "Well, Spook, looks like you get to tell me another bedtime story."

Gordon jumped from the bed to turn the lights off. Then he slid under the covers, placed the *Nigrum Nigrius Nigro* atop his chest, and then folded his arms over it like a prayer book. Gordon closed his eyes and was ferried to sleep.

Before there was a vivid image, there appeared a lilac mist.

Give Me Your Eyes

"I promise."

Edsel Friedman had such a long-winded, professional title: General of Colonial African Military Affairs of the German-Tanzanian Colony. But all who he commanded called him "General." He was hardened by war, but after surviving so many of its skirmishes, and just as many close brushes with death, he knew how to enjoy life and smile.

Africa had changed him much the same, stationed in the German colony of Tanzania, overseeing its value. The Tanzanian atmosphere had permanently burned a reddish-dusky color into his skin, especially on his square, war-chiseled face. It gave the illusion that he was on the verge of breaking out into a sweat, but it never made him look anxious. Even while seated inside the small, windowless room lit by fiery lamp and sconce, relaxed with a cigar and a glass of wine, the lean and muscular official still commanded authority.

Sitting across from the General, enjoying the same pleasures, was Belgium psychologist, Doctor Granville Coppens. He took small sips from his glass, and then politely wiped the bushy area around his mouth, keeping the salt-and-pepper hairs of his moustache and beard from being stained the color of the wine.

"Psychological imprinting, General," the doctor announced in the German language as he placed his glass on the table, "That is what will get the blacks of Africa in order."

Edsel didn't much understand psychology, but he loved to hear Doctor Coppens speak on the subject, especially as it pertained to the Africans of the Tanzanian army.

Doctor Coppens adjusted the tie on his expensive suit and leaned back in his chair to take a drag off his cigar. He looked away from the General, thinking. He exhaled smoke, and while returning his gaze toward the General, declared, "Africa might have been the birthplace of man, but there is so much infancy within her thinking. Something happened to the blacks of Africa that has made them no longer able to understand the world's politics like the civilized nations." The doctor elucidated, "The people here are in need of phase-sensitive learning." Doctor Coppens was excited about the subject, and the day's presentation that he was to give. He couldn't talk and sit, so he stood up and lectured. "Not too long ago, early eighteen-seventies, an English biologist named Douglas Spalding published his discovery of the subject, psychological imprinting. It's all about how we learn. It's the environment, how we interact with it."

Edsel grinned at Doctor Coppens' enthusiasm, which drew the General into the speech.

"There are critical moments for imprinting, but with force, an impression can always be left on the mind," the doctor continued. His enthusiasm lessened, and a stern demeanor came over him. He smoked to relax himself, and Edsel waited patiently. Doctor Coppens waved his cigar around as he spoke, looking at the floor. "Arming the black with a weapon before the black is ready to handle a weapon is irresponsible on the part of the German." He looked at Edsel and yielded to an unspoken argument, "I know the Germans are willing to create a black army—led by German officers and even some non-commissioned officers. But to keep you and other officers and German soldiers safe, and Germany's economic interests safe in its African territories, the black must acknowledge that the enemy is not the white European. The black who bends his knee to the colonists is not at war with the colonists. They are at war with, and their true enemy is, the black who is not willing to serve the interests of the colonists. When that is understood, we can even allow them to arm their children."

Doctor Coppens, cigar smoking between his fingers, planted his hands on the back of the empty chair and leaned forward. His eyes looked up as his face became pensive. He stood up straight, still thinking, and cupped his chin. "There have been rebellions. The black is good at hiding secrets. But there are tactics more useful in war that can draw out information. The blacks of your army must know these tactics. And even if the tactics are not immediately successful, they still will leave an imprint." Coppens took a pause. Then he said, "The culture here, if it can be called such, will be broken." He spoke his words carefully. "When it is broken, your army will function properly. And the black, at best, will fight the black. You will be safe."

Someone knocked on the door.

Edsel turned around. Doctor Coppens looked up.

Edsel stood and said, "We really should be on our way, Doctor. Don't waste all your energy here when it can be put into the lecture."

Both men chuckled. Edsel opened the door. An African man was on the other side. He said in German, "The auditorium is ready for the doctor's seminar, General Friedman."

"We will be there shortly," the General informed in a curt manner. "Go on."

The African man hurried down the hallway.

The General and the Belgium psychologist snuffed out their cigars into separate ashtrays, and they left their glasses partially filled with wine.

Doctor Coppens commented, "I am not here to give a lecture, General. What I spoke to you *was* a seminar, indeed. But what you will witness in this auditorium will be my words put into practice." He took his handkerchief from the table and wiped his brow. He was not quite accustomed to the African atmosphere. It was hot, and he was sweating.

Edsel left the room with Granville right beside him.

"In the Americas," the doctor spoke, "the white slave owners had the black slaves whip one another to death, sometimes for sport, and sometimes for punishment." He tapped his forehead. "This left an imprint. The black then believed his enemy was the man whipping him, the other black, or, if it was a sport, his black opponent."

Edsel nodded. "I see," said the General.

"You definitely will," Doctor Coppens responded. "In time, the blacks you command will not need you for a tutorial. In fact, if the whites leave Africa altogether, the imprint will be so deep that they will continue to act with this behavior. And this tactic I introduce to the blacks today will be their strongest. Are all my provisions in place?"

"Yes, they are," the General assured. Edsel opened the door at the end of the hall and courteously motioned for the doctor to walk through.

Doctor Coppens kindly refused, saying, "No dear, General. This is your base of operation. I shall follow you."

Edsel nodded with a smile. "Agreed," he said, and then he stepped through the door and outside into the blooming, African day. His first step was a step down, onto a sandy lot. In front of him was a large, tented canopy. He brushed aside the curtains and stepped inside. Doctor Coppens followed.

Under the canopy was a crowd of Africans. Some sat in seats. Others stood. All were dressed in a German military uniform. On sight of the General, the seated African men jumped up and stood at attention. General Edsel acknowledged them, and he waved his hand, ordering the men at ease. Some of the African men returned to their seats. The others relaxed their pose.

General Friedman yelled to the gathered crowd as he neared the front, "Alert! All of you, blacks of Africa! Listen! Listen! Today you have a lesson in interrogation. You will listen close!" General Friedman made a cool, military pivot. He faced the crowd. Doctor Coppens stood next to him. "German companies provide Africa with economic stability! Repeat!"

"German companies provide Africa with economic stability!" repeated the black audience.

"The German has given me God! The German has delivered to me salvation from the barren sands of Africa! Repeat!"

"The German has given me God! The German has delivered to me salvation from the barren sands of Africa!"

"We praise Germany. We are grateful to Germany and we fight in her name! Amen! Repeat!"

"We praise Germany. We are grateful to Germany, and we fight in her name! Amen!"

General Edsel clapped his hands hard, a signal for the audience to applaud. The black audience followed the command. "A fine group of black boys we have here! A fine group! Karl Peters be proud!" General Edsel yelled. "We have here the best! You are not growing and picking cotton. You are not building the roads for German East Africa. You are soldiers in Germany's army. You are as close to men as can be expected of you boys. The economic hardship of the black is the fault of the black. German companies provide financial stability. German companies provide jobs. Germany has given life to a barren wasteland. And you have proven among yourselves, the elite boys of Africa. Protecting the interest of the German company protects the interests of the black. And you know those who wish harm on the German providers are the enemies of the good black." Edsel paused for effect. He stretched his right arm out and pointed. "And that enemy, as black as you, is out there. They're hiding. We've had our skirmishes. But no one talks to relieve this problem." Then he lowered his arm and stepped back. He pointed an open hand to Doctor Coppens and introduced him. "This is Doctor Granville Coppens. He is a Professor of the Mind. He has journeyed here from his homeland of Belgium to teach today a tactic that will ensure to draw out all information that will lead to the capture of rebels and rebel factions. Doctor, the stage is yours."

Granville stepped up, and General Edsel stepped aside.

"Blacks of German Tanzania, I greet you," he said in German.

General Edsel raised an open palm. "Hold, Doctor," he said. "I apologize." Then he screamed, "Soldier Boy Dogo!"

An African man in his late thirties jumped to attention. His name was as the General addressed. Dogo. He had a round, smooth face and dark skin. He made several quick strides toward the General, and then stood straight. "My Good General!" soldier Dogo called. "What is your order?"

General Edsel raised a finger. "Listen, Soldier Boy Dogo. Not everyone here is fluent in German," the General yelled. "You will provide interpretation."

"Yes, Good General," Dogo shouted in military fashion.

"Do not start with Doctor Coppens' words," the General commanded. "You will translate the words I spoke earlier. Let the other boys be fully aware of what I've spoken. Go on, Soldier Boy Dogo. Speak your black dialect!"

Dogo summarized the General's earlier words in Swahili, though most of the black soldiers in attendance could speak the German language. Even among the soldiers who could not read or write the German language, it was very much understood when spoken. Dogo ended his translation. He looked at General Edsel and informed, "All soldiers understand."

"Good!" the General barked. "You are not dismissed, Soldier Boy Dogo. Translate the doctor's words." Then he ordered, "Doctor, proceed."

Doctor Coppens spoke in an informed, authoritative voice, "The black, all over the world has received a special gift from the whites." Dogo translated, and the doctor continued. "The African black is a blank slate. You all should be as grateful as you've proposed. The white man has stripped you of a savage identity. It is our duty to rebuild you properly. Riffraff rebels that wish to remain savages constantly interrupt the process of your new identity, a process that will uplift you and give you prosperity. The rebels hide among the people, people who remain quiet. War is inevitable with these blacks of Africa that put you and your families in danger. Today I will show you how to break them by breaking the woman." Doctor Coppens turned and directed General Edsel, "General Edsel, the nigger girl. Bring her in."

The General turned and left the tent through another exit. He appeared later carrying a nineteen-year-old African woman. She wore a long skirt, a loose and baggy shirt and no shoes. Two German soldiers brought in a chair, which the General sat the young African woman down upon using tremendous force. The General removed his M1879 Reichsrevolver and thumbed back the hammer, pressing the end of the barrel to the young woman's head.

"Don't move," the General ordered.

The young woman shuddered, fear prickling every nerve. Her eyes darted about. Sweat wet her brow, and she wanted to scream, but she didn't dare. The two German soldiers bound and gagged her, and they were rough in their undertaking. They tied her braided hair behind her head. One of the German soldiers asked the General, "General, permission to observe."

"Yes. We'll need you later, anyway. Go to the back," General Edsel said to them.

The two German soldiers, excited, complied with their orders.

"General," Doctor Coppens called, "you may holster your firearm." When General Edsel sheathed his gun, Doctor Coppens turned and addressed the African soldiers, "The blacks of Africa are a superstitious lot. As soldiers under Germany, your devilish superstitions no longer concern you. Now, listen. German medical doctors have examined the girl that is before us. She is a virgin. Defiled, she will be an outcast. This, she does not want. Now, listen. She knows the whereabouts of a group of rebels. She knows names. She knows plans. We will extract this information from her. We will first proceed with an interrogation of this enemy. I need a volunteer." None of the African soldiers stood up, even as Soldier Dogo translated. Doctor Coppens scanned the crowd. He spotted a young man and pointed. "You. Come. You will serve General Edsel's good army."

The young man hesitated.

Doctor Coppens waved him forward, impatient. "Come. Now."

Soldier Dogo translated, but this young man needed no interpretation.

He rose. He walked to the front.

"Your name, boy."

The young man answered in German, "My name is Hasa."

Doctor Coppens was surprised. He beamed with pride, expressing in a loud and slow manner, "Soldier. Boy. Hasa. Splendid. You speak German. Good. The girl does not. I need you to ask her where the riffraff that continue targeting German companies are hiding. Now, make that simple. Where are the rebels? Remove her gag."

Hasa bent down and started removing the gag from the young woman.

Doctor Coppens screamed, "You! Must! Be! Quicker!" Hasa jumped and stood up straight in a soldier's alert pose. "Forceful!" Then in a calm voice the Belgium doctor addressed the attentive and anxious audience, "It's okay to hurt her. This is an enemy to you. Force the gag down, not just out." He asked General Edsel, "Your firearms, please, General."

The General removed his pistol and passed it to Doctor Coppens. The doctor thanked General Edsel and then, as he cocked the pistol's hammer back, he ordered Hasa, "Yank! Understand? Yank the gag from her mouth! Pull hard! Be forceful! Your captive *must* understand that *you* are to be feared!"

Hasa bent down again. He put his hands on the rope tied into the young woman's mouth. His hands trembled. His eyes locked with the watery, trembling eyes of the scared young woman.

Doctor Coppens fired the pistol into Hasa's skull. Blood spattered everywhere on the young African woman. The crowd jumped. General Edsel was still, observant with a stoic expression. Hasa's body slumped to the ground.

"Too slow," Doctor Coppens said to the audience. "General, your soldiers."

General Edsel turned to the two German soldiers and signaled with a nod of the head to remove Hasa's body from the tent. The two soldiers scurried to the front, lifted the lifeless body, and removed him from the canopy.

Doctor Coppens scanned the audience. "Who here is true to Germany?" he inquired in a loud voice. "Who here is grateful for the prosperity that Europe, through the good German people, has brought you?" He paced the front row and came to a young African soldier. "Name?" he asked.

The man said in a hesitant voice, "G-G-Ghubari…"

Doctor Coppens fired a bullet into Ghubari's forehead. The soldier's body crumpled to the floor. "Too slow," Doctor Coppens remarked. "Are there no true boys here ready to serve the German army?"

The two German soldiers reentered the large tent. General Edsel signaled for them to remove the second slain soldier. The German soldiers did as instructed, again leaving the tent with another lifeless, African body in their arms.

Doctor Coppens asked again in the same loud manner, "Are there no true boys here ready to serve the German army?" He looked out into the audience, three rows back. He pointed. "You. Stand. Give me your name."

The African man stood and spoke clearly, "Tembo Buibui."

"To the front, Soldier Boy Tembo Buibui!" Doctor Coppens called. "To the front!"

Tembo walked the length of the row he sat in, then made his way to the front of the audience, standing at attention near Doctor Coppens. The doctor took a step toward Tembo and whispered into his ear, "This girl does not know the German language. Speak in your native tongue. Ask her where the rebels are hiding. Understood? Good. To your task."

Doctor Coppens stepped away. Tembo bent down in front of the trembling woman. Her face was spattered with blood. Her eyes, filled wide with terror, were dark brown and beautiful. With her eyes, she begged Tembo to help her in a way he believed deep down he could not. Tembo hesitated for a moment, and in that moment he anticipated his life to be extinguished by Doctor Coppens. He anticipated a split-second of thunderous noise, the jab of the bullet boring itself into his skull, and then oblivion.

But nothing happened. Tembo remained alive. He took a deep breath and tried to shut the woman's pleading eyes from his sight. He whispered to her in Swahili that he was sorry, raised his hands, grabbed the rope gagging the young woman's mouth, and pulled hard. The woman jerked forward, coughing and panting.

Tembo asked her in a soft, trembling voice, "Wh-where are th-the rebels—"

"Speak up!" Doctor Coppens screamed. He thumbed back his pistol's hammer. "I can't speak your native tongue, but even I can understand your voice is hesitant." He raised the gun to Dogo. "Is this soldier boy hesitant?"

Dogo himself was hesitant when he answered. "Yes," he spat quickly to recover from his reluctance. His eyes watched the barrel of the gun. "Yes, Doctor Coppens."

Doctor Coppens lowered the pistol and said, "And I understand why. This girl has caused such stress among us." He stepped up behind Tembo. "You must be forceful with your words. You must be as forceful with your words as you would be with any other weapon! Shout your question! There is no time to be soft. Let her know!" He said to Tembo, "Hold your tongue, boy. Hold your tongue." Then Doctor Coppens turned to his audience and addressed them as the two German soldiers reentered the tent. "There is no need to give her a threat. It will be in your voice. Even if you do not pull your weapon, she will see it." He raised a finger, shook it, and lowered his face. "But there is more to her. She is a tricky girl." To Tembo, he ordered, "Speak your command. Loud."

Tembo shouted in Swahili, "Where are the rebels that threaten the German companies and armies?"

The woman answered with tears. Her nose ran as well as the tears from her eyes. She managed to speak, "I don't know anything…"

Tembo turned to Doctor Coppens and informed, "She does not know…"

"And you believe her?" Doctor Coppens yelled. He pointed his gun toward the young woman. "Hit her. Go on. Hard. She will talk."

Tembo looked the woman in the eyes. *Her beautiful, watery, dark eyes.* He wished there was a smile there under her eyes. Under different circumstances, perhaps another life and time, he would have courted a woman like her. He dreamed a dream in his last moments, having decided he would die instead of continuing with the interrogation. So he daydreamed a moment, walking hand-in-hand with the young woman. She was smiling now, happy in Tembo's daydream. Happy in another place. The both of them. The sun was kissing her rich, dark skin. Tembo continued the daydream, waiting for the loud, thunderous bang from the gun to cut the vision short.

But Doctor Coppens only moved Tembo aside.

"I cannot ask much of you, boy. You're not a proper soldier," said Doctor Coppens, holstering his firearm. He said to the audience, "None of you are yet. But you will learn. Look. Observe. I am a former Commander. Listen. This is what you do." He balled his fist tight. "Right. Look. Look." He slapped Tembo with his other hand, and when the African soldier recovered, Doctor Coppens showed him his balled fist. He showed it to the audience. Then he cocked his fist back and slammed it into the bound woman's beautiful face. Tembo flinched, but he controlled his body from breaking out into uncontrollable tremors.

The strike's impact split the woman's lip, broke her nose, crushed her cheekbone, and drew blood. Then Doctor Coppens turned to the audience and advised in a calm voice, "It might take more than one blow, but just drawing blood will do as a start. This is for either a male or female captive. People get frightened when they see blood, especially if it's their own." He turned around and struck the woman twice more, just as hard, and once with the side of the revolver. Then he said to the audience, "An extra hit or two, unexpected, will make the subject aware that anything can happen at any time. Hit with the gun so that they will know a firearm can be used in more than one way." He instructed Tembo, "Ask her again. Same question."

Tembo, eyes wide, turned his head from the doctor to the woman. He breathed in, latched onto the dragon of an angry memory, and then exhaled in a loud voice, "You lie, woman! So I will ask again! Where are the rebels that threaten the German companies and armies?"

The woman swallowed her tears. She became strong, though it hurt to speak. "I don't know," she hissed back. Her face mixed with her tears and blood, and the blood of the dead Hasa.

Tembo grit his teeth to keep himself from crying. The woman looked at him with fiery hatred in her eyes. It was as hurtful to Tembo to see such scorn as any of the pain dealt to her. The doctor drawled with a chuckle, "Oh, I know a defiant tone of voice when I hear one. I don't even have to understand the language."

Tembo said to Doctor Coppens, "She still says she doesn't know."

Doctor Coppens fired a bullet into the young woman's leg.

The woman muted a scream, though the attack burned. Her body jumped, and all the nerves in her leg quaked with searing agony as if her appendage was on fire. Doctor Coppens pushed Tembo aside and jammed his thumb hard into the bullet wound. The woman hollered through gritted teeth, screamed for a moment, and then she passed out. Doctor Coppens slapped her face. He called for the two German soldiers to revive her with smelling salts.

"Come on, nigger girl," Doctor Coppens said as if talking to a child. He continued to slap the young woman. "Stay awake. Come on!"

One of the German soldiers held a can of smelling salts under the woman's nose. Doctor Coppens moved aside. The woman started to revive. The two German soldiers began inspecting her to see if she would remain awake.

Doctor Coppens said as Dogo translated, "This form of interrogation can be repetitive. Over and over, it can be done. You may find yourself getting nowhere. After a while, a man will break. But the female is a very resilient creature. Understand the woman endures an experience that no man will ever undergo. It is an excruciating ordeal, and her body, because of it, can withstand a great deal of pain. That is childbirth." Doctor Coppens screamed, "We men have strength here!" he pounded his chest. "But women, physically delicate creatures as they are, have strength here." He pointed to his heart. Then he turned to the two German soldiers and ordered, "Bring in the table."

The two soldiers moved away from the woman, left the tent, and after a while, dragged in a rectangular table. General Edsel moved out of the way, giving room for the men to place the table next to the woman bound to the chair.

"Unbind her," Doctor Coppens directed. "Put her on the table and hold her down."

The two German soldiers went about the task of untying the ropes binding the young African woman to the chair. The woman struggled, twisting left and right, rocking the chair back and forth. The two German soldiers continued with the woman's bindings, as if unaware of her motions in the chair. Untied, the two German soldiers grappled her legs and arms. The woman flailed about and screamed as the German soldiers carried her and slammed her body onto the table. One man held her down at the arms. The other pressed down on her legs, which hung over the table's end.

The African woman continued screaming.

Doctor Coppens asked of the soldiers, "Put her body completely on the table. Dogo, help the young man restrain and open her legs. Hold one leg as the young man holds the other." He turned to the crowd as his orders were carried out. Tembo stared wide-eyed. The doctor said, "You see? Immediately she reacts. Immediately she screams. All this through the pain we have already put her through. This is the true weapon against her. Now stand! All of you will have a taste. Stand up. She will know every one of you this day. And by the time we've all sampled her, she will give us our information. If not, she will return to her family, her friends, her community as an outcast. A whore." He turned to Tembo and told the young man, "The honor goes first to you, little boy. Have her."

The woman screamed in Swahili, *"I don't know anything!"*

Tembo stared. The woman turned to him and their eyes locked. Her face was bloody. The left side of her face was swelling with purple and reddish-brown bruises.

"I don't know anything," she pleaded again in a quieter voice.

Tembo stared. Her eyes. Watery. Beautiful. Terrified.

Tembo stepped to the end of the table where Dogo and the German soldier held the woman's legs pinned and opened. Tembo heard Doctor Coppens tell him, "She has no undergarments. Proceed to penetrate her." The woman exhaled. Her body went limp. Doctor Coppens commented, "She appears broken. But we must continue. Go on, Soldier Boy Tembo. Now, another note: age is no factor. There should be no discrimination with age. The youngest of girls, if she can speak, knows something. Gender should be no issue either. These tactics can be used on boys. The younger the boy, the better. With his manhood defiled, he will be an outcast to the society and class he comes from. He will give any information asked, and in an attempt to regain his manhood, he will beg to join your ranks." Doctor Coppens informed, "We also have today a sixteen-year-old boy to practice on."

Tembo turned his head toward the doctor and held out a hand. "I have seen these circumstances before. A gun must stay at her head at all times. It keeps the victim docile."

Doctor Coppens smiled. "Your vocabulary is profound, little boy." He slapped his firearms into Tembo's hand. "Let us make this practice as real as possible. Continue, young boy."

Tembo gripped the gun. His hand trembled. Anger tightened his throat as his eyes stayed on Doctor Coppens' crooked grin. Tembo's finger twitched, tensing around the weapon's trigger and firing into Doctor Coppens' shoulder. The psychologist buckled. Tembo flinched with the action, and all around him jumped. They froze in place, surprise shackling their hands and feet. Doctor Coppens, bent over, held his shoulder and screamed.

Something moved in Tembo's peripheral. He turned and fired another round. Everyone jumped again, and Tembo was immediately drenched with horror.

His face dripped shock as he witnessed she was dead, and it was his bullet that took her life. She had rose up, the soldiers' grip on her loose. She was prepared to fight back at Tembo's side. But her sudden movement against a still background startled Tembo. He reacted, and he'd killed her.

Fragments of the woman's skull, and splashes of her blood and flesh, were now spattered against the clothes of the German soldier who had been standing over the woman and pinning down her arms. In reaction, the German soldier backed away. He looked at his clothes in disbelief and cursed. That's where time and surprise had frozen him.

The soldier holding down the woman's right leg went for his gun. Tembo shot the German soldier in the gut; and in a swift motion, grabbed the soldier's holstered pistol and yanked it free. The gun procured from Doctor Coppens was now empty. Tembo turned and fired his newly acquired gun at the German soldier he'd wounded and taken the weapon from, hitting him in the jaw.

Tembo aimed the second gun at the German soldier whose clothes were now smattered with blood and shot him in the stomach. He turned and shot Dogo, hitting him in the collarbone. He turned and fired at General Edsel, hitting him in the arm. He fired randomly into the crowd of African trainees, and then he ran from the tent, tossing his empty weapons aside.

The thick Tanzanian heat smothered Tembo so fiercely that at first he believed someone had grabbed him. He took a moment to recover. A breath. He ran straight, passing the German military installation. He saw an unoccupied cavalry horse and increased his speed. He slowed his strides, almost tripping in his steps. He extended his arms and planted his hands on the heavy beast's body. He panted, frantic and eyes wide. He unhitched the horse, his arms and hands wild, upsetting the animal and causing it to buck and shout. The noise alerted armed German soldiers. They turned their heads to investigate.

Tembo, face caked with sweat and desperation, grabbed the reins and hauled himself onto the horse. He tugged and tried to steer the mighty steed, but it continued to jump and holler. Tembo shouted both German and Swahili commands at the horse.

The German soldiers raised their rifles and screamed a warning!

Tembo didn't hear them, but he saw them. Rifles aimed.

First warning unheard. Second warning unheard. Third warning unheard.

The soldiers fired their rifles. Tembo launched himself from the horse as bullets tore through the beast's body. Blood sprayed from the wild, bucking animal like red glittering mist and then, soon after, drained thick from its wounds. Air-popping gunfire buzzed past Tembo's head. His body slapped the dusty earth floor, and he rolled away as the horse's legs buckled and its body dropped.

Tembo jumped behind the side of a building as the German soldiers prepared to fire off another round of bullets. He rose, tired and aching, back pressed hard against the wall. He decided not to peek around the building's corner, and he ran. He saw the African trainees scattering from the large tent. General Edsel, holding his wound, emerged from the tent cursing and calling for assistance. Doctor Coppens staggered behind him.

Tembo had an idea. He would run forward and choke the life out of one of the two men. *But which one?* he asked himself. Aloud, but to himself, he answered, "Whoever is closest when I make my strides is who God has decided will die."

A soldier galloped up to Tembo, blocking his path. The soldier aimed a rifle down at him and ordered, "Stay still, soldier boy. Give your title."

Tembo clenched his teeth and snarled. He grabbed the rifle's barrel and dragged the soldier from his horse. The German soldier let go of his firearm as he slammed against the ground, the wind knocked from him. Tembo snatched the soldier's holstered pistol, tucked it down the front of his pants, and jumped to the horse. He fired his rifle at General Edsel and hit him in the lower right of his abdomen. The General fell back, but was not expired. Tembo cocked the weapon and shot at Doctor Coppens. The doctor buckled as the bullet broke through his cheekbone and upper jaw. He slapped the ground, blood spilling in a pool from his face.

Tembo, with one hand, steered the horse away and slapped the reins. He escaped farther into the desert. Grasslands, villages and life were behind him. He dropped his rifle and grabbed the reins with both hands. He wanted to go home and inform his family that he was never going to be seen again. He closed his eyes and screamed! A picture of his older sister and younger brother developed behind his eyes. His mother and father were standing there too.

Tembo opened his eyes, teeth tight against one another. He groaned as the horse continued to soar forward into the desert. He slowly opened his mouth and his groan crawled free as a loud cry to the heavens. He pulled on the reins and commanded the horse to halt! The horse responded immediately, and with a roar, ceased its run. Tembo's body lurched forward from the horse's immediate break in speed, and was almost thrown from the beast. His face slapped against the back of the horse's neck, and he rested it there.

Crying, coughing, and screaming.

A happy image of the woman Tembo was forced to torture popped into his mind.

It eased his emotions as he saw the woman smiling, twirling playfully in a green, Tanzanian field with an African sunrise behind her. She slowly faded in and out of silhouette. There was a rhythm to the flux of shade that shrouded her.

To her, Tembo spoke a prayer and asked for forgiveness. He reached for the gun tucked inside his pants and he gripped hard the curved, cylindrical handle. He decided he would join her, and he removed the gun, thumbing back its hammer. He would say a prayer first before ending his life and dancing for eternity with a woman he hoped would forgive him. But his eyes caught something peculiar. He looked up, watery vision spying the sun. The celestial brilliance appeared as if it was giving birth to another shining, heavenly body. Tembo looked on in wonder. He wiped away the tears gathered at the underside of his eyelids, sniffed, and squinted his eyes to observe the heavenly spectacle.

A bullet buzzed by him. There was no telling how close the projectile was from hitting him. He'd only heard the cut of the air made by the speeding projectile. Tembo turned his head in the direction he'd just escaped from. A wave of mounted German soldiers flooded the horizon.

More pops of bullet fire sliced the air.

Tembo turned the horse to face the incoming soldiers. He cocked the gun and uttered in a determined voice, "Your name, good woman, I call Adla, The Beautiful. And I will kill six of these men for you. I seek your name in their deaths."

Tembo lifted his arm and held the gun out straight. More bullets sped by him. He aimed and waited as the riders moved closer to him. He steadied his hand. He needed only a few more paces until they were close enough for the gunfire to make an impact.

Then the riders came to a sudden arrest.

Tembo kept his aim on the stopped, mounted soldiers. He considered his targets still out of range. His hand started trembling. His open eye, fixed on the men in front of him, started to water. Then something curious occurred. The riders turned and darted away. Tembo looked on in wonder. *"Cowards!"* he screamed. He fired three shots and hit nothing. "Would you rather me tied to a chair or table?" he yelled. "I will hunt you when I am a ghost! I will kill you all!"

Feeling disgusted, Tembo turned to ride away into the desert. Then he noticed the streaking, cobalt-blue-colored, fiery ball falling from the sky and speeding toward the desert sands. Tembo glimpsed the phenomenon for only a moment before it impacted. The force of the crash spat walls of desert sand high into the air. A thunderous force pushed Tembo from the horse. It also pushed the horse to the ground. The mount hollered as sand, earth and ash smacked against it like a cloud of locusts.

Tembo was partially buried under a thin layer of sand. His stolen horse jumped to its feet and limped away before breaking out into strides. Tembo wanted to pass out, rest. But more noise interrupted his pass into unconsciousness. Loud, volcanic noise burst from below the desert's surface and up into the air. The explosive rabble was successive. Tembo considered that heavy artillery rounds from African rebels were pounding the earth. He kept his head down, covered by his arms, as the concussive blasts continued. When the noise of the blasts ceased, Tembo uncovered and lifted his head. Tired and battered, he turned over on his back and looked in the direction of the impact. Tembo saw before him the marvelous display of a thick forest sprouted in the desert. He sat up, mouth agape, and eyes wide. He looked up and down, scoping the tall, mighty trees in the distance. The circumference of the phenomenon didn't expand wide, but the awesome sight didn't need to be large to create an effect.

Tembo crawled a few paces away from the scene. Another concussive burst happened. A tree jumped up through the earth and joined the others that made up the forest. Tembo gasped and stared. He moved his body to stand. On his feet, he realized how much he was trembling and he tried to relax. He started first with his breathing, and when he managed to get it under control, the tremors rattling his arms and legs ceased.

A bullet tunneled through the air and grazed his ear.

Tembo felt the blood collecting on the small wound. He turned his head and saw that the German riders had returned. They aimed their rifles at him. Tembo jumped to his feet and fired his remaining shots at the riders and hit nothing. He turned and ran toward the forest in the distance.

The riders charged him, shooting.

Bullets passed by him or smacked against his heels.

Tembo ran harder and harder, faster and faster, drawing nearer to the forest. Emanating from deep inside the clustered trees, Tembo could see a faint cobalt-blue glow. The light inspired him to move faster. And though his breath was expended, Tembo pushed himself harder.

The riders closed in. The massive trees bent forward and then stood up straight. A mighty brush of wind knocked several riders from their mounts. Cavalrymen following close behind toppled over the tumbled soldiers.

Tembo didn't bother to observe. He ran into the forest and only slowed his speed when he saw the glowing, feminine figure hunched over and on her knees. She looked up at him and reached out her hand, speaking in a hollow, echoing voice. Tembo's tremors returned. He stepped away from the woman as she reached for him. She spoke in a language of which he had no understanding. The sound of her voice ceased his tremors, but did not ease him any. Tembo did not move.

The glowing woman collapsed, exhausted.

Tembo's pause melted, and by reflex, he jumped to aid her. He touched her arm. Her glowing flesh felt like warm water. And by reflex of her own, the glowing woman jumped up and wrapped her arms around Tembo. The woman's light covered him as she held him tight. Tembo believed he could hear her crying. He embraced her, the palms of his hands feeling the strange, watery, glowing texture of her flesh.

Then the light dropped away, and all that remained was a beautiful black radiance of skin on the woman. Tembo could feel against his neck the wide, woolly crown that was the woman's hair. The woman whispered in Swahili, "How many moons circle our world? What color are the moons?"

Tembo stepped back to look at the woman.

She looked at him, eyes wide with curiosity and anticipation for an answer.

Tembo stepped back farther. The tremors returned. His mouth quivered, and his eyes watered. Tembo dropped to his knees and looked up at the woman, hands clasped together. "A dream…perhaps…" questioned Tembo, his voice like a sigh. "Did I die and meet judgment? Have I been killed?" The woman he addressed resembled the young African woman he was forced to torture, and whose life he took. The woman he called Adla, The Beautiful. "I was ready to kill them for you. Send me back so that I may strike down a good number for you, and then I will join you in the next life."

The woman only stared with a blank expression. Then large wings like that of a dove grew from her back and spread wide. The wings flapped once, and the naked black woman lifted into the air. Her eyes expanded and glowed with a cobalt-blue glimmer. Her wings flapped again and she soared over Tembo, gliding in the direction of Tembo's entrance into her conjured forest.

Tembo followed the woman with his eyes and head. He watched as her wings flapped twice more as she flew. Then her wings folded and a single leg, foot turned down, touched the earth floor. Her feet planted, and without losing momentum, continued moving toward the entrance. Tembo jumped up and hurried to the winged woman's side. He attempted a look at her face. Images of the ordeal he assisted in putting the young woman through attacked his vision like gunshots. He looked away, choosing instead to inspect the majestic and broad trees. Despite the entangled branches and leaves creating a dense, organic canopy, the area bubbled bright with the slightest amount of sunlight that penetrated the cracks in the natural shade.

But the unanticipated sprout of overgrown flora held Tembo's attention for only a moment before his eyes returned to the naked, winged woman. She was proceeding to walk out into the desert. Tembo raised a hand and yelled, "No! Beautiful Adla, they are out there. They will capture you a second time."

The winged woman stopped her steps and pivoted in a calm manner. She simply nodded her head at Tembo before turning around and continuing her walk out of the realm of trees. Tembo followed her out of the woods, onto the desert, and into the hazy African day.

The winged woman looked up at the sky. Her glowing eyes scanned the light-blue firmament. She appeared calm, but Tembo sensed a subtle presence of urgency in her character. She turned to Tembo and stated in an echoing voice, "The moon remains single in the heavens. Sick and pale. I fear Ahmes failed in his task." Tembo was surprised the woman spoke in his native language. He looked up at the moon to observe its faint body. It was faded in composition against the pale blue sky like a ship sinking into the ocean. His vision was then pulled away as he witnessed the winged woman look out into the desert, raise her hands, and close her glowing eyes. The palm of her hand shined with a cobalt-blue aura.

Tembo backed away.

The woman opened her eyes. Tears snaked free as all of history played for her. She swung her hand toward Tembo. He backed away until a tree blocked his path. But Tembo continued moving his feet. He inched up the tree as his feet scraped its thick base, sliding down and digging into the border of where the gravelly sand blended with the forest's rich soil.

The naked, winged woman caressed his face like a blind person searching for familiarity. But things became too familiar as the events that transpired earlier in Tembo's day appeared to her. There came the face of the winged woman. It was worn by another. She was gagged and bound. She was beaten bloody. There were gunshots. She was pleading. A man's shadow crawled over her. Thunder, loud and shaking, boomed on a clear day. The woman's beautiful face was made ugly, fragmented and shattered.

Tembo trembled as the woman fondled his features. He watched, gasping, as the woman's expression turned angry. A glowing palm wrapped around Tembo's neck, and the winged woman lifted Tembo off the ground. His back scratched against the tree. The fabric of his uniform was not torn, but his skin tore and bled. Pain bit into him, pricking the nerves of his back. The naked woman tightened her grip, anger illuminating her face like the glow she wore when Tembo first came upon her.

Tembo retched, gurgling the last of his air. She loosened her grip for an instant only to pull his body toward her and slam it hard against the tree. She said through tears, "*You* helped them hold her down!" Her grip tightened. "She was strong and beautiful, even as you extinguished her life! Your mercy was not warranted!" The winged woman growled, "I have been in the form of light for so long, but I will wear her face with dignity!" Tembo choked. The world blurred to him, but the winged woman's face remained clear. Tembo decided to not fight against the judgment he was receiving, holding onto what little breath he could inhale. "And what's worse is that I know you!" the naked woman hissed. *"Scholar. Warrior. Governor. King. Father. Brother. Lover. All the good of Alkebulan made masculine and dressed in its finest, most perfect black suit. You, Ausar, the praises of masculinity that my mother and her sisters sang to me about with hands to chest, eyes a flutter, and breath as a gasp. Your light faded, perverted, and I should quiet your light now."*

The naked woman's clasp on Tembo's neck loosened. He breathed deep and desperate, appealing his acceptance of judgment. He knew what he'd done was wrong, and he was ready to accept his fate for it. Killing the woman as he'd done. Was it an accident or was it on purpose? Had he'd considered the poor woman broken and dead anyway? He'd believed she was. And that was his purpose when Doctor Coppens put the gun in his hands. He was going to put the woman out of her misery, and then take as many soldiers with him before they killed him. Instead, things turned out different. But here was an angel sent as judgment to extinguish the last of his life.

But the winged woman coughed as if a hand squeezed her neck. Her eyes lost their light, rolled back into her head, and then her strength evaporated. Her legs buckled and she passed out. Tembo and the woman dropped to the earth, Tembo toppling over her. He remained conscious. The winged woman was struggling to do so as she coughed and wheezed.

Tembo got to his feet and scooped the woman into an awkward cradle, her wings making the ordeal of carrying her cumbersome. Tembo took a moment to survey the African land. No German cavalry soldiers pursued. The ones who chased him as he ran into the sprouted forest were nowhere to be seen. Tembo carried the winged woman inside the woods. Her breathing eased. He approached the spot where he'd found her and laid her down. He sat on the ground next to her and felt her chest. She coughed a bit and Tembo said to her, "Easy, angel. Easy."

Her eyes opened. Their glow was dim. She put her hand over Tembo's. She asked in a disappointed tone, "What have my black men become?"

Tembo didn't know how to answer her. He looked away, asking himself the same question.

"I felt the history as I descended," the woman told him. "We have fallen harder than I from the sky."

"Are you an angel?" Tembo asked still looking away from her.

"I am Sekhet Nefer," she answered. "I am of the House of Ka Mauri. I was chosen to be configured in the alchemical chamber. I arrived too early. The sad pulse of the Earth pulled me to her. Here I am again. I have failed in my mission to destroy the world. My impact was not heavy enough."

Tembo looked down at the winged woman. "Destroy the world?" he asked. "Are you a demon or a devil?"

Sekhet looked at Tembo with a perplexed expression. "You inquire as if these words are interchangeable. Even so, you do not speak these words the way they are properly used. Under your definitions, as I can sense, I must answer, 'neither'."

Tembo didn't understand, but he accepted Sekhet's answer. He continued to interrogate her. "You have an Egyptian name—an ancient Egyptian name. Is that where you are from?"

"Yes, I am from Khem," she answered. "Its borders and boundaries are far different from what I sense, but it is the same land." She looked up at the canopy. "It is the year eighteen-eighty-three," she said as she closed her eyes. "The time counted from the birth of Lord and Savior Jesus the Christ, the falcon turned dove. The man of one-thousand years, and the changer of faces." She chuckled.

The sunlight scurried away. Darkness bloomed. Sekhet's body glowed with its cobalt-blue aura and provided light. Tembo looked around. He got to his feet, and just as he did, the sunlight reappeared. He looked down at Sekhet. The glow of her body dropped away again. There laid the naked and beautiful, winged, black woman.

"Well, can you explain this?" Tembo heard a voice speak in the German language.

Tembo spun around, looking for German officials walking into the forest.

"I can say this," a familiar voice answered. *"I would call this Germany's claim to Africa."* It was General Edsel. *"This will make things interesting. It will be a scramble for Africa."* The General continued. *"This cannot get out. Not this. Germany must maintain its claim to this area at all cost, even if that puts us at war with all of Europe, the world. From this day marked. Understood?"*

"Yessir."

"They are outside," Sekhet warned.

Tembo looked back at her. "They will make their way in here."

Sekhet shook her head. "We are protected. If they enter, they will not see us."

"Kill them!" Tembo ordered.

"I have another task," Sekhet said in a tired voice. "I must give you my eyes, and for that, I must rest."

"You wish to give me your eyes? Keep them. For now, know your place as an angel. These are devils—in my term and definition. It is your duty to smite them."

Sekhet bubbled with laughter. She covered her mouth.

Darkness swallowed the light. Sekhet's body glowed. Then the light consumed the darkness, and the winged woman's glow faded. She said to Tembo, "When the darkness comes, time has no meaning. It could be days, weeks, or months, or years that have passed."

Tembo opened his mouth to question, but someone else spoke.

"It's magnificent, General Edsel!" a man exclaimed.

"Yes, Chancellor," Tembo heard General Edsel's voice reply. *"We were holding a demonstration of sorts, and a black boy led us here."*

"That's when the rebels attacked?" the other inquired.

"Yes. And they killed Doctor Coppens," General Edsel reiterated with remorse. *"Not immediately, as reported, Chancellor Bismarck. He suffered excruciating pain for two days before he died of a terrible infection."*

"Ah, good," Tembo sneered. "I got you, bastard Coppens."

Sekhet asked, "You are happy?"

"Only if Adla The Beautiful can accept my offering to her," Tembo told her. "I have slain a demon in her honor."

"But what of all this, Chancellor?" General Edsel's question interrupted Sekhet's response to Tembo.

"The Portuguese have been calling for a conference laying out a proper divide of Africa among the European nations," the Chancellor answered the General. *"I believe we should entertain those black-blooded mongrels, the Portuguese. We should secure this land as ours. Make it legal. Is anyone else aware of this phenomenon?"*

"Only two others," the General explained. *"The soldiers that came across the find have been sequestered, and they will be neutralized to keep this knowledge hushed."*

"Just keep this out of the ears and sight of the British," ordered the Chancellor. *"Is that understood, General Edsel?"*

"I have to leave," said Sekhet, her voice breaking into the General and Chancellor's conversation. Tembo wanted to listen as the two German men discussed various legends and mythologies concerning "lilac comets" and "cobalt-blue falling stars." But Sekhet's voice overwhelmed their conversation. "I must fade and take the forest with me. Staying here brings suspicion. I put all of Alkebulan in even greater danger than she has seen and felt."

Tembo returned to Sekhet's side. He lifted her hand with both of his. He rubbed her hand against his cheek, humbly lowering his head. "I cannot accept a gift of any kind," he sighed. "Your eyes or otherwise. I am stained with sin. I am not clean. I have killed a woman. She wore your face. I have helped scar Africa. I deserve no prize."

"Your devils will do worse," Sekhet said to him.

"If I am to accept anything, please, give me the strength to kill the man named General Edsel. Give me strength to kill the entire army!"

"There is no need," Sekhet said with urgency. "You have made your offering to your Adla. Doctor Coppens, this demon's name," the winged woman reminded. "But if you wish to redeem Alkebulan, Africa as you call her now, you will do as I say. You will take my eyes." Sekhet pulled on Tembo's arm, bringing him close to her. "I ordain you, *Djedhi Khepri*, Keeper of Wisdom. And I will give you my eyes to keep."

Tembo started weeping. Sekhet embraced him.

"I have done so much wrong in so little time," he cried.

Sekhet comforted him, "Become my Wisdom Keeper, good man, and your burden will lift." Darkness came. Sekhet's body glowed. Tembo closed his eyes tight, his face close to her body. The darkness faded, and light returned. Sekhet's body ceased glowing. "The trees live because of me. I must fade them. All that will be left behind will be my eyes. You will guard them. You will create a lineage that closely guards them until the day they find use again."

"Will then you forgive me, dear angel?" Tembo asked. "Will your spirit fly to heaven and beg God for my forgiveness?"

Sekhet nodded. "I will," she said. "I will deliver your forgiveness to your Adla and all the gods and goddesses of the cosmos. You will find heaven when you pass."

Tembo believed Sekhet was teasing him. He lifted his head and retracted his hands. "Don't patronize me!" he hollered. He jumped to his feet and walked away. Sekhet watched him stomp off. She found the strength to rise and follow him. She called him, but Tembo continued through the woods. After ignoring several calls, Tembo heard a rushing sound like that of wings flapping. He turned and Sekhet snatched him up and lifted him high. She held him by the collar. Tembo felt his feet leave the ground. The woman's grip defied gravity as his body stayed level.

"Forgive me," Sekhet cried as her eyes became ablaze. "I have known you as infallible. Even when you made mistakes it was never so brutal, and never so violent against my image." Sekhet embraced Tembo. Her wings fluttered and she began to descend.

Tembo inspected the new area of the woods. There was a crystal-clean pond. Water ran down a massive rock, caressing its side and cascading below into the pond. Sekhet placed Tembo down into the sparkling waters. The water came up to his thighs. Tembo looked at Sekhet and perceived that she would follow him into the water, but the winged woman stayed afloat in the air. The tip of her left foot pointed down, and Sekhet lowered her body enough for the single foot to dip beneath the pond's waters. Two jeweled chalices made of gold appeared in Sekhet's hands. One of the cups was filled with water. The other was empty. Sekhet, while humming a haunting harmony, poured the water back and forth between the elegant chalices. Then one cup, empty, disappeared. Sekhet poured the contents of the remaining cup over Tembo. He tilted his head back and allowed the water to run over his face and down his neck.

Blood and scars washed away.

Sekhet's wings fluttered. A cool breeze swept over Tembo and his face dried. The naked, winged woman landed in the lake. She scooped water inside the chalice and then circled her finger over it. She continued her hum. Even when she ceased her harmony it still remained, resonating throughout the serene atmosphere.

Sekhet presented the chalice to Tembo. "Sip," Sekhet instructed. "A sip is all you need. I promise."

Tembo accepted the chalice and drew it to his lips, He tipped the chalice toward his mouth and swallowed the crystal-clear water. The water tasted like sweet wine to Tembo. He took large gulps to keep the taste alive on his tongue. The water's cool rush slipped down into him, and euphoria hugged him from the inside out. Tembo closed his eyes, tilted his head back and exhaled a wide smile. He dropped the chalice, and Sekhet caught the wine-cup before it hit the water. She took a moment to concentrate, and then the chalice disappeared. With her open palm, now empty, she caressed Tembo's face.

"I still feel the memory," said Tembo, eyes still shut.

"You will not forget," Sekhet said to him. "The memory will not cripple you, but you will remember."

Tembo opened his eyes. "I understand my judgment," he told Sekhet in a calm and accepting voice.

"This is no judgment," Sekhet replied. "Even if you are no longer innocent, you are not guilty." She then informed, "Adla will return to you in time. You will see her again. She will wear another black shape, but her spirit will be the same. You treat her well or your memory *will* cripple you. I swear that."

"I will treat her well," Tembo declared. "I will protect her. I will do better by her. I will stand up for her. She will not be mistreated. I, Tembo the Khepri, promise. I promise."

Sekhet smiled. Her wings flapped, and she lifted into the air and away.

Tembo followed her. He waded through the water, trudged up to the bank, and sprinted back through the woods. He returned to where he'd first encountered the winged woman. There she was, landing her feet against the earth with a soft touch. She lay flat on her back, and her wings folded around her like a cocoon. Inside the wrapping of her wings, Sekhet's body started to glow.

Tembo crawled through the remaining brush and sat by Sekhet's side.

The sun's light faded twice, and darkness greeted Tembo. He heard voices belonging to spectators of the sprouted phenomenon in the desert. Sekhet's body never ceased glowing. Darkness covered Tembo a third time. There were voices when the light returned, and Sekhet's body lost its glow. The voices disappeared.

Sekhet's wings opened. There was no glow in her eyes, but she was smiling, and it was bright enough to compensate for the loss. She reached up toward Tembo, and he embraced her hand with both of his. She closed her eyes, and she took one last breath. Light poured from underneath the lids of her eyes. Tembo watched as her body faded from existence. The soft, physical touch of her hand disappeared. Only two glowing spheres remained bobbing in the air where Sekhet's eyes would've been.

Tree by tree, the forest vanished.

The land sank and seared.

African sand poured into the wide, deep crater. The abundance collected under Tembo as he sat. He was lifted as the rise of gravelly sand filled the pit. He jumped to his feet but remained fixed. Africa's sands flooded the deep and giant scar and healed the land.

The two spheres of glowing light floated at Tembo's knees. They lifted until they were at the height of his chest. He watched as their glow twisted upward like the flames of a candle and then popped away leaving behind two precious, black gemstones. Tembo plucked them from the air and put them in his pocket.

Gunfire and rockets popped in the distance. Tembo turned in the direction of the sound. A riderless black horse galloped up to him. The animal was saddled and strapped with provisions, including a rifle. Tembo grabbed the reins and looked up at the sky. He nodded his head, and then he jumped atop the mount.

He felt inside his pockets. The angel's eyes were there. His experience was real. But he didn't know what to do next, or even how much time had passed. He wasn't hungry or thirsty, but he believed he had been outside of time for months, years. Maybe it was just a few days. He considered his options. "My uncle knows of such things. That crazy old wizard spooks everybody with his talk," he said to no one in particular. "I pray it hasn't been too long. I pray he's alive." He said to the horse, "To my uncle. That is where I will ride." He galloped away, but after a few strides he stopped and turned to where the sand had filled the earth's wound in absence of the sprouted forest.

Tembo thought about the winged woman and Adla, the beautiful.

"I promise," he said, and then continued toward the horizon.

Lilac smoke fell onto the scene like a curtain closing an act.

The lilac haze dissolved into a blurry darkness as Gordon opened his eyes, waking up from his vivid, history-driven dream. He clutched the *Nigrum Nigrius Nigro*, the ancient tome he now referred to as *'Spook'*. He swallowed once and opened his eyes wide, remembering his dream. His skin became cold, and his brow moist with small beads of sweat. He blinked and exhaled the sleep from his head.

Gordon loosened the grip on Spook and moved the book from his chest to the mattress. He sat up and breathed in and out to relax the emotions grappling him. When he was calm, he opened Spook and removed the goggles tucked inside. Gordon turned on the lamp next to his bed and stood. He made a quick glance at the clock. He was surprised to see that only forty minutes had passed while he dreamed of the last set of historical events. He didn't linger on the time passed. Instead, he put the goggles around his eyes, a daunting feat as he navigated around the wild bush of hair crowning him. But Gordon managed to slip the dark eyewear on his face.

He saw nothing special, but he was amazed at how clear he could see through the pitch black, shaded lenses made from the precious gems of the angel's eyes. Gordon lifted the lenses, resting them on his forehead. He exited with Spook in hand and returned to the basement. Gordon came upon the two glowing figures hard at work. He observed them from the stairs. The female made herself comfortable in the old, tattered chair. She was knitting what Gordon perceived as a black, elastic garment. He watched her dip a threading needle into the copper jar she'd brought with her through the glowing portal. A long, gooey, black stream was drawn out of the jar, dangling from the tip of the needle. Then the glowing woman sewed the substance into the elastic garment. Gordon realized that the garment was made from the gooey material, somehow made solid as the woman knitted with it.

Gordon turned his head and spotted the glowing man. His palms were held out to the floor, and as his body vibrated with an incantation, light issuing from his palms shaped the large mass of stone and other raw materials around him. Gordon's gaze went back and forth between the glowing man and the glowing woman, watching them work and craft. He pondered a theory about the two glowing beings, wondering if somehow they were Sekhet and Tembo. Even before Gordon placed the goggles back around his eyes, he knew that was unlikely. But he looked through the lenses anyway.

The light surrounding the man and woman disappeared. There in front of Gordon were two naked, black figures. Both the man and the woman appeared to be in their late thirties. The man was stocky and muscular with dark skin and a low, tightly curled cut of hair atop his head. The woman was the same color as the man. Her hair was thick, dark dreadlocks, however, and her feminine physique was voluptuous. Gordon felt uneasy peering at her, seeing every inch of her curve and figure. She was not Sekhet, and the man was not Tembo.

The glowing woman looked up just as Gordon turned to observe her. He flinched not so much at being caught staring at her naked body, but because of the thick, white, painted design on her face. The woman's face was drawn up to look like a skull. Beauty and terror were wrapped into a cosmetic mix on her countenance. She stood with a graceful movement, black elastic garment dangling from her arms like a deflated body removed of head and appendages. The threading needles stayed in her grip. The man, realizing the woman's movements, stopped his activity. Gordon saw that his face was painted just the same.

The woman walked away from Gordon. He watched her bare bottom and hips sway back and forth. Her dark, naked figure was just as bright as her glow. Gordon looked at the man. He thought he'd seen a scowl on the man's face as Gordon ogled what may have been his wife. Gordon, embarrassed, lifted the goggles from his eyes, moving them again to his forehead. The man and woman's glow returned the moment Gordon no longer viewed them through the goggles' shaded lenses.

The glowing woman placed the unfinished black garment and her knitting tools on the workbench. She turned and approached Gordon. She reached out a hand to him, and Gordon accepted. She led him off the remaining stairs and brought him to the chair, taking Spook from him. Her glowing flesh sang, insisting Gordon sit. Gordon complied. Again, she alerted Gordon to the far wall. Strands of glowing energy shaped as characters from an ancient language, swirled from her lighted fingertip. The ancient letters fluttered toward the far wall where they gathered into a bright ball that exploded into a scene of wonder and rhyme. Gordon watched attentive, eyes now ablaze with lilac brilliance. A new voice poetically narrated the scene. Gordon listened close, concentrating on the voice's sound. It was his voice, maybe an octave higher.

The nighttime animals walk the cosmos-pasture backwards
A maiden and water bearer as their shepherds
They hide behind the sun's shine, high in the sky
Glittering pricked out points in the firmament's cloth
We watch and decode their glimmer, eyes like moths to their flames

Them animals frolic with the sun and the moon's movement
Earth's rotation, we evolve around their influence
Degeneration after generation, them animals' emotions mock us
As they play tricks that pluck the chords of heart strings
Bubbling music bursts too loud for the soul to sleep
Single eyes, blurry with dust not blessed from the desert golem's touch
Wide awake, we shake restless and go breathless
Pondering the proper rites to help dim the nighttime animals' influence
Make starry animal sacrifice
We even look to the water bearer and his virgin wife to get the knife

Work, work, work to please the heavens and ease the ego
Make the most of the desert, tilling and tempering civilization
Architecture aligned properly with astronomy
City buildings' shapes and interiors mirror the body
All sounds ring through our temples
Perfect pitch and harmony
Clothes stitched to display the soul and humor the body
In mythology, we speak simultaneous – of gods and goddesses
Astrophysics and biophysical equations
Double triples the meaning, interpretation after mathematical interpretation
Methodical is obsessive. Meticulous mocks intelligence.
Nothing is done unless it pleases the heavenly black body
          Or Her stars, the moon, and sun

For this work, we drink our smiles. Pride becomes drunk.
Stumbles our ego – vanity remains among us – restless
The heavens gasp and are breathless
Thousands of tithes have us swimming against the tide
But in time, we spread our mathematics to the world
Civilization blossoms high and perfumes the heavens
We believe, without bended knee, that charity is in our presence
And the nighttime animals continue to frolic and mock us

We forget
Punishment

Neglect of Motherland covenant
Magic squandered. Magic only flickers. Sputters soft.
We sow our oaths
Growth civilized pride
We shed responsibility
And give culpability to superstitions
The ego blamed on bipedal reptilians
Tsetse, the leopard of Mbomba, from sky to earth
The clever leopard puts fire into mountains
Where birthed and set free, Tokoloshe and the red-eyed wolves

Cursed language created, banished and isolated
Unspoken in the cold, desolated – civilization disrupted
By spotted lambs fleeced of black wool
Superstitions take the physical
Mitered materiality – the reality of the matter at hand
That rocks the cradle of our civilizations
Open mouth, from the mount, pale shadows march as whirlwinds
With heart, we give lessons to tame them
Overtime, we are paid with enslavement
Chained to pale shadow system – our rebellion only changes the scenery of the system
A concrete jungle springs up among us
A grave where the living dead reside
Hollowed buildings, unaligned, stare blank with glassy eyes
A city of puzzles and mazes and tricks and riddles
Boggled dance, we limp and trip as pale shadows shade black from heaven's light
Further unravels the degeneration – black generation after black denigration
Whether absent or present, scarred black parents maim their children

Here I stand as tall as I sit, back bent
Watery, weak conjures as tricks
I daydream and grin
Of superstitions as a wish
Infatuated, I think of the water bearer's daughter, and I wish her no harm
She is heir to his firmament flagon of fermented waters
Her steps are dances, prancing across the sky
She smiles the sun and she exhales the stars in a breath
She wears her mother's cosmic color as her flesh
Her hair is a locked mystery with many twists
Black, puffy smoke that reflects the universe's abyss
They say
she will one day

dance with a king
as black as me
This story keeps my head and glory above the clouds
But I see the city riddled with puzzles when I look down
And the height of my circumstances scares me
I come down to Earth
Birthed through the clouds
My eyes pry answers from my environment
A puzzled city stares back at me, oblivious
Its bloodstream: confused colored citizens
Little black boys kill their youth to become men
Their speech a chorus of revenge on fathers absent
Little black girls too young for pangs of labor
Mimic absent father and absent-minded mother's behavior
A prison cycle worth its weight in slave wagers
Other colors are given green to grow in our gardens
While we sleep and eat our daily bread – baked in savagery
The lack of nutrients poisons us deep
Buried is the history. The system of slavery. The pale shadow's trick and ruse.
Buried so low as our souls hang low,
Our history can no longer be used as an excuse

I escape the city's loud landscape
And go where the traffic travels slow
Too much pride in the city's vibe
Keeps other black minds tied to the city
I ponder the water bearer's daughter's mythology
And so, my mind grows. I come to know:
There is something better than the current weather

Here I stand as tall as I sit, back bent
The sky, filled with turbulent clouds, assists the wind
with haunting the trees in the background
Shake! Shake! Shake!
The sun and the blue peek to give beauty to the day
Rough waters stream – scream tumultuous energy
A conflict outside
And within me
I am surrounded by passion and enthusiasm

I carry heavy sword that weighs more
Than my wiry frame

I, a slender black flame
Doused in doubt from the words
Dripped from my Father Zero
And my Mother Nothing's mouth

Gordon turned away from the wall. He pulled against a force, groaning until he let out a scream. The scene formed by the hieroglyphs vanished in a bright flash. Gordon looked at the cement floor, upper body hanging over the chair's left arm. The glowing woman's feet stepped into his view. Gordon looked up as she bent down to his level. He looked deep into the glow veiling her features. His eyes strained to make out the subtle contours of her face. He found her eyes and aligned his with hers. He asked, "Is that me?" His voice trembled with annoyance. "That weak…man-child?" he clarified. "I got too much heart to be interpreted like that," he said in defense. He managed a smile, but his voice remained defensive as he addressed, "Where's my muscle? Where's the representation of my spirit that kept me out of that knuckleheaded activity some of these fools find themselves in? C'mon, now!"

The glowing woman returned a smile that Gordon could barely see. She pointed to the wall and her illumination sang, "This is just the beginning. Watch and listen along."

Gordon returned his attention to the wall. A bright sphere of light twirled in midair. Gordon focused on the glowing ball. His eyes became bright with lilac luminescence. A bright flash jumped at him, and the poetically narrated scene returned to his vision.

I stand youthful as The Fool
With sword instead of stick
No home and parentless
The silence is loud
Far away. Here. The city is quiet.
I can think
So I drink and eat inspiration
And I vomit plans and ideas

I spy behind the blue
The twinkling hues
Of nighttime animals
I tame them with a glance
Instead of frolicking, they dance
More rhythm in them to move
And I'm in sync,

rather than at odds,
With their groove

Up to the sky, through the air
I, to the maiden and water bearer, declare
"I will serve your daughter. She, conceived in Heaven,
Born on Earth, the perfect Queen.
I will wear the galaxy around me and be
The blackest of light – I will become her knight.
We will walk hand-in-hand, civilizing the untamed land."

Too much past time – daydream pastime
Too much past the city's line
Devil swine take me away

I, surrounded by coppers
My mind thinks mercury and silver
My thoughts shine like a mirror
Conduct electricity, stir alchemy
I think of myself as deadly poison – I am five deadly venoms
And the proper medicine
My wiry, weak frame is not the true temperament
I am candle and wick. I am a slender, black flame
My black is gold
I know my proper rites
I lift eyes to the sky and declare,
"I will find your daughter. I will walk hand in hand with her,
And I will become her knight."

The scene broke away into hieroglyphs, and the basement's environment expanded into existence. Gordon sat up in the chair. A contemplative expression ran across his face. There was determination in his brittle, wiry-framed doppelganger, and he liked that. Gordon realized the glowing woman stood at his left, and he wondered how deep in thought had he been to miss her blazing physique. The glowing man stood at his right. In a deep bass tone, the glowing man's flesh ordered in song for Gordon to rise. Even after the heavy tone in the glowing man's 'voice' dissipated, there still remained a heavy beat like that of African drums.

Gordon rose. The glowing woman stepped in front of him. She held the black, elastic garment up to Gordon as if she was a tailor. The garment resembled a wetsuit to Gordon, and when he looked closer at the alchemically stitched apparel, he saw a moving galaxy with glimmering stars and cosmic clouds swirling on its face. Then the glowing woman moved aside. Both she and the glowing man stretched out a hand toward the sarcophagus-like structure in front of him. Their glow sang to Gordon, *"Alchemy for you. Alchemy for you. This suit stitched as one is for two."*

The black and gold structure, with thick, jungle vines attached to it like electrical wires and chords, opened. Gordon stepped forward, inspecting the pod's framework. Symbols of all sorts were carved into its side. The chamber's lid resembled the face of a West African mask. Gordon finished his approach and wiped his hand over the smooth exterior. He had seen the stone from which he believed this was carved, and he was impressed by the glowing man's craftsmanship. The stone had been transmuted. The chamber was black like onyx, and the gold was so well inlaid that Gordon considered the glowing man's power changed the stone's physical chemistry before shaping it into the capsule before him.

Gordon looked inside. The palm boughs, down feathers, and the many skins that were delivered earlier by the glowing man and woman lined the interior. It looked comfortable, and Gordon hoped it was, especially when the woman instructed in a pleasing consonance, *"Strip and get in. Strip and get in. Use your eyes inside. Use your eyes inside."*

Gordon hesitated. He didn't feel comfortable stripping naked in front of the glowing man and woman. Then he decided to equalize the situation as the two blazing figures walked closer to him. Gordon pulled the goggles over his eyes and grinned as their glow dulled to the color of their dark flesh. He felt better about stripping, though there was still awkwardness to it all. He expected the woman to hand him the cosmic-stitched garment. But she again directed for him to slip into the chamber.

Gordon took another peek inside. He noticed seven empty slots carved into the comfortable bedding. The slots aligned to his spine. The glowing woman's flesh sang, "There are seven missing. Find them. Find them." And then she again instructed, "Get in."

Gordon slipped into the chamber, a comfortable fit. The glowing woman and the glowing man stood over him. The chamber's lid opened wider, and Gordon wondered how its weight hadn't caused it to drop away.

Then he wondered why he was questioning mystical elements.

The glowing woman laid the cosmic garment over Gordon as if it was a blanket, and then she backed away. The chamber's lid slid shut on its own. Before the lid closed, Gordon heard the illuminated figures' flesh sing to him in unison, "Goodbye, new spirit. We must return to our children."

Gordon was about to speak when the chamber's lid closed. On the other side, the glowing figures walked back through the ovate, shimmering doorway. Once they exited the basement, the bright portal shrank from existence. The vines connected to the chamber, running up and through the walls, and also down through the floor, started resonating in various colors.

It was like a tanning booth inside the chamber. A lustrous, lilac light brightened the interior, wrapping Gordon in intense warmth, but never becoming too hot. The fabric of the garment laying over him started to bubble and liquefy, however. Melting, the garment washed over his body like a thick lather of soap. It spread and seeped into his pours.

Then Gordon heard a buzzing noise accompanied by a small prick tickling his shoulders. He didn't flinch from the sharp pokes. He turned his head as best he could, first looking at his right shoulder, and then looking at his left. A pale-purple light scratched the symbols of the Ka Mauri house on his right shoulder. There etched on Gordon's flesh was a black circle engraved with a black panther ready to strike. Behind the large, wild cat was a veiled, African woman swinging a whip made of horsetail. Next to her was an African man with a heavy sword held above his head.

On Gordon's left shoulder was drawn the symbol of the house of Dii Mauri. Again there was a large black circle incised into his flesh, covering his shoulder. Centered into the circular layout was an Egyptian, Sekhem scepter, the head of which resembled the crown of Osiris. Three seated men and three seated women, plus one androgynous seated person, were etched like numbers on a clock around the Egyptian scepter.

Gordon's flesh absorbed the remaining melted garment. The pale-purple beams finished their sketch. The bright lilac light dimmed and faded. The chamber opened, and Gordon rose, lifting the goggles off his eyes and to his forehead. Lilac smoke rose with him. Gordon hopped out of the chamber, his bare feet hitting the basement's hard cement floor. He stood tall, glancing at the tattoos drawn on either shoulder.

The vines attached to the chamber lit up. The basement shifted into a finished and furnished area. The subterranean room's cold murkiness dissolved and gave way to a pleasant and bright atmosphere. Gordon, standing naked, marveled at the change. Then he started thinking. The room was not the only thing that changed. Gordon lowered the goggles to his eyes. All but the lenses disappeared. The cut stone that remained, like the cosmic garment, liquefied and ran painless into his eyes like tears crawling backwards.

Gordon looked down at the floor, now covered with a lush carpet. He felt light, without weight. He lifted up as if standing on his tiptoes, and his body hovered a few inches off the ground. The black, cosmic garment seeped from his flesh like a ghost, airy and smoke-like. It swirled around him like a shadow, covering him, beginning at his feet and working its way up his body quickly. Gordon's blazing eyes widened in fear as the black smoke inched up his neck, nearing his mouth. He took one last breath, but then relaxed when he realized the black matter left an opening around his mouth and chin. The smoky garment solidified, wrapping around Gordon's frame as a tight, dark matter outfit. The dark garment, with a faint hint of a moving cosmos in its fabric, swirled up the rest of his frame, covering his face. White patterns appeared over his concealed countenance, giving the appearance of an African, male Chokwe mask. Though his nose was covered, he could breathe through the fabric.

Two lilac-glowing orbs burst through the mandorla-shaped eyes, combining into one. As a single orb, it positioned itself in the center of Gordon's forehead, resting atop a diamond shaped pattern where the pointed edges looped into circles. With his eyes covered by the cosmic cloth, Gordon kept them closed. His ability to see came through the lilac-colored orb swirling at the center of his forehead. His wild hair remained uncovered, sprouting up like a flame. Gordon's body dropped from midair. He landed on the floor, palms against the ground, crouched like a wild cat ready to spring on its prey.

Gordon stood up and inspected himself, admiring with a childish glee the skintight garment covering him. It hugged his body so close that he considered it might as well have been his skin. His fingertips glowed with a violet hum, widening his smile. He looked at the chamber and noticed Spook fastened to a shelf at the head of the sarcophagus. Spook's black mirror was up. Gordon walked over to the head of the chamber and folded his arms.

"Weak, wiry frame, huh, Spook?" Gordon said to the ancient, techno-mystical device. Behind the black garment, Gordon gestured with the raise of an eyebrow. "I'd rather call this nimble." Then Gordon looked up at the ceiling. "And I got instincts, Spook. Watch this. Watch what this spirit can do. Watch and see what this dark hero has to offer." He grinned and jumped into the air, arms out wide, hands limp at the wrists but fists balled tight. His legs bent upward.

Gordon's body flattened and expanded into black strands that spun around like charged particles orbiting an atom. There was a pop! Gordon's shadowy strands vanished, leaving behind a glittering burst of lilac-colored dust, and he reappeared on the garden level above. Gordon's suited and solid form appeared out of the black strands and glittering dust clouds. He flipped forward and landed soundly on his feet. He looked around, amazed at his mode of transportation from the basement, out of existence, and up into the garden floor.

Gordon looked up at the ceiling. He jumped up and struck the same pose as before. His body again shifted into black matter strands, swirling around like neutrons. A pop and a puff of lilac smoke signaled Gordon's disappearance. He again flipped forward into existence. He was now standing in the second-floor hall, having bypassed the parlor level altogether. Gordon walked into the front guestroom, over to the window, and moved the curtains aside, looking down on Fable Avenue.

Gordon stepped on the radiator stationed in front of the window. He crouched down and pressed his fingers against the glass. He pushed. Once. Twice. A third and fourth time. His fingers became impalpable like air, and they passed through the window's glass. Gordon extended his entire arm through, and then he tried the rest of his body, slipping through the window as if it was open. He stepped out onto the ledge, solid again, and stood tall.

Gordon looked up. He jumped, posed, shifted, and popped out of existence.

Now he was on the roof of the brownstone.

Gordon looked up at the clear sky. He crouched down and whispered a quote, *"Dooley is a lilac flame, fluttering and flickering and shooting up into the sky."* He grinned and recited Jimi Hendrix, *"Excuse me while I kiss the sky!"*

Gordon's body burst into a scorching, lilac flame. He lifted into the night sky with a dazzling streak of smokeless fire swirling behind him as a tail. He didn't care who might see him, though it was too late at night for spectators. The few people populating the streets mistook Gordon's flight as a shooting star, and they marveled at the spectacle just the same. *"Look,"* some of them said. *"Make a wish!"*

Like the previous night, the cosmic backdrop of stars played music for Gordon, now Dooley. The rhythm pounded against him as if he was in attendance to a rocking funk concert. His body turned into a billowing, ghostly form as he penetrated the boundary of Earth's atmosphere and Earth itself dropped away. His legs were as one, straight and swirling into a long, lilac stream. As Dooley flew up higher and higher, the sun greeted him. But the stars seemed to back further away from his approach.

Dooley slowed his ascent to a pause. He hovered in space at peace, bobbing as if in water. He saw the moon. It was craggily, looking brittle and sickly. Gordon soared higher. Up, up, and up until Earth became a distant memory, a tiny speck miniscule to all of creation.

Dooley again slowed his ascent to a pause. He did not move as a black hole opened in front of him. It twirled with black energy. Lighted beings, no different from him, drifted from the cosmic aperture. They were male and female figures alike. Their bodies shimmered black with a gold lining. They too had one single, glowing eye centered on their foreheads. Instinct informed Dooley that he could mimic their appearance, but he decided to remain with his smokeless, ghostly mien.

The dark, cosmic spirits encircled Dooley and danced around him. They sang in a language that could only be described as mathematics. When they finished, they bowed. Then they returned to the black hole, and as the last of the dark spirits entered, it swirled from existence.

Dooley peered down. Even from his great height, he spotted Earth. An instinct tickled the back of his neck. He dived, streaking through space as a shooting star. Dawn was just beginning to bloom when he returned to Earth. But Fable Avenue was not his destination. Dooley's essence streaked across the early morning sky, blazing over the Caribbean Sea, Jamaica bound. He landed high in the hills at an altar dedicated to the Jamaican-national hero Queen Nanny. He was greeted by a congregation of wayfarers come to pay homage. But there was a family waiting specifically for Dooley's arrival.

The five-year-old daughter, held by her father, pointed to the sky and yelled joyously, *"Kibaru! Kibaru!"* The father set the little girl down as Dooley's lilac-glowing spirit hovered above the people.

The mother, standing next to their seven-year-old son, handed the little boy a tattered book. She patted the young boy on the back, signaling him to move forward. "With your sister," the mother instructed.

The little boy waited for his sister to join him. She grabbed the book with one hand as her brother held it with the other. They raised the book up, issuing it to the glowing spirit above them.

Dooley looked down, inspecting the book. He descended closer. His eyes never left the book. With his fiery tail flapping and aimed toward the sky, Dooley put his face close to the old, leather-bound tome. His instinct pricked the back of his neck. "Seshat's Songbook…?" he asked.

The children, son looking anxious and the daughter giggling, turned to their parents. The mother answered, "Yes, good spirit. My family has held onto that book for generations, now. A woman, Haitian, on travel, performed a ritual two nights ago and said a spirit will be in the sky on this mornin'. Her say him will greet our hero, Queen Nanny. Her tell I to greet you here with the book. Because I am of the great Nanny line."

"For me?"

"Yes, good spirit," the mother said. "To aid you and all them on the Fable Avenue street there. Not all that heard the music come there. Some stay where they are, waiting for their time. All the islands of this sea have them their own Fable Avenue communities. All the islands of this sea, seen and unseen alike have their rites. Tonight, them politics of this island don't hold us back from celebrating the good spirit. We dance for the Grand Wish, the Great Conjure Work."

Dooley accepted the tome. He turned his body upright, tail whipping against the ground. He made a courteous bow with his head as he held the book close to him with both glowing hands. "Thank you," he said to the family. "Thank you," he said again to all the people gathered.

"Thank *you*, good spirit" said the mother back to Dooley. "Go, and be loved."

Dooley nodded and then flew away. Across the sea and up the eastern coastline he went. He returned to the roof of his Fable Avenue brownstone. The smokeless fire dropped away, and he returned to his black suited form. He made a single thought, and his body shifted into the wildly whipping strands of black matter. There came a pop followed by a burst of glittering lilac dust. Dooley flipped into existence inside the brownstone basement. He placed the songbook atop the chamber and began putting on his clothes before making a single thought to dissipate the ghostly, silk and skintight suit from his body.

Gordon Goodspeed opened his physical eyes and took a deep breath. Something stirred in him. He was anxious, excited by the night's events. But he took long breaths in and out to relax. He remembered the calm of space, the stars, the dark spirits and how they danced around him. He focused on how small he was to the universe's womb, even with this new great power he possessed. With this, Gordon's excited spirit settled, and the stir inside him simmered down. He opened his eyes, walked to the chamber and took up the songbook. He opened it and saw written in an ancient and forgotten text, the poetic narrative shown to him by the glowing woman.

The back of Gordon's neck tingled as an instinct occurred. Gordon took two steps back. He extended his arms and let the book go. It dangled in the air, opened to the last scripted page. Gordon took one more step back and dropped to his knees. His eyes flickered and flashed with an intense brilliance. He bowed, putting his forehead against the ground. Raising upright, Gordon spoke, "I am humbled by the stars and all of heaven. I am humbled to be embraced by the black body. I understand. I am a wiry frame. But I am a Kibaru. I am a Zin Kibaru. I swim the cosmic waters of Nun. I am an astral djinn, a Lwa of music and words. Tell me my story. Tell me my mythology."

The floating book flipped to empty pages that didn't remain empty for long. An invisible pen scrawled a script in a glowing lilac-colored ink. The bright characters swirled together as if a heavy wind blew across the page. They gathered into a furious and nebulous cloud of sparkling energy. A bright flash jumped into Gordon's eyes, and then he heard and saw the continuing poetic, story of his wiry-framed doppelganger.

I arrive
Inside the city
With devil swine
I am calm. Not kicking.
Delivered to my cage
Disguised as a building
It houses so many

In house. A cage. In room. Just the same.
My thoughts sweat my brow
Wet weather knocks on window
Drops from sky, I believe the tears
In my eyes are distant cousins to the rain,
The clouds cry for reasons just the same

I understand. I am.
A wiry frame of a man.
I am. My circumstance.
Circumcised blind of my manhood
Mother Nothing and Father Zero
Broke my hands good
And they healed limp

Mother Nothing shouts obscenities
That sound as absurdities
She walks away, nose up at her history
Skeptical that she was ever a queen
Her head hangs and swings low like a sweet chariot
It's humility of slavery that possesses her memories
She bows to pale shadow authority
And asks how much they're willing to pay
For all fourteen of her husband's pieces
His penis is priceless
Mother Nothing walks backwards through the story of Isis
Littering the world with her husband's parts – mocking man and wife
One flesh, my mother

Father Zero believes himself a circle
A revolution
He is a cycle of abuse
A black, paler shade of shadow
Double duty, acting like devil swine

He polices family
Iron fist, and I know personally
His alchemy makes me golden
Shine black and blue
The system injects him with possessions
Breaking his family earns him protection
A good example, outstanding black citizen

I count my blessings
At least my Father Zero is here
Other father zeroes are superheroes
With powers to disappear
But still I blush green with envy

Maybe I should be grateful
For the lessons my parents taught me:
Question no authority
The foundation here is family
Slavery is not slavery
Bow gracefully to my enemy that shows no mercy
Only attack when the perpetrator looks like me

I take seat – rain-blurred window
I have a first class view to watch
Black cage-city residents walk in sleep
Speech, in circles – feet walk the same pattern
My throat cries a soft sigh

My heavy sword
Hidden before
Devil swine marched me
Here

My imagination donates a sword to me
Same make and shape, but lighter in weight
I swipe the air and watch the mirror
Warrior pose perfect
Reversed reflection, I begin to question
Is the world beyond the mirror perfect?

Right hand is left hand
Sleep walking, sleep deprived black citizens

Conscious and rested?
Father Zero
Mother Nothing
Less of the same; more of their forgotten titles
And names?
Pale shadows, ghosts and memories
For this I melt the mirror to a liquid
And drink the reflection for inspiration

Liquid looking glass refreshed
I see all that came before me – our story
Forgotten covenant to Motherland
I understand now that I am the mystery
I am the deeper meaning
Locked inside all mythologies

My body, the temple, I stand at my altar
Change through ritual, and alter my image
Electrolyte liquid looking glass candle magic
I sweat oil, lather baldhead
Liquid mirror inside me
I reflect on tangled, dreaded thoughts
Set them ablaze
My sprouted puffs of smoke scream coiled
Natural hair hollers tangled, dreaded – loud
Makes black hippie-gypsy guitar players proud
I beam sunshine all the same

I look through rain that stains
The windowpane
The blurry cage-city sleeps wide awake
No light, even with sunshine
I gaze up into the rainy, gray sky
I wait. The clouds part before my eyes.
Sunshine bows humble, stepping away
The day fades to night
And I ponder, curious, the stars' light
Still configured as is
To the agreement we live under,
And have cosigned with
But I decode a new alignment

The stars' light glows
A soft voice
No shouts. No growls from nighttime animals.
A pleasant purr
Voices sing, softer
A new testament from the stars
Their light croons a conjure
They chant, "You see us stars as we are.
Who are you?"

I think in mind
Song and rhyme
Up to the stars
Little daughters and suns of night

"I am Kibaru."

A bright light devoured the scene, and then it retracted, leaving behind the magically renovated basement. Gordon bowed again, eyes closed. Upright, with eyes open, the bright light possessing his eyes faded to the soft swirl of pale-purple in his irises and pupils. Gordon stood and reached out to catch the book as it descended slowly from where it floated. He observed the new script before placing it closed atop the chamber.

"I know I'm supposed to be humble, and all, Spook," Gordon said to his ancient, technological companion. "But this funk got more than a three on it," he grinned. "I mean, can you imagine Dooley in your funk?"

Gordon stepped away from the chamber. He decided to do things the old fashion way and walk up the stairs to the bathroom on the second floor. His steps were hurried, however, and when he arrived in the bathroom he removed his sweatshirt and tank top and washed. *A quick wash at the sink,* he thought to himself. *I'll take a shower later. Papa Solomon and the matriarchs have to hear about this first.* He brushed his teeth, rinsed his mouth, and put his tank top and sweatshirt back on. Gordon collected his wallet and keys, and then he left the house to tell his story.

The weekend passed. Gordon recalled all its moments, eyes on the sky out the window as he sat in his European Literature class. Professor James Brede, so most of his students believed, prattled on about Samuel Beckett's *Waiting for Godot*. Gordon paid no mind to anything around him, teacher or student. He grinned, thinking about having gone beyond the blue illusion of Earth's sky. He'd seen the calm black backdrop of space, hovered through it, floating as a celestial spirit. He'd gotten that much closer to the stars. He had spirits dance around him. He was a spirit himself, and he used his newfound aptness not only to greet and become initiated by the heavens, but also to play tricks to create superstition around the area. As Dooley, and as invisible as he was intangible, he flew through various neighborhoods and sabotaged criminal activities.

He stopped muggings. He stopped gang violence. He stopped assaults. Sometimes he showed himself, scaring the perpetrators. But he never allowed them to tell their tales. He influenced their minds to do better with their lives, and then he made sure they would forget his presence as his spirit departed. Some crimes were unforgivable, and after interrupting them, he convinced the victims to testify, and the assailants he made too weak to retaliate. Again, he disappeared without a memory of himself to linger.

But the most fun Gordon had was against the numerous youths who wore sagging pants far below their waist. He whirled around them like wind and dropped their pants all the way to their ankles, one after the other. He then spirited away, the only detectable element of having been at the scene was his gust of wind.

Papa Solomon and all three matriarchs warned Gordon about playing hero. He would exhaust himself said Maman Anansi, and the others agreed. Indeed, with every trickster act he performed, once he'd returned to his house on Fable Avenue, the spirit that brewed inside him stirred his senses. He sought his chamber, but it offered little relief, though he did find better rest there than in his bed. Madame Jeliya performed more rituals on him, but like any form of relief, the rituals' strength dulled.

Sunday night he popped home to Harlem. Without either his father or brother being aware, he gathered several piles of comic books and popped back to Brooklyn to study his childhood heroes. Popping that great a distance riled the spirit within him. He rested in his chamber, but he hadn't been to sleep since receiving his complete change and journey to the stars. Gordon wasn't tired, though. Instead he daydreamed about going again beyond the illusion of the sky. He was addicted to the heavenly black body and all her stars.

Professor Brede's voice played ever so faint to Gordon. "The play opens with Estragon sitting on a mound. He's struggling to remove a boot," said the professor, his back to his students, writing on the blackboard the names of characters from the famous play by Samuel Beckett. He turned and faced his class, adjusting his glasses on his forty-two year-old olive-skinned, chiseled face. He scratched his forehead, appearing nervous, but it was just his way. He made a slight adjustment to his raven locks that curled at his brow. "Now he, Estragon, eventually gives up. He tries again, but is still unsuccessful. As Vladimir enters, Estragon mutters, '*Nothing to be done.*' Now, what could he mean by this?" Professor Brede stood upright with a boyish smile. He peered through his glasses at the class, looking at them with a desperate gaze. His students squirmed and ducked away, trying not to be noticed. He spotted Gordon whose attention was captured by the sky outside.

Gordon's instinct tingled and buzzed up and down his neck. He turned his head. Alert, he sat up. A quick focus using his instinct replayed time's audio. He heard Professor Brede speaking about the play's subject matter. He reheard the question, but it wasn't quick enough.

"Mister Goodspeed," Professor Brede asked with a smile, walking closer to him. "Are you with us? We're waiting for you, for your answer."

Gordon wriggled in his seat, playing up the fact that he was distracted rather than instantly answering the question. He responded, "That answer can be found in what happens next, I believe."

"And what happens next, Mister Goodspeed?" Professor Brede asked with curiosity.

"Vladimir says he's come 'round to the same conclusion," Gordon continued as prompted. "Nothing must be done, and that's how the two spend their time for the rest of the play. The motif of doing and finding nothing repeats with Estragon finally removing his boot, looking inside and finding nothing. Vladimir does the same with his hat; he takes it off and looks inside to find nothing."

"Excellent, Mister Goodspeed!" beamed Professor Brede. "I was beginning to think I was teaching high schoolers, everyone looking so disinterested." He quipped to the class, "Is this class just a requirement for some of you? And you all wonder why I keep a glass of wine on my desk, sipping on it through the day." To the students' knowledge, it was doctor's orders. Professor Brede played up a sigh. "Ah, they don't allow prayer in school, but I say a prayer for you all every day. And if not for you, for me."

Low chuckles bubbled up around the room.

Then Professor Brede noticed a curiosity about Gordon. He stepped closer to him, focused on Gordon's lilac eyes. His face expressed his perplexity, and Gordon backed away in his seat. Professor Brede wasn't the first outsider to notice his eyes and inquire in a voice hovering between curiosity and concern, "Are you feeling okay, Mister Goodspeed?"

Gordon's instinct quivered. A thought not his own played in his head. It was a voice. *His weird people probably burned his eyes in some devil ritual,* it said. Gordon turned his head and spotted a male student looking at him. Doug Wallace.

Gordon turned back to Professor Brede, who was now standing over him, and answered, "I didn't burn my eyes, or something weird," he paraphrased Doug's intrusive thought. He saw, in his peripheral, Doug's face contort with a guilty look. "Just an odd happening," he continued. "I went to the doctor for it. He had nothing to say except that I was healthy. But what does he know? It's all guesswork in a white coat. There's nothing to be done here."

There came mild laughter from Gordon's fellow students. Professor Brede ignored it, taken by the soft-purple color of Gordon's eyes. The professor exhaled, "Magnificent, aren't they? Few people have violet eyes. Actress Elizabeth Taylor was one."

Gordon's instinct tightened like a collar around his neck as Professor Brede's image wiggled like a bad television transmission. This odd visual occurred when curious outsiders to the Fable Avenue community were inches away from overstepping their bounds. But Professor Brede instead took a step back. His image stopped wavering and became solid. He turned and said, continuing his lecture, "Further along in the play, these two characters, Estragon and Vladimir discuss repentance." He pivoted and faced the class as he passed the front row of desks. He was talking, but no longer in the excitement of his lecture. His voice returned to normal after a moment. He continued, "Their discussion includes the topic of the two thieves crucified on either side of Jesus Christ. Now, make note about this discussion, class. The play has numerous Biblical references. This is the first to stand out." He took a breath and said in an assuring voice, "This isn't about what you believe in. Now, I'm not trying to convert any of you who may not be Christian, or of any particular faith. I'm showing you the zeitgeist of Samuel Beckett's time. These are clues to his thoughts and ponderings in what some have said is a nonsensical play about two guys sitting around shooting the shit and waiting for some guy named Godot."

More laughter bubbled from the students, waking them up.

Professor Brede jested in a charming way, "Hey, while I'm here, I might as well teach you some things; and while you're here you may as well learn why someone takes the time out to write all this."

A female student asked, "Why disguise all this in some vague, nonsensical play? Was there a threat to have a view or talk about God?"

Professor Brede answered, "That's a good question, Anna. And that could be the answer: the fear of being ridiculed, or worse, for a thought an author, or any artist for that matter, wants to express. Miller did this with his work *The Crucible*, using the Salem witch trials as a way to talk about the McCarthyism witch hunts for the House of Un-American Activities." He raised his shoulders and hypothesized, "Or, maybe the author is just trying to be creative. Maybe the author doesn't even believe in what he or she is writing, but, they know it's the hot topic of the day—and they have a creative way of presenting it. An easy cash grab. Whatever the reason, it's within these Biblical allusions that we find the evident central theme of the search for and reconciliation with God or finding salvation. There is more than one occurrence of the characters yelling, *'We're saved!'* when they feel that Godot may be near. You can even look at the title and see 'God' in 'Godot'."

Gordon returned his attention to the sky. His instinct would alert him of any academic distractions should they present themselves. The distractions did come, but Gordon's answers were prompt this time around. One of his answers started a debate in class. Professor Brede was happy to see his students engaged.

Class ended. Professor Brede, while taking a sip of his wine, thanked Gordon for providing an engaging debate in class. Gordon walked away with a grin and feeling free. He wandered through campus, using his instinct to find his purpose in meandering. He came to the wide, grassy field where the students gathered between classes. A few trees populated the area. He chose a tree that was bright with sunset-colored leaves. He stepped into its shade, spotting another tree not too far off.

There was Fey Forrester. Her dark skin glistened as bright as the sunset-colored leaves of the tree she sat under, almost as if she reflected their glimmer. Her dark afro was cut low, looking like a woolly sun just beginning its peek over the horizon. Circular reading glasses covered her brown eyes.

Fey curled up with her sketchbook. Gordon's instinct deduced that she had just gotten situated, and his instinct also stayed his movement. He leaned against the tree and observed Fey. He saw her look around. He looked away, setting his book bag on the ground and taking a book from it. He pretended to read. He focused, and an incant veiled him. He wasn't invisible, but he didn't stick out.

Fey put headphones in her ears that were attached to an MP3 player. She looked around again. Gordon put his spying eyes on the open book in his hands, peering up and over the top of the book every-so-often. Fey was whispering words. He didn't consider that she was singing along to whatever tune was playing. It was as if she was talking to the sketchbook. A prayer or incant perhaps, Gordon considered.

Fey opened her sketchbook and four colorful sprites leapt out of the book. Purple. Blue. Jade green. The largest yumbo was silver with cobalt-blue wings. It perched on Fey's shoulder as the other three took to the sky, spiraling unseen through the field. Fey spoke as she bobbed her head. Gordon knew she wasn't singing a song. He doubted if her MP3 player was even playing. It was all a disguise. A cover for her to converse with the otherworldly creatures she conjured from her sketchbook.

Gordon shoved the book back into his school bag. He gripped the straps and jumped to his feet. One step forward and his instinct paused him. He did not move. Instead, he thought a moment. Gordon considered that if Fey was shielding even his eyes with an incant, then this was her private moment. His blessed, lilac-colored eyes intruded on that moment. But Gordon couldn't help but steal unseen glances, taking joy in her moment, despite the imposition. Gordon stepped away, walking to the library.

Fey spied Gordon retreating. She watched as his frame became smaller and smaller in the distance. She called her airborne yumboes to her. They dived into a blank, open page, and then the silver yumbo with the cobalt-blue wings followed. Fey tucked her sketchbook away inside a bag. She wrapped her headphone wires around her MP3 player and placed it next to her sketchbook. She put her reading glasses in a case, stuffed that too into her bag, and then stood to pace after Gordon.

Gordon sat in the library at an unoccupied computer at the end of a row. He signed into the computer using his college ID and loaded up the Internet. To pass time he, typed *'Joseph Pepper'* into a search engine. Articles expressing what he already knew popped up. Joseph Pepper's birth and background and death were in bulk. His life as a spiritual advisor was typed up with a cynical tone coursing through the few articles he read. The articles described the *'alleged philosopher'* as chasing tall tales and legends. Gordon changed his search. He typed *'alchemical chamber'*. Nothing specific popped up. He scrolled through a list of articles containing both words, but never were they paired together or did they explain what he possessed in his newly furnished basement. Gordon thought of other happenings he'd experienced through vivid dreams or wide awake, but he figured no search would give him any more insight than his own experiences.

"This machine sure ain't Spook," Gordon remarked to himself.

A shadow stepped into his peripheral view. Gordon's instinct didn't stir or buzz. His head turned slowly, and he looked up. Fey Forrester was standing over him. A thin, radiant glow of sunlight outlined the left side of her body. The sun's wide beam, coming through the glass window at the far end of the library, looked like two glowing arms presenting Fey Forrester like a butler would an arriving guest at a lavish estate. Even brighter was the look of surprise on her face. Her eyes and mouth widened as the emotion, which Gordon interpreted as shock, crossed over her in what appeared to be slow motion.

But Gordon stared instead of stirred. He wondered had he done something wrong to her. Had she known he'd peeked into her private moment with her yumboes? Had she calculated that he'd looked beyond her incant to hide them from the world?

Fey's astonished appearance paused. She bent forward. Her eyes looked up and scanned the sea of people busy at their computers. Then she straightened. Gordon realized she had been, and continued to be, inspecting his lilac-colored eyes.

"Happy birthday, Mister Goodspeed," she said to him. She paused between each word as if they were separate sentences. She was so transfixed by his eyes.

Gordon stood, slow as it was, and put his arms around her. "Thank you, Fey. Thank you." Fey didn't move. She kept her arms close to her chest, holding a book. But Gordon hadn't given her much time to react to his embrace. He backed away and said, "I thought I was in trouble by the look on your face. All types of things were going on in my mind."

"Your eyes, Gordon," Fey expressed in a whisper. In an even lower voice she said, "You got the brew in you. My grandmother talks about such things that are supposed to happen."

"Good," Gordon responded. "I'm glad to hear that. Please, have a seat."

Fey swiped an empty chair and pulled it close to Gordon's computer station. Both sat. Fey became attentive, but her eyes continued to inspect Gordon's. "What you been tellin' the regular folk 'round here 'bout them eyes, Mister Goodspeed?"

Gordon exhaled and smiled. "I've fielded the same question over and over since I got up on campus. I just tell 'em I don't know. Went to the doctor, he said I was fine. It can happen, eye color change."

Fey reached out a hand. Then she retracted. "Is it okay?"

"Yes. Go ahead," Gordon assured. "Outsiders reaching for a touch gives me the shakes, though."

"Oh," Fey said, defeat in her voice. "I'm not exactly…"

"You're not an outsider to the community, Fey," Gordon said to soothe her. "I'm talkin' about regular folks." He took her hand and guided it to his face. "There. Not even a tingle."

"Brew!" sang a child-like voice.

Fey sat back and rolled her eyes. "Oh, God," she said.

Fey's bag started to wiggle. It opened. The silver yumbo with the cobalt-blue wings crawled free. She climbed up Fey's back and perched on her shoulder. Panic splashed on Gordon's face. He looked around, waiting to see odd or frightened reactions to the yumbo's bright appearance.

"Relax," Fey told Gordon. "Silver has an incant around her," she whispered. "No one can see her." Gordon looked at the yumbo named Silver. She smiled at him, lost in his lilac eyes. "But I guess you can see through the incant with them eyes, Mister Goodspeed." Then she turned to Silver and scolded playfully, "However, trying to explain why my bag was moving like I got a puppy in it is another story." Silver looked apologetic. "And she's supposed to be the older, more mature one," Fey started her wording looking at Gordon, but turned to Silver and emphasized her last words with the same playful scold in her tone.

Gordon nodded and grinned with his eyes fixed on the yumbo. Then he said to Fey, "I need your help, sister." He suggested, "Let's talk outside."

Fey said to her yumbo, "Silver, stay perched." The yumbo remained still, gripped to Fey's shoulder as she stood. She and Gordon left the library and made their way back to the wide-open field.

Away from regular folk, Gordon told her, "Fable Avenue needs your grandmother's help, Fey." His words fell onto one another, jumbled and garbled. Fey took a moment to catch up with them. The statement made sense after her mind separated the words into distinct sounds. Gordon stopped walking. He saw Silver react to his words, looking at Fey and waiting for her reaction. Her face was like stone as she pondered bringing this information to her grandmother. "I know your grandmother's angry. She's been upset for going on thirteen years now. I remember…" then Gordon considered that Fey remembered too, even more so. He changed his words. "The spirit inside me can be unstable. You know spirits; they don't like to be trapped. When this spirit stirs, I get excited, overwhelmed. My emotions become tenfold on top of tenfold *multiplied* by tenfold. It's like a panic attack on top of a panic attack *multiplied* by a panic attack."

"I get it," Fey said grinning at Gordon and shaking her head. She again inspected Gordon's eyes. Her grin disappeared, and her demeanor became a still emotion. Then her eyes were sad as if she felt sorry for Gordon. "You need a ritual to soothe you."

Gordon nodded. "Yes, I do," he admitted. "Madame Jeliya asked me to seek out your grandmother for a personal ritual," he continued. "She will help, right?"

Fey paused, again thinking. She said after a while, "I don't know all the politics, but I know it all ended with bad happenings in my family, to say the least." Silver put sad eyes on Gordon as the little sprite remembered her steps into that tragic night, conjured by Fey's tears. She tried hard not to remember all that happened, but she did. The yumbo knew, however, that because of a lingering incant, Fey only had feelings, blurred recollections. "My father disappeared," Fey stated. "My mother was affected terribly. My grandmother, she…"

"I know, Fey," Gordon interrupted as Fey's words quickened with rising emotions. "And I mean no disrespect, sister. I just need you to talk to your grandmother. Please."

Fey looked away from Gordon. He expected the grim air to continue haunting her, but instead, a warm smile appeared on her face. She looked up and admitted, "I wanted to live in the old house when I started school here in Brooklyn. It's the whole reason I chose this school." She said looking at Gordon, "You know I come all the way here from Mount Vernon? Talk about a commute, even if I drive." She chuckled, and Gordon smiled at the sentiment.

"You still can," urged Gordon. "Live here," he clarified. "At your old place. No one's lived there. It hasn't even been rented out."

"My grandmother still owns it," Fey informed as a matter-of-fact. "She pays the taxes on it. She needs to rent it out. It's not like she can sell it."

"She could," Gordon stated. "She could sell it to Maman Anansi or Papa Solomon."

Fey made a face at Gordon. She retorted, "You know my grandmamma ain't gonna do that." Then Fey retreated back to her contemplation, eyes on the ground. Silver looked at the both of them. Back and forth went her large eyes until the perched yumbo's gaze remained on Fey. The young woman said to Gordon, "I'll talk to her. I'll tell her about Fable Avenue's progress. Your eyes. But I can't make any guarantees about what she'll do."

Gordon said relieved, "As long as you talk to her, Fey. Thank you."

Then Fey mentioned, "I have to run. I have Professor Brede."

Gordon snapped his fingers. "Just came from y'man's class."

"Not y'mans," corrected Fey. "Y'girl. His wife. Jacquelyn Brede. Art History."

"Oh, yeah. Right," Gordon replied. "She's always popping into class, bringing him something he's forgotten. Smart guy, but absent minded."

Fey agreed, though she'd never taken Professor James Brede's course or interacted with him, so she didn't know exactly what she was agreeing to. But she considered Gordon must've known what he was talking about. She ordered Silver back into her bag and into the sketchbook. "And don't show yourself during class. That incant around you will probably have faded by then, you hear." Silver did as told. Fey assured Gordon that she would be in touch. They exchanged phone numbers, and Fey walked away.

Gordon watched her. His eyes locked to her feminine frame's sway. Fey's bag ruffled. Up popped Silver with a scowl on her face, waking Gordon from his stare. He looked away, grinning guilty. He'd traveled to the stars, but there were still some things that kept a growing boy grounded.

Professor James Brede knocked on the open door of his wife's empty lecture hall. He stepped inside after she looked up and noticed him. He closed the door behind him and tapped three times against it.

The door locked.

James walked down one of the aisles, leather jacket slung over his arm, and a bag in his grip. He removed his glasses and his face changed. It widened and became bereft of its olive pigment. He swiped at the single, dark curl hanging against his forehead, and there again was a change. His straight, raven locks shifted to loose curls and bled their color away to a strawberry-blonde tint.

"Stanley," Lucretia called to her husband from behind her Jacquelyn Brede charade, which consisted of glasses, long white hair and wrinkles where her preserved flesh had none. Her façade wasn't an old crone. She was beautified with wisdom lines and grace.

Stanley Fallows rested his bag and jacket atop a desk. He folded his glasses and tucked them into his shirt pocket. He kissed his wife on the cheek and she warned, "Someone could see through that window on the door, Stanley. They'd think I was having an affair with a strange man."

"It's a gentle kiss, Lucretia," Stanley said to her. "I'm not having my way with you on the desk, for goodness sake." The two of them chuckled at his commentary. Stanley was relieved to see his wife relaxed, considering the news he was bringing her. He mixed in a groan with his laughter, pulled up a stool, and propped himself down. "Ah, I've become lazy, Lucretia."

Jacquelyn addressed her husband, "How so, Stanley?" She glanced at the doors. There was fifteen minutes before her class began. She was thankful not to see students gathering at the door, peeking in on them. She then faced her husband.

Stanley never lost his grin, even when he informed his wife, "Gordon Goodspeed has lilac eyes."

Jacquelyn was perplexed. "That can't be, Stanley. The boy's birthday was last week. Nineteen days hasn't passed since."

"And I got so damn comfortable," Stanley said aloud but to himself. He shook his head, cursing himself. "Our strikes on the Fable Avenue community have been too random when it comes to the Goodspeed boys and girls and their nineteenth birthdays. Oh, well," he conceded.

"Did we get the day wrong?" Jacquelyn questioned. "No. We're right? October the eighth."

Stanley ignored his wife's words. He told her, "I'll call Willie. I'll tell him to keep an eye on the crossroads. We have our doctors in place from here to Jakobiville, and our clients who owe us favors. You and I will make ritual tonight. I'll go under, into sleep, and I'll make a read of more of this story. Don't you worry now, Lucretia. We'll rewrite the script. Keep it under our direction."

"Yes..." Jacquelyn expressed.

Stanley jumped from the stool, arms reaching for his wife. He rubbed her shoulders and comforted her. "Don't worry, beautiful woman." He planted a kiss on Jacquelyn's forehead. "The Fable Avenue community figured something out. They made some progress. It's okay. It's fine. We have our own progress to make. Forward with focus, right? We have Brice moving our items from Turkey," he ran down. "Though, I think he's stopping off in London. But, regardless, the items are on their way. My contacts are on schedule. Brice will oversee the trade. Okay? Okay, sweet dove?"

Jacquelyn nodded her head. "Okay..." she said in a low voice. Her accent was coming through. Her concentrated efforts to keep her mask started receding, color coming to her white locks, and her wisdom lines filling in.

"Hey, now," Stanley said, warning his wife of her change. "Be careful. You have a class coming in here. Keep focus." Stanley kissed his wife on the lips. They both looked up at the doors. No students gathered. They were safe. Stanley reiterated to his wife, "The Fable Avenue community don't know who we are; they don't know where we are. They'll never see us coming. Their spirits will fulfill *our* grand wish. This had to happen at some point. Right?" Stanley saw his wife nod her head agreeing, but she was still taken aback by the news. "They got over on us. So be it. They are far from prepared to write their story or remove us from it. We're the heroes, here. They're the villains." He tapped her nose and added, "You taught me that."

Stanley stepped away from Jacquelyn. She fixed herself, mask coming back. Stanley took out his glasses and put them on. His face changed. The olive tone returned to color his skin. He swiped at his hair. Strawberry-blonde yielded to pitch raven color, and all but one of his curls stretched straight. The single, thick curl resumed its place on Stanley's forehead.

Professor Brede gathered his things. Jacket folded over his arm and bag in his grip. "Keep watch on the Forrester girl. How's she coming?"

"She's a remarkable student. Gifted," Jacquelyn emphasized. "I've taken an interest in her art. She's taken an interest in me."

"Good." Professor Brede walked up to the doors. He tapped against the door in front of him and all the doors unlocked. He turned and smiled at his wife. "And here come your students now," he said. "I'll see you at home. I'll go now, see what I can meditate on. I'll take the train. You have your car keys?"

"Yes," Jacquelyn answered up to her husband as the first few of her students came through the doors. James greeted the students as they entered the class. He wished his wife well, and then disappeared as he pushed through the rush of entering students.

He didn't soar to the heavens and streak across the sky while being invisible to the world. He didn't dip inconspicuously into an alley filled with shadows for cover and pop from existence to end up back on Fable Avenue. No. Gordon Goodspeed instead took the long way home when his classes were finished for the day. He took the 2-Train to its Hoyt Street stop and then transferred to the Eight. He hopped out at the last stop, Bedford, and then walked up Fable Avenue.

Gordon didn't go home. He stopped by Papa Solomon and Madame Jeliya's house. After ringing the doorbell, Madame Jeliya appeared and opened the door. "Hello, Gordon," she smiled, though Gordon sensed tension as her body remained stiff.

"Hello, Madame Jeliya," Gordon responded. "I spoke with Fey Forrester. She's going to talk to her grandmother."

"That's wonderful, Gordon," Madame Jeliya said as she exhaled relief. "I've been pacing all day. My instinct turned into nerves. Papa Solomon kept telling me to sit and relax. I couldn't, honey. Come on in. You in a rush?"

"No, Madame Jeliya," Gordon said, hoping she would offer to make one of her sandwiches for him.

"I have some spicy lamb shanks heating up. Come and get a bite."

That was just as good, if not better. Gordon accepted the offer and stepped inside. His sense of smell caught the aroma of Madame Jeliya's meal. Gordon's stomach bubbled. His mouth watered, and his spirit danced.

"Set your bag down in Papa Solomon's study," Madame Jeliya politely ordered.

"Yes ma'am," Gordon acknowledged, moving into Papa Solomon's study and stowing his bag. The doorbell rang and Madame Jeliya shouted from the kitchen for Gordon to answer the door. He stepped back into the hall. Through the door's windows he could see Oliver outside. He opened the door and Oliver attacked him with a hug and hand embrace. "What's good, kid?" asked Gordon.

"Nothing, since I didn't get to scratch you up," Oliver joked as the two backed away from their brotherly embrace.

"You gon' keep harpin' on that!" Gordon joked back to Oliver. "You want to give me a third tat' just to feel like you've done somethin'?" They both laughed. "Your mom's got a meal cookin' up. Come on."

"I know," said Oliver. "That's why I'm here. And how you gon' invite me into my own house, where I grew up."

Gordon grabbed Oliver by the arm and gave a loose tug at him. "Negro, getcho complainin' ass in here." Gordon turned around while laughing. He walked inside, Oliver behind him. "Madame Jeliya," Gordon called. "It's that no-good son of yours."

Oliver jumped on Gordon, bending him down and placing him in a headlock. "You might got some incants that bring the spirit out in you and take you to the stars, but I will whip yo' ass good right here on Earth, sun!"

Gordon fought back, laughing. The two stumbled into the kitchen where Madame Jeliya scolded them both for the horseplay. Papa Solomon came up from the garden floor and separated the two with a stern, deep-voiced command. Gordon and Oliver took seats. Papa Solomon smacked both of them on the head with a rolled newspaper. It only caused the two to laugh, stirred with mischief as they were.

"Hey, you fly home or pop straight over here?" Oliver asked settling down.

"Neither," Gordon answered. "Takes a lot out of me. My chamber rests me up some, but I'm still coming down from the weekend. I've rested, but I'm on no sleep. *No sleep!* I'm good though. Trust and believe. I wanted to pop here or take flight, especially since I had news."

"And I was going to call you, Gordon," said Madame Jeliya as she prepared dinner and Papa Solomon planted a kiss on her cheek. "But I didn't want to hound you," she concluded. Papa Solomon made an attempt to lend a hand, but Madame Jeliya shooed him away.

"Grandmamma Forrester gonna lend a hand?" Oliver asked.

Gordon lifted his shoulders. "Fey's going to at least talk to her. Probably happening right now as we speak." There was silence as everyone considered Gordon's thought. "You were right, Papa Solomon," Gordon cut into the silence. "Fey ain't as weird as I thought she was. She was using an incant to hide some conjured yumboes. Incant had enough kick to block someone from Fable Avenue. But I could see through her incant with my brew-stirred eyes. She has yumboes, all right. She draws them to life—like you can do when it comes to some things, Ollie," Gordon commented.

"Is that right?" Oliver asked with a smile, observing Gordon's demeanor as he spoke of Fey Forrester. Gordon's excited mannerisms was also not lost on Papa Solomon and Madame Jeliya as they observed him beam and light up while speaking of the conjure he witnessed from Fey Forrester. Madame Jeliya looked over her shoulder and gave Papa Solomon an eye and a smile. Papa Solomon returned the gesture and added a nod of his head. Then the two of them returned their attention to Gordon.

"She talks to them," he said speaking of Fey and her colorful sprites. "They fly out of her sketchbook," continued Gordon, smile widening. His eyes looked down at the table placemat in front of him, but they saw the scene he described. "She's slick. She has her MP3 player's headphones in her ears while sitting under a tree. She pretends to be mouthing the lyrics, but she's talking to her yumboes. And she's sitting and sketching and talkin'. The yumboes are flying all around her. She's got four. One is named Silver."

Papa Solomon reflected aloud, "A yumbo alerted us to what happened that night. The little thing helped keep that girl's mind right. Kept her eyes blinded so she couldn't see her mother's body." Papa Solomon hated to speak about the grim happening, but he decided to state fact.

"That was Silver," said Gordon excited and looking up. "I got an instinct about the little sprite. She's close to Fey in a way the others aren't."

"More like a guardian?" Papa Solomon suggested.

"Yeah," Gordon agreed.

The patriarch shook his head. "That's what I told the little yumbo to do," he said, burdensome memories heavy in his voice.

Madame Jeliya gave her husband a look. She said to clear the air, "You say you admire this young woman, Gordon. Well, that's all you need, when it comes to a woman," she opined, causing Gordon to turn his bright beaming smile into a bashful grin. She addressed Papa Solomon, "Wouldn't that be somethin', Papa? Gordon might behold this young woman."

Oliver asked while chuckling, "You startin' to like her, Gordon, now that she ain't as weird as you think?"

Gordon rolled his eyes, leaned back and exhaled hard. "Aw, you all just gon' call a brutha out on some feelings. Just be like, *'Hey, Gordon, ya skirt is up and ya slip is showin'.'*" Oliver broke into laughter. Gordon continued making a face.

Papa Solomon advised through the playfulness, "Just be careful with that brew stirrin' in you, talkin' about all this beholdin' a woman." He and Madame Jeliya set out plates of food on the counter. "You behold her, especially with the brew in your eyes, it'll take a lot to get your heart away from her should she not comply. So hope she got the same feelings. Don't make a mistake, hear?"

Gordon considered the advice.

Madame Jeliya smacked Papa Solomon on the arm and scolded, "Come now, with all that careful talk, Papa. That's a grown boy. He's been courtin' a few girls in his short time."

"But we're talkin' 'bout beholdin'," Papa Solomon expressed as a reminder. "He can't make mistakes with that. Not with that kind of power. You think your spirit's stirred now."

Madame Jeliya exhaled, cocking her head to the side and giving her husband a look. "Papa…" she said.

Papa Solomon embraced Madame Jeliya's hand. "You know I didn't make a mistake with you, Thelema-baby."

Madame Jeliya swiped her hand away before Papa Solomon could kiss the back of it. "Please, old fool! I am not that sensitive. I know we're aligned in our beholding." She made another face, eyebrows raised and lips pursed. "Some others might not know, but *I* know. Shit!"

Papa Solomon lifted his hands and backed away. "Go 'head on, withcho bad self, mamma." The two started laughing. Papa Solomon still reminded Gordon with a stern finger aimed in his direction, "Don't take beholdin' a woman lightly, boy."

"He's right," backed Madame Jeliya as Papa Solomon hugged her close and they rocked back and forth.

"Oh, great, they flirtin' now," said Oliver as he rolled his eyes.

"Boy, hush up!" Madame Jeliya yelled to her son. "If you weren't so influenced by the Concheroot spirit, hangin' with Wilson and all, you'd have beheld yourself a proper woman by now."

"Hey, I like what I like. And I like 'em all," Oliver countered.

"And if the two of you would like to eat, you both will have to come up here and get it. This a buffet tonight," Madame Jeliya announced. She moved to the cupboard, slipping from Papa Solomon's embrace. "Come on now," she ordered Gordon and her son. "Ollie, I'll put out some Tupperware so you can take food for your shift tonight."

Oliver thanked his mother. Gordon stood and followed Oliver to the counter. Everyone prepared a plate and sat down at the dinner table. Gordon fielded questions about his spirit form, much of which were the same as asked over the weekend. He considered that his company, and others on Fable Avenue, just liked to hear about it. His spirit form was called *Dooley*. Over the weekend, Gordon showed it off to some of the street's residents, and to all three matriarchs and Papa Solomon. He remained in the flesh while at the dinner table, however, unsuited and without the full glow of the lilac spirit. Oliver inquired about the spirits he'd seen in space. He wanted to know if they would come to visit. Gordon answered that he didn't know.

"We matriarchs believe this is a gateway opening, Gordon," Madame Jeliya annotated. She ate in a regal manner as she scooped up cubed bits of lamb and sautéed string beans. She chewed and swallowed before clarifying, "Magic will be more opaque, no longer intangible. You won't be the only spirit. And some of us that can already scribble with magic's ink, our mastery will increase. We expect a long line of folk for *stitching* and *webbing* rites come this Spirit Festival." Madame Jeliya rolled her eyes and mocked, *"The spirit's here! Time to have the Elders whip our conjures and incants up a level!"*

"Yeah," Oliver took up as he ate. "All leads to one thing, this Grand Conjure and Wish will be achieved, once we figure out the details on what the hell it is, and what we're supposed to do to bring it about."

Gordon thought about the mythology brought to him through glowing hieroglyphs and rhymed narration, but he didn't say a word about it. Too much of its narrative reflected what he was feeling. But he considered the prologue, which showcased the march of three, grand armies toward a mysterious, female archetype called Motherland. That particular telling of the tale seemed to Gordon more historical and less mythological. He guessed it was history expressed as legend, symbolic. Perhaps a hint of the long ago events called the Pious Wars, a series of sanguinary battles only whispered about among the dispersed conjure folk of the world. Nothing in modern books recalled the great, ancient bloody affair where conjure was grand and the world was different with three moons in its sky. Red. Black. Green. Most in the conjure community dismissed the occurrence as simple myth. And stories were so reworked among generations, and mostly told to entertain the children of the conjure community, that it was nothing more than folktales. Conjure historians swore up and down that hieroglyphs on temples from Africa to India spoke of those times. Narratives pulled from Sanskrit, where large-scale wars with terrifying powers and weaponry used, were also pointed to as proof among believers of the legendary epoch.

Gordon loved hearing the stories growing up. He and Cedron gravitated toward one legendary hero or another concerning that era. Like many conjure-folk children, they would charge around the house absorbed in imagination, recreating themselves in the image of the great champions recorded only in oral history, or even create heroes of their own to be among that speculated age.

There were two curiosities that connected the beginning of Gordon's composed mythology to the supposed Pious Wars. The motive for war was the first. Conflict supposedly erupted among the original conjure people of the world over a dispute concerning destiny and fate. The second was the loss of the original three moons of the world, faded, and leaving behind the single, pale moon hanging like an unpolished medallion in the heavens.

This ancient, stellar formation was, however, an agreed upon phenomenon in the dispersed, African conjure world, even if the Pious Wars and the reason for the loss of the three, glorious moons was not.

Gordon mentioned his hypothesis to the Elders. They took note, but said, and concluded, nothing more on the matter. Maman Anansi declared that as of now, with the lilac spirit manifested, all things should be considered possible. And Gordon even pondered now, wondering how he could bring that section of the tale to the Fable Avenue community. Perhaps he could show it during The Four Days of the Spirit Festival that took place between the final two days of October and the first two days of November.

Gordon's thoughts on the narrative segued into thoughts of his father. He'd seen his father only by way of a video chat through his phone. Their talk was cordial, and Gordon even showed his father his spirit form. Maximilian was proud. He was too busy with his job to stop into Brooklyn, but Gordon didn't mind. He still had his feelings that had been roused up since he'd seen his mother's shade. Gordon did want to see his brother. And he'd heard nothing from his friend Benny-Jah, not even through Dajon.

These thoughts stayed with him even as he finished his meal and engaged in deep discussion. His thoughts walked with him as he made his way home, down Fable Avenue. Then someone cut into his thoughts by yelling, *"Hey, spirit boy!"*

Gordon was at the gate to his house, ready to open it when he heard the voice. He turned and watched Benny-Jah walk up through the darkness sporting a wide, charming smile. Gordon charged him, and the two friends embraced.

"I've been wonderin' where you been, Negro!" Gordon hollered.

"My bad, kid!" Benny replied. "Been caught up," he said as an excuse.

"Dare I ask…?"

Benny waved his hand. "Aw, man," he retorted still smiling. "It's good, man. Don't worry." He looked at Gordon's face. He covered his open mouth with a balled fist and said with exuberance, "Them eyes, sun! Them eyes! I was told, but the reality is somethin' different."

"Yeah," Gordon remarked, breath condensing in the chilled air. "Let's get inside. It's kinda cold out here, and I got stuff to show you."

"Yeah," Benny agreed.

Gordon again embraced his friend. Reality instantly warped and shrank in Benny's view, taking him off guard as Gordon popped them from existence. When reality corrected itself, Benny and Gordon were in the Goodspeed's mystically renovated basement. Gordon stepped toward his chamber, dropping his bag on the chair. Benny focused to stop the disorienting spin of the room. Looking at the chamber helped Benny orient himself. Balanced, Benny asked, "What's all this?"

"A retreat," Gordon answered. "This thing relaxes me through the sleepless nights I've been having. I've gotten plenty rest, but no real sleep. The brewed spirit inside me got me anxious, even when I do a quick pop from one spot to another."

"You okay now?" asked Benny.

"Yeah," Gordon drawled. "I'm cool. I still got focus, but it's like a daydream, kind of. That's the best way I can describe it." Gordon put his back against the chamber. Benny moved Gordon's bag from the chair to the floor and took a seat. "How's Dajon?" Gordon asked him.

"He's fine. Servin' his time well. He finishin' up his block duty. I came to pick him up and bring him home. Pops is usually on pickup duty, but I thought this was an opportunity to see you, man. Give a congrats."

"That's cool. I was wonderin' when I'd hear from you."

"Yeah," Benny said in a low voice. He told Gordon, "Hey, our pops calmed down after he found out what Dajon was fightin' for. He still got into his ass a little more on how he handled the situation." Benny added, "Papa Solomon talked to my pops about it all."

"Said he would," Gordon noted. He put his hands in his pockets and asked, "What's ya pops gonna do when he find out you runnin' around doin' knuckleheaded shit with my brother?"

Benny squirmed in his seat. "C'mon, Gordy," he said maintaining a grin, "we misfits in trainin'. Somethin' righteous will come down the pipeline, until then, what's the problem makin' a few dollars on the side? You ain't goin' all goody-two-shoes on me, is you? We're taking from a couple rich business guys. And we got protection."

Gordon reflected on Benny's words. "I guess," he answered. "I just ain't seen you in a minute. I wanted some kind of grounding on my day of rites—and birthday."

Benny cocked his head to the side, made a face and teased, "Awww." Then he said, "Cut me some slack. I was at y'house that day."

"I'mo cut you all right. And you was schemin' and plotin'," Gordon reminded. "My day of rites had nothing to do with that. Did you ask Cedron to meet up there so you could take the opportunity to give a hug and pound?"

"*Whoa!*" hollered Benny, arms raised. "What's with the interrogation, Mister Law and Order?"

Gordon pushed himself off the chamber, feeling the stir of the spirit inside him. "You know what I told Neyeli?" he asked, his question only rhetorical. "I told her you've been protectin' y'self."

Benny's face contorted. "Protectin' myself?" he repeated, confused. "She been providing protection on our schemes…"

Gordon shook his head and told Benny, "No, sun. I'm talkin' about the closer I got to my nineteenth birthday and my second gateway rites, the more danger I was in. We all know what's happened to my cousins, to Cedron." Gordon relaxed himself so as not to start an actual argument. His voice became less accusing and angry and more sympathetic. "I saw you side up with Cedron not too long after he was shot. I had some years before my time. I always thought it was because, hey, the danger over Cedron already got him. Bein' close to me might get you—"

Benny interrupted, "Sun, you didn't really think that dumb shit, did you?" Gordon's instinct tingled on the back of his neck. He deciphered in an instant that Benny's tone, though rough, was neither defensive nor angry. He was surprised. Gordon relaxed even more. Benny did the same, taking the street out of his voice. "No, Gordon." Benny sounded apologetic. "It wasn't that. Sorry if you thought it was."

"Okay. So what's up?"

"Let that be on hold, if you don't mind. Let's catch up on the spirit, and your rights being successful."

Gordon could've pried. His instinct tingled to do so. But he left Benny's private thoughts alone. "Okay," he told Benny. "When you're ready. But promise me this: keep Tap far from that trouble, or just watch him close."

"We all under protection, Gordy," Benny assured. "Don't worry."

Gordon then lightened the mood by throwing the subject of women at his friend. He scratched his ear and his face. "Well I ain't lettin' you off the hook altogether." Gordon looked at his friend, retaking his leaning stance against the chamber. "Speakin' of you and all that protection, what's with you and Neyeli? You know she like you? Why you think she's been throwin' her protection around you. That's heart, sun."

Again, Benny's face contorted, though this time he was less upset. "Really? Please. We good friends. We more like brother and sister."

Gordon flipped Benny's words around. "Well, brutha, the sista wanna get with you."

Benny looked at his arm, glancing at a watch that wasn't there. "Well, look at the time. I gotta get Dajon. We gotta get back to Harlem. It's late. You know Negroes get ra-ra right about now."

Gordon rolled his eyes, hands in his pockets. "Yeah, she said much the same. Come on. I'll walk you out."

Benny's grin returned. He stood and said, "Hey, Neyeli is a settle down type of sista. I might have somethin' for her. But when have I not had somethin' for a cute sista walkin' about. But, if I jump on that, I ain't gettin' up." He lifted his shoulders. "In time, maybe we'll behold one another."

Gordon bubbled with laughter. He said as they walked up the stairs, "For all you and Cedron's schemin', Neyeli said you all gettin' good practice in."

"Oh, yeah," Benny said up to Gordon. "You know a blind eye is turned away from us. And when an eye is peekin' in on what we doin', they seein' how we got it down."

"Well, I been hearin' that the Elders need a smash and grab soon. The old crew is gettin' old, and an incant can't stop that. Wilson sayin' Lady Arachne need somethin'. A set of cards, I think. Said once the location is pinned down, Wilson will be tasked to get it." They stepped onto the garden floor. Gordon turned around and told Benny. "He's got his eye on Cedron's misfits. He need you all to help him."

Benny stated in a stern manner, "That's what I'm waitin' for. Community service. Make our schemes righteous."

Gordon stepped to the front door. He flipped light switches as he walked through the room, turning on interior and exterior lights alike. "I'll keep you posted." Gordon opened the door and walked out, allowing Benny to lead. Outside, Benny looked at Gordon's blessed eyes and commented, "So you got the eyes. What've you seen with 'em?"

"A lot. Been above the world, seen cosmic spirits," Gordon listed. "Seen history. I opened gateways. There was a glowing man and a glowing woman that rebuilt the basement."

Benny bent over laughing. Standing straight and easing his manner, he said, "See this is how you know you from Fable Ave'. You hear something like that and you be like, *'And…?'* All straight faced and shit." He started laughing again.

Gordon challenged his friend, asking, "You want to see the 'and'?"

Benny blinked. Gordon's clothes were gone, substituted with the skintight, black, silky suit custom stitched by the glowing woman. His African-like mask and glowing, spherical eye had Benny in awe. Benny blinked again. Dooley shifted to the glowing, intangible spirit. He swirled around his friend and then landed, clothed and as Gordon.

"That's an 'and' for you," Benny remarked. Gordon agreed. They walked through the gate, and Benny continued his comments. "A change like this brings things," he said, sounding like a warning.

"We know there are villains about. Keep practice with incants," Gordon said like an order. "Madame Jeliya told me that she and the other matriarchs believe that if this spirit has come through, then it's possible that more will come through. We'll be able to tap into them. We'll all be able to do this, they think. Expect the stitching and webbing rites to increase, people lookin' to see what kind of conjure they got. What power they can get out of the incants they already have." Gordon added, "People ain't worked with a personal conjure in a mean minute."

Benny stepped through the gate. He turned and asked Gordon, "Oh, what about your ink? Which house you marked up with?"

"Both," said Gordon.

Benny's eyes widened. "Word?"

Gordon pointed to either shoulder. "Here and here. Dii Mauri and Ka Mauri."

"How'd that go down?" Benny asked.

"My chamber tagged me," Gordon summarized. He chuckled, "Ollie never touched me. He all sore too. I tease him about it."

Benny rolled his eyes. "That's a sensitive dude, sometimes."

"I know, man. I mean, he takes it in stride and smiles, but I got a heightened instinct now. He hurt, like I did this on purpose." The two of them laughed.

"That's that Brooklynism, right. Cats around here, they tough. They not soft. At all." Then Benny annunciated, "*T'at t'all!* But they sensitive. *Shhh,* don't tell 'em that."

"Yeah, you'll get knocked on your ass, talkin' like that around here."

"Right, cuz they sensitive in Brooklyn," he reiterated in a matter-of-fact tone. Benny and Gordon's laughter burst all over again. They tried to keep their voices low, Benny signaling for them to shush. Soon after, they exchanged a brotherly embrace and a fist bump. They said their goodbyes and then Benny walked down the street to retrieve his brother and vehicle. Gordon kept his eyes on Benny until his friend turned the corner and merged with the darkness. Two Fable Avenue residents walking on the sidewalk stopped and admired Gordon's eyes. They made light talk, and then they continued on. Gordon popped from existence and into his basement. He lifted Seshat's Songbook from the chamber, stepped back, and let go. The book dangled in the air, suspended by its own magic.

"I should have an ally, because I do have them. The other world can't be that bleak," he said to the book that he dubbed *The Written.* He took his position on the floor. His eyes filled with lilac light. The book opened to a new page.

The first few lines spoke before a picture came.

Father Zeroes are too absent for me to find an ally

Even when at side
Heart gone. Ab. Sent. Away.
None in the cage-city can I spy
Comrades of mine, Bwa, Phour, and Cimetiere (we call he, Baron C)
Too many spirit-drinks haze their eye

Gordon sighed. No ally, for now. The next lines recited brought forth the glow of ancient characters that swirled to make a picture. Gordon peeked in on his wiry, slender doppelganger as he traveled across a blanched sidewalk winding through a gray city below a gray day.

So, I look for a feminine eye
To see eye-to-eye
Detect like minds
I look for black's harmony
In a proper, pitched queen carved of cosmic ebony
To rule the state of lonely with me – equal by my side

Gordon found this quest interesting. His bright eyes observed, and his ears listened close to the narrative.

I wander riddled streets for answers
Cracked, broken – leeks like flowers
Power potential pedestrians planted seeds
Cemented – stiff competition
Medusa gazed madam-damsels
Stoned distress signal
Stagnant even in movement
Destiny tells me I have appointments
With four disappointments

The first. I enter her web.
Bow and pay respect to her shadow
Though her memory is pale
And dead
Maybe she will remember
Sun and moon romances, civilized dances
On bare feet against the sands
Covenant to Motherland
Rituals to the stars – diadems, singing jewelry and hymns
Hair locked with secrets

But her hair is perverse
Upside down, she is reversed
Drinker of savior's blood,
Drunk off religion, her spirit stumbles;
She is the Queen of Clubs shaking her hypocrisy
At the rave
She plays chess with her environment
Manipulative – her medicine for ailment of anger, jealousy, and resentment
No apology with how she behaves
Narrow-minded corridor, focused on her gold chains – this slave
Newsmonger, she speaks liquid lies
Poured over her eyes, lathered lens – brain washed and cleansed
Rinse, repeat after pale shadow
Drink deep and become shallow

She is shy to her ancient light of lime
Her heart shrinks violets
Her face masks her fall from grace
Pride and ego hardened chemically
She speaks rough
"You cannot dance with me," she says.
"You remind me of another life too much.
I fell from grace. Leave me falling."
She dances. Volume high as she. Loud deafens already
She passes anger to her son. Lets her daughter inherit her Nothing
As mother
Soft memories. She stays forgetful. I walk away, scathed and burnt.

The sidewalk bends
I'm quiet. I wear an introvert's satchel
Keeping my thoughts close
Ponder wishes and hopes
And there she is, beautiful sable
Behind the wall
"Stand just there!" she shouts to me.
Out of sight, and in reach of queen

"My cup is out of touch
My chalice wants nothing more
Than to own your phallus
I can be you times two."

The world is tough enough
She restricts her feminine caress
Gives womanly attire to dress as a man
She wears manhood around her neck
She wears a king's crown
And hates what the mirror reflects
Believes her strength by taking a man's breath
"You cannot be what I already am.
I can be without you. My shadow is a man.
I am man as woman. Redundant and independent."
She wears the suit inherited from the father that abandoned her
She burns her mother's silk, and I move forward

A broom sweeps around me
"Keep clean. Clean. Clean."
Her beauty shines through dust
Sparkling. A diamond, rough.
Her children run wild as their fathers do
She's smothered, life is their life
Sons and daughters, all fathered by zero
"Cook. Clean. Nurture and care for," she repeats
And repeats. Rapid. Repeat.
She looks past me. Eight months, full sails – her belly
Her inner child borne physical
"I will eat and eat until I am full with responsibilities."
She still looks past me. Her age still climbs in the twenties.
"I will be this night's duty, and hand you child for a reward."
Father Zeroes haunt her
Cloak and scowl. Not protective. Competitive.
Lips drip savage. Sharp teeth licked. My image,
Wiry frame, satiates these Father Zeroes violent palate
I will remember her, as the dogs surround her

The next plausible I see
Believes in everything
She wears clouds as a crown
It rains smog in her eyes
Blurry head
Her heart paves her movement
A walk down Honor Road that leads to a fiery place
She fits ancient robes
But she believes everything

Whispers and rumors about her
Pale shadows have saved her
She is a volunteer gravedigger
Burying her rites, ancient rituals of life
Covenant to Motherland, her reflection
Buried proper black definition
Her resentment is her skin
Light is not light enough
Pale shadow can help her birth self-hatred as love

The four I spy
Are multiplied
A house of mirrored
Horrors
I harden to cope
Speak with hope as I speak up to the water bearer and his maiden wife
"Your daughter down here resides
I will kiss her to open proper all the mansions in the sky, far and near."

Pale shadow property
Properly propagates propaganda
Our family tree – leaflets drop in the fall
Gentrification
Gene infiltration
Brain washed
And clean
Mother Nothings are everything they are not supposed to be
Winter comes early – they see blurry
And blizzards cover their hearts
Coldly they speak to tease and baptize me as Don Quixote
Because of how I see reality – see clearly my duty

I say, "Windmills are not giants
Neighbors are not squires
I am dissatisfied with pale shadow liars
And our walk reflects their talk
Am I an idealist
To want to strive to find
The ideal brother ally and a black queen at my side?
For neighborhoods to remove the hoods
And for the same to happen in the mind?
To shut the two physical eyes and see thru

The centered glow of the trine?
Let the third eye become aligned
A favorable astrological aspect
Two celestial bodies degreed in lessons
One-twenty. Three-Sixty. Cipher our divine.
Should we not look past our enslaved past
Far back where we can find how we are truly defined?
Ye are gods, let me remind
Children of the Most High
You sit there high in a low state
We are that which is most high
We are the blackness of the sky
We are all the stars that inside reside
We are the spiral and the galactic wave
All that is creation, and all that creates
I will no longer be afraid of the heights I will obtain
Even in our imperfection,
We fit the perception of the ideal
Worship no idol, but your ideal.
That will keep
It
Real."

I sneak. Leave the city.
Only the black of night
And the moon's light
My trustworthy companions

The lilac light retracted into a calm swirl inside Gordon's eyes. The picture around him dwindled into the ancient characters that fluttered back to the page. *The Written* closed. Gordon stood and took the book from its midair bob and placed it on the chamber. Another somber chapter was presented to him, he thought.

"No allies, huh," he commented to the book. "And I can't even find a decent girl? Come on, now. What kind of bullsh—"

His phone buzzed in his pocket. He took it out. It was a text message. Fey Forrester's name and number was there. Gordon looked at the chamber and all it's individual parts. He looked at the phone and thought about the timing of the text. He considered magic and technology were walking hand-in-hand. Gordon looked at Fey's text to see what his fate was.

He had an instinct about it, and it made him smile.

Fey Forrester wasn't greeted with a return holler from her grandmother when she walked into the house and announced, *"Home, Nana!"* It was her Uncle Daryl that called back to her, jumping up from the kitchen table and entering the hallway to give Fey a hug. However, the heavy aroma of cooked food reached Fey before her Uncle Daryl. She inhaled the succulent scent mere seconds before her uncle wrapped his arms around her.

"Little Junior," Fey said with a voice full of surprise. She stepped away from his embrace, smiled up at her uncle and asked, "What brings you from Jersey?"

"He checkin' up on me," Fey's grandmother's voice yelled from the kitchen. "On orders of his damned sister that can't give a call," she huffed.

Fey and Daryl gave one another a look; with Fey mouthing the question *Is that true?* Daryl nodded in the affirmative. But still he yelled over his shoulder and denied, "Mamma, I told you that ain't true. *I'm* checkin' up on you. *Me.*"

"How's Aunt Kaia?" Fey inquired.

Daryl kept his arm around his niece as they walked toward the kitchen. "She's doing fine. Keeps threatening to move back East after she and her husband retire. Your cousin Armand will be graduating college soon. Next year. He's already lookin' for a job, but that's been a struggle. Your aunt's giving him a break, letting him take time off from his search."

"Nothing a good and proper incant couldn't solve," Savannah huffed.

Daryl rolled his eyes. "All that superstitious talk. Let the boy earn his way."

Before things could escalate, even in a playful manner, Fey continued her interrogation. "How are you all in Jersey? How's the family?"

They stepped into the kitchen as Daryl answered, "Michelle and I are doin' fine. Your cousins are fine. Derrick's enjoying his first year in high school. Milton misses his big brother being at the same school."

Fey had it wrong. Her grandmother wasn't cooking in the kitchen, she was watering plants. Savannah spoke while concentrating on her plant care, "We got leftovers, li'l lady. I can warm you up some. Other than that, it's a gopher night. *Go-for* what you find."

"Last night's meal was lovely, Nana," said Fey, laying down her bag in a chair. She removed her jacket and swung it around the same piece of furniture.

"Ah, ah, ah!" Savannah yelled at her granddaughter. "You know that coat don't go there."

"Yes, Nana," Fey drawled. She swiped her jacket, stepped into the front room, and hung it up properly inside the closet. She walked over to her grandmother and kissed her on the cheek. "Let me heat up last night's wonderful stew so you can continue to tend to your plants."

"Thank you, girl," Savannah said to Fey. "I'm not hungry. I just ate."

"So that's what I smell," Fey commented. "Uncle Daryl? You?"

"Just warm up what's to eat. I'll make my own plate. It'll be heavy," he said taking a seat at the table. "Michelle's taking the boys out."

Fey opened the refrigerator door and removed a large pot of steak and squash stew. She placed it on the stove and turned burners on high. She opened the pot and swapped a wooden spoon off the counter. "Nana, is this clean?"

Savannah peeked over her shoulder. "Yep, I just washed that. Forgot to put it away," she told her granddaughter.

Fey stirred the pot.

Small talk was made between Fey, her uncle and grandmother. Fey talked, but her concentration was on other things. She heard her uncle and grandmother's voices, and she responded, especially when her uncle turned the conversation's focus to her college studies. But the conversation was hollow sounding as Fey rested inside her head, thinking. Gordon Goodspeed and the marvel of his second gateway rites had her attention. Her thoughts didn't conjure up his plea for her grandmother's help. Fey thought about the lilac hue of his eyes, and she wondered what it was like to have gone through the Fable Avenue community's cultural rites. As a Goodspeed, Fey understood that Gordon had a second gateway ritual that took place on his birthday, but there were rites that every Fable Avenue boy and girl had to go through. Her memory was fuzzy, but not the emotions they carried. Fey recalled the coming of age rituals that she was supposed to experience at the ages of nine and thirteen. Her mother talked so much about them. The dances, the chants, and the intimate feel of the ceremonies. Seeing Gordon's eyes, proof of some cultural ceremony held in his honor, reminded Fey how much she wanted to have that experience. She was reminded how much she loved hearing her mother talk about them. It was then that Fey focused on blurry images of her mother. She believed her mother was smiling in the memory's imagery. Fey was a little girl, and it was before the dark times, and before there were only fuzzy memories with pricks of emotion.

Fey stirred the pot, not facing her grandmother and uncle. Her eyes became heavy and wet, but she sniffed and wiped her hand across them, making nothing of it. *Maybe they'll believe it was the stew's aroma*, she told herself. She put her focus on her grandmother and uncle's voices. The conversation's audio became full. Fey's participation in small talk was steady rather than sporadic. But through dinner, she crawled back inside her head and cuddled up to her thoughts. This time, however, she addressed Gordon Goodspeed's concern and became anxious. She didn't want to discuss the matter with her uncle present. Fey knew that talk of Fable Avenue and incants and conjures was a sensitive issue for her uncle, much the same as her Aunt Kaia who had moved to California. And the death of her mother, their baby sister, was only the beginning of the issue.

There were times during the conversation when Fey's uncle unknowingly tested her patience. He scooped up a hefty bowl of stew and nursed it while meandering on mundane topics. Then he went back for seconds. Fey kept her smile and the fire of conversation burning, engaging him. It had been several months since she'd last seen or spoken to her uncle; and it was always good to connect with family besides her grandmother or conjured yumboes. Fey often believed she existed in a bubble. She liked when life offered a pin for her to prick that bubble and run free a bit. But at the moment, she did so wish that her uncle could handle the subjects Fable Avenue had the ability to conjure.

Fey encountered a second challenge, and that was when her uncle, again unknowingly, capitulated to her wishes. He made his way to the door, saying his goodbyes, giving kisses and hugs. He had parting words to his mother, telling her to stay healthy, centered and safe. He extended his kind, departing words to Fey and made his exit. That's when the second challenge presented itself. Savannah mentioned to her son how tired she was, and that she was all ready for bed even at the early hour of nine o'clock. But Fey needed to talk to her.

Both Fey and her grandmother walked Daryl to the door and out of the house. They waved him away as he started his car, backed out of the driveway, and made his way to New Jersey. Fey turned her second challenge into an opportunity. Right there on the porch, as they watched Daryl's car disappear down the road, she stated, "Nana, I saw Gordon Goodspeed today on campus. He had his second gateway rites performed." She turned to her grandmother and informed, "He has the brew in his eyes. There's a stir in him, and it's made his eyes turn lilac." Fey put her grandmother's hands in her own. "That brings up a few things I remember my mom talking about, and it goes with the things you've talked about." Fey took a deep breath. She looked down and spoke, "He needs your help, Nana." She lifted her head and saw surprise sculpting her grandmother's features, sprinkled with concern. "I was waiting for Little Junior to make his way out. I know this kind of talk agitates him," Fey acknowledged, feeling awkward addressing it. "But, Gordon's stir, the brew in him, he says he can be unstable, Nana. He needs you to give him a ritual; help him make an altar for his spirit. He says he hasn't slept. And there ain't a conjure woman I know who can tame a spirit with an altar like you."

Savannah didn't say anything, still caught in her expression of surprise. Fey understood. She let her grandmother go and made a pivot to the door. "I know there's a lot there. Your memories are better than mine, Nana. But think about it. Fable Avenue has made progress." Fey walked inside, leaving her grandmother on the porch. There still remained surprise on Savannah's face. She placed one hand over her heart, and the other hand she used to balance on the rail as she took a seat on the first step. Her lips expressed little sound, almost mouthing the incant she spoke. Her voice was just as subtle, giving a whisper mighty strength if compared. But her body warmed, shielded from the crisp autumn air.

Fey walked back to the kitchen and lifted her bag and put it over her shoulder. She went upstairs to her room, tossing the bag to her bed as she flipped on the lights and closed the door. She opened her bag and removed her sketchbook, flipping to a page sketched with a penciled drawing of her four yumboes. She removed the jewelry from her neck and from her fingers and wrists and placed them in a jewelry case located on her dresser next to her altar.

Fey didn't attend to her altar. She left the candles unlit and the incense holder empty. For the moment, anyway. She closed her eyes, focused, and mouthed an incant over the opened sketchbook. Her yumboes came to life, swirling around in vibrant colors. Silver led the charge up and off the page. Then the yumbo hovered in front of Fey as if awaiting orders. Fey just smiled at her while the other three sprites darted around the room as quick streams of light with fluttering wings. Silver followed Fey to the bed as the young woman sat down on the mattress, legs folded. The yumbo turned her head toward the window.

"Don't disturb, Nana, Silver," Fey ordered, losing her smile. "Let her be. She's thinking." Fey sighed, "So am I." She looked at Silver's face and saw concern in the yumbo's eyes. Silver then looked at the unattended altar on Fey's dresser. Fey exhaled, "Okay, okay. Goodness." She unfolded her legs and got out of the bed, all with an exaggerated strain as if it was a strenuous activity. "I do need to relax," she said going into her drawer and pulling out a wooden box. She opened it and removed one incense stick.

Fey closed the box and tucked it back into the drawer. She put the stick into its holder, closed her eyes and took a deep breath. The other yumboes ceased flying. They gathered behind Fey as she spoke a short prayer and chanted the rhythm of an incant. The incense stick and scented candles lit as a result of the mystical utterance. The scented smoke swirled around Fey's altar and into her senses. The yumboes too inhaled the flowery aroma. Fey opened a single eye, turning her head to see the glowing yumboes behind her.

"Puff, puff, give," she joked to them. The yumboes giggled, more influenced by, what was to them, the intoxicating scent than Fey's joke.

Fey relaxed, and her sprites took that as a cue to dive back into flight around the room, Silver among them. Fey walked to her desk situated under the room's window. She moved the curtain aside and looked up at the moon's light, blurred by the gathering clouds. She turned and looked at her bag on the bed. "Let me get started on some reading assignments," she said to no one in particular. She removed a small pad and flipped to the latest page of notes, scanning it to see the night's assignments. Three of four had been crossed out, having been completed while she was still on campus. But there was a reading assignment to complete for an art class. Fey looked to see which pages she needed to cover when her grandmother knocked on the door.

"Come in, Nana," Fey permitted.

Savannah opened the door, slow, as if being cautious. The yumboes stopped their flight, paused as Savannah poked her head in and said, "Bring that Goodspeed boy to the house this weekend. If those other Fable Avenue fools—"

"Nana!"

Savannah reiterated to her granddaughter, "*If those other Fable Avenue fools* such as Papa Solomon, his sister and them other women leadin' the charge want to come, they can too. This has been a long time coming."

Fey didn't push. "Thank you, Nana," she said.

Savannah nodded her head. She said to Fey, "Lilac eyes, huh? Glowing?"

"Not all lighted up," answered Fey. "But I'm sure they can. They're pretty."

"Well, I'm gon' have a shot of somethin' strong and a cigarette before I call it a night," Savannah remarked. "Shit!" Savannah closed the door.

Fey looked up at the floating yumboes and told them, "Oh, I'd love to use you four as carrier pigeons to deliver Gordon the message." She dug into her pocket and pulled out her phone. "But technology is gon' do for now." She started typing Gordon a text message.

Harlem. It was good to be home, and Gordon was welcomed at the door by his father and older brother. His father dragged him inside, clutched in a tight hug. Maximilian shut the door and pulled Gordon farther into the front room. Gordon dropped his book bag and quipped, "Nice to see you, Pop." Cedron rolled up with a hard push on his wheelchair. Gordon's older brother wore a grin. Gordon, held close inside his father's arms, opened one eye and observed Cedron's approach. Cedron held an expression that looked, to Gordon, like someone plotting a crafty move in his head. Gordon ignored the look and his interpretation of it.

"My son with the spirit!" exclaimed Maximilian. Cedron's grin was wiped away by half. Maximilian opened his embrace but kept a grip on Gordon's shoulders. He held his son out and yelled, "Ain't that about somethin'! I wish your mother could see this. Look at you. Look at those eyes, little man! It's a whole other experience in person, and I've seen 'em already."

"Let me see them gems, kid," Cedron requested, signaling with his hand for Gordon to come closer as if he held more authority than their father.

Maximilian moved out of the way and pushed Gordon toward Cedron. "Go on," he said. "Let your brother have a look at your eyes."

Gordon stepped up to his brother. Cedron reached out with his mighty hands and pulled Gordon closer. Cedron's tug was like the sudden jolt of a starting vehicle. Gordon almost lost his footing. Cedron inspected Gordon's lilac eyes, looking deep. He pushed Gordon away, and Gordon caught his balance.

"The color's a little feminine," Cedron remarked. He grinned at his joke and said to their father, "Ain't it, Pop?" He chuckled, saying to Gordon, "I'm just playin' witchu, man."

The stir inside Gordon struck him. He remained still. He still hadn't slept, and his body trembled with energy, writhing through him like his body was a snake pit. He took a moment, inhaling, and calmed. He swallowed the urge to retort to his brother, "*Why don't you stand up and tell me that.*" Instead, Gordon laughed off the comment. But he turned to his father and the sting returned. His father's statement about wishing his mother to have been around to witness the blessing in his eyes stirred up his spirit and the sting.

She was, Gordon thought to himself. *And she's none too pleased with you.* Gordon took another breath, and he no longer entertained his thoughts.

"Madame Jeliya says you need to take it easy," Maximilian said, his statement halfway between a question and a reminder.

Gordon breathed out heavy. "I haven't slept, Pop. Not real sleep. Not in days." He assured his father, "I've rested. Madame Jeliya relaxes me with incants. I have a chamber that I rest in—I don't know if you've told Cedron," he said to his father. He informed his brother, "My eyes conjured a gateway for some spirits. They built a chamber for me. The magic rearranged the whole basement. It's all new, renovated."

Maximilian walked up behind his youngest son and threw an arm around him. He slapped Gordon on the chest and said to Cedron, "And he got both houses tattooed on him. I ain't tell you that! Hot damn!" He tightened his arm around Gordon, shaking him. "Ain't that something? Dii Mauri and Ka Mauri."

Cedron made another demand. "Let me see that," he said to Gordon.

Gordon hesitated for a moment. He didn't want to reveal his sacred, ceremonial designs for fear of another remark. But after breathing in and out again to calm himself, Gordon yielded to his brother's request. He grabbed the back of his sweatshirt and pulled it over his head, uncovering his shoulders and revealing the intricate sketch illustrated on his flesh.

"The chamber did it," Gordon explained.

Cedron grinned and partially quoted, *"A plague on both them houses."* He chuckled with a teasing tone. He rolled back and turned away from Gordon, pushing his way to the kitchen. "That's nice," he said with a hint of disinterest.

A stinging anger pricked Gordon's heart. He ignored the sensation, and set his sweatshirt on properly. He walked up behind Cedron, and reached out for his brother's wheelchair. Cedron barked before Gordon put his hands on the handles, "You know I don't need help, kid. This is my throne. Keep y' distance." He stopped and pushed hard, twirling his wheelchair around to face his brother. "You might got a brew in you; you might have a spirit or two. But *I'm* the king 'round here. Understand?"

Maximilian walked up behind Gordon. "You king after me," he reminded his son with a stern voice. "Got that?" He smiled shortly after.

"Of course, Pop," Cedron assured his father. He turned his wheelchair around, and with a few, strong pushes, rolled into the kitchen and dining area. "You stayin' here tonight, or are you heading back to the Avenue?" he asked his brother.

"I got to get back," he answered, looking at his father as if he had asked the question. "My chamber," he clarified. "I can't sleep, but that keeps me calm and rested."

Cedron again spun around. He advised his brother, "Sleep here in your room, kid. It's been blessed. It's familiar. You got family 'round you, not an empty house."

Gordon remarked, thinking of his time spent at the family Fable Avenue residence, "That house ain't exactly empty."

Maximilian told his youngest son, "I'm sure it isn't, Gordon. But your brother's right. Try staying here a night." He put his hands on Gordon's shoulders. "No random spirits. Like your brother said, we got the spirit of family."

Gordon thought about his mother's presence and responded, "There's family there too." He spoke without thinking. His father reacted, removing his hands from his shoulders.

"Who'd you see?" he asked.

Gordon squirmed away from the question. But he quickly rebounded, telling his father, "Great-granddad. Saw him in London. I saw some of his history with Joseph Pepper. I saw the Fable brothers too. I saw the beginning of the Street. Vivid dreams happening. Sometimes while wide awake. Walking through the house and seein' history."

"Oh," his father responded.

Gordon looked at his brother. "But I'll give it a shot. I'll stay here tonight."

Maximilian slapped his hands together and hollered, "Alright! This all works out. I got the night off. I'mo spend it with my two boys. We gon' play some good rounds of both Majestic and Samedi's Tarot," he grabbed Gordon and tugged at him close, "and some *dragon spit*—heavy on the rum, huh? You've earned it."

Gordon grinned. "Okay, Pop. Not a problem. Had some for the rites."

Maximilian let his son go. "Alright," he repeated. He aimed a stern finger, "But don't go too crazy on the drink, now, hear?" He said to Cedron, "Get us an order of pizza. I know the Elders got this boy jacked up on grains and vegetables, all that righteous food." He threw an air punch at Gordon. "Get some junk food in this kid. You restless with that spirit cuz the Elders got it bored with bein' all right and decent." Then Maximilian gave his eldest son another order to place. "Call around the way too," he commanded. "The bakery—Miss Marjorie's. Get us a cream-filled, dark chocolate cake and a salty caramel cake. Those is y'alls favorite, right?" He looked at both his sons for an answer. "Right?" he repeated sternly.

Gordon and Cedron dropped their heads. They answered their father, "Yeah…"

Maximilian raised his shoulders as he looked at his sons. "Why y'all sound so down?" He turned his head to Cedron and huffed. He ran around the back of his son's wheelchair and wrapped his arms around his body. He balled his hand into a fist and rubbed his knuckles atop Cedron's head. "What? You too cool to have some fun? Huh? You too cool, Second-King-In-Command?" Cedron squirmed, starting to laugh at his father's antics.

Gordon watched his father and brother wrestle. Then Maximilian looked up at him and said as he struggled with Cedron, "You next, understand." He let go of Cedron. The two of them inhaled and exhaled, laughing and throwing air punches. Maximilian walked past Gordon, and Gordon anticipated an attack. His father smacked him on the back and then made his way upstairs. "I'll be back," he said to them. "Cedron, place that order, Mister King." Maximilian's presence turned into creaking footsteps up the stairs.

Gordon and Cedron faced one another, broad smiles on their faces. "Pop sure is happy 'bout all this," said Cedron. Gordon responded with a nod of his head and a simple, *"Yeah. I guess he is."* Cedron locked his hands together. "He been real tense for the last couple days, thinkin' 'bout your second gateway rites, and all." Gordon responded by repeating much the same words to his brother. *"Yeah, I guess he has been,"* he said. "He upstairs now phonin' some honey he was gettin' with tonight that he can't make it." Then Cedron jibbed, "That's magic. That's love." Cedron rolled out of the kitchen toward Gordon. Gordon expected a congratulatory sentiment from Cedron. Instead, Cedron made a sharp turn with his wheelchair, and pushed up onto the ramp leading down into the garden level. "You heard Pop," he said to Gordon. "Make that call."

Gordon tried holding onto his smile, but it dropped away in a slow, defeated manner. He exhaled and shook his head, removing his phone from his pocket. He ordered the pizza first and then the cakes. The remainder of the night passed in fun and excess, as Maximilian Goodspeed intended and had demanded from his sons. Pizza, cake and rum-spiced *dragon spit* were indulged in round after round of cards. Gordon did as his father instructed, however, and took it easy with the alcoholic version of the cultural beverage. A little buzz still tickled his senses after a glass and a half. He felt good in the company of his father and brother.

Through the chatter of taunts, while playing cards, Gordon talked about his upcoming reading with Fey Forrester's grandmother. Maximilian responded to his son that Papa Solomon already informed him about the reading. Gordon kept quiet on the matter about Wilson possibly seeking Cedron and his small crew to help with an assigned grab for Lady Arachne. However, he considered his brother might've already known.

Cedron teased Gordon, accusing him of using a blessing or an incant as a cheat with every round of cards he'd won. Maximilian won the most rounds by night's end. Cedron and Gordon ended the night with a win separating them, Cedron in the lead. But, Gordon took the last hand of cards and joked to his father and brother, "You're only as good as your last game."

Maximilian stood and patted his son on the shoulder. "Good game," he said as he walked out of the dining area. "You two clean up," he ordered his sons, making his way to the stairs.

Gordon looked across the table at his brother. "I heard him," he said with a sardonic tone. "I got this. Go on ahead and do what you gotta do."

Cedron rolled away from the table. "Glad you startin' to learn," he grinned. He pivoted his wheelchair and pushed forward, out into the front room.

Gordon watched his brother's massive frame roll away. He wanted to tell Cedron that his old flame, Leah Kimberly Peters would be visiting at the end of the month, but decided against it. He got up and started cleaning the space, hearing the front door open and then close. He peeked into the front room. Curiosity guided Gordon away from cleaning and to the window where he moved the curtain aside just enough for a sliver of space to see through. Gordon looked out the window at his brother, seeing him light a cigar. His dark, hefty frame was outlined in the moon's fluorescence, keeping Cedron from blending into the night. Cedron was a cool, blue-black specter, blowing smoke and looking skyward. Gordon considered his brother was using an incant to guard him from the autumn night's chill. He backed away from the window and returned to the kitchen to finish cleaning the area. His instinct and spirit frolicked inside him as he tidied the space. He focused on his task, taking deep breaths to calm the stir within. He felt the stars calling to him, excited to have his presence among them again. But Gordon stayed focused on cleaning, ignoring the cosmic pull and the snap of his instinct to join the stars and free his lilac spirit. The junk food only made the spirit more restless. The vegetables and grains were more calming. Gordon tried to pay it all no mind.

Finished, he walked to the front room and opened the door. He asked his brother, "You okay, man?"

Cedron took a puff. "I'm cool, little brother," he answered in a sly way. "Go get some rest. Let that spirit inside you settle a little."

"Don't stay out too long," Gordon warned his brother. "It's cold."

Cedron took another puff on his cigar. He exhaled and said, "Can't feel much of the cold anyway. It can't bother me. No need for an incant." He turned to Gordon and said again, "Now, go get some rest."

"Yeah, man," Gordon said back to his brother. He closed the door and resisted the urge to lock it. He turned around and hurried up the stairs to his room. He turned on the lights and smiled at the sight of his personal belongings having been returned. There was his laptop. There was his television and video game console. His Yankees and music posters covered his wall. There again hung family photos. There were also his model toy figures. One in particular, he was always fond of. The figure stood nine inches with a massive frame, bald head, and jet-black skin with a gold design running around his body like wild circuitry. Gordon stepped toward the toy figure remarking, "I gotta take you back to the Avenue. You definitely have to be a part of my altar, whether called for or not."

"Son," interrupted Maximilian as he knocked against the open door.

Gordon spun around. "Pop…"

"Is it alright if I come in?" Gordon's father asked him.

"Yeah, Pop," Gordon answered. "Come on in."

"Great," Maximilian said, word sounding mumbled. "Thanks, son. Have a seat with me."

Gordon joined his father on the bed. He observed his father trying to settle. Gordon didn't need his acute instinct to buzz or tingle to know that his father was stalling to find the right words to begin the conversation. Nonetheless, the feeling came to Gordon. He remained silent, letting his father stir until easing.

"Gordon," his father said to him. "You ain't seen nobody else besides your great-grandfather? No one came to you. No spirit or vision." Then Gordon's father made it clear to him by asking, "Your mother…?"

Now Gordon fell silent. He heard Cedron enter the house. The door opened. The door closed, and Cedron locked it. Gordon concentrated on the wheels on his brother's wheelchair gliding across the wooden floor of the front room, them pivoting onto the ramp, and going down into the garden level.

"I saw Mom on the first night," Gordon confessed to his father.

"She talk to you?"

Gordon shook his head, no. "No," he expressed aloud. "But there were feelings. I could connect with her feelings." He looked away from his father. He stood and walked to where his favorite toy figure was placed. "She ain't too happy about you burying your sorrows by burying yourself into any female that walks by." Gordon couldn't believe how he'd phrased it. His instinct felt the various emotions washing over his father.

Maximilian's outer demeanor remained calm. He asked his son, "Was that what your silent treatment was about the day I came to visit you?"

Gordon turned around and nodded affirmatively. "Yessir," he said looking back to his toy figure. Maximilian got up. He hesitated to speak, searching for the proper words. Gordon turned and said in a soft voice, "Just sleep on it, Pop."

Maximilian shook his head. "Yeah…I will," he said. He walked out of the room, shutting the door.

Gordon put his attention back on his favorite, childhood toy figure. A warm feeling came over him. It wasn't a wave of sentiment, but an actual increase in temperature. A cool and comforting breeze followed it. Something pressed against Gordon's back, a feeling. His instinct piqued, but instead of the tingle or buzz, the pressure against his back increased.

Something was behind him.

"I knew, Gordon," said a woman's voice.

The pressure lifted. Gordon turned around and saw his mother.

"I always knew," she emphasized. She sat down on the bed. "Either you or Cedron would receive the blessing. I knew." She chuckled through a smile. "It was more than a mother's hope. There was a certainty about it."

A vision came to Gordon. It was Cedron. He was downstairs, on the garden floor, and it was at this very moment. He was observing a favorite childhood toy of his own, taking it from his altar and admiring it. The nine-inch figure was a ghostly spirit with a billowing tail and a single eye made from a violet, transparent plastic to imply a glowing effect.

The vision disappeared.

Gordon turned and looked at his favorite toy figure.

"I think you gave us the wrong totems," he remarked to his mother.

"Did I?" she retorted through a sly smile.

Gordon didn't think on it. He asked, "What about dad?"

His mother replied, "Goodnight, Gordon." Then she faded away.

Gordon's anger felt like a giant hand shaking him. He closed his eyes and took deep breaths. He couldn't afford to be upset, not while being so far away from his chamber. Popping into the Goodspeed residence on Fable Avenue was out of the question as well. The 'pop' would exhaust him greater than his chamber could relax. He'd already spent enough energy popping halfway to Harlem, which forced him to take the train the rest of the way.

Gordon opened a drawer on his dresser, sifting through it for nightclothes. Finding a pair of loose sweatpants, he decided to wear that to bed instead of proper bedclothes. He removed his clothes, slipped on the sweatpants, and kept on his tank top. He slid into his bed, under the covers. He could feel the blessing Maman Anansi put upon his room. Its intangible essence wrapped around Gordon, putting him at ease. His brother was right. It was familiar territory, and he felt no different than if he'd been inside his chamber.

There was no sleep for Gordon Goodspeed. But it felt good to be home in bed.

Fey Forrester watched her grandmother with a subtle disquiet expression while sitting next to her at the table. Savannah, legs crossed, and with her overlapping leg bouncing rapidly, tapped the ashes of her cigarette into the ashtray. Fey observed her grandmother staring eagle-eyed at Gordon Goodspeed. She hadn't said a word since Fey introduced the two of them. Fey considered her grandmother was trying to pry answers from Gordon without asking any questions, just watching, plucking the answers from Gordon's brain without him speaking.

Savannah puffed on her cigarette. She blew out a cloud of smoke, being courteous enough to exhale away from Fey and Gordon. The smoke's billowing trail disintegrating into a thin, curvy stream that filtered through the slightly raised kitchen window. Gordon cleared his throat, and as if it was a cue for Savannah to speak, she finally talked to him, stating, "We Forrester women are from a long line of superstitious female folk."

Gordon nodded. He appeared more relaxed than Fey, but Fey knew Gordon was very anxious to receive his reading and altar instructions. He'd admitted to her that the spirit brewing inside him was striking him like a lightning storm. But he sat patient, and Gordon's calm demeanor helped Fey relax as well, albeit only a little.

"We Forresters can trace our ancestry back to the woods around this area—hence our name," she continued to inform. Gordon again nodded. "Kumi and Kendra Forrester are the names of our ancestors in this country. It was they who took the name. They were the 'forest dwellers'—free blacks living in the woods. Kumi's father was an African man," Savannah smiled and said with soul and passion, "dark and beautiful as the continent itself." She took a drag, blew, and tapped the ashes into the ashtray. "Kumi's mother, a slave woman of mixed heritage, called him *Talisman.* He was sold, used as a buck in Southern slave-breeding pens." Savannah paused to let the thought sink in. "Kumi's mother had inside her a conjure of sorts. It was a blessing, and she was kind enough to give that blessing to her two boys upon her passing. The oldest was named James. He could pass for white. He and Kumi had different fathers. James' father was mixed too. The boys and their mother worked for a storeowner down in the city. But as her blessing would have it, when their master died—not too soon after his wife, and the murder of his two older boys by way of a gang fight—James inherited that family's business. No one batted an eye, because, like I said, James could pass for white."

"Wow," Gordon remarked.

"There's more to the story," Savannah said as she blew a stream of smoke and unintentionally moved it about when she waved her hand to signal a change in subject, "But it all comes down to this. Settling on Fable Avenue was nothing less than appropriate. My family moved to Fable Avenue from Mount Vernon in the early sixties. I was eleven at the time. My father didn't believe in Fable Avenue's ideals, and it split him and my mother apart. But my sister and brother and I got to see him on occasion. And there was no real bad blood between him and my mother. There was just a difference in opinion about where black folks need to be when it comes to our culture." Savannah crushed her cigarette out in the ashtray. Her expression became sullen. "That influenced me a lot more than I expected when I went off to college. Despite my best efforts to marry a good Fable Avenue boy, or a conjure man of some nature there was no blessing that would accord me that. Never thought to do a blessing myself, not with my gift. But of course, such is the curse of the Forrester family."

Fey didn't like her grandmother's last words. She made a face and sighed, "Nana…"

"It's true child," Savannah said back to Fey. "Shit. We got to acknowledge it. That's part of gettin' around it. I didn't curse us. You got to blame your ancestor for that." She turned to Gordon and said, "Kendra Forrester's mother set that on us. Shit! Don't acknowledge the Most High's gift to you, then that gift will turn against you. I didn't seek what I wanted through my own gift, and instead of a good Fable Avenue man, I met Daryl Turman. It was my third year attending Howard University. He was handsome," Savannah said in deep reflection. "Just a fine, brown skinned young man," she continued. "He was from Maryland. Lord, did I fall in love with him. Child, a curse was never so much a blessing. And he was a good man. Gave me three good children," she stated her fact. She relaxed and said, "His family knew nothing of incants or conjures, and they were strict Southern Baptists."

Gordon grinned and remarked, "Uh, oh!"

"You ain't ever said nothing more proper, Mister Gordon Goodspeed," Savannah replied. "Shit. Never did you." She asked Gordon, "You want something to drink? I got some cranberry juice up in that refrigerator."

"Yes, ma'am," said Gordon. "Please."

Fey moved to stand. Savannah waved her down. "I'll get it child. Don't you worry about gettin' up. You know I need to move about when I run my mouth." Savannah rose from her seat.

Gordon chuckled, and Fey rolled her eyes. But a smile did break through her expression, and it washed away most of her anxiety. Savannah walked toward the refrigerator. Gordon looked up at Fey, beaming at her. She smiled back. Savannah continued her story, "We moved to Mount Vernon soon after graduating college. Had a small wedding first in Maryland. Both our families showed up. I took my husband's last name not so much out of love or traditional obligation, but to shield him from the Fable Avenue culture, removing the reminder that I was from it. I made little mention about the goings-on of the people. But my Daryl had his suspicions. His thoughts and opinions stirred while visiting Fable Avenue, listening all attentive to how the people of the street spoke and of the topics. His strict Baptist upbringing took over and changed his demeanor." She removed a tall glass from the cupboard and a jug of cranberry juice from the refrigerator. She asked Fey if she wanted any, and Fey responded politely that she did not. "My Daryl was more devout in family," Savannah said as she poured. "But that devotion to family extended to his mother and father and how they raised him. I didn't want my Daryl and me to be separated. I wasn't going to raise my children the way I had to be raised. Parents all apart and what not." She finished pouring the cranberry juice and put the jug back inside the refrigerator. Before returning to her seat, Savannah made a grab for a bottle of gin resting atop the refrigerator. The tips of her fingers slid against the bottle as she made quick grabs at it. Savannah lifted herself on the tips of her toes for a better reach.

Fey asked her grandmother, "Nana, you need me to help?"

This prompted Gordon to turn around. "I can get that for you, Miss Forrester."

"Ain't a need," Savannah insisted, bouncing on the tips of her toes for a better reach. "Why do I make things so difficult for myself?" She balanced Gordon's drink so as not to spill a drop. "Damn! Fey, them overgrown lightning bugs of yours been gettin' into my gin again?"

"I don't think so, Nana. But I'll give a scolding, just in case."

Savannah snatched the bottle on a hop. "Precious Lord!" she blurted with a scowl. She made her way back to the table, set the filled glass in front of Gordon, and sat back down in her seat. She placed the bottle of gin beside her ashtray.

"Now where was I? Oh, yes. I was making fewer and fewer visits to Fable Avenue; that was my point." She exhaled and looked at the bottle of gin. "My children rarely saw much of my side of the family. My Daryl referred to Fable Avenue as the 'Devil's Den'. He was only joking," she assured. Then she continued, "Soon my mother passed away. I thought it was our curse, and me not being a part of Fable Avenue. I mean, not all Fable Avenue families are raised on that street."

"That's right, ma'am," Gordon interjected. "I grew up in Harlem."

"See? That's what I know. Shit," Savannah said in a rough voice, but with a smile. Then she concluded, "My siblings moved out of New York or to other boroughs. I didn't mind much. But then there was my youngest child. Emma." She turned to Fey and said, "Your mother. There was something in that child's eye, a gleam that shined the instant she was birthed into the world." Her attention was on Fey. "The first time I rocked your mother to sleep, I recounted historical, whimsical tales of ancient Africa, incants and conjures assisting African slave rebellions in America. And I told her about the jazz of Fable Avenue. Daryl didn't seem to mind." Her voice turned melancholy. "Then, after a time, he got sick. There was no blessing that could stop that. I thought it was the curse again, giving me a sign I wasn't doing enough." She smiled at Gordon. "Like I said, superstitious." Savannah composed herself. "When my Daryl passed, I took up the name Forrester again. I moved to Fable Avenue. By that time, Fey's aunt and uncle were too old for any coming-of-age rites. They kept their last name as Turman. But I changed my little Emma's name. She was going to be something else." Her voice trailed away. Savannah shook her head, eyes looking disappointed.

Fey noticed Gordon's uneasy look.

"I know there's politics between the Elders and you," Gordon stated.

"Don't say no more, Gordon," Savannah said to him. "Fey," she called. "Go upstairs, please. I need some privacy to give Mister Goodspeed his reading."

"Yes, Nana," Fey complied. She stood, giving Gordon one last look. Her eyes said, *'Good luck'.* Gordon made a slight nod, his smile cut to half. And then Fey was gone.

There was Gordon. He and Savannah again stared eye-to-eye in silence. But only seconds passed before Savannah presented a calming, sincere smile. "Such lovely eyes, Gordon," she said to him. "I always told my daughter that the spirit would come through, and a boy would have lilac eyes." She chuckled. "I'm no seer. Hell, we all expected that. But I loved telling my baby about those eyes that I see before me now." She paused and then asked of Gordon, "Give me your palm, Mister Goodspeed."

Gordon complied.

Savannah spread his fingers out wide and told him to keep them that way. She reached into the ashtray and scooped up a good amount of ashes, and sprinkled them into Gordon's palm. "I don't smoke for my health," Savannah remarked, making Gordon chuckle. She curled Gordon's fingers into a fist and squeezed. "Now, let's wait a moment."

"Yes, ma'am," said Gordon.

Savannah cupped both her hands tight over Gordon's fist. "Gordon," Savannah began. "There's something I want for my granddaughter, and it's something she would like too."

"Yes, Miss Forrester?"

"I know she's older, but I want her to have the proper rites of a Fable Avenue child. This is something I'm going to suggest when the Elders come inside from waiting in their car out there—and they may or may not agree with my demands. But I want you to put a strong word in should they not."

"I will, Miss Forrester," Gordon responded. "But I don't think they'd have any trouble with that."

"I know they probably won't, especially Lady Arachne." Then Savannah admitted, "I call her every-so-often. We speak, but I tell her not to let the other Elders know we've spoken. I do believe she's kept her word. She's the most sensible of them," Savannah opined. "Papa Solomon and she used to be sweet on one another before Madame Jeliya came into the picture."

Gordon didn't say anything.

"Oh, yeah," Savannah drawled. "But you ain't hear none of that from me, hear."

Gordon pondered for only a moment the love politics between Papa Solomon, Lady Arachne, and Madame Jeliya. But he mostly wondered how Fey's grandmother felt addressing the Fable Avenue matriarchs and patriarch as Elders, considering she was a little under ten years their senior. But such things were titles, and said out of respect. He also didn't mention that Lady Arachne had not come with the other Elders, and now had a good guess as to why his instinct stopped him from doing so earlier.

Savannah opened Gordon's hand and made a quick blow of breath against the compacted ash. Most of the residue disappeared rather than having been blown away. The ash left behind dug into the lines on Gordon's palm. Savannah opened the bottle of gin and poured it into Gordon's hand. Smoke rose, and Gordon flinched as his hand stung with heat. It didn't hurt too much, but Gordon wasn't expecting the sensation. Savannah held Gordon's hand in place. The ash dissipated into smoke, and Gordon's palm returned to normal temperature.

Savannah peered into his palm. She asked while gazing at the lines, "Miss Ross still run the apothecary shop?" Gordon replied with a *"yes,"* and also emphasized that her daughter had taken up most of the work. Savannah looked up at Gordon. "Her oldest? Lavette?" Gordon responded with another *"yes."* "What about Miss Barnes with the curio shop?" Gordon informed that it was her son Wilson that ran the shop at present. "That boy still anything like his father?" asked Savannah, making a face.

Gordon laughed in an attempt to dodge the question. But he answered, "He's cool. He's settled, enough."

Savannah raised an eyebrow. "Well you'll need to pay them both a visit," she insisted. "Take Fey with you. Let her go see the house. It won't be easy, but take her there."

"I will, Miss Forrester," Gordon complied in a sincere voice.

Savannah returned her attention to Gordon's palm. She inspected it for a moment. "Keep your hand out," she said to him. Gordon stayed steady as Savannah retrieved a pencil and paper. She sat back down, made a quick peek at Gordon's palm, and informed as she wrote, "You get yourself a fern-pattern cloth, any color. Place that over a small, wooden altar. The altar ain't gotta be fancy, just something to use as a foundation. Understood?" Gordon nodded. "Get yourself a ceremonial dagger, some type of cup—chalice or goblet. Break off a thin tree branch. Make sure it ain't longer than fourteen inches. Last primary item you need for this altar is a Seal of Solomon amulet or coin. Make sure it has an inscription from them old books called the sixth and seventh Books of Moses. That seal there will allow you to render that spirit inside you obedient, calm it down. You can wear the amulet if you want to, but not until it's charged through ritual."

"Yes, ma'am," Gordon replied.

Savannah continued writing down her instructions for Gordon, taking a peek at his palm every so often. She proceeded, "Get you a small, Moroccan lamp, with blue glass filters. Purchase three, small crystal balls: ruby-red, violet, and black. Put the red ball inside the lamp, put the other two at opposite corners of your altar. You'll need a tiger-eye bracelet," she continued. "Not to wear, but to put on the altar. The last necessary item for your altar is a polished lodestone, a mercury color. " She closed Gordon's hand, again holding his balled fist with both her hands. "Monday is your day. You can perform this ritual whenever you are feeling tired, but Monday will rejuvenate you. Fridays will make you feel amorous." Her voice sounded playful, but her warning was still stern. "So you just watch yourself on Fridays when you got your spirit around my granddaughter, hear."

Gordon again chuckled. "Yes, ma'am," he answered.

"You ain't gotta do much, but you do this here, Gordon," Savannah continued. "You light yourself some musk-scented incense, okay? Make sure it's coated with lemongrass oil. With that, you recite a prayer, any prayer. You can write one up, look in a Bible or some other Holy Book, or even a movie quote that calms you down. But disappear into yourself, and you will sleep well and be rested."

"Thank you, Miss Forrester," Gordon said.

"You welcome, boy. Now, I'll—" There came a knock on the front door. Both Savannah and Gordon reacted, turning their heads to view the door at the end of the hall. Savannah rose from her seat. "That's them damn fools now, Papa Solomon and the matriarchs," she said to Gordon. "They probably had an instinct that we've finished up here, or they just getting impatient in their old age." She tore out the paper she'd been writing on and handed it to Gordon. Savannah told him as he accepted the page, "Go on upstairs. You and Fey make a day together. Take her back to Fable Avenue. Tell her she can take my car."

Gordon jumped up. "Yes, ma'am," he said, walking close behind Savannah.

Fey's grandmother opened the door as Gordon passed her and hurried up the stairs. Maman Anansi was front and center on the porch. Papa Solomon and Madame Jeliya were behind her, flanking. Savannah looked around for Lady Arachne's presence. She was absent. "Where's Lena?" she asked Maman Anansi.

"Business came up," said Maman Anansi as an apology.

"We ain't good enough for you, Savannah?" Papa Solomon said, testing the waters for a joke.

Savannah gave Papa Solomon a look. "You fools got older," she teased. She opened her arms and leaned forward to embrace Maman Anansi, "Come here, you all. It's been long."

"Too long," said Maman Anansi, accepting Savannah's hug, closing her arms around her. The two exchanged kisses on the cheek.

Savannah stepped back and invited the Fable Avenue Elders into her house. "The kids are upstairs," Savannah informed. "I told them to head out. I've already done a reading for Gordon." Just as she spoke her words, Fey and Gordon shuffled down the stairs and into the hall. Savannah and the Elders entered the kitchen and dining area. Savannah offered the Elders a drink or a bite to eat, but each of them expressed a polite decline.

"Nana," Fey called as she lifted her grandmother's car keys from a small, wicker bowl. "Gordon and I are going to Sleepy Orchard for some apple picking. We'll probably head to Brooklyn later." She addressed her grandmother but glanced between the Elders of Fable Avenue, trying to recall their familiarity. They appeared to be doing the same to her, holding smiles and awaiting something from the moment.

Savannah looked at her granddaughter. Fey had her book bag strapped over her shoulder, carrying her sketchbook inside. Savannah answered her granddaughter, "That's fine, Fey. You two go ahead. Gordon, you be well."

"Will be, Miss Forrester," Gordon said, beaming an appreciative smile. "Thank you, again." He waved to her, and then he waved to each of the Elders. Fey and Gordon left the house.

Savannah sat down at the table. She exhaled. Papa Solomon and the matriarchs were courteous to let Savannah speak first. She pondered a moment what she would say, creating a little tension while searching for the right words to lessen thirteen years of anxiety.

"You all mind if I smoke?" she asked the Elders. They did not. Savannah lit up a cigarette. She took a drag. "I don't want much," she said, exhaling her first puff. "Not for myself, anyway." She tapped ashes into the ashtray. "I would like my granddaughter to have access to our house on Fable Avenue, should she choose to stay there. You all know I still pay them taxes."

Maman Anansi blurted, "Well, of course, Savannah. That will always be your family's place."

Savannah took another drag. She paused. Smoke filtered from her nostrils. "I want my Fey to receive her ceremonial rites. Both of them," she insisted. She became quiet, waiting for an answer, but not for long. The Elders agreed. Papa Solomon suggested Fey's rites be held during The Four Days of the Spirit Festival. Savannah tapped ashes into the ashtray. She was prepared for a fight, and not such an easy agreement from the Elders. She gritted her teeth to keep her anger in her throat, to yell, to scream. But instead, her eyes welled with tears. "Thank you," she expressed to the Elders. She wiped her eyes. "I know how folk do," she carried on while smoking. "Stanley Fallows and his kind of folk," she clarified. "His type of bad haunt always makin' a mess among us, and somehow got us fightin' one another while they continue doin' damage on the outside." This broke the ice. Savannah again offered drinks, and this time they were accepted. Savannah got up to supply her guests with refreshments.

At the same moment, Fey Forrester and Gordon Goodspeed drove up toward North Tarrytown to a place called Sleepy Orchard. Fey's yumboes darted around the back of the car, squeaking taunts and insults as they played tag in the air. Gordon watched the lighted creatures, mostly to make sure their play wouldn't roll into the front of the car and disturb Fey's driving. Gordon inquired about the conjured sprites, and Fey answered, "Silver was drawn by my mother. I drew the rest." She turned onto I-287 as she stated, "Their conjure was instinctive. Just a thought would draw their sketch from the page. At first I thought it was my mother's sketchbook, but Silver embedded herself in a sketchbook my grandmother gave me when I was nine. Nana never told me if she put a blessing on it, and I've never asked. When Silver was conjured from that notebook, her wings became different colors. I drew Zee, Em, and Jade into existence soon after."

"You were drawing like a pro when you were nine?" Gordon asked in disbelief.

"I got my skill down by the time I was thirteen," Fey noted. "That's when Zee, Em, and Jade popped up. The sketch had to be right, I guess. Silver kept telling me about them and tasking me with perfecting their image."

The yumboes stopped their playing and gathered on the back of Fey's headrest. Fey shooed them away. "Come on, now! I'm driving!" The yumboes scattered, giggling. They settled on the backseat and started chatting in a language unfamiliar to Gordon. He faced forward, small smile on his face. Fey continued, "Don't be fooled by them pint-sized pixies either. They grown." Fey pursed her lips and rolled her eyes. "You heard my Nana. They drink. They *love* to get into her liquor. They like to cuss. And when they dive back onto the page they go into another world. Their world. Their home."

"Really?" said Gordon excited.

"Oh, yeah," confirmed Fey. "They tell me about it, all their little misadventures there. The politics of their people. Silver says it's like a tropical island where the water surrounding them looks like a mercurial cosmos." Fey made a quick look at Gordon as she stated, "And they got yumbo menfolk there. And all four of them got more than one suitor."

"What?" Gordon questioned with playful disbelief in his voice. "You got yumbo hoes back there?"

Fey almost lost control of the car as a burst of laughter spilled out of her mouth. Silver and the other yumboes lifted in the air, wings flapping rapidly, and with scowls on their faces. They soared toward Gordon, bodies turned to streams of light that bounced against his person and provided a slight stung. Gordon laughed as if tickled, though there was pinching pain pricking at his nerves.

"My bad!" he hollered as he laughed. "You all ain't hoes," he apologized. The yumboes returned to the back seat, their bodies materializing out of the streams of light. "Just a joke," Gordon assured.

"Oh, they was just playing," Fey noted. "You'd know when they weren't messing around, regardless of what spirit you got brewin' in you, Mister Goodspeed."

Gordon made a face. "Oh, really," he said as if accepting a challenge. He turned to the yumboes and said, "Hey!" They turned their attention to Gordon and smiled as he brightened the glow of his eyes. Gordon winked, and the yumboes giggled. He calmed the intensity of the lilac glow and faced forward again. "Your grandmother's reading simmered the stir inside me. I feel okay. Still can't wait to put my altar together and get some sleep. Hope I can find all I need at Wilson's shop."

Fey and Gordon's journey ended at Sleepy Orchard. Fey parked the car. Gordon jumped out as Fey spoke an incant that cloaked her four glowing sprites from watchful eyes. She undid her seatbelt, opened the door, and stepped out. Her yumboes followed, blazing bright, but invisible to the world.

Autumn burned bright at its peak. Leaves enkindled with various sunset shades enlivened the orchard. Apples littered the ground, but many still hung from trees waiting to be plucked by visitors. Fey's yumboes mixed with the ambiance. Gordon surveyed his surroundings as Fey locked the car and came around to meet him. Gordon wanted to take her hand and head toward the store that was staged as a shanty place. But he stayed his hand, putting them in his pockets. Fey observed Gordon's posture. She smiled at him, and motioned for Gordon to follow her toward the store.

"Let's go get a basket," she suggested.

Gordon followed.

They walked into the store, took a moderate-size basket, and told a young man working at the orchard which paths they would be taking. They left to walk the orchard's trails. As soon as they turned onto the new path, Fey reached up and started plucking low-hanging apples, dropping any non-bruised grabs into her basket. "The Forresters were born here. Our name, I mean."

Gordon didn't want to sound too condescending when he spoke his inquiry. He was conscious of his tone when he asked, "And…the curse?"

Fey bubbled with laughter through closed lips. She covered her mouth with a hand and then said, "I'm sorry, Gordon." Gordon was staring at her in wonder. His eyes appeared to ask if there really was a curse. Fey answered the question Gordon's expression was asking. "It's not that there isn't a curse over the Forresters," she started to say as she calmed her chuckle. "It's just that I don't believe it controls us so much. There are ways around it. I find it silly when it's acknowledged with such fear."

"So what's it about?" Gordon asked, reaching for an apple and plucking it from its branch. He tossed it into the basket.

Fey informed, "An ancestor, on my mother's side, her name was Kendra—if you remember."

"Yes."

"It was her mother, really," Fey corrected.

"Yes."

"She was born a slave," Fey explained. "I believe she was in one of the Carolinas. I always forget." She took another apple. "She was very powerful with her incants, but the wrath of her master terrified her. He was an occultist with trinkets to aid him in tricks to silence conjures and incants. He reveled in the subjugation of slaves that carried the ancient power. He was brutal, and many superstitious slave masters went to him for help with conjurors among their stock. Kendra's mother grew up watching other slaves be beaten or raped. She was beaten, most likely raped too, and definitely tinkered and doctored on. As a result, she came to hate herself because of the things she could do. She buried her power deep, but it started to express itself within her children when she gave birth. But it only manifested in the baby girls she birthed. They were born with a glow, and when she saw that glow, she would kill her newborn child."

"Oh, wow…" exhaled Gordon.

Fey had heard and spoken the story too many times to be phased, but a remorseful expression crawled onto her visage by reflex. "Her daughters would be born with a glow, and she would kill them in front of her master to show she harbored no 'special' children."

"He was that powerful?"

"It's been said that he was a Night Doctor," Fey revealed. "A needlemen as they're often called."

Gordon nodded his head. He'd heard the legends and rumors of such nightmares shaped as cruel men. Gordon grew up with his mother and father's warnings of them. Fable Avenue Elders, including Papa Solomon and the matriarchs, spoke on how they would carry African-American incantors or potential conjurors of any age off into the night in the early days of emancipation. They were also used by slave masters to null conjures or incants in slaves, just as Fey was recounting. Hypodermic needles injected a hex into their victims, bodies lulled to sleep, taken and experimented on with more needles to extract conjure and soul. Their beginnings could be traced back to the fourteenth century in Portugal, undoing the spells of Moorish conjurors in al-Andalusia, and used by King Ferdinand and Queen Isabella in the *Reconquista of Spain* from the African Moors. Their needles at that time were the hexed ends of sharpened instruments made of metal or wood.

"He also had the system of slavery on his side," continued Fey. "It empowered and allowed him to be his natural, brutal self. He was so bad, his overseer showed more mercy than him."

"I can't imagine," Gordon commented.

"But then came her seventh child, Kendra," Fey announced with a smile, jumping back into her family's story. "But, by this time, the curse was all up in our bloodline. But this supposed cloudy curse sure was a blessing for great grandmamma Kendra. It's said that she glowed the brightest of all the daughter's born to her mother. Our curse settled into Kendra's mother, making her too tired after giving birth to take her daughter's life. She slept, and she died, blamed on heartache and exhaustion. The midwife raised great grandmamma Kendra, and she kept her safe. She didn't know much of incants or conjures, but she knew how to pray for this newborn child."

A shadow stirred in the woods. Gordon turned his head to the right, eyes blazing. "Uh, Fey, I don't think we're alone."

Fey ignored Gordon and continued telling her tale. "Magic evolves, and the evolution of this magic became a curse that could be avoided. It's simple. Should one choose to ignore his or her power, they would be struck down by it. The magic adapted to its own killing, granting its neglector's wish. Great Grandmamma Kendra accepted her power, using it to commune and control nature and its spirits. She wasn't stupid though. She hid her abilities until she was brought up here along with twenty or so slaves. Her master came up here on a trade deal with a store in the city, and a warehouse up here. Great Granddaddy Kumi's brother, who passed for white, owned the store in the city. I think this was around seventeen-ninety-nine, or it was eighteen hundred. It was a few decades or so before blacks were free in New York. My great granddaddy Kumi acted as his brother's servant."

Gordon saw the shadow stir again, still on his right. The black specter darted between trees and brush. Gordon's bright eyes scanned the woods, trying to follow the shade's path, but it was gone. Behind Fey and he, people flocked, chuckling, picking apples, and sharing stories just the same, but different.

"This way, Gordon," Fey beckoned, taking the left hand path. "Come on. Follow."

Gordon was hesitant. He gave one last look to the area, and then followed. He retracted the glow of his eyes as more people entered the orchard. No one followed them down their new path.

"I think there's something in the woods, Fey," Gordon whispered, looking around.

"Of course there is," Fey said. "It's an indigenous spirit. The Native Americans used it to fight off trouble. But a colonizer with tricks removed the spirit of its head. Then it was wild. Many colonizers with tricks tried to control it for personal gain. Grandmamma Kendra's slave master tried to control the spirit, but he was defeated by her conjures. Granddaddy Kumi played a part too." The shadow glided through the woods again. "They restored the spirit's head, and it again defended the land." Fey stopped walking. She turned to Gordon and said with a sly smile, "Needless to say, my ancestors, Kendra and Kumi were free after that incident. They settled these woods, and called themselves Forresters, They who live Among the Trees."

Gordon had more questions, but he never asked them. Instead he froze when noticing the tall, massive, black-armor clad warrior standing in their path. Three of Fey's yumboes sat atop its shoulders while Silver was perched on its black-armored head. It carried sharp sickles in either hand, and a ghostly aura billowed around its person. Gordon faced the specter. Amazement brightened his expression as well as the lilac-colored glow of his eyes. Though the armor-clad specter presented no resemblance to Gordon's favorite toy figure, with the exception of its pitch color, it was as if his childhood hero had sprung to life. His open-mouth smile widened. He shifted into his black, cosmic attire. His single eye blazed lilac, swirling.

Fey backed away from him, mouth agape and eyes filled with awe.

Then Dooley blazed into the lilac spirit, and Fey checked her surroundings so that no one was witness. Dooley bowed with humility toward the iron giant. The spirit bowed back. Its armored frame made the gesture appear more ominous than humble. But neither Fey nor Dooley were frightened.

The spirit burst into black dust, shifted together from individual particles that formed a shadow and dived back into the woods. Fey's yumboes scattered, following the mobile shade, playing a game of chase.

Gordon shifted out of his spirit form. He was on the ground, in his regular attire, one knee bent, torso bowed. He stood and dusted himself off. Fey again checked to see if there were any witnesses. A trail of people trickled past the path they had turned down, talking and laughing and paying no attention to them.

"Well, look at you, Mister Goodspeed," said Fey, awe still exploding on her face. "Will you go ahead and look at you."

Gordon reached out a hand to Fey. She, in turn, looped their rented basket around her left arm, and accepted Gordon's hand with her right.

"You can put pen to paper, Miss Forrester, and bring your imagination into existence," Gordon told her as they continued walking their path.

"Yes, I can," she acknowledged.

"I can turn into a spirit and fly to the stars to commune with others like me," Gordon continued. He looked at Fey and smiled as he said, "I'm sure everyone in our culture will be able to do that soon. You included."

Fey beamed and retorted, "Let's finish apple picking for now."

"Of course."

They continued on their path, both reaching up and plucking apples from their surroundings.

After finishing their time in the orchard picking apples, Fey Forrester and Gordon Goodspeed paid for what they'd picked and sat in the small park located near the parking lot. They drank cider and munched on apple-cider donuts. Autumn's atmosphere and color hugged them. Hot cider and conversation kept them warm, and after spending time in the orchard's park, they enjoyed an afternoon at the cinema. Fey's yumboes joined them, invisible to the world the whole time. At the cinema, Gordon discovered the creatures could control their flesh's luminescence. Fey had to renew her incant to keep her yumboes discreet, hidden from the eye of normal folk. The whole time, however, Gordon couldn't ignore Fey's glow, her beautiful dark skin glimmering with the light of the screen. Also consuming his attention was Fey's loose sweatshirt hanging off her shoulder, exposing it. It was enticing, arousing his spirit. He kept an eye on the movie, but the best picture sat next to him, a preview at every curve.

Fey kept her eyes forward, pretending not to notice Gordon's glances, and being more discreet with her scrutiny of his presence.

Fey decided not to visit Fable Avenue, and Gordon understood. There was so much good that happened in the day, she didn't want to smear it by visiting the house where tragedy struck her family. Fey dropped Gordon off at the Metro North train after the movie and a small bite to eat. She teased him that he could just 'pop' home, but here he was opting to take 'the long route.' Gordon found it amusing too, but he explained how the act would heighten the already excited spirit inside him, and that he was desperate to render it still with her grandmother's altar. He also made mention that he was going to stop in Harlem and pick up a few items before continuing to Fable Avenue and procuring items for his altar. Before parting, Gordon and Fey split the apples evenly.

Fey returned home, greeted by her grandmother in the hall as she walked through the front door. Savannah was smiling, a gesture Fey had not seen in a long time. Then her grandmother said to her, "I had a good talk with them Elders. Not everything is reconciled, but I got what I wanted." Fey looked at her grandmother. Her perplexity demanded answers. "You can stay at our residence on Fable Avenue, should you choose." Fey nodded, but guessed that there was more news. Her grandmother obliged her silent inquiry by stating, "And you, should you so choose, will receive your rites within the Fable Avenue community."

Fey's face lit up, and she blurted, "Nana! Really! Are you serious?"

Savannah bubbled with laughter and hugged Fey.

Fey pulled away from the embrace to repeat, *"Nana! Really! Are you serious?"*

"Yes, little girl. I am. You. Will. Receive. Your. Rites."

Fey jumped up and down, taking her grandmother with her as she wrapped her arms around her. Settling, she backed away, trying to stay still. She inquired, "I'm not too old or nothin'?"

"No, child!" barked Savannah. "Shit. Even if you were too old, the Elders agreed."

Fey took a breath. She closed her eyes and tried to relax. She couldn't. Her body stiffened, and she wobbled back and forth with a toothy grin on her face. *"Nan-na!"*

"Now, child, listen. I've told you about The Four Days of the Spirit festival. Fable Avenue does it big. Not like the little somethin' we do around here. It's a block party. A couple of them days are held outside of time."

Fey looked around in wonder. She said aloud, "I've never been outside time before."

"It don't feel no different than being along with time," Savannah said, pursing her lips and waving off Fey's sentiments. "Now, I told that Goodspeed boy to argue in my favor should the Elders disagree with the proposal. So, I guess that's one less thing for him to worry about. Did you all go to Fable Avenue today?"

"No, Nana," Fey admitted, voice full of regret. "We had such a wonderful time up at Sleepy Orchard. We saw the guardian! And Gordon showed me the spirit inside him. He just turned into it. It was a sight. You should've seen it." Then, as if it carried the same weight, Fey added, "We talked. We had a bite to eat. We even went to a movie."

Savannah raised an eyebrow. "Oh. Oh-kay, little girl," she commented with a look on her face.

Fey slapped her grandmother on the arm. *"Nana!"* she exclaimed. "Gordon is handsome, and he's a good man. But, to be honest…" Fey hesitated. She exhaled. "I'm not using him, under any circumstances. But I've always been curious about Fable Avenue, the culture. Our culture. My culture." She tilted her head back and again exhaled hard. "Oh, it was such a relief when he approached me on campus." She walked past her grandmother and to the table. She pulled a chair out and dropped her bag in it, putting the bag of apples on the table. She pulled out another chair and took a seat. Savannah joined Fey, taking a seat at the table. "I've never been able to talk to my closest of friends the way I've been able to talk to him." Fey admitted, "And he's handsome, and that makes it fun when we flirt a little. I mean, that's going to be natural, especially having so much in common. But I'm sure being able to talk about incants and conjures and my yumboes, even my past, to anyone on Fable Avenue, or attached to the community, would be just as easy."

Savannah nodded. She put her hand over Fey's.

Fey thought about it all, the last few days. "Necessary, Nana, is something I can't do without," Fey stated, stressing her words. "I don't think I can be a proper 'me' and 'self' without being a part of Fable Avenue." Her eyes watered. One tear slipped, and she wiped her cheek of its stream. "I don't blame you, Nana. You were protecting me."

Savannah tightened the grip on Fey's hand. Her voice compressed in her throat, but she spoke through it. "I was. But I'll admit it was a little selfish of me, guarding you from your heritage for so long, or the people of it." She aimed a finger and using a stern voice she reminded, "I taught you much, and I taught you well, little girl."

"Yes, Nana," Fey agreed. "You did." She looked around the room, but saw more than the dining area and the kitchen. She saw all of Mount Vernon, and her past growing up in it. She said to her grandmother, "This has been our home, Nana, but in some ways it hasn't, really. Circumstances made this a safe haven, and I *have* felt safe, and I've had good times growing up here. I've been raised right and well among family, and you've done a wonderful job being everything to me. But our culture is calling, and it needs our help, yours more than mine. I just have some rites that rightfully belong to me. No more seclusion. After all, I have too much of this magic in me. Even all the way here in Mount Vernon, I am Fable Avenue." Fey lifted her grandmother's hand to her lips and gave it a kiss. "Thank you, Nana, for securing *my* grand wish."

Savannah's grip on her granddaughter loosened.

Fey excused herself from the table. She stood up, snatched her bag from the table, and walked into the hallway.

"Little girl," Savannah called over her shoulder. Fey paused, attentive to her grandmother's call. "This may be difficult, but you ain't got to cut yourself off from the friends you made 'round here."

"Oh, I know that, Nana," said Fey. "But graduating high school has already done that. Most of my friends are gone. And other issues have scattered certain friends to the wind. On the flipside, you don't have to cut yourself off from Fable Avenue, considering I'll be taking up residence there."

Savannah chuckled. "I know that, little girl. That's my home."

"Yes, Nana," responded Fey before turning and walking away.

"Little girl," Savanna called again. Fey twirled around. "Gordon is a good Fable Avenue boy," Savannah stressed to her granddaughter.

"Yes, Nana," Fey conceded. She laughed, turned around, and walked upstairs to her room. She tossed her bag to her bed and burned incense at her altar. She removed her phone and texted Gordon. Her note read: *You sure can keep a secret. My grandmother told me she was going to use you as a mouthpiece to argue for me to have my rites.*

She waited for a moment. Gordon replied: *Day was so fun, that whole thing slipped my mind. Congratulations, Fey. That mean I'll see you on the Avenue soon?*

Fey responded, *Yes, but I'm still apprehensive. I have to do this, though. I hope you sleep well, Mister Goodspeed.*

Thank you, Fey. See you on campus Monday.

Fey raised an eyebrow. She thought to herself, *Why not tomorrow?* Then she figured Gordon's ritual at his altar would bring him into a deep, well-deserved sleep. Fey wrote back: *See you Monday.*

...if I'm not still in a coma, that is. If I am, will Sleeping Beauty kiss the Prince awake?

Did he just write that, thought Fey. She laughed and rolled her eyes. *Goodnight, Mister Goodspeed!* she typed and sent.

It was worth a shot, Gordon's response came up on her phone.

Fey rolled her eyes again, smile on her face. She set her phone down and sat on her bed. She pulled out her sketchbook, opening to the page where her yumboes were sketched. She called them forth with an incant recited in her head.

"Guess what?" Fey asked the sprites as they hovered at attention in front of her. "I will be receiving my rites at the end of this month." The yumboes gasped, clapped and danced in the air. "I'm happy too. There's much to do, my little, winged women. Much to do." Fey stood. She put one hand on her hip and her other hand flat against her chest and declared, "I will be the flyest sister on the block that day. Believe that if you don't believe nothing else." She walked with an exaggerated, regal step toward the window. She lifted it and said an incant toward her yumboes, cloaking them from sight. "Take flight in the night, you four. Have fun."

The yumboes ghosted through the window instead of ducking under where Fey had opened it. She closed the window behind them, making a face. The yumboes sang in an excited harmony, diving into the night. Fey returned to her bed. She took up her sketchbook again and flipped through it. Her smile faded, page by flipped page. She stopped on a three-year-old sketch she drew of a broken-winged faerie flanked by two figures. Fey's mother was one figure. Fey's father was the other. She'd drawn their likeness from an old photograph.

Fey inspected the drawing with her eyes and the tips of her fingers. Course, thick paper was all she felt. Inanimate sketches were all she saw. Fey looked up at the window as her yumboes in colorful flight streamed by. She wondered how real she could make her drawings.

It was at this time that Gordon Goodspeed was boarding the 8-Train. He'd picked up a few items at his house, stuffed them in his book bag, made small talk with his father and brother, and left before any emotional issues arose with either of them. Gordon received five hundred dollars from his father to purchase the items needed for his altar. It was probably more than enough, but Gordon was grateful, and his father told him the money came from community members in honor of his rites.

It was close to nine o'clock when he returned to Fable Avenue. He stopped at Lavette Ross' apothecary shop and purchased the oils and incense he was tasked to obtain. She like everyone else marveled at the color of his eyes. It didn't bother Gordon. He knew that people's draw to his eyes wasn't just about their glow and look, it was also about what his new eyes symbolized. Miss Ross also inquired what more would be asked of him now that a spirit brewed in him. Gordon had no answer for her. He only offered that the Elders were engaged in strenuous research to discover the answer, reaching out to, and also informing, conjure communities around the nation and world. Gordon left an apple for Miss Ross, and after exiting her apothecary outlet, he phoned Wilson Barnes. Gordon caught Wilson still at his curio store, readying to lock up. Gordon told him to wait, and that he needed a few items.

"Ceremonial dagger?" asked Gordon over the phone, his steps quick and in a hurry down the block.

"Yeah, sun," Wilson replied. "I gotchu, man. What else you need?"

Gordon unfolded the paper with the list. He huffed at the fine, cursive writing scribbled onto the page. He hated cursive. It was always so hard to read, especially if it was fancy. He stopped walking, not needing to hurry, considering Wilson was willing to stay open for his purchase. He stood under a streetlamp and read off the items he needed.

"Come on, come on. Let me see," he said. He brought the paper closer to his eyes and the light. Then he remembered the color of his eyes and their glow as something he could adjust. "I could probably use my glow to see this," he huffed, rolling his eyes.

"What?"

"Nothing," Gordon said back to Wilson. "Just forgetting I can do things, you know. Hold up," said Gordon scanning his list. "I need a fern-patterned cloth, any color."

"I got an altar cloth," Wilson confirmed.

"Does it got ferns on it, or whatever?" Gordon asked annoyed.

"Yeah, my dude, I gotchu. I got to have stuff at the ready, kna'mean?"

"Right." Gordon relaxed. He continued, "Okay, I got myself a small altar. I'm good there."

"Don't tell me what you got, tell me what you need!"

"Sun!" Gordon yelled. "You know I can shift into a spirit and take yer ass into space, right? I just leave you for the cosmos to take care of y' ass." He heard Wilson giggle over the phone. The teasing chuckle made Gordon relax his mood, but he still warned Wilson, "Sun, I swear."

"Yeah, you real ornery, my dude. Got that brew stirred in you."

"Anyway…" Gordon scanned his list. He didn't need a cup, already procuring one from his home in Harlem. He'd also taken a twelve-inch twig from the tree outside his family's Harlem residence. "I need a Seal of Solomon coin with an inscription from the sixth and seventh Books of Moses."

"A seal to render a spirit obedient…" Wilson spoke aloud, writing it down.

Gordon took the comment differently. "Yeah, thanks for summing up the plot, Mister Expository."

Wilson teased, "Yeah, that spirit you got need some obedience, sun." More light laughter followed. "You need to calm y' ass down."

Gordon chuckled, but he still barked, "I will take that ceremonial dagger and…ugh! Anyway, man. You got them small, Moroccan lamps? I need one with blue glass filters."

"You good. I gotchu."

"I need three crystal balls: ruby, violet, and black, sixty millimeters in diameter. And a tiger-eye bracelet," Gordon continued. "And the last necessary item is a polished lodestone, mercury in color."

"Would you like fries with that?" joked Wilson. Gordon rolled his eyes on his end of the phone conversation. "Getcho ass over here, man," Wilson ordered. "I got all that."

"You about to have a fight," Gordon said walking down the street.

"Bring it, bruh!" Wilson retaliated with sarcasm.

"On my way. Have my shit ready," Gordon played. He hung up the phone and jogged down the street to Wilson's shop, which was located at the corner of Fable Avenue and Marcy. Gordon came upon the store and knocked on the door. Wilson opened.

"Items all ready, man," Wilson noted with a proud smile.

"How much is all this gonna be?"

"A buck sixty-eight."

"Put it on the Elders' tab," Gordon joked.

Wilson retorted, "Whatever, sun. I'll have them pay you back. How 'bout that?"

Gordon handed Wilson two, hundred dollar bills. Wilson accepted. He went to his register to retrieve Gordon's change. "You went up to see Savannah Forrester today? How she doin'?"

"She got a lot on her mind," Gordon answered. "Especially with all this. It opens up a whole lotta things for her, to say the least. She was goin' on about her family, about how it's possibly cursed. She believe it too, but she ain't held down by it."

"Yeah," was how Wilson responded. "I remember Emma used to talk about her family's curse." He recalled the memories as he punched the numbered keys on the register. The drawer opened, and Wilson exchanged the bills given to him with the amount of change to hand back to Gordon. "That's you, sun," he told Gordon, handing him the change. "How's the granddaughter?"

"She's real cool," Gordon said with a wide smile. "She's receiving her rites. Ain't that somethin'? After all this time."

"Okay, alright," Wilson replied. He and Gordon walked to the door, materials gathered.

"We spent the day together. Went apple picking." Gordon showed his bag holding half of the apple-picking prize.

"Oh-kay!" Wilson's voice went up. "You gon' be hangin' out with her more often?" He wrapped his arm around Gordon and shook him.

"Hey, if I can. She's good people. She's *our* people." Gordon added, "She's like her grandmother, but different. You know? She's got a lot on her mind because of all this, but there's more life to Fey. Her grandmother's still torn up, and that affects everything, her and Fey."

"I understand. Keep your distance, but don't look like you keepin' your distance."

"And make a signal to get a signal."

"Ha! Yeah, right." He slapped Gordon on the arm.

Gordon and Wilson exchanged goodbyes. Gordon left the shop and went home. Two steps down the street, he popped out of existence. Quicker than a blink, he was in his basement. It felt good to use his spirit for convenience. But, he immediately realized how much it took out of him. Gordon turned on the lights, inhaling as if he'd been knocked in the gut by a heavy punch. The room was spinning, and he was dizzy. He took a moment, hand on the wall, keeping him standing. He closed his eyes and breathed slowly. After a few breaths, he opened his eyes and observed the room. There was no spin. He took his hand off the wall and made a cautious step forward. The disorienting dizziness was gone. He set everything down and went to work constructing his altar. A moderate-sized and intricately designed side table acted as the base. He draped the pale-purple, fern-patterned cloth over the top of the table. He set upon it the items he'd procured, arranged with his own design. In addition to the necessary items, Gordon also placed upon his altar his favorite toy figure and a set of Tarot cards designed by an Afro-Cuban man who lived up the street. He loved the drawings on the cards. They spoke so much with their detail.

Then Gordon lit the incense. He sat crossed legged on the floor in front of the altar, eyes closed and his hands on his knees. He breathed in and out, the scent of musk and lemongrass filling his nostrils. The aroma tickled the back of his neck. He tasted the scents in his throat, felt the perfumed air fill his lungs.

He needed to chant a prayer. Gordon considered a passage from the poetic narrative scribed in *The Written*. But so much of it was gloomy. He wanted to relax, without mention of his poetic doppelganger. In his mind, he chanted: *Dooley is a lilac flame, extinguished and at rest. Let the flame rise another time.*

Nine times he chanted in his head. Then all the restless energy bubbling inside him dropped like water cascading over a fall. Gordon opened his eyes. He was tired. He attempted to stand, but his body wobbled, intoxicated with fatigue. He turned his head, the movement sluggish. His vision blurred. He looked at his chamber and decided he didn't want to sleep in a box. He wanted a bed.

Gordon tipped over, making a haphazard plant with his elbow against the floor. Gordon collapsed onto his back. He maintained consciousness long enough to pop from his basement and up to his bedroom. He felt the soft embrace of the bed underneath him, and he kicked off his shoes at the end of the bed. His footwear rolled onto the floor, their thud sounding as heavy and tired as he. Gordon managed to slip under the covers, an ordeal that was slow. Lethargy possessed Gordon now.

Eyes closed. In the bed. Under the covers. Still as Gordon was, he felt as if he was being dragged somewhere. He made no attempts to resist the pull. Sleep was too good and long overdue.

Private investigator Martin Kimball didn't just knock on Lady Arachne's residence at seven-thirty in the morning. He pounded a hard fist several times against her parlor-floor entrance door. Two days ago, Martin believed he had something. He called for Lady Arachne's time, but his lead went cold. Now he had concrete news for her, and he was anxious to deliver said news, as his heavy hammering against the door proved. He knew the matriarch wouldn't approve of his feverish knocks, but she would understand once she heard what he'd uncovered.

Next to Martin was his partner, Macario Montez, a Puerto Rican man in his late-thirties, of average height and slender build. Both men wore suits, no tie, and pea coats. Lady Arachne answered the door dressed in a night robe, her locks draped past her shoulders. On her face was a scowl that backed Martin away from the door. He and Macario stood at attention.

Lady Arachne cleared the scowl from her face, huffing. And though she opened the door with regal elegance, her scowl sat subtly in her voice when she addressed the two men, "You found something?"

Martin nodded. "Talk about our story coming together, Lady A. Our bait got a bite."

Lady Arachne looked up and down the block. Then she told the two men, "Come in."

Macario allowed Martin to enter first. Martin stepped into the house, following Lady Arachne, and with Macario in tow. "We found your cards, Lady A."

Lady Arachne opened the sliding doors leading to her study. She walked inside, walked up to one of her Victorian-styled chairs, but did not take a seat. She finally smiled. "Thank you, Martin, Macario," she congratulated, propping up on her toes as she bowed her head forward. "But I don't want to get too excited. I know it will take a good deal of action to secure them." Martin and Macario affirmed by nodding their heads. "Well, what do we have on our hands?"

Martin looked at Macario as a signal for him to begin. Macario stepped forward, gesturing with his hands as he spoke, "My guy, Lady Arachne. You know, the one that calls himself Small Time, but everybody else calls him All Talk. Well it ain't because he only talks a good game. It's because he says it all, talks too damn much. Stay around this guy long enough he'll tell you he jerks off with his mother's blue, silk panties."

Lady Arachne made a face. *"Oh-kay,"* she said, giving Macario's words a chuckle. "That picturesque detail aside, did he let slip the whereabouts of the cards I seek?"

Martin moved in front of Macario and took up the tale. "All Talk is connected to a glorified crew, the Marcello crime family. Not really that big. Not really that organized. They're more of a hop-along gang that wouldn't be anywhere without an Italian last name."

"Just a glorified crew," Macario repeated boisterous. "Like he said."

"They do contract work," Martin specified. "A lot of protection. Never dug up anything on them that tied them to a hit. A couple of robberies, some impressive heists. Drugs, mostly." Martin moved on, saying, "Their resume aside, they're connected to a front, as Macario's contact tells us. He's started running with them, and with that, he's running his mouth. They're overseeing some items shipped from overseas. All Talk says nothing too fancy, so he thinks he's good to ramble on about it. He thinks it's weird because all the items seem legit. Nothing stolen. His bosses don't even seem interested in taking them. It's all about guarding them. He says he doesn't understand the big deal, but hey, a job is a job. Guy by the name of Brice Cadogan is overseeing this. I did a background check on Mister Cadogan, found something odd about him."

"And that would be?" Lady Arachne inquired.

"Records of this guy go back a long time in London. I figure it's a family name," Martin brushed off. "But, it's a family with a tradition. They're collectors with a taste for objects that got ties to myth and legend. I thought, great, but it didn't raise much of an eyebrow. I told Macario to keep prying at his man All Talk. I didn't expect to get much of a hit, but I wanted to see what things are coming through this Brice's pipeline." Martin started listing off, using his fingers. "He's got artwork coming, paintings mostly, from Eastern Europe. He's got an old spear from Arabia. All Talk says it's from the early thirteenth century. There's also some fancy bottle from Turkey. Don't know its date of origin. This load of trinkets doesn't seem like much." Martin raised a finger, brightened his expression, and piqued Lady Arachne's interest. "But, he says the prize that's worth the most is a set of old Tarot cards. Says they come from Africa, scribbled up around the time of the Ptolemy rulers in Egypt."

"Yeah," voiced Macario. "All Talk says they must be a forgery because the Tarot didn't originate in Africa." Macario chuckled.

Lady Arachne conjured another scowl. She waved her hand, swatting Macario's statement's away. "Let them folk believe that. He'd be partially correct. The cards I need have been handed down from a Kenyan family to a family in Mauritania. They're recreations, but they're as old as the tenth century. They're not just any old Tarot." Then she asked, "What other news do we have? Where will this delivery be?"

"Still lookin' for a delivery hub," Macario answered her. "They don't want to look too seedy."

"Oh," responded Lady Arachne, eyebrow raised.

Macario continued, "Lanz Marcello, head of the Marcello crew, got a shipment of cocaine riding along. He's using the items and the delivery as a cover. They'll be a meeting and an exchange."

Martin jumped in, informing Lady Arachne, "But Lanz is a superstitious lot. He doesn't want to use a front or some abandoned warehouse. He believes the Feds' All-Seeing-Eye is on him."

Lady Arachne pondered for only a moment. "Good," she said. "His superstition will be our blessing. We'll steer this delivery into our hands. Cedron Goodspeed is connected to a young man named Edmond Shaw. He works at the Wolverhampton Hotel." She looked at Macario and ordered, "Have the delivery steered there. There're rumors about the people who own the place. They like getting involved in things of this nature, seedy exchanges happening while taking a little money for letting it go on. Let this All Talk boy give the suggestion with the promise that if it works out, it'll be good for his reputation in this gang or crew—or whatever them boys call themselves. We'll take what we need then. I'll tell Wilson to be loud with the robbery, and then slip away. We'll have the police arrive, arrest the riffraff. We'll use that as *our* cover. Our marks will be too busy with legal matters to track us down. This Lanz Marcello thug will be too busy blaming—what was that other man's name? Kobe Bryant?"

"Brice Cadogan," Martin corrected, chuckling a bit.

"Well, whatever. Those two will be at each other's throats. Keep them off our radar. Do you have a time for this delivery?"

"They're going for November fifteenth," Macario reported.

Lady Arachne's smile returned. "Wilson and Top Hat will do the rest. Keep an eye on your tailed parties. In the meantime, keep close to this All Talk boy. Should anything change, tell me immediately."

Martin and Macario bowed. "Yes, Lady Arachne," they said together.

"Your work here is finished, my handsome investigators, and I am grateful. But your time here is not," Lady Arachne told the two men. "Let us celebrate your findings with a drink." She disappeared from her study, stowed away into her kitchen, and retrieved a bottle of champagne and three glasses. She returned, placed the glasses on a side table, and popped the champagne bottle with an incant. She brought the cork to her hand with the same magic, stopping its wild spring outward, keeping it from cracking against empty bottles placed on shelves. She dropped it onto the table, and then she poured and handed Martin and Macario their drinks. The two private investigators accepted. Lady Arachne raised her glass and said, "To your hard work, Martin, Macario."

"Yes, Lady Arachne," said Martin.

"And to love," Lady Arachne concluded.

They tapped glasses and drank.

Top Hat, a thirty-eight year-old man with cinnamon-colored skin, of average height and stocky build, walked down Fable Avenue early on the first morning of the Four Days of the Spirit Festival. His face was bent with a scowl. Atop his head was an old, tall and flat-crowned, broad-brimmed topper hat. Around his person was a long, gray coat. He wore black jeans and a white, silk shirt. His steps were hurried, pacing away from a man that had been trailing him for half a block. The day was gray, with a peek of sun breaking through small cracks in the gathered clouds.

"But, please, take my card," insisted the man following Top Hat.

Top Hat stopped his hurried steps. With a quick pivot he turned to the man who was dressed in tight, black leather pants, black boots and a black leather jacket. Thick-rimmed glasses covered the man's eyes, and a shaggy, blonde-goatee surrounded his upper lip and chin. A dark gray winter hat rested loose over his crown, tuffs of dirty-blonde hair creeping through.

"I told you, there's no need," Top Hat said to the man with an aggressive tone. "People on this street are stubborn. Nobody's selling."

"Maybe not today," the man insisted in a condescending tone that was poorly covered by a soft voice. "Property taxes are not going down. It's getting hard to afford—"

Top Hat tucked chin to chest and grinned. He reached out a hand. "Give me your card, man." The man placed his card between Top Hat's pointer and middle fingers. Top Hat took the card. He inspected it. "Norman Phillips. Okay. I got your number." Top Hat looked up, chuckling to calm himself. "And to be honest, I'm looking to get out. I leave my spot, you might have an open place, but I doubt it. You think you can give me an exit strategy?"

"Well, definitely," said Norman, voice up and demeanor piqued. "What are you looking for? And please, call me Lee. I prefer Lee."

Top Hat said as a warning, "I'll call you Norman. I prefer to call you that. It's on your card, after all." His smile reappeared and he jabbed Norman's card at him. "But that's the thing—my wants. I don't care, something nice, obviously. I still want to remain in this neighborhood," he demanded, pointing to the ground with Norman's business card.

"Okay…"

Top Hat explained, stepping closer to Norman, "Now, if I'm not on this street anymore, my boundaries are nothing past Ralph Avenue and nothing past Jefferson Avenue." He pointed in the directions of the streets he named. "Brownstone too, no apartment units. Can you handle that?"

"What's your budget?"

"Twenty-one hundred. My top."

"Sorry. No."

A menacing grin appeared on Top Hat's face. "Is that too low for what you got?"

"I'm afraid it is, if you want to stay here."

"To meet my demands?" asked Top Hat.

"Yes."

"Okay. Let me compromise," Top Hat challenged. "I'll do third floor of a brownstone. What do you have past my boundaries?"

"Still nothing, sir."

Top Hat squeezed Norman's business card between his fingers. Images of apartments came to him. Rent prices and addresses appeared too. The images were of apartments stationed within the boundaries of Top Hat's request. All had rents less than Top Hat's budget. Norman's face appeared over the images. Top Hat kept his smile. He pocketed Norman's card. "Be careful with your answer, now, Norman. Do. You. Have. *Anything*…within my budget?"

"No," he said again.

"Okay," Top Hat yielded. He warned, "But if I do research, and I find otherwise, I'm going to report you for discrimination. That clear? Or I'll beat you senseless. Take that as a promise, not a threat. There's a lot of folks coming in here and doin' their best to move niggers out and white folks in. Bed-Stuy seen a lot of that as of late. We've all heard the stories and shit. But if you cool, I'm cool."

"There's no need for that, sir."

"Yes, there is," Top Hat countered. "Because I know your boss."

Norman was perplexed, and he expressed, "My boss?"

"Yeah, Gohen."

"Gohen…?"

Top Hat nodded. "Yeah, Gohen," he repeated. "Go-hen-fuck-yourself." Top Hat hit Norman hard in the gut. Norman buckled, keeling over. Top Hat drove his fist across Norman's face, grabbed his collar and yanked him close. "Guess what I learned within the few moments you and I were talking?" Top Hat slammed his forehead hard against Norman's face.

Blood spurt from Norman's nose. Top Hat tossed him to the ground and kicked him twice in the gut, once in the face. "It's a wonderful, quick and handy thing, this information age," Top Hat taunted. "Let me guess. You got places outside this area to move me to?" He kicked Norman again. "Is that your game?" Top Hat lifted Norman by the collar and listed the apartments that came to him in his vision. He growled the apartments' addresses and rent prices. "Those places sound familiar to you, Norman? How come you got 'em but you ain't showin' 'em to me?" He held Norman up by the collar with one hand and struck him with the other. He let go and allowed Norman's body to drop against the sidewalk.

Norman's lip split and began bleeding from Top Hat's strike.

Top Hat watched Norman. The broker was curled on the sidewalk, holding his stomach and wincing in pain. Then Top Hat blinked. Concern washed over his face, and he bent down, arms reaching for Norman. "Mister, Mister! Are you okay?" he asked. He grabbed Norman's jacket tight at the shoulder. Norman used what little strength he had to grab at Top Hat's grip on him. Top Hat slammed another fist into Norman's face. Then he wiped his hand over Norman's brow, rubbing it as he suggested to him, "You fell down, Mister. It looked like a nasty fall. You okay?" He tapped three times on Norman's forehead.

Norman's eyes rolled back. His head jerked, and he came to as if waking from sleep. "Oh, God…" he expressed.

Top Hat assisted Norman to his feet. He helped dust him off, slapping Norman's person harder than necessary. He eased up and said, "You took a fall, man. You need to get to a hospital?"

"No, thank you," said Norman, wincing in pain and limping to his feet. "I'm okay. Just a fall. I've had those, and I've had worse." He leaned against a brownstone's iron gate. He stood up straight and on his own when his balance returned to him. He breathed out hard. "I'm okay," he exclaimed, tapping his fingers against his split lip, blood running from his nose.

Top Hat, a well-acted concern in his voice, said to him, "Not to brush your accident off, I know I stopped short when you were handing me your card. That might've tripped you up. But, I got your card. And I'll call you if anything comes up."

"Yeah," said the man, disconnected to Top Hat's words. He looked around, peering as if trying to make sense of where he was. "Sure. Call me." He pivoted and walked away, turning the first corner off Fable Avenue.

Top Hat sneered, "Jerkoff racist-in-hipster-clothing." Gordon Goodspeed and Fey Forrester walked up behind Top Hat. Not out of any preternatural instinct, but just to carry on his day, Top Hat turned around to greet them. "Gordon," he said giving a tug on his topper. He turned to Fey, again tugged on his hat's brim, and said, "Ma'am."

"What was up with that guy?" Gordon asked.

"Another outsider tryin' to buy niggers out and his way in," Top Hat said with a smile. "They come lookin' hip and cool now."

Gordon rolled his eyes. "Top Hat, did you incant him and send him away, or did you do your thing?"

Top Hat again tucked his chin to his chest. He rolled his eyes. "I did my thing," he admitted. "But he don't remember. But there's a bit of bad news. I can't report this one for his practices." He explained, "Had to erase part of our conversation in order to erase the ordeal I put him through."

"You feel better?" asked Gordon, disappointment in his voice. "Now he's gonna take his strategies elsewhere instead of gettin' his license revoked, a situation we could've had Maman Anansi or Stephanie incant in our favor to make it definite."

"I'll fix that," Top Hat responded, making a face. "I got his name and number. I'll go through our whole spiel with him at a later date. No need to break out the rule book like you Papa Solomon or Maman Anansi."

"They won't find out what ya did. Not from me," Gordon assured.

"Yeah, well, Lady Arachne got me on orders to give something these hucksters will feel but won't remember…of course, so does Papa Solomon." He started thinking. "And in truth, Madame Jeliya backed up Papa Solomon's secret order. And so did Maman Anansi with her own nod and wink to me. All four of 'em whispered in my ear. But still, right? Beatin' 'em down doesn't always dismantle 'em."

"A little somethin' extra, huh?" said Gordon. Top Hat answered by again addressing both Gordon and Fey with a tug of his brim, and then he walked on about his day. Gordon turned to Fey, "Still gotta have a line of defense against people tryin' to move us off the street. Our street."

"Yeah, my grandmother talks about those defenses."

"So, you nervous?" he asked his question, directed at different matters.

Fey looked down the road. "Yes. But I want to get this over with."

"Okay. Come on."

Gordon escorted Fey to her former residence. When they arrived, Fey looked up at the brownstone and commented, "It doesn't look tall, ominous, and haunted." She removed her house keys from the bag slung over her shoulder as she walked through the gate. Gordon followed.

Up the stairs.

Fey unlocked the doors.

Walking inside.

The house was cold, but it was pristine. Fey allowed Gordon entrance and then closed the doors. She sniffed and shivered, remarking that the space was cold. She spoke an incant in a soft voice, and she and Gordon were no longer bothered by the house's chill.

Fey looked up the stairs. The flight up looked shorter than she remembered. Her head turned to face the dining area on her right. She stared at the empty table and unoccupied chairs. She stepped up to the table, eyes still fixed. Gordon followed her. He paused when Fey stopped walking, standing some distance behind her to allow her space. He watched Fey as her eyes traced the room. He wanted to ask her a question, but he remained silent.

Fey pulled out a chair and sat down. "Gordon," she called. "Come sit with me."

Gordon took a seat. Fey took a moment. Then she spoke.

"My mother sat across from me," informed Fey. She pointed and said, "Right there. She was very upset about something. She was hurt. She was hurting herself. She was drinking and smoking." She looked at Gordon and stated, "I remember it as if someone told it to me, not because I can see it or because I was there, you know." Gordon nodded. The day his mother passed felt much the same. "She left the room and went upstairs. She killed herself in her room. I ran to the stairs—" Fey jumped up. She left the dining area, went into the kitchen, and then returned to the front hall. Gordon followed. Fey stopped at the base of the stairs. "I got here. Silver appeared. I think that's how it went. I ran up the stairs, she blocked my path a few times. Then she blinded me with light, but that didn't stop me. I continued on. Silver went to get Papa Solomon. The light in my eyes faded. But then all went black. I woke up in Madame Jeliya's laboratory. My grandmother had arrived by then. There was screaming. Loud." Fey shook her head. "She was something furious, and I was so scared. The memory is blurry, but my grandmother's voice is loud." She said, facing Gordon, "It was a long time before I believed everything was all right. I kept asking my grandmother if she was going to hurt herself. She always assured me she wouldn't, or let any harm come to me."

"Yeah," said Gordon, not knowing what else to say. "Up?" he suggested, pointing.

Fey shook her head. "Not yet. My grandmother's coming tomorrow to oversee the gas and lights turned on. I'll finish this journey with her then. No offense, Gordon."

"None taken, Fey," he told her. He pointed over his shoulder and asked, "My house, then?"

Fey nodded. "Yes, and some tea if you have any," she asked.

Gordon smiled at Fey's comment. He and she exited the house. Fey locked up, and then followed Gordon down the stairs and back up the road to the Goodspeed residence. Gordon asked Fey about what she'd just experienced. She answered, "It wasn't as weird as I thought it would be. The place was familiar. It was real, you know. It wasn't just a blurred memory. It was like I got my sight back. Papa Solomon cast an incant that put me out. Madame Jeliya did a ritual to calm my mind. Everything about that night is fuzzy. Plus age. I mean, I was six. It wasn't like it was yesterday. And like I said, it came back to me, but like I was recalling something someone told me."

"Right," Gordon replied. He asked as he unlocked the garden floor to his family's Fable Avenue residence, "You excited about your rites?" Gordon aimed a smile at Fey.

"Oh, yes! You know I am. Many reasons to be excited about that. I'm not even nervous about the tattoo. I can't wait."

They walked inside. Gordon turned on the lights and went to the kitchen to do the same. He started tea for Fey, and then the two went into the dining room to relax. There they conversed about Fey's ceremonial rites while they waited for the water to heat up. During the conversation, Fey conjured Silver from her page. After Fey's tea was prepared and given to her, they continued speaking about the matters of ceremony and rites. Gordon had a cup of apple juice. Silver appeared with a small cup in hand, which she dipped into Fey's tea, and scooped out a portion of the drink. She sat on Fey's shoulder, drinking. Fey commented as she sipped the last of her delicious tea, "Ah, tea is like a liquid incant." She then asked Gordon to show her his chamber in the basement. "If it's okay. I don't want to be intrusive."

"Far from, sister," Gordon assured her. "I've run my mouth about it long enough." He stood and motioned for Fey to follow him to the basement. The lights came aglow as they entered the lower level. The illumination hummed. It was bright but pleasant to the eyes. Fey stopped just two steps before the floor. She was awestruck, taking in the site. She'd never seen an altar displayed in such magnitude. Gordon moved farther into the room. Silver flew off Fey's shoulder and zipped toward Gordon's sarcophagus-like chamber, landing atop Spook's gemmed console. The sprite inspected the precious stones, but did not press against them. She was careful to walk around them. The yumbo's large eyes scanned the black mirror. She flew up and over Spook and landed on the closed chamber.

"Silver!" scolded Fey.

"It's okay," said Gordon. He turned and waved for Fey to step all the way inside the basement. "Come on. Don't get shy on me. Take a look at all this."

Fey stepped down into the basement. She walked toward the chamber. Her steps were slow, but not cautious. She was curious, her eyes swallowing every detail of the chamber. She wondered how she might pencil the structure on paper. But piles of comic books lying around the floor distracted her inspection of the grand altar. She looked at Gordon and asked, "What's all this?"

Gordon tried to smile through his embarrassment. "Study material…?" he admitted.

"What?"

Gordon scratched the side of his head and looked away for a moment. "I've been…making sure the streets are safe." He looked back at Fey. An eyebrow was raised on her face. "Not every night. It gets overwhelming. Something is always going on."

"So you're trying to be a superhero?"

"It passes the time," he exhaled. "No one else seems to know what I'm supposed to do with this spirit. I might as well help out some folks in the meantime and between time."

"Superheroes attract super villains," Fey remarked, showing concern.

Gordon put his hands in his pockets. "Yes," he agreed. "And Fable Avenue has its share of boogiemen and boogiewomen. But I go out and make sure that Negroes ain't doin' knuckleheaded stuff around the city." Then he included, "Jersey. Been over to Philly. I hit up Chicago and Detroit a couple of nights ago. Been plannin' on gettin' at L.A." He then assured Fey, "They don't remember. I do leave an impression to do better, especially with these younger cats. I'm that spirit, y'know."

Fey understood. "That's good work, Gordon," she told him in a sincere voice. "Just don't get a complex. You can't save everybody."

"I know. I do what I can." He then remarked as he raised his shoulders, hands still in his pockets, "I feel odd that I can't hand out any cash to help, but I can hand out some ass whippings."

Fey burst with laughter. She covered her mouth and relaxed to remind Gordon, "You do hand out some wisdom, though. Leave the impression as you vanish from their memory. Hopefully that's all they need."

"It's all I got."

The tattered tome, which Gordon had dubbed *The Written*, caught Fey's eye. It rested atop the chamber, Silver perched next to it. Fey walked over to the book. "Well this is an old, curious thing," she said aloud. Looking at Gordon she asked, "Can I open it?"

"Don't see the harm," Gordon replied. "A strong incant keeps the old book from crumbling into dust."

Fey put her hand on the book, but before she could get a fine grip to lift it, the book jumped into the air, opened to the first page, and bobbed as if without weight. The book's movement startled Fey. She retracted her hand and backed away. "Gordon," she called over her shoulder.

Gordon came up behind her. He placed his hands on Fey's shoulders, drawing an inquisitive glance from Fey. She looked up at him, and he let go of her and backed away. "Sorry," he said. "I-I-I've never seen the book react to anyone else but me."

"Gordon," Fey said again. She pointed to him. "Your eyes," she alerted.

Gordon blinked. "What about them?"

"They're blazing. You okay…?"

"I'm fine," he addressed. "The book tells and shows a story, Fey," Gordon explained, acting as if the brilliant, lilac glow of his eyes was nothing out of the ordinary. Fey pointed at her own eyes, waving her finger back and forth as if somehow the action would return Gordon's attention to the wild, loud glow of his own. But he only continued speaking on the matter of the floating tome. "I tried to show the Elders once, but it didn't do anything. I guessed it was a private thing, something only for me."

Fey glanced at the book, then back to Gordon. "What kind of story does it show?" she asked him, attentive and curious. "Is it history? Like Papa Solomon and Maman Anansi's father's horn could show. A past life? I've heard so much about that slave rebellion their parents participated in."

Gordon shook his head. "It's not history," Gordon spoke, eyes still ablaze. "It's a story all the same, but this is more like a mythology. Its beginning feels historical—symbolic of history, ancient history. I think the Pious Wars, the ending to them. That's what makes sense to me."

"The Pious Wars?" Fey repeated in the form of a question. Her eyes slimmed in disbelief. "My grandmother believes in those old tales…but that's very ancient history among conjure folk, Gordon—nothing recorded in this day and age. That's all oral history. Maybe it's more symbolism, y'know. Like the tales of that epoch of conjure suggest."

"The Elders are undecided," said Gordon. "It's put a smile on me and my boy Benny's face—childhood tales, y'know." Fey smiled. "But, that aside, this story then becomes something else, and I'm there in that something-else-of-the-story. I'm very wea—" Gordon's bright eyes locked on the book. Fey flinched as Gordon stiffened and went silent. She turned around and faced the open tome. The ancient characters glimmered lilac.

Tendrils of light writhed from the script and reached out toward Fey. Silver flapped her wings and hovered, but she made no move to protect Fey from the protruding light. The yumbo watched, her instinct perceiving no threat. Fey also made no attempt to move as the stream of light bore into her eyes. Fey tightened, anticipating some form of stinging prick. But only a warm feeling surrounded her eyes, and as she stared longer, the light dissolved and there came the narrative from the beginning, recounting each astounding image and poetic verse. Fey's eyes swallowed every moving frame as her ears listened closely to the poetic narration. Sight and sound coupled together within the story, bombarding Fey and causing her to gush a motley of emotions.

The story finished, and the light and all its images retracted from Fey's eyes. The book closed but continued dangling in the air. Gordon stepped closer to Fey. "You saw it?" he asked. "You saw it."

Fey turned around and faced Gordon. "All of it, Gordon," Fey told him, voice low and wavy. "It seems to be guided by your thoughts" She asked in a sarcastic tone, "What's on *your* mind?"

"But you saw it?" Gordon again remarked.

Fey looked at the book as it bobbed in the air, sorrow clouded her eyes. "It's like a guide, Gordon. You get to sort out everything in your head." She glanced over her shoulder at Gordon and said, "Your shadow self seems very pessimistic."

Gordon answered defensively, "Well, I wouldn't say pessimistic. I'm anxious to find out what all this—" His voice trailed away as Fey left the basement. He started following her but stopped when he heard Fey's voice call down that she would return. Gordon looked at Silver. "You know what's going on? She okay?"

The yumbo, once again sitting on the chamber, lifted her shoulders.

Fey returned to the basement with her sketchbook in hand. She opened it, conjuring her remaining yumboes. Fey spoke her usual incant to cloak the yumboes physical appearance. Gordon noticed a difference in Fey's inflection when speaking the incant. She ordered her colorful sprites to play outside. "Stay on Fable Avenue. Regular folk can't see you, but the people of the street can. It's okay." The yumboes didn't argue, and led by Silver, they fluttered up the stairs and ghosted through the closed, garden-floor entrance.

Fey faced the floating book. Of her sketchbook, she flipped to the page containing her three-year-old sketch of a broken-winged faerie flanked by her parents. Gordon approached Fey, but stopped when he heard her sniff back tears. Fey believed her tears threatened to drip all her anger away. And she wanted to keep her anger as motivation. She took out a sharpened pencil that was tucked into the springs binding the sketchbook. She harmonized an incant upon its whetted end and then said to the floating book, "Open." Then she humbly added, "Please."

The tome flipped to a blank page.

Gordon wanted to call Fey, get her attention. But he stayed his action.

Fey put the tip of her incanted pencil against the blank page. "I have a Father Zero and a Mother Nothing," Fey declared through clenched teeth, a heavy emotion of anger and hurt in her voice. Her hand raced across the blank page, reconstructing the sketch of the broken-winged faerie. There was no resistance from the book, even with nothing bracing it to stay in place. It lowered only a bit, accepting Fey's sketched impression, leveling to make it easier for her to draw.

Gordon's eyes resumed their bright glow.

Fey's eyes glowed as well, but with a dark, cobalt-blue iridescence.

"I have for you, Gordon Goodspeed, the perfect queen," Fey said like a growl.

Her hands were wild across the page as she drew and drew. But despite the feral movements of her strokes, a sharp image came through. The broken-winged faerie was reproduced, flanked by the sketches of Fey's long-absent parents.

Fey stood with her eyes wide with glow and wonder. She and Gordon watched as the outline of her sketch lit up with a glow that matched her eyes. Then the line broke apart and reshaped into the lighted characters from an ancient script. A bright light cast over Fey and Gordon's vision. It dissolved into a scene. Gordon's wiry, slender doppelganger walked into view. The sky was a brightly lit night. *Moon, full and beaming. The stars, bright and twinkling.* Contrasted against the night above, there below was a field of bright green grass. Strong, brown trees bloomed with leaves just as emerald-green as the grass surrounding them. A clear river rushed heavy and loud. At its banks, wearing a brown cloak and sitting upon a throne with wheels, there was she.

Narration colored the scene.

Moon, full and beaming
The stars, bright and twinkling
Kibaru sees she
That is I in his eye
Broken beauty wrapped in a tattered cloak
Hidden in hood, head made of smoke
A faint shadow, a glimmer
Black butterfly crowned in entangled web, silk cocoon
Smothers I, worn like pride
Shame of smoke-choked form, behind I hide
Time spent crying, as the Prince predicted and sang
Over seventeen mountains that stood so high

Clear, I now think – as a knight with sense of duty steps to me
My syntax intact. My voice speaks complete, "Do I spy
A knight here to bring me sunshine?
A perfect black here to deliver light?
O' handsome king
Wiry frame, a slender beam
I am for thee
The perfect queen
Like you, I am broken perfectly, as perfect as fragmented can be
Black as the cosmic sea
I hold my celestial parents in my belly, give birth to my creators
Star by star – I am physical, the water-bearer and the maiden's daughter
They are not as the stars would have you believe
My parents are pale shadow collaborators
My Mother Nothing? A maiden? No. A whore.
My Father Zero? Wisdom water bearer? A carrier of plague and poison.
I was shattered for pale shadow enjoyment
My head, severed, held under black galaxy
Liquid universe, they make me drown within me, heir blocked from lungs,
I barely breathe
And I am barely a breath
So I whisper, voice like a slither, the way I wear my hair
Body plagued with tribulation, time heavy on my shoulders
This is my dis-ease
Legs and spine broken
Thrown to throne
My spine a decaying tree – broken oak – cracked like a parental oath
From base to throat, rotted curse
This lady's malady? Blistered words, syllabic cancers

My Mother Nothing and Father Zero
Play as dancers on a grave
Filled with pieces of me
Thirteen makes me complete
Fixed to me, stars churn to make the moon dust
Split. Up. The compacted, solid celestial sickly satellite
False shine only by stealing the sun's light
Cracked open by Mawu's knife, and up into my sky
Three moons will rise and reside
Restore Motherland's covenant?
Smite my parents, and this action will bring balance

I am in thirteen pieces
Less than half a spirit lingers,
Much missing
From root to head
I would cry for my parents passing
If I had tears left to shed

Cold I sound as the space
Where heart once beat
Rhythmic
A drum in my chest
Dear knight, I task you
Put my parents out of my misery
Release them from my agony
Lay them to rest."

So much missing
Beauty radiates still
Like the hint of sunlight's rise
Behind closed eyes
Her words are alchemy
Trans-muting the sounds
That ground Kibaru in doubt
He. Hears. Her.
His wiry frame believes in its strength
Nimble. Lightsome.
In his words, "This is where
I lay my sword."
At. Her. Feet.
He bows

My ghostly, smoke-trail hand
Commands him to stand
"Up. On two feet. Quickly, quickly!
Where I point,
You strike
And return my thirteen pieces to me.
My Mother Nothing
And my Father Zero
Dissolved of haloes
They don't reside in the sky
They prance in graveyards in the daytime

Behind the cage-city they hide
Bury them where they have buried me
Thirteen of me – my spirit taken physically."

He holds his heart up, heavy in his chest
With heavy task
Beat pumps cautious
His eyes serpentine my dismembered stars
Thirteen missing, black holes, wholly holy missing
Held by my Father Zero and Mother Nothing

I plead, "Restore to me
Thru violent alchemy, if need be,
My thirteen.
Father Zero and Mother Nothing to grave
Bed of roses
Lay my anger to rest
Return to me, my name."

Heart on the horizon, bright with what little light shines
Lithesome warrior
Heavy sword strapped to back
Pivots from this broken maiden
Forward to task

"I pledge, this is for the flesh of you
I will return, task fulfilled
You complete with the rest of you…"

Light washed over the scene. The basement's environment returned to Fey and Gordon's sight, developing like a photograph in front of them. *The Written* closed as the new script dimmed its glow. The book lowered onto the chamber, settling down atop the gold and onyx coated structure. Fey noticed words appear on the aged tome's cover. *In Thirteen Pieces*, it read. Fey pointed this out to Gordon. He walked over and read the inscription for himself.

"I'm sorry," said Fey standing behind Gordon as he continued inspecting the book. He straightened and turned around to her, a perplexed look on his face. "That was intrusive," she commented. "I didn't ask for permission. I made your story about me."

"It's okay…" Gordon assured. "Maybe it's supposed to be. It doesn't open up for anyone else I've shown it to." Then he asked Fey, "You feel okay? You feel like you got something off your chest?"

Fey considered what had transpired in the piece. She felt a little embarrassed. "I don't hate my parents!" blurted Fey, causing Gordon to flinch. It was as if Fey's voice had weight, and its sound moved him back. She relaxed and said, "I'm upset at them, I guess."

"It's okay to be," Gordon consoled. "You have a right to be angry."

Fey nodded mechanically, eyes on the floor. She looked up, face changed. "Well, maybe there will be more for the story to say after my rites." She stepped forward and guided Gordon to face the stairs, wrapping her arm around his. "Come on, Mister Goodspeed. Show me around the old neighborhood. What's the agenda for tonight's festivities?"

Fey's question was answered through the remaining hours of the day. There wasn't much for the first day of the Four Days of the Spirit Festival. Fable Avenue's residents mingled inside and on the street. Community members from other boroughs, downstate and upstate, and a few representatives of conjure families from around the United States were in attendance. One important conjure family had its representatives front and center, surrounding Gordon at every turn. They were of the Gwuinee family, a large conjure network from the Midwest who were considered the oldest in America behind the Eledas family, of which some intermarried. Many people called the Gwuinee family *"the rin kakiri oju"* or *"the wandering eye"* as they were the overseers of conjure family affairs, and were considered nomadic—as they started off as runaway slaves during the late period of colonial America. They sought freedom in the territories of the American Midwest, moving around in accordance to slave hunters' or white explorers' movements. But the family, throughout its long lineage, had been aligned with what was called the *rada* spirit, and therefore peaceful and just. The two representatives, a husband and wife, were not intrusive, and Gordon was polite to them. It was business, but it was cordial.

A pleasant surprise was the arrival of Lillian Eledas-Ghedemere, called *Voodoo Lily*. She was one of many children fathered by Satchel Eledas, known as The Old Goon, and the current master of the invisible, locked real estate located at the Mississippi crossroads. Her mother, Simaetha Ghedemere, was from Saint Louis, but currently resided in New Orleans working as a nurse to blend in with regular folk. She was a carver of incanted African masks by true trade.

Legend may have labeled Lillian's father as old, but she herself was only twenty-four. Her hair was peppercorn; tightly curled tufts that resembled the short hairstyles of the African Saan people. There was a curiosity to her skin color. Almost symmetrically down her body, one half was lighter than the other, a difference between midnight and dawn. It didn't take away from her allure, rather it added to it. She had the attention of many Fable Avenue young men, especially when word traveled around that she was single. She wore a lengthy skirt and a royal blue blouse. She walked with a regal step, her father's legends in her gait, as she appeared wise beyond her years. But there was nothing pretentious about her, very friendly, mostly interacting with the Fable Avenue Elders, surprisingly with little talk concerning access to the crossroads. She'd said her father was out west, but said he'd sent his regards, and her mother did as well.

By the day's end, more guests from local areas arrived. By the weekend, conjure folk from far and wide would arrive. Maximilian and Cedron Goodspeed came from Harlem. The Brickhouse family showed up too. The Shaw family also paid a visit. Fey was invited into the circle of community members, Gordon taking her around and introducing her. The people were polite and kind toward her, though, she believed many stared in wonder about the aftermath of the night her mother died. Out of respect, no one brought up the matter. However, Fey felt conscious of the subject, believing it haunted the atmosphere of introductions and smiles. But there was so much alive about the street, and she wished her grandmother was here to enjoy it with her.

The street was loud with the sounds of jazz and blues. It mixed with the variety of music from younger generations, and a form of music unheard by 'regular folk' ears called *conjure 'n' soul.* Chatter chirped in the crisp air as the day went on. Twice, Fey became separated from Gordon. The first time was by the Elders, giving her a formal introduction and a briefing on how her rites would be carried out. She was captured by Neyeli on the second occasion and brought into a group of young women welcoming her return to the Fable Avenue community.

Backyard barbeque and cigars perfumed the air.

Gordon, with a non-alcoholic form of *dragon spit* in his hand, stood outside his family's brownstone, surrounded by his brother and friends. Cedron, Oliver, the Shaw brothers, and Wilson Barnes sipped on liquor-laced *dragon spit.* The same men puffed on cigars, cracked raucous jokes, and traded even bawdier stories. Conversation was forced inside as the night drew on and the cold flexed a might that no incant could keep away. Nature always proved Herself the more powerful conjuror.

Wheeling toward the couch, Cedron asked Wilson, "What's this righteous hit Lady Arachne got for us?" He coolly rolled his chair around to face Wilson. "Heard you seekin' my kingdom's help."

Wilson tapped Cedron on the shoulder and told him, "In time, sun, in time. Let's have a party first. Besides, I ain't got all the details from Lady

Arachne." Wilson cocked his head and pointed at Cedron. "But I want to know, if I need your crew, I got you. And you got tribute."

"A tribute is cool," said Cedron thinking of the reward. "It's mandatory. But I just want to know this grab is community sanctioned."

Wilson shook his head. "It's righteous, sun. Bet. I wouldn't come to you with knucklehead shit…anymore." The two of them laughed and remembered older grabs without saying a word.

Cedron aimed a finger at Gordon and remarked, "Just send this kid in. Let him conjure his spirit. In and out without a hitch."

Gordon beamed at his brother's words.

Wilson took a sip and a puff. He said, "Elders got him on lock. Ain't lookin' for harm to come to him. Martin's investigation might've picked up Fable Ave' villains on his scout." Cedron raised an eyebrow. Wilson addressed, "Nothing solid. But the package we goin' in for ain't the only old trinket we lookin' at. Lady Arachne guesses that anybody shippin' these kinds of items definitely got some real knowledge about 'em. But we only interested in one item: a set of Tarot cards."

"Forget me, just send in Tap over there!" Gordon called out, pointing at the young man. "He a army of many by himself," Gordon said with a grin.

Jamie beamed, but still shied away from Gordon's words and the attention he received. Wilson asked, "What's he hollerin' about, Tap?"

"Show 'em, Tap," Gordon shouted. "Show 'em!"

"I ain't got my shoes, man," Jamie said, fingers snapping to keep from stuttering.

"Shoes don't make your power," Gordon said to him.

Quiet possessed the room. Jamie considered the conversation's pause a sign of respect and a cue. He accepted the silence and lightly tapped a routine on the hardwood floor. A few moves into his dance, Jamie slammed a foot against the floor on a hard beat. A shadow jumped from under the sole of his shoe, taking shape next to him, tapping in synch with his rhythm. Gordon grinned as the rest of the onlookers hollered in excitement. Jamie continued dancing, his shadow self in step with him. There was another hard tap, and another, and another. Jamie was surrounded by more shadows, jumped from his person and taking shape to join him in the dance.

Wilson and Cedron led the applause coming from the excited onlookers. Jamie ended his routine. He and his shadows bowed to applause. Then the shadows jumped back under his feet. "Th-th-that's g-g-g-gon' be on d-d-display S-S-Saturday." A giant grin washed over Jamie's face as his head bobbed.

"Shit," Wilson remarked. "That's gon' be on display when we pull this grab off." He asked Jamie, "How you do that, Tap? You been practicin'?"

"Th-th-this is…Gordon's ffff-fault," Jamie answered, grin still wide on his face, finger aimed at Gordon.

Gordon raised his arms as if surrendering to arrest. "It was an accident. We was chillin' a couple days back. I was showin' Tap the machinery downstairs. I shifted into spirit, and he gets inspired to dance. Then *POOF!* His shadows jump out."

"And that's it?" Wilson asked in disbelief. "There go the neighborhood. Everybody gonna come runnin', tryin' to bring out a unique conjure and shit." He shook his head and shouted, "Stitching rites about to go up, everybody invest in the stock."

"True," Gordon said. "The matriarchs been talkin' about it. I told them about Tap, and they informed Maman Anansi. They got a theory," and then he corrected, "They *been* had a theory. They said get ready for more old spirits bringing out people's inner conjure. That old, black magic. *Pretos-Velhos cosmicos!*" Gordon then said snapping everyone to attention, "Hey! No one tell Fey. All of what you saw will be a part of her rites on Saturday. It's something special. Keep y'mouths shut."

Wilson remarked, "Yeah, everybody keep it a surprise for Gordon's new girl."

"What?" Gordon said in defense.

"No, no, no, man. It's cool," Wilson replied patting the air with both hands, gesturing for Gordon to relax. "We all rootin' for you on this one."

Gordon rolled his eyes. "Whatever, man. She and I will double date with Benny and Neyeli." Everyone hollered at the comeback. Raymond and Jamie grappled Benny, giving him a shake. "Cuz it's true, right? It's true!" yelled out Gordon over the playful, teasing laughter directed at Benny.

Benny attempted to retort against the accusation, but the door opened, and Maximilian Goodspeed pushed half his body through and announced, "Food up and down the block for you mystical, magical, misfit Negroes. Let's get some grub. Come on!"

Everyone filed out. Benny made his remark, but Cedron and Raymond continued teasing him. Jamie beamed a shit-eating grin at Benny. The conversation up ahead, Wilson commented to Maximilian that he needed to get his grill going in the backyard. Maximilian retorted that he'd been up the street grilling at Mister Ricks' residence. Then Wilson, in a low voice, bombarded Jamie with questions about his newfound conjure. Could he control each individual shadow? How many could he conjure? Jamie confirmed the shadows obeyed his command, and that he'd produced twenty-four before feeling exhausted.

It wasn't long before conversation, drink, the fine aroma of food, and a mix of music filled the night air. The sounds and activity faded around midnight. Gordon, his father, and his brother retired to their Fable Avenue residence for sleep. Fey Forrester returned to Mount Vernon, despite Gordon's protests against her driving home. He offered Fey a room, but she declined. He asked for her to text him when she was safe at home, and she did.

Soft piano music stirred Gordon awake at dawn. He thought nothing of it, having been used to the haunting jazz melodies that often played in the morning. But by reflex, Gordon opened his eyes. His lips were laced with cold as the house's central heat, on a timer, was just beginning its assault on the chill. Gordon sat up in bed, his movements sluggish. But the more he moved, the more his senses awakened. He turned his ear and realized the soft piano playing was coming from outside, below his window. Gordon snapped awake and leapt from the bed and looked down into the backyard. There was the specter of his mother dancing a slow routine. His breath fogged the window, and after a moment, Gordon wiped away the condensate and watched his mother dance. A subtle smile appeared on his face. He backed away from the window and hurried down to the garden level like a child on Christmas morning.

Downstairs, Gordon stopped his hastened pace. He did not move, observing the garden level's front room. The couch was empty, bare of his slumbering brother. The blanket and pillow were all the evidence that remained of Cedron's stay. The soft melody continued playing, and Gordon moved into the dining area where he saw his brother in the open doorway, watching their mother dance while seated in his wheelchair. The floor creaked as Gordon walked over it. Cedron turned his head, noticing his brother.

"Go get pop," Cedron ordered. "Now," he demanded.

Gordon ignored his brother's order and moved closer to the doorway.

Cedron made a face.

"What?" the goliath hissed. "You didn't hear me?"

Gordon watched his mother dance her routine, purposely ignoring Cedron.

Cedron tightened his scowl. "You Mister Big Shot with them eyes, huh?" he spat. "This ain't for you. This for pop. He been waitin' on this for—"

"And I've already seen this," Gordon growled in a whisper. "I'm waiting for—"

"You waitin' for? *You* waitin' for? What *you* waitin' for?"

Althea came to a stop in her dance. The music ceased as if dependent on her graceful movements. She faced her bickering children and scolded, "The two of you stop, now!" Her age may have been preserved in her mid-thirties, but she was still their mother. Gordon and Cedron straightened up. Althea presented a gentle smile, pleased more by her still active authority over her children. "Gordon," she said, "Go get your father. It's okay, baby. I'll see him now." Her voice was the same; but there was a melodious, haunting echo in her tone. And it was strange for Cedron and Gordon to hear their mother's voice at all. Gordon acknowledged his mother with a nod and ran to his father's room to retrieve him. Althea stepped closer to Cedron. She bent down and touched his lifeless legs.

Cedron flinched from the waist up. Physically he felt nothing. But his mother's touch upon his legs was deeper than physical. She was there. Her spirit was there, her specter.

Althea's eyes watered. "My boy," she said. "My big boy," she exclaimed with pride.

"Mom…"

Gordon returned with his father behind him. Maximilian, barefoot and dressed in his nightclothes, gasped at the sight of his deceased wife's spirit. His legs buckled, and he used the dining room chairs and table to keep balanced and on his feet. "Baby…" he said in a low voice. "Althea-baby…"

Althea Goodspeed stood. Her face was flush with emotion, holding back the anger she'd intended to express at her husband.

Cedron looked at his father. He rolled back into the house, moving aside and giving his father space to pass. But Maximilian stayed any movement, and when he did eventually take steps toward his wife, they were slow. He approached Althea as if he was a child and she was a small, skittish bird, ready to take flight should danger come too close. His anxious eyes were locked on his wife's spirit, hoping she wouldn't fly away. Through the door, Maximilian spoke an incant to keep warm. His steps increased, and soon he found himself standing in front of his departed wife's spirit. He said nothing, and again he remained still. He looked her specter up and down, examining her dress and her features that were now full and in front of him. Her presence was not a restful and noiseless photograph, and it wasn't a faint memory. Her spirit was there, haunting the backyard.

"You have memories, Maximilian? You think of me?" interrogated Althea, ire rising in her otherworldly voice. Maximilian reached for her, to put his arms around her, but she disappeared from his reach. Maximilian dropped his head, eyes closed. He became angry with himself. Althea appeared farther back, her head low and her face expressing disappointment. She turned her back to him. Gordon and Cedron watched, waiting, possessed with their own anxiety.

Maximilian called her, "Althea-baby…"

Ghostly, shimmering tears trailed down Althea's face.

Cedron pushed his chair forward. He reached out and closed the door. "This ain't for us," he said, wheeling away and giving his parents privacy. "Come on from there," he barked at Gordon.

Cedron wheeled back to the side of the couch. He was silent. Gordon sat down on one of the room's plush chairs. They both could hear the murmur of conversation between their mother and father. Gordon decided not to use his instinct to enhance his hearing, keeping his mother and father's conversation private. Gordon said, after a moment, "Mom came to me the first night of my rites." Cedron rolled his eyes and huffed. Gordon ignored him and continued, "She didn't speak, but she was upset. I guessed that—"

"Shut up," said Cedron in a disgusted voice. "This ain't about you."

Gordon moved his eyes around, perplexed. "I was tryin' to explain—"

"Shut up, Gordon! God!"

Gordon stood and walked away, returning to his room. He looked outside the window, peaking down on his parents. His mother and father were locked in an embrace, his mother having formed solid. He saw their lips moving, but still Gordon didn't intrude on their time. He backed away from the window, feeling intrusive anyway. He prepared for the second day of the Four Days of the Spirit Festival. While he washed and dressed, Fey sent a text that she was on her way with her grandmother. He peeked in on his mother and father as he dressed. They remained outside. Now they were sitting, holding hands and talking with smiles on their faces. Gordon still didn't listen in, but he was glad to see his parents happier.

The Shaw brothers showed up at the house, but Gordon didn't stay long to entertain them with Cedron. Instead, he met Fey and her grandmother after receiving a text they had arrived at the Forrester residence. Savannah attended to appointments concerning the electricity and the gas. Legal as Fable Avenue liked to do things, using incants to supply the house with such utilities was considered a strict no-no, believing it would arouse outside suspicions. Older folks would often say, *"We do everything by* they *books, can't no one traipse in here like Miss Fallows did with Water Bug Hollow, lying that outsiders don't like what we do here on the Avenue."*

Gordon and Fey spent little time together during the day. The matriarchs and Savannah Forrester separated Fey for preparation concerning her rites, though later Gordon was called upon for a private ceremony with Fey. It raised his eyebrow at first, wondering what he was to do with Fey in private. But Maman Anansi asked for Gordon to take on the form of his lilac spirit and shower Fey with a blessing of spirit particles. Possessing the active mind of a young nineteen-year-old college man, Gordon still twisted the meaning of the lead-matriarch's words, and by the look on Fey Forrester's face—a look that snapped Gordon's thoughts out of the gutter—he felt she could read his mind. So, with his mind wiped of salacious thoughts, Gordon took to a blazing lilac form, swirled around Fey and popped out of existence, leaving behind a dusting of lilac particles that melted against Fey's skin.

Later, Gordon informed Fey about his mother's specter returning and meeting his father. He also spoke of his brother's attitude. Fey politely reminded Gordon that his brother, though rude, was entitled to his emotions, which were no different than the feelings Gordon had gone through when his mother first appeared. Gordon conceded to Fey's words.

She too had news to share, and she told him of her and her grandmother's walk up the stairs in her old house. She remarked about having the same feelings as the day before. The house was again real to her, palpable, but the memory of the night her mother took her life was still fuzzy and with little emotion. Savannah was far more shaken then she was, and Fey told Gordon that she found herself consoling her grandmother.

The second day of festivities fell on Halloween, as always. Again music and conversation mixed with good food, much of which was leftovers, but no one complained. The other streets, celebrating the holiday, expanded the gaiety. More Fable Avenue community members from around the northeast were in attendance, some bringing prepared meals. Children, from babies to teenagers, and some adults dressed up in silly or ghoulish costumes, traveled the entirety of the Brooklyn Bedford-Stuyvesant neighborhood. Martin, Top Hat, Wilson and other adults paroled the streets in plain clothes, keeping a cautious eye for troublesome hoods. Fable Avenue glowed with festivities from Haitian stick fighting going on in some of the garden levels to Tarot and regular card games for money. There also could be found chess and even West African wrestling that was performed on mats in garden-floor areas of several brownstones.

Gordon, as Dooley, took to the sky. He flew up as a single, lilac beam, seen by all. His body burst into bright spectacles, mirroring fireworks, entertaining the children and raining blessings down on Stuyvesant Heights. He tired after twenty minutes of the activity, and retired to his altar to restore himself. Fey's yumboes darted up and down Fable Avenue, incanted with a cloak against outsiders' eyes. Other conjured sprites and small creatures joined in chase, chat, and dance.

As the night wore on, Gordon, Cedron, Jamie, the Shaw brothers, Benny, Dajon, and other young boys engaged in card game matches using candy as bets. Neyeli and other young women of the community barged their way into the boys' activity. Benny made jest they should play strip versions of the games at hand. Neyeli rolled her eyes at his comment and Gordon jibed by telling her, "Don't act like you don't love him."

Neyeli changed the subject, inquiring about Fey who was still engaging in practice for her ceremony in the morning. Gordon answered, though aware of Neyeli's verbal maneuver. He informed his party of friends that he watched over Fey's stone and oil, and baptismal rites in a private ceremony with the Elders and Fey's grandmother. His expression brightened when he described raining a blessing on Fey. Everyone around him expressed the very salacious thoughts Gordon entertained to himself earlier, and Gordon fell silent, eyes looking away and a flush of red in his cheeks. Wilson reminded, "We rootin' for you on this one, kid." And laughter filled the room.

Maximilian remained secluded with his wife in the brownstone's master bedroom. They talked and held one another in the bed, Althea pushing her spirit's focus to remain physical. It would get easier with practice. Wilson inquired about Maximilian's absence, but neither Gordon nor Cedron revealed where their father was, or the company he was keeping. Gordon made attempts, but he was always shutdown by his older brother. Maximilian did make an appearance at the house where he'd heard his sons and friends were gathered. It was eleven o'clock. He was surprised that neither of his sons relayed the news of Althea's visit.

"She's still here," Maximilian said with a lighted expression. "She's upstairs, getting to know the house again and talking with her folks."

"We know what you'll be doin' tonight," Wilson remarked taking a swig of *dragon spit.* "Gettin' your spirit-freak on," he joked.

Maximilian shook the comment aside, grin on his face. He pulled Oliver from the group and walked up the street with him, holding him close and whispering, "I need a tat', man. I need some of that incanted ink. I know all things magical got a li'l more potency since my son got that spirit stirred and brewed inside him."

"Whatchu got planned, Mister Goodspeed?" Oliver asked.

Maximilian stopped his pace. He let go of Oliver, came around in front of him and said, "I give you a photo of my wife, and you put a tat' on me of the photo—on my arm. I want her close." Maximilian looked up the street, hands in his pockets. To Oliver, he said, "This ain't a once-a-year visit. It's somethin' more. She said so. Althea can come and go as she pleases. I want the tat' to be a doorway for her, something easier. She said she gets a little loopy comin' through, but it's cool, because she gotta dance to get her head straight."

"She bound to the house?"

"Both houses," Maximilian specified. "Here and Harlem. She's going to appear in Harlem later on tonight. I'm going back there. Cedron and Gordon will stay here. I'll be back in the morning. But I want to try and undo that binding."

"Okay," Oliver nodded. He reminded Maximilian, "That Forrester girl gets her mystic ink tomorrow. I got her ritual ready. It's gonna take something outta me to have it finished for her, y'know. I gotta have my hand and arm blessed to stay steady and move quickly. My moms is helpin' with that."

Maximilian waved his arms and shook his head. "That's cool, Ollie. Take your time. Rest up. Maybe next weekend, or so. I got my baby either way. As long as it can be done."

"Yeah, it's cool. I'll have to mull over the details with my mom, so we can get the incant right, make the sketch an actual doorway. I've never done it before, but it's been done...hundreds of years ago." He made a face. "It'll take a lot, but yeah, I got you," he said, inspired. "With the brew and the spirit, we gettin' more potent with our works."

Maximilian slapped Oliver on the arm. "Good look, my man. Let me get back to my baby. Tell Gordon and Cedron they wanted at the house so we can have some family time." Maximilian turned around and walked back to his house. Oliver ran on and delivered Maximilian's message to his sons. Cedron and Gordon returned home, and the family gathered in the dining room. Cedron remained silent for most of the time. Gordon observed his mother, smiling at her, rekindling memories that were now more prominent. Late into the night, Althea's parents dismissed themselves, heading back to Harlem. Althea faded after announcing she was going to haunt their Harlem residence, and Maximilian left to join her. He said to Gordon before leaving the house, "I'm talking things out with your mom." He fumbled with his keys, looking down at them instead of at his son. He stated, "She came through every year since she was gone. But she never knocked on the door…and I…was busy sometimes—to say the least." He still played with his keys. "That spirit in you sure has opened things." But he finally looked at Gordon when he expressed, "This has always been my grand conjure and wish." He patted Gordon on the shoulder and left. "I'll see you and your brother tomorrow."

"Bye, Pop."

Gordon locked the door. He turned around and saw Cedron making his move from his wheelchair to the couch. He wrapped himself up inside his blanket and said to Gordon, "Turn the lights off."

Gordon did as his brother asked. He walked upstairs and went to sleep. He understood Cedron was dealing with a lot, but Gordon figured Cedron was most upset at the fact his old flame, Leah Kimberly Peters, was avoiding him on her visit to the festival. Gordon pried into his brother's thoughts, and his instincts were confirmed. Things played out between Cedron and Leah much the way Oliver expressed weeks ago after Gordon's ceremonial rites. And with that conversation, Gordon knew something his brother didn't. Leah Peters still held strong feelings for him. Gordon took the information to bed with him. If Cedron was as brave toward her as he was with his schemes and knuckleheaded business, he'd find out soon enough.

The third day of the festival took place outside of time. Papa Solomon had been practicing with the mystical family horn played by his father and grandfather before him. He played a series of preternatural notes that faded the street from reality, warmed the outside atmosphere, and pushed the clouds aside making way for the bright sun and blue sky. A stage with a microphone and stand was centered at Fable Avenue and Malcolm X Boulevard. Many people were gathered, even more than the two previous days. There were onlookers atop brownstones and some peering through open windows. First, Maman Anansi led a prayer and spoke a blessing to the gathered people. She segued from the blessing to announcing Gordon Goodspeed's successful rites. She commented, "With the spirit in him, our mystery has only gotten bigger. But with research, work and ritual, we are narrowing down the proper path for our story to take." She then spoke on Fable Avenue's history, focusing on rites and traditions within the community.

"Thirteen years ago, tragedy struck our community," Maman Anansi said to the audience with a heavy sadness. "We have known great loss before and after, but there among us is a family that left our community after experiencing a terrible loss. I am happy to announce, that on this day, they have returned." Maman Anansi beamed. There still was sadness in her eyes as she looked down at Savannah Forrester. "Savannah, please join me on this stage."

Savannah got up from her seat and walked to the stage, climbing the stairs. She stood by Maman Anansi's side, wearing a long, yellow floral skirt with a sky blue blouse, hair up in a purple wrap that was printed with African veves. Maman Anansi removed the microphone from its stand and passed it to her. Savannah pondered for a moment on the words. She wasn't trying to think about the right words to say. She already had the right words. It was just about controlling the emotions they conjured. Her eyes watered a bit, but Savannah said to herself, *To hell with it. I'm here now,* and so she spoke to the audience, "I lost my daughter thirteen years ago.

Something happened, and she took her life." It wasn't easy saying it. Savannah struggled with talking about the past while blocking its imagery, but her voice remained clear, and it never faltered. "I took my granddaughter away, and I wouldn't be telling the whole truth if I said it was only for her safety. I was angry. I was very angry because I was so hurt. But I kept my granddaughter knowledgeable about her heritage. I have superstitions about such things. But I did alienate her from her rites—rites she should have gone through at nine and thirteen." She turned to Maman Anansi and addressed, "Thank you, Maman Anansi—and the other community Elders—" she then added, "—though I'm older than you all." She made a face to the audience that drew light laughter. Turning back to Maman Anansi she concluded, "But I thank you all for allowing my granddaughter to receive these rites on this day and after all these years." Savannah gave Maman Anansi a hug. Papa Solomon, Madame Jeliya, and Lady Arachne joined them on the stage and huddled into the embrace.

Then Maman Anansi broke it all up, taking the microphone from Savannah and placing it back on the stand. She picked up the stand, moved it to the far corner of the stage, and lowered it down to a young man. The Elders and Savannah then cleared the stage, making room for the ceremony set to begin.

Drums pounded! Four young men walked onto the stage, djembe drums strapped to them. Their beats announced their presence. Jamie 'Tap' Ryan walked up behind them. He was dressed in navy-blue pants, a white, long-sleeve shirt, and his tap shoes on his feet. The drummers took the corners, simmering their rattle to a soft beat.

Jamie started tapping a simple dance. But he increased the complexity before stomping hard, conjuring a shadow, and returning to the soft tap. *Simple! Complex! Hard stomp! A shadow!* He repeated this six times to the crowd's applause. Jamie's shadow dancers flanked him, three on either side and angled in a v-shaped pattern, Jamie at the apex. He stomped a seventh time and a shadow jumped from him and tapped in synch, dancing in front of Jamie, shielding his movements from the audience. The shadow dancers continued their routine. Jamie tapped, moving backward toward the stage's rear stairs. When he reached them, he turned around, and walked down.

The shadows continued their tap routine. All seven faced the audience. The drummers' soft beat in synch with their dance. There came a pause in rhythm and movement. Then the beat picked up again, and the dance continued. The shadows broke into two rows of three, flanking the seventh who continued facing the crowd. It danced backward near the rear stairs. Then it stopped and stood straight. The other shadows were still too. The drummers continued, increasing their rhythm. A fourteen-year old boy stepped onto the stage. Jamie's shadow dancer covered him and imitated his movements as he dived into an intense, African dance. The fourteen-year old dancer wore the shadow like armor, the black smoky frame dancing in step with him. He traded places with another shadow, and a thirteen-year old girl walked onto the stage and danced the same, a shade in step with her. Two shadows broke from the line and a twelve-year old boy and girl stepped into them and began dancing. The last three shadows danced to the back of the stage, stiffened, and waited for three nine-year old girls to cover and dance with.

Shades and young Fable Avenue dancers formed a circle of dance on the stage. From the sky came Dooley. His lilac form blazed like a comet as he descended. In his hands was an elaborate ebony chair. He lowered the chair onto the stage in the middle of the dancers' circle, and then he soared back into the sky, all eyes on his every movement until he could no longer be seen.

Fey Forrester ascended the stage. Her feet were bare, and a gold-beaded veil covered her face. She wore a long, red, shoulderless gown made from fabric incanted with a charm. Her gown shifted through the colors of the rainbow as she moved closer to the ebony chair. She held a gold mirror in one hand, and a wooden scepter carved and colored as lightning in the other. The young, shaded dancers danced away from the center of the stage, allowing Fey to pass to the ebony chair. She sat down. Her gown was now violet, and remained so.

The drumming and dancing met a crescendo. The shades surrounding the young dancers burst into a cloud of black smoke on the final clap of the drums and the final stomp of the feet. The audience thundered with applause. Fey peered at the crowd through the beads draping over her face. She smiled, tears forming a translucent seal over her eyes.

Then it was quiet. The Fable Avenue dancers left the stage, each passing in front of Fey and bowing in her direction. She nodded in return. As the young dancers exited, the Elders returned to the stage and surrounded Fey. The matriarchs held microphones, and hummed in unison as Papa Solomon carried a tray holding an indigo candle, two cups, and a jug of cranberry juice spiced with a little rum. He laid the tray at Fey's feet. He picked up the jug of rum-accented juice and filled both cups to half. He returned the jug to the tray and gave Fey one of the cups as she set down her gold mirror and scepter of lightning. Then Papa Solomon lifted the candle, speaking an incant that set its wick aflame. He passed the candle to Fey.

Papa Solomon stood. He lifted his cup, tilted back his head, and yelled, "Your head restored, Fey Forrester. Your bones strong, they will carry you. Your shade and cloud in breath and soul. The ancestors sing inside you. The Orisha, the Lwa, the Neteru all dance inside you; they see through your eyes. In your cup is the spirit. Drink, and let Ayizan bless these rites in the name of the cosmic Ixu and Gira." Silver and the yumbo named Zee floated next to Fey's head and lifted her beaded veil high off her face. Fey and Papa Solomon swallowed their cups' contents in one gulp and in unison. Then Papa Solomon said, "You are, as you always have been, a member of the Fable Avenue community. Incant to blessing, you will be shaded. The fire of life inside you. To the air, with this flame. You are everywhere and you are here. You are Fey Forrester of Fable Avenue. May your conjure be summoned."

Fey blew out the candle in one quick breath. Papa Solomon took the candle from Fey and signaled for her to stand. Her yumboes lowered her veil and returned her mirror and scepter to her. The matriarchs surrounded Fey and each spoke a blessing to her. Then the drums resumed. The young dancers, shadowed by shade, took the stage. They resumed their dance around Fey. And then, with Fey at the head of the line, drummers, youthful and shadow-covered dancers, and Elders exited. Fey's grandmother met her at the back of the stage, taking her arm, and walking on, entourage in tow. The crowd thundered applause. The cheers dampened when the stage was empty. Fey and her grandmother parted the crowd that had been gathered behind the stage. With shaded dancers, the matriarchs and the drummers walked up the street, leaving the stage and the gathered members of the community behind.

Quiet.

The gathered residents looked up. Dooley descended from the sky. He came to a stop just above the stage, hovering with his tail whipping underneath him. Papa Solomon returned with horn in hand, taking a place next to Dooley. His voice was clear as he spoke to the crowd. "Fable Avenue's story does not begin in one place. With so many people from the African Diaspora, its origins are many. But *this* is the story that brought us here." Papa Solomon put the mystical horn to his lips and blew. His notes weren't correct, but they formed the images of the *Son Dial Tone* story composed by his father and grandfather. Dooley took flight, gliding around the stage, guiding Papa Solomon's notes and being the adhesive that kept the images together to show the entirety of Papa Solomon and Maman Anansi's mother and father's struggle through two lifetimes, culminating in bringing Fable Avenue into physical existence. Images accompanied by music entertained the crowd.

Dooley popped from existence at the close of the story. The music of Horatio Peters' band faded into Papa Solomon's soft notes. The story was concluded. Papa Solomon took a bow as Fable Avenue's residents hollered and applauded. He signaled for the crowd to simmer down, and then he projected, "Excuse my playing. I've been practicin', but I'm far from the musicians my father and grandfather were."

"That's all right, now, Papa Solomon!" declared a man from the crowd.

"You did your family proud, there!" a woman hollered up to him.

Other people chimed in with happy sentiments. Papa Solomon nodded and smiled, acknowledging his audience. He again signaled for quiet. "There's still a little more to our story. Something brought through by the lilac spirit. It's a symbol of our history. It's a symbol of where we lost our way as a people. It happens far before our recorded greatness and grand fall in history. And as I play, watch close the lilac spirit." Audience quiet, Papa Solomon played again as practiced, and Dooley flew in, showering the gathered community members in spirit that put on display the mythology he and Fey were now composing together.

There marched the three armies through a sandy wasteland, and there sat Motherland. Her disappointment and words resonated through the audience. The melancholy notes Papa Solomon played expressed the wave of emotions echoing through the armies and the woman to whom they pleaded. Dooley and Papa Solomon played into existence the story leading up to the entrance of the cage-city. The story came to a close before Dooley's mythological doppelganger was introduced, but from Motherland's speech to the forming of the caged city that now trapped her descendants, the audience understood all the symbolism.

Papa Solomon ceased playing. Dooley rose back to the sky and disappeared, and the images faded away with him. Papa Solomon wiped his brow and remarked, "And here we are. Here we stand ready to restore Motherland's covenant, and be as a whole people. Our ancient spirit, manifested through incants and conjures—our awareness of the hexes this system tries to haunt us with—does not make us better than those normal folk that are not conscious of such things, and who are out there getting by through their struggles day-by-day. But what it makes us is protectors. It makes us responsible. We've handed out blessings, kept things safe, and I know many of you believe it doesn't feel as if we've made any difference. I know many have disagreed with politics when we have stayed our hands of incant and conjure. But disagreement has remained civil. There has not been, and will not be, any Pious Wars held in this age—legends or not. The day is coming when the world will know us; and our Earthly and cosmic Motherland's covenant will be made intact, unified, and no longer at odds with the Earthly and cosmic Father source."

Sentiments were made up to the stage from the crowd below. Papa Solomon accepted them. He led the audience in a final prayer, and then they were dismissed. "Okay, now. Okay," said Papa Solomon trying to instill order from the people dispersing. "We're breaking things up a bit. Mingle on about. Be careful as I put us back in time. Stay out of the roads so no cars traveling along this way will hit you when I ease us all back into things." He lifted a finger and said, "First, we need to deconstruct this stage and get it back in storage. Where are my handlers?" he looked around and saw the voluntary men and women standing at the ready. "Okay, that will take some time. So everyone just mingle about. I'll blow a heavy note as a signal that we're easing back into time so we can clear the streets. Once we're done, I've already got the names of people that are receiving a blessing, including some community outsiders not present. We'll be at Lady Arachne's house holding counsel on that. If that concerns you, that's where we'll be. Thank you all."

Papa Solomon left the stage, and the stage handlers went to work. The crowd broke away from the gathering, some returning home. The people atop the brownstones filtered back into the buildings, as the people watching from their windows retracted into their houses. Papa Solomon's heavy note was blown a few minutes after the stage was deconstructed. The streets emptied. People huddled on the sidewalk, still engaged in conversation. Papa Solomon sounded the proper notes and Fable Avenue was once again with time, a part of the mundane reality, snapped back into place like a puzzle piece. Autumn's temperature and pedestrian activity returned. Cars appeared on the street, zooming through, up, down, and across. Outsiders passed through, walking from one street or block to the next, unaware of the ceremony that had taken place.

Maman Anansi and Madame Jeliya retired to Oliver Peters' tattoo parlor, *Magic Ink, Inc.* There, with Savannah Forrester and Leah Peters, the two matriarchs watched over Fey's ceremonial tattooing. Fey had changed to a long, ruffled skirt and a blouse that exposed her shoulders. She lay with her stomach against the reclined tattoo chair. Oliver, sitting down next to Fey, lit and puffed a cigar. He scooped up ashes from an ashtray held by his mother, and he tossed the ashes to either of Fey's exposed shoulders, covering both of them. Some of the ash darkened her white blouse, but she didn't mind. Oliver blew smoke on both her shoulders and sat back, waiting.

"You nervous?" asked Oliver, holding the needle in one hand and the burning cigar in the other.

"Not at all," said Fey. "I've done this before." She pointed to her bare feet, proud smile on her face. Oliver looked down. He saw a design on the outside of her left ankle. It was a sketch of an angel's wing. She lifted her right leg and twirled it. "Got one there, too," she said in a whimsical tone. "Other side. You can't see."

"That's tight," Oliver remarked. He put his cigar into the ashtray.

"Yeah, much to Nana's chagrin, I got that when I was sixt—" Fey arched her back, reacting as if cold water had been poured down her spine. *"Ah!"* she exhaled. The ash on her shoulders loosened, and as if they were funneled through an hourglass, they trailed from her shoulders, down the valley of her back. The sensation went from cool to warm, to burning. The arch in Fey's back grew. She placed her hands on the mechanical chair's arms and stretched, bending hard to compensate for the sensation burning her.

Savannah and Maman Anansi came to Fey's aid, holding her arms and telling her in a gentle voice to relax. Madame Jeliya whispered an incant to relieve Fey of the ashes' sting. The pain dulled, but a heavy weight remained against her back. Fey loosened. She attempted to sit back, but Maman Anansi stopped her. "Stay forward," said the matriarch.

Fey did as told, straining against her instinct to do the opposite. Maman Anansi and Savannah lifted her blouse, revealing four circles made from ash going down her spine.

Oliver repositioned the mechanical chair to get a better angle to start the mystical sketches on Fey's skin. Oliver inspected the circles on her back. Maman Anansi undid Fey's bra and stepped away. Oliver blew away the ash with a powerful breath. Images remained, but they were visible only to Oliver's eyes. Each image was of the yumboes Fey conjured from her sketchbook. Inside every other sketch were symbols from both the house of Dii Mauri and the house of Ka Mauri.

"Well, Miss Fey Forrester, your ink will definitely be something special," Oliver commented as he anointed his needle with incanted ink prepared by his sister Leah.

Fey looked up at her grandmother. The two exchanged smiles. Fey asked Oliver, "So, in which house do I reside, Oliver?"

"Well," Oliver started, "you got both images in all four tattoos."

"Oh!" Fey perked up.

"But the dominant images are your yumboes," Oliver continued. "Each one has a separate sketch."

Fey rolled her eyes. "They *would* follow me everywhere," she remarked.

Oliver had his own sentiment, sighing over the work he had to do, "Everybody gotta one-up everybody else in the special department since Gordon got that lilac spirit all brewed up in him. Seems like we all gettin' stirred up somehow, someway."

Oliver went to work. His blessed hands traced the images on Fey's back with the needle gun. Fey felt the moderate stings and pricks of the needle, but they didn't bother her. She remained calm even when there was a knock at the door. Madame Jeliya answered. It was Top Hat. "Hit a snag with the blessings," he spoke as the door opened.

Madame Jeliya asked in a sigh, "Garret?"

Top Hat nodded, which only made Madame Jeliya huff more. "Mister Rojo is upset. He says his blessing didn't work, shouting between English and Spanish. Calling us frauds, but it ain't like he's paid for the service yet. Says his boss overlooked his promotion. Gave it to someone else, and was close to letting him go. Says now his boss is hostile toward him."

Madame Jeliya rolled her eyes.

"He's admitted to not sticking to the ritual you gave him," Top Hat reported.

"What?"

"Says he felt silly reciting some of the prayers and using the oils and—"

"That damned, stubborn man!" interrupted Madame Jeliya. "We shouldn't do a damned thing—him not following the good, orderly ritual we prepared for him."

"He also tried something from one of them high-huckster gurus," Top Hat noted.

Madame Jeliya scoffed, "Don't he know them guru fools use methods that don't apply to our time and place? Those rituals will get him messed up if not tinkered with by a real *mai dabo* or conjuror."

Top Hat nodded. "I know. I know." Then he steered the conversation to conclusion, saying, "Papa Solomon said you'd take him through the complete ritual," Top Hat continued. "Stay with him, bath and all."

Madame Jeliya turned around and asked Savannah and Maman Anansi, "You all okay here?"

"We'll be fine, Thelema," Maman Anansi assured. "Go handle this foolishness."

She said to her daughter, "Leah, come along. I'm so happy you're home to oversee this. Your power has been missed." But Madame Jeliya's happiness centered on her daughter's presence to assist didn't stop her from huffing, "You know it'll take more than the ritual to make his blessing go through now?"

"Yes, Madame Jeliya," he said to her. "I'm well prepared and well rested. Once the ritual's done, I'll pay Mister Rojo's boss a visit." Top Hat smiled wide. He, Leah and Madame Jeliya walked out of Oliver's parlor.

Madame Jeliya's last words could be heard. "I know you're excited to have a little dreamscape fun, I guess now," she said to Top Hat.

"Was kind of looking forward to it," Top Hat admitted. "Oh, also Mister Connors is here. He needs protection from his boss. He just got a new car, and his boss is quick to envy."

The door closed. Oliver continued working, and even with a hand blessed with precision and speed, from outline to color, it took over eight hours to finish Fey's tattoos. Leah returned to help incant the ink to settle into Fey's flesh. Lady Arachne, Papa Solomon, and Dooley joined the ceremony. Fey was tired afterward. She was granted a few breaks while Oliver worked on her, but she longed for a bed. While incants were applied to lessen tension, her back still ached for holding the angled position in the mechanical chair for so long. Dooley asked if she needed assistance home, but Fey assured she was fine. Despite that, Savannah drove her daughter to their Fable Avenue residence and helped her up to one of the bedrooms. Fey fell fast asleep. Activities carried on through the night, but the noise outside never woke Fey. The Elders performed numerous *stitching* and *webbing rites*, giving a boost to people already blessed with conjures or incants.

The final day of the Spirit Festival was a cool down for the Fable Avenue residents. There was little activity outside, especially early in the day. Parents gathered their kids into family areas and recounted history lessons, from Africa to the diaspora, from ancient to modern times, from broad tales to personal, and even the mythology passed from African generation to African generation, and to the world. People paid respect to the dead, those that had passed over the year, and a call upon ancestors' spirits to help on the newly transitioned to the cosmic realm. People also came to Papa Solomon and the matriarchs for final appreciation and payment for blessings given and received.

Awake, washed, and dressed, Fey Forrester stepped outside into a clear, chilly day. It was the afternoon. Automotive and pedestrian traffic were mild. Fey wore a brown and tanned waist-length coat with faux fur at the cuffs and collar. She was too exhausted to speak an incant to help keep her warm, but with a freshly brewed cup of tea, and drinking its warmth, she assisted her coat in keeping nature at bay. She sat on the landing outside the door with her yumbo named Em. The sprite's wings fluttered, keeping it hovering, flesh glowing blue. Fey sipped and watched the block, up and down the road. When she was finished with her tea, she passed the mug to Em to take inside. The little, blue sprite whisked away, back inside the house, and placed the mug in the kitchen sink. She returned to Fey, who had now wrestled a wool hat from her coat pocket, and placed it on her head.

"Come on, Em," ordered Fey with a happy smile on her face. "Let's get to know this place all over again." Em was also excited. She zipped up and around as Fey walked down the street looking at Fable Avenue's housing and corner stores with a bright smile.

Community members passed Fey by, wishing her well and calling her 'sister'. Fey's smile widened with the compliments. She noticed Em smiling at her. The sprite landed on her head and started dancing. "Em!" Fey laughed, shooing the sprite away. Em flew up, then hovered crossed-legged, crossed-armed, and upside down in front of Fey's face, floating backward as Fey walked forward. The yumbo turned right-side up, keeping her same crossed-limbed position. "Yes, I'm happy, Em. That don't give you permission to act a damn fool!" Em simply smiled, then buzzed away, up and around. When she flew down near Fey's head, Fey said to her, "If you want to go home, go through the sketchbook. Going through the tattoos on my back still feels weird." The yumbo sang an acknowledgement. "How's Silver?" Em sang a reply. "Still tired, huh? She's not trying to avoid the house, is she?" Em shook her head, no. "Good."

Lady Arachne, coming from the corner store, walked up to Fey with a bag of groceries dangling on her arm. "Good afternoon, Miss Forrester," Lady Arachne greeted as she stopped Fey on the sidewalk. "And how is the woman after her ceremonial rites and ink?"

"I'm doing fine, Lady Arachne," Fey responded, giving a slight bow of her head. "Thank you." Em hovered over Fey's shoulder.

Lady Arachne noted, "Such lovely and splendid creatures you can conjure, Miss Forrester. I saw my first yumbo when I was five—probably before that, but that's my first memory. That was in South Carolina, where I grew up. Down there we called them *azizas*. But, a sprite all the same."

"Yes, Lady Arachne," Fey replied. "I'm aware of other names."

The matriarch rested a hand on Fey's shoulder. "Now, I would gladly give you a proper reading, Miss Forrester. But a set of Tarot, sketched long, long, *long* ago, will be in my possession soon. They were blessed by conjurors from Ethiopia and passed through the ages to conjurors in West Africa and Moorish Spain, receiving more and more blessings. I can feel the set brimming with all its old magic and energy." Lady Arachne shivered for play.

"That sounds exciting," Fey remarked.

The Fable Avenue Elder nodded. "It is exciting, *chil'*," she said. "And when I have them, Miss Forrester, I would like for you to sit in on the first reading. As well, afterward, I would like for you to receive a personal reading."

"Thank you, Lady Arachne," Fey said, beaming. "I would love that."

Lady Arachne tapped Fey on the shoulder. "Of course, you know that Gordon Goodspeed has got to be there, now that he got the brew all up in him." Her smile was wicked as she whispered, "You know the men folk have to ruin all the fun for us ladies."

Fey chuckled. Em nodded her head approvingly, making a face and taking the sentiment to heart. "You too much, Lady Arachne," Fey said, making a playful swipe at the Elder.

The matriarch cocked an eyebrow. "I certainly will be, with these cards at last in my possession. Good day, Miss Forrester. Enjoy your time back on the Avenue." She bowed her head and walked away, a triumphant kick in her step.

Fey continued on, eventually crossing paths with Neyeli Kimball and a group of young women. Fey was invited to join them, Em too, and Fey happily accepted. The group ended up at Neyeli's family restaurant, and Fey was treated to a complimentary meal, which she could not turn down at the insistence of Neyeli's mother. Gordon and Benny showed up. They joined the group, being invited, and Fey remarked to Em, "I guess Lady Arachne was right, huh, Em?" Em made a face, nodding her head.

"What's that mean?" Benny inquired.

But Fey kept silent, presenting a sly grin and a wink to Em. The yumbo returned the gesture.

As the day progressed, non-resident, Fable Avenue community members drove off back to their homes. Even Savannah decided to return to Mount Vernon. The Brickhouse family returned to Harlem. Maximilian Goodspeed also left Fable Avenue for Harlem. The Elders spent a long while seeing people on their way home. Gordon retired early, as did Fey. There was school tomorrow. It was a little after ten o'clock when Gordon dressed for bed. Wilson and Top Hat remained downstairs, making light conversation with Cedron. Gordon had gone through his ritual at his altar. A lot had been stirred inside him since the beginning of the festival, but his spirit wasn't as jumpy as it had been before Savannah Forrester had done his reading for an altar. Gordon hit the bed and fell fast asleep.

A dull headache dragged Gordon from slumber several hours later. He massaged his temples, trying to wipe away his grogginess as well as the uncomfortable, and growing, throbbing sensation. He sat up in the darkness. Peering into the black void only increased his headache's pulse. Gordon looked toward the window, a faint source of light, but it didn't soothe his headache.

A flash of light burst from the darkness, quick like a camera's flash. Gordon flinched. His eyes bloomed with a lilac glow. The dark scenery around him broke away like falling shards of glass. In its place came Fey Forrester's Fable Avenue bedroom. Her bed was across from Gordon's, and she lay there still.

There was another flash of light. Gordon again flinched, and he saw Fey arch her back. Her eyelids opened, and a blazing, cobalt-blue light could be seen emitting from them. Fey's mouth was agape, but neither loud scream nor soft sound was audible. Gordon's head beat like an excited heart. He ducked to brace against the pain, trying to dodge the pulsing ache grappling his dome. Despite the throbbing agony, he kept his eyes on the scene cast before him. One of his eyes closed halfway, the lid wavering. Gordon's vision blurred for a moment, and he reached out with his instinct to feel if what was in front of him was a dream or real. Like a reverberating, acoustic sound, Gordon's instinct jumped back to him, relaying a message that Fey Forrester, several blocks up the street, was playing out the scene in front of him. It was indeed real.

Gordon blinked. The scene flickered away. He took a deep breath and looked around the room, eyes aglow. He jumped from his bed, headache dissipating to his relief. His feet hit the floor, and his shadowy garment wrapped around his body like a cloud, becoming solid. Single eye blazing, physical eyes covered by cosmic fabric, Dooley looked at the ceiling for a brief moment, and then he jumped up toward it. His body shifted and twisted into thin, black strands resembling particles orbiting around an atom. Then there was a pop, and all of Dooley was gone.

The roof. There he was. Dooley popped into existence, staring down the street in the direction of Fey Forrester's Fable Avenue brownstone. Dooley focused on a destination far away. Then his body zipped up into the glowing sphere that was his eye, and like a slingshot, was tossed as a single, black beam down the street. The thin, comet-like particle with the glowing lilac sphere as its head stopped abruptly over Fey Forrester's house. The cosmic strand poured out of the eye, and Dooley again came into existence, standing on the roof of Fey Forrester's home.

A high-pitched scream broke through the roof, sounding like rusted nails scraping against glass. The sound molded into words, calling, *"Help me! Help me…"* It was Fey's voice, the tone of which sounded as if the shrill of winter's winds were speaking. Dooley braced against the scratching pitch. He looked down and then jumped up. His body again formed the wild, black atom until it popped away.

Dooley was in Fey Forrester's room, watching her just as he did when he awoke from sleep. Now the scene was real. Fey's inaudible scream had sound. It was biting, and it was laced with fear. Dooley's instinct reached out and connected to her. He absorbed the emotion possessing her. It felt like taking in a large gulp of hot water. He swallowed Fey's fear, but Dooley's actions did nothing to curb Fey's possession. Fear's presence reached up and gripped Dooley, sharing Fey's fright with him. He struggled with the emotion, but he realized he had little to no time to be afraid. He allowed instinct to guide him. He walked through the noise as if it was a heavy wind. His arms shielded his face. His body was arched, and he dug his feet into the floor to push forward against the force of Fey's squeal. He reached out for her arched stomach, laying a hand over it. She was trembling, and so he started trembling. Her icy screams muted, retracting into her body. A thin aura of light surrounded her, cobalt blue as the glow in her eyes. The light slapped Dooley's knuckles. He pulled away and rubbed the back of his hand. He looked around, wondering what to do. He reached out with his instinct.

Fey called to her mother. Her voice was like a little girl. *"Mamma!"* she yelled.

Dooley turned his head in the direction of his house. An image of the chamber in his basement flickered bright through the surrounding darkness. Dooley understood what his instinct was telling him. He looked at Fey, her body still arched and trembling, mouth still agape. Dooley backed away. He lifted his legs off the ground and crossed them, floating next to Fey's bed in a meditative pose. He put his hands together as if in prayer, and he concentrated, aiming his glowing eye at Fey.

Relax, he said. He didn't speak through his lips but rather as a mental thought coming through the glowing sphere at the center of his forehead. ***Relax, Fey. Just relax.***

Fey's body responded. A sigh escaped Fey as her mouth closed. Her arch dissolved away, and like a feather making a gentle descent to earth, her back lowered until she was flat against the bed. Dooley uncrossed his legs, stepping onto the ground, ceasing to float. He stepped forward and reached out his hand, holding it over Fey's now relaxed body.

Control that power, Fey, he said, voice again emanating from his single, glowing eye. ***Retract that glow for now.*** The thin aura of light surrounding her body faded, and Fey turned to her side, back to Dooley. He took a moment to relax, and then he scooped Fey into his arms. Fey, eyes closed and returned to slumber, put her arms around Dooley as he cradled her. She never woke, even when Dooley whisked the two of them away, popping from existence, and solidifying in his basement next to his chamber.

It was dark in the basement, but not for long. The lights turned on seconds after Dooley's arrival.

"Spook," Dooley hollered. "I need the chamber open."

Spook's face lifted, black-mirror monitor lighting up with ancient symbols. The top slab of the chamber disconnected from the lower body, sliding down and giving enough space for Dooley to slip Fey Forrester's unconscious body inside.

"Spook," Dooley called again, "close up."

He backed away, keeping his blazing eye on the chamber as it closed shut, Fey Forrester inside. He dropped into the chair behind him, his cosmic, African mask dissolved away. The spherical, lilac third eye faded. Gordon put his hands together, elbows on the arms of the chair. He rested his chin against his fingers and watched with his physical eyes. He heard a hum coming from the chamber. The inscribed symbols lit up, brightening and dimming in rhythm with the hum. The sound muted, and the light dimmed out of existence.

Gordon watched, pensive. His cosmic mask molded back around his face. His bright eye gleamed. The chamber opened, and remnants of light shifted into foggy smoke. Dooley rose in his chair, but never straightened. His hands remained on the chair's arms, body arched forward in anticipation, and mouth agape.

Fey rose, her nightclothes gone. Her eyes widened, gazing at her naked form. She bent down, wrapping her arms around herself to shield her bare body. She looked at Dooley. Her eyes lit up with a cobalt-blue fire.

"Gordon!" she hollered. "Turn away." There was an occurrence as Fey hissed her command. Black smoke perspired from her flesh. Fey giggled as the sensation tickled her. Dooley stared in awe as the tarry, phantom substance covered her, beginning at her arms and working its way around her body. And then, there she stood, mystically fitted with a tight, black suit like Dooley's. Her mask was much the same, but there was a feminine accent to its African mask facial features.

Dooley noticed a few design differences in Fey's cosmic outfit. Her mask covered the top of her head, as her low cut hair allowed. A gray, v-line pattern dropped below her neck in the front and back of the cosmic suit like a bent diamond. The mandorla shapes at the center of her eyepieces blazed cobalt blue. And above her hair was a light-blue flame. The body of fire sprouted wide like a woolly star atop Fey's head. It was like a crown, acting as extensions of the dome of her hair. She felt the need to stay in her stance, arms wrapped around her, ducking low. Dooley watched her.

"Gordon!" Fey hissed again. "Turn away," she repeated the order. Dooley's mask fell away, and the spherical light dissolved as his physical eyes were revealed. Fey dropped her head and held out a hand. "Please, Gordon, stay there," she said in a doleful voice.

Gordon did not move. He watched Fey's body shift into small, black strands that whirled erratic. She popped away. Gordon's mask wrapped around him again. His eye blazed, and he too popped away, following Fey to the roof of her house. She had her back to him.

"It's okay, Fey," said Dooley in a comforting voice. He walked up beside her. Fey sat down, legs dangling over the brownstone's edge. Dooley sat next to her. His mask dissolved away. His cosmic suit kept him warm. "You look beautiful," he said.

Fey beamed a shy smile. The fiery, blue crown atop her head faded away. The glow in her eyes relaxed, and her mask peeled away as smoke. She turned from Gordon. "I've never had a nightmare like that," she said. "I saw it all again, but it's fading as I'm trying to remember it. It was my mother, and her death. Her suicide." She looked at Gordon, eyes watering. "My father was there. He was screaming. He was screaming at her. No real words. He was just screaming." She wiped her eyes. "I can feel it, but the scene is gone." She concluded, "Ah, my *Bat Ge*. A war beats within me, no?"

Gordon said nothing, because he didn't know what to say.

Fey stated, sniffing back her tears, "I could see you, Gordon. I saw you over me. I felt you calming me."

"I woke up," interjected Gordon. "I saw a vision of you. I saw you in trouble."

"Thank you, Gordon." She smiled and kissed his cheek. "Thank you."

Gordon inspected the young, cosmic-suited woman in front of him. "Look at you now, Fey."

Fey rolled her eyes. "Yeah, look at me," she said examining herself. "This thing is so tight. *Good-ness!* It feels fine." She paused, and her eyes brightened, and her lips curled into a warm smile. She chuckled playfully and hugged herself, expressing aloud, "Nature's cosmic, crushed leaves all over me. *Pile fey!*" Then she opened her embrace and remarked, looking at her attire, "But I keep thinking I should have whips and chains to go with it."

Gordon, voice a little sterner, complimented again, "You look beautiful."

Fey continued examining her outfit, touching the fabric with fingertips that were now radiating a cobalt-blue glow. "I can see the stars on me if I look close enough," she said in a relaxed, curious tone. A smile appeared on her face.

Gordon had an idea. His mask and glowing eye resurfaced. He jumped to his feet and asked Fey, "You have any instincts in you, Fey?"

Fey looked up at Dooley. Her eyes blazed cobalt blue. The blue-white crown of fire swirled atop the dome of her low-cut afro, whipping wild like strands of coiled hair. "I don't know if I'm as fancy as you, Mister Goodspeed, but I have an instinct or two. I feel all types of conjures dancing in my blood."

Dooley let go of her and shifted into his blazing spirit form. "Got an instinct to do this?"

Fey concentrated for a moment. First her mask reappeared, and then her body burst into a smoky, cobalt-blue feminine spirit. She looked around at the world with new eyes that could see the wind. Objects pulsed with light surrounding them. She could gauge the life inside everything, and everything she'd seen before was new again. Fey couldn't stop looking everywhere. Fable Avenue's light was the brightest, but the world beamed in harmony, like a choir of backup singers to the main voice.

Dooley said to her, "Follow me." Then he soared upwards like an ascending comet.

Fey followed behind, matching Dooley's speed.

Up and up they went. The city dropped away. All of New York dropped away. The continent fell as Dooley and Fey ascended. The sky extended and became the heavens, and the Earth fell away too. Fey's throat closed, a reflex occurring under the belief that her breath would not exist. But she was spirit, and the cosmos fed her its winds. In and out, the cosmos provided. Fey relaxed and continued up with Dooley. She examined all of space, her eyes devouring the cosmic scene. She followed next to Dooley. Space was like water, and she swam through it like a dolphin. She stopped when Dooley stopped. He pointed, and Fey looked in the direction he signaled. She witnessed space open, spinning wild as a vortex. Out danced black, cosmic spirits. Around and around they danced, encircling Fey and Dooley.

Fey marveled at the spectacle. At first, she did not move, but then the cosmic festivities possessed her. She twisted her body, following every movement of dance. Music hummed throughout the cosmos. Instinct took over, and Fey ascended, fast like a bullet. She then dove into the circle of dance and joined. The spirits surrounded her, joyous. Cosmic jazz played and mixed with the reverberation of space djembe drums. Galactic horns blared, and Fey stomped and grooved with the celestial spirits. Dooley just watched, but Fey would have none of that. She soared to him, grabbed his arms, and pulled him into the dance. Dooley accepted.

Their fiery tails dissolved away, and out came their lighted legs. All cosmic instruments, save the drums, dropped their sound. Fey wrapped her arms around Dooley and swiveled her hips to the beat of the drums. Forward and back, their steps went, like cosmic salsa. The drums increased their rhythm. The dark, smoke-like bodies of the celestial spirits stretched back inside the black opening, as if sucked inside. The spinning opening shrank and popped away, and the drumming stopped in that instant.

Space was again silent.

Fey smiled. She cried human tears that iced and then dissolved in space as quick as they came. She bubbled with emotion, holding Dooley's spirit tight. He held her as she sobbed.

"I want answers," Fey cried. Her lips moved, but her voice resonated in the mental.

"We all do," Dooley replied, tone between being matter-of-fact and sympathetic.

Fey lifted her head off his shoulder, shaking it. "No," she stated. "I want answers about my mother and father. I want to know what happened. I want to remember. I have that right. Papa Solomon and Madame Jeliya's protection haunts me, Gordon. Yes, I said haunts. I have a right to know what I saw that night."

"You know what you saw," Dooley told her.

"But I don't know why," Fey pleaded. "Nana says that my father was friends with Stanley Fallows who befriended our community and then betrayed us. They were close. My father helped him come to peace. I know he's the son of the Red-Haired Harpy, called Sarinda Fallows, but he has answers."

"Stanley Fallows is a dangerous man," Dooley warned Fey. "He has tricks. He's done damage to my family as well. He worked hard to keep us from the spirit that brews inside me—that now stirs inside all of us."

Fey looked at Dooley, a curious expression on her face. A smile broke through her somber demeanor. "Gordon," she stated with her sly grin. "We're having a conversation far above the Earth. The cosmos surrounds us as we glow with spirit. How dangerous can mortal Stanley Fallows be to us now? We got the brew. Trick that man's tricks. Trick him and all his trick friends and trickin' allies. Shit, I can tap dance on cosmic clouds and supernovas now. What can that man do to me?" Dooley was about to answer when Fey lifted her hand in front of his face. "*Ah, ah, ah!* I don't want to hear it." Dooley tried again. Fey clasped her fingers and thumb together. *"Zip it!"* she ordered. Then she became serious again. "Now, listen. After school, we go to the one Elder we know will give us some answers: Lady Arachne. She will be helpful." Fey hugged Dooley again. She breathed out a relieving sigh. "I don't want that nightmare again, even if I have to go through something worse to get it out. I still feel it. It's subtle, but all over me. Please, Gordon, let me ask these questions."

"Absolutely, beautiful lightning bug."

Fey beamed warm and spirited. "Then we compose and play." She whispered into his ear, "And come this weekend, we fly ourselves to a nightclub in Brazil and dance until the sun shows." Dooley nodded, accepting Fey's offer. She let go of him and dived toward Earth, her body a cobalt-blue comet. Dooley followed, catching up to her.

Cobalt-blue comet and pale-purple comet soared side by side.

Space was like water, and Fey and Dooley swam through it like dolphins.

"*Hold that door, please!*" Thomas Bertram, a well-dressed middle-aged man with thin, graying hair, heard someone yell while rushing toward the closing elevator doors.

Thomas, the elevator's only occupant, held out his arm and kept the doors from closing. The doors sensed the barrier, and parted. A black man jump inside. He thanked Thomas as the doors closed, and Thomas replied, "No problem." The black man made an attempt to press the button for the fourteenth floor, but it was already glowing. The man chuckled to himself while scanning the numbers on the elevator's console. One through twelve were all present and labeled. Thirteen was skipped, fourteen written in its stead. The man turned to Thomas and said, "It's still the thirteenth floor, no matter if you skip it by number. Crazy superstitions, huh?"

Thomas only replied with a smile and a nod, but he had nothing more to offer. He held his briefcase and cup of coffee close and away from the man who retained his playful smile. Thomas inspected the man beside him, a gesture made obvious once the man looked straight ahead at their warped and blurred reflections in the closed elevator doors.

The black man, with cinnamon-colored skin, wore a long, thick overcoat, and was of average height and stocky build. In his gloved hands was an old, tall and flat-crowned, broad-brimmed topper hat. Thomas lifted an eyebrow and was drawn to ask, "Do you work here?"

The man turned toward Thomas in a swift motion. His hand was held out. Thomas, in quick reflex, shoved his briefcase under his arm and dropped his hand into the man's gloved one. "Wallace Bard is my name, sir," the man said. "People call me Top Hat on account that I carry this here lucky charm." He lifted the topper hat in his grip, putting it on display for Thomas to see. "Got my own superstitions, I suppose. I have in my family a great-great-great," he waved his hand, "*many* great-relative of some kind. Not a grandfather, but a relative of some sort. He also called himself Top Hat. He was a gunslinger in the Old West. Wore somethin' quite like this."

Thomas was intrigued, losing the focus of his interrogation. "Is that right?" he said.

"Yes, he did," answered Top Hat. "He's a big deal in my family. I got many family members who honor him by wearing a hat just the same." He nodded his head at Thomas and added, "My aunt wore something a little more elaborate. Her cat." Thomas spied Top Hat with a strange expression, holding back a curious smile. "Yes, she did. Her cat, black as midnight, would climb her back and sit atop her head, straight and tall, and without movement. Stiff. Tail was so long it looped around her head like one of Saturn's rings, made for the brim."

Thomas kept his strange expression, and then he burst into laughter. Top Hat did too. "You almost had me," said Thomas.

"My father had me too, until I was eleven," Top Hat said through his laughter. "He'd tell my mother every chance he'd get that her sister was strange. He swore by it, even when I got old enough not to believe him. I tell you, Mister…" Top Hat searched for a name.

"Thomas Bertram," Thomas answered. His laughter subsided. "I'm one of the directors here at Bradley and Crest Financials." His authoritative, interrogative voice returned as he cleared his throat. "I ask again, do you work here?" He noticed there was no proper suit beneath Top Hat's long overcoat, only a collar shirt, buttoned all the way up and draping past his waist, and black slacks.

"No, man," Top Hat answered. "I'm just a guest in your house today." Top Hat removed a guest pass, a piece of paper with a printed barcode and Top Hat's picture on it for him to pass, for the day, through a few of the building's magnetically sealed doors. "I'm here to see a friend. Garrett Rojo. You might know him."

"I do," said Thomas.

"Yeah, you do." Top Hat nudged Thomas in the ribs. It was a playful gesture, but hard enough for Thomas to wriggle his smile, and shake his coffee around in the mug. Top Hat pointed at Thomas and said, "Because you're the guy that promoted my friend to…" Top Hat's voice trailed off as he tried to recall Garrett Rojo's new title. Thomas stared, his eyes filled with anxiety. Top Hat snapped his fingers. The noise echoed inside the elevator, like a bullet ricocheting off the walls. Thomas flinched. "Senior Media Relations Director," Top Hat recalled. "That's it," he said in an excited manner, smile wide.

Thomas tried to maintain a pleasant demeanor, but his expression melted into concern. "He told you that?"

"Sure did," Top Hat replied.

"Garrett didn't get the job," Thomas admitted.

"Really?"

"I think he jumped the gun telling you he did."

"What was the problem?"

The door opened. "I can't discuss that," said Thomas stepping out.

"Understood," conceded Top Hat, following Thomas out of the elevator. "I guess my conversation will be a little different this morning with Garrett."

"I guess," said Thomas squirming his way out of the conversation.

"Heard you guys have a helluva cafeteria," Top Hat expressed as if that was a consolation prize.

Thomas walked away, steps quick. He hurried through a sea of cubicles and scurried into his corner office. He closed the door, relieved to be free of the situation. He dropped his briefcase next to his desk as he approached it, came around to his chair, and set his coffee down between two, small stacks of folders. He turned around and watched the city through a large, corner window. After taking in the sight, he turned and sat down. He reached for his mug and took a large gulp of coffee.

"All right," he expressed putting his mug back on his desk. "Let's begin the day here with—"

Someone knocked at the door.

Thomas looked up. His face molded perplexity. "Laurel?" he called the name of his personal assistant. No one answered. He looked at his office phone, pushed a button and asked, "Laurel? Is someone at the door? Can you announce them please?"

No one answered.

Someone knocked at the door. Three times the knocks came. And then nothing. Stop. The door handle jiggled. Thomas sat back, looking at the door handle as the person on the other side played with it. He heard a voice whispering to him. It was low, icy, and mechanical. The door handle turned again. Around it went, but this time, the door opened.

Top Hat walked in, topper on his crown.

"Excuse me!" Thomas barked, putting all threat and authority into his voice.

Top Hat closed the door, ignoring Thomas. He turned around, grabbed a seat near the door, and dragged it to Thomas' desk. He rolled it around in front of the desk and sat down.

"Mister Bertram?" Top Hat said as a question.

"What the hell do you want?"

"I'm your conscious, motherfucker," Top Hat growled.

Thomas sat up straight and yelled, "Garrett didn't get the job!"

"I know," said Top Hat. "Guy name Chad Amerling plucked it from him."

"So. What."

"Chad comes in near eleven o'clock—late for work, is my point," Top Hat stated as a matter-of-fact. "Then, after twenty minutes on the

Internet, he jaunts off to a damn-near two hour lunch. Hardly director material."

"He's a good, kid," Thomas retorted. "Shows initiative. I'm not aware of these accusations. This company invested in that kid. We paid for him to take classes for a mandatory certificate—a certificate, by the way, that Garrett never looked into. He's lucky he still has the job he's got without that thing."

"He's got a masters degree," Top Hat countered. "He don't need a certificate for what he's doing." Top Hat cocked an eye and jabbed the air toward Thomas as he clarified for argument's sake, "And you *never* spoke about him needing a certificate for the job." Top Hat bounced up from the chair. He put his hands on Thomas' desk and leaned forward. "C'mon. Let's be honest. How much money you saving proppin' that kid up in that position? He got no master's degree, and a simple certificate sayin' it's okay for him to be there?"

Thomas huffed. "Who are you?" he growled at Top Hat. "Mister Rojo's lawyer?"

Top Hat shook his head. "No. I don't get called in to handle law." Pause. A devious pride appeared on Top Hat's countenance, there in his grin and eyes.

Thomas' face crumpled with disgust. "You little shit!" he spat. "I'll have your thug ass thrown in jail. You come in here threatening me."

"Promising," Top Hat corrected.

"What?"

"Promising," Top Hat repeated. "I *promise you,* that I won't lose my shit if you take the easily-controlled-pawn down and put up a guy deserving of the job—*and* with a proper salary."

"Excuse me?"

Top Hat remained silent. His devious grin spoke for him, and so did the next action. Thomas watched horrified as the skin on either side of Top Hat's forehead bubbled, wrinkling in a circular pattern. The patterns split and cracked, and up sprouted two ram-like horns, growing and coiling, propping up the sides of the brim on his silk hat.

Thomas' legs shook like a newborn calf.

Top Hat's eyes burst into flames, and as he cackled, yellowish-red fire could be seen growing in his throat. Smoke billowed out of his mouth. Top Hat stood up straight, and Thomas' mouth dropped as he saw the lower half of Top Hat's body was now a set of fury goat legs and hooves.

Thomas kept staring at the creature, fear caught in his throat and choking him with what should've been his screams.

Top Hat grabbed him and flung his body against the office's large window. It cracked in a web-like, concentric pattern. Thomas dropped to the floor, the impact jarring him. He heard the stomp of hooves approach him. He looked up. Top Hat appeared tall, so tall. Thomas wondered why the bulky beast's extended frame didn't break through the ceiling.

Top Hat grabbed him again and slammed him into the glass.

"Why can't you leave well enough alone?" he growled. "What's wrong with you?"

He pressed Thomas' body hard against the glass with one hand. Thomas choked as Top Hat's balled fist pressed into his chest. The pressure increased. Thomas believed Top Hat's fist was going to break through his rib cage, but he couldn't scream, he could only experience the pain of the compounding pressure.

Then a thing occurred. The glass seemed to melt away as the outside wind tickled Thomas' backside. Top Hat pushed and pushed. Thomas' body pressed and pressed through the glass as if it was made of gelatin. The cold, elevated winds lashed at Thomas' body as he was held out over the Manhattan streets. Thomas kicked his feet as if in water. He hollered over the winds, pleading for Top Hat not to drop him.

"Do we—" Top Hat screamed, bringing Thomas' body forward and slamming his face against the rehardened glass. "—have a deal?" He held him out again. "Do we?" Top Hat asked again. He pulled Thomas in, harder this time, and the business executive smacked his face against the glass again. "Answer me, Thomas. My arm is getting tired." Top Hat then reiterated the terms of the deal he offered. "Drop Chad, replace with Mister Rojo, and pay a proper salary. Yes?" He shook Thomas. "Yes?"

Thomas was too frightened to speak. He kept looking down, holding on to Top Hat's forearm.

"Look at me!" Top Hat screamed, shaking Thomas. "Eyes on me!"

He didn't want to. He didn't want to look into those fiery eyes, or that face with the horns.

Top Hat loosened a finger. "Getting hard to hold you up, Thomas! What's it going to be?"

Thomas used all his strength to keep from passing out. He shook his head, gasping, almost crying. But his nod wasn't an answer. It was a wild movement to stay conscious. He yelled, "We have a deal! Goddamnit! We have a deal!"

Top Hat pulled Thomas back in. His body molded through the glass. His office's interior embraced him with a warm hug all over his body. Top Hat placed Thomas in his chair.

"Breathe," Top Hat instructed as his horns retracted into his head, and the flames in his eyes, and the fiery storm billowing in his throat, dissolved. His legs were normal as he walked back around the desk.

Thomas inhaled. He exhaled. His breathing became normal.

"Good," said Top Hat. Then he slammed his hands on Thomas' desk, causing Thomas to jump in fright. "Now *WAKE UP!*" he screamed.

Thomas sat up in bed. He inhaled. His panting was loud enough to wake his wife in much the same fervor. But unlike Thomas, she quickly gained composure, turned to her husband, and put a hand against his chest. "Thomas!" she exclaimed.

Thomas exhaled, matching the excitement in his wife's voice. His body was drenched with enough sweat for him to be mistaken for having taken a bath while fully clothed.

It was morning.

"Breathe, Thomas. Relax."

Thomas jumped at his wife's voice and choice of words. "Wh-wh-why are you telling me to breath," he said still panting.

Thomas' wife slapped him on the back of the head.

"So you can live, you idiot! What's wrong with you, Thomas?"

Thomas put his head back against the headboard, still trying to catch his breath. "Made a mistake at work." He coughed. "Gotta play chess with people's positions. Wrong man got the job." His breath was coming to him.

Far away from Thomas Bertram's Westchester County home, Top Hat was also waking up. He sat up and reached for the pad and pen on the nightstand. He rubbed the sleep from his eyes as he worked his grip around the pen. He lifted the pad to his eyes, trying to focus. He shook his head and blinked until the writing on the page came in focus in the morning sun.

Top Hat scratched off Thomas Bertram's name.

Below Thomas' name, there was another name and some notes. *Ronald Hertz, Supervisor to Edmond Connors. Jealous of Edmond's new car.*

Top Hat circled the name. He closed his eyes, said an incant, and placed the notepad and pen back on the nightstand. He returned his head to the pillow and dreamed inside another man's dream. He was on a commercial airliner that was preparing for takeoff.

"Excuse me," Top Hat said to a well-dressed man seated next to him. "*Are you Mister Ronald Hertz?*"

Lady Arachne chuckled as she sat down, relaxed in her study. Her laughter was a response to Fey Forrester's description of the tea that she prepared and presented to the young woman. The matriarch sipped her hot beverage and then repeated Fey's words while still chuckling, "*A liquid incant.* Your grandmother does have a way with words," she recalled with a grin and a raised eyebrow aimed at Fey. Lady Arachne sipped her tea some more.

Fey swallowed wrong, but caught herself before she choked. She cleared her throat and responded with dampened laughter, "...Yes, she does."

"Emma, your mother, was a little more reserved," Lady Arachne noted. "She would've smiled at the sentiment, but wouldn't have said much, or made such a comment. Your father made short work of that. She opened herself up to him."

Fey took another sip and then asked, "What about Stanley Fallows? What was his relationship to my father?"

Lady Arachne set her tea down. She fixed her dress over her crossed legs and fiddled with the wrap around her locked hair. Fey waited still and patient through all this. She and Lady Arachne stared at one another for a while. Then Lady Arachne asked, "How much has your grandmother told you?"

Fey answered, "She said Fable Avenue took in a man it should never have trusted."

"That's true," Lady Arachne acknowledged with a contemplative nod. She reached for her tea, but then decided against the action, sitting back in her chair. "But in our community's defense, Stanley came to us with a sincere heart. He renounced his mother, cursed her actions, and was very honest about helping us procure the grand wish. If anything, we were more suspicious of his wife, Lucretia." Then Lady Arachne grabbed her tea and took a sip. She sighed after she swallowed, and then she said to Fey, "All those politics were before my time, young lady. The anxiety Stanley's presence created was exercised by the time I joined the community. Stanley was a regular member. He stuck out, because he and his wife were part of the few whites inside Fable Avenue, but we were all preoccupied by finding our way, our greater purpose."

"Procuring the grand conjure?" Fey inquired.

"Yes, young lady," answered the matriarch. After another sip, Lady Arachne continued, "But Stanley's focus changed when your father's family entered our community—much like the cobalt-blue spirit in you changes our focus now."

Word had spread of Fey's cobalt-blue cosmic spirit, a compliment to Gordon's lilac flame. There were already conjure communities worldwide that worshipped what was called *'The Unseen Blue Spirit-Fire'.* Many affixed the unseen blue spirit to the lilac flame, and now these distinct spirits possessed two members of the Fable Avenue conjure community.

Was it luck, or was it destined?

Either way, research was required to understand their place in the larger narrative. This prompted Lady Arachne and others of the African Conjure Diaspora to consult cards, bones, or shells.

But conjure conjecture aside, Lady Arachne returned to the subject matter at hand, Fey's paternal lineage. "They were from Philadelphia, your father's family."

Fey nodded, though she'd known that much about her paternal side. Out of respect, she didn't inform Lady Arachne of this already known tidbit.

Lady Arachne reminisced, "Lewis—your father—we sure did wish his last name was Goodspeed." She leaned forward, and said as her smile shifted into a devious grin, "Don't tell that to your boyfriend, Gordon."

"Oh, ma'am, Gordon's not—"

But Lady Arachne kept on talking, cutting into Fey's defense. The matriarch leaned back and spoke, "Everyone knew your father was a codebreaker. He had this sense of knowing the world around him, understanding unseen details to see the whole picture. We were so happy to have someone of his talents among us."

Fey beamed. She exhaled a touch of relief while looking at the floor and seeing an image of her father in her head.

"Your mother and he didn't start dating until she was in college," Lady Arachne's voice punctured Fey's thoughts. "Your father was in grad-school at the time, studying psychology. That's where he wanted to take his talents, helping people ease the stresses on their minds. He could read people so well. Stanley Fallows encouraged your father's studies for his own purposes."

"Oh," blurted Fey, an inquisitive tone in her short reply.

Lady Arachne nodded. "Yes, indeed, young lady," she said. "Yes, indeed. Your father was pulled in so many directions because of his talents.

Building on my earlier description, Miss Forrester, your father could see things others couldn't. He could see things before they happened. And if not that, he could use his incant to put together the proper variables to see the potential of what *could* happen. He always said the world is not as limitless in possibilities as optimists would have us think." Lady Arachne chuckled. "But he understood. He followed Stanley Fallows' advice not because of anything against Fable Avenue, but, he honestly enjoyed helping people out of their anxiety. He loved codebreaking the mind, behaviors. But he also focused his gift on piecing together our community's story, understanding who we are." Lady Arachne clarified, "Even with all our knowledge, a lot has been lost to the ages through colonialism, slavery, oppression. And then there are the deeds we do to one another, and the ebb and flow of our magic." Lady Arachne shook her head and said, "Three steps forward and six steps back."

Both Fey and Lady Arachne sipped their tea, pausing to ponder.

"Your father helped focus the Goodspeed's ritual," Lady Arachne proclaimed. "Some of our rites weren't performed properly before your father came along. Until Lewis' appearance, we were just performing a series of movements out of tradition. But he decoded the proper movements, dances, and rituals. He got us to align with the magic, become stronger with our incants and conjures. We weren't able to avoid magic's ebb and flow, but we weren't affected so much by it. He worked closely with us matriarchs and Papa Solomon. And at the same time, he tended to his schooling. But then Stanley took a great deal of interest in your father. He got closer to him, and trouble started."

"What kind of trouble?"

"Your mother and father started fighting," Lady Arachne answered. "It was so odd to see, but not unusual. We believed it was just reality slipping into their relationship. The honeymoon phase, as long as it lasted, was over. You were a little under a year old then. They would settle, be in love again, and then trouble would come again."

"Yes," said Fey. "I can feel a familiarity with that. What was my father doing with Stanley?"

"Stanley had dreams about his mother," Lady Arachne told Fey. "It was a haunting, but Stanley didn't seek an expulsion for it, though. He did at first. That was his reason for reaching out to Fable Avenue all them years ago. Then he reached out to your father. He didn't seek out us matriarchs or Papa Solomon. He wanted to commune with the haunting. He thought it was purposeful to know the imprint and shade his mother left behind." Lady Arachne shook her head. "Somewhere in his sessions with your father, Stanley crumbled into the man he is today, striking from the shadows. Your father disappeared, most likely a victim of Stanley's deviltry. Your mother was broken, and…and you know how that story ends."

Fey nodded. "Yes, ma'am," she uttered.

"After I procure the cards I seek, Miss Forrester, I'll be able to do a proper reading for you," Lady Arachne assured. In a humble voice she added, "I could give you one now, but I'm too excited about the real cards." Lady Arachne thought about the prize she sought. "I'll be equal to your father," she declared aloud. "My reading will show you your path to follow, your place in the Grand Narrative. We will answer the question: Who is the Cobalt-Blue Flame?"

"Thank you," Fey expressed, appreciative.

The two women finished their tea. Lady Arachne continued to spin tales of Fey's father and his contributions to Fable Avenue, her mother's too. She learned that her mother interpreted what her father would see for people—proper paths and choices. She would make elaborate sketches, often creating embroidery on handkerchiefs that people could keep on their person as a charm that kept them walking their genuine path. Fey listened, invested in every detail of her parents' lives. The faint memories that haunted her yielded to the stories of love between her mother and father. She held these new understandings close to her, even when she left Lady Arachne's residence.

Outside, Fey's body lost its color, shifting into a shadow and gliding on the night wind. She made her way to Gordon Goodspeed's house where her body became solid again. She rang the doorbell, standing outside his garden-floor entrance. Gordon came to the door with his legs and feet covered in his cosmic fabric and a Yankees t-shirt over his body.

"Hey, lightning bug," Gordon greeted. "You learn anything?"

"Plenty," Fey answered in a satisfied voice. "Can I come in? I don't mean to bother you."

"Not bothering me at all," Gordon exclaimed, unlocking the iron door blocking the entrance. "You look happy."

"I am," she beamed.

"Well, I gotta say," started Gordon as he stepped aside to give Fey space to walk through, "I ain't jauntin' off to Brazil again to go clubbin'—no offense. Give me a couple more days to rest."

Fey threw her arms around Gordon and hugged him tight. It was unexpected, and it caused Gordon to stumble back a bit. "Lady Arachne talked and talked and talked about my mother and father," Fey said like a sigh of relief. "And I could see them. They were happy. She told me their contributions to Fable Avenue, Gordon. My grandmother never told me so much."

Gordon hesitated in putting his arms around Fey. He tried once, twice, and then, on the third try, he relaxed his body and embraced her. "That's great, Fey," were the only words he could think to say.

Fey looked at Gordon and expressed in an excited voice, "I know where my father's people are in Philly. They're originally from North Carolina," she added. "But, I don't know if I could visit them. They were as shaken by all that happened as my grandmother. I'll take my time." A thought came to her, and her expression dropped. "Shit! I should've reached out to them for the festival. They could've come through."

Gordon said in a soft voice, "Don't worry, lightning bug. When you're ready, we'll pay them a visit. All in time."

Fey pushed the iron door close. "It's freezing out there," she said. "I glided here with my body shifted and looking as clear as the wind, but *lawdy* did it treat me like an outsider."

"Tea…?" offered Gordon.

Fey let go of him and locked the iron door. "No, thank you. Too impatient," she said. Then she spoke an incant and her body warmed. She stepped inside the house.

Gordon followed Fey inside after locking the inner door. He watched Fey remove her coat and toss it to a chair. His eyes became wide when Fey removed her pants. His heart jumped several, excited beats, but then he noticed the cosmic fabric wrapped tight around her legs and feet. Fey tossed her pants onto the same chair as her coat. She kept her sweater around her, turning toward Gordon with all the grace and elegance of a ballerina. She said, "I can strut my cosmic stuff too, Mister Goodspeed." Then she asked, "Have you eaten?"

"No," Gordon said, hesitant and shaking his head.

Fey slapped her hands together. "I know you don't want to jaunt off to a club in Brazil, but how about our spirits glide across the night and hit up a café in Morocco?"

"That I can do," Gordon agreed to the proposal.

Fey took a step toward him, bouncing up. "I'm just so excited, Gordon." She wrapped her arms around him again.

"Well, I was about to take a peek at our composition—"

"That's an excellent idea!" Fey shouted. "Let's go!" She grabbed Gordon's arm and hurried to the basement only to make a sudden stop at the top of the stairs. Anxiety washed away her smile, and she hesitated while looking down into the dark. "I told you to kill them…" she said. She sounded contemplative, though she addressed Gordon.

"Fey…?"

She turned and faced him, his wrist still in her grip. "My parents," she clarified. "I told you to bring me their heads." She let go of Gordon and walked away from the basement stairs toward the couch. "That was a selfish move."

"It was an honest move, Fey," Gordon told her. "I understand it."

Fey slumped onto the couch. "Thank you, Gordon," she voiced, sounding sarcastic.

Gordon didn't like her tone, and he barked, *"Hey!"* Fey looked up at him, alerted by the weight of his voice. "You're not killing your parents. It's about washing away the pain of what happened." He relaxed himself, believing he was being too forceful with her. He knelt down in front of her and held her hands with a soft embrace. "It's okay. You're happy now. Don't lose that."

Fey did her best to smile. It took a moment for it to be authentic. She kissed Gordon on the forehead.

"Let's go see what happens," Gordon suggested with a sly grin. "Let's bring your emotions up to the surface, and then bury them outside of you."

Gordon stood, and in the same motion, helped Fey to her feet. He guided her down into the basement where the light came on of its own accord. He led Fey to the seat facing the chamber, and took a spot on the floor, crossed legged, next to the chair. Both of them focused their eyes on the ancient tome resting atop the sarcophagus.

Cobalt-blue light lit up Fey's eyes.

Lilac light lit up Gordon's eyes.

The book jumped into the air and opened, flipping and flipping until it came to a page half-written in ancient script, where last their story was written. Lilac and cobalt-blue strands writhed from Gordon and Fey's wide opened and focused eyes, scribbling ancient text and drawing on the page. Then a scene blossomed into existence.

Soft foot prints light the wasteland
Behind caged city
Lingers dust bowls, billowing sand
Scraps, graveyard grit
Of broken bits and tossed aside lives
Strewn out in crumpled mounds
Ash by the pound
A perfect place for nothing and zero to hide

One hand carries weapon for task
Dragging edge, sword tip kisses ground
Sketches scratched waves of snakes

I walk against the tide of walking dead
Who walk aimless and only fed conscious costumes
So cage city mouths can consume them, dubwana-burdened
They are nameless but numbered
Soft pale shadow voices sound like thunder to them
They are at command – their minds covered in forgetful snow
Memories melt
They are heavy wave, wind and flow
Determined to stop my go

I have memorized my stars
Jump
Up! Highest mound and look down
See where my stars hide and constellate
My Heru eye blurs reality blind
Static haze twists my gaze gray
While marks glitter yellow with intent

Poison-bearer and his madam wife,
Crippler of daughter's life
Down – I creep to kill, closer
Not deterred in deed
Determined in this need – strength heavy
As heavy sword dampens its weight
Two lives to take
This day, noted in memory
A day long remembered
A Mother Nothing and Father Zero
Will fall, accordingly

Fey struggled to keep her glowing eyes on the images in front of her. Cobalt-blue tears streaked down her face as she watched Gordon's poetic doppelganger inch closer to the doppelganger images of her parents.

Damaged daughter
Inspired
I grip sword
Leap
Off beat
Madam wife hears my silent creep
Sickle, beaming blade
Swipes and shields my fatal strike

Sharpened ice, thrown like knives, cut air
My nimble frame – supreme, zig zags
Arm, leg, leg, arm, head
Sharpened ice misses
Sickle, beaming blade, makes raids on my person
Her Mother Nothing is something in a fight
Her Father Zero turns the rain into knives
Duck. Dodge. Weave.
Sickle, blade a beam
Swipe! And swish!
Each dodge, barely a miss
Move and twist, heavy sword rips air
Blades clink and clash, eyes locked in stare – mouths an arrogant sneer
Father Zero turns rain to ash
I inhale smoke
Cough – concentration broke
Mother Nothing, anger at her command
Cuts a snake on my arm
Bleed, drip – heavy sword knocked from grip
I, kicked back to the wasteland

Constellations stand above me
Physical mythology
Come to life, childhood stories that don't live up
To their view up close – Images broken

I yell to them, "You are lies!
Criminals! Breaking your daughter, your crime!
I am under her will to kill you.
Her candle, bright and broken,
You left her heart frozen, a void closed wide open
And love cannot fill it
You are harlot and buffoon. Water-bearer and maiden wife.
You are poison and strife
Dead to me. Dead to rites. Kill me?
I'll resurrect, pursue you, and still end your life."

Eyes pregnant with perplexity
These black figures of mythology
Look back to me
Rain turns to ash, clouds my eyes, and
Lulls me to sleep

Fey was relieved. No blood was shed. There was no guilt to harbor. But there now was the worry for the fate of Gordon's poetic shadow. How would he fare, captured by the very parents she tasked him to kill?

I awake, days gone in sleepy haze
I am still in defeat
Wrapped. Head to feet.
Mother Nothing next to me
Gentle hand rubs my brow
Father Nothing stands over me

A room. A candle. Shadows dancing.
Father Nothing kneels and speaks,
"We are surrounded by lies at all times
The truth takes root in the ground 'round here
Our little shy fire has never burned so bright,
Signaling desperate knights
Our Sirene screamed to you a task to dispatch us
To her, this is justice."

Mother Nothing speaks through tears,
"We broke her, our daughter
Cruelty's kindness
Governor Tubal ordered
Death and slaughter
Of new children with old souls
Nu ancients
Mother Nothings and Father Zeroes
Obeyed, preyed on their own children
Mind pale like the shadows, perverted from lynched lessons
Black generation after generation, black did as told
Bold, we broke her to spare her
Removed her alchemy, performing mystic surgery
We hid her properties, buried

Her thirteen pieces were found
Cursed and bound to the walking titans
Governor Tubal, King of Golems,
Lord over the caged city
He manipulates all that is black
Through the thirteen pieces of our daughter's beauty."

Her Father Zero voices,
"You have allies
Young, but broken
Great spirits reside inside them
Your parents too did this to you
Wiry and weak
Words frail when you speak
All for a purpose
To hide you from the giants with a sky's view
To spot the children that will plot their crumble.
You misfits today will be messiahs tomorrow."

Wraps dissolve. Heavy sword
Falls against me
Father Nothing takes it from me
Placed in the fires of a forge
Hefty puff dissolves the heft of the sword
Carved from its dark matter, dipped in dark energy
An invisible influence and the unseen, on shadow movement of the cosmos
Shaken and stirred
Straight and sharp, there comes born from heavy sword, a black sun spear
Dear to any warrior's heart

Mother Nothing blesses me with the weapon
"You will restore her
Sirene, our daughter
The Shades be your allies – no one can conjure and cast shade against you
You were born from cosmic shadow, and rest in flesh made of dusk
Black galactic dust is your breath – add their shade to your house
As decoration – make black declaration
Align and fight against pale shadows' strife
Bring down the thirteen towers
That corrupt my daughter's power
Our ruse is no excuse on how we as mothers and fathers
Have treated you
Our spirits are solid
As Mother Wisdom
And Father Knowledge,
We are the last of the last of a failed generation
We, the last, give you task to restore the head
To the Great Mother, our daughter

Medu-Sa
Motherland covenant, give us redemption."

Her mother and father dissolve, but stay in thought
I stare at spear
Weapon as slender and nimble as I
I hold my soul
Out—into the world
Into caged city
I Heru eye view tattered buildings
I view my Mother Wisdom and Father Knowledge
Disguised in bondage

They are new to me
Complex in their villainous heroics
Stoic, wooden performance
Disserves applause
But there are still scars on the children
Can I forgive them?

Speaking aloud to the sun and stars behind the clouds,
"A generation failed because of passed down failure
Few spark new labors, disguised as despair
Parents wear masks to shadow their tasks
Open world curtain, trotted out on global stage
Whispered love, hidden under cloud of loud shouts
Lips sink in watered-down, mouthed curses
Mother Wisdom? Father Knowledge repent, cry verses behind closed doors
Re-verse-us—all of this
Sister's hand to brother's neck
Mother and father in distressed and unnamed
Ghettoes swallow themselves—Cannan-ballistics recovered at the scene
Self-inflicted gunshot wounds neighborhoods dressed in hoods, come burning crosses
Orders taken from pale shadow bosses
We are now the hood wearers and cross bearers

I am disgusted with disguises
But now I seek alliances
To dissolve pale shadow systems
Hunt devil swine's pork barrel politics."

I flee city, and watch from afar, a ghostly black beauty

Her subtle fire
Barely burning
Ducking
Low
To escape the attention
Of her own light
A subtle fire that never burned so bright
Cloaked in smoke to hide her beautiful shade of the night
It only makes her glimmer shine
What marvelous beauty
Burns bright there once whole again
This wondrous, black, feminine flame as she be – subtle and broken

A burst of white light pushed away the scene, puffing it away as a gust of wind does smoke. The cobalt-blue and lilac tendrils of light retracted into Fey and Gordon's eyes. Fey's eyes returned to their natural brown color, as Gordon's eyes continued to hum with the residue of lilac tones. He looked at Fey and asked, "You okay?"

Fey bobbed her head, going over her thoughts concerning what she'd seen. She coughed up a chuckle, closed her eyes, and sighed. Gordon watched as Fey rested her elbow against the arm of the chair, and then leaned her head onto stiffened fingers. "Humbling," she said. Gordon didn't say a word. Fey rubbed her forehead, eyes remaining closed. "I have gone through my rites. I have been blessed to become a spirit. And still this narrative shows I am not whole. Humbling," she repeated, putting her initial utterance into context. She lifted her legs off the floor and curled up in the chair. "And what's its inspiration?" she asked. "My own thoughts," she answered. She groaned a heavier sigh and rubbed her forehead again. "But I humbly disagree that I'm some kind of victim in my story."

The gentle touch of her fingers stimulated her senses. Fey's instinct leapt from her crown, up through the ceiling, and out of the brownstone like one of her conjured yumbo. The invisible line snaked through the Brooklyn streets and connected with violent sounds. Threats. Fights. Gunshots.

Fey opened her eyes, a cobalt-blue light blazing from them.

"Gordon," she said in a calm manner. "I want to haunt the streets tonight."

Fey's body burst into its spirit form and sprung up. She traced her instinct's path, ghosting through all the levels of the brownstone. Gordon too shifted into spirit. Dooley followed Fey, a streaking spirit of lilac. The two colored spirits zigzagged unseen through Brooklyn. They reached first a violent scenario of a woman crying out for help against three male assailants. One of the men silenced her with a quick hit from his fist that knocked her to the ground. The other two dragged her deeper into the alley. Fey's spirit became solid and visible, gliding as a beam and then seamlessly running on the ground, costumed and masked in the tight cosmic fabric.

"You gon' leave me for that dude?" yelled the man who hit the woman, his friends standing on either side of her. Fey ran up behind the man, grabbed the back of his head, and slammed it into the brick wall.

Fey used the man's body to steady her next strike. Hands planted firm on the back of the man's head, Fey jumped up and struck the second thug located on her left. Her feet connected with his chest, knocking him back. She flipped backwards, grabbing the back of the first man's collar and pulled him away from the wall. She let him go, and he dropped, broken nose and shattered cheekbones. Fey's gift to him.

The second thug smacked against piles of wooden and metal scrap. The back of his head broke through a worn, wooden pallet leaning against the wall. He was back on his feet, but that had more to do with the momentum of Fey's sudden blow to his person rather than stabilizing himself. The impact of it all kept him in a daze, and he shook his head to center and still his vision. A lilac beam slammed into the thug's forehead, knocking him unconscious. Dooley's beam slapped the wall, ricocheted, and slammed into the remaining thug, striking him in the chest with a hard, concussive force. Dooley's ethereal stream bounced off the thug on impact, and out from the lilac stream jumped Dooley in physical form.

Fey vaulted over Dooley, planting her hands on his shoulders. She landed in front of the final thug and knocked him unconscious with a single punch. She watched him collapse, and then she turned toward Dooley. "You handle the idiots, I'll see to the woman," she ordered.

Dooley knelt down and grabbed the first thug by the collar. The unconscious man was the woman's ex-boyfriend. The lilac, glowing sphere rotating on Dooley's forehead projected an instinct to wake him up. The man's eyes rolled, still staggering, but his mind was opened. Dooley's instinct jumped into the man's head and culled his name.

"Listen close, Douglas," Dooley growled. "She's moving on, and you're going to accept it along with whatever jail time you and your friends receive. And after what you planned on doing, and how far you got, I got no problem if this system throws the book at you bruthas. Now go back to sleep." Douglas closed his eyes and slipped back into unconsciousness. Dooley stood and said much the same to his friends.

Fey comforted the attacked woman. "He's not going to hurt you anymore," she informed the woman, whose name she received through her instinct as Talitha. "And you will be brave, sister."

Dooley reached out with his instinct and found the closest police car on patrol. He disappeared from the alley and appeared in front of the vehicle just as it stopped at a red light. A wraithlike, red fog surrounded his black, cosmic-clothed frame. The officers stared wide-eyed and vacant at Dooley's presence. Transfixed and subservient to Dooley's command, the lilac spirit pointed, commanding the officers to make a left. They turned left as the light changed green. Dooley disappeared in a puff of red and lilac smoke, appearing again at another intersection. He was visible only to the hypnotic gaze of the officers in the car. He pointed again, instructing to take a right this time. Dooley continued to disappear and reappear, giving the officers direction at each turn until they came to the alley.

The officers got out of the car.

Dooley popped away into the alley. "Come on, Fey," he said to her. "The police are here, and these two cops can be trusted," he assured. "But my instinct touched upon a couple of cops that can't. Let's pay them a visit. They won't remember us here." Dooley saw Fey's subtle response, the nod of her head as she continued to look upon the half-conscious woman in front of her. "Fey!" he called.

"Yes, Gordon," she said. "I'm coming."

Both of them popped from the alley as the cops entered. They watched, perched above on the edge of one of the buildings.

"There's more?" asked Fey.

"You know there's always more, lightning bug," answered Dooley. "Too much for us to keep up with, but let's deal with what we can," he proclaimed.

They turned into their spirit forms. Fey this time followed Dooley as they crossed into the Crown Heights neighborhood. Dooley's instinct lead them to two, bulky cops harassing a fourteen-year-old black boy who was subdued on the ground, hands over his head, guns aimed at him.

"I'm…I'm just trying to get home," he whimpered. "I swear. I was getting something from the store."

"We'll tell you what you were doing!" screamed one cop. "Now stay down and keep quiet. If you're going to explain anything, explain why we got a report of a young, black male running with a bag of cash in one hand and a gun in the other from the store you claim to be coming from."

"Sir, there's many stores—"

"Excuse me?" the cop yelled, moving his gun closer to the boy's head. "Didn't I tell you to keep quiet?"

Dooley appeared. He knocked the gun from the aggressive officer and used an invisible force to disarm the other. He grabbed the cop by the collar and brought him close, spherical eye rotating bright, illuminating the snarl on his face.

Fey appeared. Silver and Zee jumped from her back. They flew around the second officer who was stunned at their presence. The nimble, glowing sprites blew kisses at him. Glittering dust drifted off the palms of their hands and filled the officer's eyes and nose. He dropped unconscious.

"Not tonight!" growled Dooley at the first cop, an aura of lilac surrounding his black, cosmic form. "If we only stop this act once, right here and right now." Dooley said to Fey, "Get the boy home." He turned his head and said to the young man. "This you will remember tonight, little man. You will be careful on these streets. And keep in mind that there is a system at war with you." He looked back at the cop and sneered, "And they have soldiers." Back to the boy he said, "You mind your steps and manner. Pay close attention to your surroundings. The spirits won't always be haunting the streets to help you."

The young man gave a nervous nod, lips quivering, and body shivering as if cold.

Fey and her yumboes escorted the boy the rest of the way home.

Dooley said to the officer, "You and your partner will be good for the rest of the night. But I will remember you—" Dooley reached out with his instinct and retrieved the officer's name from his mind. "Officer Scott Reinhold," he hissed. He also dragged another fact from the officer's mind. There was no robbery or report of one. He heard the officer's voice suggest in a snicker, *"Let's go make a quota."* Dooley hit the officer across the jaw. It didn't feel good enough, so he hit him twice more, and he felt better because of it. He shook the officer by the collar, yanking him close to his face. "The spirits won't deal with you tonight, but an ally with a top hat will come knocking on your doors soon enough." Dooley loosened his grip on the officer and stepped back. "Now go," he snapped. He turned to the unconscious officer and said, "Get up and go."

The unconscious officer's body stood. He retrieved and holstered his weapon. Both cops made their way back to their car and got inside.

Fey appeared. "The boy's safe at home," she reported. Her yumboes had been dismissed, jumping back into the tattoos on her back. "Are you—" her instinct jumped. "Gordon," she alerted. "Gordon, we're too late, but…" her voice trailed away. Her body blazed cobalt blue, and Fey launched into the air.

Dooley soared after her, a lilac streak. They flew to the Bronx. Fey landed near a dumpster where there stood a little black girl crying. Dooley touched down next to Fey.

"Are you lost little girl?" Fey asked. "What's your name?"

"Charlotte," the little girl answered. "Mommy's friend hit me," the little girl cried. "He wouldn't stop."

Fey knelt down next to the little girl, comforting her. Dooley's instinct tugged at him, drawing his attention to the dumpster. He stepped closer to it, his instinct calling for him to open it. His heart quickened. The girl's crying softened, muted by an onset of vertigo. Dooley put the palms of his hands on the dumpster's lid and lifted. His single, glowing eye brightened, and his mouth hung open.

"Fey!" called Dooley turning to her and the little girl.

"I already know, Gordon," she replied, trying to mask the sadness in her voice. "I felt it before we arrived."

Dooley looked back inside the dumpster at the little girl's physical body, beaten, bloody, and lifeless. He closed the dumpster's lid. He clenched his teeth and started grinding them.

"Charlotte, honey, I want you to come with me," Fey told the child. "Is that okay?" she asked. Charlotte nodded her head. Fey conjured Silver and the other yumboes. The little girl smiled at the sprites' appearance. To Dooley, Fey notified, "I'll take her spirit to my grandmother in Mount Vernon. She's crossed many children before."

"I'll find her mother's boyfriend," Dooley sneered.

"He's upstairs," said the little girl.

Fey cautioned, "Hurt him, yes, Gordon. But, do nothing more. Please, Gordon."

"I gotchu, sista," assured Dooley as he choked down his anger. "But he will be hurt."

Fey sighed, looking away from Dooley. She put her arms around Charlotte's spirit, and with the little girl in her arms, vanished. Dooley looked up at the apartment complex. He sent out his instinct. He saw Warren Pollard sitting relaxed and reclined on a couch, drinking beer and watching television, music blaring around him. Charlotte's mother wasn't home, no clue her daughter was dead.

Dooley popped away, leaving behind a cloud of lilac dust. A black cloud signaled his introduction inside apartment 303-A. He was behind the couch, looking down on Warren. Hand outstretched to channel his power, Dooley used an invisible force to silence the music.

Warren turned, disgusted. "What the fu—" He jumped up at the sight of Dooley. He stepped away from the couch and screamed in slurred speech, "The fuck you is, nigga?" He was drunk and high.

Dooley balled his fist, and it glowed bright with lilac spirit. He jumped the couch and punched Warren in the side, breaking three ribs. Warren screamed. Dooley hit him in the chin and broke his jaw. Warren's body dropped back, but Dooley didn't let him fall. He caught Warren by the shirt and pulled him close. He threw a punch that shattered the cartilage in his nose. He opened his grip on Warren's shirt and caught his arm, twisting it until broken.

Warren groaned. Dooley smacked an open palm against Warren's chest. Warren's sternum cracked. Warren started wheezing, dropping to his knees. Dooley wanted to take the man's fingers and break them, but he stayed his action. He watched Warren crumple to the floor.

Fey appeared and put her hands on Dooley's shoulders. "Charlotte will be fine, Gordon," she told him.

"Her mother isn't here," he replied to Fey as he caught his breath. "She's at work."

"I'll work with her, Gordon. It will be very hard, but I'll have my grandmother's guidance, as well as the matriarchs."

"So much damage done, and there's more."

"You know there's always more, Gordon" responded Fey. "Too much for us to keep up with, but let's deal with what we can," she quoted.

"I hurt him bad," Dooley said in a trembling voice. "Can't have him like this when the police find him. They'll think he wasn't responsible. Part of an attack that left him crippled and his girlfriend's daughter dead." He looked at Fey. "I got nothing," he said. "No conjures to heal him. No will to allow my spirit to do so, if it can."

Fey inspected Warren's broken body. Her four yumboes jumped from her back and Fey commanded, "Heal him as best you can. Keep him unconscious. Keep his substances inside him." Her yumboes fluttered toward Warren, flying around him and dropping glittering dust on him. Broken bones mended. Wounds healed. His blood was washed from his person, but splotches of blood from the little girl remained for evidence. Dooley lifted the hoodlum's body and placed him back on the couch. Fey's yumboes returned to her, and then she and Dooley vanished.

There were sirens in the distance, called by their instinct. They watched from atop the building, perched on the edge of the roof. Then as colorful, but invisible spirits, they hurried away in flight, off to Manhattan where they settled on one of the Chrysler building's sixty-first-floor eagle heads. Dooley's cosmic mask dissolved into his flesh, and his spherical eye faded as his two physical eyes were exposed. Fey too retracted her mask. Both sat with their backs to the other, sitting on either side of the eagle's neck, legs dangling over the edge.

"So much, huh?" remarked Gordon.

"Those were your words, Gordon-baby," Fey reminded in a nonchalant tone.

Gordon noticed the attachment of the word 'baby' to his name. It soothed him, especially as he thought to himself, *Is this relationship moving forward?* But all he said back to Fey was, "Yeah…" Not even his high cosmic instinct picked up that Fey so wished for him to be more responsive to how she addressed him. His own insecurity blocked the signals she sent.

Fey was silent for a while, pondering her involvement in Charlotte's mother's spiritual consoling. Her eyes panned all the lights below, both mobile and stationary. Then she thought about the poetic narrative of *In Thirteen Pieces.* "I have to disagree," Fey said aloud.

"Excuse me?" Gordon asked.

"Sorry, Gordon," Fey apologized. "I was thinking about our composition. I'm trying to see its relevance to my reality, and I just don't believe my circumstances have been purposefully plotted by crafty parents to keep me safe."

Gordon pondered Fey's words and then responded, "Maybe not in the way this narrative tells it. Maybe it's a metaphor for being purposeful to…a destiny."

Fey shook her head. "I don't think so, Gordon," she replied to his comment. She lifted her left knee to her chin, embracing it. "Stanley Fallows rewrote my story to keep his going. His mother, as we've been told growing up, did the same. And they were only keepers of an oppressive tradition upheld by so many evil men and evil women before them."

"His father too," Gordon added. "Stanley's father," he clarified. "His mother's mother. His wife. His grandparents, both maternal and paternal." He spun around, embracing Fey, sitting behind her with his legs opened. "And they didn't throw anyone off their path. They made us take a detour, sure, but we takin' the scenic route."

Fey curled up into Gordon's embrace. *This will do,* she thought to herself. If Gordon didn't fasten 'baby' to her name, she could at least be in his arms. For all their power, in this moment, these two blooming sweethearts felt most safe in one another's arms. Fey's eyes still graced all the lights below. There twinkled a cold reality. "There *is* so much, Gordon. I can feel it all. The pain. The gangs and community collapse."

"Yeah," said Gordon.

"And I can't shake the feeling that at the center of it all is Stanley Fallows," Fey professed. "I can feel his influence. Does that sound strange? Even with what we experienced tonight, situations you could never pin to him or his tricks and curses."

"Doesn't sound strange at all, Fey-baby," assured Gordon, attaching the word 'baby' to Fey's name. He waited for her to make a fuss or protest about the affectionate nomenclature, but she embraced it as tight as he held her. So he continued, "Especially since he's haunted you for so long. His haunt over you is even stronger than his haunt over the Fable Avenue community."

"It's all the same now," expressed Fey. "And again, my instinct says our community is not exclusive to Stanley Fallows' oppressive haunting."

Gordon thought for a moment and then said, "We give him too much credit with our choice of words. Stanley Fallows ain't haunting, he's hiding. I like that. It means at the end of the day, for all his tricks, he's scared."

Fey grinned. "I like that notion too, Gordon. Now, you're thinking like me."

"Like you?"

"Yes!" Fey said with force. "I said a couple days ago that we're spirits. There's nothing he can do to us. He's no threat anymore. We find him, and we take control of our story. We take him out of it." She took a moment to reflect, and then she said, "I know the mythology we're crafting has its symbolisms. My parents in the story are no angels—even if their wicked ways have a purpose. But I know who the devil is." She nodded at her sentiment. Gordon did to, feeling the need to say 'amen'. But Fey spoke instead, "In reality, my parents paid the price for helping Stanley Fallows. I learned from my nana as I got older that Stanley had a hexing hand in my mother's suicide and my father's disappearance. It's safe to assume my father is dead. Stanley tore my mother and father's love apart as payment, and tore me away from knowing that love, as a little girl, as someone's daughter. A mother's love, a father's love, taken from me, and I'm going to kill him for that."

Gordon didn't argue. "Yes, Fey-baby," he told her. "But you won't do it alone. You don't have to do it alone."

"If I have to, Gordon, I will," Fey responded, welling up with emotion.

"You're back among your community, Fey-baby. You don't have to carry this burden alone anymore. *We* will end Stanley Fallows' story."

Fey pushed away from Gordon, off of the eagle's head, out into the air. She floated, turned, and faced Gordon. Her mask covered her head and face. Gordon's eyes admired her floating figure, and Fey basked in Gordon's bright gaze. "Let's forget Stanley Fallows and all his caused troubles, the effects of his haunt." Her body became a cobalt-blue spirit.

"I'll race you to the Brooklyn Bridge," Gordon suggested.

"Have some imagination, Mister Goodspeed. I'll take you up on that offer, but the race ends at the Great Pyramid of Giza."

Gordon jumped to his feet, and then he floated several inches off the eagle's head. "Double back for dinner in Morocco?"

"Don't tell anyone," Fey grinned. "We'll be a little bad with our spirits and make off with some proper clothes once we get there."

Gordon's mask covered his face, and his lilac-glowing, spherical eye flashed into existence, rotating against his forehead.

Dooley's lilac spirit shined.

"One," he began.

"Two," Fey continued the count.

"Three!" Dooley finished.

"Go!" he and Fey shouted together.

Up and across the sky their spirits took flight. Cityscape gave way to the Atlantic Ocean. Fey yelled, "Through Stonehenge!"

"Not a problem!" Dooley shouted back.

Their spirits soared above commercial jets' flight paths. Their instincts guided them to their first checkpoint in the race. Gliding around the massive structure of Stonehenge, Fey and Dooley were neck-and-neck.

"What's the next checkpoint, Fey-baby?" asked Dooley.

"Can your spirit keep up, brutha? Let's dive through Europe and break our way into the Motherland through Algeria."

"If that's where you want to lose the little lead I've allowed you to have, then let's go!"

Dooley pulled ahead as he laughed. He and Fey's spirit left sound behind. They moved higher into the sky, at the edge of the atmosphere. Then their comet-like bodies straightened their flight path. They passed over Europe, straight to France, where Fey recommended the Eiffel Tower as a checkpoint.

Such a tourist! commented Dooley telepathically.

I don't take offense, Fey countered with her thoughts resonating in Gordon's head. **I'm a free spirit of the cosmos, Gordon-baby. I'm only visiting this physical place.** They dived low, and their spirits passed through the piece of grand architecture like a gust of wind. Fey pulled ahead as their spirits jumped back to the highest point of the sky. Then they cut through Spain, over Barcelona, and down into Algeria. They didn't move straight to Egypt. Their spirits visited the African states of Mali, flying low to observe the land. Their spirits traveled to the western countries of Senegal, back to Ghana and Nigeria. To those that could see, they were noticed, praised and sung to. Down through Cameroon and into the Congo, they made their way to the Sudan, soaring down into Uganda. Then Kenya came, up to Ethiopia and Eritrea.

And then there was Egypt.

The grand pyramid of Giza stood in a glow in the Egyptian night, its limestone façade washed white by bright spotlight. Closer and closer they neared the ancient structure. Dooley was ahead, but he slowed, allowing Fey the lead. He grabbed her arm and pulled her back. His lilac, smokeless form dissipated. Fey's cobalt-blue flame also faded. They hovered in place a long ways from the magnificent wonders. Dooley drew Fey closer, but much of her approach toward him was by her own will. He grinned as their masks dwindled away, and he and Fey elevated higher against the night, camouflaged by their black outfits as much as a cloaking incant.

Fey caressed Gordon's face, her eyes blazing as bright as his. They extinguished the light of their eyes by closing them, and then kissed one another. It lasted for only a moment, but long enough. They pulled away for a breath, and Fey giggled. She spied the sphinx and called it by its proper name, *"Her-em-Akhet."* She turned to Gordon and proposed, "Let us go there. No race."

Fey slipped from Gordon's embrace, and she flew away. Gordon trailed after her. They landed with a soft touch upon the back of the marvelous structure and tiptoed into the shadows. They looked up at the stars and remained fixed for a moment. "Too late for dinner," Gordon commented. "Perhaps *breakfast* in Morocco," he suggested.

"I have class," Fey dismissed. She held herself in an embrace, as if cold. Her back was to Gordon. "Can you feel that, Gordon?" she asked.

"Yes," he told Fey. "I can." He looked around.

"There's so much sorrow here in Africa. There's so much tragedy engineered."

"But there's so much spirit here too," Gordon told Fey. "This is where it all began."

"I can feel all the strife," Fey spoke, her voice trembling. Gordon walked up behind her and put his hands on her shoulders. She welcomed his touch, and she smothered the terrible scenes of Africa's current state. "There's more and always more, right?" Fey commented.

"True," answered Gordon. "But I can feel the pull of hidden chambers. I can feel the meaning of the hieroglyphs. There's more sorrow and always more, plus *and* multiplied by strife. But there's also knowledge just the same. We have to remain strong for Africa's sake."

Fey liked Gordon's sentiment, but the cries of the land that she could hear and feel resurfaced. All the grand history of Africa was muted by its historical and current plights and struggles. But Fey tried to find solace in Gordon's opinion.

"You do understand, Gordon," Fey said facing him. He was surprised to see a smile on her face, a sly grin. "I would've won the race."

"Keep tellin' yourself that, sista," Gordon retorted.

"Home?" she suggested to him.

"Another race?" Gordon asked.

Fey kissed him sweetly and then said, "Home. Just home."

"A quick thought and a pop, and we'll be there."

Fey shook her head. "No. I like the air around me when in flight. It's like spirits giving me a massage." She smiled wide, and then she lifted into the air, mask embracing her face. Gordon watched Fey fly away. His mask wrapped about his eyes, and his glowing eye appeared. Up he went, after her. He moved alongside her and the two of them crossed Africa, high up in the sky. Their black suited bodies faded against the night, becoming subtle waves of movement. Out over the Atlantic, they changed directions heading to Fable Avenue. Never did they slip into their colorful, ethereal forms.

It was two in the morning when they arrived at the Goodspeed residence, landing on the rooftop, dissolving their masks. Gordon took Fey's hands in his. "I'll fly you home, lightning bug."

Fey hesitated and then said, "That's okay, Gordon. I'll just pop into my room."

"You left some clothes in the house," Gordon reminded.

"I'll be over tomorrow to get them."

"Okay."

Fey nodded. "Goodnight, Dooley."

"Goodnight, pretty lightning bug."

Fey kissed Gordon on the cheek. She stepped away from him and then popped from existence. She kept Gordon in mind, even as she performed a resting ritual at her altar. She continued to think about Gordon, prompting her to conjure Silver from the tattoo of the yumbo etched on her back.

"So much happened tonight, Silver," Fey told the sprite as she dissolved her cosmic suit down to the sweater she wore and her undergarments. She removed and tossed away her sweater. She changed to a nightshirt, out of her bra, and then slipped into bed. "So many feelings. Despair. Anger. Loss. So much travel. The world is so big, even when you fly far, far away from it. And there's so much hurt inside it." But still she couldn't shake the thought of Gordon Goodspeed. Dooley. The dark spirit. "I like him, Silver. I like Gordon Goodspeed." The sprite beamed and flew around in a celebratory manner. "Back you go, Silver. My altar ritual is taking effect," she yawned. Silver jumped into Fey's tattoo. Fey spoke an incant that put out the light, and then she fell asleep.

Gordon did much the same. He popped from rooftop to basement. He thought about Fey as he completed his ritual at his altar. "Saw so much tonight, Spook," he told the ancient device. "Fey was connected to a lot more emotions haunting this place. I did my best to comfort her. I guess that's that mama energy in her. The protector spirit in me. I dunno." He grinned. "But I like her, Spook," he admitted. "I like Fey Forrester." He chuckled. "Used to think she was weird."

Gordon walked to the stairs. "Goodnight, Spook," he said as the light faded by its own accord. He made his way up to his bedroom, using the stairs instead of popping his way through all the levels of the house. He did so to keep Fey in his thoughts longer.

Gordon wanted to reach out with his instinct and connect with Fey, but he decided against it. He didn't want to disturb her, and he considered that missing her would add that much more to seeing her again. He changed into nightclothes, got into bed, and turned out the light.

Fey had an early class the next day. She didn't get to see Gordon on her way to school, as his courses didn't begin until noon. Gordon first met with Top Hat before making his way to campus. He informed the mystical enforcer about the abusive police officers he and Fey encountered. Top Hat raised his eyebrow at Gordon's suggestion to handle them and any other officers abusing their badges.

Top Hat assured, "You ain't gotta worry, sun. I'm gonna have fun with this. I like fuckin' with the real gangs of New York."

Gordon and Fey's paths crossed only once on campus, just long enough for Fey to inform Gordon that she was going to Mount Vernon after classes. Madame Jeliya and her grandmother were preparing to console the little girl's mother. The incident was in the news. Maman Anansi's daughter, Stephanie Dumas, had already positioned herself into Charlotte's mother's life as a lawyer. Fey divulged to Gordon, that when the moment was right, Stephanie revealed her true purpose to the girl's mother.

"I need to be there for a time," said Fey. "A couple of days until my grandmother and Madame Jeliya can hold Charlotte's spirit without my presence. She locked onto me because of the yumboes. She likes them. I'll release Silver and the others every day after class when I'm no longer needed, so that Charlotte's spirit can play with them."

Gordon understood. Two days passed before he and Fey convened at his house. It was six o'clock at night. Thursday. Fey left her school items at her residence up the street, and then she popped to Gordon's house and knocked on the garden-floor entrance. Gordon opened the door shortly after.

"How is everything?" Gordon asked Fey as she stepped through the door.

"As good as they can be," she answered.

Gordon clarified the real intent of his question. "What about you?"

"I'm doing well."

"Good. Tea?"

"Yes, please."

Gordon closed and locked the doors. Fey stripped down to sweater and cosmic-fabric leggings, tossing her jeans onto the couch, next to the jeans she'd tossed there days earlier. She walked into the kitchen with Gordon following her. She said, "Don't worry about prepping the tea for me, Gordon. I'll get it. Making tea relaxes me, especially after what's been going on."

Gordon kept out of Fey's way while they were in the kitchen. He opened the refrigerator and removed a jug of cranberry juice. He opened the cupboard and took out a tall glass. He walked into the dining room with both, and he poured himself a cup as Fey moved about the kitchen preparing her tea. "How's Charlotte's mother?" he asked after taking a sip.

"Not doing well," Fey called back to him. "She's shaken. There's no getting around the impact of her daughter's death. Not even with our incants consoling or even seeing her daughter's spirit and knowing she's okay." Gordon heard the running water filling the pot. Then he heard the low click of the stove as Fey turned a burner's dial. Ignition billowed like a hot gust of wind. Fey walked into the doorway, leaned her head and shoulder against it, and folded her arms. "The world was as normal as it could be for her, and then in one night it was broken." She sighed. "Her boyfriend was in a gang. They'd been together for a couple of months. Charlotte stumbled on Warren testing some of his paraphernalia. He started hitting her. He was in his thug mode, heightened by drugs." Fey stood up straight and walked back into the kitchen. "We have incants blessing Charlotte's mother for protection while Warren is being processed and prosecuted," Fey informed.

Gordon heard the clink and clank of cups as Fey looked through the cupboards for a proper mug. Cabinets opened and closed as she pulled out honey and a tin box filled with tea bags.

"Should we continue our narrative after you've had your tea?" asked Gordon.

"Sure," Fey replied. "What should we eat tonight?"

"Something from around here," Gordon suggested. "Maybe even the kitchen this time. No exotic flights or jaunts to other countries."

Fey walked into the room with tea prepared. She sat down opposite Gordon. "Yes, Mister Goodspeed," she responded.

They both took several sips of their beverages, enjoying the quiet. But something tugged on their instincts, interrupting their drink and solace. Gordon and Fey looked up. Their instincts jumped from their heads and hastened from the house, through the walls, winding up and down streets until it came to five black boys arguing on the sidewalk. One was hollering while showing a gun tucked into his pants. Another yelled curses back to him, showing he had the same.

Gordon slammed his glass down. *"Goddamnit!"* he cursed.

Fey's eyes brightened cobalt blue. Gordon's eyes blazed lilac.

Their cosmic fabric covered their bodies, and their earthly clothes faded. Both popped away from their seats, materializing on the roof. Dooley leapt into the air first, body changed to a fiery, lilac spirit. Fey followed, her body a cobalt blue, comet-like specter.

They traced their instincts' path. Dooley passed by one of the teenage boys who was revealing the gun still tucked inside the front of his pants. Dooley's spirit snatched the weapon, crushed it, and materialized as a cosmic-suited specter in front of the young boy. He grabbed his collar and yanked him close.

Fey did the same with the second teenage boy flaunting his pistol.

"No one move!" snarled Dooley.

Nothing moved. Fey and Dooley took the five boys outside of time. A cobalt-blue beam snaked from Fey's forehead, split into three tendrils, and held the other three boys in place.

"No one's mother is crying tonight," Dooley sneered as his single eye flashed a light that filled the teenage boy's sight. Dooley yanked the boy again. "You hear me?"

The boy was stubborn, resisting Dooley's suggestion, his eyes trying to pull away from the influential light humming in his eyes. "This a block dispute!" he spat.

Dooley yanked the boy a third time. "You don't own these streets. None of you do. Whatever street you live on is where you lay your head, and it's nothing more! You want to own something? You own some responsibility, because from what I see, these streets own you."

"The one thing all of you will remember is that these streets are haunted," Fey ordered with force. "And you will tell everyone these streets are haunted."

Dooley stared hard into the teenager's eyes. The boy submitted. "No more. You find a good hobby to keep you busy. And if anyone has trouble with your change in life, you let your instinct reach out to us spirits. We'll guide them right." Dooley let go.

Fey backed away from the teenager she held in her grip. She and Dooley vanished. Time moved around the young boys. They looked at one another, exchanging angry glances, but walking away.

Fey popped into existence cloaked inside a shadow in Fulton Park. Gordon was next to her wearing pedestrian clothes. "Wait for me back at the house," he told her. "I'll go get us something to eat at the Kimball's spot. Anything specific you want?"

"Lamb pita with cucumbers and yogurt sauce," Fey requested.

"Got that."

"I—" Fey's instinct paused her speech. Two blocks away, a corner store was being robbed. She looked at Gordon.

"Handle it," he said. "I'll get the food."

Fey popped away. Gordon stepped out of the shadow and walked up to the Kimball's restaurant on Fable Avenue. Fey appeared inside the store, a cloud of black smoke preceding her cosmic-clothed figure. From behind the register, the Indian storeowner, hands in the air, flinched at her unexpected intrusion. The gunman turned. Fey sighed at the sight of his young, twenty-something year-old black face.

Fey's yumboes charged, too fast for the young man to retaliate with gunfire. Their varicolored bodies first attacked the young man's gun, deteriorating the weapon until it decayed into a pile of metal ash. The clerk ducked away, not knowing if he was an intended target of the radiant, harlequin assault. The yumboes' beams whipped and whirled around the young man, smacking his face and slamming into his stomach. Silver's beam knocked the man unconscious, and then all four lights soared back to Fey. She walked up to the man and opened her palm. He was drawn awake.

Fey's cobalt-blue eyes met the young man's. "Only noble spirits will haunt this neighborhood. Be one or be gone." He shook his head, face drenched with fright. Fey turned to the register. The clerk had since risen from behind it. She raised the palm of her hand to him. "He gets another chance, and then he gets hurt."

The clerk agreed.

Fey's glowing eyes returned to the young man. "Next time, I'll toss you to this cruel system looking to make a servant of you. *Go!*"

The young black man jumped up and hurried from the store. His encounter with Fey's spirit slipped from his memory, but not its impact.

Fey turned to the store clerk and said, "You get to setup shop in this neighborhood to stop us from doing so. You give back in some way, or the next time my instinct senses distress, I won't interrupt."

The clerk agreed with a swift, affirmative nod.

Fey popped from existence. Her encounter faded from the store owner's memory, but the impact was there. She materialized next to Gordon as he walked up to his residence, keys in one hand to unlock the garden entrance, and a bag of food in the other.

"Everything good, beautiful spirit?" he asked Fey moments after her appearance.

Her sweater appeared over her torso, but her leggings remained. "As good as it will be," she answered. "Something tells me our jobs are not done for the night."

Gordon unlocked the doors and walked inside. Fey walked in after him, locking the doors as she entered the house. She turned and noticed Gordon paused in his steps.

"What's the prob—" Her speech halted at the sight of Papa Solomon sitting on the couch.

"You two been playin' superheroes again?" he asked with a hint of agitation in his voice. Gordon and Fey let go a heavy breath at the same time. Papa Solomon pointed to the chairs in the room. "You two have a seat." Fey and Gordon fulfilled the request, squirming to get comfortable. Papa Solomon said to them, "Don't worry. I wont' be long. Won't keep you from your food." He rubbed his hands for a moment. His brow furrowed and he began his story, "On the very night you two went out, gallivanting as spirits, a woman was raped over there on Broadway." Gordon and Fey became alert, and Papa Solomon lifted his hand. "Settle your instincts. The young man was arrested about a day ago. But, on the same night, a man suffering from mental trouble stabbed his sixty-two-year-old father. Cops came to the scene. One officer moved in, he was stabbed fatally, and died at the hospital an hour later. Farther up the street, at the same time, a young woman shot and killed her eight-year-old son. She was aiming for her boyfriend, who was grazed. He managed to get out and call the police to the scene. She was arrested. Another woman up over on Albany Avenue has been arrested for pimping out two teenage girls left in her care."

Fey pleaded to the community patriarch, "We understand, Papa Solomon. We can't be everywhere. We were saying that very thing the other night. And the little we covered doesn't even begin to describe other cities, countries or Africa. There's no way we can haunt all the places where our people are suffering. We know," she stressed, not sounding dismissive.

Papa Solomon agreed, but he had something to add. "The two of you gon' wear yourselves out trying to regulate what little parts of the city you can." Then he listed, "You sap yourself haunting the place in all your forms. You use conjures to keep your presence unseen. You use conjures to leave an imprint of your interactions, but remove the memories of your appearance."

"We have our altar rituals to rest us," assured Gordon.

Papa Solomon warned in an austere voice, "We are watched, and your incants can't blot out your images from Stanley Fallows. In fact, it might alert him. It puts us all at risk. We're just coming out of minor incants, and starting to deal with personal conjures. Real, inner, unique powers."

Gordon and Fey looked at one another.

Fey's eyes moved to Papa Solomon as she admitted, "We know."

Papa Solomon blinked, surprise on his face. "You wish to dangle yourselves out like bait?" Fey and Gordon remained silent. "I admire your zeal. Your influence is felt. You leave quite an impression. It will spread and inspire." He said to them, "We have said that the spirits stirred inside the both of you has us all open. Our incants are more potent, and our personal conjures are coming through. We have plans for that. We do. I'm just asking, and also representing the voice of the matriarchs—and your grandmother, Fey—lay low."

"But we have an insight when something happens," Gordon voiced. "It pulls at us." The room was silent as Papa Solomon pondered. After a moment, Gordon asked, "Papa Solomon, you thinking something?"

The old man made a face while bobbing his head. "It's possible your actions have purpose." He gritted his teeth, making another face, head continuing to bob. "We'll know better once we make this move on these Tarot cards Lady Arachne is so anxious to get a hold of." He looked at Gordon, and then he looked at Fey. "Who has the first tug of the instinct?"

Gordon pointed to Fey, and she answered Papa Solomon, "I usually do. Gordon's instinct aligns with mine, as if concurring."

Papa Solomon nodded. He told Fey, "Your father was a codebreaker."

"I'm aware, Papa Solomon," Fey said, not meaning to sound disrespectful.

The community Elder stood. "Be careful," he told Fey, walking away from the couch. "Stanley took his gift." A cold feeling bore into Fey, but she made no reaction to it, save a subtle tremble of her lower lip. Papa Solomon continued to the door. Gordon jumped up and saw him out. "Miss Forrester," Papa Solomon called back to her, "Curb that instinct a bit." He turned around to tell her, "You two got spirit. Listen to this lesson: all spirits can be conjured and controlled. Understand that."

"We got that, Papa Solomon." Gordon promised. He nudged the community patriarch and said, "And I'll keep this one out of trouble."

"Boy, you too much of an enabler to keep anyone out of trouble," Papa Solomon verbally jabbed. Gordon and Fey chuckled, but Papa Solomon brought the conversation back to a serious tone when he said, "Look, us grown folk often make the mistake of actin' like we know best because of some false notion of Almighty wisdom with age. But I'm gonna confess a secret—don't tell no other older folks I said this: We don't know a damn thing. We're trying to keep this one step at a time, and under our control, because we don't know. I'm not gonna tell you to be careful. I'm gonna tell you, for now, to stay your spirits, until we got the direction of all this understood." Papa Solomon raised an eyebrow and question with a gentle authority in his voice, "Understood?"

"Yes, Papa Solomon," Gordon acknowledged.

Fey stayed silent.

Papa Solomon looked at her. "Miss Forrester?" he asked. "Am I understood?" The authority in his voice was no longer gentle.

"Understood…" she replied in a soft voice, eyes looking at the floor.

Papa Solomon nodded in return, and then Gordon saw him from the house, returning to his seat thereafter. He picked up the bag of food. Fey suggested they eat in the dining room. Gordon agreed. He got up, and with Fey, he went into the next room. Fey spoke an incant over her tea and it heated as if fresh from the pot. Gordon reached into the bag and pulled out Fey's order, handing it to her.

"Spirit got to eat," Gordon said to her.

Fey took her food, unwrapped it, and lightly picked at it. Her appetite had subsided a little. *We could find Stanley Fallows with our power and bring his haunt out of hiding,* she thought to herself, wishing she'd spoken the words to Papa Solomon. *His error in our story could be erased.* But in two breaths she decided to keep the mood light. "You see what I saw?" she asked Gordon in an upbeat voice. "Old Papa Solomon just went on 'head and broke into yo' house. Ain't that somethin' there, Mister Goodspeed?"

Gordon hummed. "Yes," he said. "Some incants should still be called tricks."

"I'm sure Madame Jeliya and he keep a third eye on our activities," Fey postulated. "But I understand why."

"Perhaps we'll just have to go to the stars to get out of their reach," Gordon recommended.

Fey grinned at the notion.

They finished their meals and moved to the basement. The light beamed bright as they entered. Fey took her seat on the chair, and Gordon sat down on the floor next to her, legs crossed. Their lighted gaze focused on the aged tome. The book jumped into the air and opened to the latest inscribed page, telling the tale of *In Thirteen Pieces.*

Gordon reached his hand up to Fey. She took his hand in hers.

Light filled the basement, and the story continued.

There tiptoes my knight
Clad in confidence
Heavy sword no more
He plays new instrument
Spear dipped in sun and the galactic core
Hands clean
Deed of judgment washed away
Ducking in shadow
He whispers to me when he says,

"Your Mother is nothing

Your Father, reduced to zero
That existence among the dead."

Carefully said
To hide what I don't spy
No thirteen pieces of me
Collected

"Where am I? The thirteen of me?
The pieces of my feminine degrees?
Anxious to kiss myself as grand conjure and wish
To be black whole
And absorb all light matter around me."

From shadow my knight parades, spear gripped
He holds his masculinity, flexing cocksureness – conviction
My knight, black warrior at my command
At the ready, at my attention
Stiff and still he makes my waters run
Auto-somatic – my nature does what's natural
Cloaked in smoke, but not muted
My eyes trace him as he traces our circumference, pointing
My ears open. His voice. Penetrates with bass.

"All around, strong and invisible – like winds and hurricanes
Stomp and step, not seventeen mountains, but thirteen towers
Your pieces of beauty power them
Possessing giants that possess them
Four stand at the four corners, split your air
They breathe your breath and live by you
Nine more seduce, curse and scar
They keep the fog rolling, using nature to control our nature."

I beam a ghostly grin
"This is where
My whole body begins
Thirteen giants
You will slay them
Bring my pieces to me

Oh, but let us ponder this equation, matter-mathematical
The towers step quiet

They whirl invisible
You need proper lens to sight them
Proper speech
To cite them
I know of a woman with blessings
A great old one, wise woman with no eyes that can help you see
She comforted me. Made my separated, physical body unseen.
Mama Gran
We'll drink rum for her, cast cowrie shells – light a white candle."

I dance standing still
My inner electric lady snakes up my spine
Maîtresse Hounon'gon pupils my sight
I blink and light our campfire
Inner electric says we cannot chant without choir

My knight answers
"I will have thirteen allies by my side."

Smoke trails my words
"Mama Gran, great old one
Has and loves herself a great old man
Captain, conjuror of shades
Debas, he will recruit your army
Plucked from whatchu know no-goods and knaves
No problems, but 99 allies will number your shades."

Dancing nude in the naked night
Pole star points
Gives my black warrior sight
Pole star sings
"This is where Mama Gran resides
Follow, follow
And when the sky turns bright and blue
You will still see me, pointing. Rest for the night.
I will meet you on the morrow."

I blow my smoke over him
A blanket and bed
To sleep
I lean back on cracked throne
A faint shade of fog

Soon whole with the thirteen pieces of me
A song from my body
Hums happy

Light flooded the scene, and folding over the brilliance was the basement's scenery. The radiant characters scripted in the book faded into ink. The aged book closed and floated back to rest atop the chamber. Fey's eyes lost their cobalt-blue fluorescence, and the light in Gordon's eyes faded to a simple lilac tone.

"We have a giant task ahead of us," Gordon said looking up at Fey. The tone of his voice revealed his pun was thoroughly intended.

Fey turned her head to Gordon and asked, "Will you do a grand task for me, my nimble knight?"

Gordon jumped to his feet and performed a bow. "And what is it that you ask for? Shall my spirit fly to the distant stars and retrieve for you exotic fruits on another world?"

Fey lifted an eyebrow, telling Gordon, "And risk poison from a strange fruit…?"

Gordon lifted his head, body still bent in a bow. "Sista, will you play along?" he groaned. "For once?" he continued. "Play along. Indulge me."

Fey curled up in the chair. "What? I ain't takin' a bite of some crazy fruit from some far off world."

Gordon straightened. "Aight, then. Whatchu want?"

Fey giggled. "I would like for you to get me my sketchbook."

"Where is it?"

"In my room," she smiled with guilt. "At my house," she clarified, as if Gordon wasn't aware.

Gordon rolled his eyes. His body popped away, first pulled into a strand that zipped around in a merkeba pattern. Then he was gone. He appeared moments later with Fey's sketchbook. "Here," he said handing it to her.

She took the item, guilt still on her face. She cowered.

Gordon asked, "What…?"

"My pencils and pens…?"

Gordon huffed.

"They're on the table next to my bed."

Gordon vanished, returning seconds later with Fey's requested items.

"Thank you, Sir Gordon-Dooley-Kibaru," she teased in a snooty tone. "Now, was that so bad, brutha?"

Gordon rolled his eyes again. He turned and said, "I'll give you some privacy. I'll be upstairs playing video games."

Fey made a face and questioned, "You can fly to the stars as a spirit and you gon' play video games?"

"Oh, what is the world coming to," Gordon said over his shoulder, stepping upstairs.

Fey chuckled. She dropped all but one of her pencils on the ground, her pens too. Then she turned her attention to her sketchbook and opened it to a blank page. Resting the book on her knee, she started drawing. Her simple sketches and lines began taking shape, and before long, a rough etching of her broken-winged faerie was visible. This new sketch of the sprite filled in parts of her wounded wings, and Fey gave her a smile, though her eyes remained teary. Fey made a quick sketch of a figure walking in the distance, not sure if the person was coming toward the broken-winged faerie or walking away. She also drew a sun on the horizon. Sunrise or sunset, she didn't know.

Fey didn't finish the image, keeping it as a shadowy sketch. She dropped her sketchbook over the arm of the chair and also dropped her pencil atop it. Curled up on the chair, Fey drifted to sleep. Gordon woke her several hours later, coming down to check on her.

"I let you sleep for a little while, Fey-baby," said Gordon in a soft voice as Fey's senses heightened, bringing her from sleep. "You want to stay the night and pop home in the morning?"

Fey fired an accusing grin up at Gordon, "And where would you have me sleep, Mister Goodspeed?"

Gordon assured, "Hey, I'd be a gentleman. You could jump into one of the other rooms upstairs."

Still groggy, Fey replied, "Sorry, Gordon. Besides, I have to meet my yumboes when they return from consoling. And my altar is there. I need my nighttime ritual."

"Of course, Fey-baby," said Gordon, a little wind taken from his sails.

Fey ignored Gordon's tone. She leaned over the arm of the chair and picked up her pens and pencils that were on the floor. Scooping them up, she said to Gordon, "Goodnight, Mister Goodspeed. We'll do this again tomorrow."

"Hauntings too?"

Fey considered the question. "I know Papa Solomon said to relax the instincts we have, but we'll see." She sat up in the chair, raising her face high enough to kiss Gordon on the cheek. Then Fey popped away, back to her home.

Gordon thought for a moment. He made a face, turned to his chamber and said, "She left another pair of jeans, Spook. Oh, well." He walked to his altar and performed a ritual to calm the spirit inside him. He popped away to his bedroom soon after, and fell fast asleep.

The next day almost followed the same routine between Gordon and Fey. There was class. There was their quick meet on campus. But today, Fey ended her schooling early. She retired to her house on Fable Avenue and continued sketching the new drawing of her broken-winged faerie. Gordon called around five o'clock that evening, informing Fey that he'd gotten a meal for them. Fey asked Gordon if it was okay for her to pop in. Gordon gave her permission, and not too long after Fey packed her art supplies into her schoolbag did she appear on the garden-floor couch in Gordon's house. Gordon was upstairs in his room, changing clothes. Fey called up to him, "On the couch, Gordon."

Gordon left his room and galloped down the steps. "Food's ready in the dining room," he told Fey as he sauntered to the couch and dropped down next to her. Again they were dressed in their cosmic-fabric leggings and a casual shirt. "Oh, good," Gordon noted looking Fey up and down. "You won't be leavin' more jeans here."

Fey smiled at Gordon's sentiment. "Tea?" she inquired.

"Already ready for the queen," Gordon relayed.

Fey put her art supplies down and hopped off the couch. Gordon followed her into the dining room. They sat down and enjoyed their meal, making light conversation about classes and revealing their desire to use their spirits to cheat.

"See," Gordon drawled, "that's how villainy begins."

"I haven't done so," Fey defended. "Besides, you said you would do the same thing."

Gordon grinned. He put his head down and indulged in his meal to hide his mischievous expression. After a moment, their gazes went around the room, trying to look beyond its walls. Fey looked at Gordon and said, "Nothing. No call."

"I'm sure someone needs our help out there," Gordon noted.

Fey nodded. "But, if our instincts aren't calling us, let's obey Papa Solomon and the matriarchs' word. Keep us out of trouble."

Gordon agreed. He stood and began cleaning his area. Fey did the same. Once everything was put away, they walked downstairs and took their places in a chair and on the floor. "Dinner and a movie," Gordon joked as he took Fey's hand in his.

Their eyes lit up with color. The tome resting on the chamber lifted into the air and turned to the latest page scripted with their mystical composition. Tendrils of light projected from their eyes and acted as ink to continue *In Thirteen Pieces.* The basement melted into a bright brilliance, and light faded into images of the story's continuance.

To my eye
Against the blue of the day's sky
There still shines
The light of the pole star
"Follow, follow," the star beckons bright
I track the point of light
Traipse through lands covered in sand
And snows
Fire, winds, and cold
To another forest lush and flushed with green
This is where pole star's light taps – atop quaint cottage – modest housing
Mama Gran in kitchen, stirring blessings
Her man, Captain Debas, outside
His imagination at his command to deliver him to battles passed
Glory days once had
He sees me
"A fool on an errand, a warrior at task
I am familiar with the math of you
The sum of you
I recognize your attire, because I once wore those boots."

I spear the ground
Hand out, and declare peace
"Venerable spirit, Grand Captain, I am Zin Kibaru
I seek to see unnatural thunders
That step in silence, walking unseen
Golems, solid columns upholding
Chains scripted as laws
I come in the name of Motherland's broken covenant
Turned ghostly beauty
Her radiant thirteen pieces power mobile, invisible towers."

I see the glory days in his eyes
My task is a present of the past, a pleasant surprise
Captain Debas claps, his reactions put aside
"You serve mythologies, legends
Your golems, giants and towers are tall stories. Wẹ've all looked to decode
Ancient odes
To find prophecies and judgment days

Locked inside long-lived lessons – let them go
Governor Tubal's laws are the way
Bring your beautiful ghost here to stay
Live with a smile that you have escaped the city's cage."

Mama Gran steps outside, eyes in the lines of her hand
She reminds her man
That he too once wore and walked in the shoes
Of a younger man anxious for command
Anxious to dissolve the fog from the land
"You remember the chase you gave to mythology?
The search for the grand key to unlock the caged city?
How strong my man you did so believe
Recall that memory. Recall your fire to set the cosmic black free." To me she asks,
"What do you wish your eyes to see?"

"Thirteen giants," I plead. "In the distance,
Their unseen presence curses me
Constructed not of love, but blasphemy
They move with the energy of a black queen's thirteen pieces
She sits broken on broken throne
Her tone resonates with skipped beats that pump the heart
Of femininity that misspeaks, walks of feminine nzambi – caged in caged city
Her true image is shattered, but there glows great beauty in this shade
A shy fire bright enough to cower the sun
She is Motherland's covenant given flesh
But she chokes on her own visitant smoke
I am tasked to restore proper heir to her to give her life and breath."

Glory days haze Captain Debas
Possessed, he dances
"I'll prance, praise and sing, if I can raise and lead an army
You will have allies in great numbers and might
Mama Gran, give this boy sight
Let giants' blood run when we strike."

Mama Gran's grin closes my eyes
She breathes stardust on forehead
Taps blessed watered fingertip
Three times
Light shines
Open

No longer blind to giants roaming
All in my sight can see
Four stand still, cornered – possessed by the four breaths
Taken in from my shy fire's chest
A continent, Alcyrion, a land living off the keys
Of the caged chained in the city
The four, most massive of the thirteen
But their height shrinks as I blink

Captain Debas shouts, "An army! An army of shades!
We'll pull from the drunkards, those in a haze
The misfits will be our messiahs today."

We journey back to the cage
To gather
Sneaking through devil swine patrols
Governor Tubal's soldiers and troops
There, sprawled in alley, are men and women drunk with fermented dreams
Age young to old
The life of nightmares
They rest their souls
Captain Debas culls the shadows of their brighter selves
Souls stand upright, we leave the bodies – shades and spirits in our army
I see three comrades stumbling
I pluck them like fruit, these recruits
Bwa, Phour, and Baron C
Allies to me
They now see clearly, Mama Gran clears their heads

We are a disturbance felt
Healed scars among the welts
First lady, Queen Malady
Governor Tubal's wife and wicked knife
She cuts through city streets
Devil swine flanked
She screams, "Shades have been pulled up,
And souls stand upright
Like windows, pristine and exposed, they beam bright with light."

Mama Gran has stitched ether
Making gossamer fabric
Knits cloaks

She covers the sleeping bodies recruited as shades
Fabric so unseen that all it covers becomes unseen
Mama Gran stays to keep safe unseen bodies
She on the streets a disguised hag in rags

Captain and I, with allies and shaded army – we leave the city
On waters rough, pale shadow pirate infested
We sink ships, recover provisions and weapons
Travel to Alcyrion
The land expands and expands and expands
Grand to giants
We are red ants, moving, and with claws wide open
But there are wulvz here, created creatures
Twisted and feral
Bristly bodies seep fog to creep, and howl as our army sweeps
Devil swine occupied, red areas restricted
There are wild animals in this land – some come from the caged city

Phour points our path
Bwa carves weapons from earth and ash, discard pirated weapon stash
Baron C curses the air against our enemies' breath
We exhale revolution while they inhale death
The fog, like a mouth, opens
Wulvz and devil swine assail and beset
My spear whet for blood – wet with blood

Shades and Captain help wulvz and swine breathe Baron C's conjure
Choked

Fate teases me
Plays chess with me
Guides my spear toss
Taps on devil swine's foot, gives him rhythm
He sidesteps, dives into fog
Spear cuts and cuts and cuts and cuts air
Sliver, slice – tears into giant's flesh
Small as a pin
Sun and galaxy inner-g injected within

Thunder shivers when giant hollers
Single scream billows and rumbles
Mountains tumble

Earth quakes
Shakes the battleground
Tower bends knee to ground

Cry wounded! Giant summons brothers.
The corners of the land close in

I run, jump, pounce
Hand around spear
Dislodge – stab – climb by prick and pierce, up and up
Spear penetrated, sun and cosmic touched
Rough screams ripple the air
Ascend, giant's legs bend
Stab spine at root – pierce, wind up to crown
Atop head, I stab down
Planted flag of victory
Screams cease
The breath of a queen escapes silently
Floats as pleasant wind, gentle and free
Breath swirls in place as one, waiting for three
Her siblings

Spear free. I, waiting.
A corner tower moves closer
Brother falling
I run, pounce
I up as giant down
Dead tower turns to dust
Straight, dive – glide through the air
Stab eye and blind second giant's stare
Hold tight as thunders might escapes in wounded roar
Up on spear – perched, planted as plank
I look into blind eye, let the winds of his screaming cry
Die
Before final strike
Spear wrest from eye, as I pounce and glide over head
Slide down spine, turn and rest spear into giant's neck
There escapes Sirene's second breath
Twirling around the first it goes, entangled – twist
Giant tumbles to death, bursts to dust, body thundered to the ground
I am grounded, spear in grip
Battle sounds of wulvz and devil swine, earth drenched in blood and grime

War stains
Purpose remains
Captain and shades control the rain of battle
Small army floods the field

Two giants infringe
Toss fire to singe the battlefield
Shades dive and sway
Move away from attacks
Bwa at my back
Phour gives a path
Devil swine and wulvz close in with pack
Baron C speaks death as incant

Captain commands shades with battle plans and the warrior's way
Wulvz and devil swine rush with fangs, boomsticks and blades
Giants attempt to crush our numbers
I pounce, leave sound behind

At the foot of the giant
I stand tall
Look up and up
And underneath this mass of beast, I understand
It is nothing more than puffs of smoke, mirrors and tricks
Size enormous, this tower cowers
I stab, it kicks – swings hand to swat and hit
Miss, and I pierce its palm – read lifeline and know
Its time has come – with final strike, its oppression undone
Remove spear from where poked – jump, pivot and float
Airstrike, thrust to throat
This giant doesn't get to scream – no release, except
For breath number three – somewhere a queen is no longer weeping
But waiting, anticipating breath trapped by these tall spires
Inhale. Inspired.

Giant falls forward – backflip
I retract with spear
Push
Off
Soar through air like the lark
Transpierce the fourth giant's heart
No scream coughed, expressive or resistant

Death is instant

Breath four adds to the core
Her cosmic winds are sovereign again
Gliding high
They first assist me
Gently down, to battle-worn ground
Captain and shades have chased away
Devil swine and wulvz
Land of giants and little light
Shines bright – stolen sun in land
As we have taken the day

The cosmic winds, once trapped within giants,
Find their way to ghostly, smoky broken black queen

'Do. I. Dream?
This proper breath I breathe?
With this fresh heir
I can now speak whole,
Black complete, back to the days of when my covenant was complete
Ancient syllables tap like feet
The cosmic winds of me
I taste laughter and every word I speak
Honey and rose are the flavors I sing
My melodies in the ol' skool company
The hymns of my hers
The suns of my daughters
The black, cosmic community
Ear up! Hear me! Enemies, listen and be frightened.
Do not be fooled by my sweet verses
To you I growl and spit rough curses
The brightest darkness
Warriors made of promise have slain four of your most monstrous
The nine that remain? Disregard their height.
To my black men, and the shaded feminine warriors that walk with them
To the Captain, his shades and my knight – warriors made of Motherland covenant
Walk as giants over that distant continent."

Light collapsed onto the scene, and then the basement's décor emerged. Gordon wore a grin on his face. He looked up at Fey, and she turned to him. Her eyes continued to resonate with a cobalt-blue light.

She winked at him. "To the roof, Gordon," she said breathing deep. She hopped up from the chair, letting go of Gordon's hand. She hummed an incant to warm her body, and then she faded away to the brownstone's roof.

Gordon stood. He too spoke an incant to keep him warm, and then his body stretched and zigzagged until he popped away. On the roof, he was clothed in his skin-tight, cosmic garb. Fey too was dressed in her cosmic attire. She was looking up at the cloudy sky. A light mix of rain and snow fell onto the Brooklyn neighborhood, accenting the November night. Fey's breath condensed in the air like a spirit conjured through her lips. Behind the clouds, the stars sang a slow melody heard by only Dooley and Fey.

In the air hung the smell of chimney smoke exhaled into the seasonal atmosphere. Fey couldn't stop taking deep breaths. In. Out. Inhale. Exhale. Long breaths, taken in like a meal. Fey could feel everything.

Dooley walked up beside her and commented, "Familiar territory, lightning bug."

Fey went through her exercise of deep inhale and long exhale. She replied to Gordon, "Not familiar enough. To the stars?"

Dooley took Fey's hands. They made a slow lift into the air. The light, wintry mix of rain and snow showered their bodies like a blessing. High, high, and high into the air they ascended. Just as they reached the clouds, Dooley reached for Fey's face, and he leaned in to kiss her. She accepted, but before moving deeper into the kiss, Dooley pulled away, retracting his cosmic mask into his flesh to have a better kiss. Peculiar, however, was the fact that the glowing, lilac orb remained spinning against his forehead. Fey stared at the triangular pattern of the glowing orb in conjunction with the bright, lilac glow in Gordon's eyes. Fey's eyes shone brilliant as a response. A cobalt-blue sphere appeared on her forehead. Cobalt-blue and lilac hues, and their triads of light, leapt from their bearers and mingled and twisted around one another. An electric hiss crackled like a furious lightning storm. The vibrant fusion snapped with a hefty push, propelling both Gordon and Fey in opposite directions.

Gordon arced over the Atlantic Ocean, his body limp. His descent was too quick, and he was unable to gain control of his faculties. Gordon smacked against the ocean's surface, skipping on the face of the water like a well-tossed flat stone. When his body's bounce and momentum halted, he dropped through the surface and sank. Gordon flailed his arms and legs. He breathed out and regained composure, swimming up. He inhaled air when he broke through the water's wavy surface. He rose out of the water, looking in all directions and calling out to Fey with his instinct.

A deep bass sound reverberated through the water and rippled it. Gordon turned and looked east. A cobalt-blue light domed over the horizon, and a single line of light emerged from it, shooting up into the sky. Cosmic smoke secreted from Gordon's flesh and masked his forehead and eyes. His spinning, spherical, lilac eye twinkled. He grinned as he looked upward, following Fey's ascent.

"There's my beautiful lightning bug," he said aloud. Dooley soared after her, leaving behind a luminous, lilac stream.

Closer and closer he climbed toward her, his speed increasing. When Dooley neared Fey, he reached for her. She looked down and accepted his charge, opening her arms and embracing him. Their bodies on touch burst into respective lilac and cobalt-blue spirits. Locked in embrace and kiss, they broke through the atmosphere, up and up and up until Earth was no longer visible, even as a speck on the cosmic scale.

The colors of their spirits bounced off one another and then jumped off their bodies, leaving them naked and constructing a large, translucent sphere of spirit around them. Gordon and Fey floated in the center of the glimmering sphere. Fey lifted her legs and wrapped them around Gordon's waist. She said to him as he continued kissing her neck, "It's okay, Gordon." He stopped kissing Fey's neck. He looked at her, eyes filled with a question. Fey repeated, permitting Gordon, "It's okay."

Gordon kissed Fey's lips, and then he slipped inside her. Fey inhaled, in, in, and in, accepting Gordon's penetration as he moved ever deeper insider her. Fey embraced Gordon in a tight, loving squeeze. He clenched his teeth and exhaled. He positioned Fey's legs to drape over his arms, and then he thrust in and out of her body. Fey leaned back, eyes closed and mouth open. When Gordon pushed up into her, she exhaled delight. He moved out, and Fey inhaled a sensual breath. Gordon continued his rhythm as he descended to the floor. He pivoted, placing Fey's back against the bubble, and for a moment, the two fumbled about to find their rhythm again. They chuckled, not allowing the awkwardness to dilute the moment. Gordon relaxed, as did Fey. They continued making love.

Fey whispered Gordon's name as she beamed an open-mouthed smile. She could see the stars behind her closed eyes. She beamed as Gordon concentrated on loving her, "I wonder if the spirits are watching?" Gordon didn't answer, remaining focused on his carnal affection for Fey. Fey sent to him in mind, ***Can it be carnal if it's spirit?*** Her body ruffled with waves of lush glee. She felt Gordon's forehead against hers, and behind her closed eyes, there was a soft brilliance coming through. Gordon huffed hard, and Fey knew he was near climax. She was not ready for this cosmic lovemaking to end.

Fey twisted, both with pleasure and with purpose. She put her hand on Gordon's shoulder and gently pushed. Gordon took her cue, assuming her position, prone against the bubble. Fey followed his every move to keep him inside her. He held the side of Fey's torso with one hand and her thigh with the other, assisting her movement.

Fey lifted and settled on Gordon. He held his breath to keep from peaking. Gordon traveled through Fey with spirit that coiled with hers, curling at the base of her spine. Up they twisted, dancing on Fey's senses, quickening her movement as she rose and settled atop Gordon. Their intertwined spirits stretched. Half of the coiled spirit ran through Gordon, scurrying up along his spine, the other half possessed Fey's body, taking the same route. Both of their brains were tickled, heightening their sense of the sensual pleasure.

A crown of light swirled above their heads. Fey dropped her head back and cried out. She and Gordon climaxed together, crying loud in a rejuvenating exhale. The force of their voices penetrated through the bubble of glimmering glow that encapsulated them. Their voices defied space and resonated sound, and the noise brimmed with bass and thunder, pushing out in all directions to become ubiquitous. Then, like a dying fire, their thunderous, collective voice, faded into the deep. Fey collapsed onto Gordon. Both were breathing heavy, but Fey was giggling the rest of her energy away. "I can honestly say, none of the men I've been with has taken me to space when it comes to sex," she continued giggling.

Gordon grinned. Fey slipped off him, and they both remained naked, hovering through the cosmos in the giant bubble made of their spirits. Gordon held Fey close. He chuckled at her comment, but was drained of spirit. Fey cuddled up to him, and eventually both were lulled to sleep. Their spirit bubble roamed space, gliding down closer to Earth. The stars hummed soft music as they slept, and three black spirits appeared from a dark, swirling opening to speak a blessing over the two lovers. From the gossamer fabric of space and magic, the black spirits stitched a blanket for the two lovers, simply for comfort, as they were neither cold nor ashamed of their nakedness. After laying the enchanted comforter across Gordon Goodspeed and Fey Forrester, the black spirits returned to the swirling, dark portal as it closed. Gordon and Fey slumbered in peace.

Fey awoke first, hours later. Sitting up, and observing Earth, gazing at her home planet with wide, sad eyes. Gordon stirred minutes later. He turned to Fey, regarding her sad look. He wiped a finger along her cheek and asked, "Why so glum, pretty lightning bug?"

Fey replied, "Look at our world, Gordon." Then she quoted, *"A once faithful world has become a prostitute! She once was full of justice; righteousness used to dwell in her—but now murderers!"*

Gordon kissed her cheek. "True, but far too grim after the time we've had."

Fey aimed a wicked grin at Gordon, forgetting Earth.

Gordon winked at her. He observed the shimmering blanket that lay across them and he commented, "I see the cosmic spirits have left us a gift. How thoughtful of them." Then he asked Fey, "So, are you my girlfriend now?"

"I better be *somethin'* to you, Mister Goodspeed!" She hit him in the ribs.

Gordon buckled, coughing up laughter as he held his side. "Oh, damn!" he winced. He held out his hand as if surrendering, saying to Fey, "In all honesty, you've always been something to me."

Fey raised an eyebrow. "Have I?"

Gordon recovered from her hit. "Yeah…" he said, hiding his face. "I admired you from afar on campus. I wanted to get to know you, but I wasn't sure how you felt about the community, having been pulled away from it. I was curious about you. When it comes down to it, I like you, Fey Forrester," he admitted in a funny voice.

Fey moved her face close to Gordon's. She rubbed her nose against his. "I like *you*, Mister Gordon Goodspeed."

Gordon snickered, "Ain't that somethin'? After stripping naked and knocking our body parts together, we have the nerve to be shy."

Fey joined Gordon in laughter. She quieted after a time and turned away from him, inspecting the glimmering floor she rested upon. She thought for a moment, putting the tips of her fingers against the bubble. She pushed against its rubbery texture with no results. Then she pushed harder, and her hand slipped through the bubble like a wet wall of mud. Gordon yelled in protest. Fey's arm lit up with cobalt-blue spirit as she pierced through to space. She smirked and marveled at her glowing appendage as it touched space. She lay fully against the bubble to stretch her reach, like a child dipping its hand into a lake from a pier. She said to Gordon, "Let's take our time returning home."

Gordon crawled on top of Fey. "I got no protests against that suggestion, Miss Forrester," he agreed. Fey retracted her arm and reached up to rub Gordon's neck as he planted kisses on hers. They inspected one another's tattoos, tracing the body art with their fingers, and making commentary on the designs. Together they tossed the blanket aside, deciding to wear one another. Fey opened her legs, and Gordon pushed himself inside her with ease.

Fey released a sensual moan, and as if on cue, the bubble rose high, leaving Earth behind until the planet was but a speck on the cosmic scene.

Card heist. Day of. The day was gray and breezy. Light drops of freezing rain trickled ever so often, pelting the bare branches of trees that lined the streets. The drab day didn't deter Dajon Brickhouse from playing a soft, beautiful melody on his violin. The drizzle tapped against an invisible dome conjured by the incanted notes the twelve-year-old boy pulled from his instrument. He stopped at the corner of Stuyvesant and Fable Avenue, continuing to play the gentle tune on his violin.

A lilac streak descended from the sky, arcing over the horizon and swooping down toward Dajon. The young boy kept his eyes shut, chin resting against his violin, and playing. Dooley landed next to him, and Gordon popped out of a puff of lilac dust on impact. He was dressed in jeans, brown leather shoes, a green sweatshirt and a waist-length jacket fitted with a hood. Dajon remained playing, eyes never opening. Gordon listened to the young boy's music. He flipped on his hood to shield himself from the increasing taps of freezing rain. Gordon engaged Dajon when the song came to an end. The boy's conjured aegis continued resonating.

"How you doin', little man?" asked Gordon. "Any trouble at school?"

Dajon squirmed. "There's been some shouts back and forth. But them cats ain't gonna engage. My mom put a blessing on me."

"Okay," Gordon replied, not pushing any further. "What're you doing here?"

The young violinist perked up. "I could ask you the same," he joked, pointing his bow at Gordon. "I heard you land. Where you been?"

"Mount Vernon," Gordon answered. "Fey's at her grandmother's. Now, your turn, little man."

Dajon pointed up the street. "My brother and your brother are talking to Lady Arachne. Some business. I guess she needs something done. The Shaw brothers and Wilson are there. Tap too."

Gordon put his hands in his pockets. "Yeah," he said. "I know what they're getting into today." He started walking up the street. He motioned for Dajon to follow. "Come on. Let's drop in on 'em."

Dajon followed alongside and the two of them walked to Lady Arachne's brownstone. Gordon rang the doorbell at the parlor floor entrance. Martin came from the garden level and shouted up to Gordon and Dajon, "Oh, was expecting Papa Solomon and Madame Jeliya," Martin admitted. "But why don't you come on down. We're goin' over the plot. Gordon, you might want to hear this." The private detective pointed to Dajon and said in an apologetic tone, "The little one has to be scarce. Sorry 'bout that, kid."

Dajon huffed.

"My house is unlocked," Gordon consoled Dajon. "Go there and chill. I got some new games. Blaze 'em up."

"Ugh, okay…" Dajon mumbled with defeat, trudging down the stairs and back onto the street. Gordon watched as Dajon made his way to his house. He yelled to him, "Chin up, kid." But Dajon just waved him off. Gordon exhaled. He rushed down the stairs and into the garden entrance. "Gang's all here," Gordon remarked, observing his brother, Benny, the Shaw brothers, Martin's partner Macario, Tap, Wilson and Top Hat all huddled inside, seated or standing. He was surprised to see Neyeli a part of the meeting. Lady Arachne stood to address them.

Papa Solomon and Madame Jeliya arrived just as Martin was preparing to shut the door. He stepped aside and bowed his head. "My apologies," he said. He bowed his head again, respectful, as he spoke their names, "Papa Solomon, Madame Jeliya."

The community Elders walked inside, returning a gracious bow at their necks to Martin. He asked to take their coats and hat. Papa Solomon declined, though he removed his hat from his head. Madame Jeliya allowed Martin to take her things. Her coat and hat were dry, and Martin suspected an incant used to keep the two of them shielded from nature as they crossed the street. He hung her items on a coat rack and then escorted the two community Elders into the circle of conversation. Wilson and Benny jumped from their seats and motioned for Papa Solomon and Madame Jeliya to have them. The Elders sat down, saying *"thank you"* to the two gentlemen. Papa Solomon motioned for Lady Arachne to continue.

Lady Arachne asked Madame Jeliya, "Are you rested, Thelema?" Madame Jeliya nodded in the affirmative. "Top Hat and Neyeli will be aiding you with protection."

"We'll use my quarters," Madame Jeliya insisted.

"Very well," Lady Arachne responded, holding her smile together. She turned and addressed Wilson and the rest of the crew. "In and out, understand. Make enough noise for the police to arrive, use Jamie's shadows to slip in and out."

"We got it worked out, Lady Arachne," Wilson assured.

Lady Arachne asked Edmond Shaw, "What time does that delivery come through the hotel?"

"They got the arrival coded," answered the bald-headed, goatee sporting Filipino man. "But the hotel is only expecting three deliveries today, all at two o'clock this afternoon. Things are supposed to be legit, considering the things that have happened at the hotel before. So, this delivery we're looking out for *has* to be on record."

Lady Arachne stressed, "Using Jamie's shadow conjure, we can have eyes on all three deliveries. Use an incant to signal the others if your eyes are on the proper delivery. Do *not* use phone earpieces to communicate. Understood?"

"Understood," the crew of misfits repeated.

Lady Arachne asked, "Everyone up on our marks? Who they are and what they look like?" Lady Arachne observed silent nods. "Good. Lanz Marcello. Brice Cadogan."

Gordon perked up at the sound of the second name. He interjected, "Brice Cadogan?" He leaned forward and emphasized, "*The* Brice Cadogan? As in Brice, first name? Cadogan, last name?"

"Is this guy some celebrity we're not aware of?" Cedron asked through a teasing grin.

Gordon made a face at his brother, but quickly straightened his expression. Papa Solomon asked, "You've heard of this fellow?"

"Heard of him? I saw him," Gordon answered. "The black mirror, fastened to the old book you gave me. It revealed some history to me a while back. Brice Cadogan was a Brit from the early nineteen-hundreds. He dabbled in secret auctions held by a group referred to as The Line. Old, and often occult, objects were rented out to the highest bidders. Joseph Pepper and my great grandfather, Madison, robbed him of the tomes I got in my chamber. Mister Cadogan was a business partner with Ethan Cassidy."

Lady Arachne turned to Martin. The detective took his cue to speak. "I thought there was something funny about this cat," he said. "He's got a long history. Too long. Suspiciously long. I passed it off as a common family name, and I'm sure that's the way things were made to look. Pretty good," Martin praised. "It worked, even against my detective insight. But I had a feeling," he said, not yielding to defeat. He walked over to the long table and lifted a surveillance photo he'd taken of Brice Cadogan. He handed the photo to Gordon.

"It's him," Gordon confirmed.

"So what're we looking at with this guy?" Wilson inquired.

"For starters, his partner, Ethan Cassidy, was an associate of Sarinda Fallows," Gordon informed. There was only a minor stir from the shared information, but Gordon could feel the people around him become uneasy with the mention of the wicked, red-haired mother of their culture's nemesis. "From the history I witnessed, Brice Cadogan was very interested in getting to know her. If he's still walking upright, it's every bit possible that he did get to know her, and he's living off a trick to keep him going."

Papa Solomon rubbed his hands, thinking. "That makes this run a little different," the old man grumbled. He furrowed his brow and pursed his lips, breathing hard. "Damnit," he cursed under his breath.

Madame Jeliya rubbed her husband's back. "Papa…"

Papa Solomon tried to relax. He said to Gordon while continuing to rub his hands, "I know you want in on this run, but I'd like to keep you out of this. Let this band of gypsies handle things."

Gordon smothered his instinct to protest. "I understand, Papa Solomon," he conceded.

"And if you're grounded, that also grounds Miss Forrester," Papa Solomon continued.

"Yes…sir," Gordon replied, not doing a good job with hiding his frustration.

Madame Jeliya connected with Gordon's turn in mood. She spoke soothingly, "It buys us a little time, Gordon. Now that we understand Stanley Fallows' possible connection to this, we know for sure they'll be an investigation—one outside the law, on our level."

"I know, Madame Jeliya," said Gordon.

Papa Solomon addressed Wilson and Jamie when he said, "Be careful with them shadows. This Cadogan fellow might be able to feel an incant if he has a blessing keeping him walking past his time. Switch up the plan a bit. Make a little more noise. Reveal yourselves, create some confusion. Step out them shadows." He asked Jamie, "There a way your conjures can drop away from a command other than yours?"

Jamie nodded his head. "Y-y-yessir," he told Papa Solomon. "We a-a-al-already p-p-practiced that."

"Good," replied Papa Solomon, a bit of anxiety lifted.

Martin brought up another point. "There're other items coming in. Should we grab them too? They're definitely something. There's an old spear from Arabia, and a bottle from Turkey. Professor Khepri and I could drum up some research on 'em."

"Do that research," Papa Solomon seconded. "But let's stay our hand on nabbing them. We'd draw too much suspicion if we go and snatch everything in this grab."

Lady Arachne reminded, "Research will be minimal once I have the cards in my possession. I'll make an inquiry about the items we leave behind." She clapped her hands rapidly. "If we're done, let's get to our task.

Come on. No need for a quick prayer, you'll have Top Hat, Neyeli, and Madame Jeliya's blessing over you."

Everyone stood. Madame Jeliya led the procession out of the house. Martin passed her, snatched her coat and hat from the coat rack, and placed it around her. She thanked him as he opened the door for her.

Martin and Macario stayed behind. Madame Jeliya went across the street to her house, Papa Solomon, Neyeli and Top Hat in tow. Gordon and the others walked up the street toward the Goodspeed residence, where the Brickhouse minivan was parked a few houses down. The rain had stopped.

"Keep an eye on my brother," Benny whispered to Gordon.

"Will do," replied Gordon, head down and hands in his pockets.

Approaching the van, Benny unlocked the doors with the remote attached to his keychain. He pulled open the side door once he reached the van, dipped his body inside, and pushed down half the first row of seats. He turned around and assisted Raymond, Wilson and Edmond in helping Cedron into the backseat.

Jamie asked, concentrating to keep his stutter minimal, "Y-y-you g-guys need help with King?"

"Nah," Cedron said back to Jamie. "They used to this. Relax y' wiry frame 'til things is ready." Then he ordered, "You can fold my throne, put it in the back." Jamie did as Cedron directed.

Gordon exhaled surprise, asking his brother, "You going out on this run?"

Wilson raised an eyebrow at Gordon as he jumped from the van, his assistance no longer needed.

"Yeah," Cedron said back to his younger brother as he strapped himself in. "I'm overlookin' this. It's a righteous grab. I'm coordinatin' this on the field." Benny propped the backseat back up as Raymond jumped out. Benny followed, and Edmond and Jamie hopped into the back seat, sitting behind Cedron. Wilson sat next to him. He removed a .38 caliber revolver and checked its chambers. When his inspection was finished, he checked a nine millimeter handgun's clip.

"We'll all be fine," assured Benny.

Gordon nodded, but still said, "You guys be careful."

"We got conjures and blessings on our side, kid," Wilson hollered from inside.

"Really?" questioned Gordon. "Then what're the boomsticks for?"

Benny slapped Gordon on the shoulder. "Theatrics!" he grinned.

Raymond entered the passenger's seat. Benny went around the car and slid into the driver's side. He started the van. Gordon watched them pull off and drive away. He looked down the block toward Papa Solomon and Madame Jeliya's house. In her sanctuary, lit by colored candles, Gordon knew she, Neyeli and Top Hat were scribing incanted circles on the floor, scripting veves, and then sitting inside them, meditating on providing a blessing for the band of misfit gypsies.

Gordon turned around, walked through the gate and entered the house at the garden entrance. He spotted Dajon seated at a chair that was turned toward the television, a wireless console controller in his hands. The twelve-year-old boy was engrossed in a video game. Gordon hollered to him, "Dajon, get up! Get your fiddle."

Dajon jumped, just noticing Gordon's intrusion. He paused the video game and turned his head toward Gordon. "What?" he asked.

"Come on," Gordon yelled, voice stern. "Outside!" he demanded. "Get your violin."

Dajon groaned and put the controller down. He got up from the chair and swiped his violin and bow off the couch. He approached Gordon, and Gordon motioned for him to continue outside. He did, and Gordon followed.

"To the sidewalk," Gordon ordered.

Dajon walked through the gate and stopped his paces at the sidewalk. Gordon came up on his left. "How 'bout a blessing?" he asked Dajon. He looked down at the young boy, eyes lighting up with an intense glow of lilac. "Play from your heart. Give a blessing in a string of chords, kid." Gordon stood up straight. He backed away to give Dajon space.

Dajon looked at Gordon's eyes and became inspired by their glow. He waited for several Fable Avenue residents to pass them by, and then he assumed a playing stance. He closed his eyes, but kept the glow of Gordon's eyes in his head. Using them as inspiration, the young violinist began playing. The music sounded like the first break of morning sun. Gordon stared, the glow in his eyes billowing like thunder clouds.

A deep growl murmured and smoke billowed over the brownstones on the other side of the street. There was movement stirring across several backyards. The few Fable Avenue residents walking the streets in the early morning stopped to observe Dajon's playing, and they also stopped to observe its effects. A large, scaly head rose over the horizon of brownstones. The long-necked creature stretched its serpentine face over the Fable Avenue houses and peered down onto the street. The slits of its nostrils rippled with smoke that blew against Gordon and Dajon as the creature sniffed at their presence. Gordon turned around, and Dajon stopped playing. The boy opened his eyes and his face burst with surprise. The conjured creature's bat-like wings spread wide behind it.

"Wow!" Dajon expressed as he lowered his violin and bow to his sides.

Gordon's glowing eyes met the scaly creature's slender, orange eyes. He shifted into his Dooley-spirit form, and hovered off the ground, daring an outstretched hand to touch the mighty beast. His hand ghosted through its image.

"Oh," said Dooley. "Okay…" He turned and said to Dajon, "I…guess this is what your blessing looks like. It's just a construct. This is your protection for the street, kid."

The beast hollered. Dooley braced himself against a wild wind. Dajon did the same as gathered residents plugged their ears. The dragon retracted its head, closed its wings, and disappeared behind the houses. Dooley landed, Gordon again popping out of a burst of lilac dust. "Some things about the beast are tangible, I guess. That doesn't seem fair."

"It ain't a beast," Dajon snapped, defending the conjured construct. *"Nyami,"* the young boy corrected. "That's *her* name."

"Nyami," Gordon respected. "You and it make sure this street is safe."

Dajon stated with pride, "My job."

"Your job," Gordon emphasized.

Fable Avenue residents congratulated the young violinist on the impressive conjure. Dajon accepted their praise, but he had to question something. "Hey," he called Gordon. "How'd you know I could do that?"

"I knew, but I didn't know," Gordon beamed.

Dajon made a face. "Who're you? Wilson?"

Gordon volleyed up laughter. He put his arm around Dajon and guided him back to the house. "At the end of the day, it was instinct, kid. Let's get back inside. I'll whoop yo' butt in some video games."

Far from Fable Avenue, passing through the Midtown Tunnel, Benny steered into Manhattan. Wilson remarked to Cedron, "Your brother gets to play superhero with that Forrester sister while we get to play mystic hoods." There was a roll of light laughter that moved through the van. "No, seriously," Wilson continued. "We're like a mystical hit squad. The Mystic Mafia." The bubbling laughter increased, muting the tension. Then Wilson said, "Yo, Benny, that boom cannon you got under the seat ain't loaded. That's yours." He slapped Raymond on the shoulder and passed him the .38.

Raymond checked the chambers. It was empty. "Me too?" he remarked, baffled. He turned to Wilson and complained, "C'mon, I'm older than this little one here."

Wilson put his hand on his chest. "I'm the adult," he told them. "I'm the one who gets the loaded gun. Benny, what would your father think if I had his son carryin' about a loaded firearm?"

"Considering the fact he okayed my being here…?" Benny offered up as food for thought.

Cedron swiped his hand, dismissing Benny and Wilson's back and forth. He declared, "In all seriousness—playtime aside. Regardless of what we learned back at Fable Ave'—old-time tricksters and enemies bein' indirectly involved, and what not and what have you. We got protection over us. We good. We go in, make some noise to drum up some sirens, swipe what we came for. We out. Bet." He asked, "We good? We hood?"

Everyone nodded.

"Raymond, Benny, follow Wilson's moves and signals," Cedron continued. "Wear Tap's shadows. Keep still, eyes on your mark. Give alert through incant. Understood?"

Everyone nodded again, coupled with a wave of the affirmative, *"Understood, King."*

Wilson commented, "Damn, you Goodspeeds is some serious cats."

Cedron agreed and retorted, "Somebody gotta keep y'all dudes in check."

Benny pulled up to the sidewalk a block away from the Wolverhampton Hotel. Cedron spoke up. He said, "Edmond, it's your go."

Edmond slid off the backseat, moving toward the door. Wilson opened the van's side door and slid it open for Edmond to hop out. Edmond thanked Wilson as he passed him and stepped out of the van. He turned and told Cedron, "I'll give you a call at time." Cedron nodded his head, still in profile, and barely moving his eye to glance at Edmond who walked off after receiving Cedron's consent. Wilson closed the door.

There was a murmur of conversation in the van just to keep noise running beside the engine. Benny made the block to keep from looking suspicious. He pulled to the curb in the same spot after two passes, and after Cedron suggested their loops could also look suspicious. Cedron's phone rang, playing a female pop star's song as a ringtone. It was Edmond calling. Before Cedron picked up, Wilson asked why he chose that song for Edmond's call, to which Cedron answered, "I made that my ringtone in general, sun. It's funny and unexpected. I mean, what's a big nigga like me look like having his phone buzz playing that goofy shit?" He gave a rare chuckle. He shook his head, smiling and saying to himself, "That shit is too funny, yo." Wilson remarked that the Goodspeeds were also weird on top of being so serious. Cedron spoke to Edmond on the phone, "Whatchu got? You're on speaker," he told Edmond.

"I got things narrowed down," replied Edmond. "Two of the three deliveries we got today are from a postal service. One ain't. It's going to a docking bay far away from the other deliveries." Then he specified, "Docking bay ninety-four, off hallway one-one-three-eight."

"Got it," said Wilson.

"Wilson, I'll leave you the details in an envelope at the front desk," advised Edmond. "I'll be right there. Come in and snatch it."

"We'll be shaded, but you should still be able to see us," added Wilson.

"Anything else?" asked Cedron.

"You might want to get a move on," Edmond's voice came through. "The show starts in twenty."

"Gotchu," Cedron copied. "Radio silence starts now. Out." He hung up. Cedron looked at everyone. "Shadow up."

"Let's play seventy-eight card pickup," jibed Wilson as he slid open the side door. "Benny, reach under the seat. Tuck the cannon in your jacket." Benny did as instructed, removing the sawed-off shotgun from under the van's driver seat. He checked its barrels, which were indeed empty of shells, just like Wilson had previously mentioned. He tucked the weapon down one sleeve and zipped up his jacket.

Cedron ordered, "Tap, conjure up these boys some shadows and then get back here."

"Right, King," responded Jamie.

Wilson shimmied off the backseat and hopped onto the sidewalk. He turned and closed the van's side door, telling Cedron they'd be back soon. Benny, Raymond, and Jamie exited the van and gathered around Wilson. He motioned for them to walk into the closest alley. The party moved forward, ducking into a shaded back lane. Wilson motioned for Jamie to start his conjure ritual, and Jamie started to tap. He slammed his foot to a hard beat three times, and three times shadows with elongated, human shapes, leapt from under his foot. Wilson, Benny, and Raymond stepped inside the shades, and their presence blended with the air and dissolved from sight of the regular folk of the world. Benny removed the sawed-off shotgun from his sleeve, carrying it out in the open.

Jamie walked back to the still running van as the shaded men moved up the sidewalk to the Wolverhampton hotel. Jamie hopped into the driver's side. Cedron told him to drive around. He pulled into traffic and moved forward.

Wilson, Benny, and Raymond angled in-and-out of pedestrian traffic, no one aware of their presence. A few times, Raymond had close calls, knocking into passersby. His image rippled into existence for a moment, and then disappeared again. No one noticed. Raymond thanked aloud the disposition of New Yorkers to be so detached from their environment when hurrying from one destination to the next.

Inside the hotel, the three of them passed through the lobby. Wilson snatched the envelope sitting at the edge of the front desk. He gestured to Edmond whose eyes were focused on his presence. Edmond nodded back, and then he returned to addressing a guest.

Wilson opened the envelope as he continued his strides through the hotel lobby. He removed a keycard from the envelope and a piece of paper with the docking bay and hallway number scribbled on it. Also included was a set of instructions to guide Wilson and his party to the docking area. Benny and Raymond followed close behind as Wilson led the way. Though unseen by regular eyes, Wilson and his young, shaded cohorts kept lookout as they used the keycard to swipe into the hotel's restricted areas. Again they dodged people unaware of their presence, but the traffic was far more maneuverable than the clouds of pedestrians cluttering the Manhattan sidewalk.

Wilson led the three-man group down the empty hallway designated as one-one-three-eight and to a door marked *Garage 94*. He stopped at the door, tucked the envelope with instructions and keycard inside his jacket, and gave a soft turn of the knob to see if the door was locked. The knob turned all the way, and Wilson quietly twisted it back to its original position. He removed his sidearm and looked at the other two, signaling for them to do the same. Benny clutched the already exposed sawed-off weapon, his hands shaking. Raymond removed the .38 given to him earlier.

Wilson opened the door slightly, making no noise. His eye observed the scene through the narrow crack. He saw a large garage and men interacting next to a delivery truck. Wilson's eye focused on three well-dressed, middle-aged men speaking to one another. He recognized two of the men from Martin's surveillance photographs. The man wearing the blue suit covered by a long winter coat, with raven-colored hair atop his head and across his lip was Brice Cadogan. A blessing bestowed on him sealed his look to his mid-forties, while the rest of him was forever of athletic build and health.

The second man Wilson recognized was Lanz Marcello. He was a tall man, of average build, with an olive skin tone and dark eyes set into an oval-shaped head. The third man, Wilson didn't know. He wore a gray suit, also covered by a long winter coat, glasses, and had a bulk to his body. His hair was thin, white and receding.

Wilson turned to Benny and Raymond. Benny eased his shaking. Wilson gestured that it was time. They put on masks, and then Wilson readied himself, gripping the doorknob hard. Benny watched and waited. Raymond did the same. Wilson took three breaths and then charged in. All three whispered, *"Shadows up! Cover their eyes!"* and the shades masking them from the world lifted and revealed them out of thin air. The conjured shadows raised and covered the security cameras.

Wilson screamed, "Everybody be cool! This is a robbery!"

Lanz, Brice, and the third businessman turned around in haste, caught off guard. The deliverymen stopped, boxes in their grips, and their guns too many motions out of reach, even while at their hips.

Benny raised his empty weapon. He was now on stage, acting his part.

Raymond yelled, "Suited gentlemen on the ground! Knees to the floor! Hands behind your heads! Now! Now!" The men did as Raymond instructed, all in their own fashion. The man unrecognized by Wilson looked nervous. Lanz looked disgusted, and Brice kept cool.

Wilson fired a shot in the air then aimed his gun at the four deliverymen, one of which was Macario's unintentional informant. The young man nicknamed All Talk. *"Eat the floor!"* Wilson demanded. *"Guns out and tossed."*

The deliverymen followed Wilson's orders.

Wilson turned his gun back to the suited men. "On the floor, flat," he yelled. "B, hold these men here," Wilson instructed Benny. "I'll check the truck."

Benny stepped closer and kept his weapon raised at the men who were on their knees. Raymond came up next to him. "No one look up," he ordered. The men obeyed. It was a ploy Raymond used so that no one would spot that his revolver wasn't loaded. To be safe, he walked around to the back of the men, keeping his gun on them. He whispered an incant bestowed on him by Madame Jeliya to contact his brother.

Brice stirred, head cocking and eyes looking around.

Raymond yelled to him, "Stay still, old man!"

Brice became still, but his curiosity toward the men robbing him was already piqued.

At the moment, Wilson was ransacking crates stacked behind the delivery truck. He found a small, plain wooden box the size and width of a set of Tarot cards resting inside one of the crates. He peeked back at the scene. Benny and Raymond had everything under control. No one moved. No one talked. Wilson put his attention back on the small box. He put his gun down and picked up the box. There was no lock to the case's hinge, allowing Wilson to open it with ease. He found a time-worn, leather pouch inside, and his lip curled into a sly, satisfied grin. Wilson lifted the bag from the box, and he could feel more than the weight of the incanted cards inside. A tingle writhed from the palm of his hand, through his arm, and up to his shoulder. The cards were real, but Wilson furthered his inspection. He set the box down, opened the bag, and sifted through the cards. He not only sensed the card's potency, but also the incant keeping the aged deck from turning brittle and crumbling into dust. The ink on the faces of the cards was fading but still filled with radiance. The cards themselves were fabricated from thin paper, but still had an inflexible feel.

Wilson repackaged the cards. He attempted to tuck the box into his jacket, but his inside pocket was too small. Wilson grabbed its edges and pulled, ripping the fabric, giving him enough space to shove the box inside. He zipped up his jacket and cursed for dramatic effect. He came from around the truck and shouted, "No money! Nothing! There's only coke and some old shit!"

"Maybe the old shit's got value," said Raymond, delivering the lines of their script.

Wilson retorted with his set of memorized words, scolding, "Man, I ain't takin' a hot item some collector or museum is waitin' for. We came here for the money." He aimed his gun at the well-dressed man he didn't recognize. "You!" called Wilson. "In this exchange, who was gettin' the money?" He bent down and put the muzzle of the gun to the man's head.

"No money. All favors," said the man. "Just favors."

"I don't know who sent you out here, buddy, but you got the wrong idea," Lanz interjected.

"Something paid for these suits," Wilson said to the men.

"I own the hotel!" yelled the unrecognized man. "My name is Nicholas Wolverhampton. We have a vault."

"Wolverhampton," Wilson chuckled. "That's a name and a half, son!" He pressed his gun to Nicholas' head. "Get up, Saint Nick. It's time for you to deliver up some Christmas gifts."

The door crashed open. Security rushed through followed by a squad of cops that had been called in. *"Freeze!"* screamed an officer. "Federal officers are on the other side of that garage door."

Wilson fired several shots, aiming far above the officers' and security guards' heads. Benny spoke an incant that reached out to the protection cast over them by Neyeli, Top Hat, and Madame Jeliya. Some officers and security guards returned fire while diving for cover. Their aim hit nothing.

Wilson, Benny, and Raymond charged behind the truck. They only needed to whisper the phrase, *"Shaded and covered,"* and they were gone from sight. Benny pressed the button for the garage door to open. On the other side were federal officers. One was named David Townley, an associate to Private Investigator Martin Kimball. And he'd waited all his life to make a bust like this.

Wilson, Benny, and Raymond walked away in a calm fashion. All three turned around and grinned at the scene of confusion and screaming that no longer focused on them but on the gangster, his business associates, and their trade. They pocketed their masks and remained shaded all the way to where they'd left Jamie and Cedron inside the van. They returned, but the van was no longer there.

Wilson called Cedron's phone. "It's over. We back, kid."

"Package?" inquired Cedron.

"Secured," Wilson answered.

"We on our way. Just a couple blocks from the spot."

"Aight, my dude. You'll see us, the rest of the world can't," spoke Wilson before hanging up. He looked at Benny and Raymond. He was grinning. "We *did* that shit, sun!" Wilson congratulated. He tucked his gun away, safety on, and then he started throwing light punches at Raymond and Benny. They retaliated, joining in on the play fight.

"There's a lot of trouble back there," noted Raymond. "Hope Edmond's job is secured. A lot of marks come out of that place."

"He gon' be a'ight," Wilson remarked. "He straight, man."

"Naw, you don't understand," protested Ray. "Wolverhampton already slipped out of some finance schemes a couple years back. He damn near lost his hotel, but he was able to make proper moves to keep from doin' time. But he ain't gettin' outta this one."

"He shady, but we in the shade," Benny consoled. "Somebody with that last name gonna run the hotel. They got heirs on top of heirs. Besides, if somethin' happen, you know we got Edmond covered."

"Yeah, but I don't think he wanna go back to driving taxis," said Raymond.

"We got him, sun," Wilson assured through tightened teeth. "Don't worry. Let's just celebrate."

"You right," yielded Raymond.

The van pulled up. Benny stepped up to it and opened the door. "Stay on the wheel," he told Jamie as he hopped inside, taking the seat behind Cedron. Raymond jumped in next, seated next to Cedron as Wilson took the passenger's seat. Raymond closed the door, Jamie's conjured shadows lifted from them, and their images were again present to the world. Jamie pulled onto the road and steered the car through Manhattan and back to Brooklyn. He parked outside Lady Arachne's brownstone. Cedron was helped out of the van first, lowered into his wheelchair. Gordon and Dajon walked up to greet them. "I'm sure you had an instinct we was comin' home," Cedron remarked. "You keepin' an all-seein' eye on us?"

"Nah, man," said Gordon to his brother. "I figured you'd be okay."

"You got that right," Cedron agreed. "Mission accomplished."

Gordon offered his brother a cigar. "To celebrate," he told Cedron.

Cedron accepted. "Absolutely," he beamed. "Been waitin' to get home for this."

Martin and Macario surfaced from Lady Arachne's house, coming from the parlor-floor entrance. "Well, if it ain't the newsmakers!" Macario yelled with a smile. He and Martin walked closer before he said in a lower voice, "Nothing but confusion when it comes to the Wolverhampton bust."

"Lanz Marcello is the focus," Martin added. He said, looking at Gordon, "Your friend Brice must have some tricks. No mention of a robbery. No mention of any stolen objects. No mention of anything but cocaine. The hotel's owner is being questioned, and he already has suspicions on him."

"Raymond figured as much," noted Wilson.

Papa Solomon, Top Hat, and Neyeli came from across the street. "Madame Jeliya is resting," Papa Solomon informed.

Neyeli walked through everyone to get to Benny. She put her arms around him, and he accepted her embrace, hugging her in return. "I was a little nervous when I saw those guns on you all…"

"That's why I reached out," Benny told her, accepting a kiss on his cheek from Neyeli.

She stepped away. "I flinched a little, but Madame Jeliya picked me up. I put an extra breath to conjure a wind to move the bullets up and away from you…all." She leaned in and whispered into his ear, "I need a drink. Join me? Some dragon spit." Then she whispered in a quieter voice, "with a kick of rum?"

Benny grinned. "I'm in, sister."

Cedron knocked his elbow into Benny's side. "Say her name, kid. Add 'baby' to it. You know how we do here," he teased.

Benny rolled his eyes and huffed, a rare, bashful grin was on his face.

Dajon said, trying to sound innocent, "Hey, Benny, once you're finished with your date with your girlfriend, I can tell you about the dragon I conjured." Then Dajon summoned a devious smirk.

Benny tried to hold onto his expression.

Cedron chuckled and verbally poked at Benny, "Your brother just called you out, sun."

Benny responded, pointing to Dajon, "How 'bout I follow you to school and rat you out to your little crush, Melinda?"

"Please," said Dajon. "I wish a Negro would. I've *been* workin' on her."

Everyone lit up. "Look at little man," Wilson commented.

Benny wrapped an arm around his brother and dragged him close to him. "Come on, kid. You tell me about this dragon." He, Neyeli and Dajon walked off after politely dismissing themselves.

"Who's got the cards?" Papa Solomon asked.

Wilson lifted a hand. "I do, Papa Solomon."

The community patriarch motioned to Lady Arachne's house. "Take 'em on in. She's waiting."

"Professor Khepri is in there with her," Martin added.

Wilson walked through the gate and up the steps, through the parlor-floor doors, and into the house. He walked through Lady Arachne's front hall and made his way to the stairs leading to the garden level. Professor Khepri was there, sitting with drink in hand. He pointed to the closed door of Lady Arachne's reading sanctuary.

Wilson approached and knocked three times. Lady Arachne answered with a quiet grace that masked her anxious spirit. Wilson presented the box holding the ancient deck.

Lady Arachne allowed her reserve to fall off as the box met her hands. Her demeanor brightened. "Thank you, Wilson. To all of you. Give my regards to King and the other boys. Those young men did a dangerous thing today."

"They're aware, Lady Arachne," Wilson said, a bow to his head. "And you're welcome, good woman." He winked.

"Stop it," she replied, winking back and conjuring a charge through Wilson's body. "Go, little boy. Mamma has work to do. The deck still needs a proper wash with a blessing. And I have to allow it to get to know me so that its potency will trust me to properly wield it." She stepped back and shut the door. Wilson flinched from another charge conjured through his person.

Inside.

Lady Arachne went to her table and placed the wooden box down. She was delighted to see there was no lock, and she opened the box with ease. Her smile brightened at the sight of the tattered bag holding the grizzled deck she'd sought for thirty years. There was no need to savor the moment. Her wait had been long enough. She handled the deck with care. The power brimming from the cards reached up to her like a newborn child for its mother. Lady Arachne's eyes watered. Her hands trembled while she sorted the deck into its four suits and Major Arcana. The cards were beautiful, and she was enamored that they were out of order. She felt connected to the past because of it. Someone had touched and used them before her, maybe an ancestor, hers or a mentor's. As her hands went through the cards, she could feel the variety of spirits that had used the deck before her. She saw a different face with every flip of a card, and she smiled at them and saw their names.

Lady Arachne believed the deck of cards she created in faithful detail with all of her masterful, artistic skill and powerful incants, did not compare to their inspiration that she now possessed, even with this ancient deck's faded images. She marveled at the cards as she sorted them into their proper suits of wands, coins, swords, and cups. All cards were present. Then she sorted the Major Arcana in numerical order.

One was missing.

Lady Arachne gasped, her spirits dropping away in panic that funneled into her stomach and stung her. She shuffled through the Major Arcana's twenty-one present cards. Not once, not twice, and not only three times. Lady Arachne sifted through the cards a total of eight times. Nothing. One was missing, and she hadn't overlooked it. Of this she was certain. Defeat was all she could admit. Hurt lay over her like a thick, wool blanket on a burning summer's day. It took time, but Lady Arachne yielded to the terrible fact. The Lovers card was absent from the deck.

Lady Arachne collapsed against her bench. Her tears were uncontrollable, but the sounds of her sobs were muted. She could hear Wilson and Professor Khepri holding a low conversation beyond the door.

She swallowed an incant and wished to cough it into her hand and rub it like lotion all over her body. Oiled with this lustful incant, she wanted to expose herself to the men beyond the door and draw them inside herself, smother them as they drowned in her. Devoured. Show the world that there were no webs like those spun by this mistress.

But Lady Arachne only swallowed her potential.

Deep.

Once again.

She continued crying.

But like the potential brewing inside her, she eventually swallowed her tears, lifted her head, and wiped her face clean. She spoke an incant that dissolved the dizziness brought on by her sobbing and sadness. Composed, she turned around and opened her sanctuary's door. "Gentlemen," she said, snake-like eyes bearing down on Professor Khepri and Wilson Barnes. "Please excuse me. I have much work to do. You are dismissed. Please lock the door on your way out."

The men stared at her, mouths agape.

Lady Arachne opened the door wider. Her grin curled just the same as she exposed the lush, enchanted potential swirling inside of her, letting it drip as a faint aura that tugged at the men sitting in front of her. Wilson and Professor Khepri continued staring. Lady Arachne raised an eyebrow. "Gentlemen…"

Professor Khepri and Wilson jumped up.

"Yes, of course, Lady Arachne," both men said at the same time. "Apologies," they continued their simultaneous speech.

Lady Arachne watched the men fumble over each other as they readied themselves to leave. A chuckle bubbled between her grin, but she cooled her demeanor. The men continued fumbling over themselves making their way to the exit. Lady Arachne suppressed a cackle of laughter. The matriarch shook her head, and as the men exited her house and locked the door behind them with an incant, she muted her potential's faint glow. She closed the door and returned her attention to the cards.

"My name is Lena Franklin," she introduced herself to the ancient deck, talking to them like a horticulturist talks to plants while watering them. "I have been anointed as *Lady Arachne*." She paced closer to the separated cards. She straightened the haphazard way the stacks of cards lay on her table. "My mother, Hanna Franklin, was of feather and blood. Her maiden name was Fields. My father, Clinton Franklin, was called The King of Skulls. I was raised in the divination, or rather *afọṣẹ* arts by both parents. I was inducted into the *Asase Ya Afua* order, mentored by the luscious Maman Wura Ekuru—praise her wild spirit. As a little girl growing up in South Carolina, I watched a long line of Franklin women on my father's side throw cowry shells, stones and read bones. My mother's people used feathers dipped in ink to scribe prophecies and the possibilities of time-to-come. But I was attracted to the cards. Your numbers and your pictures told such wonderful stories, and they gave me sublime insight. You have helped me guide people through difficult times and onto better paths."

Then Lady Arachne paced around her sanctuary. Her eyes never left the ancient, separated cards on her reading table. The ambiance was like a web made of intertwined streams of light and shadow. The elongated, waving shadows acted as subjects surrounding their queen.

She stopped and breathed in deep. Then she exhaled, stared at the cards she'd long sought after, and took a seat. Her eyes paced each suit of the Minor Arcana staring up at her, the Ace of each deck stacked on top. Her hand moved over the Major Arcana. An old and fading image of The Fool sat atop the stack of twenty-one aged cards. Lady Arachne sighed a smile down on the image and spoke, "Oh, how I am always humbled to be your reflection, little Fool." She lifted the Fool's card and positioned it above the four stacks of Minor Arcana suits. "My Fool's Errand begins here. I walk through all four lands, solving your puzzles and riddles, and reclaiming your treasures of knowledge, wisdom, and understanding."

Lady Arachne spied the next card in the Major Arcana. The Magician. She said with a humble tone, "High Father, your power is great." And she plucked The Magician from the stack, laying him over The Fool, but only covering the card partially. She took up the third card of the Major Arcana, The High Priestess. "But, Great and Good Father, your power cannot shine without Her Majesty, the Great Mother." There she was in all her glory, faded as her image had become. There shined a black woman, crowned and anointed as queen, wearing the cosmos as her flesh. The stars were her eyes. Sitting, she was, between two pillars, and with the scrolls of her magic clasped in her grip.

Lady Arachne sang an incant, and the card rose on its own. She continued singing the mystical notes, moving her eyes to where The Magician and Fool cards were positioned. There floated The High Priestess, following Lady Arachne's eyes. Over The Magician card settled The High Priestess, offset from completely covering it. Lady Arachne's song ended. She stood up, beaming a relieved smile, eyes on her cards.

"The full moon does not shine," she said to the cards. "And the sun is often veiled by the clouds," she continued. "But I know a song of moon and sun that will charge you. I know a cosmic song too. I will lather you in the ethers, and your potential will be set free. You will be charged." She sighed again, her smile dropping away. "I have questions for you."

Lady Arachne stood straight and cleared her throat. She closed her eyes and crooned a soft melody dedicated to the moon. The flames dancing on the candles gleamed bright with a white-hot, otherworldly fluorescence. Lady Arachne continued humming the melody as she prepared a large African Abalone shell with sage. In the same melody as the song she sang, Lady Arachne hummed an incant that started a gentle burn over the sage. She carried the shell to the table and set it down near the cards. The enchanted smoke rising from the burning sage passed over the deck of cards and cleansed them.

The matriarch sat down. "This is your first bath," she said to the cards. "Let me get to know you. I will clean you with the full moon, and later the sun. I will sprinkle sea salt on you, and you will charge. My voice will be silk enough to wipe you off. This is Lady Arachne's web, little cards. You're safe with me here."

A day later, the same ritual was performed. This time, Lady Arachne sang the song of the sun, making the candles mimic the bright yellows, oranges, and red hues of the radiant celestial body. Sunrise to sunset they shined. Lady Arachne continued to talk and bind herself to the cards, knowing each of its seventy-seven personalities. The Fable Avenue matriarch focused her intent and questions in her hands as she spoke to the deck about her life and family. She was happy as she talked to the deck of cards, one missing. But Lady Arachne was determined to find out where The Lovers could be.

Winter hurried autumn off the northeast stage a month ahead of schedule. There was nothing particularly harsh about the late November weather, but winter barged in, blowing thin carpets of snow to cape the city streets and sidewalks from time to time.

Gordon and Fey found little time for each other. There were only short-lived bump-ins on campus. The final days of their semester permeated their lives and took their focus away from meta-scripting *In Thirteen Pieces* or the occasional haunting of the streets. Fey even spent her days at her grandmother's in Mount Vernon so as not to be distracted by Gordon being down the street. Though, it wasn't as if she couldn't use the spirit inside her to simply pop from Mount Vernon to Brooklyn. But it was the illusion of distance that Fey consciously bought into in order to focus on her studies.

Gordon didn't pay much mind to the illusion, but he respected Fey's decision to not be steered away from her studies. This included the last several weekends. But to fill the void of her absence, he too concentrated on his studies. Talks on the phone and occasional texting were all the time they shared outside of the sporadic meet-ups on campus.

Gordon, at the moment, was taking a break from studies, losing himself in a video game. Behind him, Cedron explained again, and with great delight, the exploits he coordinated to secure Lady Arachne's much sought after conjure cards. His audience was Maximilian Goodspeed and the specter of their mother, Althea Goodspeed.

"Well, Cedron, these boys need to call you 'coach' instead of 'king'," suggested Althea, proud smile on her face. Then her tone changed as she scolded, "And please put that cigar out."

"Aw, Mom!" bellowed Cedron. "It ain't doin' you no harm."

"No, young man, but it's doing you some harm," Althea pressed, eyebrows raised over widening eyes. Cedron snuck in one last puff before extinguishing the cigar in an ashtray. "Uh, young man! You gon' sit there and try to sneak a taste while I'm looking right at you?"

Cedron kept his grin as smoke billowed through his teeth and smile. "Aw, Mom," he repeated.

"Boy, you will be on the other side of the ether with me you keep that behavior up," Althea noted. "What's with the cigars anyway? I watched over you and saw you go from healthy to smoker."

Cedron cleared his throat. "Coach always let us smoke after a win," he admitted through a guilty smile. "Not everybody indulged, but…"

"No. He. Didn't!" Althea expressed.

Cedron shrugged his shoulders. "Mom!" he pleaded, "we were of age. Some cats were a little under, but c'mon. We was okay."

"And now you all are hooked," Althea said, rolling her eyes. She looked at Maximilian. "You hearin' this?" she asked her husband. Maximilian did, but he only sat at his chair, beaming at his wife and enjoying watching her chastise their eldest son.

But then he did think of something to add. He scratched the back of his head and commented, "I'm at a bit of a loss, Althea-baby, over you bein' upset about the cigar smoke—especially in our culture. Hell, both our family's alone could be considered chimney stacks."

"Rituals," Althea continued her playful protest. "Spiritual blessings. Time and place," she reminded.

"Celebration is a ritual," Cedron pointed out through a bubble of laughter.

Gordon paused his game, turned, and commented, "So you have no trouble with the fact he helped coordinate the robbery of one of Manhattan's luxurious hotels?"

Althea turned to her youngest son and retorted, "A corrupt corporation allowing the secret laundering of a known stolen piece of our culture—that's what that was. That wasn't robbin', my baby boy, that was taking back." Althea huffed and rolled her eyes, folding her arms. "Please, folk want to be angry cuz we takin' back what's rightfully ours. Shit, we need to make more moves, like in them old days. The Fable Brothers and Horatio days."

Gordon forgot how fiery his mother could be. He didn't understand her reactions when he was growing up, having had a strong, sensitive connection with her emotions. It scared him, rattling his heart when his mother was irritated at the world. Now he understood.

The doorbell rang on the parlor floor just as laughter came through Gordon's expression. He got up and said, "I'll get that." And up the stairs he went, answering the door to see his friend Benjamin Brickhouse on the other side. "Cedron's downstairs with my mom and dad," Gordon said motioning over his shoulder.

"Naw, my dude," said Benny. "I'm here for *you*."

"Okay…"

"I was just up the street with Neyeli. She need some peace for her studies. Got me thinkin' about somethin', and I'm here. I need some advice, O' Great Spirit."

Gordon grabbed Benny by the collar and dragged him inside. "Getcho ass in here!"

Benny maneuvered out of Gordon's hold. "Too slick for the spirit," he teased.

"Please!" Gordon snapped. He walked back down to the garden floor with Benny in tow. Gordon led them to the kitchen, introducing Benny's presence to his family. Benny greeted Max and Althea Goodspeed in a polite tone, and he threw a 'wassup' to Cedron who nodded with a friendly nod of the head.

"How's your mother, Benny?" asked Althea.

Benny answered, "She's doing fine, Miss Althea."

"Oliver is still working on my husband's incanted tattoo, but when it's finalized, I'll pay her a visit." Then she emphasized, "At *your* residence. She doesn't have to keep coming over to ours."

Benny responded, "Okay, Miss Althea. She was just asking about your progress."

"Oh, good. Tell her it's coming along fine."

Gordon grabbed Benny again, this time on the back of his jacket's collar. "Getcho Eddie Haskell-ass in here."

"Uh, excuse me, Mister Gordon Goodspeed?" Althea reprimanded. "Boy, being dragged into my ether and getting an incanted ass whuppin' is not exclusive to your cigar-smoking brother."

"See this, Miss Althea," Benny spoke up. "I come here for advice, I get abuse. All spirit, no manners."

Gordon ignored his friend. He reacted to his mother's chastisement with a sigh. "Yes, Mom…" He gritted his teeth at Benny and sneered, "Getcho butt in here—makin' me get in trouble all up in my own house." Then he asked in a livelier manner, "You want a drink, man?"

"Nah, bruh. Thanks, though. I was just having lunch with Neyeli."

"Okay," said Gordon. He opened the refrigerator and pulled out a jug of non-alcoholic *dragon spit* for him. He set the jug on the counter and opened a cabinet door to retrieve a short glass. "So what's up, sun?" he asked Benny as he filled the short glass.

"I know I could've asked Neyeli, but I want to surprise her," Benny started.

Gordon inquired as he turned around and leaned on the counter, "With what?"

"Registration for next semester at the college," Benny answered. "Is it still going on?"

Gordon took a swig. "No," he told Benny as he swallowed. The cold drink hit hard against the back of his throat. He said an incant in his head to recover from the icy sting. "But, they'll have late registration early January. Keep up on the website. They might have it going on a little before Christmas."

"Okay. I'm gonna do some business courses. See how I like that. Neyeli changed up to psychology as a major since her empathy conjure appeared." Benny made a face. "Me? I'm sure I'll be helpin' my pops—*and your pops*—run the taxi service. Maybe I'll help run one of them farms we got upstate. Help direct the trade to the corner stores we got here on the block and in Harlem. Might think of some other things to study. I like Drama."

"Don't I know it…" Gordon quipped turning back to the counter and refilling his glass. He put the jug back in the refrigerator.

"Man, forget you!" Benny retorted.

Gordon smiled, turning back to his friend. "So, a kiss from a cute girl got you to do something I've been tellin' you to do for the last two years."

"Hey, sometimes a prince needs a kiss to wake up," Benny commented. "Besides, I snuck a course or two in. Give me credit."

"Not college credit," Gordon continued joking as he sat down at the table. "You got a conjure yet?" he asked in a whisper.

Benny replied, making a face, "Why you askin' like there's regular folks in the next room?" Gordon didn't have an answer. Benny sat back. "I'm workin' on something. Been askin' Tap about his conjures, the shades." He circled a finger against the table, a shy chuckle coming from him as he looked down. "I've been…workin' close with Neyeli to see what might be stirred inside me—inside both of us."

"How much work is actually getting done?" Gordon asked, arching a single eyebrow.

"Right…"

"Your conjure come through, it'll be something and nothing."

"Whatchu mean by that?"

Gordon shook his head. His eyes looked everywhere as he searched for the proper words. "Fey and I, when we haunt the neighborhood—hell, the city—all the emotion we feel coming from…our people."

Benny huffed, "Shoot, these niggas ain't my people—dumb as they can be. They done forgot heart. They filled with smog and fog. Babylon's words on they tongue. Too scared to speak they spirit, and to know incant and conjure. Them regular folk. Worldwide, not just in this city, this state. *Your folk*. Not mine."

"Nah, Benny. They are ours."

Benny shook his head, continuing to disagree. "Them regular folk scared of what's here," he said tapping on his chest at his heart. "We got incants and conjures, and they too busy believing the lie that our culture is devil worship—told to them by folk that don't look like them and used to enslave them. We got promises to keep. Puff away with 'em," declared Benny as he waved his hand in dismissal. "I got no respect for people so afraid of their own shadows. Hell, you gotta wash they minds of your haunt when you save they asses from doin' knuckleheaded stuff."

"You gotta stop hangin' with Wilson," Gordon noted. "Besides, the understanding of it all remains here." He tapped a finger against his head.

Benny rolled his eyes. "Minds washed but still brainwashed."

"Clever," Gordon retorted. He took a moment to think, and then he said to his friend, "I can go to the stars. I want that acknowledged."

"Acknowledged how? That it's something special?"

Gordon shook his head. "Yes."

"You're special," Benny teased.

"Not me."

"Then who?"

"All of us. Anybody can do this."

"Awww..." Benny continued teasing. He clapped and said, "O' wise philosopher, tell me more. Please...more."

Gordon balled his fist and shook it at Benny, looking at his friend with one eye. Then he leaned back in his chair. "I miss Fey," he admitted. *She would understand what I mean*, he thought to himself. He told Benny, "I'm in the same predicament as you. She's studying, needs her space."

"Yeah, but you got some studying to do yourself."

"I'm taking a break. I was considering going out, getting some air."

"Where?"

"Mars."

Benny rolled his eyes. "Special," he observed. "Go teach that. Cats probably look at you and ask, *'What about black-on-black crime?'* and it ain't even got..." he slowed his words and considered Mister and Missus Goodspeed in the next room. "...stuff," he chose the word to use, "to do with what's here." He tapped on his heart again.

Gordon didn't care. "So what? What's the answer to that?" Gordon asked. "System against us, black-on-black crime?"

Benny didn't hesitate. "They both the same thing. But these fools you tryin' to convince are my people don't see it. Black-on-black crime originates from the same tyranny that Babylon's system traps us and kills us with. You know," Benny jabbed Gordon with his words. "You've saved your share of kids from this system's soldiers."

"I have," Gordon nodded. "And like you say, they don't know that. They don't know the spirit saved them. A black spirit. They don't know they spirit called it forth. African, but indigenous to every land. But *you* know that? And you might not got a conjure yet, my dude, but you got incant and you got knowledge. Bet. So what that make you?" asked Gordon.

"Special? Better…?"

Gordon shook his head. "Nah," he told his friend. "Your clearance is above special. It's above better. It makes you—it makes all of us—responsible for these regular folk out here."

"You conjure Brother Malcolm's spirit and have a conversation or somethin'…"

"Nah, I'm just from that Fable Avenue conjure culture, sun."

Gordon and Benny burst into laughter.

Hard pounds knocked against the door. Gordon turned. His instinct reached out. "It's Top Hat," he said to Benny. Maximilian answered the door.

"Lady Arachne needs to see Gordon," Top Hat could be heard saying as he stood outside. "Gordon here?"

"Yeah," answered Maximilian, gesturing an invite inside for Top Hat. "He's taking a break from studying."

Top Hat walked inside. He turned to the kitchen as Gordon was caught in his peripheral. Maximilian closed the door "Getcha self together, kid. Lady Arachne's had a breakthrough with them cards. They're charged and ready for a read. She says she needs you at her house now."

Gordon jumped up from the table. He turned and asked Benny, "You in?"

"Yeah," he answered.

"Come on," Gordon motioned. He and Benny made their way to the door. Althea spoke an incant that wrapped warmth around Gordon and Benny as the two made their way outside. "Thanks, Mom," Gordon yelled over his shoulder as he slipped his sneakers on. His father and brother stayed behind.

"She been at them cards since she got 'em," explained Top Hat as they walked down the street to Lady Arachne's brownstone. It was snowing hard. Thick flakes fell from the sky, pelting the earth and the three young men walking through it. They were forced to hide their faces away from the falling snow. "She finally got those cards charged," reiterated Top Hat. "They're not at full potential with one card missing, but something has her excited."

Gordon asked, "Papa Solomon and Madame Jeliya there?"

"No," Top Hat answered. "Papa Solomon is glued to the Wolverhampton coverage. He's uneasy at the fact no robbery is mentioned. He thinks it means our adversaries will deal with us quiet-like." He added, "I'll head over there when I drop you all off."

"Any insight on the missing card?" asked Gordon.

Top Hat shook his head and sighed, "None."

Lady Arachne's brownstone. Top Hat led them through the iron gate and knocked on the garden-floor door. The woman of the manor answered. A stoic but elegant demeanor disguised her excitement.

"Gordon," she said as she moved aside and allowed entrance.

Top Hat remained outside. "I'll go get Papa Solomon and Madame Jeliya," he said.

Lady Arachne instructed, "Top Hat, have them call Maman Anansi. We may need her. She's reported that her personal conjure has come through. We may need that."

"Yes, Lady Arachne," he replied with a bow.

Lady Arachne closed the door. Gordon and Benny moved farther inside.

"Mister Brickhouse, please wait out here while I conduct Gordon's reading."

"Yes, Lady Arachne," said Benny. He took a seat and removed his wool hat.

"You need a drink or anything, young man?"

"No, Lady Arachne. Thank you."

Lady Arachne shuffled Gordon into her sanctuary. The dancing flames of lighted candles lit the room summoning an army of shadows on the walls. A thin stream of incense smoke haunted Lady Arachne's sanctuary, perfuming the area with its spirit. The matriarch closed the door and instructed Gordon to sit. He did as told, and watched her round the divination table and take a seat on the other side. Though there remained the carnal tug generated from Lady Arachne's slithery movements, her countenance appeared tired. Gordon's instinct sensed a buried, despondent emotion. He retracted his instinct from prying any further. Drawing back on his foresight, Gordon felt Lady Arachne's excitement at the surface of her poise, and he aligned with her foremost emotion.

She lifted her newly acquired deck of Tarot cards.

"Shall I shuffle and cut the deck?" Gordon asked.

Lady Arachne didn't look up at Gordon when she answered, "There's no need with this deck. I'll take care of that." She looked at him and disclosed, "It humbles me. All the power I put in recreating this very deck, and not even close to imitating its potential." Her sadness crept to the surface, pouring through her eyes not as tears but as expression, and it shadowed her excitement, slowly covering her face. All the while, she held her smile through the emotional usurping. "I might've fibbed a little, Gordon, when it came to the work I've been doing with this deck as of late. My work did have me exhausted, but I was recovering from my initial disappointment of not finding The Lovers card within it, seeing the deck incomplete."

Gordon responded, "Oh. I'm sorry about that, Lady Arachne. I know having the complete deck was something you were looking forward to."

"Thank you for your sympathy, Gordon," the Elder replied. "I have engaged in intense, and tiring, meditation. But it wasn't always to bring out the deck's potential. I was also searching for answers as to where the missing card may be." She added with an assured tone, peppered with what Gordon believed was the slightest spice of doubt, "It does exist." Then Lady Arachne's voice stuttered, "Th-th-that I do know. I am sure. I've already found out through inquiry with the cards. But it's missing..." Perplexity then covered her face, shaking away all other emotions.

"I could use Spook to locate it," Gordon suggested.

Lady Arachne's spirits lifted. "Your black mirror?" she asked, countenance brightening.

"There has to be some story concerning those cards," continued Gordon, now relieved that Lady Arachne had vibrancy restored to her.

"That would be wonderful," Lady Arachne complimented. She laid a hand on the table and said, "Let's now concentrate on the reading before us."

"Yes."

"I asked questions, Mister Goodspeed," she told Gordon. "I asked a lot of questions. With one question, you were its answer," she told Gordon. She tapped her finger against the table. "Chil', let me tell you, this deck might be incomplete, but it gives me insight to fill in the blanks. I swear."

"It's good to see you happy, Lady Arachne."

She ignored Gordon's sentiment and commenced shuffling the cards as a child-like grin crept onto her visage. She raised an eyebrow, eyes on Gordon, and stated, "And now it's time for your answers." Lady Arachne's shuffling came to an abrupt stop, and she revealed four cards: The Two of Cups, The Moon, The Star, and The Tower.

Gordon looked up from the cards at Lady Arachne, waiting for an answer. She was stiff like a mannequin. An instinct jumped up inside her and assisted in deciphering the cards' meaning. When she moved, it startled Gordon.

"Is Miss Forrester down the street, Gordon?" she asked.

Gordon shook his head. "Fey?" he answered. "No. She's in Mount Vernon. Do we need her?"

Lady Arachne, eyes still on the cards, held a timid expression. She shook her head. "Let her be, Gordon. Her absence might be all we need to avoid something terrible." Her eyes moved to him. "Take Mister Brickhouse with you. Be cautious or conflict will take place." She said to herself, "The cards have served my instinct well. Maman Anansi will be needed. I hope her conjure has kick."

"Where to, Miss Arachne?"

Lady Arachne came from her thought and stood. Her movement was sudden and unexpected. "To Jackson and Gaston Fables' houses. Take these cards with you," she instructed. She pointed as she clarified, "The Moon and The Star. Lay one at each of their doorsteps. The doors will unlock. Then cross over, Mister Goodspeed. Walk through the house to the other side. You through Jackson's brownstone, and Mister Brickhouse through Gaston's brownstone."

Gordon got up. Lady Arachne picked up The Moon and The Star cards. She handed them to Gordon, and he accepted. He handled the cards with as much care as their new master would. Gordon turned, made his way to the door, opened it, and walked through to find Papa Solomon, Madame Jeliya, and Top Hat in company with Benny. "Maman Anansi is on her way," Madame Jeliya informed. "What is the news, Lady Arachne?"

"Our answers lay beyond Jackson and Gaston's houses," briefed Lady Arachne. "Let us keep a close eye here."

"Benny," Gordon called. "Let's be out."

Benny jumped up, slapped his hat back on, and followed Gordon through the door. The snow had calmed, but late autumn's wintry snap whipped Gordon as he stepped outside. He didn't bother revitalizing his mother's warming incant. He trudged through the gelid air, passing The Star card to Benny. "Take this. Go to Mister Gaston's. Lay it on the doorstep. Lady Arachne says the door should unlock."

"Got it," said Benny as he accepted the card. "You know what we'll find?"

"Possibly trouble," Gordon admitted. "And since your conjure ain't come through, you keep a good, defensive incant at the ready." He looked over his shoulder, checking. He then said to Benny, "And hell, a trick if you got 'em."

"Yeah…" Benny said, voice trailing away as they neared the Fable brother's old and locked brownstones.

It was at the end of the street, near Bedford Avenue, where Gordon and Benny stopped in front of Gaston Fable's house. "This is your stop," Gordon remarked. He made a slow turn, looking across the street at Jackson Fable's brownstone-façade homestead. "At the doorstep, Mister Benny-Jah," he reminded shaking The Moon card. Benny remained hushed. Gordon asked, "You okay?"

"Yeah..." Benny said, voice again trailing away. "I was just thinking about Neyeli...her protection."

"You'll be fine," Gordon promised. He put out his hand. "Shake my hand, sun. My spirit will get you." He lied just to calm Benny's anxiety. Benny shook Gordon's hand and a warm feeling passed from Gordon's palm to Benny, relaxing the young man.

Benny took a deep breath. "Thanks," he said to Gordon.

Gordon nodded his head. He put his attention back on Jackson Fable's residence. His mind went to Fey, but he didn't let his thoughts of her linger too long, concerned his instinct would reach out and call her. He put a foot forward, and then both he and Benny stepped toward their respective houses. Benny hustled up Gaston Fable's brownstone steps, and Gordon crossed the street, and hastened up the stairs. Both Benny and Gordon placed their cards at the doorstep and backed away, waiting. It wasn't too long before a thin, black light surrounded The Star card and a fluorescent, white light surrounded The Moon card.

The Fable houses unlocked.

Gordon looked over his shoulder at Benny, and he saw Benny doing the same to him. They shared a nod of their heads toward one another, and then turned their attentions back to the now unlocked entrances. Gordon reached for the knob. Benny did too. They walked inside, stepping into identical rustic and charming kitchens and dining spaces. Nothing within the two interiors were like brownstone houses. And what appeared to be the front entrance from the brownstone façade side, was truly the backdoor of the houses. Moving forward, Gordon and Benny came to similar circular front rooms that featured white walls and winsome décor. Not everything was identical, however. The scenery beyond the genuine front doors, as observed by Gordon and Benny, were quite distinct.

Benny opened his front door and wandered onto the front porch and into an area that looked like regurgitated wreckage from the collapse of a civilization. But this was modern times, and a modern area. It was a ghetto stirred with ruination, a trash heap piled with broken lives and spirits that walked the cracked streets while hunched over, slow, and dragging their burdens. The backdrop was of rundown properties the area's population called housing. Nature whispered attempts at coloring the locale with trees, but the flora were gray and bare. There were willow trees, piteous and bent. It was early afternoon, but it was dark.

A party of three rough-looking, young black boys approached Benny, looking him up and down. "Who dis, dude?" one asked, gold plated, fake grills shining on his teeth. "Walkin' up in the Hollow, here." His words were muddled together, sounding like the sloshing of mud. The boys were in their late teens, wearing tanktops and sagging pants.

Benny ambled down the stairs. "I'm just visiting my grandpops," he said. "All the way from Harlem to…the Hollow." He looked around and spotted a sign. *Water Bug Hollow of Jakobiville.* "I'll be damned…" Benny said to himself. His eyes swept the area again. A haunting image of the past shimmered and disappeared. The young boys moved closer to him, surrounding Benny. An incant sat at the ready on the tip of his tongue. He spoke its soft, African syllables and the young men surrounding him backed away, turning around and returning to where they first congregated. Benny stepped forward, eyes exploring the rundown area. He remembered the stories told to him of Water Bug Hollow's once grand past. He also remembered it was hexed by Sarinda Fallows, and years upon years later, it crumbled into the state he saw before him now.

Five hours and thirteen minutes away, and just across the street, Gordon stood on Jackson Fable's front porch. He was at the crossroads in Clarksdale, Mississippi. The golden, grassy fields were dulled like unpolished brass. A gas station was built on the lot adjacent to Jackson's house. Gordon sauntered down the stairs, a curious expression on his face, eyes sweeping the scenery. A scraggily, scrawny man wearing a red cap and overalls with smudges of soot and oil covering his face walked out of the gas station. He fiddled with a grimy rag, wiping off a component come from under a car's hood.

Gordon strolled to the intersection of the crossroads. He and the gas station attendant stared at one another. A grin enlivened the yokel's face, exposing both missing and dirtied teeth. Gordon moved his lips to speak, but the noise of a fleet of cars coming down the road stalled his words. He turned his attention to the armada of vehicles. The fleet consisted of four, 1970s-style Bonnevilles. They kicked up dust and dirt from the country road. They came to a cloudy, dusty halt, and the engines died. The front doors opened on a golden-brown colored car. From the passenger's side came a familiar face to Gordon. It was Brice Cadogan, traveled from London to Manhattan and now to Mississippi's sacred crossroads. He was wearing slacks and a tucked in dress shirt. Clasped around his right forearm was a piece of armor. Engraved on its side was the number nine.

The yokel backed away and moved inside the gas station, face smacked up against the glass door.

Gordon's vision was fixed on the man with the blessing that locked him at a youthful age. But his attention was drawn away when from the driver's side ejected a tall, brawny, white man wearing a straw hat, a buttoned up collar shirt, and suspenders holding up a pair of jeans. A thick, Dutch-style beard framed his chin. Gordon's eyes spied on the man's hip an old, tattered bullwhip curled up like a rattlesnake. Its once dark-brown body was weathered to a light tan, with faint, red speckles spattered around it. The man was also equipped with a gun holstered on the other hip.

Parties of six stepped out of the remaining cars, two in the front and four in the back. Medical masks covered the men's faces, and they wore scrubs and white medical coats. They clutched in their hands hypodermic needles, gripped like daggers. These men were night doctors, also called needlemen. Here now was Gordon, facing off with whispered rumors made real, but the conspiracy was no theory. Gordon scrutinized the masked men and their hypodermic weapons. He wasn't sizing them up. He was just aware of a suspected victim of one of their attacks: his mother, Althea Goodspeed, injected with hex and plagued until death. His father said it was a warning to stay away from the second gateway rites ritual. Maximilian disclosed this to his son the morning after Gordon confessed to have seen his mother's specter. All Althea's death provided was a strengthening in his family's resolve, divulged Maximilian to Gordon. And now, his mother's possible murderer may have been among the lot. His eyes scanned and scowled upon each needleman. Their dress was the same, but they were not the same man hidden under masks and medical garb. He'd have to hurt them all equally just to be sure, and to send his own message.

They did not move, awaiting orders from the man with the thick beard who was clearly the leader of this pack of wolves. He addressed Gordon. "Don't be alarmed, boy," he said in a gravelly voice. "I just want to talk. The name's Willie." Gordon remained still, but his posture shifted, bracing for action. "Hell," Willie continued, "we've been waiting for you. We've been waiting for you a good while, now." His chuckle sounded like a low, maniacal grumble. "I was beginnin' to doubt Master Fallows' word. But, he insisted you'd be here on this day at this time." Willie shrugged. "Me and the boys here been comin' 'round this way for a while now, just-a waitin' for you to crop up. And here you are: the spoils of the harvest for us to reap."

Gordon flinched. His movement was subtle. His instinct reached out and touched Willie. There was something familiar about his presence, like a description of a childhood monster come to life. Willie swiped the air as if shooing off a pesky mosquito. Gordon retracted his instinct.

Willie carried on. "There's a problem, though, boy," he insisted. "You see, I respect Master Fallows' tricks to see what time might bring. But

I get a tickle when there are those rare moments he ain't got it all right. There was supposed to be a girl with you. Me and my boys were more so lookin' forward to her bein' here than we was you. We was goin' on about how much fun we'd have with her."

The phantom fabric dissolved away Gordon's clothes and wrapped around his skin. His spherical, lilac eye blazed against his forehead. Dooley balled his fists. The needlemen took a stance.

Willie grinned. He examined the phenomenon in front of him, mouth agape and drawing in an exaggerated, dramatic breath. He uttered, "My, my, boy! Take a pretty look at you. Maybe we can do without the girl." He stroked the whip at his side, and then he took it up, holding it tight for it not to unravel. Willie quoted, grin still alive on his face, *"He put on righteousness like a breastplate, and a helmet of salvation on His head; and He put on garments of vengeance for clothing and wrapped Himself with zeal as a mantle."*

Dooley waited.

Willie let the whip unravel and slap against the road. "Don't try fighting me, boy," he warned Dooley. "I got just as much spirit as you, and I got a long list of experience hurtin' your type of jungle spirit." Willie looked at Brice who was rubbing the piece of armor on his forearm. He said, eyes back on Dooley, "You ain't got a lick of knowledge on who we are or what we're capable of, boy. But we keep our studies up on you—all you Jungle Avenue folk. From Brooklyn to the world, we've been killing your kind the moment that bitch Mamma Indigo spoke of your demonic, lilac, grand wish-granting self. We know you. We know you celebrate the death of my employer's mother. Yep. We know you all inside and out, eye on you all like a magnifying glass. Sometimes we blink, and BOOM! A conjured spirit such as yourself evades our pryin' eyes. Either way, boy, you all can only guess about us." Willie chuckled again. "Master Fallows sure did believe he had you all in check. But I guess not, and I can confirm it. Far as I can see, you all been gettin' on with them rituals and old ways Master Fallows warned your folk about. And I know you all been gettin' on in them old ways, boy. Even before your little conjure trick, dressin' up in that pretty, cosmic color. I saw that you got them special eyes."

Dooley grit his teeth as he took the offensive. He focused on Willie's chest, and his body turned into a beam of light that zipped up into the glowing, lilac sphere. In the same motion, he was tossed as a single, black beam at the man taunting him and holding the whip. The thin, comet-like particle, with the glowing lilac sphere as its head, smacked into Willie's chest and knocked him to the ground. The black, cosmic strand bore through Willie as he toppled over, falling to the dusty crossroads.

An image came to Dooley as his essence slammed through the man. He saw Stanley Fallows standing over a grave marked *Cornelius "Curly"*

Burnside, holding the whip now wielded by Willie, and reciting a prayer from an aged parchment. The scene faded as the burial ground bubbled and pulsed with life. Dooley came into existence, standing over Willie, panting.

Willie was unscathed from the impact, save a burning feeling coursing through him. But the sensation didn't curb Willie from laughing, or making an attempt at a strike. He whirled his arm around, bringing up the whip, and aimed a blow at the spirit. Dooley evaded the strike as he launched an assault on the needlemen. Up, into a black beam with a lilac sphere for a head, Dooley struck. He collided into a needleman's chest, ricocheted off another's chin, and bounced into the nose of a third.

Dooley popped out of the black stream, throwing punches, tussling with a fourth needleman. He dodged a stab made at him, caught the needleman's arm with both hands, and broke the bone over his knee. A swift chop to the man's face knocked the needleman unconscious.

A blow smacked against Dooley's stomach, a jab caught his chin. The attack pushed a burning, electric charge through him. He grit his teeth and jumped back, steadying himself for a fight. Brice Cadogan was in front of him, readying another strike. Dooley burst into his lilac spirit and dived forward. Brice maneuvered away, quicker than Dooley expected, and caught the spirit by the neck. He slammed Dooley against the ground. The lilac glow, upon impact, dispersed from Dooley in a cloud of dust.

Needlemen inched in as Dooley lay on the ground, but Willie took the moment to make a second attempt to slap Dooley with his whip. Again Dooley's actions were too quick. He slipped into a beam, his essence shooting up into his spherical eye and charging Brice. Willie's whip smacked the road, billowing dust. Dooley's black, comet-like beam crashed through Brice, pushing the Englishman to the ground.

Another scene flashed in front of Dooley's eyes. In it, an elderly man resembling an old Brice Cadogan was sitting inside a posh Manhattan hotel suite. Further inspection noted that it was indeed Brice Cadogan, aged in proper time. Sitting opposite him, relaxed on a sofa, was a voluptuous red-haired woman wearing an emerald gown. Sarinda Fallows, villainy wrapped up in devilishly alluring beauty. Old Man Brice was giving her every last bit of attention his eyes could afford, almost forgetting the piece of armor in his hand. He said to Sarinda, speaking in a humble voice, *"It's old, but there's something in it. A charm, an enchantment of sorts, Miss Fallows,"* he explained. He looked up and told Sarinda, *"I've heard so much about you, Miss Fallows."*

"As I have you, Mister Cadogan," Sarinda responded, a charming and seductive smile running across her face. *"Though, it took a lot to pry information about you from little, ol' Ethan. And just the same, that damned Curly kept information of a good soldier like you out of my reach. I will talk to him about that, I*

will—best believe. He's always had a little jealous streak in him; worried someone else would be my number two. There's only been a small mention or two from either of them boys." She chuckled, and Brice sighed like a schoolboy meeting his crush. *"But, we're here now, aren't we, Mister Cadogan. Tell me about this piece you've brought me. It has such an allure. I can feel its pull."*

Brice perked up. *"Oh, yes, Miss Fallows. Indeed."* He presented the object. *"It's from a Templar who was killed by his own after they discovered his armor was blessed by a Blackamoor conjuror."* Brice hung his head, taking a moment to gather confidence before he asked, *"Good lady, Miss Fallows, I ask of you to give me a blessing with your tricks like you did Ethan. I will serve your interests overseas."*

Sarinda grinned. Devious. *"I can't have an old fool at my command, Mister Cadogan,"* she said in such a charming tone that it made Brice forget the sentiment's offensive facet. Instead, he only smiled wider to hear Sarinda speak. *"But with this new veil I've acquired, I can easily conjure a trick to restore a little youth to you. Not too much youth, now. Not every man's prime is in his twenties, or even in his thirties. No. I want something I can use. A mature man I can taste."*

Brice grinned. Devious.

The scene blew away in a cloud of smoke, and through the cloud came a clinched fist. Dooley dodged, coming back into awareness. Brice lost balance, but gained his footing long enough to swing the same armored arm into Dooley's back. The electric charge stunned the cosmic-clad spirit, allowing Brice to wrap his arms around him. A needleman charged, hypodermic weapon gripped sideways like a shank. Dooley tossed Brice over his shoulders, the Englishman's legs cracked against the needleman's face, knocking him unconscious.

More needlemen advanced. Dooley zipped away as a comet, plowing into and ricocheting off four of them. He formed solid again and wrestled with two more needlemen, slapping their needles away as they moved in to strike. Dooley swept one off his feet, turned, and slammed his fist into the next, knocking the needleman out.

Dooley's instinct scratched the back of his neck! He turned his body around and saw Brice rushing at him. He stepped aside, grabbed Brice's collar, and tossed him again to the dusty road. Brice tumbled, but he managed to use his arms to stabilize his movement, and jump up onto his feet.

Dooley braced for a strike, but Brice stayed his attack. Dooley's instinct reached out, alerting him. He turned. Willie was in mid-swing with his whip, too quick for Dooley to move. The thick and tight, hexed-laced leather weapon slapped across Dooley's chest, and the cosmic spirit screamed loud enough to shake the sky!

"I gotchu," growled Willie. "I gotchu, you filthy, jungle spirit."

Dooley dropped to his knees.

Willie whipped him again, and Dooley hollered, head back and voice terrorizing the sky.

"That's right," Willie grinned. "You scream when I hurt you, boy. I like that. Always have." He whipped Dooley again and again, and Dooley smacked the ground, lifeless. Willie cracked his whip against Dooley's back manifold, until the cosmic fabric ripped away and Gordon's flesh was exposed. Willie continued whipping Gordon, scratching an assortment of deep, bloody, serpentine scars into his back. Gordon's cosmic fabric retreated into his flesh like a limping, wounded animal.

Willie stepped back to admire his work. He waved Brice and the needlemen to stand down. "Look at this," he said to no one in particular. "The naked flesh of a spirit is so pretty. It's sensual." He looked up at Brice and the needlemen. "Boy or girl, a naked jungle spirit, you could just kiss it, lay with it." Willie caught his breath, watching Gordon struggle to straighten his arms and crawl on the dusty road. "Hurting one is better than any ball you can attend. It's better than making love to anyone you've ever fancied." The faint image of Gordon's earthly clothes covered the young man. Willie whipped Gordon again, and the earthly clothes faded, leaving Gordon bare. "Look here! Look here!" shouted Willie. And then he quoted, *"So justice is driven back, and righteousness stands at a distance; truth has stumbled in the streets, and honesty cannot enter."* He took two steps and made a swift kick to Gordon's ribs. *"Truth is nowhere to be found, and whoever shuns my presence becomes a prey."* Willie knelt down and grabbed Gordon's wooly hair. "Where is that pretty spirit Master Fallows said you fly with?" He leaned close to Gordon's ear and whispered, "The love I've shown you will not compare to the love I show her; and I'm not even done loving you yet, boy." Willie shoved Gordon's head away. He stood and whipped Gordon hard!

Gordon aimed his head to heaven and shouted an electric cry!

His instinct escaped and raced north, leaving light and sound behind. It arced across the sky and outraced nature's wind. Its speed disappeared from time, coming into existence inside a room in a house in Mount Vernon, New York. There it pierced Fey Forrester's forehead as she studied a history book upstairs in her bedroom. She flinched as the instinct presented itself to her. It played in rapid succession the images of Gordon's reading, trek into Jackson Fable's house, and his current foray with Willie, Brice, and the needlemen. She dropped her highlighter and turned her head to the window. She stood and gasped, *"Gordon-baby!"*

The cosmic fabric poured from her flesh at the speed of thought. She conjured her yumboes from her spine and commanded, "To the Avenue. Alert the Elders. Em, to Water Bug Hollow. Find Benny and call him back through that house."

She popped from her room onto her grandmother's roof. She burst into a cobalt-blue spirit and soared up into the air, arcing across the sky and flying south at a blinding speed. Her yumboes, lower in altitude, streaked toward Fable Avenue.

Fey's racing spirit appeared as a cobalt-blue vein across the sky, no care if she was seen by anyone below. She pushed her spirit's speed. Gordon's instinct continued playing images for Fey. Her eyes were closed to watch them. She used her instinct to guide her to Gordon's location. Behind her eyes, she saw through Gordon's sight. Willie was over him, whipping and drawing excitement from Gordon's screams. She saw her *Gordon-baby* catch a glimpse of a cobalt-blue trail soaring up and over the horizon as sight and time caught up with one another.

Fey's radiant spirit landed hard in the middle of a gathered party of needlemen, the ground rumbling on impact. The cobalt-blue flame whisked from her, producing a strong, whipping wind. The needlemen braced against the gale, and as the fierce wind died, they encircled the newly arrived spirit. They closed in on her. Fey moved swiftly into an assault, punching and jabbing two needlemen nearing her. She conjured another heavy force that pushed away the remaining needlemen around her.

Fey turned and spied Willie.

His grin melted into an expression of awe. His eyes traced every inch of her body, up and down and around. He commented, words slowed by his admiration of Fey. "The love I'm going to show you, little girl." He gripped his whip and sneered, "I'm gonna strip your jungle spirit, and after I whip you into defeat, I'm going to hold you down and worship you."

A bullet whizzed by Willie's head, cutting his ear. He turned and saw Wilson coming from Jackson Fable's house firing at him. Maman Anansi and Papa Solomon accompanied the Fable Avenue rogue. Maman Anansi, dress flowing, bodice strapped with conjured, pale-purple throwing knives tucked into small pockets lining the garment. She grabbed a few of her weapons and tossed them with lethal accuracy. She struck four needlemen in the chest. A small burst of spirit exploded on impact, lifting the needlemen and casting them a great distance.

Papa Solomon, equipped with his father's horn, played several hard notes that spat heavy exertions strong enough to turn two of the parked cars over. Their roofs collapsed into their cabins, glass shattered, and Papa Solomon blew an extra note to light the vehicles ablaze.

Willie grimaced, spitting a curse. He took out his gun and fired shots at the house, scattering Papa Solomon, Maman Anansi, and Wilson. As they separated, ducking away from Willie's gunfire, Fey's yumboes zipped through the open door of Jackson Fable's house. Their bodies turned to streams of light, and they struck Willie, slapping him with the irritation of bee stings. He hollered and backed away to his car, slipping inside and shutting the door.

Brice followed Willie, commanding the needlemen to rush the Fable Avenue conjurors. Fey tackled him as he hurried back to the car. The Englishman fought back, grabbing Fey by the throat with his armored arm. He slammed her against the ground, jumped to his feet, balled his fist hard, and threw it into Fey's cheek.

Gordon's blurry vision witnessed the tussle. He screamed, and though wounded, his spirit's instinct took over. The torn, cosmic fabric folded over him, and he shot forward. His dull, comet-shaped spirit punched through Brice's body, hard and painful. A lilac glow chomped at Brice's body, forcing the Englishman to the ground. Gordon popped out of the comet shape and slid naked against the ground.

Brice lay motionless. A few, wheezing breaths proved his body kicked with life. Willie lowered his window and fired to cover Brice as the Englishman staggered toward the car, crawling, digging his fingers into the dusty road. Fey grabbed Gordon's naked body and lifted him into her arms. Gordon's earthly garments folded over him as Fey ducked behind an overturned car. She heard Papa Solomon play otherworldly notes from his horn, and the ground started rumbling.

Willie sped away with Brice back in the passenger seat.

Fey looked up. There came a large, destructive vortex of violent, rotating wind ready to cleanse the crossroads. Maman Anansi hollered for her. With Gordon's unconscious body cradled close to her, she ran toward Jackson Fable's porch. Her yumboes dived into her back and were again a part of her tattoos. Retreating needlemen ran by her, all trying to fit into the remaining cars. Fey and the Elders and Wilson ran through the door. The house's image faded from the lot, and the storm swept the crossroads clean of all its stains. Only Willie's car and the gas station escaped nature's otherworldly and wrathful twist.

Fey passed through Jackson Fable's homestead with long, quick strides. Wilson and the Elders were behind her, keeping up. She exited through the kitchen, coming out onto the brownstone steps of Fable Avenue.

Benny met her at the bottom of the stairs.

"Is he okay?" he asked Fey, The Star card in his grip.

"Meet me at his house, Benny," Fey said, words blended together.

She popped away, appearing in Gordon's basement seconds later. The lights came on, and Fey ordered, "Spook, open the chamber. Gordon's hurt."

The *Nigrum Nigrius Nigro* rose, and its black mirror stirred with ancient symbols. The chamber slid open, and Fey placed Gordon's body inside. She backed away as the chamber closed.

"Mister Goodspeed. Miss Althea! Cedron!" Fey called from the basement.

"Fey?" Maximilian yelled in response. "Fey, is that you?"

The chamber hummed. Its symbols bright with white-hot light.

Fey's mask retracted as Maximilian rushed into the basement, Althea gliding down behind him. Fey looked at them, mouth covered, and eyes watered. Maximilian walked up beside her.

"Fey…?" he asked, worry in his voice and expression.

A downcast emotion drenched Althea's spirit. She shuddered, gasping as she drifted closer to the chamber. "My baby!" she hollered. *"My baby!"*

Fey stared at the chamber, expression quivering with sadness and coated with streaming tears. Maximilian inquired about what had transpired, but Fey couldn't answer. She only cried harder, falling into Maximilian's arms, choking on her tears.

Maximilian held Fey tight. He looked at his wife, hoping her spirit had an answer. She turned to him and expressed, "He's hurt, Max. They hurt my baby boy."

Maximilian looked at the chamber. He listened to its hum and watched the light flickering from it. "He'll be fine, Althea-baby. That bracket will work its incant."

Fey's eyes opened, looking past the blur of tears. She spotted the black mirror attached to the *Nigrum Nigrius Nigro.* Ancient script was scrawled across it. She could read it, and it said: *Seven missing. Incomplete. Scars remain.*

Fey closed her eyes and continued crying.

Benny stood at the top of the stairs with Cedron next to him. Gordon's brother shook his head in frustration. He rolled back and away from the basement, pushing hard. Benny followed him.

Far away from Fable Avenue, at a gas station a few miles away from the crossroads, Willie made a call on a public phone. He uttered a trick that allowed him to bypass dropping coinage to place the call. He dialed the number of a house in Long Island, New York, and he leaned against the station watching Brice squirm in the passenger's seat of his car. The other line rang twice and then someone picked up.

"Willie?" Stanley Fallows' voice came through.

"Uh, yes Master Fallows," Willie responded, fumbling over his words and turning away from his car.

"Don't worry, Willie. The missus and I saw everything."

"I'm sorry, Master Fallows."

"It's okay, Willie," Stanley assured. "It's not exactly as I believed things would happen, but it served its purpose. Relax."

"If it's any incentive, Master Fallows, I believe I have some of the boy's blood and fabric on my whip." But Stanley didn't respond with excitement, as the brutish overseer would've liked.

"Get on a plane," Stanley instructed him. "You and Brice. We'll see what we can salvage from the scrimmage."

"We need any doctors, Master Fallows?"

"No, Willie. We got boys up here. Come on up. Waste no time. How's Brice?"

Willie looked at Brice shivering with pain inside the car. "Nothing a quick trick can't fix, I believe."

"Okay. Let him rest for a day, then come up. I'll put your tickets through and give you a call when they're ready."

"Yes, Master Fallows."

"You did good, Willie. You did. Again, it wasn't how I believed this would transpire, but it's all the same. And, yes, for the record, I would've appreciated if both spirits had been whipped properly, but we got him. That's fine, for now. We'll have a talk with Miss Forrester when the moment comes." He paused for a beat. "Let me ask, Willie. Was she beautiful? Her spirit."

Willie closed his eyes, recalling Fey Forrester's cosmic-clothed physique. He breathed in through his nose and smiled. "Oh, Master Fallows, she was magnificent. I tell you that I saw *among the captives a beautiful woman, and hast a desire unto her, that thou wouldest have her to* my *wife.*"

"Good," Stanley replied. "Good, and goodbye, Willie. I'll see you in a day or two."

"Yes, Master Fallows. Goodbye, and thank you."

Stanley was gone. Willie put the phone back on the receiver and ambled back to his car. He slid inside and inspected Brice. "We're gonna get you rest, Englishman. Master Fallows thinks we did well enough. He's given us some rest before going up. My tricks ain't strong, but they should ease some of that sufferin'."

Willie started the car. Brice continued writhing in agony.

"That jungle spirit hit you hard with that last one," Willie commented as he put the car in reverse and maneuvered out from where he'd parked. He shifted into drive and pulled away from the gas station.

The day was a little more than half over.

Undead, thought Gordon. *That's what he was. Willie was a lich. Willie the Lich.*

He shivered, eyes looking straight ahead at his chamber but seeing a dream. He was wrapped tight in a blanket, sitting in his basement on the mystically refurbished plush chair. Benny was seated next to him in a chair from the kitchen. Althea Goodspeed's specter glimmered near her son, watching with anxious, hopeful eyes.

None of this existed to Gordon. Not Benny. Not his mother. Not the chamber, or the chair he sat in, or anything in the basement's surroundings. Gordon was standing and at the crossroads. He was swathed in his cosmic suit that was ripped and tattered everywhere but his mask. He watched with a curious glimmer Brice Cadogan crawling toward him. Gordon's head was tilted downward, and his spherical, lilac eye glowed with a muted shine. Brice's attire was just as ragged, and he was missing a shoe.

There was an image of Fey's spirit flying toward an island in the Caribbean. She landed. People rejoiced, but there was news she had to deliver to them.

The crossroads. Brice edged closer to Gordon, his body scraping against the dusty intersection. Gordon observed the small, slithers of blood on Brice's arm through the Englishman's torn sleeves. Reaching Gordon, Brice flopped over on his back, panting.

"So there you are again," Gordon said down to Brice. *"I'm glad to see you back. I thought you were gone forever."*

"Me too," responded Brice exhausted but through a volley of laughter. He coughed and told Gordon, *"We'll have to celebrate this."*

"But how?" Gordon asked.

Brice's body stiffened, and then it jumped up to stand straight. The movement was as if a fall caught on film had been reversed. The motion was awkward and silly looking to Gordon. Brice was up in a moment, standing on his feet. Then his body loosened, and he crumpled to one knee, still panting. Brice looked up at Gordon and said, *"You know who Stanley Fallows is, Mister Goodspeed."* It was a statement, but Gordon heard it as a question. *"Perhaps I should strap you to a chair and quote Blake in your ear behind a mask as clear as the one Stanley Fallows wears."*

"I thought we were speaking in Becketts," Gordon replied.

Brice started laughing, and his laughter caused him to cough and wince in pain. He put his arm around his stomach. *"This hurts. Oh, God, it hurts."* Blood spurt from his nose, and then it dripped with a slow, simple ease like water at the end of a melting icicle. *"But it's a lot easier when I'm asleep and dreaming, Mister Goodspeed."* He looked up at Gordon and said with a smile, *"We're in this together."*

Gordon blinked. There was his chamber in front of him. He was in the chair, a blanket around him. The specter of his mother stood near him shimmering. His childhood friend Benny was seated in a chair next to him. Gordon took a deep breath. His body jumped as he came from the dream. He oriented himself.

"It was Brice again," he said to his mother and Benny.

"You keep mumbling about that Willie guy," Benny responded.

"I know what I keep doing…" Gordon retorted in a sharp tongue. He exhaled, closing his eyes. "Sorry, Benny," he apologized. "Sorry. I just feel…" An acute sting burned over Gordon's back. He gritted his teeth to ease the pain, and it subsided after a moment. He again took deep breaths.

Althea stepped toward her son and knelt down. She asked, "Are you okay, my little man? How do you feel?" Another sharp pain crawled up Gordon's back, and he squirmed in the chair, rubbing his shoulders deep into the upholstery. Althea reached her hand out to Gordon, the glow of her haunt brushed against his cheek. The pain writhing up Gordon's back increased. Althea moved her hand away, and the pain in Gordon subsided.

Gordon started sweating as he wheezed heavy breaths.

Althea stood, keeping her desperate eyes on her youngest son.

"I'm okay…" Gordon assured in a weak breath. "Can I speak to Benny alone?"

Althea covered her mouth. Shaking her head, she started weeping. Gordon didn't want to see her cry. Her spirit had been so happy, and now he collected and carried the burden for bringing her pain once again. Before he could console her, she uttered, "Fey is here," and then her spirit faded away. Benny moved his chair closer to Gordon. He watched his friend shake off the chills and pain running through him.

Gordon turned his head, which was leaned back against the chair, toward Benny. "Stop, okay? I can feel it."

"Stop what?"

"Beating y'self up for not being there," Gordon clarified, trying to control his heavy breathing, which in turn was a reflex to the pain grappling his body once again. "Just act like you goin' to Canarsie on this one."

Benny was confused. "What?"

Gordon grinned through his pain. He asked Benny, "How do you get to Canarsie, man? What train you get on?"

Benny provided a quick answer. "You gotta take the—" and before he could finish, he understood. He swallowed and rolled his eyes. A smile came to him, figuring out Gordon's joke. Then he finished his answer with a tone reflecting a different meaning altogether, "You gotta take the L."

"Right…" Gordon said, straightening his expression. He said in a stern voice, "This loss is a minor setback. That was just a battle, not the war. Y' conjure gonna come in time, Benny. You'll have plenty of chances to swoop down and rescue me, or back me up."

Benny stayed silent, focused on a thought.

Gordon's instinct intercepted Benny's thinking. *"Hey!"* Gordon yelled, causing Benny to flinch. He moved his head closer to Benny. "Don't think that, man. There *will* be another chance." The pain came again, rough and burning.

First Benny scowled at the scolding. Then he relaxed. He set his mouth in motion to apologize to Gordon, rising a little off his seat, when he heard Fey call from upstairs, "Benny!" Her feet clanked against the creaking staircase as she made her way into the basement. "I'm back. I got him, little soldier."

Gordon and Benny stared at one another. Benny broke the silence. "Another chance?" he said.

Gordon nodded his head and managed a smile. "This ain't your fault in no way, sun," Gordon assured, struggling through pain beginning to throb and smolder on his back. "You was too busy partyin' in the bayou…" he chuckled, and it turned into a cough.

Benny stood, telling Gordon, "Ain't no parties down in Water Bug Hollow. Not for…our people, them regular folk… Its rich history is buried under its present poverty." Fey walked up next to Benny. He said to her, "We're talking about Water Bug Hollow, sista."

Fey acknowledged with a nod.

Benny continued, "But there's magic there, regardless of how rundown it is."

Gordon lifted an eyebrow. He looked up at Benny, made a face and proposed, "So…you're sayin' despite the lack of knowledge concerning its own magic, how something—perhaps a hex, or a system—has it bound against itself. You're saying, the magic is still there, correct? That's what I hear, no?"

Benny didn't know whether to smirk or scowl. His expression was somewhere between both, and he added a roll of the eyes for good measure. "Yeah…" he admitted to Gordon. "Them regular folk, our people, still got magic beneath their feet; at their…soles."

"Okay…I'm just checkin' to see if you throwin' the right signals for what you pitchin'."

Fey looked back and forth between Benny and Gordon. "Am I missing something…?"

Benny answered only by going back to the subject of Water Bug Hollow. "Somethin' got that place's spirit locked up. Like you said, Gordon, a hex, a system." He told Fey, "Maman Anansi goes on about how that place got away from us."

"That war was a generation or so ago," added Gordon. "And Papa Solomon and Madame Jeliya talk up the Hollow's glory days so much to cover up the loss, that all we can see is that," Gordon remarked. "Reality is a sonava bitch, I tell you."

"Maybe with this renewed spirit we possess, maybe we can get it back," suggested Fey.

"It looks bad, sister," Benny countered, injecting the sentiment of reality that was now Water Bug Hollow. "That's a helluva responsibility we'd be takin' on."

"Well, Gaston's house leads there for a reason. But until then…" Fey touched Benny's arm and turned her head to him. Gordon spied the gentle gesture and his eyes made a subtle bend. The pain coating his back throbbed with a dull hum, but he was distracted by the sudden pang of resentment stimulated by Fey's fingertips against Benny's arm. Gordon swallowed the thought. She was only getting Benny's attention, he told himself. But her touch on him was so soft and so sincere, he also considered. He flushed his thoughts again, and a stinging wave of discomfort washed on the shores of his back. "Neyeli's looking for you, sweetie—" Gordon caught himself from flashing a grimace inspired by Fey's choice of reference for Benny. "—go see her. She wants to know you're okay."

"Yeah," growled Gordon. "Go to *your* girl." Then he tried to hide the keen snap in his voice by stating in a well-meaning tone, "So she can stop worrying about you, or me. Tell her I'm doing fine."

"Will do," said Benny to both of them. He put a hand on Fey's shoulder, and Gordon looked away, an angry burn stirring in his stomach. "Take care of him, Fey."

"I will, brother," Fey replied. "I have something brewing upstairs for him."

Benny gestured toward Gordon, and he told his friend he would return soon. He left the basement thereafter. Fey walked in front of Gordon and knelt down. "How you doing, Gordon-baby?" she asked. Her voice rang with such sweet music that it hushed the agony pricking at Gordon's body and cooled the sweat on his forehead.

Gordon's emotions didn't ebb. He shut his eyes and asked in a sharp voice, "Where have you been?"

Fey quivered with surprise. Her instinct tugged at her, reeling in an emotion of disgust to match the sharp tone in Gordon's voice. But she inhaled the moment and buried it down deep. She instead caressed Gordon's cheek rather than follow her initial response to slap him there. Gordon quivered with her soft touch on his skin, almost as if he was trying to duck away from her. Fey continued rubbing until his trembling calmed. "Oh, Gordon-baby, I didn't abandon you," it took much to say the words. Fey paused for a moment. Her instinct felt a cold presence. It resonated from the scars on Gordon's back. More than tattered and opened flesh was in his wounds. She could feel the residual of the hex from Willie's whip. Willie the Lich, as Gordon mumbled in his sleep. "I swear," continued Fey, using the soft tone in her voice to fight against whatever was influencing Gordon's emotions. "I went to Haiti," Fey explained. "My grandmother told me of a family there with remedies that might ease your pain. I'm brewing a tea I got you."

"They have any answers?"

"Who?"

"The family in Haiti?" Gordon replied with force. He took another deep breath and tried to relax. "Sorry, Fey-baby." He returned to the matter at hand. "I…I figured you explained my condition," he said to her. "And if they gave you a remedy, they had a suggestion on what's happening to me."

"It's okay," she said, keeping her soft, understanding tone. She caressed his face, making a few warm strokes, and then she put both her hands on his legs for balance as she knelt. "I told them your spirit suffered a great attack, and the attack came from a cursed, wicked haunt. They gave me something for you to drink. It'll calm your pain, but it won't heal you."

Gordon nodded.

Fey rubbed his legs. "You still have scars on your back, Gordon-baby," she told him, voice now filled with sympathy.

"Oh, I know that," he chuckled and then winced as the pain reminded him too.

Fey described, "Maman Anansi inspected your wounds." A warm smile appeared on her face. Reminiscence struck her eyes. "You should have seen her conjure, Gordon. It was a spectacular show. She conjured throwing knives laced with spirit." Fey shook her head, smile dampening, and her eyes peppered with a creeping sadness. "Where was all this during the triangle trade?" Then she shook the notion aside. "Some of us did have a spark of conjure and ritual in those days…" She guided her words back to her original thought. "Maman Anansi inspected your back while you slept in your chamber. Spook's black mirror showed you inside. Maman Anansi was able to zoom in on your scars. Your chamber plucked out thin pieces of that man's whip for her. She and her husband ran rituals on it. They found words inscribed on the fibers. A spell of sorts, they say. Mister Dumas and another Fable Avenue resident—I don't remember his name, a scholar, but not Professor Khepri. Anyway, he said the whip had paper infused into it, journal entries from old slave owners. That man with the whip is the sum of our fears, I take it."

"Willie," Gordon named. "The man with the whip was named Willie."

"Yes," Fey acknowledged. "You said his name like a title, over and over. Willie the Lich." Fey presented what her instinct had told her. "His whip left more than physical scars, Gordon-baby. My instinct can feel the trick lacing your wounds, and it's something fierce. The same types of scars you have were found on my mother's back when she took her own life, the same hex and all. We must be cautious."

Gordon winced as pain breathed through his body. He twisted, again burrowing into the chair. Fey continued rubbing his legs. Her touch settled all the erratic emotions and pain that possessed Gordon, but there still remained a jitter in him. He shivered. *"Speech made flesh,"* Gordon defined Willie, eyes bubbling bright with lilac light. *"A concept on two legs. He's the torment of history, standing upright but uncivilized."* Fey listened. Gordon was talking, but not to her. He was rambling. She saw his eyes become blank, aimed forward.

"Gordon," she called him in a gentle voice. "Gordon-baby," she said touching his face. She looked in the direction Gordon's eyes stared in. She whispered into his ear, "What do you see, Gordon-baby?" Gordon didn't answer. He continued staring. "Do you feel anything? Can you feel the presence of the men that did this to you? Look past them. They are tools, nothing more. They are not our suffering's cause. Look to their master? Can you feel Stanley's presence? Can you pinpoint where he is? I swear, Gordon-baby, if you concentrate hard enough and touch his presence to know his whereabouts, I will turn to spirit and exact revenge for you…for what that bastard has done to us all…"

Gordon flinched, looking at Fey with a perplexed expression. He wasn't aware of her words, but there was a feeling. Fey rubbed his hand and looked away.

Althea materialized beside Fey. "His remedy is ready, sister," she informed her. She looked at her son again, a spark of confidence in her eyes. Althea faded as Fey stood up straight.

"I'll be back, Gordon-baby," Fey assured, turning and leaving the basement.

"Okay…" acknowledged Gordon.

He was alone. His eyes closed, weighing heavy with fatigue. The scene of blackness faded fast, and Gordon was once again standing at the crossroads. His cosmic fabric adorned him, tattered and stringy. His mask was complete, and he stared down at Brice Cadogan who was on his back, laughing off an electric pain that ran through his body. Gordon had his own pain to feel. It was agonizing, burning his back as if the sun was taking a bite out of him. But Gordon could control the pain if he concentrated. He couldn't dampen it, but he could move the pain around. With great focus, he shuffled the sharp, unpleasant discomfort pulsating on his back and gathered it into the palms of his hands.

Brice's laughter amplified. *"Can't take it, can you?"* he yelled up at Gordon. *"You want to put it all in me, do you? Do you wish to choke me with your pain? Where's your spirit, young man?"*

Gordon's palms glowed lilac. The color darkened to purple with a faint fluorescent white shimmer glimmering at the center of the glow of his palms.

"Come on!" Brice yelled. *"Choke me, you black, jungle spirit! Send me to hell, is what you want to do! Go on! Have at it! Come along, then!"*

"Gordon…" he heard Fey calling him, voice echoing like a passing, light breeze. "Gordon," she called again.

He blinked. The crossroads disappeared. There was his basement, and more importantly, there was Fey. She was kneeling down and presenting a cup of tea to him.

"Take a sip, Gordon-baby," she enjoined, bobbing the cup in front of him. "I don't mean to be condescending, Gordon-baby, but can you hold it?"

"I can," he said wiggling his way out of the cocoon that was his blanket. He reached for the cup, taking it into his trembling hands, trying to keep them steady as he brought it to his lips. He stared at the cup for a moment, staying the draw toward his mouth. Smoke rose from the tea's surface, the heat throbbed against his hands and warmed them. He focused on the heat resonating from the cup, its soothing feel in his palm. His hands ceased to shake, and he raised the cup to his open mouth and drank.

Gordon's pain hurried away. The tea also warmed his body. He exhaled relief, taking a few more sips. Gordon could relax. He slumped into his chair, body loose and at ease. "Thank you, Fey-baby…" he said like an apology.

"Yeah…" Fey replied. She kissed his cheek.

Fey's mechanical response turned the warmth inside Gordon into a slow burn. He ignored the impulse to address Fey's drop in sentiment toward him, and his instinct couldn't penetrate her thoughts that were guarded by her strong spirit. He asked instead, "How's Lady Arachne? I know Benny feels guilty, but she gave the order to go there."

Fey sat in the chair Benny earlier occupied. "She's fine. As if nothing happened. She's consulting her cards and working with Madame Jeliya. The two of them are in rare agreement, saying that this is all part of the greater story to procure the grand wish and conjure. She's very interested in Water Bug Hollow and the crossroads."

"She knows my fate from these scars?"

"Hasn't said," expressed Fey wrapping her arms around herself as if cold. Gordon wanted to ask if Fey was okay with all that was going on with him, but he decided against it. He continued drinking the tea she prepared for him. "Since the tea has you feeling better, do your ritual at your altar. Get some proper sleep without any bad dreams."

"I feel relaxed, but not tired," Gordon responded before he took a long sip of the tea.

Fey lifted off the chair a bit and leaned forward. She took the cup from Gordon's hands. "Let's not overdo it, Gordon-baby," she told him. "This ain't regular tea."

"These ain't regular scars," he replied in a matter-of-fact tone.

"That's a good point, Gordon-baby," Fey noted, but she didn't return the cup. She set it down and asked, "How bright can your eyes glow?" Gordon looked at her, a question in his eyes. Fey answered, "I want you to focus on our tale, *In Thirteen Pieces*. Let's add that to your ritual."

Gordon tightened, bracing as if an outpouring of pain was ready to spill on him. He said to Fey, "Conjuring my spirit hurts." He took a breath and then asked her. "How do my eyes look?" He saw Fey smile at him, and that helped as much as the Haitian tea.

"They haven't lost their glow," she commented. She then assured, "If anything happens, Gordon-baby, we'll retract our glow and we'll eliminate the bedtime story before the ritual." She put a gentle hand on his shoulder. "But I want to start from the beginning. Is that okay? I want to see it all over again."

A fiery impatience twisted up Gordon's spine like an instinct. He gritted his teeth and held back the scowl trying to colonize his expression. A tingle of pain pricked the scars on his back, but the Haitian remedy kicked in and cooled the irritation. Gordon took a breath, closing his eyes. Opening them, he pushed aside the impatience and said to Fey, "Okay, Fey-baby…"

Fey was compelled to inquire, "Gordon, what's wrong?"

"My first instinct to everything is to get angry," answered Gordon, again fighting against a sudden, rising exasperation. "I'm exhausted, but can't sleep. When I do close my eyes and drift away, I'm back at the crossroads…struggling." A few beads of sweat appeared on Gordon's forehead as he spoke. Fey wiped them away with a rag that had been lying near Gordon's chair.

"That's why I want to start over, Gordon-baby," she told him. "I want you to see your poetic complement. In the beginning he was—" and Fey was careful when she chose her next word, "—fragile."

But it didn't get by Gordon. "Weak…"

"Delicate," Fey corrected with force in her voice, though she never lost her gentle sincerity. "But he gained his strength. And there I am—my counterpart in this mythology, broken. But you're there for her. For me," she stressed.

Gordon nodded, putting his eyes on *The Written* that was lying on his chamber. A vibrant, lilac light bubbled from his eyes, and there was little pain produced from the globule of spirit pouring out. Fey turned to *The Written*, and her spirit gushed from her eyes in a cobalt-blue brilliance. The aged tome jumped into the air and flipped to the first page of the poetic piece *In Thirteen Pieces*. Strands of light undulated from Gordon and Fey's eyes. They touched the open pages of the book and caressed the ancient script scribbled onto the page. White light dispersed the basement's scenery, and the colorful narrative played into existence not from where it had left off, but from its beginning.

Three armies marched the African sands, representatives of twenty-four warring states that had declared peace, and the last of a failed generation. There was Motherland waiting, sitting on a grand throne. She was disappointed, and she scolded the men and women of the armies on approach, even after they expressed their wrong doings. But sealed was their fate, scripted in the stars above. And generation after failed generation led to disintegration and enslavement by a collective unalike in nature. Pale shadows.

Culture existed in an anorexic condition, and freedom was an illusion. Around the original people of the Earth there was a cage, built long and wide, with all the façades of a city skyline. Thirteen towers were erected far away, mobile and living off the spirit of a broken covenant to Motherland. And broken generation after broken generation there scripted by the stars was to come a feeble hero.

Gordon Goodspeed watched his wiry, lurching counterpart struggle to maintain balance with a heavy sword while making as if he was the grand hero to save the land. *Fake it until you make it, kid,* thought Gordon. Zin Kibaru, his slender doppelganger, capered about the city possessed with a Don Quixote spirit. He wandered with determined adventure in his eyes, hopes high to befriend an ally and follow a childhood mythology to find the woman of his heart. She would be to him a queen to serve, as he would be to her a knight at her command. What he found in the city was a dense population of broken spirits, abusive or absent parents, and torn children aspiring to be the same or competing to outdo the uselessness of the generation before them. Mother Nothings. Father Zeroes.

A small pain nibbled at Gordon's back, and his frustration for the events of the story rose. But there was not enough pain to break his concentration. He continued watching and saw Zin Kibaru stumble across a female spirit confined to a throne with wheels. A character composed by Fey Forrester, steering the story toward its purpose. The anger that echoed from the ghostly voice of this shy fire named Sirene could quake and open the earth. And she had a task for Kibaru. She wanted her Mother Nothing and Father Zero dead, and Zin Kibaru obliged her order, heavy sword in hand.

Kibaru lost the fight, his inexperience more considerable than his focused determination, which was coupled with great naïveté. But Sirene's Mother Nothing and Father Zero showed mercy, and expressed the depth and brutality to which their mercy could extend. Sirene was dissected from spirit, her somatic body crippled to keep her safe. The pieces of her soul and body were buried, but the caged city's governor found them to help fuel the gigantic, constructed monstrosities called the Towers. Kibaru now had his true task, and with a newly forged weapon, a black sun spear, he returned to the caged city to gaze on its population with new eyes. He spied his parents too.

Kibaru returned to Sirene. She knew his task was incomplete, but he was different to her. He had new strength and a new weapon forged for him. His scrawny frame no longer walked with a bunglesome gait. He was renewed as an agile champion. Kibaru detailed to Sirene his new undertaking, the slaying of thirteen giants, and Sirene conducted a ritual to ask the stars to guide him to allies. In the morning, Kibaru, anointed as a true warrior, made voyage to an elderly woman named Mama Gran and her husband, an aged captain acting out glory days just as old. Kibaru convinced them to offer service, though the captain demanded more persuading than Mama Gran. Coupled with them, Kibaru entered the caged city, and assisted by Mama Gran's magic, plucked the shaded souls from the dregs of the street. A shaded army was created. Among their ranks, three of Kibaru's childhood friends now cleansed of their inebriated ways.

Then across a grand sea they sailed to a massive land where thirteen giants roamed. Dominated by armies of soldiers called devil swine and savage beasts called 'wulvz', Kibaru and the shaded army carved a path through the landmass and eventually confronted one of the four largest towers. The towering behemoth called three larger titans to battle. Inside these four constructs were held the breaths of Sirene, Motherland's covenant in the flesh. In the field of battle, the giants succumbed to the ants. Kibaru's nimble moves, his pounce, and his spear fell one after the other, and the land trembled when the colossi fell. Sirene's four breaths fled the giants' bodies, rushed to her, and filled her with air she had not tasted in ages. She spoke with authority to all of her enemies, shouting for them to cower before her shaded army, and she declared that all would be free when her thirteen pieces were restored to her.

There was more to the story, but the narrative's scenery gave way to the basement. The tendrils of light protruding from Fey and Gordon's eyes retracted. Fey's eyes returned to brown. Gordon's eyes faded to a dull lilac shimmer. The aged tome continued floating in place.

Fey asked Gordon, "How do you feel? Is there any pain?"

"I'm okay…" he said relieved. He looked at her and continued, "I know I'm not healed—I can feel that—but having my spirit read the story from its pages didn't pain me."

"Shall we continue…?"

Gordon nodded, yes. They returned their attention to the floating book. Lilac and cobalt-blue light fled their eyes. The strands of luminosity acted as ink, scripting ancient glyphs that burst into the environment of the mythology. And thus, the saga continued.

Queen Malady stares me down
As I dream inside her dream
And she dreams inside my dream
She stares me down
We stare each other down
And she scowls, frowns
Images behind closed eyes, at rest
With renewed breath
When the sun goes down

Queen Malady taunts me,
"All the shades of nature cannot hide you
I will find you
And cut the breath that fires you anew
I will use your breath to burn your natural retreat
You, child, will never be thirteen complete

We run on the weakness of warriors
And the heads of you Medusas – Medu Sa
Medicinal mothers of the sea, birthing glorious family trees

Whose leaves we've worked so hard to cut
Grown and sewn, woven – weaved, roped up
Hung from branches anointed and sacred
Used to scare the population of you
Hang you from your family tree
Bodies swung, kissed by the sun
Swinging dead, hating the roots they come from
You think we'll let you nick and prick
The trick we've planted, tilled, plucked and pulled?"

I open eyes
Ritual in my throat
Pitch perfect
Harmonize cosmic notes
I sing to the sky
The morning blue opens,
Just a little
Small circle of pitch perfect black of night

My four breaths
Up to heaven
And pole star listens to my song
"Call Mama Gran to me," I sing.
"Call her to me, again I must be unseen."

Pole star spins my voice
To caged city
Spin and spin on the wind
The breeze sings my warning for Mama Gran to hear
Voice of me dancing in her ear
Faint
The garble of devil swine rhythms
Boots' drivel march – march – march
Onto city streets
At command of Governor Tubal
And Queen Malady
Searching for glimpses of me

My warning song
In Mama Gran's ear
Volume up, she hears me

"From the city streets," Queen Malady screams.
"Beyond this caged city,
A ghost child – she possesed by the devil's covenant
From the untamed darkness of an abusive, abandoning
Motherland."

Mama Gran
Cloaked, unseen
Slips past devil swine march
Glides on gale
And leaves caged city
Knit and stich
Stich and knit
Unseen cloth, fabric fabricated
Conjured cloth
Made as cloak
Thrown over she and I
Masked unseen, we hide

And on the horizon
March devil swine
They come through the dense trees
Like a breeze
They flood the forest
Sweeping
They flow past Mama Gran and me
We are silent, tucked comfortable in our invisibility

Enter Queen Malady
Beautifully robed in disease and intention
Determined to see what she cannot see
But she believes
I'm here
She creeps around our cloaked unseen
Grin bright as she begins speaking,

"I am a covenant too
My husband scripts laws on my back
And I uphold them
My smile regulates, and I seduce
I bring shaded men to forget you
I devise makeup dipped in your thirteen pieces

To walk as you
I was born to keep you broken
Shaded men frozen, stoned in gaze so that I
Might wear the crown of Medusa
Your writhing wisdom slithering atop my head."

She kneels – her back to me
But her imagination
Accords her a desired effect
I am there to her
Fashioned to be her reflection in a mirror

At the call of her husband
She leaves
The devil swine persist
To search for us, Mama Gran and me
Out in the open – unseen

The basement's setting popped out of a sudden bright flash. Gordon and Fey's tendrils of light withdrew from the open pages, to their eyes, and then faded away. Fey asked Gordon as she rubbed his arm, "You feel fine to continue?"

Gordon's back resonated with sharp tingles, inspiring his response, "I do, but let me get a swig of that tea." Fey handed him the cup of what was now lukewarm tea, and Gordon took a careful, but long and deep swallow. "Ah," he exhaled as the needling sensation numbed by way of the remedy he drank. After taking a few more sips, he passed the cup to Fey. "Thank you, beautiful woman," he told her.

Fey took the cup and set it down. "Another journey, shaded, nimble warrior?" she inquired.

Gordon's eyes blazed with light. He grinned and said to Fey, "Let's see bold and determined ants take down the might of elephants."

Fey looked at the floating book. Her eyes lit up, and her tendrils of light reached out and mingled with Gordon's. Together they intertwined on the face of the page, continuing the story.

Spear, swords and arrows
Point the way for determined eyes
Phour prongs position,
There, the horizon, our port of call
We believe giants cower behind mountains

Cover themselves with earth and snow
But plots and tricks
Tickle their ears on purred wisps of speech

Confidence allows us to walk tall
But through this massive land
We creep
Crawl through fog
The night plays a haunting song
Wulvz snarl in the distance
And the wind accompanies the feral chorus
There spirals and stirs the sound of the gales' hulking bays
Trying to keep our courage at bay

Devil swine patrol
Boast boots
Marching
Over marsh and mud
Their rhythm and stomp
A gravelly choir of subjugation

But tyranny's song fades
Mutes
As we hear singing a beguiling beauty bouncing as voluptuous ballads
Prancing vocabulary ballet dances in our ears
Hymned and hummed
Honey-sweet voices lick us
Attentive
Bass moistens feminine shades
Vibrating drums on their thighs
While the masculine shades of our army
Hold smiles filled dreamy, eyes just as sleepy
But willing
Listening to the alluring swivels of trills
We men
Stand
Erect
Stiff and at attention
We walk with an aimless gaze

We see
The perfect

Giants
Two voices intertwined
From single throat
Janus-gendered voice, rendered notes
Of man and woman
As the second dances like a pendulum
Back and forth
Feminine shades see a man chiseled from desire
We men see a woman, dripping with the ocean
Bewitched and bothered – enticed

Captain Debas wears the veil
Of Mama Gran on his eyes
Her voice in his ears
He is still – unmoved by dance and song
We go by, go by, go by, and go by him – 20 times 10
Shaded line, long

Sword to sky
Captain Debas yells high,
"Sorcery, tricks! Voice and sight
Negate growls that seethe through fog
And night
And we believe the giants sweet
Cover your eyes!
Listen close – hear that their rhythms are off beat, off key
Motherland's covenant, close to your heart and eyes, keep."

I blink
Exhale illusion
And rub the fool's deception and dream from my eyes
Three allies and I
Few shades see the giants' true

Synthetic solids, moldable
Grafted incant
They continue to prance closer
Spell cast
Huldra, the body
Sirin, the voice
They throw picture shows that stroke
Black shades' egos

Lull to sleep with hallowed scandals
Bojangles, unchained conjured with rattled bangles
Fallacious covens fellating once conscious men
Now entranced
As are the shaded women warriors
Cunning cunilingus from all of this – transfixed, spellbound
Some shades wave white flags, surrendering to sight and sound
Believing their enemies validate them proper
As Huldra and Sirin
Cast images of Legba and Samedi
For corporate cooperation
Some of our shades are fooled
Draw closer and closer – consciousness pushed away far
Some shades speak in happy dream, "They know who we are…"

Large eye smiles, beholder of shades
Titan Thunlibiri creeps from behind the fog
Flare, flash and streak – eye yells a beam
Many shades turn to ash as seduction reveals itself
A trap
Ensnared
Thunlibiri's single eye glares
Yells bright flash
Motherland covenant, these conscious shades failed to remember
Turned to cinder and embers
Bodies burned up, erased
Remaining shades shake awake!

Huldra and Sirin
Dance and chant
Swivel and sing
Frolic in front of smoke turned screen
To give the make of shade and shape
Their rhythms quicken, and they lull more true shades back to sleep
Flash to ash bursts Thunlibiri's beam
They give us speeding race cards to play
To charge a ploy, a gambit – and they react because we're conscious of this
Chance to chants – a strategy laced with incant
Captain Debas commands
And we follow order
Baron C conjures fog, thick around the ears
Bwa blinds our eyes with leaves

Phour lights bright our third eyes' sights
We see clear, and we hear nothing sweet

Phour throws a cosmic cloud, washing Thunlibiri's eye
The titan screams, writhes
Dark matter water stings his sight
Time becomes our unreliable ally as the giant goes blind

By our will, we move closer and closer
Bwa sings nature into the air
where Sirin breathes
Her mouth sprouts thistle, crabgrass, and pigweed
"Soon, she will too push up daisies!"
For now, silence becomes her song

Baron C binds Huldra's feet and wrists
With rope fabricated from cosmic mist
Huldra's fluid dance becomes stiff
Closer we drift
To giants high and tall, approximate feet of twenty-six
Crippled, these towers cannot signal a cry
to devil swine or wulvz reinforcements

Captain Debas
Stabs the giant Huldra
Legs bleed as she screams
Falls to knees
Uncompromised shades helix-twist around her frame
Fighting and stabbing

Bwa's vegetation fills Sirin's mouth
And throat
Until she chokes
Now I pounce for fatal stab
Black sun spear through the back
Spring through fog, shove and press
Spear through Huldra's chest
Lunge high
Pierce Thunlibiri's stolen third eye
And kill its physical form

Three giants. Pimp and prostitutes.

They explode. Silent.
Essence, three of thirteen
Abused body, voice, and eye
Arc across the sky
And find, unlike patrol of devil swine,
True Sirene
Her constellation reveals three more stars
All that surrounds her is her sky, her kingdom

She now speaks in seasons
Her body restored
Though missing head
And hands
But under unseen fabric, still unseen
She stands
Up from broken throne
With proper tone she wants to speak
But even a whisper would be a scream

Her voice, it is hard for her to swallow
When introduced to surprise
By the glow of her third eye
Her parents, and their true names
Come into sight
She even fights
Against anger for me, for what I did not keep
There stands evidence of my broken promise

Her thoughts think:
***I narrow third eye*
But struggle with truth
Of what I see
Blending all I have known
And come to believe
My rotted family tree
Dissected of heart
My Father Zero and Mother Nothing
Cruel images fade and shrink
But here stands benevolence

Knowing I'm unable to speak
They step to me

And confess their cruelty
A blessing of their affection

It will take time
Before they earn my smile
But lips quiver in reflex
When my Mother Wisdom
And Father Knowledge
Speak my proper name
"Ashaba," they say. "Ashaba-Sirene."
I flicker a smile, but hold stern emotion in place
I am whole
Without thirteen
All comes together better than I had dreamed
Six towers remain
My sentiments unchanged
To my black men, and the shaded feminine warriors that walk with them
To the Captain, his shades and my knight
Continue to disregard these towers' height
My warriors made of Motherland covenant
*Walk as giants over that distant continent***

White light faded the scene. The basement's setting consumed the light, and Gordon and Fey's eyes returned to normal. Fey noticed Gordon held a sly grin on his face as he unwrapped himself from his blanket.

"Tea?" she asked.

Gordon nodded, yes. Fey handed him the cup again. "I could sleep," he commented as he finished the drink. "Fey-baby, could you get me to the bed upstairs when I collapse? Thank you."

"Yes, Gordon-baby," Fey replied, watching Gordon attempt to stand. She jumped to her feet and assisted him. He was slow and stiff, but she was patient, guiding him to his altar.

"You're coming together nicely, Miss Ashaba-Sirene," Gordon praised, voice wavering to steady a groan from the pain he felt. "I'm like an old man," he remarked.

"I was about to say," Fey began. "We have to make sure *you* come together."

"A little rest and I'll be fine," Gordon responded. At his altar, he bent his knees, slow and careful. A dull throbbing scratched his back. "But I know I'll keep dreaming about the crossroads and the fight that happened there. It'll be whittled down to our friend Brice Cadogan. That last hit I gave him, we like this now." Gordon crossed his fingers. "I got an instinct he's having the same dream. We're in it together. He my nigger if I don't get no bigger"

"You think he's hurt?"

"Far more than myself," said Gordon to Fey, groaning heavy with his knees to the floor. "The trick in his blood keeps him fit and ageless, but it ain't got nothin' on what this pain is putting him through. It's beyond the trick in his blood." Gordon proceeded with his ritual at the altar. Fey asked if he needed to be alone, and Gordon told her no. He wanted her to stay. When he finished, he started to wobble as sleep crawled over him like living vines, squeezing consciousness out of him like water from a sponge.

Gordon's eyes closed, and he fell back. Fey caught him, easing his body against the floor. Four colorful streams of smoke and light swiveled from Fey's back. Silver and the other yumboes configured from the light and smoke, wings fluttering wild and with a pleasant buzz. Fey ordered, "Go up to Gordon's room and prepare his bed, please."

The yumboes' bodies twisted back into smoke and light and soared through the ceiling, ending up in the bedroom Gordon took as his own, several floors above. Solidifying out of puff and brilliance, their activity of preparing Gordon's bed was immediate, pulling back the comforter and fluffing the pillows, readying them for the placement of Gordon's head. Silver dissipated again, and tunneled her way back to the basement. She found Fey kneeling on the floor, over Gordon's sleeping body. Silver informed her that Gordon's bed was ready.

"Thank you, Silver," Fey said over her shoulder. She reached down, gently took up Gordon's arm, and closed her eyes to focus on a thought, *Gordon on the bed. Gordon on the bed,* she repeated to herself. Then there was a soft whisk of air as Fey's body whirled away with a mystical pop, taking Gordon with her. Silver flew up through the floors, rising back to Gordon's bedroom.

Gordon's body snapped into existence on the bed, head snug against the pillow that curled around his sudden presence. Fey put his arm down and stepped away. Her yumboes dragged the comforter over Gordon, tucking him in.

"Rest, dark hero," Fey whispered to him.

Althea Goodspeed appeared, watching over her son. "Thank you, Miss Forrester," she expressed.

Fey's yumboes, turned to colorful light and exhaust, seeped into her back. "You are welcome, Miss Goodspeed. I care for Gordon greatly."

"Oh, I know, Fey," smiled Althea. "And I can feel you have work to do."

"Yes, Miss Goodspeed."

"I will watch over my son," Althea told Fey. "Mister Goodspeed is in Harlem at his job. I'll tell him later how our son is doing."

"Yes," said Fey.

"Go on, young woman. Everything is fine here."

Fey popped away to the basement. There she stood in front of Gordon's chamber. After a moment, she spoke aloud, "We're trying to find answers here." Her eyes panned the chamber. "Spook," called Fey. *"Seven missing. Incomplete. Scars remain,"* she quoted. "What's that mean? Give me something." She turned her head to the *Nigrum Nigrius Nigro* as it crept open, the black mirror lifting up to address her question with words lit across its face. The characters were an ancient language, and their presence brought a brilliant blaze of cobalt-blue light from her eyes, allowing Fey to read the words.

Look inside chamber, Spook directed.

The light didn't leave Fey's eyes as she returned her attention to the chamber. The capsule slid open. Fey peeped inside and spotted seven empty, circular slots aligned along the bottom. She reached inside and felt the empty spaces with two fingers. "Spook," she called again. "What's supposed to complete this chamber?" She became upright, looking at the black mirror through brightly lit eyes.

Ancient words scrawled across the black mirror. Spook explained in text and Fey read along, *Djed Pillar Jewels: Used in alchemical chambers for specific, curative properties for the Lwa resting inside. Originating in Alkebulan, called Africa, sets of gems have been carried around the world.*

"Mirror, mirror," joked Fey in a deadpan voice. Spook started closing. Fey scowled and expressed, "Really, Spook? You're offended by that?" She huffed, "Gordon was right. You *are* sensitive." The aged tome raised again, the face of the black mirror upright. Fey read aloud the words that scrawled across it, *I can joke too.* She smiled and rolled her eyes, a short burst of laughter escaping her. "At a time like this?" she inquired. "Well, thank you for lightening the mood, Spook." Fey relaxed, but she still needed answers. She interrogated, "Any knowledge on the whereabouts of a set of Djed Pillar Jewels here in America or abroad?"

Spook responded in ancient text. Water collected at the edge of Fey's eyes, and her face was filled with surprise as she studied the text that appeared character-by-character. *The Sunset Gems are believed to be a set of Djed Pillar Jewels. Legend speaks of the Amazons of Queen Califia having the responsibility of guarding the precious stones in the American Southwest. The jewels were possibly brought over to the Americas through a Malian voyage in the late 1200s or early 1300s, or even longer ago.*

Fey inhaled and covered her mouth. She asked the black mirror, "Can you give me a specific location?"

Spook returned a set of words: *Cannot decipher without connection.*

The words were like anvils tied to her emotions and pushed from the highest of cliffs. Fey's face dropped. "What's that mean?" she whispered in such a low voice that it was barely audible. "Spook, what's that mean?" she asked again, her voice loud for Spook to hear.

Spook repeated the text, *Cannot decipher without connection.*

Fey exhaled. The tears that had gathered in her eyes, fell, but no longer did they express happiness. Her knees bent and touched the floor. She turned and put her back against the chamber. Wiping her face of tears, Fey concluded, "We're close. We're close. My spirit is close to you, Mister Fallows. I have questions to ask before I end your long, diabolical life." She stood and conjured from her back the youngest of her yumboes. It was the jade-green colored sprite aptly named Jade. "Go tell Miss Goodspeed that I'm heading out. If she fades, you watch over Gordon. Understood?" The yumbo nodded her head in the affirmative, happy to receive a mission. In a streak of smoke and light, the yumbo traveled up through the house.

Fey's cosmic attire wrapped around her frame, and she popped away, up onto the brownstone's roof. She tilted her head skyward, eyeing her escape route. She needed to get away. Fable Avenue and all its politics were too much for her at the moment. Even caring for Gordon added a weight she needed to shake off, especially if she were to tackle the entirety of the task of restoring him to health, so she said to herself. She sighed, feeling a little guilty. But her absence would only be temporary.

And so her body blazed with cobalt-blue spirit, and she soared into the sky, racing toward the boundary of Earth's atmosphere and space. Beyond, she would find solace among the cosmos and all its beautiful, black spirits.

Are you kidding me? Gordon thought with such intensity that he believed he'd said the words aloud. Gordon moved forward, taking small steps toward the train-car doors, making an attempt to walk through them. His steps were slow, but not because of any pedestrian pain clinging to his back and burning his legs, which was active as he moved. But Gordon's slow pace could be explained, and was at the mercy of, a young man wearing a heavy coat, sagging jeans, and headphones in his ears sauntering at a relaxed speed in front of him. *All the room on this train and you're taking your time like it's crowded!* Gordon huffed inside his head. *What're you too hard and too street to have an ounce of common courtesy? I bet you any amount of money you'd have a shit fit if the situation was reversed, actin' all hard like you about anything other than the ignorance in you.*

Then the man committed a sin that raised Gordon's frustration, causing his body to flinch. The young man stopped in the doorway, blocking an entire half of the opening, and without moving aside and flattening up against the chair rail to allow the flow of traffic to continue onto the train.

Gordon's thoughts became audible by way of a reflex he couldn't rein in. "Son, you kiddin', right?" But the man couldn't hear him because of the headphones. Gordon wanted to slam into him, give him a slight bump to wake him up about the world around him. He opted to do otherwise, however. Gordon instead moved around him, and as a kind gesture, allowed two women to go before him. He moved into the subway car and found a seat. He closed his eyes and put his head back against the wall. But Gordon wouldn't find solace on his way to campus as the man next to him bumped his arm and said, "It's cold out there, ain't it, bruh?"

Gordon made a face, looking at his arm where the man had nudged him. *Whaddya wanna sing a duet about it?* he kept to himself. Gordon fixed his expression with a smile, replying in a sardonic tone unnoticed by the man, "Tends to happen around this time of year."

"Nah, bruh," said the man in a hushed voice and looking around. The train started up, all passengers aboard and announcements made previewing the next stop. Gordon looked around, mimicking the man. Again, Gordon's sarcasm was lost on the man as he was focused on conversation. "It's colder than normal."

Normal—that's rich, I'll say, Gordon considered. *A word I don't need heightened instinct to know that's never been used to describe you, my dude.*

"That's the shadow government at work," the man warned in a hushed voice. "That's that secret government."

Gordon teased, "Really? If it's a secret, why do you know about it, Jimmy?"

The man again missed Gordon's snarky tone. "I read up," he answered. "I'm learned."

"I'm sure you are…" Gordon chuckled.

"They got that HAARP machine stirring things up. You ever hear of HAARP?"

"I'd bet a dying man's last minutes that I'm about to," Gordon replied.

And then the man dived into an explanation, filling Gordon's ear with the numerous conspiracy theories that had been conjured up concerning the High Frequency Active Auroral Research Program that operated on a major sub-arctic facility in Gakona, Alaska, acronym HAARP and pronounced just like the stringed instrument. Gordon knew the basic purpose of the research program was to analyze the upper atmosphere, or so was the official story. But many armchair scholars, such as the man addressing Gordon at the moment, felt there was something more sinister to the government-sponsored project, helping influence weather patterns and the cause for major catastrophes from devastating hurricanes and tsunamis, earthquakes, and even tragedies surrounding downed airliners. And Gordon was getting an earful.

"So this is how it breaks down," Gordon began to summarize what he'd just been told. "Never mind the fact that it's late November in the northeast—me and my lying eyes be damned, and all that. Astrophysics and that hocus pocus called science be damned with it. Forget the Earth's closer proximity to the sun during fall and winter, which causes the earth to spin more quickly on its axis, causing the days to be shorter and the cold air to flux into the northern hemisphere between October and March—truthfully starting around the end of July, but really feeling these affects by mid-September—but anyway, just ignore all that, because it's a machine that has Mother Nature totally in control."

Now the man made a face, backing away from Gordon. He waved his hand and cursed, "Aw, shit, boy. You Negroes don't want to know the truth. You all want to be caught up in this devil's lie. I'm trying to give you some knowledge."

Gordon exhaled. He closed his eyes and leaned his head against the train. *I know,* he said in his head, sounding like an apology. *But I've been to the stars, so I don't care.* Mild irritations scratched his back, causing Gordon to squirm a bit. He concentrated on the pain, trying to smother it by flexing his back muscles. The discomfort eased, and Gordon continued his thoughts. *I got your number, Willie. The scars you've given me by way of your hexed whip might have my New York irritability and sarcasm past ten. Mine now goes to eleven—hell, beyond. But I refuse to bend to its will and aim my anger toward anyone but you, Brice, Stanley and his little wench. With all your tricks, who's to say my friend here ain't got the right knowledge?*

Gordon decided to apologize to the man talking to him. He opened his eyes, lifted his head, and turned toward him. There again came the pain, like stabbings from a thousand maniacs. The man's voice glided into his ears. He was spouting more of his conspiracy theories to a gray-haired Latino woman. Gordon's arms trembled. He looked down at them, suppressing the urge to reach out and wrap his fingers around the man's neck. Gordon closed his eyes again. He relaxed, head back against the train.

The train stopped. The doors opened. People flooded the car, yelling at one another to move. But it was one voice that Gordon heard. It was the voice of a woman cursing out her child for not walking fast enough. "Move, you little motherfucker!" she yelled. "Every *got-damned* time with you! Sitcho ass down over here! Go!"

Her voice scratched Gordon's heart, and broke it a little too. There also came a heavy pressure slamming against both sides of his head when she spoke. He opened his eyes to a crowded car. Through lines of people, Gordon could see the mother standing across from him. The little black boy, her son, was sitting down, eyes wide and staring up at his mother. Gordon held back an urge to scream at the woman. His instinct jumped around, latching onto the mother's thoughts, digging deep inside her head and traveling back through her past. Her despair and broken self-image dragged Gordon's instinct deeper into her unconscious thoughts that were now expressed as behavior. The origin of her anger was like a blurry image coming into focus. Its date of birth came far before the little boy's father abandoned her and their son.

Gordon clenched his teeth and closed his eyes. He struggled to draw back his instinct from prying any further, but an image of the woman's past came into focus. Other distorted, kaleidoscopic pictures from the woman's past accompanied it, speeding by in a rapid montage. Clear was one word etched somewhere in the running memories. Its letters burned. *Fallows.* Gordon saw the choices the woman administered in her life, made incognizant on a blurred moment coming more and more into focus. Gordon retracted his instinct before the picture came into focus. He clenched his teeth to ease the pain, taking breaths to calm himself.

Three rough-looking men were loud. Gordon opened his eyes to them. Their voices hacked at his nerves. Again his instinct jumped out. It split like a multi-tailed whip, and the invisible stream of Gordon's projectile consciousness penetrated the men's foreheads. It happened all over again. There came the picture shows of their lives. Different, but the same. Instances in the past stringing them along to make choices like a puppeteer manipulator. He saw the burning word again stamped on their memories. *Fallows.* Now they were loud, Gordon concluded, looking for attention and a fight. *Better yet,* Gordon corrected, *hoping for some attention, someone to challenge them, and* then *a fight.*

The train stopped. Gordon watched as a short white man in a business suit and long coat pushed his way through the rough men. They parted for him as if they were the Red Sea and he was Moses. The people they bumped up against to give the man room shouted at them, giving the men the attention and challenge they were looking for. They yelled back, shouting curses and threats.

"I'm tryna let this man through, stupid bitch!"

"Fuck you, nigga. No good motherfucker!"

Gordon's back blazed as if the sun set all its burning weight on him.

More people backed away to give the man room, something they had a problem doing for one another just one stop earlier. The doors closed, and the train started. Gordon watched the well-dressed white man's face. He looked just as comfortable pushing his way through the crowd of black faces, as they were to accommodate his passing, fighting one another to give him space. He neared Gordon, and Gordon stretched out his leg through the crowd of people. The man tripped. Gordon retracted his leg without notice. The man hadn't a clue as to what he'd stumbled over. He was too busy catching himself on the mother standing across from Gordon.

"Excuse me," said the man. "Forgive me," he pleaded in a polite tone that rattled Gordon's instinct.

The woman smiled at the man. "It's fine. You want a seat?" She turned to her son before the man answered. She yelled at the little boy with the wide eyes, "Getcho ass up and let this man sit!"

The man was about to thank the woman. But Gordon thought otherwise. *You don't wanna do that,* Gordon said in his head, projecting the thought through his instinct. *Don't take that little kid's seat.*

The man straightened himself, reaching out for the bar above the seats. "No, thank you, Miss," he addressed. "Thank you, though. Thank you. Too kind." His smile made Gordon's instinct squirm. The man looked at the little boy. "Listen to your mother," he said through nervous laughter.

Gordon concentrated on smothering the fiery distress rippling through his back. He started by blocking out the noise around him, and then he closed his eyes. But there remained a noisy pollutant coming from his right. He balled his fist. Irritated, he opened one eye and moved it to the right. At some point the man he was talking to earlier had gotten up and moved, or got off the train all together. But in his place was a boy in his late teens listening to a song blaring from a device held in his hands, bobbing his head and dancing around in his seat.

Gordon's instinct perceived the young man was also looking to be noticed. He looked around every-so-often from his antics, head low, and smile on his face, looking to see if anyone was paying him any attention.

Gordon was.

"Whatchu lookin' at?" he asked.

"I'm just thinkin' you got psychic powers," Gordon remarked with a grin. "You're listening to the very song I wanted to hear blasted throughout this place, son. I was sittin' here thinkin', I wish someone would blast that irritating and annoying, shitty new song that's out there. But I couldn't think of the name, 'cause there's so many of those types of songs nowadays." Gordon kept his teasing grin as he asked, "So, what's the name of that copy and paste, shitty lyric-laden song again?"

The young man turned off his device. The train was quieter than quiet. "Fuck you say, nigga?"

Gordon put his hands on his chest. "I'm sorry, my dude. I was just wondering why with all the flashy things you got on, why you couldn't invest in a pair of ten dollar headphones."

"Fuck you think you are?"

Gordon's instinct tunneled its way into the young man's head. He extracted what he needed and said, "I'm a cop, Trevelle. I look young, but that's the point. Now listen close, for the first time in y' life, kid." Gordon motioned for Trevelle to come closer. He did. "I know you've been through some rough shit in this system. But what you're going to step into tonight is going to be worse, far worse. It's a mistake to go. Eight o'clock. Amersfort. *We* know about it. *You* stay out of it. And get as far away from it as possible, and wherever that faraway place is, you stay there. Move on." Gordon put emphasis in his words, but made no attempt to lace them with an incant to push his points. His words would have to be enough, or he'd suffer a pain greater than he was already going through.

Trevelle leaned away, face possessed with disdain masking confusion. The train stopped. Gordon maneuvered his way through a crowd of people. He looked back at Trevelle and reiterated, "Stay away!"

He hopped off the train, grateful to have avoided an actual physical confrontation. All the potential for a fight was there. What did bog Gordon down was the miserable pain in his back. As he walked, the pain dwindled to the sensation of soft, manageable needle pricks. It was enough for Gordon as he then transferred to the 2-Train and continued his way to school. He arrived at his campus after a short three-block walk, once above ground from the subway.

He had two finals on this day, and he was looking forward to them. Gordon's anticipation wasn't because he was prepared for the tests, which he was. But it was because the tests offered distractions. The Elders of the community, his mother, and Fey, were against his leaving. But he felt obligated to finish his semester, and he didn't want to file for an extension. Gordon's best argument came when he told the truth. He explained to Papa Solomon and the matriarchs that when he slept he was riddled with dreams of fighting Brice Cadogan at the crossroads. Even with a goodnight's sleep, he woke up exhausted, whether he engaged in simple conversation or fisticuffs with Brice. Awake, Willie's painful scars flared up. When he concentrated on studying, the pain would go away. He'd hoped the tests proved to be the same. The Elders allowed him leave, and before he'd left the avenue for the day, he'd had some of the incanted Haitian tea.

His first test was *Introduction to Statistics.* Focused on the exam, the world and the pain dropped away. Gordon finished, confident he'd scored a good grade. He then moved to his British Literature exam, facilitated by Professor James Brede. A calm swept over Gordon the minute he sat down in the classroom. There was no need to spend a moment concentrating on pushing the pain aside. A cooling sensation poured over Gordon's back as Professor Brede entered the room. He embraced the relief, smiling as Professor Brede addressed the class before handing out the exams.

"Here you go, Mister Goodspeed," Professor Brede said, placing a test on Gordon's desk. "There's no need to wish you luck, Gordon. You've been good at taking my tests, even when I deal out my toughest exams for you."

"Personally, for me, Professor Brede?" joked Gordon. The professor replied with a chuckle. "We'll see what this one gives me," Gordon remarked, taking the blue-covered test booklet and the stapled question sheets.

"It's the big one," Professor Brede said. "The final," he continued, eyebrows arching up with excitement. He continued handing out the exams to the remaining students as he told Gordon in a teasing tone, "But it won't leave scars like my last one."

Gordon's irises and pupils pulsed with their lilac glow, but Gordon wasn't aware, and the phenomenon lasted for only a moment's notice. His instinct buzzed up the back of his neck, shot through his brain, and tickled his pineal. Again the sensation was for only a moment. Gordon even suppressed it, believing it might reignite the pain in his back. But he was aware of his instinct's buzz, dismissing it as Professor Brede's words triggering the memory of the scars and the battle where he'd received them. It was nothing more, and so he dived into his test as Professor Brede ordered the class to begin.

The professor took his seat and watched his students, his eyes remaining on Gordon the longest. He took a sip of his wine, and a small grin came to him. His eyes changed colors and his countenance shifted. Away fell the veil of Professor Brede. Stanley Fallows observed the class, eyes focused on Gordon. *Look up, Mister Goodspeed. I'm right here. Your friend, Stanley Fallows.* Gordon maintained his focus. No buzzing instinct alerted him of his professor's change. Stanley mumbled a hushed trick to keep the students in front of him engaged in their tests. Gordon was not entangled in Stanley's otherworldly lacework, but neither he nor the other students lifted their head to peek at their professor, face anew.

"Take your time," Stanley told the eager test takers in the voice of Professor Brede. "This is designed to be a three-hour exam. It will whip you if you let it."

Gordon looked up. Professor Brede was looking down at a newspaper spread open on his desk. There was a hint of a smile on the professor's face. Gordon's instinct hummed with a faint buzz, gone as soon as it came. Gordon dived back into his test, scripting away with short and long answers. He finished a little over two-hours in, taking the remaining time to look over his answers. He reworded a few sentences in two of his short essays, and also modified a short-winded answer appearing early in the test. Gordon liked what he saw, smiling to himself as Professor Brede called time. Eleven students remained in the class, the rest having left early upon finishing. Professor Brede stayed in his chair as the students brought their tests to him, including Gordon.

"Any nightmares, Mister Goodspeed?" he asked Gordon. "Or will you sleep soundly now that this test is over?"

Gordon paused. He chuckled, looking around perplexed, reacting to a sudden, faint buzz in his instinct.

"Something the matter, Mister Goodspeed?"

Gordon shook his head, which was more about brushing off the sensation of instinct writhing up his neck and throughout his head. He turned to his professor and acknowledged, "No, Professor Brede. I guess I keep hearing what I want to hear in things."

"Anything I've said?"

Gordon nodded. "Yeah. Just reminded me of the test. Hope I got all the answers."

"I'm sure you did fine, Mister Goodspeed. Like many a-student when taking a test, you are called to arms. And like I said, this is the big and final one. The fire is falling, but you are not helpless and naked when leaping into my dangerous exams." Professor Brede smiled.

"So dramatic, Professor Brede," Gordon said shifting his book bag on his shoulder.

"I'm an English Professor, Mister Goodspeed. T'is my nature," he winked. "Good semester, Gordon. It was a pleasure to have you in my class. Now, go on. Get some rest. I'm sure there will be more tests in your future."

"Yes, Professor Brede." Gordon exited the class, leaving Professor Brede with legs crossed at the ankles atop his desk and continuing his read of the newspaper. The farther Gordon walked away from campus, the more his concentration broke on holding back the pain. The burning sting came like the fury of a screaming, runaway train. The pain felt new, fresh, as if Willie was there to give the lashes all over again. Gordon had to endure every scratch as he made his way up the block and to the subway, wobbling in his walk. He put his hands in his pockets and hunched over, moving along the sidewalk as if fighting against the day's windy chill. Despite the pain, Gordon pressed forward, rushing into the subway as he approached the entrance. He removed his wallet, and from it, his MetroCard. Making a swipe, he moved through the turnstile and pocketed the card in his wallet, and then placed his wallet back inside his pocket.

Gordon sat at a bench and waited for the next train. Sitting didn't ease the pain any, but Gordon could bare it more seated than standing. The train rushed through, bringing wind and a loud holler of metal scraping against metal. Gordon shrugged as he observed a crowded train. He got up and boarded as the doors opened. The train was filled with the depressed souls staggering around the Brooklyn borough. Gordon was forced to stand. He was smashed up against people, and so face-to-face with a young, black man that they could've been mistaken for lovers. Gordon didn't like it, and the young man didn't look like he appreciated the circumstances either.

Gordon looked left. He looked right. Anywhere but forward at the young man who, for some reason, held a peculiar look of resentment aimed at Gordon. Gordon noticed the look before he'd stepped onto the train. Scowl-faced and mean. Now it was directed at Gordon's proximity. *Really?* Gordon thought. *You're going to look angry like I'm the one who's got everyone bunched up? What are you, from Ohio? You never been on a crowded train before? It's* New York, *son!* Gordon wanted to stare the young man down, but his instinct spoke against such an action, so he only rolled his eyes. *Whatchu mad at, man?* Gordon asked in his head. *Tryin' to look all tough and hard. I'm getting sick of this! What's the cause of that scowl, 'cause it can't just be me. We just met. Why you so angry, tryin' to scare the world so they don't see you just as scared inside. What's your problem man? We in this ride together.*

Then Gordon's instinct jumped from his head, tunneling into the young man standing close and opposite him. Images transferred to Gordon, and he was surprised to see most were happy, even with half a family. Dad not in any of the pictures, but there were close cousins, half-siblings and friends. A good time on the block, the occasional fight, and not too much dodging of school work. If the young black man standing in front of Gordon was a hustler, he was hustling in the right direction. But there was pain, and Gordon noted it before making an angry judgment berating the young man for putting on the thug act. There was legitimate anger. And Gordon saw the image that answered the question why.

The young man was four. It was dark, but a door swung open to let light in from a hallway. There stepped inside an older man so close to the young man's family that he was called uncle. He was drunk, and Gordon could smell the liquor on him as he was dragged inside the memory. He called the four-year-old boy Scotty, whispering the name as he shut the door. Then it was dark again, and the older man inducted Scotty into a long line of tradition that this play-uncle had been initiated into by his mother's sister when he was a boy. And she her father. And her father by his grandfather. Gordon looked deep inside the gruesome scenes to find the burning letters that spelled *Fallows*. It never came aflame despite Gordon feeling a presence. He stopped in traversing the lineage, refusing to walk down the terrible deed's entire genealogy.

But there was a timeline for Scotty's maltreatment. Ten years, and then the older man died one day of heart failure. There was Scotty attending the older man's funeral upset that the people around him mourned the older man's passing instead of praising it. He was alone in that.

Gordon pulled back his instinct before he drowned inside the memory, smothered to the point where he would've carried the experience inside him long after retracting from it. But his instinct did not leave unscathed. There came with it a stream of awareness like a fisherman reeling in a catch. *Moms knew,* he heard Scotty say. *That was my punishment for reminding her of my pops.*

Gordon's expression contorted, scowl-faced and mean. He and Scotty stared at one another, bonding with only Gordon being conscious of the connection. Gordon blinked, exhaling a low, mournful sigh. The doors opened at his stop, and Gordon stepped off the train, tears welling up, and possessed with the feeling of wanting to strike something. Anything. He gritted his teeth, pain biting him, and emotion devouring him. He walked different, legs limping in a rhythmic swagger. Then he straightened and became himself, all while he transferred to the 8-Train, getting off at the last stop and walking up Fable Avenue.

If someone had told Gordon there was a cloud raining sharp glass and rusted nails on his back, he would've believed them. He would've also asked if there was lava poured into his wounds. A community member drove by and slowed down in his car, his wife with him. He offered Gordon a ride home, seeing him struggling down the street. Gordon accepted the kind gesture, and thanked both the man and the woman as he crawled inside their car. His name was Manny, short for Manuel. His wife's name was Diana, and she was pregnant with their first child.

"You okay, Gordon?" he asked. "Word's been creepin' 'round the Avenue your spirit wrestled a mean haunt and a crew of night doctors. Ain't heard 'bout their kind in a long time. They lookin' for spirit to extract. Spirit and blood," he told Gordon. "They get you with a needle?"

"No," Gordon answered. "But I got a few bruises, Mister De Sousa," he continued through a rough wave of pain.

"Gordon," Diana called his attention. "My grandfather knows incants to cleanse the scars fiery haunts can give." She turned around and looked at Gordon as he squirmed in the backseat. "He's out in Saint Louis. He's old, but I've been studying the writings he's sent to me. The Elders, this past Spirit Festival, took me through the stitching ritual. My incant has greater strength now. I can work an uncrossing."

"That's just fine Miss Diana," Gordon replied to her. "Strong as your family's incants might be, we're dealing with something a little stronger." He winced and added, "I don't mean to be dismissive. I apologize."

"That's fine, Gordon," Diana told him. "To be honest, I was hoping you would turn me down. I just wouldn't want to take on so much responsibility reigniting the lilac flame."

"It ain't extinguished yet," Gordon remarked in a sly voice.

Manny gave Diana a quick, sharp look. Gordon caught the action.

"It's okay," said Gordon relieving the tension. "I'm going through some things. I'm down but I ain't out. It's good that you all have found some incants to extend a hand. We'll need 'em. The block has tangible enemies again." Manny slowed the car in front of the Goodspeed residence. Gordon exhaled, "You two stay strong for the sake of that little girl comin' up in here…in what? The next three months?" He saw Manny and Diana exchange open-mouthed, surprised looks. They turned their expressions on Gordon. He made a face and apologized, "I'm sorry. Did I ruin the surprise of the child's gender?"

Diana chuckled. "I had an instinct telling me it was such," she admitted. She looked at Manny and told him, "I'm sorry, baby. This isn't much of a surprise to me."

Manny coughed up excitement, sounding like a car struggling to come alive in the winter. He went from sputtering happiness through a smile to a loud excited howl. "A princess?" he exclaimed. "We're going to have a little princess? Oh, this is wonderful! All my sisters have had boys. Oh, this will make my mother stop complaining that there are no little girls running around!" He and Diana kissed. "And *I* can give her that!" Then he corrected while still embracing his wife, "We, I mean, we."

Gordon struggled to smile. He made efforts to dig into Manny and Diana's happiness, reverting to a mildly assertive voice garbled with pain, "That's lovely, wonderful and all that. Can someone give me a hand inside, please?"

Manny pulled away from Diana and looked at Gordon. "Oh, my goodness, I'm sorry, Gordon." He unclipped his seatbelt and opened the car door, checking first for oncoming traffic. Manny came around to the passenger's side and opened the door, reaching in for Gordon. "Come on, Gordon." Manny assisted the wounded Gordon from the backseat. He guided him to the garden-floor entrance after closing the car's rear door.

Gordon reached into his pocket and removed his keys. "I got it from here," he told Manny. "Thank you, Mister De Sousa."

"You sure, Gordon?"

"I'm sure," Gordon insisted. "Go celebrate with your wife."

Manny patted Gordon on the shoulder. A slight jolt of pain wrestled Gordon's nerves, but he managed to keep down a howl. He unlocked the garden-floor entrance and walked inside, turning for a slight moment to again extend his gratitude for Manny and Diana's help. Manny accepted, and when he could see Gordon was safe inside, he turned around, returned to his car, and drove away.

Inside, Gordon dropped his bag and staggered into the kitchen to prepare some of the healing tea Fey brought him. He wished he could speak a simple incant to speed up the water's heating, but the slightest use of his spirit increased the pain he felt. He had the stove on high, however, and his wait was no longer than five minutes. He assembled the ingredients, dipped it into an empty mug, and poured hot water over it. Gordon gave time for the cup to cool before taking a sip. He didn't bother stirring honey or anything else into his tea. He drank it straight.

The drink took effect, lathering his lacerations with a numbing sensation. He finished the cup of tea and placed the mug in the sink. He felt better, improved in his posture, standing straighter. But as he made his way upstairs to his room, some of the pain crept back in. It felt as if he was climbing the steepest of mountains equipped with a truck on his back, one that was grinding its tires into his flesh. The medicinal, incanted tea alleviated some of the pain, but it was losing some of its quality as it sat in his house.

But Gordon persisted, trudging up the flights of stairs and into his room. There, he changed into nightclothes, bottoms and a t-shirt. He faced his dresser where lay his altar brought up from the basement. Before he started his ritual, he sent a text message to Fey.

Home, Fey-Baby, he sent. *About to get well-needed rest.*

Good, came her instant reply. *I'm still studying for my tests tomorrow. How did your tests go?*

My tests went well. Won't have another one until after this short, holiday break. Let me not keep you from studying, and let me get some rest. Good night, Fey-Baby. And good luck on your tests tomorrow.

Thank you, Gordon-baby. Goodnight, my dark hero.

Gordon put his phone down and then started his ritual at the altar, speaking an incant to lull him to peaceful sleep. It was almost instantaneous, a blanket of fatigue thrown over him. Even the pain in his back had to yield. He had enough strength to crawl into bed, and before long, he was fast asleep.

When he awoke, it was early in the morning, 5:30, and it was still dark. Gordon believed it was the middle of the night until his eyes confirmed otherwise by glancing at the clock. Moving his neck caused the pain on his back to stretch out in a dull web, pulsing from the scars made by Willie's strikes. The healing tea brought from Haiti put in overtime on his scars. He was glad to be awake, as dark as the house was, even with his enhanced eyesight. Conversing with Brice was getting old. He desired action, something more than only holding his anger in the palms of his hands. He wanted to choke Brice with it, kill him with it. And Brice continued taunting him to do so. But Gordon's instinct deciphered that action would kill Brice, and not just in the dream.

Gordon's ponderings were broken by his instinct telling him to go downstairs. His travel downstairs was sluggish, and when he arrived, his instinct caused him to reach for the remote and turn on the television. An image of the local morning news popped on, a grim report already in progress. The volume was too low to hear, but all Gordon had to do was read and watch to identify the horror announced by the broadcasters. He first saw the picture of Trevelle Stevens, the young man he'd interacted with on the train at the beginning of the day. Scrolling across the bottom of the screen were the words: *Gang-related killing in Amersfort Park.* Trevelle was the hit. The young man's life was extinguished.

Gordon's eyes burst aflame with a lilac inferno, widening at the horror he was witnessing. He dropped to his knees and started screaming, and then his body hit the floor, unconscious and convulsing. His instinct leapt out, soared up through the house and down the block where it dragged Fey Forrester from sleep. She saw an image of Gordon's body shaking on the floor on the garden-level of his house. His eyes were wide open, spewing a radiant lilac light that lit the dark room. Fey jumped from bed, her tight galactic garb spilling over her. She blinked from her room, reappearing inside Gordon's house. She rushed to him, reaching out with her instinct, trying to calm the wild gyrations in his body.

Gordon was back in his dream. The crossroads. The sun was overhead. His cosmic wear was so tattered that he may as well have been bare of clothes. There was Brice Cadogan, standing at the ready, equipped with his brace of armor clasped around his forearm. He looked to have strength, but as he stepped forward, he wobbled.

"We're in the same boat," Brice reminded Gordon. *"This will be interesting."*

Gordon concentrated his angry thoughts into the palm of his hands until he felt them burning. He made fists. His mask covered his face, and a dull, spherical, lilac-colored orb comprised of swirling light appeared at his forehead.

"We're going to play a little game, Brice," Dooley sneered. *"It's called, 'You can get it too'."* He charged the Englishman, the strength of his motivation and the weakness of his scars battling for supremacy as he maintained balance. He swung a fist and connected against Brice's jaw. The Englishman just laughed. Dooley growled, *"Take that with you, Bricey-boy! Report back to Mister Fallows with it. More is coming."*

Brice caught his step, recovered, and threw a quick jab to Dooley's ribs. Dooley buckled. A biting sting coursed through him and carried a curse dispensed by the incanted piece of armor around Brice's forearm. Brice didn't spare the moment. He swung again at Dooley, connecting at the cheek.

"I've got a trick in this fight, boy," he snarled as he landed another fist against Dooley's face. *"I got some aid by Miss Lucretia, Stanley's wife. What're you doing in the conscious world, Mister Goodspeed?"*

Gordon was upright, his eyes wide and burning with lilac spirit. He was fighting, throwing hard punches at Fey as she tried to move in close to calm his unconscious movements. None of his swings landed against her as she used her spirit to dodge his attacks. Up and over him she leapt, landing soft and crouched atop the coffee table. "Gordon-baby, this isn't you. It's those scars. They got a hex dancin' in your head like a horse."

Gordon had his back to Fey, catching his breath, still operating unconscious. The scars on his back, laced with a curse from Willie's whip, reached out and attacked Fey's instinct. She didn't buckle, fighting back in her head. But the influence of the scars wrapped around her neck, squeezing and causing the empathy she had for Gordon to twist into anger against him.

"Goddamnit, Gordon!" Fey yelled. The scars hex loosened from around her neck. *"You listen here!"* She lunged as he turned his body around. Her fist knocked against his jaw, but Gordon caught himself before falling back. He jumped toward Fey, and he and she locked arms, two forces colliding, pushing and resisting, trying to gain balance over the other.

Dooley landed a hit inside the dream, knocking Brice to the gravelly crossroads. Brice bounced, and then crawled away a few paces. *"I can see through your eyes, jungle spirit,"* Brice laughed while wiping his bleeding lip. He spat at Dooley, *"We got you right where we want you—you and that lightning bug of yours."* Brice concluded in a rough manner, *"At each other's throats."*

Dooley rushed Brice, and the Englishman swung his right leg around in an attempt to swipe Dooley off his feet. But Dooley jumped up, letting Brice's motion swing under him. Brice didn't suffer the loss. In fact, he thought quickly, planting his hands at the sides of his head, and leaping upward with a deft push. Feet pointing straight at Dooley, Brice slammed against his upper chest and chin, knocking the cosmic-clad spirit out of the air. Dooley landed hard on his shoulder.

Gordon blinked, a flinch in consciousness occurring. He recognized his surroundings, dark as it was. He was on the garden-level of the Goodspeed Brooklyn residence, and he was wrestling with Fey Forrester. She was clothed in her cosmic uniform. Both had a strong grapple and forceful push against the other. Gordon didn't need a signal from his instinct to inform him this was neither practice nor for fun, especially when Fey loosened her grip, cocked back her arm, and hit him hard in the face. Gordon fell back against the wall.

Dooley looked up at Brice. He clenched his teeth and pounced like a wild a cat. He grabbed Brice's armor-clasped forearm with one hand, and he grabbed the Englishman's neck with the other. Dooley lifted Brice a few inches, and then he slammed him to the ground. A quick focus allowed Dooley to conjure his pain and anger into the palms of his hands. He squeezed Brice's neck, planting a foot on his incapacitated foe's arm.

"C'mon, little jungle spirit," Brice taunted, his voice squeaking through the tightening grip Dooley had on his neck. *"End me with all that pain you got,"* he spat. Dooley squeezed harder.

Fey blinked her bright, cobalt-blue eyes. Gordon was snarling at her, using the wall she had just knocked him against to regain balance. She writhed as if struggling against an invisible net wrapped around her. But there was something there, battling her instinct. She used a burst of her spirit to push away the unseen influence of Gordon's hexed scars that reached out to her. Fey stepped back and focused, clear and conscious. A swirling, spherical, cobalt-blue light appeared at the center of her forehead.

Dooley continued squeezing, teeth bared and clenched.

"Gordon-baby…" said Fey to Gordon, voice filled with sadness.

Dooley squeezed!

Fey's body zipped up into the glowing sphere on her forehead. The tail of her essence swirled around the sphere and then snapped, projecting the ball of light forward. The thin, comet-like particle hit Gordon in the chest, knocking him to the floor and unconscious.

Dooley's image disappeared. Brice panted, no longer blocked from air. He looked around for his adversary, but Dooley was gone. The pain Brice garnered at the physical crossroads battle washed over him. He screamed! His image faded from the crossroads dreamscape as he too awoke.

The sphere ricocheted, and out of it came Fey's corporeal form. The lighted globe was attached to her forehead. Her landing was soft, feet against the floor. She put a hand over her heart and sorrowful eyes on Gordon. He was still. Eyes closed. A smoky, silver stream spiraled from her back and materialized into the yumbo Silver. The sprite took notice of the scene, the television screen providing light in the room, flickering as the images on the screen changed. Silver's eyes went wide, and she clasped her hands over her mouth.

"Silver," Fey called. "Go to Madame Jeliya's. Wake her. Tell her I'll be bringing Gordon to her altar-sanctuary." Silver dashed away, ghosting through curtain and window, scurrying in flight to the outside. Fey walked over to Gordon and knelt down, eyes still dripping with melancholy. She put her hand over his chest and reached out with her instinct. She could feel that Gordon was at rest. She closed her eyes, bowed her head, and said an ancient prayer over his body. Silver appeared a few moments later. She flew through the wall from the outside and informed Fey that Madame Jeliya's altar-sanctuary had been prepared for Gordon. "Thank you, Silver," Fey told the yumbo. She grabbed Gordon's arm and popped away with him.

Silver snapped her fingers and the television turned off, leaving the house dark. She dashed forward, wings flapping. Through the wall and outside, she flew down the street and straight into the ground once arriving at the Peters' residence, tunneling into Madame Jeliya's sanctuary located in the basement. The matriarch was already working an incant over Gordon's body, standing at the head of the chaise lounge where Gordon rested. Fey, still suited in cosmic attire, stood over Gordon at the side of the lounge. Papa Solomon was next to her, comforting arm around her shoulders. Silver floated over to them and watched as Madame Jeliya applied the incant and ritual.

"I thought my Art History final would be the hardest thing I did today," Fey attempted a joke. It didn't help. Papa Solomon tightened his embrace. At least the sun was making the day brighter, which was hard to tell in the basement of the Peters' brownstone.

"He'll be just fine," Madame Jeliya announced after speaking the last of her incant. She straightened and said to Fey, "Let him rest. You do the same, and then get to that exam, Miss Forrester."

Silver became a lighted, slither of smoke that seeped back into Fey.

Fey thanked the Elders and then popped away.

Gordon rested with no nightmares of the crossroads.

A memory never experienced was recalled in the final moments of Gordon's rest. A tussle with Fey Forrester was worse than any nightmare, and as his instinct buzzed at him in an intuitive form of Morse code, it was confirmed that it all happened. It was early this morning. It took place after seeing the morning news report the death of a young man he'd warned not to get involved in a series of events. It happened after a day of being force-fed the emotions of people burdened with personal history. It was concurrent with a rough-and-tumble fracas on a crossroads dreamscape with a man he attempted to kill.

Emotion welled as Gordon came from sleep. He lay on Madame Jeliya's lounge with a blanket over him. His blurred vision cleared and he looked around to bring the room into view, setting his bearings straight. Papa Solomon, seated in a chair, watched over him. The pain on Gordon's back was numb, and euphoria battled with the weight of emotions and histories he'd stolen the previous day. Gordon took a moment to let the emotions inside him wrestle until tired. Settled, and feeling relaxed, Gordon sat up and took a deep breath.

Papa Solomon remained quiet, allowing Gordon to shake off sleep and whatever spirit brewed like an electric charge inside him. But that didn't stop the Fable Avenue patriarch from having a little fun. He believed the spirit could always use some fun to straighten out the tight knots it often experienced.

"You been keeping up with your studies, young man?" Papa Solomon asked, sounding sincere. "How many tests you got left 'fore the semester ends?"

Gordon presented a soft smile, appreciating Papa Solomon's attempt to lighten the mood. "I had a couple tests yesterday," he answered his elder. But then he became somber as he stated, "I think I failed one of them." The pain of yesterday started setting in on his back as the memories of his unconscious skirmish with Fey came to the surface in quick, unbearable flashes. Then the memories came of his train rides to and from campus and the news report his instinct pulled him from sleep to see. It was a deluge, but Gordon held back his despair.

"We're not doing enough," he told Papa Solomon, thinking about all the memories he'd experienced from the people that surrounded him on the train. "If we're doing anything at all," he added.

Papa Solomon was serious when he asked Gordon, "How's the pain?" But before Gordon answered, Papa Solomon notified, "Madame Jeliya's on standby to apply an incant—she's at the funeral home in Harlem, helping with an embalming. But she's at the ready if you need anything. Maman Anansi and her husband are still trying to research the hex that man Willie hit you with." Gordon nodded his head, acknowledging Papa Solomon. Then the patriarch concluded, "I've been on the phone with the Old Goon, Satchel—Mister Eledas, down in Savannah. Told him Jackson and Gaston's houses are open. If his family wants to claim them, they can select new crossroad guardians at their leisure. And, Lady Arachne keeps getting a reading pointing to Fey."

"Oh, you'll have to see Fey about that," Gordon uttered, looking at the ground and thinking about something else. "She said she was scrying with the *Nigrum Nigrius Nigro*." He got up. "I'm sorry, Papa Solomon," he said looking at the Elder. "I need to go into Harlem and ask my father about something."

Papa Solomon looked up at Gordon. "You okay to do so? Could a simple phone call do? That's a long ways to go, farther than your campus."

Gordon considered Papa Solomon's suggestion, taking into account the population of the city trying to fit onto a train, and all the emotions and histories his instinct would try and bring to him. He sat back down on the lounge, looked at Papa Solomon and confessed, "I can get rid of a lot of this pain I carry, Papa Solomon."

The patriarch's expression became curious. "How so?" he asked. Gordon rubbed his hands together, contemplating and stalling. "Gordon?" Papa Solomon prodded.

Gordon snapped out of his sidetracking activity. He described, "When I sleep, Papa Solomon, I dream I'm back at the crossroads. I'm back in that fight."

"Yeah, just you and that British boy having a tussle," Papa Solomon finished Gordon's account. There was a quick beat. Now he was rubbing his hands together with a hard rub like a pitcher getting the ball ready for a deft toss. "Both of you share that pain, his nature and your spirit. You both there at the crossroads."

Gordon nodded. "It's a dream, but it's real." Gordon balled his fists. "And everything I feel is right here. I can focus, and I can put it all right here. And with these scars making me more empathetic, absorbing the hurt around me…" His eyes glowed brighter. The effect was subtle, but brighter still. Gordon bared clenched teeth. The pain on his back was biting, like a pack of wolves gnawing with all their ferocity. "I. Can. Hurt. Him. I can give it all to him."

"But you'll kill him on this physical landscape," Papa Solomon deduced.

Gordon was honest in his response. "That's not the problem I got with it, Papa Solomon. The problem is the pain won't get back to Stanley Fallows. It won't make a difference." Gordon attempted a grin, but it wavered. "He'll do his heartless villain thing and find himself another crony. He won't suffer. He'll clasp that tricked out armor onto someone else's arm—maybe promote a generic night doctor in place of Brice."

"Probably…" said Papa Solomon, head dropping. He shook a finger, raised his head and said, "But there's a possibility that this British boy is a great asset to him. It might set old Stanley back some in his plans."

"It might," Gordon agreed. "It just might."

Papa Solomon weighed another option, and then spoke it aloud. "Then, of course, maybe it's just the right time we fight back. Send a message to the Fallows family."

Gordon went stiff with only a subtle shake in his frame. His eyes drained of brightness, fading into a simple lilac hue. He'd heard the stern sound of a command in Papa Solomon's suggestion. "You want me to take a life, Papa Solomon?" he inquired, almost choking on his words.

The old man sat up straight. He rubbed his knees as if wiping his hands clean of a foreign substance. "Fable Avenue gets its stigma not because of the traditional Afro-spiritualism we honor," he stated. "Ad-hoc as we decipher the concepts to produce magic like we do 'round here," he added. "We see the magic in it all. Hell, some folks 'round here recite certain passages from the Bible in ancient Cushitic tongue to perform their incants." Then he asked Gordon, "Your father ever tell you about Dwayne Wilmore?" Gordon shook his head, no. "Cedron probably knows about this, being a little older. But I thought you'd be old enough to tell it to. Maybe your father has just blown it off."

"Oh," Gordon responded.

"I don't want to step on Max's toes, but I'm going to tell you." Then Papa Solomon explained, "Dwayne Wilmore was a thug in this neighborhood. Wasn't the only one, but he was someone we caught wind of. You know Tabitha Johnson, right? Well, her friend's daughter—outside the community—was being hurt by this Dwayne fellow." Gordon nodded. "But that was only one of many offenses on his resume."

"Right," said Gordon, picking up his cue to show attentiveness to the story.

"He ain't around," continued Papa Solomon. "But he ain't in prison either, dig?" He waited for Gordon to nod before carrying on. "The matriarchs tried to conjure justice by way of the law against him, but that only stirred me up." Papa Solomon reflected. "I gave your father the order. He went to Martin, Top Hat and Wilson."

"People got scared after that, huh?"

Papa Solomon shook his head, no. "No one knew, but," he made a face, "they knew. You know?"

"Details?"

"Your father picked him up. Wilson knocked him out. Top Hat tapped into his head, and Martin helped cover it all up." Papa Solomon brushed it away. "People don't know those details. But they suspected it was some people on Fable Avenue that handled that one. But I begin there because that's where and when we had a small crew haunting the neighborhoods, tryin' to regulate the everyday problems. This crew was a little more than misfit thievery of our ancient items."

"Okay," Gordon grinned, liking what he heard.

"People suspected things after we dealt with a situation of a woman pimping out her twelve-year-old daughter," Papa Solomon informed. "A situation we keep seeing pop up from time-to-time. Mothers doing that to their daughters," he elucidated.

Gordon pointed to Papa Solomon and said, "Now, *that* I heard about."

"The matriarchs were behind hexing the mother's mind, getting rid of her. Top Hat and Wilson were in charge of the last boyfriend she had. Bad man," Papa Solomon shook his head, making a face. "Worse than Dwayne Wilmore, let me tell you, little spirit." Papa Solomon gritted his teeth and cursed under his breath. "The girl's grandfather, we'd given him a blessing before. So, he understood, but he didn't like that. Not how we handled it. He didn't like admitting it was going on in the first place. Made him feel weak, like he wasn't protectin' his daughter or granddaughter." Papa Solomon huffed, "His wife jumped in, was his megaphone. She spread the word quicker than a spill, talkin' about our heathen ways."

"Girl got older," Gordon commented, sounding like a question.

"Yep. She went to go find her mother. Couldn't stop or blame her."

"She find her?"

"Don't know. That was about nine or ten years ago. She left the city to track her down." Papa Solomon exhaled. "That girl won't find anything but a woman that don't remember her. Chalk up another person angry at Fable Avenue's spirit, and that was where ours was broken. Our offense stopped, so worried about the words used to describe us."

"So you are asking me to kill him," Gordon concluded.

Papa Solomon shook his head, no. "Get creative. Send a message to Stanley," the old man ordered with conviction. "You're right. He should feel it too." Then he drifted, remembering. He chuckled a bit and told Gordon, "There was a time when Stanley Fallows helped us take down boys like old Brice Cadogan."

"Ain't that somethin', Papa Solomon?"

"Oh, yeah," the patriarch answered. "Stanley and his wife were vicious tacticians." He cursed again. "Now he's got your Fey's father's conjure, and he's rallying terrible forces against us." He shook his head and said, "I tell you, invite a banished man into your house after declarin' him banished. Watch out, and be careful when he come-a-walkin' back up to your door." He scoffed, "He was sincere toward my mother and father. Then things went to hell after a time. He always kept people like Brice and that Willie fellow in his back pocket on a 'just in case' basis. I suppose that case got opened."

Gordon's thoughts focused on Papa Solomon's suggestion of getting creative. There was a long pause, silence between he and the community patriarch. Gordon took the moment to stand, a plan taking shape in his head. He patted Papa Solomon on the shoulder and said he'd see himself out. The old man remained seated. He spoke an incant that surrounded Gordon in warmth. Gordon was, after all, still dressed for bed. Papa Solomon said to him as he reached the stairs, "Fey brought your shoes and a change of clothes. They're upstairs near the door." Gordon thanked Papa Solomon and continued on.

While sitting, Gordon was fine. Moving, climbing the stairs, and stepping out into the cold after slipping on his shoes were different stories. Within a few steps up the stairs, the pain crawled out of his back like a newborn spider from its egg. It explored his body with feverish curiosity. It felt more like a heavy weight on him rather than a burning irritation. Madame Jeliya's incant made the pain dull, but it was there, waking up with each step. But he endured and made it home. Before leaving Papa Solomon's house, he'd found his house keys tucked into the jeans Fey left for him. He scooped up his clothes and didn't bother changing. At his house, Gordon used his keys to unlock the garden-floor entrance, and he walked inside, exhausted from events of which he was barely conscious.

Door closed and locked, Gordon returned to his bedroom on the second floor after taking a long look at the front room. He thought about Fey until he reached the bedroom and spotted his phone on the dresser drawer where he'd left it. He put down his change of clothes and picked up his phone. He unlocked the device and flipped through his contacts until he came to his brother. He dialed. Cedron answered.

"What?" Gordon heard his brother ask.

Gordon looked at the bed and thought about sleep. The dream he'd been having as of late spread through his thoughts. He said to his brother, voice skipping in tone, "I gotta ask you something about your activities." Before Cedron could protest, Gordon added, "I won't be direct. I know this an open line."

"You know I got an incant to counter that," Cedron replied. "Though I wasn't expecting this call to be about something like that."

"Either way," Gordon spoke up, interrupting his brother. He took a moment to think about his words. The phrasing came to him and he inquired, "As a magician, making things disappear—and what not. I know you got, uh…" Gordon kept his eyes on the bed, thoughts split between a proper phrasing of his inquiry and his dilemma at the crossroad dreamscape. "I know you got a way with making objects vanish, right. You ever pull a trick like that on a person?"

Cedron's pause was so quiet that Gordon believed his cell phone dropped the call. Cedron was still there, though, silent and incensed at the question Gordon posed to him. He interrupted Gordon's 'hello' to see if he was still there. "The hell you ask me that for?" Cedron snapped. Gordon stuttered over words explaining his dilemma, but Cedron's anger punctured and interrupted that as well. "I might be running some knuckleheaded business on the side, like you all believe—pulled by the same crew the older folks all sought after for *your* sake, may I remind—but I don't do disappearing acts like that. Considering my predicament, kid, where I am right now, I can't even believe you—"

Gordon hung up the phone and put it down. He looked at the bed and thought about his dream and dilemma. He was tired, but he didn't want to sleep. As much as it pained him, he walked to the basement, taking his phone with him. Inside his sanctuary, Gordon picked up the blanket on the floor and put it around him. Wrapped up, he sat down in the mystically refurbished chair. He lay back, looking up at the ceiling, exhaling a breath.

"Hey, Spook," he said to the reconfigured tome.

The book opened, black mirror facing Gordon.

"I'm trying my best to handle this situation like Othello, y'know," he told the sentient, ancient technology. "Just go for it. Do it." He groaned a sigh. "But reality make you Hamlet like a motherfucker, just standing there thinking about a decision." He chuckled at his own joke. Pain scratched his back. His shoulders stiffened, and Gordon took a moment to ease it away. "I told Papa Solomon that it ain't about taking a life. We're not really taking lives when it comes to Stanley and his army—his known and unknown associates. They're not natural, Spook." The pain came again, stronger, Madame Jeliya's incant subsiding. "Like this pain," Gordon winced. He cleared his throat, looked at Spook and asked, "Spook, give me everything you told Fey about my condition."

Gordon sat up. He watched as characters scrolled across the black mirror. Gordon squinted, reading while using his instinct to keep up with each word, translating them. Spook repeated the information shared between it and Fey Forrester. Gordon read. He inquired, "And there's no known location for the Djed Pillar Jewels?"

In an ancient script across Spook's black mirror came the words, *Cannot decipher without connection.*

"Spook, open the chamber," Gordon commanded. The lid atop the sarcophagus structure slid open. Gordon unwrapped himself from the blanket and stood, straining as the activity was entwined with scathing irritation. Gordon hobbled over toward Spook. He laid his phone on the bejeweled console. Gordon stated, "If Fey calls, have the chamber wake me. Understood?" Spook's black mirror glowed with script familiar to Gordon. The mirror spelled out that it would alert him. "Thanks, Spook." He slipped into the capsule and the cap sealed over him. Gordon closed his eyes. He focused, instinct jumping from the center of his forehead and communing with the chamber that enclosed him. A soft glow brightened the inside. Gordon slowed his breathing.

Get creative, he thought. Minutes passed with Gordon focusing on an idea. He smiled when it came to him, and then he continued resting, anxious for sleep and a return to the crossroads dreamscape.

"Did I wake you?" asked Fey Forrester in a trembling voice, brief pauses between her words.

"No," Gordon answered through the phone. "I was resting in the chamber, but I told Spook to alert me if you called. You home?"

"No, I'm still on campus," Fey told him, standing at the door of Aaron Douglas Hall, watching the bare trees and the final shine drain from the bright autumn day. "I'm leaving now. Is everything okay with you?"

"Still in pain, Fey-baby," she heard Gordon say. "I've been in the chamber resting."

"You needed to speak to me?" she asked, cutting into Gordon's words.

Gordon hesitated for a moment, but then queried, "Are you heading straight home?"

"Only to lay my bags down," Fey replied. "I was going to see if Lady Arachne was home from work."

"That's good," Gordon voiced with a relieving sigh. Fey was surprised by the sentiment. "I got the transcript of your scry with Spook. I want you to inquire about the Djed Pillar Jewels."

"Oh," Fey interjected, voice perking up. "Will that help us get around the message in Spook's mirror? I keep reading '*Cannot decipher without connection*'."

"Possibly," Gordon's voice came through the phone. "Spook can't scry an object without having it placed between his mirror and jeweled console. That's what he's tryin' to tell you. Find an object, make an inquiry about the object's relevance to you, then take Spook in your arms and lie down. You'll dream the object's history. But your inquiry's gotta *be specific.* Otherwise, when you're lulled to sleep and see the history in your dreams, it will be one long, historical tale concerning whatever it is you're scrying about."

Fey moved away to allow pedestrian traffic to flow in and out of the Hall. She said, frustrated, "Well if we had the gems, we wouldn't need to find them."

"I know, Fey-baby. It's frustrating. The cards we scored for Lady Arachne might give us some insight. Maybe we'll find something connected to them that we can scry with. Or we'll get the proper answer. Something…"

"Right, Gordon," Fey uttered, absent of the lively spirit once in her voice.

"Fey-baby," Gordon said, getting Fey's attention.

"Yes, Gordon?"

There was a pause. Fey waited. Then she heard Gordon tell her, "I'm sorry for what happened this morning."

Fey closed her eyes and shook her head, feeling a headache coming. She heard a sound that was accompanied by an image. An argument. Her mother. Her father. Then their two images transitioned into she and Gordon. Fey opened her eyes to escape the scene. "It's okay, Gordon…Gordon-baby," she told him, putting her attention back on the day's fading light. "I know it wasn't you. It was the scars. Willie's lashes." The excuse, though valid, did little to lessen Fey's hurt. She shut her eyes again. The images reappeared. Mother. Father. She. Gordon. An argument. But this time she watched until they went away.

"Fey? You okay? You've seemed distant this whole conversation," Gordon noted. "I'm sorry."

Fey rubbed her forehead. "You don't have to be, Gordon," she assured, having brief pauses between her words. "I've had a day, you know. Tests."

"How do you think you did?"

"Well," she answered. "I think I did well." She expounded, "But, going through what happened between us, didn't help—I admit. But I don't blame you, Gordon…baby. It was Willie's lashes." She sighed and then told him, "Uh, let me go so I can get out of here and to Lady Arachne's. I'll be over tonight after the reading. Is that okay, Gordon?"

"I'll be waiting."

"Have you had any of the tea I got from Haiti?"

"Not today. No."

"I'll make you some. Let me go, Gordon."

"Okay, Fey-baby," she heard him wince. "Hurry home. Love you."

"…Love you too." She hung up and placed her locked phone into her pocket. She walked through the door and down the steps, scurrying onto the paths that would take her off campus. Fey was too anxious to use the train or other pedestrian means for her travel back to Fable Avenue, and truthfully she didn't have to conform to regular folks' measures and norms. Fey Forrester had power, and she was not above using it.

She hiked to the first alley ahead of her, wanting to use it for cover as she popped from existence. As it was cold, few people walked the streets. The alley was not in the direction of the nearest subway entrance. There were also few cars on the road. Then, Fey's instinct vibrated, shooting from her forehead and alerting her to the presence of two men following from behind. Fey rolled her eyes and continued on. She thought nothing of it, but decided to quicken her pace. When the two men also quickened their pace, Fey rolled her eyes again. She ducked into the alley, slipping into a shadow.

The two men hurried up toward the alley, giggling. "This bitch gon' make it easy for us," cackled one of the men. But they turned into the alley and found nothing but shadows and the silhouettes of objects. "The fu—"

Hands wrapped tight in cosmic fabric extended from the darkness. They grabbed the first young man by the back of the head, the talker—the one with the comment. They slammed his face up against the brick of the building, left wall of the alley, knocking him unconscious on heavy, bloody and ferocious contact. The hands then grabbed the collar of the second man, whose face was now drenched with surprise. They dragged him into the shadows. Soon after, there came from the unlit alley a racket of grunts and knuckles pounding flesh. After a moment, the second man's unconscious body was tossed from the backstreet. A cop car pulled up, drawn to the scene by instinct.

Fey Forrester popped into existence, hurrying up Fable Avenue to her family's residence. She was now in her civilian clothing, bag slung over her shoulder. She shook her shoulders, waving off frustration and the heat of the moment. She rummaged in her pockets for her keys and pulled them out. Walking up to her door, she commented in an annoyed manner, "What do I need these for?" She shoved her keys back into her pocket and popped away, snapping into existence in her room. She spoke an incant and the lights turned on.

Fey dropped her bag and then disappeared. On the street, she made quick strides to Lady Arachne's house. Approaching, she spied the matriarch parking outside of her house and exiting her car. Lady Arachne saw Fey and acknowledged with surprise, "Miss Forrester?" She shut her car door and locked it using an incant. She shifted her large bag hanging from her shoulder as she said, "I was going to give you a call and see if you could come through on your day off tomorrow. Are you okay? I heard about your ordeal with Gordon."

Fey stepped up to her and answered, "I'm fine, Lady Arachne." She made a courteous bow of the head, and then, looking at the Elder, Fey explained her coming. "I need a reading, Lady Arachne. Do you have time?

I could come back tomorrow. You're just getting home from work, I don't want to—"

"I've been waiting for you, Miss Forrester," Lady Arachne broke into Fey's rambling of excuses. "My readings surrounding Gordon's conditions keep pointing to you. I believe you might have an answer."

"I have an inquiry that might lead to one, Lady Arachne," Fey clarified.

The slender matriarch motioned for Fey to follow her into the house. Through the gate, and with Lady Arachne chanting a quick incant to unlock the garden-floor door, inside they went. Lady Arachne turned on the lights, removed her scarf and coat, and hung both items on the coat rack. She reached her arm back and directed Fey to pass her coat. Fey did as ordered, tucking her hat into a pocket before handing her coat to Lady Arachne. Lady Arachne moved farther inside, setting her pocketbook on the table.

"Some tea, Miss Forrester?" offered Lady Arachne, voice sounding as rushed as her movements. Fey declined, just as anxious as the Elder to find answers. "Down to work then. That's fine." She beamed and noted, talking over her shoulder to Fey as the young woman followed her to the reading room, "I always relax with a round of cards, trying to peer into our story, ponder its edits, and see if we can script its final chapters." She asked of Fey as they entered the small room, "Please close the door, Miss Forrester." Fey did so. Lady Arachne conjured flame to candles and burn to incense.

Fey looked around the room in wonder. It wasn't so much the supernaturalism of the décor, but the ambience it all produced in such a tight space. It was as if she'd turned into her lighted, spirit form and dashed through the atmosphere into the heavens.

Lady Arachne asked Fey to have a seat, and she sat down on the wooden bench. She took up her cards and started shuffling.

"Dear, querent," she said to Fey, "what is your query?"

"I did some scrying with Gordon's black mirror," Fey said to Lady Arachne. "Gordon's chamber needs seven blessed stones called the Djed Pillar Jewels," Fey outlined. "Supposedly, a set were brought to America long ago. They were christened the Sunset Gems." Then Fey asked, "Where are these Sunset Gems? Where can I fly to find them?"

Lady Arachne, a serious look now on her countenance, closed her eyes and focused. She repeated Fey's question in her head and hummed the notes of a sacred, African hymn. She stopped shuffling and drew a card, flipping it down on the table. Lady Arachne announced without opening her eyes, "The Seven of Cups." And she was correct. "This is what you seek, Miss Forrester." She continued shuffling.

Fey flinched when Lady Arachne announced the first card. It was the matriarch's voice, but it boomed as if through a loud speaker. She waited, bracing herself for the moment Lady Arachne's voice rumbled the next card.

After several rounds of shuffling, Lady Arachne stopped. She lay down three more cards, announcing them in order and without opening her eyes. Her voice was again like a roll of thunder. "The Queen of Pentacles," she said flipping over the first of the next three cards. "The Knight of Pentacles. The Four of Swords." The last two cards were placed over one another.

Lady Arachne was finished. Her eyes opened, and she put the remaining cards aside on her worktable. She scanned the drawn cards, thoughts concentrated. Her instinct shifted the images on the cards. The dark woman seated on the heavy throne changed and became Maman Anansi. The image of the knight seated atop the heavy, black horse became Top Hat, as did the image of the sleeping man drawn on the Four of Swords.

Fey used all her power to keep still. It was hard, watching Lady Arachne decode the meaning of the drawn cards. The matriarch was silent, with only a hint of activity through shifting facial expressions as the meanings came to her. Fey observed this, still on the outside, crumbling on the inside. Her stomach tightened.

"I believe…" Lady Arachne started. She paused, staring at the cards.

The effect caused Fey's heart to quicken. She leaned forward, face still stoic but inside trembling with impatience.

Lady Arachne looked at Fey and continued speaking. She started again, saying, "I believe Top Hat and Maman Anansi have answers for you." She added, "The cards have given me instinct. Top Hat is home at the moment, up the street. Maman Anansi is at her home in Queens."

"Lady Arachne," Fey prompted. "Can you call Maman Anansi while I go find Top Hat?"

"Absolutely, child," Lady Arachne affirmed. "I'll take the matter across the way to Papa Solomon and Madame Jeliya."

"Thank you," Fey expressed. A cloudy stream seeped from her back. The purple yumbo named Zee fluttered into existence. A piercing sting on Fey's back accompanied Zee's appearance. Fey tightened until the pain dissipated. She ignored the sensation the moment it passed. "Zee, assist the matriarch." Fey looked at Lady Arachne and asked, "Is that okay, Lady Arachne?"

"That would be just fine, Miss Forrester," said the Elder, admiring the hovering sprite with the purple glow to her flesh.

Fey stood, but not before getting permission from Lady Arachne. Zee ghosted through the door before Fey and Lady Arachne opened it and followed the sprite into the next room. The two women gathered their things from the coat rack. Scarf around her neck, and coat around her body, Lady Arachne said to Fey, "I'll send message—" She turned to address Fey, but the young woman was gone. "—through. Your. Yum. Bo…" she finished, voice trailing away. She said looking at Zee, "Does she always do that?"

Zee nodded, yes.

Fey popped into existence a few steps from the brownstone of Top Hat's apartment. She walked up to the parlor-floor door, buzzed his apartment number and waited. She peered through the curtains on the door. She saw the frame of Top Hat's silhouette through the curtains as he walked down the stairs with all his weight in each step. He opened the door and said with a surprised expression, "Fey? Everything okay?" He looked different to Fey without his signature coat and top hat.

"I was at Lady Arachne's for a reading. Your name came up."

"Whatchu need, sister?"

"You ever heard of the Sunset Gems?" she asked. Fey, again, was impatient yet courteous as she perceived Top Hat to be thinking about the question. *Yes or no, it's not that hard,* she thought.

"Come in out the cold," he invited.

Fey walked inside. Top Hat closed and locked the door. They stood in the hall for a moment before Top Hat answered, "Supposedly the outlaw Thunder John went after the gems. A distant relative of mine mentored him, but by that time, my relative was old with an incant blessing his life. So he was old, very old. But he was still there with Thunder John." He threw his thumb over his shoulder and said, "Papa Solomon and Maman Anansi's great-grandfather led that charge. Joseph Pepper the Fourth. He hired Thunder John and the Brother Dogs for that excursion."

"Did they recover the gems?" Fey asked. A faint hint of desperation rattled her voice and widened her eyes.

Top Hat hiked his shoulders and uttered, "I. Don't. Know. I don't think so. We know of all the folklore items we have in our possession. The gems aren't cataloged as being stored upstate—or with another family out of state. Not to my knowledge. And if Lady Arachne sent you here, most likely, they're not on any conjure family's records."

Fey continued her inquiry, asking Top Hat, "Do you have any items from your relative, specifically something from his time with Thunder John? I need it for scrying. It might lead to healing Gordon."

"Yeah," he said. "I got something, Fey. Wait here."

Top Hat hurried up the stairs. Fey exhaled, relieved. She paced until Top Hat returned. He handed to her, with care in his pass, an old, rusted hunting knife.

Fey took the object, handling the knife with as much care as Top Hat. The object rattled loose in her grip. "I will respect this item, Top Hat. Thank you," she proclaimed.

Before Top Hat could acknowledge her sentiment, Fey popped away. But Top Hat, with a grin on his face, still said "You're welcome, sister." And then he went upstairs.

"Gordon!" Fey hollered as she appeared in the parlor hall of the Goodspeed residence. She kept the blade in the palm of her hands, held out like a servant delivering a plate of delicacies. "Gordon!" Fey called again. There was no answer. Fey reached out with her instinct and felt Gordon's presence in the basement. She moved to the lower level, staying careful with the hunting knife. Once there, Fey placed the hunting knife down on the coffee table, and then she rushed to the basement. *"Gordon!"* Fey cried as she entered the room.

His face was buried in the seat's cushion, knees to the floor. Fey approached him, steps quick. She stooped down and put her arms around him. He was trembling. Fey tried lifting him. Gordon turned over, eyes bright but not aflame with light. Sweat soaked his brow.

"T-t-tea…" he said to her.

"Can you stand, Gordon-baby?"

Gordon nodded, yes. He gripped Fey's arm and used her for balance. Fey assisted as Gordon pushed up to stand. It was a quick vault up, and then he turned around and plopped down in the chair. Gordon caught his breath. Fey wiped his brow with a pat.

"Oh, Gordon-baby…" she sympathized.

He smiled. "Any answers…?" he strained to ask.

"Yes. But let me get you some tea and relax that bruised spirit."

"More than bruised, Fey-baby…"

Feeling better about Gordon, Fey went to the upper floor and started water for tea. She returned when the brew was prepared. Fey handed the tea to Gordon, holding the cup as his grip trembled, guiding it to his lips. Gordon sipped. The tea was instant. His shakes and pain dispersed. His grip tightened on the cup, and when Fey was certain Gordon could handle the mug on his own, she sat down on the floor.

"Top Hat gave me an item to scry," Fey informed him. "A family heirloom connected to that old outlaw Thunder John. Supposedly he was hired by Joseph Pepper the Fourth to help procure the precious stones."

Gordon nodded. "So, a bedtime story and ritual to put me to sleep, and then you'll dream vividly of the past?"

A smile broke on Fey's face. It was as warm as the tea Gordon sipped, and it was just as healing. "Yes, Gordon-baby." She was silent thereafter, watching Gordon drink and regain strength. He didn't finish the tea. He drank enough to numb the vile scratches on his back, and then he put his drink down on the carpet. Fey slid next to Gordon and asked, "Do you want your blanket, Gordon-baby?"

Gordon reached out for Fey's hand. She took his, and he said to her, "Yes, please." She covered him with the blanket, and then they turned their heads to the *The Written* tome. It lifted by instinct and opened by the same faculty. Fey and Gordon's eyes burned bright with their signature auras. Tendrils reached out and lathered ink onto the page, continuing the story of *In Thirteen Pieces.*

Press pause
Press play
We press forward
All eyes opened
(we see more than fog)
Ears attentive
(we hear more than the taunts of devil swine and wulvz)
We hear the shackles worn by nature in this land
She, subjugated
The fog leaves us in the open
Closed off from camouflage
We wish for a veil of shadows to blanket our army of shades

Mock! Mock! Laughter buzzes our ears.
A chorus of slithering sounds is near
Hiss. Rattle. – His babble of twisted knowledge cackles
And footsteps rumble earth
We file, deep in ranks – eyes everywhere see fog

Grand hands lift gossamer gauze
Wipes away the gray day
The sun cowers at the horizon
Where pours the snarl and charge of wulvz
And devil swine

We break line
Open like lotus
Blossom war and rage
On this familiar stage

A rampage of unalike in kind
Watch our eyes dine on battle
We dive into waves of uncaged ferocity
Giants dance away
A fleet of body and blood left in our wake

Grand hands that part the fog
Point to streams of blood from leg
To arm
And motion for our earth to open
And blood to flow, deep as the ocean
The power to heal wielded backwards

Shades bleed light
The giant Ache points
Joints quake
Shades breathe lighter
He points and scripts fate
Fills hands with lines of discord
And an off key song, held in the palm

Footsteps bellow, enter Sedua
A giant crowned with knowledge
He stands proud with crown atop the head
Thirteen points point straight like pitchforks and devil's horns
They dissolve to form the body of snakes
Writhing with hiss, fangs curved from their lips
They slither backwards – stop progressive thought
Writhe and writhe and writhe from the scalp
And around the heads of shades
Thought is squeezed and policed
Subdued to obey – this giant froths the venom of his snakes

Vubrawl, her spine an electric whip
From bottom, to top of tip
Lashes turn shades to ashes
Her screams gargle the air
Spinal whip tears through her allies, unaware
Wild, erratic attacks

Baron C opens earth
And speaks

"If graves you make
Of earth and lakes
Then drown and drip
Toes that tip, stumble and trip."

Earth sinks
A bowl to cup
Trip up,
The one to fall is Ache
We shades find relief from his point and quake
And the opening wider of our wounds
Captain Debas, shades and I
Continue battle through the rattle of our bones

Phour gives
And Phour gets
Wrapping the snakes
That are wrapped against heads
Into cosmic nets
Tight! Tight! Tighter!
Cutting their breaths

I pounce
Slam spear down
Two snakes are cut to ground
An army more
Slithers from Sedua's head to the earth's
Blood drenched floor
Entangled in the waltz of war, snakes
Overrun shades
And the day goes gray again with fog
My spear punctures, sprays red haze
Invigorates the shades
Captain Debas commands a raid
His words recruit allies three,
Bwa, Cimetiere, and Phour – a reiterated triad of soldiers
"Mud against wounds – and that giant cannot harm
Phour, confuse his eye to guide his hands against
The electric whip and spine."

Soaked earth kisses our scars
And hugs tight

Deflects hexing point of finger
That would widen wounds
Phour moves in rush, tosses stardust into his hands
And crowns the eyes of Ache
The giant quakes – seeing stars
Fingers aimed, hexes scratch and scathe Vubrawl
Her spinal whip lashes strikes back
Smack and crack against Ache

Captain Debas commands,
"Brother-C, bury deep and create pit
Let this giant's snakes sit there."

Ground opens deep
Snakes seep,
Their serpentine slither, slithers into the ground
Baron C's grip of earth
Drawn back like bow – let go
Let loose a wave of snakes into the air
Earth follows them there, a wave of mud and rot
Drops Vubrawl's lightning vibration
And there my cue, my indication to strike

I pounce
Up into air
Plummet
Tumble underneath
Stab stomach
Ache bleeds his last breaths
His ashes drip
And the power in his hands
Is wrestled from his fingertips
The true healing touch for Motherland's covenant
Count. Down. One more of her thirteen restored.

Sedua's crown conjures snakes to the earth floor
He commands with roar
Wind kicks up the ground
Sedua makes fatal step on the burial
Of Vubrawl's mound
The lightning whip—wild lashes grip his neck

Swift move
I stab Vubrawl at her root
Retract – stab up into roof of mouth
Agony muted, no screams aloud
Retract – spear point crash through heart
Puff to ash – spinal energies returned to Sirene

Pounce – up
High above the wave of snakes
I strike down
Spear point through Sedua's crown
Eyes roll up
Body to dust
My feet slam against the earthen bed
Twisted, locked natural snakes
Return to their natural state
Draped down, the lioness' mane and crown
Wisdom upon her head

We pause to breathe
At ease
This battle has reduced us
We are just us
An army of twenty, myself adds one
We hear wulvz whimper, humbled
They are tamed and domesticated dogs
As the winds growl through us
We carry the spirit of Anubis
Devil swine are the black pigs sacrificed to Marinette
We hear the fear pounding – a coward's heart in their chest
Assured, be rest – this army of black shades be conscious
We are the coming storm warned about
Scatter heat and cold, heavy rain and snow
– we are the climate
Our snarl mutes wulvz and the devil swine's finest
We shout to the last,
"Come out! – Let us battle, you remaining giants..."

Fade to light, and light fades to scenery of the Goodspeed basement. The bright sparks in Gordon and Fey's eyes dimmed to their natural color. The floating tome flipped close and landed with a gentle touch against the chamber. Fey looked at Gordon, spying his body shaking.

His shiver wasn't erratic, but she reached for his cup of incanted tea and presented it to him. He accepted and started sipping. Fey released Silver, Em, and Jade from her person. Again there was a slight sting upon their cloudy conjure into the world. Fey paid the discomfort no mind. She said to her conjured sprites, "Upstairs, you three. Prepare Gordon's bed. Thank you." The yumboes fluttered up, ghosting through the ceiling. She asked Gordon, "You need help getting to your altar?"

Gordon shook his head as he slurped the remainder of his tea. "No," he said aloud after swallowing. "Thank you…" He winced. He handed the cup to Fey, and she set it back to the ground just as Gordon attempted to stand. "Half this pain is because I've been taking my altar up and down the stairs, piece-by-piece."

Fey watched. Gordon struggled, but he managed to stand, though he was hunched over. She rose with him, walking alongside him as he staggered to his altar. "Stubborn as an old fool, I guess," he commented. His legs wobbled as he bent down, knees to the floor. Fey, as if she was Gordon's shadow, mimicked his movement. When Gordon, hands trembling, placed a stick of incense within the burner, she gave aid by speaking an incant that lit the stick. Gordon thanked her, and then he closed his eyes and inhaled the scent. He spoke a prayer to himself and dropped back unconscious. Fey caught him before his back hit the floor, and she popped from existence when his body fell into her arms.

Upstairs.

Fey was beside the bed, laying Gordon's body against the mattress. She had to adjust herself, standing with a wobble as she came into being in his bedroom. Silver and the other yumboes laid the comforter over Gordon as he rested, and then Fey called them to her. There was a mild discomfort as the yumboes retracted into her tattoos. Fey stiffened, and then she stretched her neck and shoulders until the ache in her back dissipated. Straightening, she paused for a moment to say a prayer over Gordon. When the prayer was finished, she disappeared to the basement.

She came to, standing in front of the *Nigrum Nigrius Nigro*, the mirror of which was already facing up. "You going to help me dream, Spook? I have an object and a query."

Then insight I will provide, ran across the face of the black mirror in an ancient script. Fey lifted Spook from the shelf where it was fastened. A quick snap separated the black-mirrored tome from its attachment. With ancient device in hand, she climbed the stairs.

"I'm not really feeling tired, Spook," she told the arcane object.

You'll sleep, Fey read the assuring words as she sat down on the couch.

She reached for the hunting knife on the coffee table, setting the antique item atop the jeweled console. She shut the black mirror over it and then flattened out on the couch, Spook to her chest. Fey, free of will, wrapped her arms around the closed tome as if it was a prayer book. She thought of her query, and then history dragged her into sleep for her viewing pleasure.

Her Six-Gun Conjure

"I want what every woman wants, Mister Cross."

A wave of cobalt-blue light erased a scene of cloudy darkness. The light lifted, revealing a location of long ago in the American Old West. It was night. Smoke hung in the air like a fog. There was dust and ash floating together as one, all part of the décor accenting the Crab's Creek mining camp. Occupied tents varying in size lined the muddy streets. Miners contracted in service or licensed as independent were inside. Some of the housing had within its leather walls whole families packed tight. A few tents glowed with a soft orange and yellow hum, giving preview of the goings on behind the tanned façades. Along the face of ten glowing walls, in flickering silhouette, there played out card games, drinking and conversation, lonely contemplation with occasional scribble of thought in journals, and mothers giving final tuck-ins to their children.

Scattered around the tents were a few finished buildings and the skeletal frames of those in progress. The finished structures, though not towering, were a sense of inspiration for the slow growing town that was trying its best to transition into a boomtown. Even the in-progress sites signaled a move forward. The completed buildings were under pressure to house more than one function. One office building of moderate size housed the headquarters for local law enforcement, lawyers, and the postal service. Posted on the building's entrance doors was a sign that mirrored the other signs stationed at all of the entrances for Crab's Creek. It read: *The Carrying of Firearms is Strictly Prohibited.* This of course did not mean that guns not being carried was absolute, and the local law enforcement was rather lax on prosecution.

Ruffians were found on the outskirts of Crab's Creek, hugging the trails used by miners, scouring for excavated quarry to seize. But with the aid of civilian posses and bounty hunters, the local law enforcement apprehended, killed, and kept some of the roughest bandits and criminals at bay. A monetary reward offered for assistance or capture helped strengthen Crab Creek's law enforcement numbers and turnout for both bounty hunters and vigilante mobs.

On this night, however, such prize-for-capture was being rescinded from a three-man group of bounty hunters. The leader of this gang was an old man named Bunk "Old Gun" Abraham, a dark skinned, seventy-three-year-old black man with a bushy, white mustache. Underneath his raggedy and bunched top hat was a receding bush of hair just as white as his mustache. His two, flanking lieutenants were the sons of a man that once served him as a soldier of sorts in an all-black gang fronted by Bunk called The Black Scarves. Bunk was of average height with a muscular build and a warrior's demeanor.

Jonathan Cross was the older of the two brothers flanking "Old Gun" Abraham, but by only three years. He was twenty-five, with smooth brown skin and a rectangular-shaped face. His round eyes were now accustomed to holding a narrow stare. Over the years of learning how to track bandits for profit, squinting in the distance through dark of night or light of day became a permanent fixture of his gaze. Jonathan didn't wear a hat. He wore a black scarf on his head that covered a bush of puffs and twists. The same scarf that was his father's when he was a soldier in service to Bunk Abraham's self-made army. Over navy-blue trousers, Jonathan wore brown, leather chaps. He wore a beige collar shirt, buttoned up and covered by an opened, black vest.

Donavan Cross was a few shades lighter than his older brother, their mother's partial indigenous blood showing more prominent in his reddish color. Donavan too had a boyish look to his face, though much like his brother, he'd seen a great deal of action in the past five years. His eyes were wide and observant, and whatever it was that he saw he only relayed to Donavan and Bunk in a low, shy whisper. His hair, like his skin, was a dark reddish-brown. It was straighter than Jonathan's, and he wore it in braids that he let grow down passed his ears. He wore a tan jacket over a plain white shirt, and dark pants tucked into his boots.

All three men were armed with various weapons of choice, and the local law allowed this to be so considering their status as bounty hunters. The three of them, at present, shared the same grimace on their faces, having come from the sheriff's office and having their reward taken from them for their latest apprehension.

"Ain't seen that before," griped Jonathan to Bunk.

Bunk just huffed.

Jonathan looked at his brother who just rolled his eyes and lifted his shoulders.

"We got something for our troubles," Jonathan continued speaking, trying to keep a bright side on the situation.

"Seventy-five dollars ain't the three hundred we were promised," Bunk snapped. "These boys better get they villains straight. Keep their board updated. We tracked Lucas McAlvy for three days. We spent sixty on the hunt. That's just fifteen dollars we made for this. And we got to restock provisions, ammunition."

They walked into the second-most important constructed building: The saloon. Things didn't look better inside. There, at the bar, was their capture. Lucas McAlvy. He was now loose and free to roam. The dirty-faced, sunburnt man waved Bunk and his lieutenants over to him, an apologetic look on his soot-stained face.

"Come this way, fellas," he said. "I got your drinks. No hard feelings."

Jonathan and Donavan didn't move. They looked at Bunk for a cue. "Come on," said the old man. "No harm in sharing a drink with this man." They pressed forward through the sea of patrons.

On approach to the bar, Lucas asked the men to name their drinks. Bunk spoke for the group. "Three whiskeys with blackberry liquor," he told Lucas, who then turned to the bartender and pushed the order.

Lucas took off his beige, crumpled cowboy hat, exposing his unkempt, dirty-blonde hair. "You know in all this, boys," Lucas told them as they settled up to the bar. "In all this, my biggest surprise was that I was worth four-hundred dollars." He swiped up his drink and took a sip. He chuckled as he said, "You boys were going to get stiffed either way. Local law was only looking to give you three hundred of that." He grinned as he commented, "I swear the Negro is but thirteen years free, but he ain't got no freedom. I mean, shit, don't you boys know they send some of the hardest bounties your way to preserve deputized men? Saves the trouble of real casualties." Their drinks were served. Lucas pointed to them coolly, as if Bunk and his lieutenants weren't aware of them. "I'm grateful you boys went for the capture rather than the kill. Still don't believe I ended up on the wanted board. They had a picture of me and all."

Bunk didn't reply. He merely grimaced. Jonathan decided to smile and play along, thinking there was something to Lucas after all. "You got anything on you, besides bad luck?" he asked not looking at Lucas until finishing a sip of his drink. "Don't worry. We wouldn't turn you in for anything other than what they want you for." Jonathan put a hand on his chest, smile remaining. "On my honor," he assured.

"Boy, I couldn't tell you," Lucas said, wondering himself.

"Come on, Lucas," Jonathan continued. "There's got to be something. I mean, I swear, I won't tell. Again, on my honor."

A little frustrated, Lucas answered, "Look, if I had the slightest clue, boy, I'd tell you. Ain't like I haven't been locked up for one thing or another in my thirty-eighty years. Shit, I was locked up when I was sixteen." Lucas' eyes spotted the guns strapped to Jonathan's belt. "Ain't that somethin'," he expressed, features widening with awe. "Now where did you come across them pair of cannons?"

"Oh, I bought these," Jonathan announced with pride. "These were purchased to commemorate a big, bad catch of ours. I'd let you hold them, but town regulations won't let me draw them out."

Lucas nodded, acknowledging John's words. He continued staring at the two, heavy LeMat revolvers holstered at Jonathan's side. "Goddamn! Color me double lucky you didn't take a shot at me," Lucas hollered, thanking the Almighty above for the derailment of alternative possibilities to his fate. "One hit from one of those, at close range? Shit, I'd be done. Glad I was worth more alive. It all don't make the sense God gave a mule. I don't know."

As the conversation between Jonathan and Lucas continued, a woman entered the saloon, though no one could tell it was a woman. Her manner of dress didn't readily draw the salacious attention from some of the more unsavory and drunken male patrons. But when they noticed she was indeed a *she*, their eyes remained glued. Her name was Ori Washta, and she was dressed for the frontier, decked in masculine clothes. A navy-blue jacket, old but well-kept with the exception of dirt and dust from recent travel, covered a white collar shirt. She wore a black scarf around her neck, tied in a knot with the ends tucked into the front of her shirt. Her beige pants were in much the same condition as the jacket. And she wore dark-brown leather boots with her pants tucked inside.

What caught some of the patrons' attention was the assortment of weapons carried on her person. Slung across her back was a bow and rifle. She wore a quiver of arrows on one hip and a cattleman's revolver on the other. Around her waist was a series of cultural trinkets, and a holstered dagger. Her wide brim hat shadowed her surprisingly clean, dark brown and ovate face. Long, black braided hair draped down from her hat and far past her shoulders. And while the people stared at her for her weapons, they noticed the feminine curves of her frame. Lucas spotted her walk to the bar, and she came between him and Jonathan, stepping up to the bar and ordering a strong drink in a soft, almost musically, feminine voice.

Lucas switched his interest from the conversation he was having with Jonathan to the young woman named Ori Washta who was fit for the frontier. "Hey," he opened his line of flirtation. "I thought you was a boy. That was making me a little nervous. Something about your walk was saying otherwise. Had me stiff, honey," he chuckled.

Ori didn't get offended. She looked up from under her wide-brim hat and beamed a smile. But she did not respond to Lucas. Instead, she flagged the bartender, and when he approached she asked, "Hey, there, mister. Can a girl find lodging around here for the night? It looks mighty cramped in this town." Her voice was polite, and there was an air of sophistication that held so much civility in it that her tone negated the rough exterior she fronted.

"You want to talk to a woman named Catherine Murray," the bartender answered, giving Ori her drink. "She's the owner of a lodge just up the street."

"Thank you," said Ori.

"Such a pretty face," Lucas continued. "Not a speck of dirt on that pretty, brown face of yours."

Bunk moved between Jonathan and Ori. Drink in hand, he offered, "Ma'am, you need an escort up the street?"

"Oh, no thank you, kind sir," Ori replied. "I'll be fine. You gentlemen can all go back to your celebration." She looked at Bunk, then at his lieutenants, and then Lucas. "I saw you all clank glasses just as I walked in."

Bunk chuckled, dropping his head. Then the old man explained, "This is far from a celebration, ma'am. We three here—" and Bunk waved his drink around, aiming at himself and his two lieutenants Jonathan and Donavan. "—We lost the collect on our capture, which would be this man standing right here." He aimed his drink at Lucas. "Three hundred dollars he was worth. We got seventy-five for our trouble."

"Oh," said Ori, intrigued. She turned and looked up at Lucas from underneath her wide-brim hat. "You must have yourself a good lawyer."

"I did," Lucas admitted. "My employer's lawyer, really," he clarified. "But he proved that I had no business being on that wanted board, sketch and all. And to show I'm a good sport, I bought these boys a drink. No harm done. They was only following what they believed to be their bounty." He rubbed a finger across Ori's face and stood tall over her, smile on his countenance. He told her, "Wasn't like these boys would've seen the entire bounty. I was actually worth four hundred dollars. Only three of that was going their ways."

"Oh, my," said Ori. She turned and looked down the bar at Jonathan. "Don't let this hurt too much." Both Jonathan and Donavan looked up at her. Ori was smiling at them, and they smiled back. "Two handsome young men such as yourselves got a lot more bounties to come your way, even if Crab's Creek's law won't relinquish the full purse for your troubles." She nudged Bunk and said up to him, "I'm sure an experienced, refined man like you seen plenty to let this one go. Keeping money out of the hands of some fine, honest and hardworking black men is no new experience, is it?"

Bunk grinned at Ori, wondering what her angle was.

Lucas barged into Ori's commentary. "Let these boys alone, little missy," he suggested to her. Ori turned and gave Lucas her full attention.

"Let me tell you about your black brothers. You see these boys? These boys right here? Your people got freedom on paper, but from where I stand I keep seeing black boys like these ones here doin' the work, struggling with nothing to show. But a good man like me? Well, I can provide for you little honey. All of life's comforts," he emphasized. "My name's Lucas." Then he asked her, "Where you come from, looking so pretty? Damn-near no speck of dirt on you. Soft, and dark brown, and pretty you are. Like a good cup of coffee," he compared. "What's your name little girl?"

"My name is Ori Washta, and I'm a worldly woman, Mister McAlvy," Ori answered. Donavan Cross perked up with Ori's words. He whispered something into Jonathan's ear. "You see, my father was a Negro, roots tied to Africa," Ori stated. "He was a slave until he ran away years before there was a war to inspire the ending of such a system. He fled west, and he was taken in by an indigenous nation."

Lucas snickered, "*Nation*… You make it sound like the savages got laws and order."

Ori ignored him and continued with her tale. "That is where he met my mother's people and established himself as a prominent member while he courted and married my mother. My mother's people are called the Qalifia Nation. Have you ever heard of them, Mister McAlvy?"

Lucas' confident grin melted away. He grabbed his drink and nursed its final sips. Finishing, he commented, "Sorry, Miss Washta. I don't keep up with what half your kind call their cluster. I just know where not to go so I can avoid them—regardless of name." He reached into his pocket and pulled out money, dropping it on the bar and signaling for the bartender that he was through, and all that was laid onto the bar was enough to pay for Bunk and his lieutenants' drinks. "Now, if you'll excuse me. It's been a long day."

Bunk was thinking about Ori's words, made apparent by the deep look of speculation on his face. "Miss Washta, did you say your mother is of Qalifia blood?"

Ori heard Bunk, but she didn't make an immediate response. Her eyes were on Lucas' departure, following his leave out of the saloon. "A tale for another day," she answered, addressing Bunk's question, and leaving him unsatisfied. She suggested to Bunk, "Perhaps early tomorrow. A packed belly like this town don't keep room for long. I'm sure someone's making a walk away from this place, getting flushed out somehow." Ori went into her pocket and dropped some coins on the bar for her drink.

Then Ori disappeared through the crowd of patrons and out of the saloon doors. She was gone before Bunk could again offer assistance in escorting her up the street. "Jonathan," Bunk called. He whispered to the older of his lieutenants, "Keep a step behind. Stay shadowed. Just make sure she gets down the road okay."

"Yessir," Jonathan said to his mentor. "Besides, Donavan noticed she addressed Lucas by his last name. He never told her what his last name was. Something don't sit right."

"Probably because it ain't," Bunk remarked. "Now get going."

Jonathan moved through the crowd, stepping outside. He saw as he walked away from the saloon that there was no one on the street, in any direction. Ori Washta was gone, and so was Lucas McAlvy. Jonathan put his hands on his hips, just above his holstered LeMat revolvers, and he contemplated. He looked over his shoulder at the saloon entrance, eyebrow raised. He walked back into the bar and whispered to Bunk, "No sign of our pretty frontier woman. I'll check the lodge to see if she's there." Bunk made a silent approval as he downed the last of his drink. Jonathan asked his brother if he wanted to trudge along, but Donavan declined. "Okay. Suit yourself. The pretty lady is all mine then," he teased his brother with the claim, slapping Donavan on the shoulder. Then Jonathan turned around, exited, and pressed down the street to the well-built, three-story lodge down the road.

He scoped all directions as he made his way to the hotel. There were few activities happening this late on the street. Most people were rushing to their tents or lodging rooms. Jonathan saw nothing out of order. He stepped inside the hotel and up to the front desk where a well-dressed gentleman was stationed. He asked the gentleman behind the desk, "Did a young, frontier woman come in here looking for lodging? I believe her name is Miss Ori Washta. I just want to know if she arrived safe."

"Oh, yes she did," the gentleman said in an excited manner. "Lovely woman, even with all of the rough garments of the frontier on her. She signed in early this afternoon. Been a long day, but she's returned. Another of our guests just now accompanied her. They seem to be getting along quite well."

"Lucas McAlvy?" Jonathan asked.

"Yes. Friend of yours?"

Jonathan grinned as he nodded his head. "Yes, he is," he replied, hands on his hips. He cleared his throat and said, "Well, thank you, good sir. I'm glad she's safe." Jonathan twirled around, and he missed the gentleman's parting words and kind tone. Outside, Jonathan kicked the muddy street and gritted his teeth. He returned to the saloon and informed Bunk and his brother that Ori Washta was okay. "That girl went and shacked up with Lucas McAlvy," Jonathan added. "And the odd thing is she's been registered at the lodge since this afternoon. She already had lodging."

"I ain't gon' pretend to understand the world," Bunk commented.

"You think his words about us not being able to provide got to her?" Jonathan asked with his face contorted.

Bunk only repeated, "I ain't going to pretend to understand the world." He looked over at Donavan, and the younger Cross brother rolled his eyes.

Jonathan whispered, "I think he's a mark. I'm going to keep a close eye. Maybe we can get some money out of all this. Or maybe they partners, playin' us some fools. For all his providin' talk, he didn't pay for her drink."

Bunk considered the notion, bobbing his head and making a face as he thought about it. He concluded, "We've had a day. Losses abound. I'm superstitious enough not to jump into a game of cards. Don't need any more grief if loss is the day's theme." He turned away from the bar and told his lieutenants, "Sheriff got us lodged up in the offices tonight. Let's take him up on the offer. Hell, it's free. Come on."

Jonathan joked, "Hope it ain't in a cell." And Donavan managed to express a chortle.

The Cross brothers followed their captain out of the saloon and across the muddy street and through the fleet of tents. Crab's Creek was now silent, and the glow of tents had been extinguished. Even the noise from the saloon was dampening. At the law building, Sheriff Robert Goddard gave a warm welcome to Bunk and his young lieutenants. He and two deputies were keeping eye on the night. He spoke of a possible game of poker, but Bunk declined, citing for the sheriff his musing on the luck the day had offered so far. After a few minutes of small banter, Sheriff Goddard had one of his deputies escort Bunk and the Cross brothers to a moderate-sized room with three beds. It was on the second floor of the two-story building, and the deputy also pointed out the bathroom area down the hall. It had a large bin filled with water from which they could make a quick wash come morning. The outhouse was in the back of the building. Bunk thanked the man and then he and his lieutenants prepared for bed.

Jonathan hopped out of bed early the next morning. He took a wash down the hall and put on the very clothes he'd worn the previous day, save the leather chaps and black vest. With his guns strapped around his waist, and his scarf wrapped around his neck rather than atop his head, he headed to the saloon for a bite to eat. Two eggs, two slices of toast, two slices of bacon, and a glass of water was his order. He waited at the bar until his breakfast was served, and then he paid and took his food to go sit at an empty table. The bartender, a Mexican-Irishman named Cal Ortiz, mentioned to Jonathan that the sheriff was posting more bounties today.

Jonathan thanked Cal for the information, and then he commented over his shoulder that he'd inform Bunk when the old man rose for the day.

Early as it was, most of Crab's Creek had already pulled out. Prospectors were starting their day beyond the town, getting their hands dirty mining for fortune. All that was left in town were a few assigned lawmen, wives awaiting the return of their husbands, prostitutes waiting for lonely miners to proposition, the local doctor and his wife the nurse, and children being homeschooled. Few patrons filled the saloon, and those that did were enjoying their breakfast in silence like Jonathan.

Ori Washta walked into the saloon while Jonathan was into his first few bites. Her presence stirred his attention away from his food. She was wearing a long-sleeved, dark jade, and princess-line dress with gold trim. Her chest and neck were fully covered. Atop her head, resting on her braided hair that was wrapped up into a sizeable bun at the back of her head, was a small cap with veil extended over the left side of her face. Her hands were gloved, and Jonathan found it peculiar that her dress' train was unblemished from the mud on the street. But her presence brightened an otherwise gray, cold day. Jonathan watched Ori step up to the bar, and it was then that he dropped his head and continued eating. He missed Ori's exchange with the bartender, ending with Cal Ortiz pointing to where Jonathan was sitting. But Jonathan noticed Ori's approach, though he kept his head down, making it appear that his attention was on his breakfast.

"Mister Jonathan Cross?" Ori said, presenting herself. "May I join you at this table?"

Jonathan stopped taking bites. He set his fork down and looked up at Ori Washta, unable to keep a grin from his face. "Yes, ma'am, you may." Ori pulled back the chair, and by instinct Jonathan made a move to stand.

"Thank you, Mister Cross," Ori said to him. "It's right kind of you to get my seat for me, but stay yourself. Please."

Jonathan watched Ori sit. "You look lovely this morning, Miss Washta," he complimented. "Bit of a change from the rough attire."

"Thank you, Mister Cross," she said with an ever-so-slight and elegant bow of her head, never losing eye contact with Jonathan. "Behind it all, I'm still a lady."

Then Jonathan shifted in his seat. His demeanor changed as he thought about why Ori would've had such a glow, considering her night with Lucas McAlvy. "I guess Mister Lucas McAlvy provided for you last night," he remarked, conjuring his smile. "I was on orders to make sure you got to the lodge all right. I was told he checked in with you."

Ori beamed a pleasant smile. "And did I show him a whirlwind of a night," she told Jonathan.

The bounty hunter went back to his meal and said with a hint of defeat, "So he did provide?"

Ori shook her head, no, but Jonathan missed the action. So she said aloud, "No, Mister Cross. I'm afraid Lucas McAlvy did not provide." Jonathan looked up, a peculiar look etched into his face. Ori continued, "And that's when the night's events took a different course from where he believed it was going, and where you believe it did." Ori lost her smile, and the stern demeanor that now ruled her facial expression burned into Jonathan. A storm was in her eyes, but she kept her composure. Jonathan swore to himself that the look she was giving would've made the roughest of bandits cower.

"Oh…" was all Jonathan could say.

Ori cleaned her expression. But though a bright smile was swapped in substitute for a stern countenance, the ambiance of her austere emotion remained. She made a quick glance around the saloon, checking carefully each of its patrons and making sure they were well engaged with one another and their meals. Once she trusted that no attention was being paid to her, she leaned across the table and in a hushed voice said to Jonathan, "Mister McAlvy is still in my room. He's not awake, but I'm hopeful that he dreams of reconsidering the fact he could not provide for me." She leaned back. Jonathan remained forward. Ori continued talking in a low voice, "He's tied up. He's beaten. He's beaten real good," Ori emphasized, and Jonathan blinked his eyes. "And he's bloody from it all."

"Did you rob him?" Jonathan asked in a very low voice, words almost mouthed.

Ori answered no with a slow shake of her head. Then she called out, "Thomas Tanner. Edward Rogers. Julius Bradshaw. Rufus Hatfield. Link Nash." She asked Jonathan, "These names sound familiar to you, Mister Cross?"

Now it was Jonathan's turn to fade into an austere manner. He again shifted in his seat. He answered, "Those men are on record as having been captured or killed by myself, my brother, and our captain who leads us."

"It's an impressive list, Mister Cross," Ori said, eyes now admiring Jonathan as she imagined he, his brother and their captain engaging in wild shootouts with the wanted bandits she listed. "Are you a mystic, Mister Cross? Or are you a skeptic?"

Jonathan thought about the question. He answered, looking at Ori, "I've been through enough things to know there's got to be a Good Lord looking out on me. But I ain't much of a church-going man, if that's what you mean, though."

"No, that's not what I mean, Mister Cross," Ori said, looking down and holding a shy smile. Then Ori confessed, "I made good with a ritual, a cultural sacrament and offering, to get our good friend Lucas McAlvy placed on that wanted board."

Jonathan grinned. "Did you now?"

"I did. And believe you me, he is guilty of the crime of jewel theft."

"Your jewels, Miss Washta?"

"No, Mister Cross. Not Mister McAlvy. But men that he works for very much have wronged me. Lucas McAlvy is a soldier in a string of instruments used by the men he's attached to. It's these men that have stolen from me." She paused for a moment and then added, "I would very much like to employ the services of you, your brother, and your captain. I need your assistance." Jonathan didn't say anything. He pondered the offer, and he wondered the reward. Ori again looked at the table, away from Jonathan. She put on a humble smile and admitted, "When I saw my ritual had put Lucas McAlvy's name up on that board, I wondered who it would be to track him down. I got wind it was your crew, Mister Cross, your captain's crew. I was glad to see that a group of black men were on the hunt. I asked around about you three. It was the bartender that spoke highly of you, some patrons too." She pointed out the window, "Some of those people stationed here for mining. I guess you did some guard and escort duty for people up on the trails."

Perplexity again sprawled onto Jonathan's face. "Miss Washta," he began. "Our hunt for Lucas McAlvy started two weeks ago. You've been around Crab's Creek all this time, asking about us?" Jonathan looked around. "I guess we can't trust a single soul around here. Not one person relayed to us about someone asking questions. Not even Cal over there."

Ori insisted, "Please, relax, Mister Cross. Don't blame the hardworking folks around here, especially Mister Ortiz. No one I interrogated has memory of my line of questions."

"Is that so?" Jonathan remarked intrigued. After a beat, he asked, "You a conjure woman, Miss Washta?"

"Of sorts," Ori answered. "And with that being so, I made some inquiries to souls not physically among us."

Jonathan chuckled. "Oh, damn! What does the afterlife have to say about us black bounty hunters?" he played along.

Ori replied, "You came here to find gold, Mister Cross. Your captain led you here. That old man, Mister Abraham—Mister Bunk "Old Gun" Abraham? Well, he was once called Top Hat, was he not? And he had himself a group of crusaders known as the Black Scarves freeing runaway slaves. But his most legendary and wicked of deeds is from his actions after the tyranny of slavery ended. He collected prizes for freed Negroes who put bounties on their former, cruel slave masters."

"You keep your voice low, ma'am," warned Jonathan. "You be hush on that."

"I apologize," said Ori in a sincere tone.

Jonathan asked, "You giving me an ultimatum, Miss Washta?" Then he recited the terms he'd deduced. "We help you, and you don't turn our Captain Abraham over to the authorities?"

Hand on her chest, and with a gasp, Ori expressed, "Heavens, no! I wouldn't do such a thing, Mister Cross. I admire Mister Abraham, and that would be the last thing I would do. My father would conjure himself up and strike the black off me!" She expressed, "Besides, among many whites, your captain is considered a Negro myth." Ori straightened herself. "I just know, Mister Cross, you three came here to find gold, but all you've collected are bounties. Would you not like to try your hand at your original intent? Perhaps combine your flare for killing with your desire to unearth riches."

Jonathan hesitated. He thought for a moment, and then he beamed a grin at Ori Washta. "You seem resourceful enough on your own, considering the fate of Lucas McAlvy."

"Indeed. But conjures can take a lot out of me, and every good queen needs herself an army, Mister Cross, no matter how small." She leaned over the table and said, "And I'd wager that you three men are an army big enough."

Jonathan kept his grin and eyes aimed at Ori. He made a quick glance up to the bartender and ordered, "Cal, prepare some hot tea for the lovely lady here."

"Coming right up, Mister Cross," said Ortiz with a smile.

"Thank you," Ori said to Jonathan.

He winked and nodded his head at her. He leaned back in his chair and asked, "What do you want, Miss Washta?"

"I want what every woman wants, Mister Cross," Ori answered. And then she listed, "I want flowers. I want gold. I want trinkets and baubles encrusted with the finest gems the world has to offer, and it wouldn't hurt for these fine items to be blessed with a soulful incant or conjure. But most importantly," she concluded, "I want dead the four men that keep me from my prizes. Your reward for helping me will be the most grand bounty you've ever scored from a hunt." It was easy for Ori to read Jonathan's intrigued expression. "I am very sincere about this, Mister Cross. I can assure you that I am not running a game on you. I did not lay with Mister McAlvy last night. That would be an insult against the women of my father's line and the women of my mother's line who had to endure brutal accosting over the many years by Mister McAlvy's people, whether his kind were dressed in suit or rags." She paused to catch herself as memories and stories came to her. "I can explain my predicament outside of town. Do you know where Copper Lyall is, Mister Cross?"

"I sure do, ma'am," Jonathan answered. "Place is sort of dead, is it not?"

"A church still stands there," Ori informed. "You, your brother, and your captain meet me there at sundown. I'll have Mister McAlvy with me." Jonathan's perplexed look widened. Ori told him, "You let me worry about dragging him from town. In brightest day, there will be no witnesses. Not with my conjure, Mister Cross." She nodded. "For now, enjoy your breakfast, and I will enjoy my tea when served."

Jonathan bowed his head as a playful gesture. "Yes, your majesty," he said. He went back to his breakfast, and before long, Ori's tea was served to her, cup on saucer. Lumps of sugar cubes were gathered at the side of the cup with a small tong and spoon for assistance. Ori thanked Cal as he put the cup and saucer in front of her and walked away. Ori requested that Jonathan recount the tales of capture of the notorious men she had named. Though not much of a storyteller, Jonathan still obliged, and Ori was entertained. When he finished his meal, Ori politely dismissed him.

"Please, Mister Cross, go and talk things over with your brother and captain," she insisted.

Jonathan stood. "Yes, your majesty," he repeated, playful grin beaming. He took his empty plate, piled with utensils and glass, and he returned them to bartender Cal Ortiz. He also paid for Ori Washta's tea.

Ortiz commented, "Switching up to be a gentleman, ain'tchu, John? Or are you trying to impress the lady?"

Jonathan winked at Ortiz. He slapped the bar with both hands, rolling a drumbeat, and then he backed away. He turned and exited the saloon, walking across the street and through the body of tents and covered wagons. At the law enforcement building, he was greeted by several deputies at the door before going inside and scurrying to the room where Bunk and his brother Donavan were still resting.

Jonathan slammed the door, waking Bunk and Donovan. *"Okay!"* he announced in a loud voice. "Up! Captain, you're old. Donavan, you got no excuse. Get up. We got ourselves a job."

Bunk rose up in the bed with a snarl on his face. "Whatchu say about me being, old, boy?" he questioned with sleep holding his eyes shut. "I will slap the cowboy piss out of you." Donavan looked as if he held the same sentiment toward his brother.

"After this job, Captain," Jonathan said with respect in his tone. "I just scored us some bounties."

Bunk and Donavan were up, rubbing sleep from their eyes. Bunk exhaled. "There something big on the day's board?"

Jonathan sat on his bed and addressed his captain, "No, sir. This is personal." Then he recounted his meeting with Ori Washta. He described her tale as best he could, trying to inject not the urgency and desperation, but the idea of taking part in an extraordinary adventure. Donavan was taken in, but Bunk had his concerns, which Jonathan guessed he would. The old gunslinger's concerns were legitimate, however. *Who were they going to kill?* Jonathan never got the names or details. But Jonathan said Ori Washta would explain her circumstances outside of town. They were to meet her in an abandoned church in the empty town called Copper Lyall.

"Well, shit," Bunk huffed. "I'm seventy-some-odd and some change in years. If it's a setup, I've had a long, good life." He got out of bed with an old man's groan and creak in his bones. "Can't say the same for you two young boys," he remarked, slapping Jonathan on the shoulder as he passed him. "We'll take two or three of the bastards before we're gunned down like dogs." He left the room, saying, "Let's wash up, Donavan. I'll go first."

Jonathan looked at his brother and proclaimed, "I'll get the horses ready."

An hour passed before every one was washed and ready. Provisions were stuffed into satchels and horse-saddle purses. Weapons were checked, loaded and strapped on. Rifles and machetes were sheathed into holsters attached to the saddles. Bathed and fully clothed, the three-man gang went to the saloon where Bunk and Donavan ordered a meal with water. Their conversation included little about their coming excursion to the dead town of Copper Lyall, but they spoke on Ori Washta.

By the afternoon, miners filtered into the saloon. Card games of all sorts started popping up. Cal's brothers, acting as dealers, hosted them. Bunk and Donavan got involved with poker, winning a few rounds. Jonathan jumped into several rounds of Twenty-One Blackjack. An argument broke out in the middle of one poker round where Donavan and Bunk sat in. Bunk tried to calm the man who initiated the argument, but the quarrel escalated, encouraged by drink. The one named Francis Brody sneered at Bunk's attempt to squash the argument and said, "Nigger, when there's a bounty on my head, then maybe your shouts carry some authority. Until then, you ain't law. So keep your guns and words holstered."

Bunk responded with a roll of his eyes. The men, who were miners, were both tired and frustrated from their hard day of turning up nothing from their expedition. They jumped up from the table, the younger man going for a gun. Donavan was quick, and he was armed. The quiet bounty hunter pulled his cattleman revolver, flipped it in the air, grabbed the barrel of the gun, and smacked the young man across the back of the head, knocking him out. Donavan holstered his gun. The patrons went silent and observed. Jonathan stayed his person, believing jumping to his brother's side would stir more trouble. But he kept his eyes close on the situation.

Ortiz came from around the bar, long-barreled shotgun aimed at the table. "What's happened here?" he demanded.

"Just a bit of an argument," Bunk grumbled. "It's finished now."

Francis looked down at Bunk and sneered again. He growled, "I don't need a nigger to speak for me." He looked at Ortiz. "Look past your bean-eating blood and talk to me as a fellow Irishman. Boy on the floor was taking his time, wasn't speeding up the game. Hand was all trembling. His eyes were wild. I got to go back on expedition in an hour. I ain't got all day."

"Take a walk from my establishment," Ortiz ordered Francis, making a motion toward the door with his shotgun. "Come back when you're calm."

"I'm calm!" Francis insisted. "Argument's over. Done. Tell these violent, trouble-making darkies to get the hell out if that's your angle, Irish bean-eater."

Bunk looked at Ortiz, again rolling his eyes.

"Bunk, there's twenty dollars in it if you get this man to the sheriff's office," said the bartender to the aged gunslinger.

Bunk nodded. He turned his attention back to the table. "I fold," he said, tossing his cards away. "That's my bounty on you," he told Francis. Bunk made a slight turn and then slammed his fist hard into Francis' stomach. The aggrieved patron buckled over. Bunk still moved fast, old as he was. He was up from his seat, grabbing the back of Francis' head, and slamming his face into the table. Blood burst from Francis' nose. The appendage wasn't broken, and Francis remained conscious, though disoriented, seeing blurred, double images of everything around him. Bunk grabbed the back of Francis' sweat and dirt-stained shirt, and tossed the drunken, belligerent miner at Donavan. The young bounty hunter caught him. It was then that Jonathan stood from the game table, taking his cash earnings with him. He walked over to the scuffle, reached down, and picked up the unconscious miner on the ground, tossing him over his shoulder.

Bunk tugged his brim at Ortiz, who was lowering his shotgun. "I appreciate the bounty, but keep your money, Cal."

Ortiz nodded. When Bunk and his lieutenants exited, he told the remaining patrons, "Go back to your games and talk. Keep it civil." Activity started up again, and Ortiz took his position behind the bar, tucking his shotgun away.

Bunk and the Cross brothers dropped the miners onto the law office porch, informing the two deputies of what had taken place inside the saloon. "They'll sleep it off in a cell," said one deputy as he dragged the one carried by Jonathan. "No need for a fine. No need to put these two further in debt." Francis Brody gave a little resistance. But he was still reeling from Bunk's attack and the alcohol he'd poured into his body.

Then Bunk and the Cross brothers, wrapped in heavy duster coats, went around the back of the law offices and unhitched their horses from their posts. They made a quick check of provisions before guiding their mounts on foot to a drier section of the road that led east of town. At the far end of the road, toward the town's exits, they hopped onto their horses and galloped away, keeping east of the trails leading to the mining areas.

Not too long after sundown, Bunk and the Cross brothers sauntered into the abandoned town of Copper Lyall. Each man had one hand on their horses' rein, and the other holding a gun for caution. Their eyes were focused, peering into the darkness and discerning distinct shapes and shadows. There was no movement, save the wind. The few, remaining, hollow buildings stood out in the desolate area that was once a town no different than Crab's Creek. But what stood out more was the modest-sized church where the three-man gang was scheduled to meet the young woman named Ori Washta. Even in the darkness, the white church looked pristine. Bunk and the Cross brothers pressed forward on horseback, eyes keeping everything in sight.

"Gentleman," said a woman's voice. "Welcome." It was Ori Washta.

Lanterns posted around the church lit up at the sound of Ori's voice. There she stood, at the corner of the holy sanctuary dressed in a sleeveless, black, cream, and gold gown. A black veil was pinned up in her hair, and the young conjure woman's left nostril was pierced with a gold, looped ring that had fastened to it a chain attached to another gold looped ring in her ear. Both ears were decorated with intricately designed earrings. Ori's presence was captivating, especially in the flickering light and waving shadows. Her dress was cut low at the neck, and all three men could clearly see the gold-colored tattoo of a chain etched around her neck. The sketch draped down to her bust where attached was a drawn pendant that spelled out a word in Ori's native language. *Soul,* was what the word read, though none of the men were fluent in Ori's indigenous tongue to know that, or close enough to see that the etching was a word at all. But they stared at the all of her, their fixed gaze making it seem as if they were staring at her breasts, pushed up by way of her corset.

Donavan was the first to look away, noticing that Ori was sleeveless and outside on such a bitter, cold evening. "Ma'am," the usually reserved bounty hunter said in a very low voice. "Your arms are exposed. You need covering."

Ori bowed her head in a respectful manner. She said to Donavan, "Thank you, young man. I am fine, but we all should come along inside." She turned. "There's a post at the front of the church where you can hitch your mounts. Come, gentlemen." Then she walked on. Bunk and the Cross brothers followed behind her, holstering their weapons and coming to the front of the church. There, just as Ori said, was a post to hitch their horses. Bunk and Donavan positioned their rides up to the post and then dismounted, strapping their mounts down. Jonathan moved his horse to the post where Ori Washta's mount was hitched. He moved his horse next to hers, dismounted, and tied his horse's rein to the post. Grouping with his brother and captain, they followed Ori Washta inside. The three men removed hats and head scarves out of respect.

The church caught the bounty hunters by surprise with how warm it was. There wasn't an explanation for the soothing heat. Only a few candles glowed near the pulpit, and their fire appeared decorative. The candles' flicker, coupled with the darkness that waved at the edge of the glow, was inviting. Occupying the front pew, right of the aisle, was Lucas McAlvy. He sat up straight and stiff. Ori guided the three men down the aisle, and they kept their eyes on Lucas. Coming up to the front, Bunk and the Cross brothers viewed Lucas McAlvy as he sat wide-eyed, staring straight ahead. His face was covered with bruises and cuts, sustained when Ori Washta interrogated him.

"You three gentlemen remember Mister McAlvy," Ori said turning around and addressing her three hired guns.

Jonathan came around, bent down, and waved a hand in front of Lucas' face. Lucas didn't move. "What's wrong with him?" he asked Ori, standing up straight.

"Mister McAlvy still wouldn't cooperate on coming forth with the information I needed from him," Ori explained. "So, I went deeper. And in doing so, I've turned him into a human compass. He will lead you to the first man to kill: His employer, Captain Bell Frank."

Jonathan and Donavan both looked at Bunk. The old man adjusted his gun belt and his hat. He cleared his throat. "That name's familiar to all of us. Captain Frank has himself a private army."

"Much like you, Mister Top Hat—if you don't mind me calling you such," said Ori, holding in her eyes a bright look of admiration for Bunk.

"No, ma'am," assured Bunk. "I don't." He looked at one of the pews and pointed. He asked, "May I have a seat?"

"Certainly, Mister Top Hat," allowed Ori, admiring eyes still aglow.

Bunk sat down, groaning as he bent. He rested his top hat next to him before saying, "I can still fight, Miss Washta—old as I am, bones creaking and all. I'll give a young whippersnapper a run, I can. These two boys? They fight just like their father—and he's still got it in him too. But going up against a man like Captain Bell Frank? That's suicide."

"He's the muscle for the Speers and Gardens faction," Jonathan noted. "Them boys is harder than the Santa Fe Ring I've heard." He felt a little embarrassed, now knowing the risk he'd gotten himself, his brother, and his captain involved in.

"They are indeed deadly expansionists," Ori said, agreeing with the sentiment on everyone's mind. "These are not gangsters disguised as prominent cattleman. These are hired guns for the United States government. They wear silk vests and fancy suits to cover their savagery. They do more damage with pens and papers and handshakes than all the bandits combined, equipped to the nines. And they have moved into Qalif territory." She patted the air, palms down, and said, "Here. Copper Lyall."

"This place is all dried up, Miss Washta," Jonathan pointed out.

Ori cupped her hands together and shook her head at Jonathan. "No, my soft-faced, handsome gunslinger," she started correcting him. "Early prospects believed as such. They left. Government interest in Copper Lyall was little then. But by that time, most of the warriors that protected this land had been slaughtered. The few who did remain were of great interest to the superstitious Donald Speers. He's captured three of them, and he's sealed my warrior-brothers up in jail cells that are made entirely of silver." Bunk and the Cross brothers gave one another peculiar glances. Ori addressed, "These men are superstitious, even if you gentlemen are not."

Bunk raised his hand, motioning for Ori to relax. He assured her, hand now on chest, "I say a prayer every time I trudge into a hunt, whether that hunt be for bounty or when I would look for our people in bondage. But I'm not—none of us I believe are—familiar with the holy arts of conjure. Forgive us. So I ask, why so specific, Miss Washta? Why silver jail cells?"

"It keeps them weak," was all Ori said. "These warrior-brothers have been held captive for twenty-six days. In two days, dictated by the laws of their specific conjure, the full moon will sketch maps on their backs, provided by the proper ritual. These maps will show the location of seven troves of gold and silver stored by the Brotherhood Nation of Muurs." Ori looked at each hired gun before concluding with orders, "On the full moon, you will attack. These warrior-brothers are being held somewhere by Captain Bell Frank. Once free from their silver cells, you will have allies like you've never known." She paused for a brief moment and then said,

"Secure their release for me and I will share the wealth of the hidden troves. That is my promise."

Bunk and the Cross brothers fell silent.

"You may rest here," Ori continued. "Don't worry about your mounts. It will get colder, but they will be warm as long as they are in proximity of this holy sanctuary. And considering they're hitched up at the post outside, they will be fine."

Jonathan took a seat next to Lucas McAlvy. "Miss Washta," he called, charming grin lighting up his face. "I'd like to have a conjure displayed." He shook his head. "Now, I'm no skeptic, but I'd like to see the power of a conjure woman before my eyes."

"It would be my pleasure to show off for you gentlemen," Ori said with a nod. She aimed a hand at the candles lighting the room. She twiddled her fingers and the flames expanded and extended from their wicks. Like threads of yarn, the bodies of fire wove together and created the shape of a winged, serpentine creature. The kindled beast lifted its head up to the ceiling and hollered a wide pillar of fire. Bunk and the Cross brothers jumped. Their excitement calmed when they realized the flames weren't setting the ceiling ablaze. Ori Washta twiddled her fingers again. Jonathan realized she was mumbling a chant of some kind, but he kept his eyes on the blazing beast as it came undone. The sinewy fibers made of fire unraveled and returned back to the gentle flickers of flame whipping atop the candles.

Ori Washta said to Jonathan, "I will be here at this church, providing a protective aegis around the three of you as you make your assault wherever my warrior-brothers are being held." Bunk and the Cross brothers nodded together. All three addressed Ori as ma'am. Donavan took a seat next to Bunk. Ori cupped her hands again and said as a desperate plea, "The gold and silver troves are secondary prizes for these men. They have superstitions. They want this land for its spirit. And when they conquer Copper Lyall and its surrounding regions, they will set their sights on the Qalif people, the sister nation to the Brotherhood of the Muurs."

Jonathan stood. He bowed, but there was no playful grin running across his face. He was sincere when he said, "We are soldiers in your army, your majesty."

Ori was happy, and she replied, "By my three chains of gold, thank you, gentlemen."

Jonathan sat. His smile returned. "Besides that pretty ornament dangling by your ear and nose, I only see one etched up around your neck, Miss Washta," he remarked.

Ori bared her wrists, and there illustrated on each arm, and colored gold, were two more chains that the three trackers appeared to miss. They were shorter than the chain drawn around her neck. They too had an intricately drawn pendant dangling from them. Each pendant was made up of letters spelling out the words *Mind,* on the right hand, and *Body* on the left. Bunk and the Cross brothers marveled at the tattoos. "I have three chains of gold, Mister Cross. And upon my cosmic flesh, they will shine forever." Then she pointed to a door in the corner behind her and noted, "There is a warrior's meal located in the first room off the hallway. Through that door," she specified. "You three may indulge." Ori looked down at Lucas McAlvy and stated, "I will bring our compass here a plate to dine on. He too needs to keep his strength"

Bunk and the Cross brothers got up. Bunk took lead toward the door with Jonathan behind him. Donavan stalled, stopping near Ori Washta. She asked if everything was okay. Before Donavan answered, both he and Ori looked up and noticed Bunk and Jonathan waiting near the door and eyeing them. Donavan played with his hat, head down. Ori gestured with a wave at Bunk and Jonathan, and the two men continued through the door.

"Donavan Cross, is it?" Ori asked. She smiled and said, "There is a woman back at my nation that sure has a crush on you, handsome devil. She's my closest friend, the sister I never had. And when my ritual gave me insight to you three going after Mister McAlvy here, I just took her on a vision to show you three off, mostly you handsome Cross brothers."

The comment pulled a sheepish grin to the surface of Donavan's face. Head still hanging, he moved his eyes to sight the young conjure woman in front of him.

"Oh, yes," Ori continued. "Her name is *skin shining like dew*, but we don't call her all that. We say all that with two words. *Izenth-Elei.*" Ori lifted Donavan's head with a single finger under his chin.

"Can your conjures heal my head?" Donavan asked in an almost inaudible voice. His eyes dropped away from looking at Ori Washta, smile lost to him. "I have bad dreams."

Ori sighed. "I know," she acknowledged. "Something you saw when you were a little boy."

Donavan nodded, remembering the attack. His uncle was killed. His eleven-year-old cousin died during the ghostly-clad men's ravaging of her. He was beaten until he was unconscious, believed to be dead by the men who had attacked him and his family members. He didn't dream about it every night, but he dreamed about it enough times to worry about sleeping.

"I can stop the dreams, Donavan," Ori told him in a comforting voice, using a finger to hook several dangling braids back behind his ear. "But the memory will always be there. We'll work with it."

Donavan shook his head, understanding. He stood straight and thanked Ori in his near-muted voice. Then he rushed off to join his brother and captain in a meal. Ori stayed for a moment, looking at Lucas McAlvy. She turned and joined her three hired guns and prepared a plate for the vacant-minded jewel thief.

Twice, up jumped the sun. Twice, down into the earth it dived. And so, two days passed. Bunk and the Cross brothers rested for the most part, and Ori Washta spoke blessings over them at sundown on each passing day. She also gathered natural ingredients to create black and white paint. At sundown, on the day of attack, while her face was veiled, she applied the coloring to Bunk and the Cross brothers, fashioning their faces as black skulls with white lips and wide, white circles around their eyes.

Ori, wearing a sleeveless, black and red gown, stood while Bunk and the Cross brothers knelt before her. Lucas McAlvy occupied the front pew, wide stare still on his face. Ori lifted the veil and tossed it back over the top of her head. Ori's face was drawn up too, black and white, in the same skull-faced pattern. Her hair was now unbraided, frizzy and wild and decorated with crow feathers and red, silk strings. Cultural trinkets and a dagger lined her belt. A six-round, cattleman revolver was tucked just right of her belt's buckle.

"A black pig bleeds away its life as a sacrifice for the war you three soldiers make tonight," Ori announced as she paced back and forth in a slow, deliberate manner. "You don't wear face paint. You wear the blessed color of nature, incanted with the souls of fallen warriors that once protected this land. Each of you is an army." Pointing to Lucas McAlvy she said, "The compass here will lead you to our mark. Captain Bell Frank." She retracted her arm and told the three hired guns, "Strike and procure the three warrior-brothers." To Bunk, Ori Washta said, "You already have a name, hallowed solider. Top Hat. You are a legend in the flesh." Her eyes went to the Cross brothers. "This night, you two men—the Cross brothers—earn your names." She commanded, "Stand." And they did. "Take the compass here," she advised, nodding her head at Lucas McAlvy. Turning to the catatonic jewel thief, Ori Washta instructed for him to stand, and Lucas McAlvy got up, standing in a mechanical, vacant fashion. "Return to Captain Bell Frank, Mister McAlvy," she asked of him.

"Yes," he said. "I will."

Ori addressed her hired guns, "Follow him. He will take my mount. She will return to me once Mister McAlvy dismounts from her. Go, my soldiers."

Bunk and the Cross brothers filed out of the church, down the aisle and out the door. Outside, in the cold night lit by the bright full moon, they mounted their horses. Lucas McAlvy was already on Ori Washta's mount, unhitched, and galloping northwest. The captain and his lieutenants turned around and rushed to follow him. Their horses stomped over fresh snow, kicking up nature's powder as they followed Lucas McAlvy onto a trail that led into a dense wooded area.

Inside the church, Ori Washta stood alone. She pulled a cigar from her belt and held it between her fingers. She removed the gun tucked between her person and her belt, and she placed it down on the pew in front of her. Then she sat next to the weapon. She closed her eyes and spoke a harmonious incant. A candle's dancing flame extended upward as a thin, fiery stream. It curled as it stretched, appearing sentient like an animal on the prowl. Its tip pointed left and right in quick motions, as if scoping for its hunt. Then it reached out, lashing at Ori Washta's cigar with a crackling snap. The end of her cigar lit up, and the slender fire retracted back to its candle as a simple flame.

Ori Washta puffed the end, taking in the cigar's smoke and taste. She bent her head back and exhaled a thick stream of smoke straight up to the ceiling. Then she stared at the pulpit again, smoking the cigar. After a moment, she stood from the pew, walked halfway down the church aisle, turned around to face the pulpit, and then took a seat on the floor. Legs folded, Ori kept the cigar between her fingers. She crossed her arms over her body, hands near her shoulders, and closed her eyes. A vision appeared.

It was this night, far from Copper Lyall. There mounted on horseback were Ori's hired guns, Bunk and the Cross brothers. They were at the edge of a dense, wooded area. Beyond the trees there lay an abandoned hunting post turned fortress for former American officer, Captain Bell Frank. Bunk and the Cross brothers' horses, though gray, brown, and painted, appeared pitch black in Ori's vision, even with the full moon shining bright upon them. Bunk tossed off his heavy coat, a warm incant hugging his body. The Cross brothers did the same. Donavan drew his short-barrel shotgun, and Jonathan removed his heavy, LeMat revolver. The old man reached down and unsheathed his machete.

Ori viewed the scene through her preternatural sight. Thick strands of smoke, swiveling off the burning cigar, glistened with a yellow glow and swirled around Ori in an elliptical pattern. Several orbiting lines of smoke coupled together and spiraled up around the conjure woman, culminating into a pillar of light that extended upward and through the church's ceiling. The smoky pillar of light split into three tendrils and traveled across the sky to Bunk and the Cross brothers' location. Unseen by the three bounty hunters, the smoky tendrils washed over them, bathing them in Ori Washta's incanted protection. From far away, Ori watched, concentrating on both vision and her conjured, protective blessing.

Bunk and the Cross brothers proceeded forward. From the darkness, and from the direction of Captain Bell Frank's fortress, emerged Ori Washta's horse, vacant of Lucas McAlvy. It dashed past Bunk and the Cross brothers, riding back through the wooded area, making a return to the holy sanctuary in Copper Lyall. The gunmen paid the horse no mind as they trotted out of the wooded area in the opposite direction.

Two men approached them, shouting questions to prompt the mounted bounty hunters to identify themselves. Bunk addressed the men, telling them, *"You have three men in your custody. You got these men locked up in cells. We've come for them."*

"Those outlaw nigger-savages?" one of the men questioned.

Eyes closed, Ori raised an eyebrow at what she'd heard in her vision. "Stomp their yard," she whispered, expressing her sentiment as a command.

Donavan's gun resounded through the night. It appeared that even the full moon's light rippled with the massive, elephantine sound. The double barrels screamed fire and projectiles, slamming into one of the armed, approaching men. His body dropped back onto the fresh, fallen snow. Small, red, glittering gushes of blood spat up from the man's fatal wounds, catching the moonlight, and then rained down to stain nature's white, powdery condensation. Donavan reloaded his weapon.

Ori took a drag of her cigar and continued watch on her vision.

Jonathan twirled his drawn firearm, caught the gun's handle in his grip, and in the same motion was able to use his thumb to cock the hammer. He fired on the second man. The blast from his gun, thunderous and with weight, propelled the bullet with such force, it broke open the man's chest and killed him. He lifted and was tossed into the air by the impact. He crashed against the snow, leaving a blood trail as his body continued its motion, hissing as it slid. Finally stopping its sail through the snow, blood from the body expanded on the ground in a thick, crimson pool, washing out the white of the thin, wintry blanket. Bunk and the Cross brothers jumped from their mounts and pressed forward to the hunting post turned fortress. Their horses remained still.

Inside the makeshift fort, Captain Bell Frank commanded his hired soldiers to take positions at windows and doors. He instructed four men to investigate the shooting and inform the soldiers outside to sweep the perimeter. Then he returned to a section of the fort that had been built onto the original structure. It was an area that housed three jail cells made of pure silver. Bars. Floors. Ceiling. All were fashioned from silver. Inside each silver-made cell there lay a man dressed in ragged pants and no shirt. Their bare backs were exposed to the ceiling. A small hole was fashioned into the top of the silver cell, ushering in the full moon's light. A native shaman was forced at gunpoint to oversee a ritual.

Bunk and the Cross brothers were already engaged in close and brutal combat with Captain Frank's exterior patrol units. Bunk made the first attack, stepping from the shadows and swinging his machete at a patrolling gunman's neck. The strike split the man where his neck met his shoulders and caused him to cough up a gush of blood. Bunk drew the blade free, pulled his gun from his holster, cocked it, and shot the man in the head. Three men advanced on the old gunslinger, shooting at him with every step they took. His protective blessing curved the bullets away from him, and after several shots, his attackers' guns jammed. They pulled hunting knives.

"Hoorah, my Captain!" The loud cry came from Donavan Cross as he jumped from the dark. High above Bunk's attackers, the young bounty hunter descended, crashing against one of the three men. Both he and the gunman toppled to the ground.

The older Cross brother came charging! He screamed at the unit's remaining men, *"Never bow! Never kneel!"* He kept pressed the gun's trigger while repeatedly slapping the weapon's hammer with the palm of his hand, allowing for rapid fire. Four bullets ripped through one of the men, dropping him. Jonathan moved his aim toward the last man standing. Three slugs, center mass, took down the third soldier in the small party.

Bunk moved away as more rifle fire veered his way. Donavan ducked low and remained crouched atop the man he'd jumped on. Bullets whizzed by him. He pulled his short barrel shotgun, aimed it and fired. Lucas McAlvy smacked against the snow, bleeding and dying. Donavan jumped up, taking the man he'd been crouched on with him, standing him up to receive an attack by Bunk. The old bounty hunter forced his machete through the dazed gunman as Donavan walked away to finish McAlvy. But his older brother got to him first as the dying jewel thief used what was left of his strength to crawl to his dropped rifle.

Jonathan fired twice into Lucas McAlvy's back, killing him. He picked up the rifle and tossed it to Bunk who strapped it around his back. The three men stepped out into the open as more men poured from the fort. They took aim and cocked their weapons, but the collective screams of three captive men shook their concentration.

Then the night went silent.

Bunk was old, but he was alive with fight and vigor. Again, he made the first attack. His machete cut the air, the blade whispering a quick preview of the deadly strike. The old man's hard chop broke through his mark's skull with a shattering crunch. Bunk was able to lodge the blade's edge a little off center in the man's forehead, inches deep. The man's body stiffened and fell back, life drained. Bunk pulled his gun and started shooting at the other men. They scattered, retaliating with cover fire as they dived for safety. The aged gunslinger pulled his machete free from his kill and took cover behind a tree.

Donavan scooped up another loose rifle from the snow. His short barrel shotgun draped around his back, he took aim with the rifle and fired on anything that moved. He caught one man in the belly, another in the side. Both men managed to take cover before they were finished off. Jonathan marched forward, the chambers in his drawn LeMat revolver reloaded. He pulled his second LeMat while spotting the men who had been wounded by his brother. He fired and killed one with a bullet to the chest. His second shot broke into the other's jaw, but the power of the LeMat shattered the man's face, and the shock of pain squeezed the remaining life out of him.

Jonathan was the closest of the three bounty hunters approaching the makeshift fort. He was near the steps, and as he lifted his foot to make the climb, gunfire riddled the stairs. Jonathan dived to his left, taking cover behind a thick wooden fence. Safe from the gunfire coming from the windows, Jonathan was still exposed to the unit combing the grounds. His presence brought men out of cover and on the attack. Bunk and Donavan kept him covered, shooting at Jonathan's attackers before they could squeeze off shots and forcing them to again find cover. One brave man continued forward, loading his rifle as he charged. Jonathan, alerted, turned and saw the man's approach. He holstered his guns, jumped up with arms extended, gripped the man's collar and pulled him close. Jonathan rolled back with a tight grip on the man. The soldier's face smashed against the thick, wooden fence, knocking him out cold. Jonathan tossed him aside and removed one of his guns. He rose from behind the fence and fired shots at the windows. Four shots, two in each window. He ducked. A volley of gunfire thwacked against the fence.

Jonathan stayed low. His eyes fell on the unconscious man lying next to him. An idea struck him. He grabbed the unconscious gunman and put the double-action revolver in his hand. He lifted the arm over the fence and fired several shots at the windows. He pulled the man's arm down as gunfire was returned. When the night became silent again, Jonathan grabbed the man's collar. He grit his teeth, counted to three, and screamed, using all his might to lift the gunman up and onto his feet. Rifle and pistol fire tore through the man's limp body. Jonathan stood, drawing his guns and taking aim. His decoy continued being riddled with bullets. The first shot to his neck woke the unconscious man long enough for him to experience his own killing.

Time slowed from Jonathan's perspective, but he was in truth reacting within the interval of split seconds. His eyes, aided by the flickering flames waving inside posted lanterns, focused and saw the silhouette of gunmen stationed in the second-floor windows of the old hunting and trade center. Jonathan lifted his guns and fired. He killed one with one shot. The gunman's body buckled with his last breaths and then dropped his weapon. His lifeless body draped over the sill, arms dangling as he hung out the window.

Jonathan fired again. The bullet crashed through the upper window, shattering the glass and breaking through another rifleman's throat. He fell back dead. Jonathan pointed both guns at the last man. Though this particular gunman was more alert, now focusing his aim at Jonathan, he was down to three shots. He fired his remaining ammunition at Jonathan, and on any other night, Jonathan might've been dead to rights. But on this night, he was blessed and protected. The bullets whooshed by him.

Jonathan emptied his guns into the window. The remaining gunman's body danced wildly as Jonathan's gunfire ripped through his body. He fell back a bloody mess. Jonathan ducked. He holstered his nine-round LeMat revolvers and snatched both double-action revolvers from the riddled body of the man he made his decoy. He marched up the stairs, stepped up onto the wide and long porch, and pilfered the rifle dropped by the dangling gunman.

Around the corner came four men. Jonathan ducked and fired the procured double-action revolver at the first man in the line. A bullet tore through his knee. Another hit his belly, burrowing deep. The man toppled onto the porch. Jonathan blasted the man behind him, two bullets in the chest. The fourth man ducked back behind the corner as the third was forced against the wall, his head drilled through by a bullet fired from the shadows by Donavan Cross. Now empty, Jonathan tossed away one of the double-action pistols and took up the rifle he'd taken. He waited as his brother used gunfire to back the fourth gunman farther away.

Bunk charged up the steps with a new weapon in hand: two sticks of dynamite he doubled-back to the horses for, removing the explosives from one of the saddle purses. Jonathan watched his brother fire off more shots. Now with Bunk and Donavan on the porch, and feeling safe, Jonathan stood and rushed over to the man he'd wounded. Captain Frank's hired gun was in too much pain to draw his second firearm and attempt a shot. Jonathan cocked the rifle and put its muzzle to his head.

"You got three men locked up in silver cells," Jonathan snarled. *"Now where would those cages be located?"*

The man answered, stuttering in pain, *"B-b-back hall."*

Donavan hustled up to Jonathan. The brothers walked away from the wounded man, leaving him to die. They moved to the fort's front door. Jonathan grabbed the knob and gave it a slow, cautious turn. Heavy bullet fire pushed the door from his grip, blowing sizeable holes in it and forcing the Cross brothers to post up at the side of the entrance, shoulder to shoulder. Jonathan looked at Bunk, kneeling on the other side of the door, stick of dynamite in his hands. He said, *"Captain, Plan-C."*

Bunk nodded. He struck a match and lit one stick, tossing it through the door. The Cross brothers backed farther away. Alarming screams from Captain Frank's hired soldiers rang through the door split seconds before the exploding dynamite shook the makeshift fortress. Bunk and the Cross brothers kept their balance, and Jonathan jumped to action. He came around in front of the door and fired into the building serried with smoke. Jonathan's shots were wild, but two, staggering men were hit in the back. Jonathan again posted up at the side of the door.

The building exhaled more smoke through the opening. The black gunmen waited, panting and listening to the soft ringing in their ears caused by the explosion. Bunk made the first move, shoving his unused stick of dynamite through his belt, and then standing directly in front of the opened, charred and splintered door. He waited for a moment. There was nothing. No threats hollered. No shots fired. The old gunslinger stepped inside the fort and waded through the smoke. Fire crackled and chewed at the wooden interior, but its swelling risk did nothing to keep the black bounty hunters from trudging through the front room's wreckage, the Cross brothers following close behind their captain.

The bounty hunters merged in formation. Backs to one another, guns out, they stepped over dead bodies, body parts, and men moaning away the last few moments of their lives. They kept their distance from the intensifying, crepitating flames. Bunk and the Cross brothers heard faint calls for retreat in the distance, coming from the back of the fortress. Bunk signaled to follow the sound, and the Cross brothers, still in formation, executed their captain's orders. Moving through the smoky interior, Jonathan spied the extension of the building he was informed about. He stopped, and the others stopped with him. He motioned toward the door. Bunk nodded, and they all made their way through it and into a large hallway lined with bright lanterns. Built into the hallway, on the right side, were three cells made of silver. From bars to floor to walls to ceiling, the jail cells were a treasure unto themselves. A dead, indigenous, shaman lay on the floor. His bare chest caked with blood streaming from the tiny hole drilled through it from a gunshot. At the end of the hall was an open door where Captain Bell Frank and the last of his men had escaped.

Bunk and Donavan inspected the silver cells. Three men were suspended upside down in the air, hanging from what appeared to be the moon's light wrapped around their feet. Two of the men had mud-brown skin, and the third, the shortest of the three, had light-brown skin. All three had, designed on their backs, and spotlighted by the moon's light, pieces of a map that collectively displayed the surrounding lands. Neither Bunk nor Donavan questioned aloud the sorcery at play, or even if they could effect the wizardry. Bunk ordered Jonathan, *"Boy, toss me that hunting knife of yours."*

Jonathan unsheathed the heavy blade and pitched it to his captain. Bunk caught the hunting knife and immediately began using its tip to jimmy the middle cell's lock. Donavan covered the back door, and Jonathan kept his rifle up at the partially opened, steel-made, heavy entrance they'd passed through. Smoke, voices and other noises filtered through the front room's entryway. Captain Bell Frank and his soldiers had returned. Jonathan heard the hiss of extinguished fire, water being tossed upon it. Bunk and Donavan heard it too, but the bounty hunters stayed focused on their jobs of keeping guard and picking the cell's locks.

"Check the captured," screamed a man that Jonathan guessed was Captain Bell Frank.

The older Cross brother backed up and cocked his rifle. He tossed a look over his shoulder, checking on Bunk's progress. He heard something click and determined Bunk had broken the cell's lock.

A gun came through the entranceway, and a man peeked inside. Jonathan shot the hand holding the gun. Bunk flinched, his effort to open the cell momentarily halted. Donavan turned around, gun up. Wounded and bleeding, Jonathan's target, with gun dropped, pulled back his hand and screamed. He ducked low and reached back inside with his other hand, swiping his gun away. He fired twice into the room but only hit the wall and ceiling. Jonathan ran toward the door and slammed his body into it, closing the heavy, steel door with his impact. Jonathan heard gunfire ricocheting off the metal from the other side. Captain Frank gave the order to circle around back to take the intruders there. Then came a second command shouted by the captain, an order for the placing of dynamite near the steel door.

"Shit," Jonathan cursed. *"We good, Captain?"*

"Going in," informed Bunk, opening the cell door. Inside the silver enclosure, the old gunslinger marveled with mouth agape at the otherworldly display of light as rope. Bunk ran his hand through the light and felt nothing but the cold air rushing into the cell. He sheathed his machete and pondered the sight for a brief moment. He took a chance in moving the suspended, indigenous warrior. The captive's body moved with surprising ease, floating away from the moon's light as if in water. The

ropes of light released the man's ankle. His weight came into play. Becoming heavy, he dropped to the silver floor. The fall woke him from unconscious slumber. He trembled, teeth grinding and anger rising. The map inscribed on his back faded away.

The braided-haired warrior growled, *"My name is Eyes Are Bright, soldier, Ori Washta's United Army of Muurs."*

Bunk told him, *"Boy, you save your breath. We're here to get you three to your General-Queen."*

Jonathan ducked into the open cell. He called for Donavan to do the same. The younger Cross brother did as ordered, scurrying into the cell moments before an explosion rattled the fortress. Jonathan, crouched down at the side of the door, stuck his head out to examine the damage. The door held onto the last of its hinges. Jonathan screamed, *"Hot damn, fellas. We got sort of a half-a-pint of luck left. But she ain't gonna hold if they give her another knock."*

On the other side of the steel door, Captain Frank and his men smacked away at it with a thick, wooden post taken from the fence outside. In several hits, the mighty men forced the steel door down. Jonathan fired on two soldiers, catching one in the shoulder and knocking him to the ground. His second bullet broke through a man's breast, backing him away and to the side of the door. Jonathan fired thrice more, scattering Captain Frank and his other soldiers.

Bunk took his concentration off the recovering warrior, removed the second stick of dynamite, and set it on the floor. He dug into his pocket and retrieved his matches. Striking one, he picked up the stick of dynamite, lit it, and flung it to Jonathan after alerting him. Jonathan cursed. Bunk yelled, *"Give it back at 'em, boy!"*

Jonathan hurled the stick at Captain Frank and his men. Shooting cover fire, the private army scattered. Jonathan ducked back inside and braced himself, as did his brother and captain. The dynamite exploded, and again the building rocked, crumbled, and sank. Bunk and the Cross brothers were taken off their feet. Eyes Are Bright reached up and snatched Bunk's machete. The old man allowed the warrior-brother to have it.

World no longer spinning, and structure no longer quaking, Jonathan got to his feet, unsteady in his crawl up the wall. Bunk asked if Jonathan could hear him, yelling over the severe ringing in his ears. When Jonathan answered affirmatively, Bunk commanded the older Cross brother to check the corridor. Jonathan moved his rifle through the door. He moved out, making cautious steps. First he checked the blown in entranceway. Though smoke clogged the area, Jonathan could see that the front room no longer existed, caved in and burning. Only one of the lanterns continued flickering in the hallway, appearing as though any moment its quick, whipping snap would be its last.

A click happened behind Jonathan. A rifle was cocked. He turned, rifle up, and without hesitation, he pulled the trigger. The hammer struck an empty chamber. The knock against emptiness, signaling defeat, sounded louder than the gunfire and explosions bursting earlier. The man holding Jonathan at rifle point and sly grin was named Tom Martin. He was thirty-one years old, and he'd been making a name for himself as Tom Rifle. Even Jonathan recognized him from bounty hunting boards across the territory. But over the passed year, interest in him had waned. Tom would've made a legendary bandit, talked about for decades to come, and ultimately achieving the prestigious form of immortality the West had to offer. But Captain Bell Frank, with his clean-shaven charm and fatherly authority put a stop to all that, taking Tom under his wing and casting him as a prominent soldier in his private army. He wasn't much of a thinker, but he could run, and he could fight.

Ori Washta opened her eyes, losing the vision but retaining her protection on the three hired guns. Lighted smoke still swirled around her, its glow more intense. She took a moment to take a puff of her cigar and exhale it toward the pulpit at the sculpted, crucified Jesus she'd painted to have brown skin. She took another hit of her cigar. Shutting her eyes, she reached out, focused, and withdrew her protective blessing from Jonathan Cross. Ori saw the moment again behind closed eyes. Tension posed as quiet. But the silence was muted by Tom Rifle's gunfire aimed straight at Jonathan Cross. And just like that, John Cross was on his back, hole in chest, and dead.

Ori reached out and turned the head of Donavan Cross, inviting the hushed bounty hunter to witness his brother's death. His screams forced Ori Washta out of the vision. Her eyes opened, and she began gasping. Rattled by the sight and sound of her visions, and her participation in the events, Ori Washta stood and walked out of the field of lighted, orbiting smoke. She balanced herself on the pews, holding her head, which was now throbbing. When her eyes closed, she saw and heard the war her hired guns waged. Now, they had allies. Hand against her chest, Ori felt the rapid pumping of her heart. She still struggled to catch her breath. Closing her eyes to regain her faculties only put her back in the war.

"Where do I want to be buried?" she heard Eyes Are Bright scream, watching him stand with machete in hand. Determination doused his face, and his eyes glowed with want of war and with a shining brilliance that continued growing. He jumped into the hall and screamed, *"BURY ME IN AFRICA!"* The light in his eyes inundated the passageway. Tom Rifle buckled and dropped his weapon. His eyes stung, as did the eyes of the men trying to pile in behind him at the command of Captain Bell Frank. With a warrior's cry, Eyes Are Bright leapt at the would-be outlaw legend. He

slammed against Tom Rifle, knocking him to the ground. Crouched over Tom's body, Eyes Are Bright made repeated, swift chops with the machete into the hired gun's person. *"Don't hesitate,"* yelled Eyes Are Bright, continuing his lacerating assault against Tom Rifle. *"I will spill on you and kill you on the battlefield—true!"* With every word he made a rhythmic chop, using Tom Rifle's body like a drum to keep rhythm. Blood painted the charred walls, thrown about by Eyes Are Bright's hacks.

Ori opened her eyes. The church's interior surrounded her, but she could still hear the sounds of battle and Donavan Cross' continuous scream for his brother. She took a hit of her cigar and said, "Let it out, young brother."

Blade cut air. Hard, rough hacks cut into flesh.

Ori blinked, and in that moment she saw Eyes Are Bright free the other two warrior-brothers and more dead soldiers lining the hall. The shorter warrior-brother, Adamus the Hawk, with the light skin and hair like knotted worms crawling from the earth of his scalp. He put his balled hands together and against his mouth as if firing a blowgun. He opened his fists and propelled a hard breath, aiming at Bunk. A short and thin, glittering, pink stream cast out and sunk into Bunk's neck. The old man dropped unconscious, asleep. Adamus did the same for Donavan, but even when the younger Cross brother fell to sleep, he continued convulsing and moaning, still expressing the trauma of watching his brother die.

"Bring them to me," said Ori. "All three of your rescuers," she said aloud.

They heard her.

Then there was the tallest warrior-brother. Dark brown skin and hair like a rooster's comb. His name was Exploding Sun. His body burned with a blaze of fire, attacking oncoming soldiers and setting them aflame. The warrior-brothers charged while yelling obscenities in both their indigenous language and English. They rhymed threats as they made kills, beating their captors in the rhythm of their words. *Bury me in Africa,* their choral war cry. Indigenous to the land for thousands of years, blood and body acclimated to the weather of this northern wilderness. Their spirits, however, stood at the eastern coastline and yearned for a continent long left by their people. With this, they fought, possessed by the warrior spirits of two lands.

But even with their conjures ablaze, the ferocity of these indigenous, warrior-brothers had yet to be displayed until they chased their adversaries outside. Now, no longer bound by the rays of the full moon's light, they ingested it, satiating on its cosmic luminescence. The power of their conjures heightened, but the air breathed in from the moonlight was for another purpose. The warrior-brothers growled a war cry in harmony. Ori heard the sounds of skin stretching and bones popping and reshaping.

Large shadows, woolly and wild, and with long snouts, stalked the wooded areas for the retreating soldiers. Ori Washta allowed her warrior-brothers privacy for their hunt, opening her eyes but keeping an ear on the tears of flesh and screams and deaths of the men that helped decimate her people and culture.

Ori didn't know which of the screams and kills was Captain Bell Frank, but he was part of her warrior-brothers' catch in their hunt. When the battle died down, she pulled away from the sight, walked to the still glowing strands of smoke that swirled in an elliptical pattern, and dismissed them with a wave of her hand.

She waited, smoking the last of her cigar. When the thick, smoke stick was but a stub, Ori blew it out with an incanted breath. Tossed into the air, the cigar stub turned to ash. Then Ori spread her arms between the aisles and leaned her weight on the pews on either side.

Time passed. Then there was commotion at the door. Horses bayed, backed up by the sound of a young man moaning. Exploding Sun kicked the door open, Jonathan Cross' limp and lifeless, bloody body in his arms. Ori stood up straight. She pointed to the door leading to the back hall. "Take his body to the altar room," she instructed with urgency. The next warrior-brother, Eyes Are Bright, entered behind Exploding Sun. In his arms he held the shivering body of Donavan Cross, squally moans coming from his unconscious body as if he was experiencing a terrible nightmare. "Eyes Are Bright, lay him on the front pew, right side." Her warrior-brother did as ordered, quickening his pace to the front of the aisle.

Adamus the Hawk assisted an awakening Bunk "Old Gun" Abraham into the church. Once all were inside, the doors closed by way of incant. Ori asked Adamus to sit Bunk on the closest pew to him. Adamus walked the aged bounty hunter up the aisle a few paces, and then sat him down on the left side. Bunk mumbled something at Ori, body slipping to the left. Adamus caught him and kept him up. Confident that Bunk could keep his balance, Adamus stepped aside.

"Adamus," called Ori. "Just put him out again."

Adamus put his hands together like a blow gun and propelled his breath through. A pink sliver of light projected out and hit Bunk in the neck. The old man went back to sleep. Adamus caught his body and set it across the pew.

Ori removed her veil and wiped it over Donavan's face. The warrior paint disappeared from his countenance, magically erased. She hushed him and spoke an incant that relieved the shakes in his body and his moans. "There you go, black warrior. It's okay," said Ori bending down and taking up her veil. She opened Donavan's mouth and put her palm above it. "See it all over again. It's okay to scream."

Donavan resumed shaking. His mouth widened as if screaming, but no sound escaped. His eyes remained closed. Ori stood straight, keeping her palm hovering over Donavan's opened mouth. His body arched and white streams of light slithered from Donavan's opened mouth and up into Ori's palm. "Louder," said Ori to Donavan. His mouth opened wider, and the streams of white light increased in speed, number, and brilliance. The up-pour of lights merged as one, collecting in Ori's palm as a cylindrical blaze. Donavan's shaking eased. His mouth closed, and to sleep he went.

Ori made a fist as a bright charge of light surrounded her hand. She put her hands together and the charge increased. Pulling one hand away from the other, she separated the light into two, fists surrounded by either aura. She bent down and grabbed Donavan's hands with hers. The light jumped from her palms to Donavan's as Ori spoke an incant. "No more bad dreams, Donavan," she told him. "But you will now speak with this light and with closed fist." She concluded, "You are now a warrior-brother. Your name—" she turned and looked up at Exploding Sun, who had returned, standing behind her.

He folded his arms and pondered. He inspected the young bounty hunter lying across the pew, looking Donavan's body up and down and appearing as if reading something written on his person. Then the dark brown warrior-brother gave name anew to the sleeping Donavan, *"Aku the Boom Stick."*

Ori nodded her approval at Exploding Sun. She looked back at Donavan, and loosened her grip on him. The aura of light remained swirling around Donavan's hands, but after a time, it faded. Ori straightened, telling Eyes Are Bright and Adamus the Hawk, "Watch these two here. I'll prepare a new life for your next captain."

The warrior-brothers bowed at the neck. She ordered Exploding Sun to follow her, and the warrior-brother stepped to his order. Ori hurried to her altar room, Exploding Sun in tow. There, Jonathan Cross' dead body lay on a cot in the middle of the ritual-casting room. Under the cot was drawn a sigil representing life and death. Ori stepped inside and closed the door. Candles blazed on the altar that lay against the wall opposite the door. She walked around the cot and prepared incense for burning. She aligned talismans into the correct configurations, preparing for an incant that would take much out of her. She picked up a large hourglass and unfastened the top at one end. She laid her enchanted, black veil over Jonathan's fatal wound and spoke an incant in her indigenous language. The veil's fabric turned into pure light and slipped inside Jonathan's wound. The blood staining Jonathan's body and clothes vanished, and the wound scarring his chest sealed, flesh mended.

The veil, as light, sprang up from Jonathan's patched chest. In midair, it lost its glow, and Ori Washta took it in her free hand and fastened it to her hair, covering her face. "Exploding Sun," she called. "Drum."

The warrior-brother began beating his chest, producing a heavy rhythm. Every few pounds to his person, he clapped his hands. With every clap, fire burst from his palm. Faster, he clapped and pounded. He hit knees and kicked his feet up and slapped them to produce a beat. His hands gleamed with fire on every beat until the fire endured.

"To ash," said Ori as a command.

Exploding Sun crouched and slammed the palm of his hands against Jonathan's chest. The body burst into flames and ash, turning into a small, gray tornado of cindered flesh. Ori held out the opened hourglass, and Jonathan's ashes filled the glass vessel. Ori set the hourglass on her altar and removed the veil from her face. She turned around, bent down, and swiped the cot with the enchanted fabric where Jonathan's body once lay. She swiped once. Twice. Thrice. And then she pulled the veil away. Exploding Sun clapped with a resounding thunder, and then appeared Jonathan Cross' body, face clean of warrior paint. Eyes closed. His heart and breath inflating and deflating his chest.

"Leave us," said Ori to Exploding Sun. The warrior-brother obliged his General-Queen. Ori sat on the floor, knees up and with her arms embracing them. She exhaled and watched Jonathan's life come back to him. "Forgive me," she told him. "I had to go to some extreme measures to ensure that conjures that reside in you, good brother, could be brought to the surface."

Jonathan blinked and looked around at the room. He sat up. A sharp pain tore into his chest. By reflex, he palmed his chest and contorted his face. "Goddamnit!" he cursed.

"Lie down, good brother," Ori told him. "You're not all whole. You need rest."

Jonathan lay on his back, groaning as he did so. He looked up at the ceiling and said to Ori Washta, "Your protection faded."

"I took it back, good brother," Ori corrected. "So you could die," she added as if obvious.

Jonathan looked at Ori with an incredulous expression. "You killed me?"

Ori nodded. "I sure did," she acknowledged. She buried her face in her knees and then turned to look at Jonathan. "But I brought you back," she grinned. Then she blessed him with a new name. "Thunder John," she titled him.

"Where's my brother?" asked Jonathan, voice growing with bass.

"He's new too, good brother." Ori rocked. She tossed her head back and exhaled a proud shout. "He's a warrior-brother now, and he has no bad dreams."

Jonathan didn't understand. But he had another concern. He inquired, "And our captain?"

"He's fine," answered Ori. "He rescued one warrior-brother. Eyes Are Bright is his name. He's all that needed releasing."

"Your other warrior-brothers?"

Ori assured, "Eyes Are Bright rescued them. They slaughtered Captain Bell Frank and the remaining soldiers in his private army." She stopped rocking and got to her feet, wiping off her dress. "You rest, Thunder John. You'll learn who you and your brother are soon enough." Jonathan said nothing. "Rest, Captain Thunder John. Sleep. I will return in the morning and we will choose which one of the wicked men we shall kill next."

Jonathan grinned. "Yes, your majesty," he said.

Ori smiled back at him, opening the door. "Goodnight my soft-faced, handsome gunslinger," she said to Jonathan. She pointed at his holstered guns and spoke, "Keep them close, Captain Thunder John. But you'll never have to load them again." Then she left to check on her warrior-brothers and the slumbering Donavan Cross and his now former captain, Bunk "Old Gun" Abraham.

Ori ordered her warrior-brothers to hunt, and bring back a splendid catch for all of them to feast on. The resting warriors needed a meal to rejuvenate them, according to the young, conjure woman. Her warrior-brothers did not hesitate to put her command into action. Out of the church they went into the cold, full moon night. They breathed in the moon's aura and heightened their personal conjures for the hunt. They disappeared into the night, howling.

Ori Washta looked at Bunk. Then she spied Donavan Cross at peace in his sleep. She thought of Jonathan resting in the backroom. She sat on a pew and looked up at the brown skin Jesus and exhaled. Her conjure and gamble had worked out, and her army had grown. On future hunts, she would follow the men into battle as their General-Queen.

Fey Forrester watched in dream as Ori Washta kept her promise. The next day the young and powerful conjure woman strode into her altar room and met Jonathan Cross as he awoke. *"Good morning, my mighty, mahogany and soft-faced gunslinger,"* she greeted him. *"Which one of the wicked men shall we kill today?"*

But that first day they killed none. The Cross brothers instead learned their specific conjures and practiced their craft. Donavan, now called *Aku the Boom Stick*, could toss a furious and concussive scream from his fists. Jonathan could take the smallest of sounds and amplify them into a heavy force. The soft click of the hammer on his heavy, LeMat revolvers slapping against an empty chamber, incanted by Jonathan's conjure, became a locomotive push of pressure unrivaled. He would never again need to reload.

The warrior-brothers initiated Donavan into their order. With his initiation came a change in his attire. The code of dress was grey-blue pants tucked into black boots. Matching, heavy jackets lined with fur in winter. In warmer weather, the same style of coat had a lighter make in its stitching. A black and red scarf was worn around the forehead with a black, wide-brim hat adorned with a crow's feather. For thirty-seven days he studied to become a true warrior-brother, learning lessons on divine mathematics, the sun and moon, and rhythmic scriptures praising nature and the animal spirit. Donavan, blessed with a new name, recited these same lessons from book until they were committed to memory. He also created poetic narratives that referenced battle cries, his inner animal spirit, and his unique conjure. This was done while on his knees in a humbled posture. He knelt before an elaborate, wooden statue of an anthropomorphic gray wolf holding a sickle in one hand and a balance in the other. Adamus the Hawk and Eyes Are Bright flanked the tall, wooden sculpture as Exploding Sun held a curved sword to the back of Donavan's neck as he recited his lessons until memorized. The sharp blade, held inches away from the back of his neck, was a reminder of the dire consequences of breaking the oath he now pledged.

Fey Forrester watched as Jonathan and Bunk led the warrior-brothers into battle with Ori Washta at their side. With every slaughter, left behind, written in coal, in large letters were the words: *THUNDER JOHN AND THE BROTHER DOGS HAVE STRUCK.* Ori didn't like for her warrior-brothers to be referred to as 'dogs', but such was the nature of the feral spirit possessing these male warriors. And the name prompted a strong bond between the young warriors, which Ori Washta appreciated. The Speers and Gardens faction were broken one corrupt business at a time, on some nights, three businesses at a time. Falling on a full moon, business tycoon Donald Speers, his banker and partner Frederick Gardens and their bulldog of a lawyer, Rudolph Fischer held a private party that conjured debauchery in all its wealthy greatness. Ori Washta, aided by Thunder John and the Brother Dogs, finished the bloody storm of war they'd started.

The barbarous days of war streamed through Fey Forrester's dream, one clash leading into another. The passage of time connected the events through fades and dissolves of cobalt-blue light. The last of the history made her a witness to the growth of Copper Lyall into a safe haven for African- and Indigenous-Americans, but all were welcomed without prejudice. The treasure troves were recovered to fuel the town's economy. That was far from the last of Ori Washta's adventures with Thunder John and the Brother Dogs, but it was all that Fey Forrester was shown.

Sleep's blackness inhaled the cobalt-blue billows. Fey Forrester opened her eyes to the environment of the Goodspeed residence. Her vision was blurred by sleep, but the spirit stirring inside her brought her surroundings into focus. She lay straight, stiff, and guessed that at no time during her sleep did she move. She still clasped Spook with her arms folded as if in prayer. Her yumbo Zee, with purple glow and smile brimming bright, sat atop her hands.

Fey lifted her head. Sleep and the emotions of the dream were still on her. Lifting her head was like coming up from being submerged in water, but she managed. The kitchen's light was the only source of illumination. Fey spotted the dark silhouette of Maman Anansi sitting in one of the chairs close to the couch. Fable Avenue's head matriarch sat quiet and observant. Her glass of rum-kissed *dragon spit* lay on the coffee table in front of her. Madame Jeliya and Lady Arachne occupied the small kitchen table. They were involved in an intense round of Samedi's Tarot, the both of them puffing on cigars and taking small sips from the glasses of wine in front of them. Madame Jeliya fussed at Lady Arachne for taking her time, contemplating her cards. "This ain't a reading, Lena," she huffed. "Show your suit or take some cards." A child-like grin brightened her face as she suggested, "Or fold."

Lady Arachne lifted an eyebrow at Madame Jeliya.

But their game came to a stop when Fey's head lifted.

"Miss Forrester," greeted Lady Arachne. "Your yumbo let us in."

"We've been watching you," spoke Maman Anansi from behind her shadow. "I don't mean to make that sound creepy," she added as a playful quip.

"What time is it?" asked Fey with a head and mouthful of sleep. She yawned and sat up. Zee fluttered into the air and landed on her shoulder. Fey put Spook on her lap.

"It's one o'clock in the morning, child," Maman Anansi answered her.

"Is Gordon okay?"

"He's resting just fine," Lady Arachne reported, swapping two cards for two from the deck.

Madame Jeliya also swapped out cards. She arranged her new cards with the one's she'd kept and suppressed a smile. "Did you see anything with your scry, Fey?"

Fey shook her head. "No," she answered. "Nothing that would help Gordon's condition," she continued, thinking of Ori Washta and her tactics and conjures. "But I was sure shown a lot." She opened Spook and removed the aged hunting knife from between the archaic and mystical technology's binding. Fey placed the antique blade on the coffee table. Maman Anansi stood, walking from her shadow and into light where Fey could better see her features. The head matriarch bent down and presented Fey with a black fabric veil that, much like her cosmic cloth, appeared to swirl with the faint glimmer of a galaxy. Fey took the garment, thanking Maman Anansi. Fey was already familiar with the enchanted shroud given to her, having seen it in her dreams worn by the young conjure woman Ori Washta.

Maman Anansi sat down on the couch. "You're looking for the Djed Pillar Jewels, is that right, Fey?" Fey nodded, and Maman Anansi tapped on the young woman's thigh. "I wish you'd come to me earlier when you learned of this." She brushed her sentiment aside and continued her tale. "They, dear woman, are a set of gems my great-grandfather, Joseph Pepper the Fourth, looked up and down for in his youth. He almost had them." She positioned her pointer finger less than an inch away from her thumb. "He came this close," she said. "He actually held them. His spirit used to entertain me with the tale." She leaned close to Fey and expressed, "He supposedly employed the services of the ruffian outlaw Thunder John and his crew called the Brother Dogs."

"You don't believe your great-grandfather's story?" inquired Fey.

Maman Anansi answered with a smile, "Oh, I believe, Fey." She reflected on the times Joseph Pepper IV spoke to her when she was a child, visiting her dreams. She recited, "He was able to keep the veil for helping protect a town out west."

"Copper Lyall!" blurted Fey with her eyes wide and expressive. Maman Anansi acknowledged, recalling the town's proper name with Fey's help. But Fey's excitement didn't last long. Her eyes fell and spied the veil. Gone was the charge in her spirit. She sighed, "But if he never recovered them, then scrying with the object won't help."

"He was able *to keep* the veil, Fey," Maman Anansi repeated with emphasis. She elucidated after noticing the befuddled look possessing Fey's facial expression. "The items are connected. He was instructed to bring the two items together. Supposedly, dear woman, both items came over from Africa on the same ancient voyage. Though I'm not entirely sure they were forged at the same time. Incanted gifts for the indigenous man and woman residing here, I suppose. Probably one set of mystical baubles for some others." Again she tapped Fey on the thigh, but this time with her whole hand rather than a single finger. "So you just go on ahead there and dream of history, dear woman." With an approving smile, Maman Anansi got up and returned to her chair, slipping back into shadow. "Now, remember, my great-grandfather was a storyteller, and he held that veil for many years before he passed it to his true love, my great-grandmother. There will be some story attached to that sacred cloth from that alone."

Fey smiled at Maman Anansi's sentiment. She opened Spook's black mirror and laid the precious veil on the bejeweled console. She closed the *Nigrum Nigrius Nigro* and laid flat on the sofa, clasping her hands around the book. She thought carefully of the question she needed answered. She heeded Maman Anansi's words coupled with the age of the veil and its relation to the Djed Pillar Jewels. The last thing Fey Forrester needed—to use the nerdy term of her dear Gordon Goodspeed—was to see an origin story for the item, ancient as it was.

The power of the *Nigrum Nigrius Nigro* reached up, wrapped itself around Fey, and dragged her to sleep to witness history.

Madame Jeliya and Lady Arachne returned their attention to their game. Lady Arachne displayed three of her cards, placing them on the table. She announced, "Knights triplet." She slapped her fourth and fifth cards down, The Sun and Four of Wands, which did nothing to strengthen her already strong hand.

"Oh," choked Madame Jeliya. She said aloud, "Huh…" She put four of her cards on the table and triumphantly declared, "*Regal House of Pentacles.*" And there lay the king, queen, knight, and page of the pentacles suit. She tossed her fifth card, the Page of Wands, which was of no consequence to her round-winning hand. Madame Jeliya chuckled. Lady Arachne gave her a stern eye. "Please, Lena," said Madame Jeliya as she got up from her chair, taking her glass of wine with her. "You're up three games on this night—out of *four*. Let me have some fun with a win."

Lady Arachne said nothing, keeping her stern gaze on Madame Jeliya while gathering the cards and reshuffling them. Madame Jeliya took a seat at the other chair near the sofa and watched Fey's peaceful rest. Lady Arachne joined the other matriarchs, glass of wine in hand. Maman Anansi took up her glass of rum-kissed *dragon spit.* The three matriarchs, taking simultaneous sips, observed Fey as she was lost in a dream that recalled history.

Copper Moon Full Over Sunrise Gems

"It's Ori Washta's three chains of gold that keep them Dogs on a leash."

Joseph Pepper IV appeared to his audience of few to be a peculiar young man of twenty-six years. It wasn't so much that he was an old-soul type of character. To the few occupants of the saloon, he looked young with his smooth, beige skin that didn't even have one speck of stubble on it. But he carried himself like a venerable, learned professor, fancy walking stick and all. He claimed he was a lecturer, and his listening audience in the scarcely occupied saloon believed him, considering his dialect. His manner of dress was far more worldly-wise than the common vestments worn by the people of the town of *Casa Negra*. Furthermore, he claimed to hail from New York City, having come west for research.

He sat at the bar with a plate of hot breakfast food in front of him. Situated left of his plate was a newspaper announcing a continued investigation into a massacre occurring several towns over. This became the current topic of conversation. A bit of chatter concerning the philosophy and politics of the western frontier, and the end of its Golden Age, passed the time between Joseph ordering his meal and it being placed in front of him. Joseph's light causerie fastened the black bartender's ears to his words, putting pause on the square-faced and burly forty-five-year old man's duty of wiping off the bar and cleaning glasses. The bartender's narrow eyes focused on young Joseph Pepper.

Joseph tapped the newspaper with his fork, stating, "Now, they say here there's been a massacre two towns up." He looked closer at the paper, adjusting his glasses to read. "Waterberry," he highlighted. "The citizens were spared, but government soldiers and a few local law enforcers were butchered, and a train was robbed of its silver. Much carnage was found at the scene—as you can imagine." Joseph looked up at the bartender, spying the two, heavy, nine-round guns strapped around his hips. He looked the bartender in the eye, examining his face filled with old scars, knowing each had a bloody and brutal story attached to them. "Word is that's the umpteenth time a train with silver has been swiped, and brutality accompanied the grab." Joseph noticed a man sneaking up behind him. Another closed the doors to the bar and locked them. Instead of addressing the issue, Joseph returned his attention to his meal, keeping his head down.

"They say it was done by indigenous men, or 'savages' as the white man continues to call them. Apparently, this is the work of thousands of warriors…or, possibly, one legendary, stealthy manslayer." He continued eating. On swallowing he reported, "Locals call this man *El Cazador de Sombra*." Then Joseph Pepper translated for his listening audience of few, *"The Shadow Hunter."* He took a sip of water and then informed, "The locals on either side of the border purportedly saw him walking the land." He looked up from his meal and expressed, "The clamorous gunfire and the slaughter of law enforcers and government troops have roused the residents of Waterberry to drag this mythological figure into imagination and wild theories to make sense of the gruesome ordeal that stained their Waterberry roads. So shaken and confused are these citizens that, as the paper chronicles, many of them report spying *Sombra* during this fray."

The bartender folded his arms. "Does seem unfathomable that one man could do all this," he agreed. The man behind Joseph moved closer, careful in his approach. But it was too late. Though ignored, Joseph had already spotted him.

"Indeed," spoke Joseph, returning to his meal, head down. "As my intellect and reason have deduced, I can tell you two things for certain, my good man."

The bartender chuckled and said to Joseph, "Never heard a Negro speak like you. Not in a long time, anyway. You're alright." He grinned and leaned his weight on the bar's counter. "What can you deduce, young man?"

Joseph said, "*Sombra* had nothing to do with this slaughter. And it was not the work of thousands of warriors."

"Is that right?" asked the bartender, grin growing wider.

"True indeed, my good man," Joseph replied. "In fact, it was only five."

Joseph lifted his head, stopping short as against his neck was pressed a six shooter's muzzle. Joseph remained calm, even when he heard the mechanized click of the weapon's hammer cocked back.

"You law?" asked the man behind him.

Joseph didn't answer. He stared at the bartender whose grin never faltered. The lecturer looked around the room, barely moving his head so as not to excite the man holding him at gunpoint. He counted only three other men, all dressed in the same rugged manner: grey-blue jacket and matching pants tucked into boots. A black and red scarf worn around the forehead, and a black, wide-brim hat with a crow's feather sticking out of the band. The man behind Joseph was dressed the same.

"So," started Joseph, eyes still locked onto the grinning bartender. "Which one of your Brother Dogs, Thunder John, has me at gunpoint?"

"That would be Adamus the Hawk," answered the bartender, admiring Joseph Pepper's use of his moniker. "And he's not too handy with an earthly firearm. So I suggest you answer his question."

"Finger sure does itch, Big Chief," growled Adamus as an added point for Joseph to consider.

The young scholar instead chuckled to himself, saying aloud, "It's the turn of the century, and you boys are living in the glory days of this western territory. Apparently, the government's expanding reach on a mission to civilize the western frontier has not met all of its corners."

Thunder John, grin intact, lifted himself up onto his arms. The former bounty-hunter shook his head. Looking up at Adamus the Hawk, he exhaled, "You want to scratch that itch you got, Adamus?"

"On your word, Big Chief," Adamus said with his eyes locked onto the back of Joseph Pepper's head.

But Thunder John raised a hand and gave a simple wave for Adamus to stand down. The Brother Dog eased the hammer from its position and holstered his gun. To Joseph, Thunder John asked, "What brings you here, boy? Now, I don't need to force a confession that you're not law—local or federal. I can see that. But I'd like some respect paid to me and my men in our saloon." He again rested his weight against the bar and told Joseph, "We don't much care for researchers coming here looking for a story either."

"I spoke in falsehoods," said Joseph, "so that I may gain your trust."

Thunder John considered the point, looking up and shaking his head left and right as he pondered. "That's a new one," he concluded. He returned his gaze to Joseph. "Care to explain?"

"I *am* from the city of New York, but I am not here for research," Joseph answered. "That part of my work is complete, and it is within that work's conclusion that I have journeyed here." Adamus came from behind Joseph and propped himself on a stool. "I am a lecturer, speaking on African customs and traditional African spirituality. I believe the Negro could use an education in the matters of knowledge of self, giving us a firm foundation to survive post-slavery in this northern wilderness called America." Thunder John and Adamus shared a look and a chuckle. "Is there something the matter with my proclamation? I assure you, I am not alone in this notion."

"Understood, Scholar Joe," said Thunder John.

"Then what causes your guffaws?" Joseph inquired.

Thunder John simmered his laughter and answered Joseph with the comment, "You're going to scare whites and Negroes alike with that type of hoodoo talk. Trust me."

"I do," admitted Joseph in a sincere voice. "That's why I've been through much to find you."

Adamus gave his captain, the Big Chief, a look. The other Brother Dogs, stationed around the saloon, did the same. Thunder John took notice, but he kept his focus on young Joseph Pepper. "And what type of all '*much*' have you been through, scholar, to track me and my brutal band of feral brothers here?" asked Thunder John, removing an already rolled cigarette from the pouch on his apron. With it he removed a box of matches and struck one, lighting the cigarette in his mouth.

"A Negro of my knowledge and investigative curiosity warrants an adversary or two," Joseph relayed. "Or three," he added. Then he thought for a moment, "Perhaps an entire government," he concluded. "Nonetheless, the curiosities I seek already have a swarm of villains closing in on them. Individually, they have nothing but disdain for one another. Collectively, however, I am their common foe. And in this tale, mighty Thunder John, they have bonded for the purpose of keeping me from my prize." Joseph recalled in question, "What type of all 'much' have I been through you ask? There is too much, at this short notice, to recount every obstacle of adventure put in my way. But make no mistakes, grand gunslingers, I'm rich with yarn to knit the narratives."

The Brother Dogs burst into laughter. Adamus, who now was enjoying a smoke and a glass of whiskey, slapped Joseph hard on the back. "You alright, scholar," he told Joseph while wearing a wide smile. He chugged his whiskey in one gulp, bracing his throat and stomach against the drink's burn. Then he continued to laugh, thinking of Joseph's words. *"Rich with yarn to knit the narratives,"* he repeated while shaking his head. To his captain, he said, "I'll follow him into a battlefield if that's what he needs. No prized purse attached to the call to action. I'm in just on the strength! Let me apologize for the gun ordeal, scholar."

Thunder John once again put his hand up at Adamus, signaling him to relax. "What's your prize, young Pepper?"

Joseph hesitated for a moment. When he spoke, the volume in his eastern-accented voice startled Thunder John and his band. "I seek a bracket of seven jewels branded by folklorists as the Sunrise Gems," he confessed. Joseph witnessed a quiet unease sweep through the saloon. The Brother Dogs seated behind Joseph Pepper stood and converged on the bar, standing behind the traveling lecturer. Joseph lit up with a grin. He smacked the bar's smooth surface and hollered an order, "Whiskey, my good man!" Thunder John slapped down a glass and filled it halfway. Joseph took a large sip to impress the ruffians around him. The burn shook him, but Joseph didn't make a face, though he braced against the fiery drink. He waited a moment before he spoke, having lost his voice to the heavy intoxicant. When his voice recovered, he informed, "True scholars know the stones as the Djed Pillar Jewels, and that the jewels hail from across the Atlantic. Their birthplace is Africa. These particular gems anyway."

Exploding Sun, the tallest Brother Dog who had a rooster comb-like hairdo, leaned on the bar with his elbow at Joseph's right. "I'm not going to take away whatever education you got, scholar," he grumbled. "But I have to correct you. You ain't got to have passed through some white man's schooling to know the stones are truly named the Djed Pillar Jewels."

Thunder John's brother, Aku the Boom Stick, patted Joseph's shoulder with a couple smacks. The one named Eyes Are Bright chimed in by saying, "Hooligans like as us are kind of connected by blood to legends such as the one you speak on."

"Indeed," said Joseph, tipping his head at Exploding Sun and lifting his glass of whiskey. "And if I've offended you all, that was not my purpose. I was not making note of my education, but merely hinting at those who do real scholarship and research would find the proper name of what they seek rather than the colloquial appellation." He drank a heavy gulp, swallowed the drink's burn, and exhaled a hard breath. "And that is why I have sought you proud, savage hoodlums." His joke culled a chuckle from his company. Putting his glass down, Joseph tapped on the newspaper. "I have more to speak on about this event—deductions concerning you all. Things you already know, having been there."

The Brother Dogs were attentive. Thunder John lost his grin and swiped a dirty cup. He started cleaning it with a wet rag. "Okay, scholar," he said. "Whatchu got?"

Joseph felt the Brother Dogs lean in close. "I have, my good man, the *true* story of this night's events." Again he tapped on the newspaper. He said, "Not the one the press wishes the blind citizens to believe."

Aku the Boom Stick's quiet voice inquired, "Whatchu know?"

Joseph answered, "I know that the federal troops riding along with that train of silver were not entirely federal. They were hired guns wearing federal clothing. I also understand—and I'm not sure how the press intends for the local residents of Waterberry to believe this story against what they witnessed—but none of the local law enforcers were killed. They were wounded, and not even near fatal." Joseph picked up his glass. He said with a smile and his drink hovering near his lips. "You boys did some damage, and there was indeed a slaughter. But the exaggeration—"

"They make no mention of us," said Adamus with a disgusted look on his face while snatching up the paper to give it a read.

"Of course not," retorted Joseph. "You all are myths for other hired guns to deal with. And *that*, savage ruffians, is the enemy *we* have in common." Joseph drank again. The whiskey's burn was occurring less and less with every sip he took. "This enemy has free reign to operate as they wish within this country and many others. Their foot soldiers are allowed to wear the military dress of the country they're operating in." To Thunder John, Joseph addressed, "Allow me to inquire. How long have you been hitting trains of silver?"

Thunder John contemplated the answer. He said to Joseph, "Almost two years."

"And why? What was the instinct that made you go after them?"

"Wasn't quite instinct," expressed Exploding Sun, taking a seat next to Joseph. "Our General-Queen had an insight. Someone was stocking up on silver. And they were coming to put down us Brother Dogs. But hell, they'd have to make way down here to find us."

Joseph looked at each of the Brother Dogs, scoping them up and down with an admiring smile beaming on his face. Legends stood before him. He said, "Silver, huh? So the stories *are* true." He turned his attention to his drink. "Is it the full moon that brings your inner beasts in bloom?"

Thunder John's grin returned. He looked down at the glass he cleaned and reminded, "We don't much care for researchers coming here looking for a story, Scholar Joe." He exhaled cigarette smoke, puffing through his mouth as he spoke each word.

Adamus the Hawk's hand clasped his holstered firearm. "I got to pull my gun on this fool again, Big Chief? I was beginning to like him—glory into battle with him and all."

Joseph finished the rest of his whiskey, shaking his head at Adamus that it wouldn't be necessary, though he understood Adamus was only playing. Joseph told Thunder John after his final gulp, "Oh, come now, you 'savage ruffians'. I'm not looking for a story." Joseph arched his shoulders and lifted his hands as if surrendering. "I'm merely trying to upturn some clarity on an existing one." He raised an eyebrow. Then he requested from Thunder John, "More whiskey, good man. The more I drink the more truth I give."

Thunder John stopped his cleaning, putting the polished glass under the bar. He first tapped the long trail of ashes on his cigarette into a small bowl resting on the counter before filling Joseph's glass. Glass filled and cigarette back in his mouth, Thunder John turned his attention to another glass that needed cleaning. Eyes Are Bright moved behind Joseph and shook him by his shoulders. "Ah, Big Chief, this young, scholarly whelp can be trusted." He put an arm around the traveling scholar and explained to Joseph in a whisper, "And the full moon, educated Moor, only strengthens our lupine spirits, it doesn't dictate our change." He winked and tapped his fingers on Joseph's shoulder, and then he stepped away from him.

"Keeps us young and pretty too," Adamus added with a grin. "For the ladies."

Thunder John huffed, "This from a guy that likes his women a little mature. But you act like a kid, so I guess you might as well look like one." The other Brother Dogs laughed. Joseph mumbled a chuckle as well as he sipped his new glass of whiskey. Thunder John looked at his brother and commented, "And you. You like that youth keeping incant, don'tchu. What happened to the dream of growing old and hardboiled out west?"

Exploding Sun jumped in and vocalized, "Him grow old while his wife maintains that pretty youth of hers? She'd toss him aside for a young whelp like this scholar here." He punched Joseph on the shoulder. Settling back onto his stool, he asked, "A whiskey, Big Chief?"

Thunder John looked at Exploding Sun and shook his head. "Not now."

Exploding Sun straightened. "Yes, Captain," he said.

Thunder John shifted his heavy frame, and the weighty weapons at his hip moved with a mighty sway. He explained to the Brother Dog, "Understand, Sun, I need your head clear to deliver written word to my wife." He placed the now clean glass under the bar to dry. He slapped the wet towel onto the bar and leaned against the counter. He assigned, "Eyes Are Bright, patrol the outer limits. Adamus, Aku, you're on border town duty." His eyes went to Adamus and his brother. "Anything suspicious, you alert me." Both Brother Dogs nodded their heads at their captain. He addressed Joseph, "We can't make a move without my wife's approval. And I'd like to see if she has any insight on you, Mister Joseph Pepper the Fourth. She's a conjure woman."

"I understand the precaution," Joseph yielded.

"Good," Thunder John stated. "Because it's the protocol we follow." He pulled a journal from his pouch and opened it on the bar. Tucked inside was a pen. He picked it up, opened to a blank page, and started writing. "Exploding Sun, you take this here note to my wife. Have her give some insight. Bring back what she sees." Everyone remained quiet as Thunder John scribed a quick note. He tore the paper from the journal, folded it once, and handed it to Exploding Sun. "Rest up now. Travel at sundown," he commanded the Brother Dog.

Exploding Sun took the note from Thunder John. "Yes, Captain," he responded in a humble voice. Without another word, the tall, wild-haired Brother Dog stepped off his stool, walked to the doors, unlocked them, and left the saloon to take rest before his travel. Thunder John started wiping down the counter with the cleaning rag. Making his way over to Adamus the Hawk, he took his glass from him and spat, "Everyone to their jobs. Now! Outer limits." Adamus took one last drag of his cigarette and then tossed it into a metal bin near his stool. Stepping down off his seat, he heard his captain add to the order, "Dog it up out there on your patrol. Not big and on your hind legs. Full canine lupus," he demanded. "And be careful for hunters looking for wild game," he shouted as Adamus made his way to the door.

"I'll give 'em a game, all right," Adamus grumbled.

"What was that?" asked his captain.

"I said, yes, Captain," Adamus replied in a respectful tone.

"That's what I figured," Thunder John boomed. "Don't go looking for a fight." Then his stern gaze went to Eyes Are Bright and his brother. "Sweep the town. Eyes up, boys." The remaining Brother Dogs bowed at the neck, addressed their captain with respect, and left the bar. "And keep them doors open so we can get paying customers in here."

The Brother Dogs did as told, and a host of patient patrons filtered inside soon after. A young Mexican man in his early twenties came behind the bar. "*Hola,* Señor Cross," he said boisterous. "I can relieve you of tending. My brother and uncle are here to watch the place and take orders too."

Thunder John finished his cigarette and snuffed it out in the bowl on the counter. "Thank you, Little Ortiz," he said, smoke streaming between his lips. He removed a few items from his pouch and put them on the bar. Then he untied his apron and handed it to Miguel Ortiz. "*Gracias*, Ortiz. There you go. How's your mother and father doing?"

Putting on the apron, Ortiz replied, "I haven't received a letter in a long time, Señor Cross. But the last one said they were doing well, settling into California just fine. They say it's peaceful out there. My dad is trying to open another saloon, maybe two."

"Is that right?" Thunder John grinned, eyes on Ortiz but scooping up the items he'd placed on the bar. "That's good. He was a tough man, your pop. He's got fifteen years on me and still going strong."

"Like I say, that's what brought me and my brother out here. Put some hair on our chest."

Thunder John and Joseph chuckled. Miguel moved into position behind the bar to take orders and drinks. "I guess," was all Thunder John said. He thought for a moment and added as he looked around the saloon, "These small towns out here stuck in the past. Just remember to get out. My brother and I headed this way for the same reasons. But we forgot to leave."

"I know Señor Cross," Miguel smiled. "But with my father getting some new saloons up and running, Cristo and I will probably go out to help him. Don't worry, you'll still have my uncle." Miguel started laughing when he added, "My father won't let him near his business. He drinks up all the profit, if you know what I mean."

Thunder John, coming around the bar and behind Joseph, returned laughter. "Well that's not that refreshing to know," he commented. He nudged Joseph. "Get your things. We got a discussion to have." He addressed Miguel as the young man was handing a drink to a patron, "I'll be upstairs if there's any trouble."

"Okay, Señor Cross," Miguel acknowledge.

Joseph slipped from his seat. He picked up the newspaper and his cane, and with his coat and satchel already around him, he followed Thunder John out of the saloon and behind the building to a set of stairs. Up onto a balcony, Thunder John strolled several doors down. He unlocked the door and stepped inside the quaint room, tossing his things onto the bed. He closed the door when Joseph entered and pulled out a chair for the young scholar while he sat at his desk. Bright sunlight shining through the window lit up the room.

"So, Scholar Joe, how do our paths coincide?" asked Thunder John.

Joseph sat, and then he rested his cane against the bed. "There is an organization of powerful men that seek curiosities from around the world, items of myth and legend. They auction these items off to one another, but not for keep. The items are on loan for a purchased amount of time. And then, the items are re-stored…" Joseph's voice and expression brightened as he concluded, "…somewhere. Somewhere I do not know of." He fixed his face and explained further, "The items sought do not always have to be inanimate objects. You and the Brother Dogs are such items. That's your part in this." He crossed his legs, and then he continued, "My part began when I did research on the legendary Queen Califia, an ancient, black queen who ruled over a tribal nation of black women indigenous to America, specifically the land of California, for which the state supposedly receives its name. Was she real or just the musings of a clever and imaginative sixteenth century, Spanish writer?"

"And what did your research conclude, scholar?" asked Thunder John, face holding curiosity.

Joseph jumped to his feet, swiping his cane. Thunder John flinched. He watched the young, erudite black man attentively. Joseph turned his back for effect, pivoting with the grace of a military solider. Over his shoulder he said to Thunder John, "I once thought *you* were a work of fiction, Thunder John." He spun around to face the outlaw. Stepping forward he said, "The idea of Califia is real, for not every black man or black woman was brought here through the odious system of slavery. Some of us came on voyages thousands of years earlier, establishing culture and interacting peacefully with the indigenous red man and woman whose spirits were already cultivating and communicating with the land." With eyebrow raised, Joseph Pepper inquired, "Your Brother Dogs. Why do whispers concerning your ruffian soldiers call them the Wild *Zulu* Indians?"

Thunder John leaned back, looking down at his lap with a grin. He chuckled as he leaned the seat back onto its hind legs and balanced. He set the chair down, locked his hands together, and put them on his stomach. "The Negro has an interesting story, doesn't he, Scholar Joe?"

Balanced on his cane, Joseph answered, "We do. We do."

Thunder John exhaled. "My wife is of the Qalif Nation—on her mother's side. To them, Queen Qalifia is quite real. Every reigning chieftess—to this day—takes the moniker." He swiped one hand out wide and noted, "They say her treasures are spread throughout this land." Then, with the same hand, he aimed a finger at Joseph. He spotted the traveling scholar through one eye and said, "And you, Scholar Joe, are close to getting a set of her treasures." He leaned back in his chair, settling his arm. He asked Joseph, "What would you have us rob, Scholar Joe?"

Joseph's countenance remained stern, but he was delighted, as it appeared the legendary outlaw agreed to aid him in his pursuit. He explained in a tone similar to his expression, "In four days, there is scheduled a train coming from California. The train is carrying ammunition. Bullets forged from silver. It also carries with it five pine boxes. Each one a specific fit for you and your warrior Brother Dogs."

"Ain't no trains run through here," remarked Thunder John.

Joseph nodded his head, acknowledging Thunder John's sentiment. He said to the rugged-faced gunslinger, "The only stop I'm interested in is over in Chapel Root. That is where a pickup will be made. It's a rundown area, void of enough people to make a pickup of such nature. Those tracks haven't been used in years, according to my research."

"They will be, for the gems you covet," Thunder John ventured a guess.

"Indeed," Joseph confirmed. Thunder John shifted in his chair. He pondered Joseph's proposition. Joseph returned to his chair. "I cannot offer much, Thunder John."

Thunder John shook his head, shaking a finger, and with a grin in place. "You don't need to offer me anything, Scholar Joe. The Brother Dogs and I live for this type of emprise—the hunt, as my soldiers and I call it." He tapped his chest with the same finger. "No, it's my wife you have to convince." He rose from the chair and walked over to the room's only window. He moved aside the thin, beige curtain and allowed more of the morning's light through. He watched the town's citizens as they filtered through the streets, in and out of buildings. "Like I said, she's of the Qalif Nation. The prize you seek, she just might lay claim to it. No hard feelings."

Joseph nodded his head, understanding Thunder John's position. Then he rocked in his chair and pondered the thought. It wouldn't matter, he concluded, and he said so aloud. "If your wife—the conjure woman you speak of—could give me a blessing using those gems, that would suffice. She may keep what is rightfully hers."

Thunder John turned around. "That sounds like a good idea, Scholar Joe. A fine plan." He walked up behind the young, New York scholar and patted him on the shoulder. "You stay here, okay. I'm going to set up a room for you. Free of charge," he added. "It'll be a while before we hear word from Exploding Sun." The rugged-faced gunslinger left the room, leaving Joseph alone with his thoughts.

"Well, my once good friend, Ethan," he addressed as if his subject was present. "You have many benefactors, and now, so do I."

Not much time passed before Thunder John returned, reporting that he'd acquired a room for Joseph at the small hotel across the street. He had with him a bottle of whiskey and two clean glasses. Pouring Joseph a glass, and handing it to him, he took a seat after filling a glass for himself and resting the bottle on a small desk in the room. Joseph gulped a fresh amount of the distilled drink, and then he and Thunder John engaged in conversation involving the organization of people called The Line. He told the outlawed gunslinger that he and his Brother Dog soldiers were not the first human trophies The Line ever sought. Joseph knew of five men in China, two of which were successfully hunted, and the others still pursued. There were a host of hunts for legendary figures throughout Asia, Arabia, and Africa. Some of the trophies had been collected. Weapons or body parts were kept as prizes.

Joseph also confessed to once having a friendship with a man named Ethan Cassidy, a man of Southern descent, and who was now part of The Line. Joseph remarked, "He traded up one Negro for another. A black man named Anderson Gunner now assists Ethan. I don't much understand that man. He does more damage to his own people than a slave owner. He travels and does lectures after me trying to negate my words. He's not good on that account. He makes himself look like a fool. He says my knowledge, wisdom and understanding of ancient Africa and its affects on all that is modern are a stretch, misguided. A shame, it is. He has such an amazing name. *Anderson Gunner.* Sounds strong. But, alas, some of us Negroes choose to be weak. He hesitates not when applauding other cultures' influence on modern society, but when it comes to the Negro and our ancient civilizations, oh, then it's a stretch to believe so. He even scoffs at the Moors and their wondrous influence keeping Europe from collapsing." Thunder John was intrigued by all Joseph had to say, and he was doubly intrigued to know that he himself was a highly sought after trophy.

"The legend of you was purposely suppressed," noted Joseph. "The Line's soldiers have now been brought in to sweep your existence away. Even without the conjures and superstitions surrounding you, your wife the conjure woman, and your Brother Dogs, you have the potential to be grand heroes in the eyes of the Negro. And that potential must be stomped out. I heard much the same was done by your mentor. Was he not the infamous plantation raider called The Top Hat?"

Thunder John nodded at Joseph. "Yes he was. But he's still kicking, thanks to a blessing. Stubborn and old, just like his story. He lives on. But, if these Line soldiers happen to succeed in their hunt, then you tell my story, Scholar Joe," he tasked. "You tell it well and with all manner of truth. My wife and sons will help you pen it."

Their talk lasted until midday. Thunder John dismissed himself, returning to work behind the bar. He first escorted Joseph across the street to his room at the hotel. Signed in, and once inside his room, Joseph was finally able to remove his coat and glasses. He lay down on the bed and went fast to sleep, first lighting the lamp near his table and making the light very dim. Joseph awoke a few minutes after nine o'clock. He sat up as fast as the remaining spell of sleep would allow him. He was dazed, in awe at how tired he'd been from his travels. He removed his pocket watch and placed it close to his eyes and saw the time. He exhaled a sigh and slipped his watch back into his pocket. He reached out for his glasses and put them on his face.

Joseph opened up his leather-bound journal and took out his pencil, stuffed in between two clean pages. After brightening the lamp's flame, he began writing about his travel to the town he presently occupied, dating the entry. He was careful not to use the names *Thunder John* or *Brother Dogs*, but his clever mind found a way to describe the ruffian crew without giving them away. He also wrote around his intentions of robbing a train from The Line. Thunder John visited him around midnight, bringing Joseph a hot plate of rice, beans, beef strips, and ginger water for a beverage. The outlaw didn't stay long, though there was a friendly exchange of history passed between them. He returned to his ruse of being bartender and cook quickly after.

Early morning brought word from Exploding Sun. Heavy pounding on Joseph's door fragmented his rest. *"Scholar Joe!"* he heard Thunder John yelling. *"Scholar Joe!"* his new moniker was shouted again.

Joseph sprang up. He checked his watch and put on his glasses. Standing, he trekked over to the door and opened it wide. Thunder John and three of the Brother Dogs stood in the hallway. "Greetings to you four," said a sleepy-eyed Joseph. "News, I take it," he continued, yawning as he spoke and rubbed his eyes. Through the fading blur of his vision, Joseph could see Thunder John's outfit had changed to fit the threads of a gunslinger on the frontier rather than a bartender. He wore a hat over a scarf that covered his low-cut bush of hair.

"We got you a horse," Thunder John informed Joseph. "Pack up, and then mount up. We're heading to Copper Lyall. My wife wants to speak directly to you."

Joseph perked up, sleep dispelled. "You've heard word?"

"Howl," corrected Eyes Are Bright. "We heard Exploding Sun's howl. It was a call to Copper Lyall."

"That's a bit of a distance," Joseph replied, turning his back to gather his things. "Come in, please. No need to wait out in the hall."

Thunder John and the three Brother Dogs stepped inside. Adamus remarked, "So all the legends about us Brother Dogs you're willing to believe, but you got a problem with our good hearing and the travel of our callings."

Joseph chuckled as he gathered his belongings and clothes. He removed a small, leather pouch from his coat, opened it and reached inside, pulling free a wad of *mentha* leaves. He stuffed the bunch in his mouth and began chewing. A burst of cool, airy mint filled Joseph's mouth and washed his breath of the tarry taste and odor accrued while he slept. He offered his pouch to Thunder John and the three Brother Dogs standing in his room, but they declined, saying they'd already freshened up.

"You need a meal?" asked Thunder John. "It's going to be a long trek."

Joseph scooped up the last of his items and answered, "I should be fine, Thunder John. I have some vittles with me. Small things like jerky."

"You need a weapon?" Aku the Boom Stick asked in a low voice.

Joseph picked up his sapphire-encrusted cane. Standing straight, and addressing the Brother Dog's question, he replied, "I'm armed. Trust me." He gave his cane a small toss up and then swiped it from the air, gripping it again and planting the end on the ground. "Had some travels through India a few years ago. I put together a trinket made for both offense and defense, with help, of course. I was assisted by a Dravidian shaman with remarkable knowledge."

"That stick got a kick?" Adamus asked eyeing Joseph's fancy walking cane.

Joseph tapped the object on the floor. "It does indeed, my Brother Dog," he told Adamus. "The power of Shango and Indra resides here. And the great, black beyond knows good and well I need them at my side. As I've acquired a great many enemies, I shall equip myself with a great deal of weapons."

Adamus jumped over to Joseph and tossed his arm around the young scholar's shoulders. "You got five, rough and tough weapons assisting you." Adamus slapped Joseph on the chest. "It's conjures and a wild animal spirit that gets the job done, Scholar Joe!"

Joseph put his eyes on Thunder John. "So is that to be my name, Thunder John?"

The hardened outlaw nodded. "Men that ride with us get a name," he said. "That's yours, Scholar Joe." He waved everyone to the outside. "Let's go, if you're packed up, then mount up." Adamus let go of Joseph and formed up with his warrior-brothers and captain. Joseph put out the light, and then shuffled into the hallway with the noble ruffians. Thunder John said over his shoulder, "Your horse's got a canteen filled with water." He tapped against the wall and said, "The hotel looks fancy from the outside, but it still ain't got indoor plumbing or electricity. The saloon's got plumbing inside, if you need to head to the bathroom before we make our way, or if you want to get a warm bath."

"I'll be fine. I'll freshen up when we make it to Copper Lyall. My sweet scent shouldn't have dissolved by then," said Joseph. He patted his pelvis. "I've come to develop an iron bladder with all my travels. Besides, I can make do with the woods should nature call."

Thunder John and the Brother Dogs laughed at the scholar's antics. When Joseph asked how long the travel was, Eyes Are Bright responded, "A nice jog for you and the Big Chief's horses. Should be about a six, seven hour ride."

"You won't be joining us?" Joseph asked the Brother Dog.

Adamus answered, "Not on horseback."

"We'll be in the shadows should we come across some undesirable company," Eyes Are Bright noted.

Once outside, Joseph and Thunder John unhitched and mounted their horses. Aku the Boom Stick, Eyes Are Bright, and Adamus the Hawk walked alongside their mounted captain, Joseph in tow. At the edge of town, the Brother Dogs dashed away into the woods where they traveled off of the trail. Joseph peered through the dense flora, but his eyes lost the shadows of the Brother Dogs to the movement of wild canines. A howl echoed through the day, and as it filtered through the air, Joseph pulled up alongside Thunder John. Both men made small talk while they journeyed.

Their horses trotted for more than an hour before being given the command to sprint hard. But after the grueling motion, Thunder John and Joseph Pepper were forced to rest their horses and make a small camp with supplies strapped to Thunder John's mount. He remarked, once camp was built, that the town of Chapel Root was only several hours north. But their route to Copper Lyall would divert many hours northwest. Thunder John joked that the two of them could make off with the gems Joseph coveted, but if his wife didn't authorize the order, there would be hell to pay. Joseph commented, "I take it she's a strong conjure woman. I look for a woman as strong as her with conjure. That is what I hope the gems will bring me." And Thunder John replied, "Indeed." But he added a strange sentiment just as he considered their rest over, "It all begs me to ask, where was all this conjure and incant while we were in chains?" He finished the last of his dried beef and took a drink from his canteen. Joseph informed that the incant and conjure existed, low in tide as the magic most often was. He also remarked that was the reason for his study. Packed up, with horses well rested, the scholar and the outlaw continued their travels.

The rest was well needed for the horses, as the mounts had to be compelled to take them the remainder of the way. Thunder John led he and Joseph Pepper into Copper Lyall an hour after midnight. Adamus the Hawk and Aku the Boom Stick greeted them at the edge of town, noting they arrived a few hours earlier.

There was little activity in the street at this hour, but Joseph could feel the aura of life emanating from the town, which was more a village with houses huddled together. There were few commercial, governing or law buildings mixed in. Thunder John noticed Joseph observing the town. The scholar was in awe. He said to Joseph, "We brought this town back from the dead. From ghost to solid, living body. Can you feel it, scholar?"

Joseph's eyes kept their wide, fixated gaze as he answered, "I definitely can, Thunder John." Led by the two Brother Dogs, Joseph and Thunder John came to the church at the center of town. "A service?" asked Joseph.

"No," said Thunder John as he and Joseph dismounted. "Not at this hour. But my wife rests here."

The two men hitched their horses to a post and then walked inside. Adamus and Aku parted from their captain, making their way up the road to their respective homes. Joseph and Thunder John proceeded through a short, wide hallway that led directly into the church's main area. Candle light danced to inaudible music, and the shadows around the room mimicked the rhythm. Seated in the pulpit was the Queen of Copper Lyall and wife to Thunder John. With wild and curly, graying hair, she was dressed in a red gown with silver linings, Ori Washta, Queen Governess of

Copper Lyall was aged with wisdom and beauty and with not a single crack or wrinkle in her dark brown skin. Time and two children added weight to her frame, but Thunder John often remarked that he loved how time fleshed her out. More curves, he'd tease. Ori stood as Thunder John and Joseph entered. Her eyes bent on her husband.

"Thunder John," Ori said to him, a nod in her head. "I did not call for you."

Thunder John stopped halfway down the aisle and leaned on a pew, grin painted on his face. He retorted to his wife, "And yet, good woman, here I am standing before you with handsomeness in full bloom." It was just a game husband and wife played with one another. She waved his retort away, continuing to play. Thunder John asked, "Where my boys at?"

"I sent them to the woods to be among the nation," Ori answered her husband. She turned her attention to Joseph and addressed the scholar, "Joseph Pepper, I presume."

"Yes, my lady," said Joseph, feeling the need to bow his head at the neck.

Ori approached him. "And you seek my people's treasures, correct?"

"I apologize, my lady," stated Joseph in an upbeat voice. "I do not *seek* your people's treasures. No, I intend to *rescue* them from the hands of villains."

Ori cocked her head to the side and remarked, "I'm afraid I can't offer you much help." She patted his shoulder and took a seat at a pew. Thunder John joined his wife's side.

Joseph looked perplexed. "Will I not have your husband and the Brother Dogs at my side?" he asked. He leaned his weight on his cane. "I understand. But, I will still move forward with my plans. I will even present you with the gems once recovered."

"Oh, no need to be dramatic, Mister Pepper," Ori said. "My husband and his Dogs will assist you. But, little protection can be offered from me." She sighed. "I do as much as I can to cast my conjure on this town, keep its residents safe. Keep government intrusion from our borders."

"I understand, my lady," said Joseph.

Thunder John nudged his wife. "What about that veil of yours?"

Ori turned to her husband and told him, "With the veil, I most certainly can." Then she turned back to Joseph and pointed up to him, "But Mister Pepper will need the veil for the gems he wishes to rescue."

Joseph stepped in front of Ori and Thunder John. "So, I have the services of your husband and his soldiers?"

Ori's face stiffened, smile still upon it, but looking pale. Joseph observed. He watched as she turned to her husband and nudged him again. She asked in a bitter-sweet tone, "One last ride, husband Thunder John?" Joseph wanted to inquire about her choice of words, but he stayed his question. Then Ori dismissed Joseph without giving him a look, eyes on her husband. "Let us be, Mister Pepper." Joseph didn't hesitate with the command. He left the husband and wife, exiting the church.

Outside, Joseph spotted a thin, elderly, bald man with a thick, gray mustache, wearing a raggedy top hat and leaning against the door. It didn't take long for him to deduce the old man's identity. Uncontained excitement exploded through Joseph and splashed on his face. He almost hugged the wizened legend, but instead, he backed away and let his charged voice embrace the bounty hunter. His arms remained wide, however. *"Bunk! Abraham!"* he blurted.

The old man managed a smile, shaking as he moved. "You sure got sharp study on you," said Bunk back to Joseph. "Them two eyes can see through all this age on me, and ain't no photograph captured how pretty I used to be."

"Oh, I know who you are, good man. I, as have many young black boys, grew up listening to tales of your exploits and rescues. As we got older, we heard more explicit stories about your raids and rescues on plantations and your collected bounties after emancipation and the war."

Bunk worked hard to think about the days of which Joseph spoke. A blessing in him pulled out some faint memories. What he recalled was not the violence, but the smiles on the black faces after having been rescued and reaching freedom. Bunk shook his head. "Yes. Yes." He took a breath, pulling up a short stool located at the side of the church. He sat down, resting his back against the church. "You come here to ask me some questions about all that?" he queried. "It's gon' take some time for me to recall much." He twirled his hand at the side of his head. "Well, shit, that's what I get for wantin' this blessin', and such. Just wanted to see my friend's boys make a name for themselves. That time's come. So I guess, sooner or later, my time will come too." He sounded tired, but ready.

Joseph kept his smile on Bunk. "No, sir," he said in an apologetic tone. "My name is Joseph Pepper, good hero, and I came here to recruit Thunder John and his Brother Dogs for a mission."

"Oh," said Bunk with curiosity widening the expression on his face. "A travelin' adventurer we got here."

"Indeed, sir."

"Where you from, young man?"

"New York City," Joseph exclaimed.

Bunk smiled. "I see you ain't no eastern tenderfoot, though." Then he asked, "Thunder John inside with Queen Washta?"

"Yes, sir."

Bunk nodded his head, thinking to himself. He remarked, "Them Brother Dogs take they orders from their captain, Thunder John. But it's Ori Washta's three chains of gold that keep them Dogs on a leash."

"Yes, sir," Joseph repeated.

"What that adventurin' spirit got you lookin' for, young man?"

"I seek a bracket of stones called the Djed Pillar Jewels," said Joseph, proud and confident. "They are often called the Sunrise Gems."

"Heard a story or two 'bout them," Bunk admitted. "Some folk say them things were molded from the Devil himself."

"Absurd!" Joseph spat, face askew in disgust.

"I know that, young man," Bunk chuckled. "I know that. But that's what folk be sayin'. Especially some of them colored folk, all scared or superstitious if it don't talk about Jesus or Abraham or Moses."

Joseph scoffed, "People that wish to believe such silliness without research deserve to be ill-informed." He relaxed, but only a little. "Considering your statement on superstitions, my good hero, I know the supposed deviltry surrounding the stones is an invention more to steer the Negro away from his and her culture. The mythology surrounding the stones is about love. The love of an African warrior and an African princess," Joseph emphasized.

"Oh," said Bunk, intrigued. "I'ma have to hear that one."

Joseph recounted the tale for the old man while inside the church, in a backroom that was beautified with shrines adorned with cultural trinkets and burning incense and candles, laid Thunder John and his wife Ori Washta in a bed fit for two. Thunder John's guns were hanging holstered over the back of a chair. Both he and his wife watched the hourglass as the last of the ashes trickled down from the top chamber to the bottom chamber. Ori's face brightened as she recollected, "I found you, Jonathan, in Crab's Creek. I saw you in my insight before I stepped through those saloon doors. And all I could wonder was how a soft-faced gentleman like you was making it in such a seedy, rough area. Turns out, you was twice as rough, Thunder John." She squeezed his arm and cuddled up to him. They continued watching the falling ashes. "I'll come with you," Ori whispered in Thunder John's ear. "Our boys will make do without us. It's time we go up. This town will be just alright. My blessing will remain behind." She unbuttoned Thunder John's shirt and rubbed his dark-brown chest. "Now you go set that scholar up in one of the hotels. There should be room. Then you come back here and make love to me, Thunder John."

Ori's words prompted Thunder John to sit up. He stood, buttoning his shirt back up. "Damn, woman," he cursed. "I ain't lay with you for a while. Don't be mad when this is over quick."

"Thunder John," purred Ori as she sat up. Raising an eyebrow she noted, "I got conjure enough to keep you strong until I want your rush shooting inside me."

Thunder John, grin in place, swiped his hat from his head and slapped it atop his wife's. He put his face close to hers and said through clenched teeth, "I'll be back to serve that honey-tail of yours proper." Then he pulled away and left the room. Salacious smile intact, Ori lay back against the bed, in wait for her husband's return.

Outside the church, Thunder John interrupted Joseph's retelling of the legend surrounding the Sunrise Gems. The outlaw asked Bunk what he was doing out so late, and the old man replied, "I'm headin' back to Miss Abigail's. Got tired, took a rest here at the stool. Started up a talk with this young man right here."

"You gettin' honey-tail from that young thing, Captain?" asked Thunder John.

Bunk made a face and replied, "Boy, please, that young thing is sixty-three years old. Let us grown-ass folk do what we grown-ass folk do."

"Says a man that needed to rest between his house and hers," Thunder John noted. "You need me to help you over there, Captain?"

Bunk got up, body shaking. "No. I don't need no assistance," he said waving his arms. "Shit. I just woke up is all. Then her friend knocks on my door and says they got to talkin' and she want me over there." The old man grinned. "I think her friend want to join in." He started chuckling and then scurried off down the road, leaving Thunder John and Joseph Pepper shaking their heads.

Thunder John commented, "So much legendary fights and battles behind that man, and he ain't no different than any of us with a rod between our legs." Joseph laughed at the observation. "Come on. This way," said Thunder John pointing up the road and taking lead to a small hotel.

No different than from the previous town, Thunder John set Joseph up in a quaint room. When the traveling scholar was settled, Thunder John returned to his wife to attend to the duty he'd been tasked with and looked forward to fulfilling. Joseph, on the other hand, found the building equipped with indoor plumbing, which he took advantage of, preparing a bath for himself after setting his things down. Clean and perfumed, Joseph changed into sleep clothes pulled from his satchel. Over the coming days, Joseph purchased new outfits and plotted with Thunder John and the Brother Dogs on their approach to take out The Line's train and make off with the gems inside. The outlaws had become experts at hitting trains, and decided not to deviate from previous attack strategies, but they did find a way to incorporate Joseph Pepper.

In the days following, Joseph Pepper met Thunder John's two sons, Aku the Boom Stick's wife, Izenth-Elei, and their two daughters and one son. They were a beautiful family rich with spirit. It was something that Joseph one day hoped to have, a good wife and wonderful children.

The night before the train's scheduled arrival, Joseph witnessed the Brother Dogs partake in a war dance. The ceremony occurred outside of town in a grassy clearing. The Dogs danced around a campfire. They shouted rhymes in their native tongue and in English. Eyes Are Bright kept rhythm with a drum while his fellow Brother Dogs danced and shouted crass, rhythmic speech describing the extent of war and the destruction of their enemies. Their rhymes were filled with clever, poetic nuance, and a smattering of curse words and harsh language. But for Joseph, it was beautiful to witness. In town, and in the back altar room of the church, Thunder John and Ori Washta spent the night together making love. In the morning, enlivened and ready for battle, Joseph Pepper, with Ori Washta and Thunder John, met the Brother Dogs at the edge of town. Joseph wore a six-round gun on his hip, nestled in its holster. On his back, strapped like a sword, was his bejeweled cane, slipped through the loops of a sheath made for a blowgun. Thunder John had his LeMat revolvers, and the Brother Dogs had their animal spirit and unique conjures.

Ori, while wearing her enchanted and ancient veil, dismounted with her husband and walked up to the Brother Dogs who were on foot. They dropped to their knees and bowed their heads as Ori spoke parting words. "The ashes have fallen," she informed. "All down. All is prepared for us to make our way down the same path. Ride strong my warrior-brothers." She turned to Thunder John and said, "My husband." Then Ori pivoted, facing Joseph. She removed the veil covering her face, folded it neatly, and presented it to the mounted scholar. Joseph accepted the garment, tucking it into his satchel. "When you find the gems, Joseph, wrap them in the veil." Behind her, Thunder John jumped back to his horse. "I will perform a ritual over you with the veil and stones when you return."

"Yes, Queen Washta," Joseph said with a respectful bow of his head. "After tonight, you will be a step closer in reclaiming all treasures that have been scattered and lost to your people."

"With more research on both your end and mine, I might be seeking your services in the future. We'd make a remarkable team," she opined. Thunder John coughed as a gesture. Ori looked up at her husband and beamed a smile. "Not as remarkable as myself and my husband—hard-headed as he is."

Thunder John chuckled. "Woman, you know I'm playing with you."

Ori walked to her husband's horse and lifted up on her toes. Thunder John bent down and kissed his wife. The Brother Dogs rose and charged into the woods, howling war cries. Again, Joseph watched them as they darted into the dense flora, and again he lost their warrior frames to the sudden appearance of large, canine silhouettes.

Ori pulled away from her husband, and Thunder John sat up on his mount. "Goodbye, my husband," she said to him. Thunder John only smiled in return. Then he and Joseph sped away. Ori walked to her horse and clutched its reins, watching her husband ride off. She mounted and rode away when his shadow disappeared over the horizon.

Their journey to Chapel Root ended two hours before the scheduled train's arrival, and just as the sun was giving off its final moments of light. Joseph and Thunder John kept their distance from the isolated and decaying town. "It's a wonder people live there," said Joseph peering through a spyglass, focusing the lens. "I can only imagine the politics that led to this town's abandonment and why some chose to stay. But I guess the latter is somewhat understandable." Continuing his philosophical banter, half-listened to by Thunder John, Joseph asked, "Where do you go when there's nowhere to go to?" He saw people in rags walking through the street. Tents filled with families were up and down the road, most of the abandoned buildings being too dangerous to squat in.

Thunder John, with his spyglass, witnessed a group of military soldiers on horse and foot approaching from the east. "Joe," he alerted the scholar. "Got some boys dressed up all military-like, coming in from the east."

Joseph, eye still peering through the spyglass, swirled east. Sunlight was fading, but his extended view could make out the cluster of armed men, appearing military. "Regular as clockwork," remarked the scholar to no one in particular. He moved the spyglass from his eye, removed his watch and checked the time. "The few citizens of Chapel Root will probably be moved off the streets when the exchange is made."

Thunder John looked at the sky. "Night and shadow are here," he stated. "Let's move closer to town."

Joseph agreed. He allowed Thunder John to take lead. He inquired about the Brother Dogs and Thunder John answered that three Brother Dogs were getting into position miles up the tracks, and Eyes Are Bright was tracking close behind, ready to assist with boarding the train. The closer they drew to Chapel Root's borders, the more the horizon swallowed the last of the sun's light. They trotted up behind a dilapidated building and waited. The legion of troops paraded through the streets, moving citizens aside and only making a slight effort to move their hefty, manmade wave around tents. Thunder John led Joseph through shadows and behind another building, keeping the army in sight. Electric lights popped on around the area, taking Joseph and Thunder John by surprise. Joseph was more impressed by the lights' sudden appearance, considering the deficient wealth of the old town. Burning lanterns hitched atop wooden posts were lit by townspeople. Joseph was no longer impressed by the presence of the light, manmade or natural. The light was a disadvantage to the sneaking scholar and bounty hunter as it narrowed paths of shadow. In the distance hollered the horn of the incoming train. Thunder John looked over his shoulder and saw the massive, black, heavy amalgam of machinery speeding down the tracks. Then came the horn again, followed by the sound of the train's brakes scraping against the rail.

Joseph kept an eye on the soldiers. Orders were shouted, but Joseph couldn't make out the words. He got Thunder John's attention and signaled to move closer toward the train's approach. Thunder John scoped a route covered by night and led them along it. Farther up, they saw the train's slowing approach. From around the corner, Joseph observed his former friend, Ethan Cassidy, exit one of the buildings that stood in fair condition. At Ethan's side was Anderson Gunner, a tall brown-skinned black man with short graying hair and goatee. He wore a brown suit with a long coat. Joseph shook his head at Anderson as he appeared.

"My brother, what do you do against us?" Joseph asked in a whisper. "You work with a group of men and women bent on suppressing our history and lore, yet you stand in disbelief of your own image present at the beginning of time." He looked at Thunder John and stated, "Blind has never been a more appropriate word."

"Right," Thunder John remarked in a disinterested tone. There were other issues at hand for the outlaw. "Come on. We got to make our way onto that train before it starts crawling with soldiers." He dismounted and waved Joseph down off his horse. "The horses will be fine. Let's go."

Joseph jumped down. He patted the horse and gave thanks to the mount. He then followed Thunder John through the shadows, up to the train that was now coming to a stop at the town. The two stayed low, siding up to the train. Thunder John removed a holstered revolver and waved for Joseph to pass. "Go," he hissed, cocking his gun. "All the way to the end of the train," he stated. "Go," he repeated. Joseph moved forward, still crouched. Thunder John walked backwards, keeping his eyes and gun on the front of the train. He saw handshakes between Ethan Cassidy and what he believed was the army's leader. Thunder John backed up a few more paces when he felt Joseph's presence near. The outlaw looked over his shoulder and observed the scholar peering through his spyglass.

"I see it, Thunder John!" he exclaimed in a whisper. "It's an oak case. Ethan is opening it and…my goodness! Behold our prize." Then Joseph collapsed the spyglass and shoved it into his satchel. "The troops are heading our way."

"Go, go, go!"

Joseph turned and hurried away, Thunder John behind him. Both men were crouched low, covered in shadow. The trot of cavalry mounts increased in volume as their distance between Thunder John and Joseph Pepper decreased. Several mounted soldiers held lanterns, lighting their path.

"In there!" alerted Thunder John as he caught up to Joseph and pointed over the scholar's shoulder. Joseph hopped onto the hitch between two cars, Thunder John mimicking the move soon after. Both men lay flat with their backs against the train's car. On either side of the train, cavalrymen rushed by in a clamorous wave. The horses came to a stop at the train's end, and Joseph and Thunder John resumed breathing, opening their eyes. "Stay pinned up," Thunder John directed. The two men did not move.

A voice shouted at the back of the train, *"Make a sweep!"* was the voice's command. *"Search under, above, and in between. Hurry, we move out soon."*

Only Joseph's eyes moved, locking with Thunder John's. The outlaw hissed a curse between gritted teeth. He removed his other holstered LeMat revolver and cocked the weapon's hammer. "Things may get loud, Scholar Joe," he notified Joseph.

Joseph eased his back off the side of the train, reached behind him, and unsheathed his sapphire-encrusted cane. He quipped, "You provide the thunder, good hero, and I'll supply the lightning." He rested the end of his cane against the ground as Thunder John aimed his guns. Then a wolf howled, and Joseph and Thunder John put their eyes back on one another.

"You hear that?" inquired a soldier in a quivering voice.

"If them the dogs we're looking for," replied a second soldier, cocking his gun. *"Then we'll get 'em."*

To the right of Joseph and Thunder John, a cloudy shadow ruffled the turf. Its pace was quick, fast approaching Joseph and Thunder John. Something jumped out of the blackness and landed in front of the scholar and the outlaw. Eyes Are Bright lifted a finger to his lips. Thunder John nodded, but Joseph was unsure. He remained still, and took his cue from the hardened outlaw.

"You see that?" the same, voice-quivered soldier asked.

"Move on up. Both sides. We'll take care of it."

Eyes Are Bright moved between Joseph and Thunder John. He pressed his palms to their chests and whispered to Joseph, "Just. Stay. Quiet." Joseph said nothing, putting faith in the Brother Dog.

A black glow bubbled out of Eyes Are Bright's irises as the Brother Dog concentrated and spoke an inaudible incant. His eyes blackened further, and light and reality bent around the three of them. Wavelengths of light folded over Joseph, Thunder John, and the Brother Dog, and as the group of four horsemen—two on either side of the train—trotted up to the hitch, all three men could not be seen. Their reflection and discernable shape were no longer visible, and the cavalrymen only held rifles at one another. Joseph looked to his right and left. He didn't know what to make of Eyes Are Bright's low muttered incant, but he hoped it worked.

"Nothing!" said one of the mounted men.

"If it was an animal, it weren't one we're lookin' for," remarked another.

The mounted soldiers continued to the front of the train. Behind them strolled soldiers, sweeping the grounds, looking under the train cars with lanterns. Four soldiers climbed atop the train at its rear. They walked along the top of the cars with their pistols, lanterns, and eyes going to and fro and down into the gaps between cars. The rooftop soldiers jumped across the gap where below hid Joseph and the two outlaws. They remained unseen with Eyes Are Bright's black-eyed incant ablaze and covering them.

"Eyes Are Bright," whispered Thunder John to his solider. "How long can you hold this blessing?"

The Brother Dog took a heavy breath and answered, "I'll be fine, Big Chief."

Thunder John holstered his guns and grabbed the steel ladder near him. He said to Joseph, "Hold tight, Scholar Joe. This train's gonna have a kick when it starts up."

Joseph sheathed his long, bejeweled wand and peeked around the side of the car, peering up to the front of the train. Joseph jumped down to the ground, crouching low, Thunder John hissing for him to get back up. He ignored the outlaw, frustrating Thunder John further and prompting him to warn the scholar that he was no longer under Eyes Are Bright's protective blessing. Joseph paid no mind, drawing out his spyglass, extending it and placing it near his eye. He adjusted the focus until he could see Ethan Cassidy and Anderson Gunner.

"We're clear!" shouted a mounted soldier as the party canvassing the train approached the front.

Joseph watched Ethan and Anderson board the train. He collapsed his eyepiece with force and an expression of pride on his face. Stuffing the spyglass into his satchel, he hopped back aboard the train and clutched a steel handle welded to the back of the car. Eyes Are Bright placed the palm of his hand on Joseph's chest, and the scholar returned inside the fold of the Brother Dog's blessing.

The train started up with a kick, jerking Joseph and Thunder John. But they held firm, keeping balance and hanging on. Eyes Are Bright, hands on Joseph and Thunder John was unfazed by the train's sudden movement. The ride was steady with one long bend until again straightening out. Mounted soldiers kept pace with the train, and Joseph and Thunder John kept their eyes on them while Eyes Are Bright concentrated to keep them unseen.

Another jerk of the train jolted Joseph and Thunder John, testing the strength of their grips. Eyes Are Bright pressed them harder against the back of the train car, keeping balance. Metal scraped against metal, squealing a high-pitched scratch against their ears. All they could do was grit their teeth and hold on until the train came to a jarring stop. Joseph turned to Thunder John, ready to inquire about the moment, but he stayed his speech when cavalry soldiers trotted up on either side of them.

"Something's burning on the track!" the squad's leader shouted. *"It looks human! All in flames,"* he continued. *"Investigate. Keep your eyes open."*

Joseph witnessed, out of the corner of his eye, Thunder John remove his guns. The outlaw turned to Joseph and nodded his head, prompting the scholar to unsheathe his cane. To Joseph's left, there waited three horsemen. Each one peered forward, trying to get a look through the darkness concerning the commotion at the front of the train. To Joseph's right, much the same was happening with another group of mounted soldiers.

Then, a pink-glowing, needle-thin conjure that was no longer than the average hammering nail, struck each of the horsemen on either side of the train. One-by-one, after a quick slap on the neck where the conjures pricked them, the men's eyes rolled up into their heads, and they dropped unconscious from their horses. Eyes Are Bright lifted his protective blessing, and light and reflection untwisted and straightened from around he, his captain, and the scholar. As if a blanket lifted, the three men came into existence. Eyes Are Bright fell against the car in front of them, catching his breath and chanting an incant to help restore his strength. Joseph let go of the steel handle and bent down to assist the exhausted Brother Dog.

Thunder John peered around the side of the train, guns aimed. He looked both ways with eyes and weapons. "They ain't noticed their boys down yet," Thunder John whispered over his shoulder. Then there came scuffling from above. Joseph and Thunder John turned their heads up, reacting to the noise. Shuffling over the roof's side, and looking down at them with a wink of his eye, was Adamus the Hawk.

"Brace yourselves, gents," he stated. "Aku is up next—"

The train shook, rattling as if cannon fire had struck its side. The massive, mechanical structure tilted up on the track, but it never turned over, coming down onto its right wheels with a jarring crash. The glass windows shattered. Adamus the Hawk was tossed from the roof, and Joseph Pepper fell to the ground on his back, Eyes Are Bright sprawled out next to him. On the other side of the train, Thunder John was lifting himself off the ground, weapons aimed up. He saw the burning body on the tracks stand up and jump to the roof of the train's locomotive, gunfire following it.

Joseph used his cane to help himself stand. Eyes Are Bright was already on his feet, watching a band of mounted soldiers charging at them. Thunder John jumped from his side of the train to Joseph and Eyes Are Bright, screaming, "Eyes Are Bright, Plan-C!"

The Brother Dog hollered an animalistic battle cry! His eyes expelled a brilliance of dazzling light, and the magnificent shine slammed the eyes of the incoming soldiers, blinding them. Though aimed away from him, the flash was so bright it even caused Joseph to look away. Thunder John followed up the action by aiming his unloaded LeMat revolvers and pulling the triggers on the sightless soldiers. Thunder John's blessing amplified the simple sound of the hammers' clicks hitting against empty chambers. The resonance was deafening and concussive, passing through the muzzle and propelling outward in a wide force of sound. Thunder John's conjured impetus battered the mounted men, pushing them from their horses, ribs and arms broken, rifles shattered.

Joseph took the moment to charge the train, finding a car with a door and entering the area. It was empty of passengers. He continued on, passing through the door at the end and crossing into the next car. It too was empty, but he heard more than the cacophony of Thunder John and the Brother Dogs' assault entertaining the night sky. Something was coming up on him. He turned, lifting his cane, thrusting it out like a sword.

"It's me!" exclaimed Adamus, arms lifted, Joseph's divine cane held inches away from his chest.

Joseph lowered his weapon, turned and proceeded forward. Sounds of thunder and gunfire rocked either side of the train. Flashes of bright light rippled through the night like a bright flicker of lightning. Exploding Sun's blazing physique rushed by, growling and assaulting soldiers mounted and on foot. Massive, beastly shadows tossed and scratched soldiers. Chilling howls and snarls sliced the night air. Exploding Sun could be heard yelling, *"Bury me in Africa!"* Adamus peeked at the battlefield, longing in his eyes.

Adamus heard a soldier yell, *"The devil's spirits are among us, but stand your ground men!"* Another cried, *"I thought these silver bullets would make things easie—argh!"* There was a growl and a thunderous sound before a crack of bones and a scratching and tearing of flesh. Adamus commented under his breath, "You gotta hit us first."

Joseph and Adamus moved into the next car. It too was empty. The seats had been removed, and stored there in their place were five coffins varying in size, each fitted for the Brother Dogs and their captain Thunder John. Behind Joseph there came a mighty growl expressing frustration followed by a startling clamor of wood breaking. Joseph spun around. Adamus' flesh was already molding back to its human physique, clothes torn and loose. "None of us will occupy their coffins tonight. We outlaws is rough, and we'll steal away with the take from this robbery."

Joseph nodded his head, and then he heard a familiar, southern-accented voice. "Impressive," said Ethan Cassidy as he and Anderson Gunner appeared from the shadow near the end of the car. They both held up pistols. The hammers were thumbed back at the ready to strike with silver bullets. "I don't think I'll see something more beautiful for the rest of my life." He shook his head, smile wide. "Wild and untamed," he continued his comments. "You are a marvelous beast. But this whole train is a coffin. And you'll be the first legend to occupy it."

Joseph put the tip of his cane on the ground and concentrated. An electrical wave snaked through the floor and wrapped itself around Ethan Cassidy and Anderson Gunner. Each man's body gave way to seizures. Their guns went off, bullets striking Adamus in the shoulder and chest. The Brother Dog buckled, screaming. A pain squeezed him as a stinging charge bit into him. He blew through tucked fingers, tossing a lighted, conjured projectile at Ethan, piercing his neck. He turned to Anderson and shot at him, but the conjure dwindled into pink dust right as it was fired outward. Adamus smacked against the floor, writhing in pain. He remained conscious, but he was sweating profusely and breathing hard.

Ethan stayed on his feet. His vision blurred, and his consciousness fought against the sleep that negotiated for supremacy inside him. He cocked his gun again and aimed at Adamus. But Joseph rocked him again with another wave of electricity. Ethan and Anderson buckled with the strike, but both men remained on their feet, able to make a run from the car. Their destination was the front of the train to give orders to the conductor.

Joseph rushed to Adamus' side, bending down. "Brother Dog Adamus, are you all right?" he asked.

"My chieftess always told me that silver stings," he said through a cough. "I'll be fine. Have to concentrate and bring out my animal spirit so I can keep playing." He grinned. "I'll take the fight outside."

"You will be fine?" Joseph asked again.

"I will, Scholar Joe. Now go track those villains down. Get our prize."

Joseph stood and dashed away. Behind him, Adamus' form was lost to shadow. A burly and bristly silhouette emerged with a long snout and pointed ears. It ignored the sting of silver coursing through its body, jumping through the window to the outside, snarling, charging through the battlefield and swiping at soldiers with tooth and claw.

Joseph came to a freight car void of a rear door. He hurried up to the roof, continuing his journey to the front of the train. Using his cane's power, he cast a blue shield around him. Stray bullets from the fray below ricocheted off its façade. But it was Joseph's immediate environment that posed a threat. The train started up, knocking Joseph off his feet. The vehicle's move forward caused Joseph to slide to the car's side. He caught onto a small wedge and held tight. The blue shield around him faded. Bullets thwacked against the train, but missed his person. A wave of sound rumbled, and a heavy volley of air lifted Joseph back onto the roof. Joseph, making sure his cane was firm in his grip, and as he again conjured the blue aegis around his person, noticed Aku the Boom Stick running alongside the train. The night's shadow folded over him as the train picked up speed. Aku's frame disappeared, replaced by the shadow of a large, canine-like animal charging on all fours. The beast took a moment, and then it leapt onto the train, two cars down from Joseph. The scholar took his eyes off the bulky beast, watching Thunder John ride up on a stolen horse. Joseph smiled, nodding his head at the legendary outlaw. He looked back at the beast, but it was gone. Aku the Boom Stick, half-naked, hopped onto the car where Joseph stood.

"Come, Brother Dog Aku," Joseph yelled over the roaring wind. "The prize we seek is somewhere at the end of this train!"

The protection glowing around Joseph's person ballooned and covered Aku. The two crossed the train, staying on the roof of its cars, and careful not to be knocked off. Thunder John kept pace next to the train. Soldiers occupying the car ahead of Joseph and Aku aimed their guns out of the window and fired on the outlaw, missing their target as he dodged away into the night.

Joseph stopped his advance. "I have a plan," he shouted to Aku. He moved around the Brother Dog and made a cautious return to the back of the car. He removed the blue shield from Aku and himself, and he made a careful effort to lie on his stomach. He aimed the end of his cane at the hitch connecting the cars. Joseph concentrated for a moment before a snaking stream of electricity crackled from his cane's tip. It latched around the hitch's pin, and Joseph used all his might, mixed with an incant, to pull the pin free and separate the cars. The train sped up from the sudden loss of weight. Aku fell back, hitting the roof hard.

Joseph apologized to the Brother Dog, hollering over the wind. He looked in the distance and spotted Thunder John riding up to the car they stood atop. The outlaw fired a shot, and his thunderous conjure blew open the back of the storage car, rocking Joseph and Aku off their balance. They remained on the car's roof, holding tight to one another and a bar welded to the car. "Well, in the name of…" Joseph blurted, frustrated at Thunder John's strike.

Thunder John holstered his gun, guided his stolen horse closer to the speeding train, and jumped from the mount to the hole he'd blown into the storage freighter. His landing was inelegant, rolling until he smacked against several crates. He stood up and dusted himself off and shook away the sting.

On the car's roof, Joseph sheathed his cane and slipped over the side, dangling from a steel bar lining the train's roof. He swung to and fro, building momentum and confidence before tossing his body forward and into the freight car. He tumbled as he hit the ground, and his body rolled into the same set of heavy crates that stopped Thunder John. Thunder John helped Joseph to his feet, remarking with a groan, "These sons-of-bitch crates knocked some wind out of me too. You okay there, Scholar Joe?"

Joseph caught his breath. "Yes," he said brushing himself off. He pointed and looked up, "Your brother remains topside."

Thunder John maneuvered through the large, wooden boxes, making his way to the car's side door. He swiped one of his guns from its holster, cocked the hammer, and blasted the door with a thunderous cry of force. The latch on the other side blew away in the wind, carried by Thunder John's power. He slid the door open, moving back, catching piercing wind.

Joseph saw Aku's legs dangling over the side of the car. He swung inside, landing against crates, but anticipating the impact better than Joseph and Thunder John before him. Aku turned and faced the open side door. He grabbed it and slid it shut. Backing up, he threw a hard fist. With the action came a quick booming sound. A wave of force broke the door off its rails enough to remain closed without its latch.

Joseph climbed atop the crates, and Thunder John and Aku followed his lead. Thunder John pressed ahead of Joseph as they neared the end of the freighter. He aimed his gun at the far wall and fired, exploding the metal outward. The next car contained eight soldiers, along with Ethan

Cassidy and Anderson Gunner, armed and ready to strike. A clap of heavy thunder splintered the door, but there came an immediate retaliation of gunfire. Joseph, Thunder John, and Aku scattered to the side of the freight car. They remained, ducked away from the salvo of bullets and curses. All went calm, but the slightest peek resulted in gunshots.

Aku put out his hand, opened with fingers wide to enlarge the target. He waited. Nothing occurred. Aku pulled his hand back around the side of the door. He ducked low, and though he believed the silence could be a trap, he took the risk to move forward. He put his stomach to the floor and crawled from the freighter to the spacious passenger car, looking like a slithering snake. He heard the murmur of clicks and clasps as the soldiers reloaded their weapons. Aku caught them off guard. He threw air punches at the soldiers. Waves of sound boomed through the cabin, slamming into soldiers' midsections, cracking their ribs, and lifting them up into the air toward the far end of the train. A strike at Ethan forced the Southern occultist to toss his gun away. He braced himself and used the blessing inside him to catch, like a heavy ball, the projected, concussive sound tossed at him. The weight spun him around, but he kept his balance. He twirled around and tossed the sound back to Aku, hitting the Brother Dog in the chest and knocking him off his feet.

Anderson Gunner slipped the last bullet into his revolver and clicked the cylinder into position. Cocking the weapon, he aimed it at the Brother Dog. Joseph jumped into the car, conjuring a blue, mystical aegis around he and Aku. All six of the black aristocrat's bullets bounced off the face of the electrical shield. Anderson cursed his luck, tossing the gun at Joseph's mystical shield out of frustration. The weapon bounced off no different than the bullets fired from it.

Thunder John leapt inside the car, shooting his clamorous booms at the remaining soldiers, tossing them through the air, breaking body parts on impact, and knocking them unconscious. Anderson ducked out of the way. Ethan kept his ground, hoping for Thunder John to make him a target. It wasn't long before the outlaw granted the former soldier his wish. And as he did with Aku's power, Ethan caught the concussive force of Thunder John's conjure and tossed it back at the outlaw. Thunder John ducked away, and his rebounded blast ripped open the passenger car at the back corner.

The train rocked back and forth, lifting off the rails. Both Thunder John and Aku projected their conjures against the wall opposite them, keeping the car tipped. One final blast from the Cross brothers knocked the car over, its weight dragging the attached cars and the locomotive with it. The earth and the car's interior rumbled with the train's mighty crash. The passengers were knocked around in an uncontrollable, dangerous and aimless toss. Anyone conscious tried to grab hold of anything, but nothing was sturdy enough to soften the rough tumble of the train crash. Joseph reached out for Thunder John and pulled him into his conjured aegis before the train toppled over. He and the Cross brothers remained safe, though they were bounced around the car like a batted ball. Only two soldiers survived, though with their bodies mangled. Once they regained consciousness, they would regret their luck. Anderson Gunner cracked most of his ribs as his stomach was slammed against a passenger seat. His head cracked against the roof and other objects tossed about the car as it tumbled, opening up a bloody gash on his forehead. Ethan, though thrashed about just the same, remained unscathed. But when the train's drag across the field ended, the once Confederate soldier was left in a daze.

Joseph banished his protective aegis and climbed his way to Ethan. He stood over the limp body of his nemesis and struck his friend-turned-adversary with the end of his cane. A shock of electricity traveled through the Southern soldier's system. Ethan hollered! Joseph yelled, "Where are they, Ethan? Where are they?" He pressed the tip of his cane harder into Ethan's stomach, increasing the shock emitted from his weapon. Ethan didn't answer, finding delight in keeping silent through Joseph's torture. Joseph smacked him between the nose and eye with the end of his cane. "Where are the gems, Ethan?" he asked again with as much potency in his anger as there was in the electricity coursing through Ethan.

"Probably…thrown from…the train…" Ethan answered in agony.

Joseph smacked him again, tip to Ethan's face. An electric surge knocked Ethan unconscious, and Joseph let him be, the intense use of his cane tiring him. He sheathed his weapon and jumped up to a broken window, crawling through it, out of the car. He stood on the train and surveyed his surroundings. The train's violent crash tumbled and skidded its way far from the tracks. Joseph could see the wide, rugged gash in the earth. He didn't inspect the violent wreck for long, lowering himself off the train. With his feet on the ground, the adventuring scholar searched through his bag and removed Ori Washta's supernatural veil. He unsheathed his cane and wrapped and tied the veil around the enchanted walking stick's handle.

Joseph lifted the cane high into the air, concentrating as he looked around through the dark. "Come on, now," hissed the scholar. "Work, you makeshift thing."

Joseph continued to focus, and soon there came a blue glow resonating from the veil wrapped atop the enchanted walking stick. Joseph's expression brightened. He closed his eyes and focused harder. His cane vibrated. The shake erupted into a beam of blue light jumping from the veil and pointing to a wooden lockbox several yards away. Joseph opened his eyes and shook his fist, giving himself praise for the quick thinking. He looked over his shoulder. He spied no movement from inside the train, and so he pressed forward in the direction of the blue beam. His pace was quick. He stopped short of the lockbox, the edge of a drop catching his eye. Joseph again looked back at the train, but not for movement. He looked beyond the wreckage. His concern was on the tracks, tracing them to their end over a cliff with no extension across the chasm.

"Ethan, you son of a bitch," Joseph said to himself. "Sometimes I envy your wicked brilliance." He pivoted, putting his attention back on the lock box. He strode over to the object cut into the earth and knelt down. The vibrant beam radiating from the cane and veil faded away as Joseph took up the lockbox. Its lock had been broken in its toss from the train. Joseph pitched his cane and set the box on the ground. He untied the veil, taking a look over his shoulder. Still nothing stirred inside the wreckage. With the veil untied from the cane, Joseph bent down and opened the lockbox.

The gems were magnificent, though they were not gems at all. They were flat, cylindrical stones an inch to an inch and a half in diameter. The stones' glow pushed away the night from around Joseph. Each stone cast a specific glimmer from the color spectrum of the rainbow, and Joseph marveled at his prize. These were the seven Djed Pillar Gems, and one by one, Joseph removed them from the box. The stones felt smooth in his hand, and Joseph relished the touch. Here he held history, and he laid each precious historical piece onto the veil spread out on the ground. He then folded the fabric over the stones.

Behind Joseph came the scraping click of a pump-action shotgun. He guessed Ethan, but Joseph's deduction failed him. When he turned around, there holding a shotgun at him, was Anderson Gunner. "Set that box down, Joseph," Anderson ordered, split lip and scratched tongue slurring his words. He limped closer to Joseph. "Those stones there are the property of—"

"I've never heard proper speech sound so ignorant, my confused brother," Joseph interrupted, frustration in his voice. "These items belong to the descendants of Califia—and those descendants only. The Negroes of the Qalif tribe."

Anderson chuckled. "You still believe in mythology, Pepper," he spat through a low, sinister huff. "This grand past of the Negro you speak of. Established here in the Americas at a time when the blacks of Africa were steeped in ignorance in the dark lands."

"Are. You. Serious, my man?" He stood, caution in his motion. He put his hand on his cane, conjuring the aegis around him. Its presence was absent of glow, and Anderson's head was still getting straight from the train's topple. The power of Joseph's walking stick had slipped his wobbling memory. But his duty to procure the stones for Ethan Cassidy remained.

"Pepper, I'll kill you if I have to." He raised the shotgun higher.

"You foolish Negro, Anderson!" barked Joseph. "Look behind you. Look at those tracks over there. They lead to a large chasm. Your precious Ethan intended to ride you all to your deaths, a ride he would've been able to survive, making off with these gems."

"His rightful property!" yelled Anderson.

"Much like your conscience," Joseph quipped.

"Excuse me?" Anderson sneered.

"My brother, did you not hear my words?" Joseph asked with an incredulous look. "He. Would. Have. Killed you." He shook his head. "Why do the living negotiate with the dead?" he asked himself. "Anderson, my bamboozled brother, I agree with the song that I should lay down my burden by the riverside. But I'll be damned if I lay my sword and shield with it." With a simple focus, Joseph conjured from his cane an undulating stream of electricity that jumped up and slapped Anderson unconscious. Joseph sighed. "Insentient is how you can best serve the world, Mister Anderson Gunner. You Negro toy of your oppressor."

Something hard slammed into Joseph. It cracked against the dimmed, mystical buckler surrounding him. But its force, coupled with determination, knocked Joseph off his feet. The New York scholar lost his grip on his cane, and his body sailed through the air. He hit the ground, scratching the earth like the train during its tumble. He rolled just the same. Digging his fingers into the ground, Joseph stopped his momentum. His coat spread wide as it caught the wind like a sail. Looking at the area from where he'd been evicted, Joseph spied Ethan, collecting the stones off the veil and putting them back into the lockbox. He closed the wooden case, and he decided to take the veil with him. But before the tips of his fingers graced the ancient cloth, a charge of thunder slammed into Ethan's chest, driving his body far across the field, near the drop into the chasm. Ethan exhaled all the wind his lungs held onto, but the grip on the lockbox never faltered.

Thunder John flipped his gun forward and cocked back the hammer.

Joseph jumped to his feet. Reaching out he yelled, *"Thunder John, no!"*

Another hard, bellow of thunder sounded. Ethan accepted the monstrous force as it collided with his chest and knocked him down into the dark chasm. Joseph's prize was now lost to him. But Thunder John had another opinion as he met Joseph halfway in a run toward one another. "We'll track him, Scholar Joe," he assured. "I can risk those gems, but not that veil."

Joseph said with a nod, "Understood, good hero."

Thunder John holstered his gun. "C'mon," he said to Joseph, slapping the scholar's shoulder. "Let's go round up my Dogs." He turned to make their way to retrieve Joseph's cane and the veil. And that's when thunder screamed loud enough to silence history. Joseph saw it. Thunder John's body buckled. There appeared upon the aged outlaw's shirt a bloody tear, a hole torn into his chest by the dense collective of projected pellets from a shotgun's powerful blast. And then thunder went silent.

Joseph couldn't scream. His anger was too thick to let out noise. Only action could be called upon, but he was nowhere near his mystical instrument. And Anderson Gunner, who was now standing up, clumsy and still shaken from the jarring train crash and Joseph's electrical lash, was too near the cane for Joseph to snatch and use. Standing straight, Anderson cocked the shotgun again.

"You. *Killed!* A legend!" Joseph was able to yell, his anger loose enough to shout.

"Wild Bill Hickok is a legend, Pepper," Anderson shouted back as he took several steps toward Joseph. "Wyatt Earp and his brothers were great men with purpose. Hell, even William Boney was a rebel with a cause. That man, Thunder John, and his Wild Zulu Indians are a scar on the face of black America. We have no legends out here. Only savages that make us all look bad in America's eyes."

"Bass Reeves!" Joseph named.

"Never heard of him," snickered Anderson. "That another one of your Negro myths, Pep—" The night growled, cutting into Anderson Gunner's words. A burly, furred shadow, a beast on its hind legs, snatched Anderson into the fade of night. Joseph couldn't see the gruesome killing, but he could hear Anderson's screams, the tearing of his flesh, and the curdling crackle of his bones.

Joseph returned his attention to Thunder John despite a small instinct to force his eyes away from the noble outlaw's lifeless body. He ignored it, however. His eyes fell to where Thunder John's body lay, but nothing was there. Joseph dropped to his knees, sifting his fingers through grass and earth to make sure the space was empty. Aku the Boom Stick walked up next to him. Joseph noticed the Brother Dog's clothes were more torn than before. Aku wiped away thick globs of blood from around his mouth and neck.

"What magic is this?" asked Joseph, as the Brother Dog's final steps toward him ended. "Your brother was killed…"

"Long ago, Scholar Joe," said Aku in a voice that was barely a whisper. "He's done it so many times he's gotten good at it." He knelt down next to Joseph. "I reckon," said the Brother Dog, a soft smile making an appearance, "this is supposed to be his last time."

Joseph's face remained painted with confusion.

"Bury me in Africa!" Exploding Sun's voice shouted as he and the other Brother Dogs galloped up on horseback to Aku and Joseph.

Aku stood. "The storm's over, my brothers. Thunder has rolled on this night."

The other Dogs were silent. Exploding Sun dropped from his horse and embraced Aku. "He and Ori told us his ashes had run their course, but I speak for all us Dogs when I say, we were not prepared for this." Stepping away from Aku, Exploding Sun announced, "This fight here was a farce. We tore the information from an enemy. They had us on a wild chase as a brigade of these men, disguised as Klansmen, carries burning crosses to Copper Lyall." He addressed Joseph, "Take my horse. We Dogs have four legs to run on." The other Brother Dogs dismounted. Each of them was torn of clothes, half naked, the blood of their enemies smeared around faces and hands. Savagery never looked more graceful to Joseph. He jumped onto Exploding Sun's horse.

"Are you okay?" Joseph asked Adamus, referring to his wounds.

"Exploding Sun numbed the silver with his heat," Adamus answered. "I'm fine enough to fight, but I'll feel it in the morning." He remarked, "And though my body loves the moon, I *will* see the sun rise."

Joseph guided his horse to his cane. He bent down and snatched the object up. Using the end of the walking stick, he picked up the veil, folded it properly, and tucked it inside his satchel. Cane lifted high in one hand, the horse's rein in the other, Joseph charged into the night with four, massive, beasts flanking him. He used his cane like a spur, snapping an electric charge against the horse for it to pick up speed.

Time and distance became abbreviated, and quicker than Joseph expected, Copper Lyall was in the distance. The flames of three burning crosses were staged at its western side. Twenty-four armed men filtered into the town, yelling and shooting. The large, wild canines charged ahead of Joseph. They passed through a dense fold of night and changed. Running upright, the Brother Dogs screamed, *"Meet 'em boys on the battlefront! Don't bow! Don't kneel!"*

The hooded soldiers turned, taken by surprise. Exploding Sun's body ignited as he grabbed limbs and snapped them, set bodies and clothes aflame, and acted as a fierce, scorching piece of the sun. Adamus the Hawk blew his incant through his hands, the projectiles a bright purple and volatile, exploding on contact. Eyes Are Bright blinded a few of their attackers, yelling, *"You ain't shit to us!"* He grabbed the blinded men's pistols, aimed them under their jaws, and pulled the trigger. Their hoods contained the explosion of brain matter. Aku the Boom Stick threw punches at the air, tossing invisible force and pressure against body and bone, leaving them broken and forever unusable. The Brother Dogs chanted and rhymed as they fought and killed without mercy.

Joseph Pepper, like a valiant knight, attacked from atop his horse. He swung his cane, electrocuting anyone he hit. Ori Washta, dressed in a green gown, fired her pistols at the attacking soldiers. Her bullets were infused with an incant, doing poisonous damage once penetrating the flesh, making any of her shots a kill shot. Her face was painted up as a skull, and she yelled the cry of Mother Earth as she fought against the town's attackers.

When all time was taken up, all twenty-four men were left dead in the streets of Copper Lyall. A few citizens were left wounded, but no casualties were suffered in the small town. With the battle's dwindled ardency, a disturbing calm passed through Copper Lyall's streets. At the command of Ori Washta, men took to the streets to clean the gruesome scene. While she pointed and gave commands, the Brother Dogs surrounded their General-Queen, feeling the heaviness on her heart. But she assured them she was fine, understanding the possible outcome of their mission. She ordered for her warrior-brothers to get rest, and then she pushed her way to Joseph Pepper who dismounted on her approach.

"My lady…" he began, reaching for her embrace.

Ori put up her hand, keeping Joseph at bay. He backed away, understanding. "I know what happened, Mister Pepper," she said. "I know my husband hunts among the spirits. We've planned for this." She asked, "Do we have our prize?"

"No, Governor Washta," Joseph addressed as he pulled the otherworldly garment from his satchel. "I had them, and I had done as you asked. But the villains won the day. Your husband was able to keep your veil safe, however."

Ori took the veil from Joseph. "Thank you, Mister Pepper. I ask, from the bottom of my heart, that you wait until we have a ceremony at the edge of town before you depart."

"My presence will be in attendance, Governor Washta."

"It has been a night for you, Mister Pepper," Ori noted. "Please, get rest. We here will see that the streets are clean. None of this will exist by the morning."

Joseph attended to the governess' orders. He returned to his room, but he didn't rush away to sleep. Instead, he opened up his journal and started writing. *Excitement and sadness fills me for many reasons at this moment. I am only twenty-six years of age, and I am convinced, even with my worldly travels, that I have just participated in the greatest adventure of my life.* However, it wouldn't be long until life would prove Joseph's grand intellect and deduction incorrect. Joseph found himself at a loss of endurance to remain awake. He lay back on the bed, still in clothes that were now tattered and seared, and went to sleep.

The morning delivered on Ori Washta's promise. The streets were clean of any stain. There was no hint marking the massacre that had taken place under the night's veil. Joseph Pepper washed and replaced his tattered and seared attire with new threads to his fancy. He didn't discard the old clothes. He folded them neatly and kept them as remembrance. Joseph got to know Copper Lyall as he walked about its streets throughout the day. There was sad word that Bunk Abraham had passed away shortly before the soldiers disguised as Klansmen attacked the town. At sundown, Exploding Sun came to Joseph and walked him to the edge of town where their ceremonies were held.

Ori Washta, dressed in red, was part of a circle that included her sons, the Brother Dogs, and Aku the Boom Stick's wife and children. The townsfolk had gathered this time. Joseph heard the drums first, their beat rich in tone. Walking closer to the circle, he realized the beat was being echoed through a simple clap from Aku the Boom Stick. Exploding Sun ignited his hands and spread fire onto a pile of wood. He kept the flames under control as the people cheered and the Brother Dogs sang in unison about the fall of their beloved captain, their Big Chief, the brave and mighty Thunder John.

Joseph smiled, but more surprises were in store for him. Joining the circle, Ori Washta embraced the scholar and presented him with the veil. "Queen Califia would love for you to have this here." Joseph was not quite sure if Ori had meant figuratively the ancient and legendary queen, or the current chieftess of the Qalif people. He didn't inquire. He simply thanked Ori Washta and accepted the veil. "Unlock its power, Joe Pepper," Ori asked of him. "It will lead you to the woman you seek." She kissed his cheek.

Joseph thanked her, backed away and stuffed the veil down between his belt and pants. He started clapping in rhythm to the singing and drumming. But Ori Washta had more to do. She reached down and picked up the large hourglass filled with her husband's ashes. She lifted it high above her head for all in attendance to see. The crowd erupted in excitement. Ori slammed the hourglass into the fire where its glass chambers shattered, and all observed an otherworldly color populate the fire. Cindered ash rose from the flames and twisted together to make the spectral form of the late Jonathan Cross, called Thunder John. He was dancing there in the fire, head back to the sky and howling out of tune but excited with life as if he was still in physical form. The fire changed from a bright orange-red to an ice-blue color. Joseph's expression widened with surprise. Adamus the Hawk and Exploding Sun swarmed Joseph, shaking him and laughing.

Thunder John's apparition tossed an object to one of his sons. The young man caught what was thrown at him and smiled when he realized it was one of his father's LeMat revolvers. "You don't use that now. You take that east. Pay homage to a place called the crossroads in Clarksdale, Mississippi. You set that there. And you two tell my story all over when you travel." His sons responded with a *'Yessir'*. He tossed his second revolver to Joseph Pepper. The scholar almost missed catching the weapon. Joseph was surprised by the weight, but not because of the gun's heft, but that it was real, tossed not from the fire to him, but from the other side into the physical world. "That cane is all right, but you strap yourself with a good luck charm, Scholar Joe," Thunder John insisted. "But you got to keep it loaded."

Joseph nodded in acceptance.

Then Thunder John reached out of the fire and toward his wife. Ori Washta accepted his hand and stepped inside. Her worldly flesh was stripped from her. Not through some hideous sight of sinewy exposure. She simply turned into a specter as sparkling ashes burned off her when she walked into the fire. Ori embraced her husband.

Thunder John, with his arms tight around his wife, opened his eyes and said to his brother, "You speak loud, little brother. And all you Dogs keep Copper Lyall safe. And be careful. Age will get the better of you now. The side I dance on has real estate for you four," he joked with a grin. But his brother and the other Dogs only celebrated harder with the news that one-by-one, their incant would dwindle and life would exhaust like all the normal folk of the world. To pass on would be the greatest blessing for the four warriors.

Thunder John and Ori's spirits rose up, dispersing into dust and spiraling toward the stars. The fire returned to its natural color, though there was a greater vibrancy in its flicker. The celebration continued until morning. Singing, drums, drinking and dance occupied all spaces in Copper Lyall.

Joseph spent one last day in town. At sundown, he packed up, mounted a steed and galloped from Copper Lyall after being wished well by the Brother Dogs. He made his way to where the night's ceremony had been held. He thought that perhaps there would be greater adventures to come.

Then Joseph Pepper IV rode away.

It felt like being embraced by family, revisiting the history of Ori Washta, her husband Thunder John, and the Brother Dogs. With Joseph Pepper IV stirred into the dream, there collided legends. But even as the story faded through a transition of cobalt-blue waves, Fey Forrester remained hibernated in history. When the waves dissolved, there was a midday scene of a nightclub in Harlem. It was the early 1960s, and the club's marquee read *The Harlem Dixie.* The cobalt-blue light filtered into the club's interior, down the hall and into an office where seated behind a desk was the handsome Stanley Fallows.

Seated in front of him was the raven-haired Englishman named Brice Cadogan. Clamped around his arm was a shiny, metal piece of armor blessed long ago by a Moorish conjuror, but worn by a European Templar. On the desk was an opened lockbox made of wood. The contents shone with a rainbow-like glow, staring up at Stanley as he stared down on them with a pensive expression. *"Tribute, Mister Fallows,"* said Brice.

Stanley didn't move. He continued staring at the seven, smooth and cylindrical gemstones resting inside the lockbox.

"I loved your mother, young Stanley," Brice stated. *"I was very much infatuated with her knowledge. I feel so lucky, having had the opportunity to court her for a time. It pained me to walk away when she refused my many marriage proposals."*

"Believe me now, Mister Cadogan," spoke Stanley. *"You made my mother happy."*

It did Brice well to hear it said. *"I visited off and on after our affair dwindled,"* he said. *"There was still business. My heart didn't move on, but I understood that I had to."* Brice sat up. *"But I'm here to join your ranks. To watch you close and make sure you're guarded well. Your mother had a purpose for you."*

Stanley closed the lockbox, suppressing the gemstones' magnificent glow. *"I don't need a babysitter, Mister Cadogan,"* he said, almost as a reminder. Brice prepared to present a polite retort, but Stanley interrupted his words. *"My mother was involved in a war. There was something not right with her spirit. She continues her fight now."* He looked wide-eyed, his gaze and hand sweeping the room. *"Somewhere, out there, beyond this physical realm we lesser beings occupy."* Stanley relaxed. *"I'm trying to understand that. And to do that, Mister Cadogan, I have to befriend people that you would rather have me make war with. I have to be at peace with people my mother might not approve of. Hell, my wife has a problem or two with it. But I remind her of the necessity for peace. I need peace in order to understand my piece and place."*

"Peace is fragile, Mister Fallows," Brice suggested.

"Let's hope," Stanley replied. *"If peace needs breaking, I will break it. But for now, I need it."*

Brice smiled. He reached over the desk, extending a hand. Stanley accepted, and as the two men shook hard, they stood from their chairs. *"I'm a phone call away, Mister Fallows. And know this—"* he retracted his hand, ending the shake. *"—I extend my service to you as a vow to your mother. And many more allies are with me. I do have a great deal of insight when it comes to your mother and her power's reach."*

"I'll remember that, Mister Cadogan," Stanley assured. He showed Brice to the door, opening it for him. Taking them by surprise, on the other side of the door, was Delia-LaRue Peters. She was dressed in a fancy skirt and blouse with a veil pinned to her hair. Stanley's countenance brightened when he saw her. He introduced Brice to her, referring to the young black woman as his cousin. *"Old, family friends, my mother with her grandmother,"* he explained. *"Delia's grandmother even wore that veil,"* he pointed out. *"My mother treated it well when she donned it for her performances."*

"I know, Stanley," said Brice, looking at Delia with disdain in one eye and lust in the other. Also there was familiarity as he looked the young black woman up and down.

There was an awkward pause. Smiles remained. Stanley broke the silence first, saying, *"Of course, Mister Cadogan."*

Brice shook Delia's hand. Then the Englishman dismissed himself, and Stanley invited Delia Peters into his office. She unfastened her veil and set it down on the desk, the garment folding over the corners of the lockbox. Stanley moved the veil aside and took up the wooden case. *"Let me move this away,"* he said turning to the picture behind him. He swung the mounted painting on its hinges, revealing the safe in the wall. He turned its dial to the proper numbers and opened the door, sliding the wooden lockbox inside and closing it up. Setting the painting back in place, he turned to Delia and asked, *"How is everything? Where's Horatio?"*

"He's in the area, visiting family," Delia answered taking the seat earlier occupied by Brice Cadogan. *"All is going well, Stanley. The album has reached the Caribbean, South America. And we always knew Europe would get in on the swing. Even communities in Africa are dancing to it, seeing its story. Fable Avenue is not just a street in Brooklyn, Stanley. Our community has grown worldwide."* Then Delia added with a laugh, *"It's still small, but it's good to know there are others."* The two of

them shared a laugh. Delia asked in a sincere voice, *"Are you ready for our session, Stanley?"*

Stanley looked down at the veil on his desk. *"No,"* he answered. *"Never am. But, let's move to the other room so I can lie down on the couch."* He picked up the veil and came from around the desk, reaching out to Delia and helping her stand. They left the office and proceeded to another room. Stanley turned on the lights, and he locked the door once Delia was inside. He walked to the couch, apologizing for the umpteenth time about his mother's actions against Delia's family. *"It was cruel,"* he said. *"She seduced your father with dreams of being a great artist. And what she had done to your mother…"*

Delia hushed him. *"Let's not have any of that, Stanley. You have to be strong for what's about to happen."*

Stanley agreed. He pushed the thoughts away and laid down flat on the couch. He placed the veil over his face, Delia pulled up a chair beside him. She hummed a haunting harmony, and Stanley fell asleep.

A cobalt-blue flicker returned the scene to The Harlem Dixie's exterior. Time hastened. Day and night faded in and out. The nightclub's marquee disappeared, but its façade remained to recall an era long passed. A sign outside the main entrance read *Harlem Area Museum of Jazz and New York Sound.*

Fey Forrester woke up.

She was panting, and her vision was wracked with fog and distortion. Her hands unlocked from one another, and the *Nigrum Nigrius Nigro* fell to the floor, opening and spilling the veil from in between its mirror and console. Lady Arachne and Fey's grandmother rushed to her. Savannah held up Fey's head, and she placed a hand on her granddaughter's chest to help Fey control her breathing. Zee, the purple glowing yumbo with the yellow wings, hovered above the scene.

Fey came to, coughing as her breathing stabilized. Her vision straightened back into focus. Lady Arachne picked up the *Nigrum Nigrius Nigro* and set it on the coffee table, opening it and laying the veil out flat.

"Fey, darling," said her grandmother. "You okay?"

Fey looked around the room, breath at ease. "There was a lot," she told her grandmother. "I know where the gemstones are. They're in Harlem. They're somewhere inside the Museum of Jazz and New York Sound." She took another deep breath, the dream at the surface of her memory.

Lady Arachne stood, saying, "Let me get you some tea. I'll put a little incant on it, get yourself at some kind of ease." she turned and strolled to the kitchen.

Savannah helped Fey sit up, back against the couch's arm, legs laid out. Zee landed on the back of the couch, staying perched and observing. "Is Gordon okay?" asked Fey to her grandmother.

"He's fine," she said. "He got up early to go to campus. He said he had a test to take."

"How was he?"

"Weak," answered Savannah, moving away from Fey and taking a seat. There was a beat before Savannah smiled and told her granddaughter, "He loves you, Fey. He said so. He stood over you, rubbing your brow. He asked us if you were doing fine." Savannah shifted. "I mean, the boy had to get up and go take his exam, but he was running on fumes. But he found strength in you, little girl—and that tea you brought from Haiti."

Fey stayed silent, giving no comment to her grandmother's words. But she internalized the feeling. "When did you arrive?" she asked before her thoughts drifted to other matters.

Savannah checked her watch. "Been here since nine this morning," she answered her granddaughter's inquiry. "It's half-past eleven, now. Lena was still here. She told me that Madame Jeliya and Maman Anansi had left early in the morning, around five or six."

"I saw him," said Fey cutting into the last of her grandmother's words.

"Who, baby?"

"Stanley Fallows."

Savannah said with a sad face, "You okay about that, baby?"

"It makes him real," was all Fey could say. "He wasn't a monster. Not yet. But there was something beneath his surface."

"He was sincere," Lady Arachne noted passing an incanted cup of tea to Fey. "You got exams today?" she asked as she backed away and took a seat.

Fey blew on the surface of the tea, shaking her head, no. The tea warmed and eased Fey as quick as the first sip. She thanked Lady Arachne and then sat properly on the couch, feet on the floor. "Zee, come to me," Fey prompted.

The yumbo jumped into the air and then dived at Fey, body changing into a thin, purple stream of smoke. It seeped into Fey's back and disappeared through the tattoo under her clothes, back to her realm until called for. Again there was a stinging sensation, but Fey chose to ignore it. Instead, she sipped her comforting tea and relaxed in the deep hug of the couch. She reflected on both visions presented to her in the scry. She thought about the sudden waking from the second dream. She looked at the *Nigrum Nigrius Nigro* and asked in a lighthearted voice, "Did I hurt you,

Spook?" The black mirror lit up with ancient script. Fey chuckled as she read Spook's answer. *I can take it.*

"What?" Savannah questioned. "That black mirror got a spirit inside it?"

"I guess, Nana," said Fey as she continued sipping her tea. "Don't know how it works, really. Maybe Gordon knows." She looked at Spook and asked, "You got a spirit in there, Spook?" More script scrawled across the black mirror, providing an answer. "It appears to have a spirit, Nana."

"You understand all them lines and such? What's that, a language?" Savannah continued to interrogate her granddaughter.

"Yes, Nana," chuckled Fey. "For both questions," she added.

Savannah folded her arms and legs. "Well, all right then. Tell me somethin'. Shit."

Lady Arachne got up and announced, "On my day off, it looks like I got work to do. I'll have Wilson and Martin run up into Harlem and case the jazz museum." She bent down and scooped up the aged hunting knife. "I'll return this to Top Hat." She made her way to the door. Savannah followed her. Fey set her cup down on a coaster and jumped up, pacing after her grandmother and the matriarch. She asked if her grandmother was heading to Mount Vernon, and Savannah told her that she was heading up the road to their Fable Avenue residence.

"I'll be there shortly. I'm going to shower here."

"Won't you need some new clothes?" Savannah asked putting on her coat and purse.

"Oh, I got spare clothes…" She tried to stop her words, but it was too late "…here…" she ended, voice trailing away with the final word. A guilty expression appeared on her face, which she tried to cover with an innocent smile.

Savannah raised her eyebrow. "Why you got spare clothes here, missy?" Her hands were on her hips. Fey remained silent with her expression still the same. "Mmm-hmm," Savannah hummed. "You and Gordon be lovin' each other up in here. Probably got that Spook-thing over there recordin' y'all on a spirit camera to preserve in one of them hooker crystals."

Lady Arachne opened the door and pulled on Savannah's arm. "Oh, hush, Savannah. You was young once. Long time ago," she joked. "Them two got matching spirits stirred up inside them. They probably been beheld one another already, and everything."

"It might've been a long time ago, Lena, but I ain't old enough to be having *great*-grandch'ren, understand."

"Oh, you don't have to worry about that, Nana," said Fey with her words laced with sass. "My spirit has me aligned with the original aspects of a woman." With her hands on her hips she declared, "I ovulate when I want to."

Lady Arachne smiled at Fey. Savannah's mouth hung low. She blinked a few times to shake off the shock. "Did you hear what this child said?" she asked looking at Lady Arachne. "Let me get outta here before I fall and all that can catch me is my late husband's arms. Chil' I tell you!" She turned away from Fey. A little through the door she spun back around and ordered, "The spirit still better wear some protection. *Somethin'! Shit!* I already got to deal with them thangs of yours buzzin' 'round my house. I can't deal with ch'ren conjurin' up a fuss."

Lady Arachne grabbed Savannah's arm and pulled her from the house. "Come on, now, you old crone. Actin' like you wasn't young and in love."

Both women continued to bicker as Fey closed and locked the door. She chuckled and shook her head, turning around and heading up to the second floor. She tossed her clothes off and prepared a hot shower. It felt good, but she wished Gordon was here, healthy and able to kiss the back of her neck. The both of them pressed against one another, him inside her. Making love through a warm shower wasn't quite like being surrounded by the stars and all of creation, but Fey considered that it ran a very good second.

Washed, perfumed, and clothed, Fey popped from existence, ending up on the roof. Her black cosmic suit washed over her, fading away the clothes she wore. With one leap into the air, her body burst into a blaze of cobalt-blue, smokeless fire. Up into the sky she soared. Across the continent her spirit arced, gaining time as she headed west, but losing the light of the morning sun. Her speed increased, outrunning sound. Instinct guided her, and when it pinpointed her destination, she landed on the spot where Copper Lyall once stood. Her fiery essence puffed away, and there she was as a cosmic-clad figure. Fey's mask dissolved into her flesh as she turned around to observe her surroundings. There was nothing there save a few roads leading to modern, small towns. Fey wondered if the inhabitants were aware of the area's history. Then she noticed the names of three towns on the green, rectangular sign up ahead. They were peculiar and familiar to her. Garden Speers, Fischer Commons, and Bellford Place.

Fey looked in either direction, up and down the road, before proceeding to the sign. Standing in front of it, she reached out with her instinct. She stared at the signs as her memory recalled the names of associates striving to take over the indigenous land. There was Donald Speers, the mouth with the silk tongue. There was his partner, the money handler and banker Frederick Gardens. There too was the pit bull of a lawyer, Rudolph Fischer. And there was their muscle, Captain Bell Frank.

No, Fey thought to herself, trying to keep her heart afloat. *They were defeated.* Her instinct tingled, and Fey said to herself, head low in defeat, "But not their heirs." Her instinct leapt from the top of her head. It traveled up the road, visiting each town. They were prosperous, and at the center of their prosperity was the names Speers, Gardens, Franks, and Fischer. They haunted the land, walking upright under businesses still involved in unjust practices. Fey stepped away from the sign. It was too painful for her to view. Stanley Fallows was her mark. Taking him would set things straight.

She backed away, turning back to her original task. She conjured up her instinct and followed a pull where once lay Ori Washta's holy sanctuary. Fey knelt down, sweeping her hand above the earth. She felt history's spirit rub against her palm like a stream of water. Keeping her hand still, there was a pulse like a beating heart. Fey dug into the earth and ladled up a bit of dirt. She didn't forget about the sign, but the piece of sacred land invigorated her spirit. Her mask folded over her face, and then, up into the sky her cobalt-blue spirit soared. Her smokeless, fiery physique preserved the spot of dirt as she arced back across the continent, increasing in speed beyond sound. Flying over Fable Avenue, Fey looked down and could see the ghostly, protective construct Nyami, its long and winged serpentine body nestled across several backyards. The dragon, invisible to the civilian world, arched her head up and hollered a greeting as Fey approached. She waved at the conjure and proceeded on down the street, landing atop her family's brownstone. On contact with the roof, Fey popped out of existence, and solidified inside her room.

Fey flipped on a light and walked to her altar, her mask dissolving into her skin. She filled a ceremonial cup with the dirt she'd taken, and she said an incant to light an incense stick. "This is for you, Ori Washta. You brave and beautiful conjure woman." Then Fey sat on her bed with arms angled back, legs crossed. She watched the scented stick burn, the smoke swiveling up and around. "I'm in my room, Nana!" she yelled after reaching out with her instinct to see if her grandmother was home.

Footsteps stomped against the stairs. Savannah knocked on the open door and peeked her head inside, puffing on a cigarette. She shook her head, remarking, "Every curve of your body is shining through that cosmic clothing. I see why Gordon likes you, girl," she joked, taking a puff of her cigarette. She said after exhaling, "That Goodspeed boy better know what he got."

"He does, Nana," Fey giggled.

"Be careful, now, child," Savannah warned. "This is still Fable Avenue. They no more progressed on understanding our story then when your mother and father where helping them along."

"Progress is being made, Nana," Fey insisted in a polite tone. "And stop talking about Fable Avenue as if you're separated from it. We have to acknowledge our culture, Nana."

"Girl, you mocking me?" Savannah said with an eyebrow raised.

Fey shook her head. "No, Nana. I wouldn't do that," she assured. "I'm just saying."

"Well, so am I," Savannah retorted. She took a hit from her cigarette. "Shit," she breathed out smoke. "Your boyfriend, Gordon, is in a spot. All mangled and bruised up. We makin' progress, and our grand adversaries are right there making sure enough to stop it."

Fey turned away from her grandmother. She watched the smoke swirling off the incense stick. "I'll set Gordon right, Nana."

Savannah fussed, shaking her cigarette at Fey, "You watch yourself on that part too. Lady Arachne said you shouldn't be anywhere near that mess when them boys break into that place. Let them rough boys handle that on they own."

Fey thought of Cedron, and she was pulled from the hypnotic moment of watching the incense smoke. Her mask appeared. "Nana!" she blurted as she stood up in haste. "I have to go to Harlem!" She burst into her cobalt-blue specter. Savannah flinched.

"Go on, child, 'fore your spirit set somethin' up in here on fire!"

Fey rolled her blazing, cobalt-blue eyes and popped from existence. Outside, she was high in the air, soaring up to the fading light in the sky. To Harlem she flew, becoming a cobalt-blue comet. She wanted to speak with Gordon's brother, helping coordinate the effort to secure the gems. But after arriving at the Goodspeed's Harlem residence, returning to civilian clothes, and speaking with Cedron, she was met with shock when there was only one thing on his mind.

"Tribute?" Fey questioned, trying to reduce the anger in her voice. "He's your brother, Cedron. He's hurt."

Cedron raised his eyebrows. Leaning forward he asked, "You don't think there ain't a wounded and sidelined soldier alive that don't know that better than me?"

Fey took a breath. "I'm just saying, this isn't a time for—"

"This is about tradition, little girl," Cedron retorted. "That's something Fable Avenue has always been about. I'm sure your grandmother taught you that after she whisked you away to the safety of Mount Vernon."

Fey continued to contain her anger, but she still spat at Cedron, "Excuse me?"

"I get a tribute when I put my crew on the line," Cedron reminded. "Simple as that," he said with a slow shake to his head. "It happens with all of us. I ain't the only king. I'm just top tier. Cedron's misfits. I coordinate the best grabs. Yeah, I make a little somethin' for myself on the side with my crew's skills. But no one says a damn thing, because I show and prove. These mystical smash and grabs ain't nothin' new. Like everything else, it's been tradition. But this hometown territory now. Callin' them small crews from out of state ain't gonna do. Not while Cedron's misfits keep showin' up. Them Jersey and Connecticut cats don't cut it anymore. Boston think they got something, but they don't. Everybody keep thinkin' I'm babysittin' these kids. I'm schoolin' them in tradition, bringing them up. Papa Solomon and Maman Anansi's great-grandfather was all about this. The Shaw brothers and I been doin' runs for the community since middle school, little girl, back when I had two legs to stand on." He sat back and lifted his cell phone. "I already got a call from Wilson to be on standby. Whatchu think the first thing out his mouth is gonna be next time he rings me up about this—whatever it is. He's gonna say, 'I got two things for you: tribute and a job for your crew.' And *then* he'll mention it's all for the better of Gordon's condition." Cedron went silent, giving Fey time to think about what he'd just said.

All Fey could say to him was, "I just thought, for your brother, you could put tradition aside."

Cedron put his hands together and said as if addressing a child, "Tradition is what got us all into this." He wheeled backwards, making his way to the ramp leading to his room in the basement. "Offer up a tribute. My services will then be for you and the community."

Fey held back tears as she watched Cedron roll away from her. She turned and said to him, "I'll see myself out." And she did. Stepping into the cold, she spoke an incant to warm her. On the sidewalk, she looked in both directions for an alley she could duck into and pop away. All she saw were pedestrians. Her conversation with Cedron stayed at the forefront. Fey considered reaching out to Mister Goodspeed, tracking him down at the cab station. But she didn't want to complicate family matters, and she didn't want to be at the center of the conflict. She also considered having one of the matriarchs conjure Althea Goodspeed's spirit, but Fey also believed that too would be intrusive. However, looking across the street, an idea came to her. She dug into her pocket and pulled out her phone. "So glad I didn't leave this in my purse," she commented to herself.

Fey looked through her contacts and called Benjamin Brickhouse.

"Fey!" Benny's voice came through after several rings. "Everything okay? How's Gordon?"

"He's fine, Benny," she said. "He's still weak, but we got a remedy. Are you home?"

"Yeah."

"I'm across the street," Fey informed. "I was talking to Cedron."

"Oh."

"Are you decent? Dressed?"

"Yeah…for the most part."

"You in your room?"

"Yeah. Why? Where you taking this conversation? You getting lonely without Gordon," Benny joked.

Fey popped away, forming solid in Benny's bedroom. She ended the call and put her phone away. "No," she answered. Then she realized Neyeli's presence. She and Benny were relaxing in his bed, curled up with arms around one another. "Oh…"

"You're not interrupting anything, sister," assured Neyeli, guilt in her voice, spilling out into a shy expression. The locks of her hair changed colors from a deep red to a cool blue.

Fey noticed. "Your hair, Neyeli," she said, pointing.

"That's my conjure coming through," Neyeli clarified, pushing on her hair with the palm of her hand. "It's just been going wild since the lilac spirit has come to our world." She slapped Benny on the shoulder. "This one keeps calling me a damn 'mood ring'."

Benny beamed a proud smile in response. Fey remarked that she liked the nickname. Neyeli just rolled her eyes. Benny invited Fey to have a seat. Fey sat at the end of the bed. She exhaled and asked, "Why is Cedron such an asshole, Benny?"

"What's wrong?"

"You all got another job coming," she answered. "The items that can heal Gordon, they're here in Harlem. With what you all did for Lady Arachne's cards, you're going to be up at bat again."

Benny whispered into Neyeli's ear, "She's using baseball metaphors. You know she been hangin' with Gordon." Neyeli chuckled. Fey slapped Benny on the leg and scolded him to be serious. "Okay," he replied to her. "What's the problem with Cedron?"

"He wants tribute."

Benny took a moment before saying anything to Fey. He inhaled and then told her, "He's not being cold. That's how things get done. He cares for Gordon—"

"Then he needs to put that aside!" Fey yelled. She jumped up and folded her arms. "You mean to tell me, if he doesn't get a tribute—*paid*—to go and help his brother, you and the rest will stay your thievin' hands?"

"I—" Benny's face went from excited to defeated. "Tribute or not, I don't think I'll be there."

"Benny…"

"Baby," pleaded Neyeli, her hair shifting pale green. "You'll be well protected."

Benny didn't say anything. He looked away, the problem unshared by his silence.

"It's scary. I know," said Fey in an attempt to be comforting.

Benny snapped, "I'm not scared. That ain't it."

"Then tell us," Neyeli insisted. "Otherwise we're going to be offending you with all our efforts in guessing at what the matter is and trying to comfort you through that."

Benny huffed. He made an attempt to speak, but he stopped. He huffed again, rolling his eyes. Then he confessed in a low voice, "All y'all got a spirit. I ain't got a conjure yet. And I've had the Elders perform the stitching ritual on me." He exhaled. "Shit, my little brother got a unique conjure, and he didn't even need a damn ritual performed on his behind. I'm walkin' around with only some Jamaican-Harlem swagger." Benny said to Fey, "Look, it's like this, when Gordon got caught up at the crossroads, I wasn't there for him. Now he got dreams bein' back there, goin' back to that fight. Shit, I got dreams haunting me too." He shook his head thinking of possible outcomes to a situation gone wrong because he was without conjure. "I can't…" Benny fell silent, sighing.

Neyeli hugged Benny tight.

Benny asked Fey, "Why can't you run up into whatever place has what Gordon needs?"

"I've already been told to stay away," said Fey. "Stanley Fallows is watching too close. Hell, I'd go right now. It's damn near right up the street at the jazz museum."

"Oh, really?" expressed Benny. He was taken out of his somber mood by Fey's revelation. "That place got tight security. Always did. But we all know the stories about it being a nightclub owned by Sarinda Unhallowed. It's supposed to be city run, but folk talk—our folk, at least. The Fallows name hasn't stopped haunting that place."

"So, you in for the challenge?" inquired Fey planting herself back down on the bed. Benny didn't answer. He thought about his promise to Gordon. There would be another chance for him to swoop in for the rescue. But he still had no conjure to him. As Benny settled into silence, Fey observed Neyeli gazing at him. Again, her hair changed colors, turning from pale green to a mix of red and yellow. The spectacle presented Fey with an idea, reminding her of the last moments of her dream. She recalled the beginning session between Delia Peters and Stanley Fallows. "Neyeli," she called, getting the young woman's attention. "Can you take Benny on a walk?" she proposed. "A journey inside," she added. "Into the *mirak* with your empathy blessing," she suggested further. Benny and Neyeli looked at one another, their shared looks holding different meanings. "C'mon, Mood Ring," Fey teased, getting up.

Neyeli's hair flared bright red. "Maybe you'll find something, Benny-baby."

"What…should I do?" asked Benny.

Neyeli moved off the bed. "Stay there," she ordered him. "Just lie down, baby. Relax yourself." She walked around the bed, standing next to Fey. "I do this to relax family members, but we'll see how this goes." She attempted to gain confidence by reminiscing. "My older brother was about to go off to college, all the way in California. He was so nervous, but I put him at ease. Please forgive me if I'm no more than a *manbo si pwen.*"

"You'll do fine, sister," Fey assured.

Neyeli walked to Benny's side and knelt down. "I don't have any materials for ritual," she asserted.

Fey repeated, "You'll do fine, sister. Your conjure is all you need."

Neyeli accepted the encouragement. She eased. Her hair brightened to orange. She picked up one of Benny's hands, holding it with both of hers. Benny straightened his posture on the bed, lying flat. He kept his eyes closed. Neyeli bowed her head, shut her eyes, and recited Genesis 24:56 as she focused. Fey observed another change in her hair's color, a deep purple in shade. At the same moment, a soft glow emitted from the palm of Neyeli's hand, putting Benny to sleep.

Benny and Neyeli opened their eyes. They were standing, hand-in-hand, at the crossroads in Clarksdale, Mississippi. The sun was at the horizon in the east, and the light it gave off revealed a serene environment. A man approached from the distance. He was of average height and build, but there seemed to be something in his walk. He had swagger. There was a confidence that made him appear bigger than he was. The man was in his early thirties. He had a round head with short cut hair and a mustache so thin it was possible for people to debate its existence against his light-brown skin. He wore World War II military flight trousers, a brown shirt with a black tie. Around his person he wore a leather bomber jacket. The man stopped and gestured to come forward.

Neyeli let go of Benny's hand.

"Benjamin!" the man yelled. *"Come on over here, boy."*

Benny turned to Neyeli. She looked at him. *"Go on,"* she said, nodding her head in the direction of the man. *"That's an ancestor ready to bless you."*

Benny's eyes looked at the man. *"I recognize him from old photos. Heard stories of him. My mother's grandfather. He was a war pilot. He flew in World War Two, a pilot with the Tuskegee Airmen,"* he continued recalling. *"He passed before I was born. Just heard him called Big Uncle or Little Wing."*

"He's a pilot," Neyeli said intrigued. She took several steps backwards, ending up behind Benny. She whispered into his ear, *"You might be able to fly, Benny Jah."* Her hair erupted into the passionate colors of purple and red.

Benny's eyes remained fixed on the man. *"Yeah,"* he said. *"Maybe I can."* Benny recalled more about the man. His family called him Little Wing. And according to family lore, the man claimed Jimi Hendrix was truly singing about him in his song of the same name. It was the way he would describe flying his plane and how she handled in the air, making him feel alive and free during a time of war. *"I don't remember his proper name,"* Benny confessed.

"Benjamin!" the man yelled again, waving his hand high and toward him. *"Come on, boy."*

Neyeli prodded, *"Go on, Benny Jah. You got a blessing coming to you."*

Benny put one foot forward, but it was sometime before he put forward the next and completed the step. Benny quickened his pace after further encouragement from Neyeli. In a few strides, he was standing before his great-grandfather. They were eye to eye. *"Hello, sir,"* Benny greeted.

The man removed his jacket and presented it to Benny. *"You been looking for this, young man?"* Benny stared at the jacket, unsure of what to do. He looked over his shoulder at Neyeli. She was smiling, hair bright with the same passionate purple and red colors. He turned back to the specter of his relative. *"You know who I am, boy?"* the man asked.

"Yessir," he said. *"Sort of. I've seen photos. I've heard stories."* Benny admitted, *"I don't remember your name, sir."* He was apologetic in his tone.

"Robert Jonas Grey," he answered in a military fashion. He retracted his coat. *"Now, you know me then. That means I'm no stranger. You're from my line, young man. I'm your great-grandfather."*

"Yessir…"

"So, the fact that this here jacket is from your great-grandfather, and the fact that's me, should make quiet any idea that you taking candy from a stranger." Robert's words made Benny laugh. *"Or any doubt you might be entertainin' in your head—"* he presented the coat again, *"—that this doesn't belong to you."*

Benny nodded his head, agreeing. *"Yessir,"* he repeated, taking the coat and slipping it on. His frame was a little too slender for the jacket, but he wore it well. He looked at his person, admiring the coat. It was a little oversized, but Benny didn't mind. He loved it. He put an eye on his great-grandfather and asked, *"You really talk about flying to Hendrix? He really write that song after you and your plane?"*

Robert grinned. *"Oh, young man,"* he said swatting the air as if knocking the question aside. *"You gotta make it sound good."*

Benny nodded. *"Yessir."*

Robert had more to tell his great-grandson. With a stern point of his finger and voice he said, *"Now, I didn't know anything about conjure and spirit when I was up in the air. I had my prayers though. But you do the same with that jacket—the same as I did when I was up in that sky."* He pointed and looked up.

Benny looked up as well. He returned his gaze to his great-grandfather. *"You want me to pray? A certain prayer?"*

Robert shook his head and said, *"No. No."* he balled his fist and made a hard, short punch to the air. *"I want you to hit hard. Strike fast. You become that sky. Day or night, however it shines or doesn't. That's your home."*

"So I can fly?" Benny stated with a grin.

"Oh, you sure as hell can. You surf them clouds."

"Absolutely, sir," Benny made a stern promise.

"Go on, now," Robert ordered. Benny pivoted. The coat disappeared from around him as he finished his turn, making his way back to Neyeli. He stopped and twisted his body to take a look at his great-grandfather. *"It's okay. It's still with you. It's still on both of us little windsurfer."*

Benny accepted the words and continued his walk back to Neyeli. She embraced him upon his approach. He hugged her in return, planting a kiss on her lips, which she happily accepted. *"Let me sleep a little longer, Mood Ring,"* he asked of her. *"I'm going to change the scenery and understand my conjure in dream. I'll be a mild expert when I wake up."*

Neyeli beamed at Benny. *"I'll let you be, Benny-baby."* She opened her embrace and slipped away from his. After two steps backward, Neyeli's image faded. Benny turned and saw the image of his great-grandfather fade. Then the new-day scenery of the crossroads dwindled away, replaced by a midnight, New York skyline. Benny was atop a tall skyscraper. He surveyed the city, charged to the edge of the building, and jumped out. Dark clouds billowed under his arms, outlining them from armpit to a little past his balled fists. He waved his arms, caught a conjured wind, and glided up high into the night sky.

Neyeli and Fey watched Benny as he slept, dreaming of practice with his newfound conjure. He was in the dreamscape called the *mirak* by some in the conjure community, and *miujiza* or *ajaba* by others. Neyeli's family referred to it as the *reverie*. It was a place that could be filled with epiphany and blessing, such as what Benny now experienced. Or it could be a place where one battled their *inawo*, or burden, such as what Gordon was experiencing when he dreamed of his fight with Brice Cadogan at the crossroads. Neyeli had guided many family members through its transcendental landscape, and now she'd done the same for Benny.

Neyeli thanked Fey for her suggestion, and she gave her a gentle hug. Fey told Neyeli she would see her after their exams on campus. Then she popped from existence. When Fey was gone, Neyeli pulled up a chair beside Benny's bed. She sat and watched him as he slept. Her hair was still a passionate purple and red. She watched him for the entire night. When he awoke, Benny sought his family to tell them of the news that he found his unique conjure.

The following night, Benny had a private conversation across the street with Cedron. He gave his oath to the wheelchair-bound goliath, boasting that he'd found his inner conjure and that he would use it to help secure what was needed for Gordon to regain his strength. He also promised Cedron tribute, to which Cedron suggested, "Just a trinket from the museum. Something good, but nothing that'll be missed. Understood? That's all." Benny reiterated his promise, and that he would pass on the suggested tribute to Lady Arachne and Wilson. "You see now," stated Cedron, "that's all I ask. That's what my little brother's girl just don't understand."

Benny didn't argue. He said his piece and left the house. At midnight, with Neyeli watching from his bedroom window, Benny climbed to the roof of his home, jumped off, and indulged in his conjure. Neyeli's hair turned into lit locks of yellow and gold, her smile just as bright as she watched Benny soar through the night, up into the clouds. She focused her conjure, and the excited state that filled Benny funneled through her. A yellow glow outlined her body, and an instinct occurred to her. She crawled through the window and jumped into the air, ascending up toward Benny. She surprised him, which made the two of them falter in flight for a moment. But Benny grabbed Neyeli's hand, summoned a flurry of air and elevated. Neyeli's glow returned, and the two of them glided hand-in-hand through the night sky.

Holidays on Fable Avenue were about the celebration of harvest and growth, change and rebirth, and fertility. Parents and Fable Avenue Elders would reiterate the more ancient lessons of each holiday when they came around. Halloween, for example, was an ancient celebration about Mother Earth being impregnated with the Father's spirit, seeded. As with many traditions, it began in Africa-East. The inception began in September, or *Pa-n-ip.t* in the Egypto-Nubian language. It was a time to sow and scatter seeds, and it was a time of ritual to protect the future harvest from malignant spirits wishing to curse the ground and spoil the yield. The rituals of planting and blessing the soil culminated on the last day of October, or *Ḥwt-ḥwr.*

Whether the harvest was bountiful or meager, during the final nights of this time, children in ancient Africa would dress as either the malicious or benevolent spirits and journey from house to house, curious about what was produced. Had the reaping been minute, then the evil spirits' trick against the growth had been successful. But had the picking been abundant, the children were offered a sample, a great treat. The tradition of the sowing of the hallowed (or even hollowed) earth spread worldwide. *Sowing Hallowed*, or *Sow-Ham* evolved into the Halloween known today. The people of the Fable Avenue community understood it as an ancient African tradition and celebrated it with that knowledge. They also incorporated the ancient understanding of acknowledging the dead.

But that was not the end of tradition and observance. This holiday was connected to the next. A plentiful or meager harvest always produced a communal *Grand Supper.* It fell toward the end of the month now known as November, anciently referred to as *Ka-ḥr-ka.* Abundant or not, all who participated in the shared feast were thankful. This is what the widespread community of Fable Avenue honored in the final days of November. It was also a month of celebration that focused on the 'blooming' of Fable Avenue into existence and the vanquishing of its adversary, the wicked Sarinda Fallows.

The Christmas festival was no different in its observance. The holiday heralded as the birth of the Christian savior by contemporaries, retained so many of its pagan traditions when it came to celebration. All the modern accents of decorations and lights adorned many of the homes along Fable Avenue. Lessons were taught about the origins of the holiday, but not every family participated in the festival. However, everyone was respectful of those who did. It wasn't about any particular spiritual philosophy, ancient or contemporary. It was a time of rejoicing, acknowledging the sun rising at the same point in the sky for three days, and then extending its stay by one minute per day following Christmas. A new sun was born out of the darkness.

While lessons were passed around concerning the various origins and mythologies of the day called Christmas, there was one Fable Avenue spoke of, but did not embrace. That aspect was Santa Claus. It was not out of any superstition regarding the jolly, red-garbed and bearded gift giver. Lessons were taught on him too. Fable Avenue instead indulged in the combined Zulu and Yoruba mythology that created the story of *Eshu's Treasure Basket.*

From the Zulu mythology was borrowed the *Basket Monster*, a creature with spiny arms and legs and a basket for a body. The basket's opening served as the creature's mouth, and according to Zulu folklore, would eat people. Its victims' brains were its favorite indulgence, snatching people inside its basket body and lulling them to sleep with magic. Later, it would spit the person out and feast on the brains. This gruesome aspect of the story was left out, so as not to scare the younger children of Fable Avenue. But, according to the story, there was one clever man who sneaked out of the basket monster's mouth when the monster was itself in slumber. To not wake the woven fiend, the man left rocks in his place that weighed as much as he. And he escaped to tell the tale. Somewhere, even before Fable Avenue was a budding culture, Eshu, the Yoruba Orisha of chance and trickery, became the young artful dodger who escaped being digested by the woven creature. But instead of rocks, Eshu left behind treasure, and when the Basket Monster woke, he had a new taste for the finer things people desired in their heads and less of an appetite for their brains.

And so on Christmas morning, the parents of children would conjure an illusion of Eshu's wild treasure basket, and the children—if of appropriate age—would happily wrestle it to the ground. When the conjure was subdued and dissipated, all gifts earlier bought and wrapped by the parents would be left behind. Not everyone participated in the event. Some children grew out of it after reaching their teenage years. Some children were too young. And it was very rare for adults to partake in the wrestling event. But there was nothing more fun for the children than tackling the conjured Basket Monster and wrestling it for their desired prizes.

But it was only Christmas Eve on Fable Avenue. The twinkle of the lights on houses brightened as the day passed, illuminating decorations of all sorts. Shoveled snow lined the sidewalks, creating an ice-melting, salted path for people to walk through. A light, winter drizzle brought a haze to the entire neighborhood. Holiday songs resonated through houses. Children waited, impatient, convinced in their stern declaration that December 24 was the longest day in existence. Strategies were planned by children on their approach to wrestle Eshu's Treasure Basket. Children participating for the first time were nervous about the talk of confronting monsters, even if treasure and gifts were involved.

Strategy extended to plans involving Fable Avenue's greater politics. Wilson, Private Investigator Martin Kimball, and his partner Macario, had been casing the Harlem Area Museum of Jazz and New York Sound. One at a time, and on separate days, the three men walked the grounds. Top Hat also took a stroll through the museum's interior one day after work. That same night, in slumber, he revisited the museum, taking a dream walk through its dark, well-guarded corridors. It was this trek through the premises that helped locate the vault where the Djed Pillar Jewels resided. No combination to the safe was culled from the spirit-reconnaissance, but its location was enough. Also learned was that the museum would close early on Christmas Eve and be the night with the lightest guard. And so Fable Avenue's sole patriarch and three matriarchs conceived a plot to wrestle the treasures from the belly of the museum. Cedron's syndicate paid close attention to detail, whether drawn or spoken.

With the help of Papa Solomon and the three matriarchs, Edmondo and Raymondo Shaw were blessed with conjures by way of the *grand stitching ritual*, also referred to as the *cosmic webbing*. This was an old ritual performed on Fable Avenue to draw out residents' potential to perform incants and conjures. First, Papa Solomon gave a blessing that prepared the brothers' bodies, minds, and spirits. At this stage, the initiate was called a *flume*, readying the body to have their unique conjure or incant flow through them. Then, Lady Arachne held a reading for the brothers. Cards were drawn that spoke to their inner conjure. With the readings' interpretations, Madame Jeliya was able to map their inner blessing, and Maman Anansi spun a web of sorts that connected the map leading to their inner blessings to the rigid lines on the palm of their hands, and then to the center of their minds. The Shaw brothers praised their conjures and called them *salamangka*, a common word for magic in the Philippines where dwelled a community of *salamangkero* or magicians. Their mother provided altars for Edmond and Ray to keep their risen conjures and spirit at rest. These rituals and altars were more aligned with the indigenous cultures and beliefs of the Philippines.

Since the lilac spirit had manifested, and Lady Arachne had retrieved her desired cards, the *grand stitching ritual* was increasing among the Fable Avenue conjure folk and the global conjure community. The goal was to either strengthen existing conjures, or draw out an innate, gestating conjures. The ritual didn't always provide instant results, and Papa Solomon and Madame Jeliya had to have close, observational sessions with people after performing the ritual. And it took so much out of the Elders for it to be performed. Each ritual was a long and arduous process. It was also not a free service, but the politics of paid service was of no matter in the community. The Shaw brothers manifested quicker than expected, their conjures coming into full bloom over the course of three weeks. However, not having the enchanted tattoos and cultural rituals performed on them, made Edmundo and Raymundo Shaw susceptible to a host of intense dreams while their conjures matured. Some were good. A lot were bad. Madame Jeliya and Maman Anansi saw the brothers through the process.

Regarding the heist's plot, Benny argued to move into the museum and perform the grab on his own. It was a hard sell, but the young man was able to pull it off. Half of his argument consisted of a fib about manipulating his newfound conjure—though he had his theories on the extent of his smoke and wind incants. The other half was a good point about too many sneaking about the museum looking for one item. Benny was given the honor, which displeased his mother. But she respected the Elders' decision. Benny's father supported it as well. Jamie's shades would not be used as invisible cover. There were other plans for his shadows, and his focus needed to be on them.

Eleven o'clock at night was the hour designated for the strike. But before then, Gordon Goodspeed and Fey Forrester spent much needed time together in his basement. He was, as usual, wrapped in a blanket with a cup of incanted tea in his hands. Fey sat on the floor with her legs crossed. Gordon had just finished a face-to-face call on his smartphone with his family in Harlem.

"You feeling okay, Gordon-baby?" she asked as Gordon clicked a button to rest his phone.

"Anxious," he answered honestly. He put the phone on the floor and handled his cup of tea with both hands.

"Oh, come on, Gordon-baby. What could go wrong?"

Gordon sipped his tea and raised an eyebrow. He set a stern gaze on Fey, looking very upset. "Don't speak of trouble, won't be no trouble," Gordon commented.

"I'm sorry, Gordon-baby," Fey said with all sincerity in her voice. She reached under his woolly cocoon and rubbed his leg. "Won't be no trouble on this run," she promised. "And when it's finished, we'll have your good spirit straight." She watched him take a breath, drink more tea, and calm. "You still have those dreams?" she asked. Gordon nodded, yes. "That will be set right too," Fey assured. "Drink that tea, Gordon-baby. We'll get you to bed, and then I'll be on my way to help Madame Jeliya and the others with projecting a blessing."

"Can't sleep," Gordon groaned. "Thinking about it all."

Fey retracted her hand and stood. She walked around in back of Gordon, leaned over the chair, and put her arms around him. "We'll get you to sleep, King Dooley," she told him. "You ask, and your queen will provide." Her eyes burst with a cobalt-blue shine. She eyed the ancient tome resting on the chamber, and it lifted into the air, its pages fluttering open to where their mythology was last scribed. Fey kissed Gordon, and his eyes brightened with an intense, lilac storm. "Make me whole, little Kibaru," Fey whispered into Gordon's ear. "And I will put you back together in this lifetime when next you awake."

Eyes on the book, tendrils of light extended out of their glowing pupils and onto the page. The swirling streams of light mixed together, spilling on the page until an ultimate burst of brilliance dissolved the scenery around Gordon and Fey and transported them back to the realm of their personal, bardic mythology.

I watch on wheeled throne
I am a garden of woman, watered and flowing
Alive, I as 1000 flowers stand at less than half broken
But there walks open the finality of me – the last three of my twisted 13
There. Walks. Fabrique. Composed of cosmic unseen
Shaped with femininity – caliginous timber,
Dark matter – haloed. On two feet. Dangerous giant.
She unmakes her adversaries, stomping with a nimbus mouth
Devouring flesh and spirit into nonexistence
She spatters warrior shades to starry matter, cosmic dust cloud disintegrates
Spirit through her is unmade – death through her
No soul in Heaven bathes

Only few warrior shades remain
And my handsome Kibaru, slender and strong
His captain
And three allies
Victory for them in reach, stretched long
Wulvz bear fangs, growl and help claim
Lives of warrior shades
Blood cloaked shields and blades

Devil swine pour from the mouths of caves
And a haze of red defines a once blanched soil

There beats and pumps
An emerald colossus that thumps
Four chambers of his person, defiled and ruined
When Yollj stomps, the sound of hate reverberates
Shades' discipline dwindles down
They long for system structure, dependent
Their spirit and love for freedom chained
Wulvz and devil swine cut them loose from life
Their screams like steam
Pump, pump through Yollj's four chamber person
He lives and breathes off the slaying of shades
And to us, the effect is monstrous

Allies and my handsome Kibaru, they fight each other
Their weapons and conjures smother – brother against allied brother
Captain Debas drowns in fright
Castrated – separated from courage

Behold a third behemoth
My mind trapped within it
Ill effect, grim scene rewarded atrophy
Chapeldamn
He is beyond reason, sick with demons – possessed
His breath fills the air
His demons seep into my warriors' hair and flesh
They are dressed in the cloth of devil swine
They mime the unalike's hate

Wulvz and devil swine pause, take in
Giggle – laughing
The sight of my beloved, his shaded warriors, allies and captain
One another, fighting, not quite yet killing
But the red stained hands of shades and my Kibaru draws closer
Shades of ally blood
The last three of the thirteen have taken the day

And so cries my third eye
In the blink of the sky
It appears all the black-lighted stars that shine

Have been prophesized to die
Mama Gran and Mother Wisdom sing a new cosmic tune
Their voices glitter many colors, and they stitch
A spiritual
"Glory! Glory! Glory! Glory! Tell me how your
Story, story, story will conclude.
What will be the question of you?
How will you remember this moment
And what you did, and will do?"

The morning sun shines on me a smile
Through haze of a new day
I return her favor,
Inhaling spirit, I, inspired, count my treasured belongings
What do I have with me
What of the thirteen are now me?
My 4 cosmic winds bless my voice
My body, my spine, and the wisdom writhing as my hair
My hands, my body—fine—my third eye

I sing praises to me
In harmony with Mama Gran
And Mother Wisdom
And with them, what is there as me
Stands
Ten of my 13 at my command
The crescendo of song gleams
My body swirls into an air stream
Double-helix flight, swirling air covered in light
Arcing across the sky, over the conflict and strife
I land on the battlefield
Physical body wrapped in shield
Nine of me split into groups of three and distract the conflict
And trick
Spoken silent from these giants' lips

My warriors exhale confusion
Handsome Kibaru blinks rapid
Thinking my presence
A rabid illusion
But I prove to him, with kiss and whisper
I am here

While my nine as three sets of 3
Penetrate the last of the colossal thirteen
Decoding weakness of structure
Pinpointing crucial spots to rupture
Pressure points to anoint with
Black sun spear tip

Wulvz and devil swine come back to life
Captain Debas commands remaining shades
Act as shield and blade against them
While allies three, on bended knee speak triangular symmetry
Combined conjure to keep at bay the giants' tricks
Nine attributes return to me, ten as whole as can be
With my body

I sing mathematically
Numbers supreme
Carved onto black sun spear point
My voice harmonizes strategy
Supreme alphabetically
Ancient script, scribbled from end to tip

I am light and rope
Wrapped around Chapeldamn
Force him to knees and bend
And my handsome, knighted, black Kibaru
Up and pounce
Down onto Chapeldamn's crown
Knowledge, wisdom, and understanding injected
Ignorance bled, actual facts and purpose resurrected
My light slips
Loose
Razor sharp,
Wrapped around neck like a noose
Head severed – Chapeldamn is ash

His death blesses me, my Medusa head story
Now restored
Onyx stone, I am crowned in glory
And the light of my spirit roars – a sound muted

The ground reverberates with hate

Yollj's stomp and gait bars my heart
I sing love
Standing before his mass, calmly
The wave of his abhorrence is hindered
"Come Bwa! Come Cimetiere! Come Phour!"
Their chants and conjures glow swords of cinder
Kibaru inspired
They pounce
Drive cindered swords to their mark
Three chambers of Yollj's heart
Up! Kibaru springs
Black sun spear – fourth chamber pierced
The emerald mass dwindles away in ash

Pump! Pump!
The green flows through me
Heightened courage
I stand determined
Third eye on Fabrique

Twelve of my 13
Reside in me
Motherland's covenant
Restored
Piece by peace
My disciples
At my command, disciplined
I can feel all that has been swallowed by Fabrique
Within – a faint existence
Twelve streams of light flow from me
Disappear into Fabrique, reaching and resurrecting
From inside
All consumed shades, those unmade – only preserved
Reborn, recreated
Her mass is inundated, overflowed with life
She bursts – broken, ashes
As remade shades escape her void and prison, risen

And there glows my halo
Dark matter
It swallows me to become me
And here I be

Whole, with all 13

I swing hand over land
All fallen shades once again stand
Our army, just as me, stands complete
Remaining devil swine and wulvz
Pulled into our gravity
Slain, no retreat
We will be the mouths that tell the tale

I, surrounded by shades
My handsome Kibaru
Captain and allies
This army that has fought for me
Restoring my thirteen
They give praise on bended knee

Gray land brightens with color, and
I turn to the sun in the sky
Smile, one hundred and twenty allies
At my side
My sight arcs to a crying city
I rise
High, stature strong
My beloved Kibaru looks up to me
Thirteen complete
In the distance, my third eye can see
Mama Gran visible
Her conjures twist and tangle
With Queen Malady's tricks – medicine dueling disease
Mother Wisdom and Father Knowledge engage devil swine
In city streets
While they shout blessings to wake minds from sleep

"Let us join them," say I
Stature colossal, head in the sky
The blue above, and sun and moon and stars, my crown
I am a tower of conjure
Shades, Captain, allies
And handsome Kibaru are blessed with flight
Forward we move
I am the force of nature – potential now blossomed in full bloom

The mythology collapsed into light, and the basement's scenery unfolded out of the brightness. The tendrils of light expelled from Gordon Goodspeed and Fey Forrester's eyes retracted to their source. Gordon took a deep breath, a hint of weariness creeping around the pain hovering over him.

Fey tightened her arms around him, kissing his cheek. She thought about what she'd just witnessed. Her mythological mirror, *Ashaba-Sirene*, with all thirteen qualities restored to her, contributed in the final battle with the remaining leviathans. Warriors surrounded her, but it was her addition to the fight that secured her remaining three of thirteen pieces and the defeat of the giants that possessed them. Fey coupled this thought with the strategies and leadership of Ori Washta. Gordon moaned, and Fey said to him, planting another kiss on his cheek, "It's time to sleep, Gordon-baby."

"Yes," he said as he groaned.

"Upstairs?" asked Fey. "Or will you sleep here?"

"Upstairs," Gordon answered. He wiggled out of his blanket, and asked for assistance to stand, making his same remark about being an old spirit. Fey indulged his words with a smile, fighting against a melancholic expression that, through her eyes, escaped concealment. Gordon witnessed the expression. He coughed as Fey guided him to his altar. Managing a grin, Gordon said to her, "Aw, Fey-baby, you don't worry about this spirit here. In less than a few hours, I'll be good as new. Best. Christmas. Ever."

Fey continued assisting Gordon as he lowered himself on the floor. All four of her yumboes swiveled as smoke from her back. She gave them a command to prepare Gordon's bed as they turned solid, wings fluttering as they hovered in place. The sprites soared up, turning into streams of smoke and light, traveling through the ceiling and up to Gordon's bedroom.

Fey knelt down next to Gordon as he performed his nightly ritual for rest. Items were arranged. Incense was lit. And Gordon spoke his incant and prayer. He collapsed. The lilac spirit inside him was pulled to sleep. Fey caught his body, and as Gordon's physical form landed in her arms, she disappeared, popping into existence two stories up. She was still kneeling and next to Gordon's bed. His body came into existence on the mattress, and Fey's arm was in an awkward position under it. She stood, slipping her arm free. When she looked up, she saw the specter of Althea Goodspeed standing on the other side of the bed. Fey flinched in her presence.

"I'm sorry, Fey," said Gordon's mother. "I didn't mean to startle you."

"It's okay, Missus Goodspeed. I was tucking Gordon in."

Althea watched Fey handle her son's sleeping body. She appreciated Fey for all she did for Gordon. "My husband and Cedron are on the way," she said. Then she looked down at Gordon and concluded, "He'll be fine by the morning if all goes well tonight."

Fey's yumboes hovered in place, each holding a corner of the comforter. Fey slipped the bed's top sheet over Gordon as he slept. She then waved the yumboes to cover Gordon with the comforter. Fey took a step back, addressing Gordon's mother, "Missus Goodspeed…?"

"Yes, Fey…"

Fey kept silent, though she didn't have time to hesitate. She shook her head and said, "I have my duties with Madame Jeliya."

Fey's yumboes twirled into smoke and seeped back into her tattoos. She nodded at Gordon's mother, and then she turned and left the room. Althea called to her, "Miss Forrester!" Fey stopped at the door and turned around. "You want to know about your mother and father's spirits, correct?" Fey nodded, yes, eyes hazy. "I can't tell you." Althea recognized a curious expression flash across Fey. It was there for only a brief moment, but long enough for Althea to catch. "I don't mean to sound as if I'm keeping information from you," Althea elucidated. "It's just that I've never felt your parents' presence or met them on my plane. I'm not quite sure if that's a good thing or a bad thing."

Fey's hazy eyes cleared, and a smile appeared. She dissolved the thought of her mother's suicide being the cause of her absence on any plane in the spirit realm. "But, it's a thing, Missus Goodspeed. Thank you," she said. Althea smiled back, and she wished Fey success as her son's sweetheart turned and walked from the room.

Althea knelt down next to her son while he rested in a deep slumber. She waved her hand over Gordon's forehead, her specter ghosting through his physical form, touching his mind. Standing, she walked to the chair in the corner and focused, sitting on the chair's physical presence. Althea continued watching her son, wondering about his dreams. Something moved her, compelling her to sing the old gospel song *Hush, Hush.*

Gordon dreamed of the crossroads. He stood there, cosmic suit more tattered than in any dream he'd dreamed before. Half his mask existed, one side of his face exposed. His spherical eye was a fading, lilac glimmer on his forehead. A cosmic loin cloth hugged his waist. His toes poked out of what could've been black slippers. The ends of his fingers popped out of black gloves, and one arm wasn't covered at all. His torso looked to be wearing a ragged, cutoff shirt from the 80s. A small piece of fabric blew in the wind behind him like a cape.

Here he was again, after again, the same dream. This might've been the South. Clarksdale, Mississippi. But this was also the Old West. It was high noon, sky and sun putting a spotlight on the dream and its setting.

Gordon stared down the barrel of many eyes. Brice Cadogan was there, and that was expected. He was still as weak as Gordon, hopping in place to stand up straight. Neither of them was prepared for another fight. But there was nothing else to do but pass the time trading blows. Maybe this time, one would kill the other.

Brice was kind enough to bring friends, or as Gordon considered, smart enough. Needlemen had followed him, cloaked in hospital scrubs, long white coats, and armed with syringes that Gordon wasn't interested in knowing the effect of had they pierced his skin. Birds flew high, announcing the showdown. A breeze accompanied them. Gordon looked up at all the sky had to offer. Then he put his eyes on Brice and his small army of twelve needlemen. Nina Simone's rendition of *Feelin' Good* serenaded the dream. And under the music, Gordon could hear the faint voice of his mother singing a gospel song.

Gordon embraced the stinging pain he felt. It was his ally now. Putting it into his palm, he could give it a handshake. The pain was his weapon, and he intended on using it. Gordon didn't care that Brice had the extra weight. But he had a message for the needlemen. *"I'll give each of you a chance to wake up before this fun begins,"* he warned. *"I'm a little achy, but I'll manage. I'll manage against all of you."* He looked at Brice and stated, *"We might be dreaming, but this is going to be the kind of heavy, spiritual ass whipping nightmares are made of. And you boys are gonna feel it when you wake up. So if nerves are haunting any of you, I'll extend my mercy and allow you to open your eyes."*

None of the needlemen made a move, or disappeared back to consciousness. Gordon didn't mind. Brice pointed to a man standing three needlemen away from him. *"Mister Fallows asked me to bring this particular chap in with me,"* he told Gordon. *"He's the man, and that's the very needle, that put your mother in the grave, Mister Goodspeed."*

Gordon didn't flinch, remaining stable and on his feet. He retorted to Brice, "*Thank you for bringing him to me. And thank whatever god you believe in that I don't have my full strength and spirit. But prepare to be amazed—and frightened—by what I can do with what little I'm workin' with.*"

Brice ordered the needlemen to strike.

Gordon braced himself, gathering what little spirit he had. He thought of his mythological counterpart, Kibaru. He thought of his wiry frame, nimble antics, and his pounce. He calculated the incoming swarm of needlemen, and he thought about all the times he'd been at the crossroads fighting Brice. He contrasted that with the fights he'd engaged in while haunting the block, and while he was absorbed in the narrative of *In Thirteen Pieces.* Nina belted her heart out about it being a *new world and a bold world.* But this was the same fight. Same dance. Same dream, different details. The pain coursing through him acted like a weight, but even still, Dooley was fluid. He dodged the first strike, catching the needleman's arm at the wrist. He kept the needle pointed away from him and slammed his elbow into the needleman's masked face. He bent the needleman's arm, and made the man stab himself in the chest, and then he kicked him away.

His mother's killer made the next strike, swiping at Dooley in every direction. *Down! Up! Right arcing strike! Left arcing strike! Jab!* Dooley dodged, managing to duck away from converging needlemen also taking stabs at him. He kept his eyes on his mother's poisoner. He tripped two oncoming attackers, dodged a third and fourth, and made his way back to his mother's killer. The needleman made another attempt at a stab. Dooley coolly shied away from the offense and made a counterstrike, a hard fist at the needleman's face, cracking nose and jaw. But the man didn't fall. Dooley chopped hard at his wrist, causing the needleman to open his grip on the needle. Dooley caught the syringe. He punched the needleman in the stomach, making him double over. And then Dooley jammed the needle in the back of his neck.

More needlemen moved in on him.

Dooley clutched the back of his mother's killer's head and pushed him to the ground, face first. With both hands planted on the back of his head, he vaulted forward. Landing on his feet, he saw himself surrounded by more needlemen. Nina Simone's rendition of *Feeling Good* reached its scatting and declarative crescendo just as Dooley jumped into battle with the new set of night doctors. The heavens put the song on repeat, and the dance continued.

Althea Goodspeed watched her son sleep. She continued singing even as her husband arrived. Maximilian didn't interrupt his wife, posting up against the dresser. Up the street, at the Peters' residence, Madame Jeliya, Top Hat, Neyeli and Fey Forrester sat in Madame Jeliya's sanctuary with their legs crossed. Rolled out beneath them was a mat with various theurgic symbols. Candles were the only source of light in the room as they concentrated with eyes closed. Savannah Forrester kept watch, sitting on the chaise lounge with her legs crossed.

The focused group of conjurors projected their blessed protection. On the receiving end was a group of preternatural goons with a purpose. At the moment, they were quiet in a van, driving toward Harlem. Wilson was behind the wheel, making roll call in his head. Benny. Cedron. The Shaw brothers. Tap. All four of Fey Forrester's yumboes were along for the ride too. The iridescent pixies shimmered with a faint glow as they sat patiently in a little space inside the van.

Wilson drove carefully through the wintry mix of snow and rain and the frosty mist they created. He parked two blocks away from the *Harlem Area Museum of Jazz and New York Sound.* Everyone in the van took notice of the street. The area was quiet with few pedestrians milling about. Only the mist was in mass. Harlem was hushed, but there still lingered business. There were always ghosts in Harlem. A tension that Papa Solomon would say was brought on by the musical jazz notes still ambling around the streets. The mystical notes played by his father and grandfather, Horatio and Pete Peters. Something was still playing the notes. Something was still trying to compose the rest of a story gone off key. Up the street, there lay the source of it all. The haunting notes weren't lingering. They were imprisoned by a lasting trick keeping them in place. Stanley Fallows mastered that trick, and kept the music and its story stagnant.

Wilson turned and looked at his crew. "Ready?" he addressed, arm around the back of the seat.

Cedron looked at his men in service. They looked at one another, Benny, Jamie and the Shaw brothers. It was Benny that answered, "We're ready." He looked at the yumboes and said, "Let's go."

Silver fluttered up first, and the others followed her lead. The yumboes dimmed their lighted flesh entirely. Benny opened the door, and the four sprites moved outside. Jamie and the Shaw brothers exited next. They didn't wait for Benny to follow. They hurried up the street with the yumboes hovering close in tow. Edmond and Ray made conversation to look inconspicuous. Jamie only listened, hands in his jacket pockets, face hiding from the wintry haze. Silver and the yumboes glided in shadow alongside them, staying clear of being seen by the few passersby that walked the street. Jamie and the Shaw brothers heard three exterior guards engaging in small talk when they arrived across the street from the museum. The three-man unit wore hooded rainwear over patrol uniforms.

The Shaw brothers turned to Jamie. Edmond said in a manner to draw attention, "Man, you think you Gene Kelly, or something." He held out his hand and looked up. Then he addressed Jamie again, "Man, this ain't rain, mostly snow and ice. I know you can't sing, but let's see you dance in it."

Jamie retorted, "M-m-man, wh-whatchu think y-y-you know 'bout this here?" He dived into a tap routine.

Edmond nodded his head. "Don't slip, now."

Jamie tapped and tapped and tapped. Then he stomped. One. Two. Three times. And from the ground beneath the conversing guards came three, black and misty shadow figures. Before the guards could react to the shadows' elongated frames and frightening ghostly shapes, the misty specters lunged their smoky bodies into the guards and possessed them. The guards stood straight. They were wide-eyed with blank stares. Mechanically, they returned to their beats, walking the museum perimeter.

Edmond patted Jamie on the chest, thanking him. He waved for Raymond to follow him. The Shaw brothers jogged across the street, around the corner where the building extended. Edmond stopped there and looked up. He looked both ways. Up the street, one possessed guard walked with his back turned to them.

"Okay," he said while exhaling a breath. He grabbed his brother by the collar. "Okay," he said, readying himself. "Hold on little brother. Madame Jeliya said you're supposed to be as light as a feather." Raymond took a breath too. Edmond crouched down, pulling his brother down with him. "And up we go!" he whispered. He jumped! Raymond held on for the ride as high up they went, shooting past the museum's roof. Edmond pushed his body forward, arcing into a position over the roof. Then they descended, landing hard on the building and taking three guards by surprise.

A yellow aura bubbled around Raymond's left hand. With his right, he reached for the yellow ambiance and drew back as if handling a bow. A golden, electric strand stretched as Raymond pulled. He let go, projecting three radiant arrows. Each magic missile smacked against a guard's forehead and knocked them unconscious. Raymond ran over to the fallen patrol and checked the guards for a pulse. He looked at his brother and nodded his head, signaling with a thumbs-up. Edmond returned the gesture, and then he waved for his brother to follow him. The Shaw brothers crept around the roof, using exterior vent shafts as cover. Never spotted, the brothers came across three more guards. Two were huddled together in conversation, walking their patrol. Raymond made short work of them, coming up from behind and knocking them out with his conjured arrows. A third came to investigate, and Edmond silenced him with an old-fashioned, swift punch to the face.

Continuing on their path, Edmond and Raymond found the building's fuse box and backup generator. Edmond asked his brother in a low voice, "Should I open them up first?"

"Nah, *kuya*, I got this," assured Raymond. His balled fist bubbled with the glow of his conjure, and he drew back a strand of its spirit. He concentrated the full potential of his conjure and discharged two shimmering arrows into the electrical system.

The museum's interior went dark. Lights and monitors went blank. Movement from security was still for a moment as all in the building waited for the backup generator to kick in. Nothing. The night watch captain radioed the unit on the roof. His voice came through, turning Edmond and Raymond's attention to the static transmission coming through a nearby, unconscious guard's radio.

"Can you give me a lift?" Raymond asked his brother as he balled his left hand and conjured a bright, billowing swirl of spirit around it. "High up?" he emphasized.

Edmond picked his brother up, tossing him over his shoulder. He bent down, told Raymond to brace himself, and then jumped high into the air. Through the wintry haze they soared. Raymond drew back a thick strand of spirit and aimed at the museum below. "Almost got it," said Raymond, teeth clenched. "Got it…and…taking the shot!" he let loose a single, massive-sized arrow. The stream of spirit dived toward the building's roof. Its impact flattened the large, golden arrow into concentric waves that spread over, around and through the building, knocking out all electrical devices. "Hits away!" exclaimed Raymond. Then something occurred, and Raymond reacted, *"Oh, boy!"*

Their ascent ended, and he and Edmond dropped. The descent was like the fall on a rollercoaster. Down. Swift. Their stomachs left them, and they both made a reflex gasp. But despite that, Edmond's landing was soft, and he set Raymond down on his feet. He rotated the shoulder where Raymond's body had been. It was stiff, but it functioned. "Not so light as a feather," he commented. Raymond ignored his brother, and instead, aimed a glowing fist upward. He drew back the conjured spirit with his other hand, and shot a flare into the sky.

Wilson spotted the glimmering projectile. He said over his shoulder, "We got us a signal, gentlemen. Benny, you're up, kid."

Benny opened the car door and hopped out. The wintry mix was now big drops of wet snow, falling rapidly and at an angle. Benny pulled his hood over his head and made his way down the street in haste, but was not conspicuous. Up the block, and at the corner, he encountered Jamie. Fey's yumboes appeared from a shadow, surrounding Benny. He addressed them. "Okay, you four," Benny said to the winged pixies, "it's time to unlock some doors." Silver and her pride of yumboes zoomed across the street, bodies shifting into a thin stream that penetrated the locks on the front door. There were multiple clicks, and then the locks gave way. The door made a slight move open. Benny took that as his cue and ran across the street, slipping inside. He heard the voices of guards scrambling, cursing that nothing electrical was working. His eyes adjusted to the darkness. Silver and the other yumboes, bodies seeping as colored smoke from the door's locks, became solid, hovering around Benny. All five quietly moved down the right path of the angled hallway, clinging to the wall and the darkness.

"Does anyone have a working flashlight?" a security guard yelled.

Benny and the yumboes stopped moving. The voices were just up the dark hallway, but they sounded muffled.

"Nothing works, sir," spoke another voice. *"My phone is off. Cameron's phone ain't workin'."*

"Yeah. We're in the dark in more ways than one."

"Shit!" cursed the man who started the conversation. *"Okay. Cameron, Carter. The both of youse take a walk outside and make a phone call from a street phone to the electric company. Jimmy, Seth, Clarke. With me. Upstairs. Let's check on our guys there. Jesus-in-Christ with all this! The rest of youse stay here and spread out. The power's probably gone to shit."*

Benny cursed. He saw the faint silhouettes of the guards come into the hallway, stepping through one of the doors. He backed away, staying pinned flat against the wall. The two named Cameron and Carter walked his way. "Can you see?" asked one of them to the other.

"Ah, shit," the other answered. "I'm gettin' use to the dark. But I know this place, y'know."

Both men used the walls for balance. Carter used the wall on their left. Cameron used the wall on their right, Benny in his path. They stepped carefully, and Benny watched them, backing up as Cameron moved closer to him. Two more steps back, and Benny put his arms out. Dark clouds billowed under him, shaped like feathers. He jumped into the air and lifted to the ceiling, gliding over the two security officers.

"You felt that breeze?" asked Carter.

"Our luck the power goes out in this cold," Cameron grimaced.

Benny glided to the floor, landing without making a sound. Silver and the other yumboes swirled into smoke and spiraled past the advancing security guards. Benny, crouched in the middle of the hallway, kept watch on Cameron and Carter. The security guards made it to the door and opened it. The dark hallway flooded with enough lights from street posts to call out Benny's presence. He looked over his shoulder, making sure the other guards had their back to him. The captain and the crew he'd assembled finished shuffling through the door that lead to the stairwell. The others were making their way down the remaining area of the hall in the opposite direction, checking the doors, peeping into the rooms. The front door shut, and Benny was relieved. Outside, Jamie tapped up two more shadows to possess Cameron and Carter.

Inside.

Benny spread his arms, conjured a wind to lift him, and floated up until his back was flat against the ceiling. He glided to the first doorway past the entrance to the stairwell and waited. A guard opened the door and walked out. Benny concentrated his conjure, removing the oxygen from around the guard until he fell unconscious. Benny swooped down and caught the man, dragging the guard into the room he'd come from. He set the man's unconscious body down, shut the door, and remained still until Silver and the other yumboes popped into existence.

"That you I hear flapping about?" Benny asked in a whisper. Silver giggled, yes, and Benny ordered, "Light up." The yumboes' flesh shimmered in all their colorful glory. Benny looked around the room, eyes taking in the sight. It was an old dressing room, staged to look busy with mannequins caught in time, rushing to prepare for a gig. Benny snatched a blanket off the couch and stuffed it at the door to keep the yumboes' light from seeping through. Standing up, he acknowledged, "This ain't the room. It's a couple doors down." He looked at the yumboes and asked, "Can one of you ghost through and meet me there? Unlock the vault behind the painting."

Zee's hand lifted first. Silver accepted her volunteering. Zee dimmed the light of her flesh and buzzed away, body turning into ghostly smoke and penetrating the wall. Benny stepped to the door and placed his ear on it. He heard nothing, and then he made an attempt to open the door. The yumboes dimmed their bodies' glimmer. Benny slipped from the room. He again glided to the ceiling and moved down the hall. Two doors down, he waited. Another security guard emerged, and before Benny could sweep down and make a move, another guard entered the hallway from two doors farther down.

"I got nothing," said the one under Benny. "We're still secure."

"Yeah," agreed the one down the hall. "I got the same here. Secure."

More emerged from various rooms. "Secure?" one asked.

"All good here," one answered. "Captain's right. Power's gone screwy."

"I feel a breeze," the one under Benny commented. "Cold gets into this place quick."

"C'mon," said a security guard walking underneath Benny. "Let's search the display halls."

"Where's Wendell?"

"He's probably already there."

The guards passed under Benny. He kept still until he heard their voices become distant, before landing on the floor without noise. He opened the door. Zee was there. She lit her body after Benny entered the room in flight and shut the door. Benny noticed Zee's expression as he landed. As bright yellow and purple as her body glowed, the look on the yumbo's face was blue.

"What's wrong?" Benny asked. Zee told him the vault was empty. "Dammit!" Benny hissed. But he kept calm, telling Zee, "Go and round up the other yumboes. You guys twist about this place until you find the stones. All of you reassemble and report back to me when they're found."

Zee zipped away, body again dimmed of color. She passed through the walls, through the next two rooms, and formed solid when meeting up with Silver and the other yumboes. She informed the sprites of the dilemma, and Benny's orders. Silver accepted the mission. She delegated which directions for the other yumboes to search. At the end of her assigning tasks, the yumboes scattered on command.

Benny waited in the dark. He stayed near the door, listening for anyone approaching. On the rooftop above, Edmond and Ray ducked behind shafts of ventilation and various objects, staying out of sight of the security team come to investigate. The unconscious bodies of the roof's patrol unit were found lightly covered with the falling snow. The captain escalated concern around the current situation. He ordered several of the men to supervise the unconscious bodies. To another group, he instructed to continue on and check the fuse boxes.

"He's fine, Captain," a man said, checking a fellow guard's body.

"Steven's got a pulse too, Cap," another informed.

The captain shook his head as more positive news was relayed to him. "Okay, okay," he said, contemplating and looking around. "Keep your eyes open. A surge might've knocked out the power…" he went silent, thinking. He looked at the wet roof, and he thought about the unconscious men. "The surge knocks out the power," he said aloud. "And maybe it went t'rough the ground here, I don't know. It knocks out our guys, but not enough to kill 'em."

"No foul play, Cap?"

The captain shook his head. "Nah," he answered, again looking around. "I don't think so. Not this time." He added to his theory, "I mean, all our electrical stuff is shut down. My watch, my phone," he named. "These guys were near the source. They're lucky they're not dead."

Edmond and Raymond listened. Edmond tapped his brother on the shoulder. Raymond looked up at him, and Edmond motioned with his thumb for them to make a move. Silent and careful were their steps, staying low as they retreated, crouched like crabs. Edmond stopped, grabbed his brother's collar, and launched the two of them up and out. None of the guards witnessed their speedy, vertical departure. But it wasn't entirely because Edmond's jump was in haste. Just as the brothers left the roof, soaring upwards and arcing out, the investigating security guards ceased moving. They were in mid-gesture. They were in mid-sentence. They were in mid-blink, and in mid-breath. Frozen, but not from the cold.

The Shaw brothers landed unnoticed in an alley. Edmond patted his brother on the chest and exclaimed, "We did it, kid!" He and Raymond stepped out of the alley and toward the van.

"It's all about Benny, now," Raymond stated. He thought for a moment as Edmond knocked against the side of the van. It slid open, and Raymond suggested, "I'll see if security still got a shadow in them. I'll keep a look out for Benny near the front doors."

Cedron and Wilson heard Raymond's proposal, van doors now open. "Just be careful," Cedron warned. "And check up on Tap. I know that dude got an incant keepin' him warm out there, but just—"

Tap ran up to the van's side. He was out of breath, but able to speak. "S-s-s-somethin' ain't r-r-r-ight." As he struggled to catch his breath, his stutter became less. "Sh-shadows j-jumped b-back in me," he briefed. "Guh-guards all stiff. Th-they ain't movin'."

"I'll check it out," Raymond volunteered, sticking to his plan.

Wilson reached under his seat for his gun. "Hold up, I'm with you," he said.

"No offense, Wilson, but conjures can be tucked away better than a piece," Raymond noted. "My conjure here got kick and stick." He said to his brother, "We ain't found an angle on your conjure to put out offense." He turned to Jamie and told him, "And we ain't got time for you to dance up an army. I meet up with Benny and the *diwata*, I'll be good. If I see trouble before I get to them, I'll fire a flare. Come in as you see fit."

Wilson looked at Cedron, and the wheelchair-bound goliath gave an affirmative nod of the head. Wilson put his gun away. "A'ight. You got this," he told Raymond.

Edmond and Tap jumped inside as Cedron said to Raymond, "We goin' to make the block like we've been doin'. Keep suspicion down from normal folk out here. Get Benny, meet back here and we'll pick you two up. Hopefully he got what we came for. Just that. I don't need a souvenir for tribute."

"Right," Raymond affirmed.

The van door closed. "I hope Madame Jeliya and crew are workin' up a strong protection," Wilson commented as he watched Raymond run up the street and cross to the other side. He pulled away from the curb and drove up the road.

Raymond watched the van go by as he stepped onto the sidewalk. He kept a casual pace as he strolled past stiffened guards, giving a quick inspection to their immobile state. Raymond slipped into the building, looking left and right down the angled hallway as the streetlights provided a moment of illumination. He shut the door, and darkness recaptured the area. He ducked low, moving down the path to his right. Behind him, the museum's front doors locked on their own and without making a sound.

"Benny," Raymond whispered. *"Benny!"* he said with more force. He kept to the side of the hall where the doors were. *"Benny,"* he repeated, whispering into the first closed door. Nothing. He moved forward, repeating Benny's name at each door he came to. Someone answered when Raymond traveled several doors down.

"Ray?" Benny whispered, head peeking through. "That you? What the hell you doin' here?"

"Something's not right, Jah," Raymond said to him. "You and the *diwata* find the rocks?"

Benny shook his head and said, "No. The yumboes are buzzing about looking for them." He opened the door wider. "Get in here," he told Raymond, and his friend slipped inside and stood up straight. "What're you doing here? I thought you'd be back in the van by now."

"Tap said his shadows jumped back at him," Raymond began explaining. "The guards they possessed were stiff, not moving. I saw them walking up here. Ed and I were back at the van. Tap runs up to us and tells us what's going down. I came back here to see about you."

"I'm fine," assured Benny, a little frustration in his voice. "But I'm waiting on the little winged ones." He asked, "You tussle with security on the roof?"

"Yeah," Raymond answered. "More came up, but we didn't touch 'em. Edmond jumped us out of there. They don't suspect anything. They think a power surge knocked everything out, including the roof's patrol unit."

"I wonder if they're immobile too," Benny pondered. "I mean, the guards outside might be an effect of Tap's shadow possession."

"He didn't say it might've been, but he also—"

Silver and the other yumboes buzzed into the room, through the wall. Their bodies brightened, and Raymond and Benny were relieved to see the light and their surroundings. Silver delivered good news. The whereabouts of the gems had been discovered. The Djed Pillar Jewels resided behind a vent under the stage in the main auditorium.

Benny exhaled, shaking his head. He told Raymond, "That's where a security crew is right now."

"When's the last time you heard a noise or something stir?" asked Raymond.

Benny pondered the answer. A peculiar thought came to him. He expressed, "It has been a while."

Raymond opened the door. "Let's take a look, Jah," he suggested. "See if these boys ain't frozen in place." He and Benny slipped into the hallway. The yumboes were behind them, glowing flesh dimmer than when in the room. But they provided enough light to see a ways down the hall, until darkness engulfed the faint shine.

Raymond balled a fist and conjured a ripple of spirit around it. He stretched back a strand and backed up as they made their way to the grand auditorium. Benny put his ear to the door when they arrived. He heard nothing, looking at Raymond and shaking his head. He put his hand on the door's handle and pulled down. He was cautious. Pulling down as far as the handle would go, Benny pushed the door open. It was dark inside. There was no movement or sound. He peeked in, seeing nothing. He opened the door wider and pushed his entire head inside. He moved into the large area, using his body to keep the door open. He looked at the yumboes behind him and said, "Add some light to this place."

Silver and her sister-sprites fluttered over Benny's head, into the room. Their flesh brightened, providing light in the pitch-black room. The security team was there. They were sitting. They were still and upright, looking forward and appearing attentive as if enjoying a performance on the stage. The yumboes dared to fly around the stiffened security guards. Visible to the world as the little winged yumboes were, the wide opened eyes of the security team never stirred to view them.

"Somethin' ain't right," Benny reported to Raymond. "Keep them conjured arrows up and aimed, Mister Shaw." Raymond nodded at Benny, and then he followed the young Jamaican man inside the auditorium. The doors closed, locking without making a sound. Benny casually walked to the stage. He said to the yumboes, "Point out the spot."

Em flew down, stopping center stage and hovering. Benny saw the grate. He lifted an arm and opened his palm. He conjured miniscule, but strong winds to rotate the screws in the grate counterclockwise. The screws loosened, and Benny manipulated his conjure to pull the grate loose. Em lowered, hovering next to the opening, allowing her glow to reveal the wooden lockbox inside. Benny rushed to the opening, ducking down and reaching inside. He snatched the lockbox and drew it to him. He lifted the top, and a smile hopped up on his face. Closing the wooden case, he turned to Raymond and said, "This is them. Let's go." He told the yumboes, "Form up. Let's get out of here." He stood and used his conjure to screw the grate back in place.

Raymond backed up to the door, conjure still drawn at the ready. Benny hurried up to him, a firm grip on the wooden lockbox. He put his free hand on the door's handle and jiggled it. It didn't move. He tried again, but it was locked in place.

"Let me fire one at it," Raymond recommended.

"Nah, nah," Benny waved him off. "Let's keep damage to a minimum." He looked at the yumboes and commanded, "Zap the lock."

Silver nodded. She shot forward, her body a beam of light. But strands of electricity, sprouting from the handle, jumped at her. She formed solid, wild sparks of hexed spirit writhing around her. When they dissipated, Silver fell to the floor, body perspiring smoke. The other yumboes rushed to her side. Zee assured Benny that Silver was okay.

It was here that all went black, but not from Benny, Raymond or the yumboes' point-of-view. It was the vision of the entire scene broadcast to Madame Jeliya and those seated around her offering protection to Cedron's crew. Their peek into the goings-on had been flickering for a time, and a cold pressure squeezed them. Now the scene faded away. Their projected blessing retracted with enough force to blow out the candles surrounding them.

Savannah jumped to her feet as Madame Jeliya opened her eyes, hastily speaking an incant that turned on the decorative, electrical lamps in the room. Neyeli was on her feet with a panicked expression draped over her face. Her hair was solid white, looking as if the winter snow had possessed her locks. Fey was next to her, arms around Neyeli, consoling the shaken woman. Madame Jeliya stood, paced over to Top Hat and said as she bent down and put her hand on his forehead, "Keep an eye on that scene, Top Hat."

"Yes, Madame Jeliya," he replied, closing his eyes and crossing his arms, placing opposite hand on opposite shoulder. Madame Jeliya spoke an ancient prayer, hand against Top Hat's forehead. He fell fast asleep. His body lay back softly against the mat, spirit projected to the scene in Harlem. But he awoke only seconds later, gasping for air. His sudden rise startled the women around him. *"Goddammit!"* he spat. "They got night doctors on them."

Neyeli pleaded, "Fey! Take your spirit and help them."

Fey looked at Madame Jeliya and her grandmother. The community Elder nodded her approval. Savannah did the same, and Fey popped away. She formed outside on the street, walking up the block. A determined expression made up her countenance, but it was soon masked as her cosmic regalia came upon her. Fey's body blazed with cobalt-blue spirit, and she launched into the air like an ascending comet of smokeless fire. Her gaze pierced the veil blanketing the scene in Harlem. A flicker of sight flashed in front of her, granting Fey observance of Raymond, Benny and her yumboes tussling with needlemen and Willie the Lich. Raymond conjured arrows and knocked down needleman after needleman. He switched hands to conjure spirit and draw back an arrow depending on the advance of an attacking needleman. Benny used his conjure of wind and gravity to push the night doctors away from him, dodge their attacks by making himself as light as air, and also gliding away from Willie's strikes. They were holding well, but Fey could feel them getting tired. Their conjures taking a toll with such use.

The scene faded away. Fey increased her speed across the sky. The rush of snow and wind were in her eyes, but did little to blind her. Instinct guided her straight to the *Harlem Area Museum of Jazz and New York Sound.* Her comet-like streak pierced an invisible aegis cast around the building. The penetrating act caused an effect, a mystical ripple of light that reverberated out, but could only be seen by the eyes of the Fable Avenue heist crew who were still making the block.

Wilson hit the brakes! He looked up at the wave of spirit cast off the building, as did the others in the van.

"What the hell is that?" Edmond asked.

"I don't know," Wilson commented. "I just hope it's for our team."

Fey's spirit ghosted through the roof and through separate floors. She landed in the middle of the fray between Raymond and Benny, her yumboes, and the needlemen and Willie the Lich. Her fiery cobalt-blue spirit dissipated as her feet hit the floor, leaving Fey in her tight, cosmic costume.

"There she is, boys," Willie grinned, "the savage, jungle wench of our dreams. And she's right on time." He cracked his whip, and then he slapped it in Fey's direction.

She dodged, and in her swift move away from Willie's attack, she tackled a needleman, rolled with him on the ground, and then tossed him into one of Raymond's mystical arrows. Planting her hands against the ground, Fey vaulted up and wrapped her arms around Raymond, disappearing on contacting. She popped into existence on the city streets, leaving Raymond in a daze as she blinked away. Next she grabbed Benny, taking him from the museum's interior before Willie's whip cracked down on him. She sprang out of the ethers, on the sidewalk with Benny in her grip. She left him next to Raymond, disappearing with a crackle and pop to her exit.

"To me!" yelled Fey to her yumboes as she formed into existence inside the grand auditorium. Silver and the other yumboes phased into smoke and light, and dived into Fey's person. Fey's instinct scanned the room, alerting her to the lockbox with the Djed Pillar Jewels inside them. She dashed toward them, narrowly dodging strikes from Willie's whip. Like a cat on the run, Fey kept low to the ground, using hands and feet to move forward. Needlemen converged on her. She slid, kicking out her legs to take

two of them off their feet. Fey spun, jumped into the air, and hit another needleman with her fist. She kicked out to knock another in the jaw.

Fey was like a lioness perusing a hunt. She landed on the floor, skittering between rows and aisles of the grand auditorium. Another needleman jumped in her path. Fey leapt at him, blocking his strike with one arm, and gripping his neck with her free hand. She drove him to the ground, using his flattened body to spring into the air. She soared toward the lockbox, snatched it, and rolled onto her knees.

But Willie was there too.

Fey hesitated for a moment, and before she could pop from existence, his whip crashed down on her back, tearing away a large, jagged area of her suit and scarring her flesh underneath. The scar bled across three of her four tattoos, and it felt as if the cosmic apparel adorning her had turned against her, scratching at her nerves. Then a searing sensation came, as if the sun birthed itself from her spine, exploding. Fey screamed! Willie only struck her once, but that was all that was needed. Fey disappeared, coming into existence on the sidewalk. Raymond and Benny stood over her. The tear in her cosmic fabric mended before they noticed the wound. Fey dissolved her mask and assured Raymond and Benny that she was okay just as Wilson pulled the van up and Jamie opened the door.

"Looks like it was for our team!" exclaimed Wilson, getting a view of Fey with the lockbox in her arms. She and Raymond and Benny piled into the car, and Wilson drove away. "What trouble brought you here?"

"Needlemen," Fey answered. "Willie the Lich. Hexes, a trap. They knew we were coming. But we got what we came for." Fey passed the wooden box to Cedron. "For your brother," she said with a light scold in her voice. "Maybe you can keep the box as tribute," she added, voice sounding a little more frustrated.

Benny shut his eyes and cursed himself. "I ain't snatch nothin', King."

"To hell with a tribute, man," Cedron consoled. "I told Raymond I didn't need it. Gettin' you out was the main concern."

"You still got yours comin' to you, King," Wilson commented. "We all do."

"Right now it's about Gordon," said Cedron as he opened the lockbox and inspected the seven gemstones.

I notice you ain't call him 'brother,' thought Fey, rolling her eyes while her face was hidden in shadow. She breathed to calm herself, thinking about the scar on her back. The fire was unnerving, but she held strong. She had to. It was for a purpose. She swallowed the pain, thinking of Ori Washta, her own personal mission, and how her scar would give her a connection and lead her to Stanley Fallows.

Needlemen lay unconscious and scattered up and down the crossroads dreamscape. The fight had whittled down to Dooley and Brice Cadogan, and it had been this way for some time. *"Now that the distractions are out of the way, let's fight,"* said Dooley to Brice after knocking out the last of the needlemen. *"You look tired,"* Brice retorted. *"We're both tired,"* Dooley noted. *"But I'm tired and know how to fight through that,"* he quipped. *"You've had it easy on the sidelines. You've been trying to hide the fear in your eyes for this moment ever since I knocked out the first night doctor."*

That conversation was forever ago in dreamtime, and now both were drained. It would be a great effort for either of them to cast a punch. Even Miss Simone's voice had faded from serenading the hostilities, and the wind now blew as an exhausted sigh. Dooley and Brice were on their knees at the center of the intersection, wobbling, swaying, and trying their best to catch their breaths and gain advantage. Dooley was first in that notion, but he didn't waste the little strength he'd regained on a light punch to Brice's jaw. Instead, he lunged at the Englishman, hands around his neck. Through clenched teeth, and with a murderous expression, Dooley growled, *"We've been here before, haven't we?"*

Brice fell back, Dooley's weight on him. He was sapped of strength, but he managed a grin. It widened when he realized Dooley hadn't the strength, or possibly the nerve, to choke the air out of him. The young spirit was too drained. *"C'mon, kid. Ain'tchu got fight enough to smother me?"*

"Whaddya think I'm doing, Brice?" Dooley exhaled, determined expression stamped on his face. But with all the vigor straining on his countenance, Brice felt nothing from Dooley. In fact, he believed his strength was returning to him. The oppressive pain that had been wracking his senses and bringing him to the edge of life while awake, and to the crossroads in dream, lifted from Brice. The Englishman couldn't feel Dooley's grip around his neck, and he felt too much as if he was breathing freely, receiving fresh air for the first time in ages. His eyes met Dooley's. The expression floating in them was of surprise. Dooley, however, remained intense, focused as he continued the gesture of choking Brice.

"You're not killing me, you damned jungle spirit!" Brice spat.

"Don't get happy yet, Brice," sneered Dooley. *"It's been my dream to snuff you out, but I'm not killing you here. I'm taking it all back. I'm taking back my pain, because how dare you live off of my plight. How dare you hijack my suffering. I went through this, not you."* He leaned closer to the Englishman's ear and whispered, *"This has only been a dream, Brice. But when we meet one another in the physical, I'll take the breath from you there."* He relieved Brice of the last bits of excruciating, burdensome pain. He took it all into his own body and spirit. He yelled up to the heavens. Dooley's cry was loud, and its sound crawled over Brice's person like an invisible spider that had razors for legs. Exhausted of his scream, Dooley looked down and knocked Brice hard in the jaw with his fist. *"Don't. Think. You got off easy,"* Dooley said to him. *"You remember the pain you felt, because you'll feel it again soon. And tell that coward in hiding, Stanley Fallows, the same is coming to him."* Dooley grabbed Brice's collar and sneered, "*They that sow the wind shall reap the whirlwind.*"

Dooley shook. The pain writhed through him like an electric snake. He coiled and jerked, but managed to stand up. Brice remained still, watching Dooley closely, anticipating anything except what happened next. With his strength regained, Brice woke up and disappeared from the crossroads. The bodies of the unconscious needlemen also faded.

Dooley dropped to his knees, screaming, arms wrapped around his body.

There was pain like he hadn't felt before.

Gordon's body breathed rapidly, cradled in Wilson's arms as he transported him from his room to the basement, Maximilian Goodspeed several steps ahead of him. Gordon's body jerked wildly while in transport, but Wilson managed to keep the young man in his cradle. Althea Goodspeed floated down the stairs behind the Fable Avenue hood.

Papa Solomon, Madame Jeliya, Lady Arachne, and Savannah Forrester waited on the garden level. Cedron, Top Hat, and the Shaw brothers were there with them. Fey Forrester was in the basement, slipping the last of the Djed Pillar Jewels into their respective slots inside Gordon's chamber. She had been following schematics and instructions scrawled as ancient text across Spook's black mirror, which lay next to her on the floor. Oliver Peters was behind her. There too was Neyeli, arms wrapped around Benny, head on his shoulder. Everyone tried to mute their anxiety. As usual, their eyes betrayed them.

Maximilian rushed down the stairs. Wilson took careful steps behind him as Gordon trembled in his arms. Fey stood. She signaled Wilson and told him, "We're ready. Put him in." She backed away, giving Wilson space. He placed Gordon into the chamber and stepped aside. The capsule sealed tight.

There came a hum from the chamber, and then a mechanical tumbling. The chamber moved, lifting upright, shaking as it did so. The surrounding witnesses remained frozen by anticipation. It was only a few seconds, and the hum and tumble ceased. The chamber opened. Gordon, eyes still shut, dropped out of the black and gold structure. His body smacked the floor, crumpled. Althea and Maximilian rushed to their son's side. Fey ran between them, kneeling down and putting her arms around Gordon. She leaned her head close to listen for breath. Gordon remained still for a moment. His breaths came first as a series of coughs, and then his breathing trembled as he stirred from rest.

"Just relax for the moment, Gordon-baby," instructed Fey in a warm tone. "You're a new born, free from hexes and scars. How do you feel?"

Gordon breathed, pondering Fey's question. Behind him, his chamber floated back into its horizontal position and closed. Gordon took another breath. The pain was gone, but even still, Gordon used his instinct to examine his person. The fiery burden of Willie's hexed lashes was no more. His sickness had dissipated. He smiled, putting his hand on Fey's shoulder and using her to get to his knees. His relieved gesture widened when he looked up at her. She was clothed in the tight, cosmic bodysuit. At the back of her neck was a flap of fabric as if her mask could be pulled off and on like a hood rather than mystically applied. He hugged her and kissed her, and the two of them stood.

"How you feel, little man?" Maximilian asked his son.

"Like I got the best sleep of my life, Pop," Gordon answered, pulling his lips from Fey's. His voice was loud, filled with euphoria.

Fey Forrester moved away, allowing Maximilian to hug his son. Gordon's father turned his head and yelled up the stairs, *"He's okay! He's together!"* The news relieved everyone on the upper level. There was no giant form of applause that erupted, only silent sighs and warm hugs shared. Maximilian tightened his embrace on Gordon and said, "My boy's spirit is back together again." He let go of his son and waved the others in the basement to come forward. "Welcome my son back," invited Maximilian.

They didn't swarm Gordon too quickly, not wanting to rush him. Althea glided over to her son. She focused her spectral form, touching Gordon's cheek with her hand. Fey also allowed for the others to approach Gordon. She scooped up Spook and slipped into the chair, watching Benny, Neyeli, and Wilson welcome Gordon back to health and whole spirit. Oliver suggested they go upstairs and reintroduce Gordon to the Elders and others waiting on the garden level. Fey stayed behind, listening to the congratulatory sounds upstairs. Her grandmother entered the basement.

Savannah bent down and hugged Fey, telling her granddaughter, "I'm so proud of you, young woman. I am so proud! We all are."

"Thank you, Nana," said Fey to her grandmother.

Savannah straightened. "It's been eventful, this Christmas Eve," she noted. "I'm headin' up the street. You comin' home or are you goin' to be using some of them extra clothes you got stored here?" A single eyebrow was raised and her lips pursed. Her arms folded. "I know your boyfriend got his spirit back. I know how these things proceed."

Fey chuckled. "I'll be home, Nana."

"Mm-hmm..." Savannah bent down and kissed her granddaughter on the cheek. She wished her well, and then went up the stairs.

Fey released Silver from her back. The yumbo appeared as a funnel of smoke first, and then she formed solid, flapping her wings and hovering just above Fey's shoulder. Silver's release was jarring. The yumbo's exhalation from Fey's body felt like a deep knife had been removed from her back.

"How are the others and yourself, Silver?" she asked the sprite, catching her breath as the pain trailed through her. Silver glided in front of Fey, answering that the other yumboes were fine, resting. Silver sounded tired too. "I didn't mean to bother you. I just wanted to know you all were doing fine, and I wanted to verify something." Silver hovered, anticipation on her face. A cobalt-blue light filled Fey's palms, and the ancient device she held in her hand disappeared. Spook was sent upstairs to Gordon's bedroom to keep private the conversation between Fey and Silver. Fey stated, "I know the others can't come through, can they, Silver?" Silver answered no, shaking her head. "My tattoos are scarred, but I'll be fine. I can still conjure Zee, Em, and Jade through the sketchbooks if I need assistance." Silver gave a concerned look at Fey. "I'm okay, Silver." Silver's concerned look intensified. "Really, I'm fine," Fey pleaded. Silver asked about Fey's acquired scar. Fey took a moment before answering, allowing her instinct to pry into the goings-on upstairs. Everyone was well distracted. She put her eyes on Silver and answered, "This is a necessary discomfort. It's just a small scar. Just one. It's not the lashes Gordon took." She leaned toward the yumbo and explained, "I'm experimenting, Silver. When the experiment is over, I will crawl into that chamber and wash this small, little scar away." Silver reminded her that the scar was hexed, coming from Willie's whip. "I'm counting on it," Fey confessed. "I allowed this to happen. I had to. I had to be my own sacrifice. Like Ori Washta did Thunder John. I told you about the history I saw." Silver nodded, slow but affirmative. There was noise from upstairs. Fey glanced up and waited, reaching out again with her instinct. The people upstairs were still preoccupied. She told Silver, "I can study the hex, and it can lead me to its master." Her eyes watered. "And then his master." Silver nodded, eyes sad, reacting to Fey's temperament. "I wear a scar like my mother. But I'm conscious of its potency. I have the cobalt-blue spirit in me. I'll be cautious. The scar will be an antenna for me to use, and I will use it. After that, we can put to rest the man who took away the woman who first penned you into the world." She laughed a bit and sniffed. "Penned us both…and the man who took my father from me, destroyed my family." Silver made a plea for Fey to tell someone of her experiment, an Elder or Gordon. Fey shook her head. "Telling anyone will only have them encouraging me to heal myself. They'll say it's too dangerous." Fey exhaled, and then she commanded Silver, "Now, go rest," and with a grin she added, "Before I banish you."

Silver attempted a smile, and it only showed partially. She was too concerned for Fey. Still, the yumbo swiveled into light and smoke, and then funneled back into Fey's body. The yumbo's penetration stung, and Fey clenched her teeth through the scathing irritation. She leaned back in the chair, exhaling the last of the pain. She listened to the conversations upstairs. Gordon was happy, and he argued in a playful tone as people announced being tired and leaving. His spirit was restless, and there was so much he wanted to do now that he was relieved of Willie's hexed lashes. His pleading persisted as people filtered from the house, Maximilian and Althea telling him to get to their Harlem residence in the morning for Christmas gift opening and the traditional breakfast. Gordon pleaded for his mother to stay, and that she couldn't be tired considering she was a spirit. Fey heard Althea chuckle at her son, and she began using her instinct to peep in on the scene playing out upstairs. Althea followed Maximilian out of the house, fading into the passenger seat of the vehicle he'd arrived in.

"It's three in the morning!" Gordon yelled. "You're going all the way to Harlem? Now? Stay here. Cedron, you're going too?"

"We don't do Christmas in Brooklyn, Gordon," Fey heard Maximilian answer for Cedron.

"Technically you do, Pop," Gordon retorted. "Look at the time."

"Go be with your girl downstairs," suggested Cedron.

And that was the end. A few seconds after the door closed, Gordon was rushing downstairs. "Fey! Fey-baby!" he said relieved that she hadn't vanished on him. Fey stood. Gordon rushed her, repeatedly planting kisses from her forehead to her cheeks. "Let's conjure our spirits and go to the stars, Fey-baby." His clothes dematerialized, substituted by his cosmic garb. Face masked, he pleaded with Fey, "I haven't touched the cosmic fibers in ages. You know that." He petitioned, "I'm up. My spirit's alive again. I want to—"

She put her hand over Dooley's rapid fire of words. Fey giggled and said to him, "Easy, lilac spirit. You're up, but we're all winded—even me. I need rest. A lot of people went through hell for you tonight." Her back burned as she spoke to him.

Dooley relaxed. The mask dissolved. Gordon exhaled.

"There you go," said Fey in a loving tone. "There you go." She took his hand and led him to the seat. "Sit down," she said, voice still warm and soft as one of her kisses. "Take a seat, Gordon-baby." He sat down, and Fey rested on his lap. "That too much?" she asked.

Her weight pressed against him. She curled up on him, and he felt the warmth of her body. "Absolutely not, beautiful spirit," Gordon answered. Fey leaned in and kissed Gordon. To him, the kiss was new. Fey tasted like a refreshing drink, and Gordon couldn't get enough of the brew of Fey Forrester's kiss. The hex from Willie's scars dulled his tastes for all things. Now he was whole, and Fey's lips were the fruit from the tree of life.

Fey pulled away from the wild, passionate lock to catch her breath. Gordon reached in for more, and she giggled. "I said easy, lilac spirit." Gordon replied that it was impossible. "We need to relax that brew in you. As usual," she chuckled.

"I have some ideas," said Gordon attempting another deep kiss.

Fey held him back with a single finger. "You put me back together, Mister Goodspeed," she said giving him a small kiss on the lips. "I did the same for you." Her eyes brimmed full with cobalt-blue light. Gordon's eyes were compelled to equal her glow, lilac in brilliance. "But there is still more to our story, isn't there?"

Gordon pulled Fey close. They cuddled for a moment. His spirit billowed into a storm, and like an unruly haunt, he wanted to possess Fey Forrester. He wanted to take her body, her spirit, and her mind. But he respected her fatigue, remembering what had been accomplished to cause it, and how it was all for him. They turned their gaze to the tome of *The Written*, the book now on the floor. It fluttered up into the air and flipped to the last page where their shared mythology of *In Thirteen Pieces* was scripted. Tendrils of light stretched from their eyes and began inking the conclusion of the tale. Light jumped from the pages of the book, and what was written became seen, heard, and experienced.

I walk complete

She is the flesh of the cosmos – ancient, black and deep

Armies of wulvz and devil swine patrols

Look up in fear of me
I outstretch my hand, but not to greet
But to cleanse the land of their ailment
My blessings assail them
And their oppression and bodies
Blaze into fire at my command

***Her growth frightens even the Heavens*
*But they embrace her – long lost daughter fallen to the Earth***

I carry with me the waves of the sea
I flood the city, drowning Tubal's armies
I bring clouds to the sleeping souls
The refugees of urban slavery
My disguised Mother Wisdom
Masked Father Knowledge
Their blessings have blossomed
Supreme alpha-mathe-magically
Slaves once in dream
They are free with rapid third eye movement
From slaves to warrior-shades, broken chains
Spirit and soul is stirred through them
The ghetto, from their brow, drips away
Spinning, spiral swims beneath the skin – they awake to revolution

***Ashaba-Sirene – my mythology queen, cosmic royalty*
I grip black sun spear as weapon
Lead allies, captain and shades into rebellion
Phour lights path,
*Insurrection mounted in every direction***

I walk on city streets
Tear buildings down with claps and beats
Ally Bwa rebuilds naturally, earth, leaves and trees
Cimetiere dwindles the concrete
I see Queen Malady, and she sees me
I am a distraction
As Captain Debas and Mama Gran are
United, hand-in-hand against her

But her gown, composed of rot and disease,
Poisons the air as the bell of her gown sweeps

She smothers the breeze
Shaded allies, Debas and Gran
Forced to knees
Queen Malady grins
Staring up and up and up and up
At me

***I don't breathe—I chant my name, Kibaru*
Ingest knowledge and wisdom
Allied with parents now awakened, if ever they were asleep
They surround and safeguard me from Queen Malady's disease
This doesn't suffice as an apology
Their parental abuse, the emaciated emancipated
That failed our generation, their children
The reflection of thought staggers my balance in battle

Mother Wisdom weeps,
"Stand child. Wipe my sins away from your brow.
Sweat away my words that weakened you."

Father Knowledge insists,
"These wulvz and devil swine,
Slave laws and whores dressed in disease
You're stronger than them. You are all their giants
Multiplied by ten
You stood up and fought the God in me
Muted the anger of my words that lashed you
Worked against the expectations expected to trap you
Stand up, my sun."
I am under
Standing
An equipoise between
Wisdom and knowledge
Regain traction, black sun spear in hand
I pounce back to action

Enter Governor Tubal's laws and hexes
His tricked speech that resurrected
City ash to ragged wulvz
A new army of devil swine pulled from the air
Governor Tubal mounted, he rides the terrible
Hexum NightMare

Parents and shades that do not breathe
And allies three
Wade through air wracked with disease
Wulvz and devil swine drip with our blood
*But I make them bleed***

I see my shaded army of Khem Trails
Slowed by chem trails
I speak an incant and lace my lungs with a veil
I, colossal queen of the cosmos, inhale
Put the cloud of disease at ease
And exhale blessings on release

***Free of cloud*
Allied shaded warriors take the weight
Of the fight
And I pounce
Black sun spear pierces Governor Tubal's mount
We topple to the ground

His head
Wigged and wild with blanched fire
Eyes bewitched with orange-yellow light
Mouth screaming exhaust, dark gray fog
His speech chokes me with legislation

My Mother Wisdom and Father Knowledge
Provide blessings, lessons
I align with cosmic ordinance and essence
Bypass Tubal's smoky bylaws, dubious regulations

Governor Tubal, this self-proclaimed giant,
Is not so tall – But he's calm, at peace
As his city falls and burns, crumbles to ash
Enslaved populace released
Free to rebel
Down to his last breath
Confident in the face of death
Or simply accepting of it

All he has as defense, an aegis of lies

His illusion of offense shaded into light
Color dampened
I thrust against hexed, domed buckler
Sparks and light express our stubborn vigor

But I think thoughts up to my grand queen: I don't fear defeat
Because they have already killed me
U and I, majestic butterfly – we as family
Our death cannot be again, by any degree
We repossess this physical flesh, with spiritual depth
Inhale cosmic soul
*And spit dark matter and inner-g as weaponized breath***

My dark hero and king, I see it all
Fights and brawls
Blessings and hexes
Focus centered, I enter I

I see clear inside I – I am made of thirteen
So I take all of me
And release myself to destiny
Kingdoms erect everywhere I touch and speak
Everywhere my eyes gaze, new life rises
I am the body that holds everybody
All the heavenly bodies
I juggle healthy sun and waxen moon
Rearrange the sky
Parents, maiden and water bearer – starry, mythological characters
Shepard shimmering, heavenly critters into the Manjet-boat
Stay instead of sail through 12 provinces – this barque of millions of years
With this, I as Motherland covenant,
Rescript the heavens to prophesize our oppressor's end time
Set to now
Pull cosmic-cleansing moisture from the milky galaxy
Condensed into clouds,
I let Mayet reign down

Tubal's aegis evaporates
My handsome Kibaru, fixed earth sign
Black sun spear he thrusts
I move winds to push Tubal away
Leaving spear point left uncorrupt

Male shades and fathers' knowledge turn Tubal into a story
Flesh as syllables, broken vocabulary
Hexes exposed as illusions, imaginary
He is something we will speak about
In past tense

Feminine umbra and mothers' wisdom
Take the last warden of this prison
Queen Malady
She is stripped down to a memory
Faded into a reminder, talked up as warning
So that we may never be bound to her disease, her infectious hatred
Toxic thinking
Feminine umbra and mothers' wisdom think clean
Lively and lovely, seen – from the 16 shades of the dark flesh,
To the dark matter halo of our bodies
We beam
No longer lives Queen Malady
But all hail to the original Queens

The sun is up to shine bright
And the day
And the battle
Are won

I reduce in size

***Her steps put beats in my heart*
Her feminine sway, waves of dark matter beauty
*Walking complete to me***

My handsome Kibaru,
The warrior-shade – the dark brightness
My black sun spear-wielding knight

***We become light*
Black bodies swirling together
*Masculine and feminine forever***

Up to the sky we soar
Our light resting on black sun spear's tip
Double black helix

A crossroads beneath us
In the cardinal directions its four roads extend
As we soar up to the heavens

With all nature we commune
To animal, to the souls of shades,
To all that is natural, we speak, "Balance,
And the end of our tale comes soon."

Above the blue
Where beautiful
Original
Creative dark spirits bloom
Our divine, intertwined spirits
Penetrate the moon
The snowy heavenly body
Glows
Pregnant with its siblings
It births moon two and moon three
Its white fades to black, golden halo wrapped
And there on either side – red and green

Motherland's hant beams
"My covenant restored
My moons and their colors reborn
There, red black and green
Golden halos gleam – the world in balance
Consciousness uplifted – satisfied am I
Rejoice in all its glory
Thirteen complete – here ends our story."

Ink lighted script
Cobalt-blue and lilac
Fade to – and return all to original Black
End this final act

Complete. The final scenes of Gordon Goodspeed and Fey Forrester's composition were overwhelmed by a splendid dazzle of lilac and cobalt-blue light. The brightness burst, and out of its silent and brilliant eruption, the basement's environment faded in. Gordon and Fey's eyes returned to normal. They said nothing. Only a deep kiss would suffice, and when it ended, Gordon was inspired to ask, "Are you sure you don't want to take to the stars, Fey-baby?"

Fey kept her face close to Gordon's, their noses touching. "The offer is tempting, Gordon. But I need rest."

Gordon answered, trying to hide his disappointment, "...I understand."

Fey kissed his forehead, an action that helped suppress a slight burn of anger inside her. She'd sensed Gordon's unhappiness with her decision to rest, and as subtle as the anger was, it stung. Fey could feel the anger's potential to become a violent storm with all its rain pouring down and aimed at the young man she was now straddling. The young man she professed to love. The kiss she planted on Gordon's forehead lasted long, as she waited for the emotion to pass. It muted, but its haunt remained. Fey leaned away from Gordon's face, smiling at him but thinking of Willie's scar and the hex she possessed. It would be different from Gordon's experiences, she believed. She was conscious of what was wrong, therefore, it could be controlled long enough for her to bond with the hex, and make it point the way to its masters.

Gordon ran his fingers along Fey's smooth, brown cheek. "Will you stay here?" he asked.

"No, Gordon," Fey answered in a soft voice.

Gordon protested in jest, "Aw, c'mon, Fey-Baby. Use your altar, but pop back beside me in bed."

She wanted to choke him. She'd made a decision, and here he was questioning it.

Fey kissed Gordon again, this time on the cheek.

She wanted to bite him, deep into his throat, and tighten her teeth hard around his neck. But she pulled away and instead said in a calm but stern voice, "Look, you might be up from being relieved of your hexes, Gordon-baby, but you need *real* sleep. No dreaming, little spirit. You need a black calm. No fights. No crossroads. No Brice Cadogan." She sighed, "You've been fighting since you were hexed. We went up against needlemen and Willie the Lich tonight. We barely got out of there. I had to fly from here to Harlem to help Raymond and Benny out of that jam."

Gordon considered Fey's points. He added, "You've also been through history, scrying answers out of Spook."

Fey became excited. "Lawd, did I ever. I saw some things," she told Gordon.

"I'm sure you did."

Fey again leaned close to Gordon. "I'll share all those experiences with you when the sun comes up," she promised. They kissed again, and Fey said to him, "Merry Christmas, lilac spirit." Then she faded from him.

Gordon felt empty without Fey's presence. He looked at his altar. It had been through as much as him, set up in his bedroom, and then moved back down here. Gordon didn't feel tired at all, but Fey made a good point to get rest. He jumped up from the chair and landed in front of his altar. The spirit in him was alive and excited. He pondered setting it free and journeying to the stars. But the idea of flying up and into the cosmos alone grounded him. So, instead, Gordon knelt down and performed the ritual that would quiet his spirit. It worked well, giving him only a moment's time to pop from existence and end up in his bed all the way in Harlem.

For Fey Forrester, fading away from Gordon and materializing in the dark of her Fable Avenue bedroom produced an excruciating pain. She formed solid on her bed, convulsing as her scar ripped at her. She felt as if every nerve in her body was set aflame. She gripped the comforter atop her bed, and she stiffened her body. Eyes closed and teeth clenched, Fey flexed every muscle she could in an attempt to fend off the pain. She breathed, keeping still until the pain lashing at her subsided. Her cosmic attire faded from her, leaving behind the clothes she wore earlier. The transition also came with a wave of irritation, but it passed quickly. Once the pain was gone, Fey got up off the bed. She thought about the tea she'd gotten for Gordon. Some was taken and stored downstairs days earlier. She wanted some of the tea now, but it was too late, and she was truly exhausted. She performed a resting ritual and was able to slide into bed before it took effect.

Fey wondered, before drowning in slumber, what dreams might come. She closed her eyes, and the answer came to her.

The nightmares began.

It was a surprise for Fey to see him, to be standing in his presence. She'd searched for a month to find another, but connecting to this faint memory of a man who was now standing before her was something she'd realized was her heart's greater desire. This was Lewis Banneker, her father. He was only an average-looking man, but there was a charm to him, a confidence. He wasn't tall, but he stood around five feet, nine inches in height. He was well groomed with brown skin, clean-shaven, but not boyish, and he knew how to wear a suit. It was in his swagger. It was in his stance. He was handsome through conjure. All of him was simple, but far from mundane. Fey Forrester immediately understood what her mother saw in him. This was her mother's Gordon Goodspeed. This man was her mother's lilac-eyed spirit, even if his eyes were brown. He was tall to Fey, and she didn't mind being as a little girl to him. It was the happiness of walking with her father that made him so grand.

How appropriate that the suit he wore was the color of the sky, Fey considered. His smile shined as bright as the sun, and it warmed Fey to be in the presence of such a phenomenon and the man who possessed it. The man she could call 'daddy'. She'd found him, or he found her. Either way, she wanted to tell him so much about being a part of the Fable Avenue community. She wanted to show him her spirit in all its bloom. She wanted to open her heart to him, forget his absence, and be a daughter to this man. Most of all, she wanted to tell her father about the young man she'd fallen in love with. Gordon Goodspeed. There was so much to say in revealing Gordon's name to her father. There was Gordon's spirit, the lilac brew inside him. There was also the story they'd composed together inside an ancient tome. Fey wanted to tell her father so much about *In Thirteen Pieces* and all its symbolism and how it related to her. She was complete again, from mythology to reality. She even helped restore Gordon's lilac spirit to health.

She wanted her father to be proud of her.

Fey had questions too, but she didn't want to spoil the moment, walking with her father as he guided her to a wide-open, grassy field in

North Carolina. The questions would come in time. For now, it was about father and daughter, reunited and happy.

There was a breeze. It was mild in force, but it was sharp enough to bite at Fey's bare shoulders. Lewis didn't shield his daughter from the elements with an incant. Fey didn't do the same, waiting to see what her father would do. He was kind enough to take off his suit jacket and put it around his daughter's shoulders. She was cold, and he saw that. And more so than with any other man, Fey Forrester did so want that action to come from her father. His smile and his kind gesture sufficed to keep her warm more than any incant or article of clothing.

They walked on, deeper into the field. The bell of her yellow, summer dress pushed the overgrown blades of grass away from her. Fey kept her head low as her father looked at her with a smile. She wanted to look up at him, begin a talk that would end with all her questions answered. She wanted to be angry and happy. She wanted all those emotions. But they kept walking instead.

"Okay, boy," yelled a voice behind them. "That there's far enough."

Lewis and Fey stopped, and they turned around at the same moment, spinning in the same direction to take a look at the man who'd called out to them. It was an older man with a Dutch-style beard. He wore a wide-brim straw hat, colonial wear with a two-tailed frock coat covering his heavy frame. His right hand held a curled whip, its brown color blanched and speckled with faint, red splotches.

"Right here is fine, Mister Willie?" Fey's father asked the man.

Willie proceeded toward Fey and her father. "I said that's far enough, didn't I boy?"

"Yes, Mister Willie," Lewis complied.

"Hold that jungle spirit tight, now," ordered Willie. "Don't let that wench go."

Fey looked up at her father. "Papa?" she said, voice sounding like a child.

At first, Lewis did not move, and Fey believed her father was standing in defiance of Willie's orders. But then her father's face turned something mean. Lewis Banneker yanked his jacket off his daughter's shoulders and grabbed her from behind at the arm and neck. "Put her on her knees, boy," Willie instructed, wading through the grass. Lewis kicked Fey's footing out from under her, and like a cruel, pitiless puppeteer, he guided her to the ground.

Fey protested, "*Papa!*"

Willie stood in front of Fey, grinning down at her. He said to Lewis, "Your daughter, boy, has been actin' like one of them troublemakin' 'coons that keep runnin' up into Master Fallows' gardens. She's been mighty mischievous." He said all this while shaking his head and keeping bent eyes on Fey. He looked up at Lewis and chuckled, "That's a devious spirit that heifer of yours pushed out, boy." Willie took two steps back. He clutched his whip hard. "Now strike your daughter, boy. She has disrespected Master Fallows' property."

Fey's eyes overflowed with tears and fright. She trembled. "Papa…" she said in a low voice.

Keeping one hand gripped around the back of Fey's neck, Lewis drew his other hand back, and slapped Fey. "Again, boy," Willie ordered. "You hit her so I won't have to."

Lewis slapped Fey twice more.

"Papa, please…"

Lewis hit Fey with a clenched fist. She fell against the grass, nose bleeding. *"Goddammit, girl!"* yelled Lewis, kicking his daughter in the stomach. *"Goddamn you!"* He dropped to his knees and slapped Fey's face hard. "Why the *hell* you do this to Master Fallows?" He smacked her with the back of his hand, and then he put his hands around her throat. He shook his daughter and squeezed. "You ain't been nothin' but a burden on me and your mother since you was born!" Fey didn't believe this was how her father spoke, but it was how he spoke at the moment. He squeezed harder, and she struggled, fighting to take in air. She took advantage of her father loosening his grip to slap her another time, but she almost lost consciousness as she exhaled and Lewis gripped her neck hard again. The air halted, its escape passage blocked. It was jarring to Fey, making her head throb and stuffing up her ears. She tried breathing through her nose, but that only made blood seep down into her throat. She spit it up in a cough, and it landed on her father's hand.

Willie walked closer, his foot stopping directly in front of Fey's line of vision. His image blurred, but looking up, she could see the grin on his face.

"Willie!" a voice called. It was faint to Fey as her ears were clogged with air. Everything was blurry, fading to darkness. Someone walked up beside Willie. Fey couldn't make out his face, but she knew whom it was. She knew the voice, its age locked in its mid-thirties by blessing and herbs. "Have our boy stop, Willie," directed Stanley Fallows.

Willie forced Lewis off his daughter, pushing him to the ground. "Okay, boy. That's enough."

Fey caught her breath through a succession of coughs and dry heaves. She buried her face in the dirt and crumpled grass. She tried to recall an incant or conjure. There was nothing. She wanted to call on

Gordon, have his Dooley spirit arc across the sky and fly down, swooping her away. But she wanted to do this on her own. What good would he be?

Lewis too caught his breath. He got to his knees and said, "Yessir, Mister Willie."

"Get up, boy," Willie scolded Lewis.

Lewis jumped up, repeating, "Yessir, Mister Willie." On his feet, he stood at attention waiting for another set of orders. He kept his eyes on Willie, surmising that the next set of directions would come from him. But it was Stanley Fallows that spoke. Lewis pivoted his body to give Stanley his full attention.

"Hold your daughter up, Lewis," instructed Stanley in a calm voice. Lewis stepped over to Fey. He bestrode her, reached down, and lifted her off the grass. He stood Fey up on her knees.

Fey's sight cleared. She turned a defiant gaze toward Stanley, but the balky look dissolved quickly. Stanley was gone. She looked left, eyes wild. She look right, eyes the same. Stanley was not there, and in her frantic search for him, she didn't notice the whip disappear from Willie's grip, replaced by a heated branding iron. The smoldering end appeared to be in the shape of an eight, but on closer inspection, it was two links in a chain.

"My property wears my mark," Stanley's voice came from behind Fey. "Hold her still, Lewis. Good boy."

Lewis wrestled with his daughter as she struggled to get free. He put his knee in her back, bending her backward. Fey winced. Her fight dampened, and her father held her head back, keeping the side of her neck exposed. Willie approached, aiming the burning brand. Its orange and white-yellow tip cackled with its heat. *"Daddy, please!"* cried Fey. *"Don't let him do this! Daddy!"* she shouted.

Willie pressed the brand against Fey's neck, and her flesh melted away. Smoke and the smell of burned meat leapt into the air. Fey screamed. She trembled as the initial shock dug into her body, starting at her neck and tunneling its way throughout her person. The chilly breeze blowing through the day could not exist near Fey. Heat possessed her body like a curious ghost. Willie pressed harder. An open-mouth grin was on his face.

Stanley informed Fey, "It was your father that brought you here. He smothered you, Miss Forrester, but I gave you air. And as cruel as it might seem now, I give you fire." Stanley signaled Willie, and the overseer released the brand from Fey's neck. He put the burning tip to his lips and spoke a trick. The rod cooled, and Willie tossed it aside.

Fey was turned around, her father forcing her to face the other direction. Stanley moved aside, and Fey was still unable to get a glimpse of him. "Your father holds you hostage, Fey," said Stanley. Fey tried looking at him, but there was a strange force that kept her eyes from looking up in

Stanley's direction. Her eyes were fixed to look straight ahead. Out in the field there were men, women, and children working the land. All of them were African-American. Some were dressed in rags, and others were clothed in the finest suits. "When you work my land, I give you earth," Stanley dictated.

Fey saw a man pull up a bushel of weeds. He began jumping up and down, celebrating his find. "I got enough to give Master Fallows, and I got enough to eat for myself." Another man jumped him, yelling to the excited man to give him some. They tussled in the grass, and then there was a gunshot. More people started fighting. There were more gunshots.

"You have to know my system, is all," Stanley commented. Fey watched as the land, where the workers tilled and fought, sank and filled with water. "When you bathe and drink, it is from the water I discovered." He asked Fey, "Why can't you be grateful for that?"

"We are, Mister Fallows," a familiar woman's voice spoke. "We are. My daughter is. I swear. You've given us so much." Emma Forrester pushed Lewis away from Fey. She knelt down and asked, "Fey, you don't cause trouble for Mister Fallows, hear. No trouble." She hugged her daughter. Fey started crying. This wasn't how her mother spoke, but it was how she spoke at the moment. "Don't cry, little girl. Don't cry." Fey's tears wet her mother's shoulder. Her comforting voice was what she remembered about her mother. Emma looked up at Lewis as he recovered from her push. Fey heard her mother say to her, "Your father is no goddamned good." Fey hid her eyes. She tried to smother the sound of her mother's scathing words. "You hear me, you bastard?" Emma scolded Lewis. "You no goddamned good!"

Lewis staggered. He spat back with words just as salty, and they started arguing. Their words after a while were so loud to Fey that they were unintelligible, save the cursing and baseless accusations. The biting scar from Willie's whip, and the scalding brand seething her skin, were small pricks compared to the sound of hate and cursing tossed back and forth between her parents. It was screaming. It was terrifying and loud and threatening. They were going to kill one another, Lewis and Emma, screaming, shaking fist and finger at one another. Fey's heart beat as the sound increased, as the cursing became viler. Her heart beat to where she believed it would burst.

A soft voice then came, appearing through the argument like a cool breeze. It muted her parents' angry exchange. "I made the yelling stop once before, Fey," said Stanley. "I can make the yelling stop now." Fey's mother disappeared. Stanley was holding her now. Her tears dripped on his shoulder, and his body became her comfort and balance. She wanted to lift her head and face him, eyes locked. But she felt so safe. "Just be grateful,"

Stanley told her. "Say, 'thank you.' That's all. We have so much in common." Stanley kissed her on the neck, a tender gesture that pressed on the brand she'd received. The heat scratched at her, and then cooled.

"Thank you," Fey exhaled.

The screaming ceased.

Stanley was no longer holding her, and she almost fell forward. Fey spied Stanley out of the corner of her eye. She tried to look at him, but she was unable to. The field was empty. No one existed except them. Stanley remarked, "Everything that I have torn apart, I can put back together." And then he was gone too. Fey closed her eyes, dropping onto her hands, and then collapsing onto the grassy field.

Fey's eyes opened. She was in bed, in her room at her grandmother's residence in Mount Vernon. The day was just beginning, but the winter sun had not yet risen. She was still. She heard her grandmother starting a bath. The muted sound of lapping water behind the closed, bathroom door entered her room from the hallway. Fey used the sound to relax herself, and it worked. Her back hummed with irritation, but it was beginning to subside. She was out of the dream, but the emotions were still on her. No bath or shower blessed with incant or soothing salts would be able to wash it away. The dream's grip loosened, but it would haunt her until it wanted to show itself again when next she slept. The dream would come at random, and as it stood, this was the sixth time Fey's cursed dream occurred since falling asleep early Christmas morning. It was the end of January, and though there were variations on the setting, the dream always played out the same. And Fey never became accustomed to the effects. But it was something she had to endure. Her nightmare wasn't just a series of happenings induced by a hexed scar. Fable Avenue's rogue gallery was there, Fey deduced. Willie the Lich and Stanley Fallows' essences were there in her dream. Fey only had to take control of the setting. Fey believed she had to make the dream lucid and make her instinct tap into their hidden location in the physical.

That's all she had to do, she believed. It was a task Gordon wasn't up for when battling Brice in his dreaming. But Gordon was too focused on his fight within the dreamscape setting, Fey pondered as she peered through the darkness, looking up at the ceiling. The fight distracted him. Fey's father distracted her. Regardless of the many incants and prayers she recited before journeying into the nightmare's realm, there was always a distraction.

Fey tried and failed to connect with her scar's potent hex. When sleep lulled her to dream, there was her father. He was perfect, if only at first. He was all the knowledge she ever wanted to know. Even now, awake, Fey concentrated on the parts of her dream where her father, Lewis

Banneker, would first appear. It was so perfect. Father and daughter. The emotion of it all had crawled out of her dream and followed her into the real world. But she refused to cry, feeling the sense of tears building in her eyes. She couldn't help but think of the dream before it turned into a nightmare. Her father walked by her side. The thought relaxed the pain emanating from the scar on her back, but it also helped flare it up if she dwelled on it too long. Even the daydream turned into a nightmare.

Fey was relieved that today would be an easy day at school. She had two art classes scheduled, and she would continue painting her works in either class in peace. Though the themes in her art classes varied, Fey was able to draw inspiration from *In Thirteen Pieces* for both her assignments. It put her at ease, especially when she was painting in Professor Jacquelyn Brede's classroom. Professor Brede was not only supportive of Fey's work, watching her paint with an admiring eye and smile, but she also engaged her after class to talk about painting. Fey said it was part of a series, a story that she and a close friend had been composing. Fey was happy around Professor Brede. Her scar cooled in the professor's presence, and the burden of Fable Avenue's culture, having been heavy on her as of late, dissipated. It was easier to concentrate on her art, and on those within the artistic community whom she found more supportive. Professor Brede was such a person. All she had to do was draw and paint. There were no cultural expectations for her to live up to or rules of responsibility to abide by. She was such a wonderful lady, inviting Fey to all the showcases and galleries New York had to offer. Gordon wasn't fond of it, as it took her away from him…and the community, as he professed.

But Professor Brede never disappointed, and there was never a burden placed on Fey to be anything but herself. Fey still couldn't believe there was a moment of hesitation to sign up for Professor Brede's Technique of Art class. It was all due to Fey's long held belief. Fey had already taken a course with her. She didn't like having the same teacher twice. It didn't feel as if she'd progressed, a feeling based on an experience in the third grade when her teacher fell ill in the middle of the year and another took his place. This new teacher received a job as a fourth grade teacher, and she requested Fey to be in her class. Fey had really liked Mrs. Depasquale, but having her for both the third and fourth grade made it seem like one, long school year, regardless of summer vacation.

But Fey went against her philosophy and took another class with Professor Brede, and she hadn't regretted the decision. It did feel different too, as the class had a different focus, and her talks with Professor Brede resumed after being stifled a bit with all of Fable Avenue's goings-on. There was no responsibility of another to consider. There were no politics of a community. There was just her. Fey believed she deserved that. It even calmed the desire to find and confront Stanley Fallows. Albeit, mildly.

The dream's impression dampened, and when the effect was at its most dull, Fey rose from bed. She didn't turn on the lights. Instead, she got up and walked to her altar, still feeling a needling tingle on her back. Fey opened her sketchbook and spoke an incant that conjured all four of her yumboes from the page. Their glowing bodies and wings provided light. Fey asked for her conjured sprites to make her some of the Haitian tea stored in the cabinet downstairs, and the pint-sized, winged creatures dashed away about their task. Then Fey turned on the lights. Her clothes had been prepared the night before, but her carrying bag needed packing. It wasn't long before Silver and the other yumboes returned, and to Fey's surprise, carrying her cup of tea.

"You guys!" she blurted. "I would've come downstairs for this." She took the tea from them. "Thank you," she said. She blew over the heated beverage, and then she took a careful sip. The sting on her back dulled, the herbal drink's anesthetic taking effect. She thanked her yumboes again. She sat on her bed, drank, and thought about the day.

Savannah Forrester emerged from the bathroom, bathed and partially primped. "I'm not done, little woman," she told Fey. "But you can jump in."

"Okay, Nana," Fey replied. "Will you need the car today?"

"I have a few errands to run," her grandmother said back to her. "I'll drive you as far as I can into the city and get you to a train."

"Thanks, Nana."

"You sure you don't want to pop your spirit there, or fly across the sky?" Savannah teased her granddaughter. "It's supposed to be a cloudy day. Ain't nobody will see you above the clouds."

"There's an incant that can keep our spirits unseen, Nana. But, no, I won't be engaging in all that spirit walking."

Savannah stepped into Fey's doorway wearing her bathrobe. She leaned against the opening and folded her arms. "You still feel overwhelmed, little woman?"

Fey drank before she answered, but she nodded her head to affirm. "Yes, Nana," she sighed while not looking at her grandmother. "I'm letting the winter pass. When spring comes, I'll walk back into the community and be a part of all their politics again."

"I understand," Savannah assured.

"Thank you, Nana."

"Does Gordon?"

Fey didn't answer immediately. She drank, and then she said while still looking forward at her altar, "He says 'yes,' but in a voice that says, 'no'." A soft smile flared as she imagined the scenarios expressed in her following statement. "He, Benny, and Neyeli have been haunting blocks from Brooklyn to Harlem," Fey chuckled and rolled her eyes. "I can only imagine." Then she thought about the tasks of haunting the grittier neighborhoods and personalities the city had to offer. "Or maybe I shouldn't imagine," she added.

"Okay, then," said Savannah, turning away and not inquiring further.

Fey placed her tea on the dresser, and then moved to the bathroom for her shower. She washed, dried, and brushed her teeth in twenty minutes time. Returning to her room, Fey prepared her skin with lotions and perfumes. She combed twists into her hair, and packed up to begin her day. Fey went into the city with her grandmother to be dropped off at the 4-Train in Harlem. It was still going to be a long ride to school, but once there she settled into her classroom and dived into her artistic work. The world fell away. The calm feeling expanded when she attended her class with Professor Brede.

Fey was at peace, absorbed in her work. The scar on her back only hummed its irritating twinge in a low vibration. But even the dampened effects of her dream washed away as she sat in front of her easel and brushed a new reality onto canvas. Sunrise colors invaded a blue sky, assisted by thirteen, black clouds stretching in a grotesque manner and appearing to have human shapes. Seated in a wheelchair below the sky was a hooded woman, her head looking skyward and her arms stretched up to the heavens. The theme Professor Brede gave to her class was 'imprisonment'. Fey knew how she would express the concept. When she first started, she had to explain to Professor Brede the smog monsters held aspects of the woman below, they had captured her essence and left her crippled. She coupled her idea with the various techniques of brushwork Professor Brede bestowed on the students. The professor was impressed with Fey's work to say the least.

It snowed outside, and the sight viewed from Fey's peripheral added to the calm. Professor Brede spoke in a soft voice as she drifted around the room, reminding the students of techniques and concepts, and to blend the two together in a cohesive expression. She paused in her steps, standing still behind Fey, observing. Fey didn't mind. She hid a smile, waiting for Professor Brede to give a compliment that would keep her warm for the rest of the snowy day.

"Excellent work, Miss Forrester," whispered Professor Brede into Fey's ear. "I would like a talk with you after class."

Fey made a slight, affirmative nod so as not to look too anxious or alert the other students in the class. She made a quick glance at the clock.

There was a long way to go before the end of the three-hour session. Indulging in her painting passed the time well enough.

Alone in the classroom, Fey's conversation with Professor Brede was brief. It was accompanied with more praises for her work, but also a proposal. "I want you to come to our house in Long Island. James and I live in Baiting Hollow, and we hold a winter showcase around Valentine's Day." Professor Brede peered over Fey's shoulder, looking at the painting. She rubbed her fingers across the emeralds inset in the silver collar strapped around her neck. The painting animated behind Fey, and Professor Brede watched as the elongated, gray clouds formed into solid giants on the ground. They marched in the background, approaching the hooded, wheelchair-bound woman. With another stroke on the emeralds, the painting reverted back to its original composition. "It would be the Saturday after Valentine's Day, the fifteenth."

Fey glowed with the proposal.

"Professor Brede, I'm flattered."

"Then that's a 'yes'?"

Fey remained silent. Her eyes fell to the floor, looking about with her mouth agape. She lifted her gaze and answered, "Yes, Professor Brede. That is indeed a 'yes'." She hugged her. "Thank you."

Professor Brede reminded, words sounding like a lesson, "It's your gift, dear, not I." Backing away from the embrace, Professor Brede asked, "A friend of yours helped you with this, correct? Or am I getting the story wrong?"

"Well," Fey started, "a friend and I composed a story which this is inspired from."

Professor Brede's face lit up with a smile. "Tell your friend to come as well," she suggested.

"I think he'll like that," Fey said, pondering if Gordon would approve. Then she changed her answer, telling her professor, "No, he *will* like that. We haven't seen one another in some time. He'll be delighted."

After an exchange of smiles and hugs, the conversation ended, and Fey left the classroom. Professor Brede's flourish of compliments kept Fey warm against the weather outside just as she predicted. No incant was needed. Her scar buzzed only a little, and her haunting nightmare was not even a fog on her conscience. Now it was time to go home and drink tea and be safe inside from the cold. She considered calling Gordon, telling him to 'pop' by. He could use a break from Fable Avenue too, she believed.

"Fey!" Gordon's voice called her.

It was so out of the blue, and with timing too perfect, that Fey believed she'd imagined the call of her name attached to Gordon's voice. She spun around, witnessing the last strides Gordon made up to her.

"Gordon," Fey expressed, eyes wide and happy to see her lilac-eyed spirit. They exchanged a polite kiss, the kind given to one another by friends. Gordon reached for more, a subtle move, but Fey stepped away. Gordon retracted, making nothing of it. "I was…just thinking about you. Would you like to join me? I'm heading back to Mount Vernon."

He watched her for a while, paying close attention to her growing afro made up with twists. She looked beautiful to him. She had on a woolly headband and a decorative pashmina wrapped around her neck and tucked under her jacket. He found it cute that a reddish color, brought on by the cold, flared up through her dark skin. The effect was most visible at her nose and cheeks. He missed her, and he wanted this small moment to never end. "How's about going to Fable Avenue, Fey-baby?" he inquired, taking a chance. "Benny's here with a car. Neyeli's with him. They're in class now, but they'll be out in an hour-and-a-half. We can wait somewhere inside. Go to the coffee shop up the street."

Fey struggled to keep her smile stationed. "I can't do Fable Avenue right now, Gordon. You know that. I'm still trying to…exhale a lot of what went on. What we went through…"

Gordon nodded. He said with a little force in his voice, "Yes, *'we'*. That's the whole point of community. We go through this together. We don't go at it alone."

Her scar burned. Her expression fended off the announcement of sudden, rising anger. She stiffened her jaw to suppress the urge to strike Gordon. She dropped her head for a moment, hiding her wrestling emotions. She looked up and exhaled, "I appreciate that, Gordon…" She stopped. He was observing her, scanning her person up and down, trying to figure her out. *Don't. Ever. Marry no damn codebreaker. You hear me?* the memory of her mother's voice came to her. She conjured her instinct, and it wrapped around her, keeping Gordon's prying intuition from giving her thoughts an audit. "Don't you dare," she called him out.

Gordon looked directly at her with his mouth agape. Guilt and concern alternated in his eyes. "I'm sorry, Fey-baby," he apologized. "I just want to know you're okay. We're from Fable Avenue," he stated. "We confront and engage, often physically, what most of these folk out here aren't aware is fighting them on all fronts every day."

"I'm okay, Gordon," Fey assured, strangling the last of her rising anger so as not to cause a scene. "I was saying to my Nana this morning, I'll walk back onto Fable Avenue when I feel ready."

"Okay…" said Gordon. What little and careful fight he had in his voice backed off. "If you get overwhelmed, however, there's my chamber for you to rest in. There're the Elders. We got people on the block."

Fey, again, contended with another swell of anger brewing inside her. She forced it down, but she was still irritated. "I don't need help, Gordon," she pushed. "I just need respect for the decisions I make, for me, independent of a culture. I'm not broken, I'm not scarred, and I don't need rescuing. I'm fine. I just need a little time for myself. Fable Avenue's culture can be very warm—yes, I get it. But it can also be smothering, and constantly on edge on what will happen next."

Gordon rolled his eyes. He'd had enough. "I didn't say you needed anything, I said *'if,'*" he noted. *"If,"* he emphasized. He jabbed a finger in Fey's direction, and with a stern voice said to her, "You know what? I don't care what you say, I *know* something's wrong. I don't need an instinct to see that."

Fey responded in a calm manner, "You can have your opinion, Gordon, but I'm fine."

Gordon huffed, "When you stop lying, you know where I'll be." He walked past her in a hurry, and Fey let him go.

She would go to Professor Brede's house by herself.

Benny listened. He did not move as Gordon ranted. It had been like this for the past two weeks. Today was worse. It was Valentine's Day. Gordon had a lot to say about Fey Forrester. A stranger with an ear on Gordon's tirade would either be able to immediately deduce that he loved the woman his scathing words were directed toward, or a war was brewing and coming to a head for his arch nemesis.

Gordon paced, yelling on about Fey's behavior and seclusion from the Fable Avenue community. When he would come around to this point, he would always add, *"And me!"* so as not to appear unaware of the fact. While sitting comfortably, Benny watched Gordon pace back and forth, left and right. He was as professional as a psychiatrist listening to a patient. And Gordon needed the therapy, he considered. Benny did so wish he'd had a license to practice psychiatry. He would've struck it rich from the long sessions of catharsis Gordon had been taking him through.

Gordon went silent. Finding a moment of pause in Gordon's philippic soliloquy, Benny raised a counterpoint, "It wasn't easy on her, man." It was a set of words he started using as a cue to wind down their sessions in Gordon's basement. "You guys tussled too."

Gordon stopped pacing, taking in Benny's words. He made a face and replied, "Nah, sun, she said she understood. That wasn't me. It was the hex." Gordon aimed a finger and a stern gaze at Benny. "But she brings that up every-so-often." Benny believed Gordon would begin pacing and ranting all over again. But he stayed still. "And now she says that she don't wanna hear all that. She said she's tired of me blaming my actions on Willie's hex. She says when it comes down to it that it was she and I in that situation. Willie was nowhere to be found." Gordon spread his arms out and yelled, "But, c'mon, sun. Technically, *I* wasn't there. I was in a dream, throwin' dogs with the Englishman."

"She don't see it like that, man," Benny said, shaking his head.

Gordon disagreed. "No," he told Benny. "Something ain't right. I know that."

"So do I," Benny remarked. His voice sounded like a confession, and Gordon's instinct caught the slight tone of admission. He reached out and tugged with his instinct, pulling more from Benny's vocal intimation.

But it wasn't about Fey. Something was on Benny's mind, or rather his shoulders.

Gordon wiped his chin. He turned around, walked to his chamber, and then leaned against it, facing Benny. He put his hands in his pockets and said, "For a long time, kid, I've sensed something on your mind—and I mean before all this too." He removed one hand from his pocket to tap on his head. "I just got a better instinct now for these things. We've talked. You've said things, but you ain't give me nothing to be cool with. And I was never cool with the way you've brushed it off for later." He made a face, returning his hand to his pocket. "Now, things transpired, things happened. What you've needed to say was put off." Then he put his hands together. "But please, I need closure from someone—some kind of explanation. Everybody's trying to hide they shit at a time when that's dangerous."

"What makes you so entitled?" The question was presented with a half-joking tone.

"Me?" blurted Gordon. "Nothing, sun. Not a lilac spirit. Not a ritual. Nothing." He pointed his hand up at the stairs and said, "But we got a villain out there able to turn your emotions against you with one crack of his whip." He smacked his hands together. "And that ain't even the dude we got to worry about. That's just a soldier." He stepped away from the chamber. "Your girl's conjure works off emotions. Imagine she feel something from you and the Lich takes advantage of that. We supposed to be better than them fools walkin' around out there, the people we tryin' to help, because *we're* conscious of the world's tricks to keep them where they at. But we can't talk about what's on our mind?" Gordon slapped his chest. "As rough as I might've been when I was hexed with Willie's scars, I expressed mine. All I ask is that someone reciprocate. Please."

Gordon had a point, Benny thought. But where could he start?

He waited for Gordon to relax, and that took some time. It helped that the span of time was in silence. Benny decided where he would begin. It was a sad story, but something made him laugh as if it was nothing. His laughter subsided as he explained, "I was a little kid, man. Y'know? I was having the time of my life. I'm spendin' time with my pops in Jamaica. It's a culture of conjure folk there. It's music, y'know. It's incants and conjures. I love my world, my island. I live there, I jaunt here. I get the same thing." Benny was excited, smile lighting up his face as he recalled his youth living between Jamaica and Harlem. He was everywhere with his words, but Gordon didn't stop him, or interject to guide Benny to a point. He let it flow. "Then one day I take candy from a stranger." He sat back, lifting his shoulders. "I'm ten. I don't know the politics of my island. I don't know about the violence, the gangs. I mean, you hear about things, but they're not in your world directly. They're stories from a radio or television box, nothing more."

"This about Sword Sinner Simon?" asked Gordon, not meaning to be rude with his interruption.

"It looked like a birthday gift, y'know," was how Benny answered. "It was a box. It was wrapped. One of his soldiers—he got a nice suit so as a ten-year-old boy, I trust him—he tells me to take it into the café. Someone needs it. I go in, and there's this well-suited brother, right. I mean, he looks more fly than the dude who gave me the gift. He's sitting across from this guy dressed in army fatigues." Gordon heard the story before, but he allowed Benny to tell it as if it was the first time. "I'm ten, but I know dude ain't a real army guy. But he look dangerous. When I walked in, I didn't even notice them at their table, scarce as the business in the place was at the time. I'm holding this wrapped box just standing there. Sword Sinner raises his hand and calls me over. I walk the box to him, he grabs it from me. He looks excited, talking to the guy in fatigues. Says he has a gift for y'boy in fatigues. I'm stupid. I'm standing there wanting to see what it is." Benny snickered and shook his head. "But you know what?" he asked rhetorically. "Sword Sinner doesn't even dismiss me. No thought to being a reasonable drug lord—or potential big boss. He opens the box—it looked wrapped, but it's just for show, he lifts the lid off—pulls out a piece and fires twice into fatigue-boy's face. Guy falls back in his chair. Sword Sinner stands and puts three more in this guy's chest. I see the whole thing."

"Yeah…" Gordon mumbled.

"It's stayed with me, but I can't always really recall it visually," Benny said, making a face to try and make sense of his words. "But it's there, and it's been there. Sometimes it's vivid. Total recall, right. But when I explain it to someone out loud, I can't really see it, like, I feel as if I can't really express it. But when I'm alone, it's there."

Gordon chose his words carefully when he asked, "You think an Elder could remedy that? The chamber behind me…?"

Benny waved his hand. "Nah, man. That's fine. It is what it is."

"C'mon, I'm tired of that defeatist bullshit," cursed Gordon. "We a culture of conjurors and incantors," he reminded. "To say, *'it is what it is'* doesn't make a dog shit worth of sense, sun. It can be anything we want it to be with a conjure or an incant."

Benny lifted his hands. "Relax, I'm just saying I can do without," he fired back. "Seriously. Besides, that's just the back story of it all." Gordon became attentive again. "Sword Sinner dropped five-hundred dollars into my ten-year-old hands. He walked away the new big boss. Old competition extinguished. Fatigues-boy was the old big boss named Oil. Sword Sinner worked Oil's soldiers against him. He promised them a bigger cut. And when Oil was put down, I gotta say, Sword Sinner was more giving. Hell, he gave to me. You better believe, five hundred dollars wiped away the trauma of seein' a man gunned down. I was ten, and he had me looking every which way for that quick grab. For two years I'm an errand boy. Fable Avenue was cool, Harlem and other borough factions. But back in Jamaica I was running small items to people. Never knew what was in the boxes. Never stayed around for anything but a slice of cash. It was never as big as the one I first received. Twenty-dollahs here. Hun'ed dollahs every-so-often there. But to an eleven and twelve year old? I'm making millions, sun. I'm keeping small gangs up on bus routes so they can rob 'em. They stay away from my pop's taxi business. Bunk a protective blessing. Their word was my assurance my dad or his cabs wouldn't get jacked."

"I gotchu."

"Then we moved here, for good to be with my moms."

"They know? Your pops at least?"

Benny shook his head. "He raised an eyebrow once, on my fourteenth birthday. I had extra cash from my ceremony. They were tucking things away into my own account. I always kept the cash I earned, rarely spent it. I told my pops I did some knuckleheaded shit back on the island, which is true. But I never went into detail. He didn't question what I'd done. It was the past as far as he was concerned. It hurt though. I could see it in his face."

"How much you have?"

"I gave him one thousand, but I still got two thousand that I slip little by little into my account so there's no suspicion. I was a kid. I didn't hustle every day, and I wasn't always on the island." Benny turned away from Gordon, eyes wide. He started trembling. His eyes started to tear up. "But that ain't it, Gordon." Benny looked possessed. Gordon reached out with his instinct and scanned Benny's body, searching for haunts and hexes. But there was only an emotion. Only guilt made him tremble. His tears collected with such intensity in his eyes that Gordon believed they were a shining light. Benny inhaled, swallowing the emotion that shook him. The teary light remained in his eyes. "I loved that rush, I won't lie. As violent as it came when I was a little boy. Getting money dropped into my lap, it was like a blessing shot into my veins, man." A few tears snaked down Benny's cheek. "I was like, thirteen, fourteen, comin' up with schemes. Sometimes, not even to pull off, just to think and plot." He sniffed, wiped his face and laughed a bit. "I had a plot to build a train, a line from Jamaica to Harlem, importin' that blessed and incanted weed them Jamaican conjurors be messin' with. I *started* to get up on that, but I said no, let me go on. That was our culture, y'know. I didn't want to pimp our shit out like that. The Elders already do that with handin' out them blessings." Both he and Gordon chuckled a bit, but it was a small pause in the confession. "I stayed away from it all." The tears regained their luminescence in Benny's eyes. "Then there was this one day, the urge for a scheme just got to me." The trembling started again. "Lamar Rogers comes up to me, says he needs a piece for protection. He tells me, Tauheed Greer got him marked over dumb shit. Lamar's a good dude, he played ball with your brother. At first I argue, stay low. He gon' graduate soon. But he scared." Benny looked at the floor. His new set of illuminated tears hung but never dripped. "I could've introduced him to the culture—I should have. But it was around Cedron's second rites. Everybody was on alert. Elders were being cautious." He faced Gordon. "So I found him someone that could get him a piece. I took a cut of the sale."

Gordon recognized the names. He put it all together, putting events in line with a string branded with Benny's name.

Benny dropped his head into his hands. He cried, letting his tears run. He screamed into his hands, words muffled but still possessing a horrifying might, "Ray *told* Cedron not to get involved. *I* told Cedron that Lamar could handle himself. But he had to go play star superhero like it was some damn regional-title game. Shots were fired. That idiot Lamar didn't hit Tauheed, but he got…" He pulled his face away from his hands. "Y'know sometimes I look at Cedron, and I think that's what you get for trying to help these regular folk fools. But most of the time, I just understand that I have to dedicate the rest of my life to his orders for arming the dude that put him in that wheelchair." He leaned back in his chair, sniffing away his tears, face molded in anger. "I don't get a rush pullin' schemes with your brother," Benny said with venom in his words. "It's a helluva thing how a debt can dull a high."

Gordon leaned against his chamber, thinking about Benny's confession. He tried using his instinct to feel an influence of Stanley Fallows in the situation presented to him. But the haunt was absent. There was nothing to blame but ghetto politics, regardless of how much influence the Fallows haunt and lineage had on it all.

"No offense. I'm just using you for practice, Gordon. I want to tell Cedron," offered Benny. "No Elders. No rituals to ease my guilt. No chamber," Benny listed. "A straight confession to the person who needs to hear it. I don't care how he reacts," he concluded.

Gordon didn't think it was such a good idea, but he said, "Okay…" He reached out with his instinct, shooting it into the sky and to his family's residence in Harlem. Cedron was home alone, smoking a cigar and watching the partly cloudy day from the window. "Let's give it some time. No need to 'pop' right there. Let's take your ride."

Benny fixed himself, sniffing and wiping away tears. He stood. "Come on," he said. He walked to the stairs and Gordon followed.

Gordon asked up to Benny as they climbed the stairs, "You think we should bring Neyeli? She could use her conjure to dampen the mood, make sure it don't get out of hand."

"I need to say what I say the way I say it," said Benny. "Your brother need to react the way he need to react."

"Yeah, well, I wasn't confident in my suggestion," Gordon noted.

They put on their coats and left the house. Gordon locked the doors, and he walked with Benny to the car. Benny unlocked the car doors with a remote, and then he and Gordon jumped inside. He started the car and pulled onto the road, driving up the street. Dajon's protective construct, the dragon Nyami, lifted its head from over the building and growled. Not much in the way of conversation transpired as Benny and Gordon made the trip uptown. Every so often, Gordon would ask Benny how he felt, and Benny would answer, "Just am." And that was all. Gordon hoped, with every stop they made at a red light, Benny would give his approach to his confession some thought, and then change his mind. It didn't happen.

It wasn't so much they pulled into Harlem, as it seemed that Harlem pulled up to them. Time and space appeared to fold, and the neighborhood was suddenly just there. There was nothing magical about it, as it was only Gordon's point-of-view. If anything, he wished he could hold back time and space and delay this meeting. But here they were, parking at the curb just outside his family's Harlem residence. He again asked Benny how he felt, and again Benny answered, "Just am."

They got out of the car and walked up to the front door. It wasn't locked, which Gordon found strange. Turning the knob and opening the door, Gordon felt a familiar, cold feeling surround him. It wasn't the wind, and it wasn't the regular chill of the winter day. It was something preternatural.

Door opened, they walked inside. The lights were off, but the setting sun provided enough shimmer through the front window. Cedron was in the front room. He was hunched over, contemplating, hands locked together. Gordon shut the door, and Benny walked in front of him.

"Pop home?" Gordon asked Cedron. There was no answer. Gordon reached out with his instinct and felt the absence of their father. He was probably at work, manning the cab depot with Benny's father.

But Benny didn't allow for the silence to become awkward. He said to Cedron, "I got something to tell you, man." His voice didn't crack, but he was nervous.

Cedron looked at Benny, eyes focused on the young Jamaican. "Whatchu gotta tell me?" he sneered. Gordon again felt the familiar, cold presence. It whisked up his spine, tingling his instinct on the back of his neck. "Huh, Jah?" barked Cedron. He put his hands on the arms of his wheelchair and pushed. *"What-the-fuck you got to tell me that I don't already know?"*

Gordon and Benny flinched. They stepped back, balancing their stance and bracing from the surprise.

Cedron stood up.

His six feet-eight inch, Herculean frame never appeared as tall as it was now. With all the time that had passed with Cedron injured and wheelchair bound, Gordon and Benny had forgotten how big the all-star sportsman could be when on his feet. Their heads tilted back to view the black titan. Noticeable was his physical change. His flesh turned pitch, and along his skin ran a gold design, looking like wild circuitry, angling through African veve symbols. Gordon stared at the mighty figure his brother became, the sentiment in his eyes shifting from admiration to dread.

Benny's gray, cloudy feathers appeared under his arms, but Cedron knocked him aside before he could conjure a breeze and take flight. The golden circuitry-like tattoo covering Cedron's body rippled with purple-colored spirit that converged on his arm. It jumped free and grappled Benny as Cedron hit him. Benny's body smacked against the wall, knocked unconscious. Cedron's spirit crackled around his frame and then dissipated.

Gordon conjured his cosmic suit. His spherical, lilac eye blazed, and he turned his head, shooting away from Cedron's strike at him. Dooley formed solid out of the lilac streak. He was crouched on the stairs. He eyed his brother, focusing on Cedron's head. "I'm not gonna hurt you, but I'm gonna put you down, big brother," Dooley snarled. His body became a beam of light, wrapped up into his spherical eye, and catapulted at Cedron's head.

The circuitry on Cedron's frame lit up. He reached out an arm and caught Dooley's beam, and Dooley's physical shape molded in Cedron's large grip. Cedron squeezed his brother's neck. He turned to the front room's window, holding Dooley out. Cedron cocked back his arm, and drove his fist forward. His circuitry writhed with spirit that collected at his fist, contributing to the strength of Cedron's already mighty punch. Dooley soared away, crashing through the front room window, passing over the sidewalk, and tumbling into the street.

Dooley wobbled, attempting to get to his feet. The world swayed and blurred, and he was unaware of several cars that ghosted through his unseen form. Cedron's strike wasn't just heavy and filled with a powerful spirit. It was framed like an argument. Cedron's voice possessed Dooley's head. It echoed. His brother screamed and yelled. They were his big brother's fears, his circumstances, and his regrets. They were vocalized, shouted at Dooley like an apoplectic confession. All of it focused in the spirit of one punch. And as Dooley looked up and spied his brother's black, colossal figure move into view at the broken window, the blurry world sharpening into focus, he knew Cedron had more to say.

Cedron's tattoo coursed with spirit as he leapt out of the window. Dooley attempted to shoot away, but Cedron caught his beam by the tail. Dooley came into shape out of the trail of light, his left leg held by Cedron.

Dooley was pulled back. He looked up. Cedron's fist was there, knocking him into the pavement. There again came Cedron's voice, echoing, hollering his life's contempt. Physically he didn't say a word. His bludgeoning strikes spoke for him. With another punch against Dooley, Cedron's telepathic rant rattled the lilac spirit's senses. Over and over, Cedron tossed furious flurries into his younger brother, and the stormy confessional continued shouting in Dooley's mind. It was too much to fight against, and so Dooley considered not fighting. His spirit kept his face from blistering, breaking or bleeding from the strikes. The pain was unbearable, but Dooley powered through it. He allowed his brother the moment, the catharsis. Dooley shut his eye, but he still saw a vision. He was in a dark room where only a single, hanging bulb provided illumination. He was strapped to a chair. Across from him sat Cedron in a wheelchair, screaming all the emotion that was inside him. Dooley listened. He felt his brother's words. Every painful syllable was a strike against his jaw or cheek. The left side of his face took a hit. The right side of his face took a hit.

The ferocious scene played out in the middle of the street, but Dooley and his brother were unseen to 'regular folk' eyes. Dark clouds moved in unexpectedly. They brought with them antagonistic winds and heavy snow. Nature's sudden change expressed the fracas between the rival siblings. Purple tears streaked down Cedron's face as his aggression increased. Dooley listened and felt his brother's physical-verbal assault. He listened. Cedron hit him, and the punches screamed! Dooley listened, and listened, and listened, being the audience his brother needed. But then came from Cedron a weary sigh.

It was out of him, and Dooley discovered a moment to give his retort.

He blazed into his lilac vitality, focused his strength and dived forward, a comet of spirit. He slammed into his brother, his essence coursing through Cedron like a jolt of lightning. The unexpected, heavy winds whirled, shattering windows at the Brickhouse residence and through the neighborhood. Street lamps sparked and burst.

Dooley's lilac-ignited spirit passed through Cedron, and there came a scene. It was the past. It was twenty minutes before he and Benny decided to take the trip into Harlem. It took place at the Goodspeed's Harlem residence. The doorbell rang, and Cedron rolled into the front room to answer it. On the other side was an Eastern European woman familiar to Dooley. She had raven-colored hair that draped in lengthy, bouncing curls that framed a dark-eyed, round face. She was tall, but under six feet in height. Around her neck was a silver neck collar decorated with smooth and round, gray flat stones speckled with red splotches. This was Lucretia Tolvaj-Fallows, wife of Stanley Fallows. And she was here, paying Cedron a visit. She looked as youthful as the day Dooley's unseen spirit visited the Peters' residence on Fable Avenue in 1958. A needleman stood next to her, at the side of the door and out of view.

Opening the door, Cedron looked the woman up and down. She wore a full-length, brown winter coat with gray and black animal fur lining the cuffs, bottom, and neck. On her arm dangled a purse.

"Can I help you, miss?" asked Cedron, his voice unconsciously gruff.

Lucretia inquired in a polite tone and smile, *"Cedron Goodspeed?"*

"Yeah," Cedron answered. *"Can I help you, miss?"* he repeated, voice now consciously gruff.

Lucretia knelt down and put her hand on Cedron's right leg. Cedron made a face just as Lucretia rubbed the stones inset in her silver neck collar. Cedron choked on a trick. *"You're such a strong man, Cedron. You remind me of an African man I once knew long, long, long ago."* The needleman came into view. Cedron's eyes looked up at him, but nothing else moved on Dooley's brother, not as long as Lucretia had her hand on his leg. *"I whisked away his strength with a kiss and a trick,"* Lucretia bragged, all smiles, eyes closed. Opening her eyes, she told Cedron, *"I ate his potency, Cedron, and to the deceptive gods I swear, I was not ready to take him into me. He was my first,"* she admitted. *"I kept his conjure inside me. It was like a bull, though I named his memory Buck. And I played with it and pet it as it ran through me. I couldn't keep it, but I could save it."* She took her hand away. Dooley felt his brother anxious to move, but he remained still as Lucretia opened her purse and removed two gray and red speckled stones. They were larger than the ones inset in her collar, roughly the size of an egg, but still flat. She laid them on Cedron's left and right leg. *"He was so potent, Cedron, it took two stones,"* she commented. She looked proud of herself, her wide smile on display. But there was also sadness in her eyes. *"I always wondered who I would give his strength to. I've taken from so many conjure men and conjure women and sold their stolen magic to the highest bidding impotent man or woman to use. But I've always kept my Buck's treasures close to me."*

Lucretia gazed longingly at Cedron as the crippled titan trembled in his chair. She tapped on the stones in a rhythm recalling a song from her culture she'd learned as a young girl. She rubbed Cedron's face as it perspired.

"I can feel *your strength, Cedron Goodspeed,"* she said. *"You hide it so well under all that anger. Let it out, and embrace my Buck. Take him into you."* The needleman's eyes looked restless. But Lucretia took her time. *"My husband, who I also blessed with the power of his best friend—a conjure boy from your Fable Avenue community—he can see things now. My husband can connect reality's web. And he knows why you're in this chair, Cedron. His strikes against your community didn't do it. This disability came from* within *your community. Your own people crippled you."* She rose and whispered into Cedron's ear the events that led to his disability. Benny's confession dripped from between her lips. Her words turned into pictures inside Cedron's head. He saw it all, and he screamed, sounding like an erupting volcano. Lucretia stood, unfazed by the thunderous sound escaping Cedron's mouth. *"There's my Buck,"* she said with a loving smile. *"Stand tall, my beautiful, black Buck."* The needleman jabbed his syringe into Cedron's arm. But he didn't expel anything into Cedron. He extracted blood and spirit. Cedron continued screaming. *"I still need something from you, Buck number two,"* said Lucretia with an apologetic tone.

Nature's holler ceased as Dooley was brought out of the memory. He rolled on the ground, lilac spirit evaporated from his person. He recovered and looked in Cedron's direction. His brother, still with pitch flesh and circuitry-like tattoo, lay in the middle of the street, unconscious. Their fight over, neither he nor his brother were cloaked from the world. The day was darkening as the sun cast its remaining rays of light over the winter horizon. Dooley stepped to his brother in haste. Cars came up the street in either direction. Dooley grabbed his brother and popped away, ending up inside his house, kneeling next to Benny's still unconscious body.

Dooley could hear commotion coming from people exiting their houses or emerging from hiding. The cars traveling up the street stopped, and their passengers ejected, looking around at the damage 'nature' had done. Dooley reached out with his instinct and replayed the scene of his and Cedron's fight into the minds of his father and Benny's parents. Benny's mother was already outside on the steps of her Harlem brownstone. She ran up to the Goodspeed residence and opened the door.

"Gordon!" she called. *"By my conjure!* Benny!"

"He's fine, Missus Brickhouse," Dooley assured. "He's fine. Just let me get him to my chamber. Both of them," he emphasized. "Please keep watch on the house. Mister Brickhouse and my father said they're on the way."

"Dajon is watching the house with his friend Melinda," Missus Brickhouse stated. "I'll stay here."

"Thank you," said Dooley. He took Benny and disappeared, popping back into his basement in Brooklyn. "Spook," he called to the ancient device. "I need the chamber opened." He lifted Benny into his arms and stood. The chamber's lid slid open. "He needs healing, okay?" Spook's black mirror displayed an ancient script that simply translated into, *'Okay.'* Dooley put his friend inside the open chamber and stepped away as it closed. His physical essence dwindled away, and he reemerged back at his family's Harlem residence. Benny's mother was on the phone, most likely with Mister Brickhouse. "Benny will be fine," Dooley assured. He knelt down, put his hand over his brother's chest and then popped away, back into the basement of his Fable Avenue address.

Benny was already coming to, the chamber having expelled him in an upright position. He didn't fall from the capsule. He walked free, but with a wobble. He put his hand on his head, rubbing it. He felt refreshed, rested, but there was still a slight weariness to him.

"You feel okay?" asked Dooley.

"Yeah," Benny answered. "I'm good."

"You in balance?" continued Dooley's questioning.

"I'm good," Benny repeated.

"Help me get Cedron into the chamber."

The chamber returned to its horizontal position. The lid floated above it, rising until it hit the ceiling. Benny scanned Cedron's body, its physical change. "Jesus Christ, this all really happened."

"Yeah, it did. C'mon, help me."

Benny bent down and scooped up Cedron's legs. Dooley lifted his brother's body from the other end. Cedron's weight was heavy with conjure, even for Dooley's otherworldly might. Benny used his conjure to lighten the load. Moving the titan's mass became easier, but was still arduous. Cedron's frame was clearly too large for the chamber. But Dooley insisted, "Put him on top." And he and Benny did so. They plopped the enormous Cedron onto the open capsule where his limbs dangled over the sides of the chamber.

It took a moment, but then it happened. The chamber let out a growl and stretched its shape. It widened like the jaws of a voracious animal. The expanding capsule swallowed Cedron, and its lid, also expanded, closed down on top of him. The chamber's familiar rumbling occurred. The cosmic, African mask dissolved from Dooley's face. Gordon blinked his eyes. He stood still, waiting with Benny as the chamber rumbled. The capsule turned upright, and as it positioned itself vertically, its lid moved aside. Cedron collapsed onto the floor with a thunderous thud. His flesh returned to normal, and he was devoid of tattoos.

Cedron wore a suit with no tie. He sat in a chair that was situated in the doorway connecting the dining room and the front room of the garden floor. The dining room was at his back as he stared into the front room. The lights were off in either room, but the day's brightness found its way into the house and cast everything in a silhouette, even the smoke Cedron exhaled as he puffed away on a cigar. His legs were crossed in a figure-four, and his focused stare held in its grip the wheelchair that had been his home for the last five years. Memories faint with image but loud in sound mixed together as he stared and smoked. He could hear the day he'd been shot. The commotion, the yelling, and the gun going off were audible to him. There were also sirens blaring from ambulance vans and police cars. The sounds of that day mixed in with the sounds of yesterday. His fight in Harlem blended with a seductive voice that spoke with an accent. But he mostly heard the commotion, the yelling, the sound of hard punches against flesh and bone that summoned Nature's wrath. The winds of incant and conjure bent trees, shattered windows, and knocked down nearby people.

The news reported the weather's unpredicted phenomenon. This was the second time in recent history that Cedron's shenanigans made the news. The hooplah at the Wolverhampton Hotel was the first. His orchestrated deeds at the *Harlem Area Museum of Jazz and New York Sound* were not reported. Of course, it was in his culture's nemesis' best interest that the robbery stay out of the news.

Cedron continued puffing on his cigar, listening to the sounds of his memories as their volume decreased, and watching the stillness of his wheelchair. He could walk again through a strong focus of his conjured spirit. But he did not move, comfortable in his chair at the moment. There would be plenty of time to walk and run.

Althea Goodspeed's spectral presence appeared behind him, accompanied by a short, whooshing breeze. Cedron extinguished his cigar with an incant, exhaling the last bulge of smoke. Althea glided next to him. "My mother doesn't possess a conjure," she stated. "Both she and my father are a little clunky with incants and such. But my mother has an instinct in her, a foreknowledge of sorts, and my father can sure work a root ritual. He uses that gift to this day to assist my mother with her instinct." She focused, making her ghostly characteristic solid, and put her hands on her son's shoulders. "When Gordon was born, my mother had an instinct, a perception about you and your brother." Althea did her best imitation of her mother when she recited, "*'They gonna oppose one another like the Lion and the Water Bearer,'* she'd say. I thought it was so strange, because, even as a boy, you took to your little brother so well." She thought for a moment, and then she added, "Of course, I have to credit your father with some of that."

Cedron smiled, and in a quiet, but upbeat tone remarked, "The whole time you was carryin' Gordon, Pop kept tellin' me that I was a man now. I had a little brother coming. I was supposed to protect him, teach him." Then his expression dropped. "But he didn't stay a little baby, did he. He grew up, got a personality." He chuckled, and so did Althea.

"I remember your first big fight," she said. "You were ten or so. Gordon was five."

"Yeah, around there," Cedron interjected, remembering the correct ages were eleven and six, but deciding not to correct his mother.

"Either way, the two of you wrecked my Grand Supper decorations," she said with a soft scolding in her voice. "And all I could think of when it was over—and I was putting things back together—was my mother's foreknowledge about you and your brother. She always just said things, but you didn't know what she was talking about until the event occurred." A self-congratulatory smile brightened Althea's countenance as she recalled, "I had an instinct of my own. I went to Jersey to visit Mister Dyack, the figurine maker. I gave him locks of your hair and Gordon's hair, and his wife did a reading on them. She saw you and your brother's spirits, and Mister Dyack made figurines expressing them. Yours was brawny, tall, pitch and had all types of symbols over it, and a gold line connecting the symbols, running all along the body. Gordon's figurine was a ghostly image, like a djinn spirit."

Cedron smirked at his mother's cleverness. And he also rolled his eyes as it all came to him.

"I paid extra money for Mister Dyack to finish the figurines in time for Christmas. And he just made it. That Christmas, I surprised you with those toy figures," she continued. "But I put your figurine inside Gordon's treasure basket."

"And you gave me his," said Cedron, smiling wider and shaking his head. He told his mother, "We still fought." Then he corrected, "We *still* fight."

"But you *appreciate* and *respect* one another," she insisted.

"Ah, that would've happened anyway, Ma. That's my brother." But then he reflected on the totem and figurine he always looked to for strength. "I got bulkier, y'know. But that totem always made me think I could still glide as if I had no weight. I was air. That's how I always got through the defense in a game. I was that spirit."

Althea declared in a soft, motherly tone, "And I know Gordon has drawn strength from what he believes is his totem. And by doing that, I rest in peace knowing the two of you draw upon one another to get through difficult times. We're a family. And within our Fable Avenue culture, that means something."

"You don't have to worry, Ma. I'll always love my little brother, even when I knock him through a window."

"A window you will pay for, Mister Cedron Goodspeed," Althea said, summoning her motherly authority. "You've made enough through tributes and some of your *other* activities with your misfits. You got the money. Our house and the Brickhouse residence," she noted.

"Aw, Mom. Seriously?"

"Absolutely, young man," Althea hollered, smacking the back of Cedron's head.

"Hey! C'mon," Cedron pleaded. "I wasn't even in my right mind. I had a hex on me, a trick. A white woman's too. You know what you told us about white women! Besides someone can just snap a finger and fix it with an incant."

"Excuse me? Taxes for your behavior, young man!"

Cedron relaxed. "Fine…" he groaned. The two of them smiled. There was silence for a moment, and the room became darker as the day started fading. "Mom," Cedron called. "Did grandma ever have foresight into your…passing?"

Althea nodded her head, "She did, actually." Then Althea expressed in a sarcastic, dramatic voice, "She said I would be dancing in heaven among the stars." Then she waved the premonition away. She admitted to Cedron, "I took that as a sign that I was going to be on Broadway." She rolled her eyes, smile still intact.

Cedron laughed. He covered his mouth and said, "I'm sorry, Ma. I can't believe I'm laughing at that."

"My spirit is here, Cedron. There's nothing wrong celebrating life and spirit."

"Yeah…"

Althea hesitated before asking, "How's it feel? All of this?"

"Using my legs takes a lot out of me," Cedron informed. "I keep them in the change so I can move them. That circuit of spirit on me, it's not complete when I just keep my legs in the change. So, I keep it up to my chest in the change, where normal folk can't see." He pounded his chest. "I'm a newborn, Ma, and I'm learning my limits and pushing them as much and as quick as I can."

"My big boy, always the athlete," proclaimed Althea.

She concentrated, substantiating her form. Althea kissed her son on his forehead. She patted his shoulders. "I'm going to check on Gordon at Lady Arachne's. You okay?" she asked.

"I'm fine, Ma."

"Good."

Althea faded. Cedron flipped his cigar back into position and used an incant to relight its end. He went back to smoking. Audio from the conversation between him and his mother played in his head. He looked at his wheelchair, smiled, and exhaled a bulge of cigar smoke.

Althea appeared on the garden level of Lady Arachne's house. Her husband and Papa Solomon sat at the long table in the room, waiting. She glided to her husband and said, "I've been talking to Cedron."

"How's he doing?"

"He's fine," Althea answered. She turned her head and looked at the closed door to Lady Arachne's reading sanctuary. "Gordon's inside?"

"Yeah," said Maximilian to his wife. "Been in there for a while now. At least that's what it feels like."

"It's been five minutes, Max," said Papa Solomon, trying to calm Maximilian. He told Althea, "Madame Jeliya and Maman Anansi are in there too. There was some fuss between my wife and Lady Arachne, but that seems to have passed."

In the reading room, all three matriarchs were staring at the cards that had been pulled from the shuffled deck. Lying on the table in front of Gordon were The World and The Judgment cards laid over one another. Laying over them horizontally was The Death card. Positioned below that configuration, the Two of Cups. The image on the card was of an African couple standing opposite one another, touching chalices. From Gordon's perspective, this card was upside down, in the reversed position. Over the Two of Cups was The Devil.

Lady Arachne studied the layout, eyes moving back and forth as if reading text. Maman Anansi looked a little impatient, but she kept her frustration from her voice when she asked, "What can you decipher, Lena?"

Lady Arachne turned to the head matriarch, beamed a polite smile, and nodded her head. "Both questions have been answered, Maman Anansi," she announced. She focused her attention on Gordon and told him, "Where is Miss Forrester right now, Gordon? She's in danger."

The revelation made Gordon flinch. His eyes swelled with concern. But he answered in a calm voice, "She's in Long Island. A professor of hers is showing off her work at a gallery held on their estate. Benny's coming to pick me up so we can go support her. Neyeli's' coming too," he added. "It's kind of a surprise. Well, it'll be a surprise for me to be there. She invited Neyeli, but not me. Even considering what happened in Harlem yesterday, I'm going to be there."

"You all be careful," Lady Arachne warned. "And you all come back here. I'll dial Miss Forrester's grandmother and tell her to come here as well."

"Lena, what's wrong?" asked Maman Anansi.

Lady Arachne put a finger on the spread containing the Two of Cups and The Devil cards. She didn't answer Maman Anansi's question. Instead, she asked Gordon, "How is your relationship with Miss Forrester?"

"Rocky," Gordon admitted, hurt as he spoke the words. "She's been overwhelmed by recent events."

"I'm sure it's been hard on her," said Madame Jeliya.

Lady Arachne pulled another card, laying it across the Two of Cups and The Devil. It was The Tower card. Her motion to flip the card onto the table was brought on by instinct. "There is something not right. Something's blocking my intuition. A feat I know only one man could do." She then revealed, looking at Gordon, "Your dear Fey's father."

Gordon spoke slowly. He asked, "Lady Arachne, is Fey in trouble?"

The matriarch didn't answer. Her instinct again moved her to flip over two more cards, creating a separate spread. She drew the Six of Cups. A happy scene where a boy and girl planted flowers in six chalices existed on its face. But placed over the card was the Ten of Swords, a gruesome sketch of a man lying on his back with ten swords piercing him. Gordon glanced at the cards. Lady Arachne looked at the door, mouth agape and eyes ballooned with fright. Gordon and the other matriarchs looked at the table as Lady Arachne put down the two cards. One hand clasped over her mouth, and the other went to her stomach. Her eyes watered as a vision tunneled into her extrasensory sight. Moving her hand from her stomach, Lady Arachne banged a fist on the table, bursting into tears. Madame Jeliya and Maman Anansi surrounded and consoled her, but she didn't calm.

"Lady Arachne!" Gordon called. "Is Fey in danger? What do you see?"

"Lena," Maman Anansi implored. "Lena, what do you see, honey?"

Muffled screams slammed against the palm of her hand that rested over her mouth. She pounded the table more and more, and then a heavy roar shook the room. Instinct guided Gordon. His cosmic suit and mask appeared, and immediately, his instinct leapt out of his swirling, spherical, lilac eye. It passed through the walls of Lady Arachne's house and landed on the street outside. The rumbling and roar was there too, and only Fable Avenue appeared effected. Regular folk walking up and down the other streets were unaware of the violent quake. But through his instinct's sight, Dooley saw the epicenter of the deafening holler. The massive blessing, expressed as a dragon named Nyami, cried up to the heavens.

Dooley drew his sight and instinct back to Lady Arachne's reading sanctuary. The roar and rumble continued, but Lady Arachne's hysteria seemed to be subsiding. She was still not talking, and all three matriarchs were trying to maintain balance. Dooley heard his parents and Papa Solomon calling to them from the next room. Althea appeared in the room. Her spectral makeup was unfazed by the shake and rattle of the house. Dooley blinked away, appearing in the middle of the street, peering up the road at the construct as the last of its explosive, earth-moving roar faded.

Then Dooley noticed the protective blessing's enormous construct dwindling away. He reached out with his instinct to speak with the conjured element before it evaporated in the cold, winter wind. Dooley's instinct bore into the construct like a fishing line tossed into deep waters. It wasn't long before Dooley pulled an image connected with the dragon. It was its reason for hollering and fading away, and the vision drove itself into Dooley's head with the force of a runaway train. He too wanted to scream like the dragon and Lady Arachne before him. But he didn't move. He just stared at the vision now in his head. A vision connected to a scene miles and miles away.

Twelve-year-old Dajon Brickhouse had been shot.

Dooley's instinct returned to Lady Arachne's sanctuary. The matriarchs were recovering from the otherworldly quake only witnessed by the people of Fable Avenue. Althea Goodspeed's spirit unlocked the door and allowed her husband and Papa Solomon entrance. Dooley's instinct focused, in a clockwise motion, closing in on the last two cards pulled by Lady Arachne. The vision faded into Dajon's body on the sidewalk, two bullets in him, and blood coming from his mouth. His friend Melinda was screaming, kneeling down over him. People were running away. Anyone of them could've been the perpetrators fleeing the scene.

Again Dooley's instinct focused, clockwise, over Dajon's body. It moved closer to the boy's forehead. An engraving of light appeared. There were the initials *S.F.* The light making up the words became brighter and brighter, flooding Dooley's vision. Then the scene washed away. All that existed was what was in front of Dooley. Nyami and her protective aegis were gone.

To Dooley, despite the people swarming from their houses, Fable Avenue appeared quiet and still.

Fey Forrester felt honored to be at the Brede Estate in Baiting Hollow, Long Island. The snow made the area beautiful, with lush piles of soft, white fluff that made it appear as if the clouds had nestled among the common folk below. A long stretch of road led into a plowed, circular driveway where The Bredes' Spanish-style country house stood at the bend. Fey looked on wide eyed, swallowing the magnificent scene in front of her as the cab pulled around. There was a castle quality to the light-yellow manor, but there was also a humble demeanor about its presence. It was grand, but not flashy. Fey considered the house to be an exact fit for the eccentric qualities of Professor Brede and her husband. And as Fey was being honest with herself, as the cab driver curved around to the front of the house, she didn't believe the Bredes could afford a place such as this. There was also something familiar about the setting. Like the faint haunt of a dream.

Professor Jacquelyn Brede stepped out of her house wearing a long, sleeveless, bright-yellow gown. She trotted up the walkway and greeted Fey as she stepped out of the cab. "Ah, Miss Forrester," she beamed. "I am so excited you have arrived. Your work is already hanging in the gallery."

Professor Brede's revelation of Fey's work already on display warmed her and soothed the irritation on her back. "I'm honored to be here, Professor Brede," she said exiting the cab. "But you must be freezing." All Professor Brede had around her was that companionable neck collar with the shiny emeralds.

"I am only out here for a short while, Miss Forrester," Professor Brede insisted. "It is nothing of the much." She grabbed Fey's arm as Fey moved back into the cab to pay the driver. "Nonsense, my student," she told Fey, moving her aside. "Back away, now." She had several bills in her hand. "Close this door," Professor Brede said to Fey as she walked around to the driver's side. Fey closed the door, smile on her face as she watched Professor Brede pay the driver. She thanked him, and then the cab sped away. Rushing by Fey, she grabbed the young woman's arm and brought her into the house.

The inside resonated the same appeal as the manor's façade, fancy but not pretentious. The entrance opened to a wide, marble-tiled hallway, with a winding staircase on the left. A well-crafted wooden bench with a high back lay at the right. Next to it was a large closet where all the coats for the current season hung behind two large, wooden doors. At the end of the hall was an archway, leading into a small nook decorated with tall, potted plants. Through the short nook was the kitchen, and Fey spied a glass door with a view of the beach far in the distance. Professor Brede led Fey to the closet, where she took her coat and winter apparel, and her purse.

"Everything will be safe here, Miss Forrester," assured Professor Brede as she hung Fey's belongings in the wide closet. She closed the doors and proceeded through the nook. Fey followed. The kitchen was large and bright, with an island countertop sculpted from the same marble as the hallway floor. On either side of the large kitchen were even larger rooms. None of them appeared to be decorated with art, which Fey was quick to observe. Like the other areas of the house, these rooms, from where Fey could see, were large and beautiful, and decorated as either living rooms or family rooms. But she did find it strange that the walls were bare of art for a house owned by a woman who taught, on a college level, the techniques and history of the subject.

"Downstairs is where the gallery is being held, Miss Forrester," Professor Brede informed.

"Shall we go?" Fey said, not caring if she sounded too eager.

"Not yet, dear," the professor replied. She moved Fey's attention to the large, sliding, glass door with the picturesque view. "There's so much to see before you're smothered by the likes of other pretentious professors and connoisseurs of art. Take time to relax. See this outside view."

Fey turned and perceived the wonderful, exterior visual. It started as a glance made only to politely entertain Professor Brede's suggestion. But Fey was drawn into it. Her eyes consumed the scene of the white winter day, the rough sands of the beach peeking through, and the waves moving in and out like a relaxing breath. There again murmured the faint familiarity of it all. Fey stepped to the door, and Professor Brede followed her.

"I would love to paint this scene, Professor Brede," Fey told her teacher. "There's a tug to it, a spirit that would be a great challenge to invoke on canvas." Fey's eyes concentrated on a spot that was bare of snow, and where snaked a paved path through the element. "May I go outside?" she asked Professor Brede.

"I encourage it, Miss Forrester. You may find inspiration."

Fey was ready to call on an incant to keep her warm, but she considered against it. She would only be a few minutes, and Professor

Brede made it known that an entrance to the basement could be reached through the back of the house. The glass door slid open, unlocked and moved by Professor Brede. Fey stepped out onto the deck. The elevated platform snaked around the back of the house. To Fey's right, the wooden path turned into a set of stairs going up to a third, wider level. It was empty at the moment, save for a large grill covered from the elements. However, Fey deduced chairs and a table were placed outside during the spring and summer seasons. On Fey's left was a path leading to a lower level, and it was this path Fey walked. Professor Brede was close behind.

Hand on the rail, Fey kept her gaze on the scene, glancing every-so-often at the stairs to keep balance. The next level beyond the stairs was only a small wooden landing, and there came another set of stairs leading down to the snow-capped lawn. Fey continued forward, stepping onto the paved path that snaked to the particular spot she was drawn to. Maybe it was the view she wanted to see from that spot, Fey didn't know. But she was compelled to walk there, and she did. Professor Brede stayed close behind.

Fey didn't suffer too much from the day's chill, and there was something very comforting about the cold. She stopped over the spot that drew her interest. Professor Brede stepped to her side. Fey looked out at the water, shaking her head. *What was it about this spot,* she asked herself. The view was no better here, she believed. In fact, without the elevated height provided from the kitchen view, the awe of the sight dampened. And it was getting cold now. Fey took a step forward, and that's when she heard a familiar voice behind her.

"Okay, now," yelled the voice. "That there's far enough."

The burn of her hexed scar flared up, and it teamed with a sharp chill that trailed her spine. Fey twirled around. When she faced the opposite direction it still felt as if the world continued spinning. There walking up to her and Professor Brede was an older man sporting a Dutch-style beard. He wore a wide-brim straw hat, winter colonial wear with a two-tailed frock coat covering his heavy frame. His right hand held a curled whip, its brown color blanched and speckled with faint, red splotches.

"Right there is fine, little girl," the man said.

Fey's eyes fixed on the man, but her thoughts ran wild. The first thing she asked herself was if she was dreaming. Her second question was if Willie the Lich was in front of her, or was she caught off guard by an illusion brought on by the anxiety of her work being on display and the hex-infected scar on her back.

The man called out, "Miss Fallows, I don't mean to be out of place with giving you an order, now. But I need you to get a good hold on that jungle spirit real tight-like. Don't let that jungle wench go."

"Absolutely, Willie," Fey heard Professor Brede speak. Her accent remained, but there was a change in the tone of her voice. There was youth seasoning the sound. Fey moved her eyes, spying a distinct, physical change in the woman's appearance. Professor Brede's façade shifted. Fey was not familiar with this new woman remolded from Professor Brede. Her height changed several inches, growing a little under six feet. Her skin turned an olive tone, and her straight, white hair draped into wavy, curls, that framed her dark-eyed, round face. This new woman's hair color bloomed with a raven's black hue, shedding its once aged color. Lucretia apologized to Fey with her eyes, but her grin announced a different sentiment.

She rubbed the gems on her bejeweled collar with one finger. Fey noticed the precious gems in this woman's choker were no longer emeralds. They were now flat, gray stones speckled with red splotches. The woman touched the stunned Fey Forrester gently on the back, right in the area where she'd received her scar. Fey screamed. She dropped to her knees, believing fire burst from the ground below her, consuming her. Lucretia took her finger away. Fey scraped her fingernails against the stone pathway, tightening her muscles in an attempt to deflect the fiery torment scratching at her. The pain took its time to subside, and before it dampened, Fey felt the sting and crack of Willie's whip around her neck. He walked in back of her, tugging hard on his whip, forcing Fey's head up. Fey tried loosening the whip wound around her neck. Her fingers struggled to create a distance between the weapon and her throat as it smothered her by way of Willie's hard tug.

"I've been waiting to hurt you since I saw you," Willie stated with a grin. "When I'm through with you, you won't know the difference between love and pain. And you'll be begging me for more of it." He pulled on his whip tighter, forcing Fey's body to bend backward. "I'll have you sell out your family and your lover just for a taste of my violence." He pulled tighter. "You won't know worth unless I'm beating you, girl. You'll seek my validation even if I spit on you."

"Ease up, there, Willie," said another man. Fey moved her eyes in the voice's direction. It was Professor Brede's husband, James Brede. He was walking up the pathway with a glass of wine in his hand and a needleman, equipped with syringe, following him. He wore a sky blue suit with a white-collar shirt and black tie. On his right was Brice Cadogan, healthy and armed with his piece of armor clasped to his forearm. Fey wasn't surprised when James' appearance changed with a simple flick of the black curl dangling at his forehead. She watched the reveal, eyes angled on the loss of Professor James Brede. His skin's olive tone melted away, and his locks curled and drained of their blackness into a strawberry-blonde color. His face changed into someone with whom she was thoroughly familiar. Stanley Fallows. "Ease up, now," he continued to scold Willie, even though it was in a polite tone. "We get it. She gets it, and she won't be any harm."

Willie flicked his wrist, apologizing with a bow toward Stanley. His whip loosened, and the weapon unwound from Fey's neck. He jiggled his wrist again, and the thick, leather instrument wound up like a snake in his hands. But the overseer couldn't quite help himself. He stepped over to Fey and kicked her in the back, forcing her to the paved pathway.

"Willie!" Stanley spat. He finished his wine and handed it to Brice. He walked up to Fey's slumped body and stared down at her. Curiosity lived in his eyes, and for a moment, he did not move. Then he knelt down and helped Fey to her knees, offering his apology for Willie's behavior. And then as quick as he was gentle, Stanley became firm with Fey in his grasp. He gripped her chin, and moved her face from side to side, examining her skin. He squeezed her jaw until Fey opened her mouth. He moved closer, looking inside Fey's mouth, down her throat. He reached inside with his free hand, feeling around her tongue and teeth. He removed his hand and wiped it on his pants. Stanley turned her head from side to side again. He widened each of her eyes with his thumb and pointer finger, one at a time, and he looked close, putting his eye near to hers. The stretch of her eyelids pained Fey, but Stanley didn't seem to care.

"What makes you so special, Miss Forrester?" he asked her, backing away. "I just can't see you," he continued. "I can see the many paths and streams of time, I can see all its probabilities, and I know which ones people will follow, but not you, Miss Forrester." He expressed with charm, "Things get all fuzzy with you." He admitted, "Even with Gordon and his lilac spirit, I can get a little sense of what he's going to do next. And Fable Avenue, they got their tricks to keep me in the dark every-now-and-then. I don't mind that, because I have my tricks to keep their eyes elsewhere. But your beauty's walk is always fuzzy," he repeated. He slapped both his hands against her cheeks, and he squeezed his hands together. "That's why I watch you so closely when I catch a dream of you. And I've been having so many dreams of you as of late. Maybe we're just dreaming of each other."

Fey's arms extended in either direction, feeling pulled as if clamped in chains. She moved her eyes to the left and right. There was nothing visible holding her arms, but she could feel the ruggedness of rusted chains tugging at her. The back of her shirt tore open, and the cool, winter air chilled her. Fey's bra unstrapped, and her bare back and lashed tattoos were exposed.

Stanley kissed Fey's forehead with tenderness and sincerity. "I had an uncle—a close friend to my mother, really. To be honest, a little bit of him makes up Willie there. Anyway, no matter how brutal of a man he was to someone, he always showed them a specific detail of respect. I'm going to show you that same level and detail of respect, Miss Forrester. I'm going to put you through the last moments of your mother's life," Stanley announced. "We're going to whip a hex into you like we did her. And then the sins of the mother will be committed by you, her lovely daughter." He looked deeper into Fey's eyes. "You don't remember being here thirteen years ago, watching your mother get whipped next to your father's lifeless body." He snickered, "You can thank me for that memory loss. But let me remind you that you screamed and screamed as Willie whipped your mother. It was so entertaining to watch her shout curses at myself, my wife, Willie and a few other associates. Willie kept hitting her with his whip, and her voice slurred and she went from cursing us to cursing your father's limp body unable to help her. But I showed mercy on you then, little girl. I took your memory from you, and I let your mother go and finish herself off. Papa Solomon took those memories from you—that brutal aftermath." He examined Fey again, but only with his eyes, a hint of worry in them. He scanned her entire body as if reading a book. "I can't see you, Miss Forrester, but you're wounded now, so, all of your intentions are dripping off you. They're an easy read." Stanley lifted his eyebrows. He looked at Fey and said to her, "I'm impressed. You risked a lot, but I'd say too much, to get to me. Like two people destined for love, though, we were looking for each other and didn't even know it. How wonderful your instinct was to walk out here to the very spot where I buried your father and tortured your mother." Fey started to scream at Stanley, but he covered her mouth and kissed the back of his hand as if it was her lips. He pulled away. "Shhh," he said in a calm manner. "Quiet."

Fey swallowed her voice. Nothing but muffled sounds came from her. She shook, trying to escape her invisible chains and lunge at Stanley. He stood, ignoring her wild movements, attempts to free herself, and attack him. Willie stepped up behind her, but Stanley motioned for him to stand down. He signaled the needleman, and the night doctor plunged his syringe into Fey's arm and took spirit and blood. "You jungle conjurors have a grand conjure and wish to make," stated Stanley. "So, do I. I too have a grand conjure and wish to bring about." A cobalt-blue light, along with Fey's blood, filled the syringe's vial. "But I don't think my grand wish is too grand, Miss Forrester. I only want to preserve the world, this physical space. Does that sound bad to you? Does that sound like something evil?" The needlepoint continued drinking Fey's blood and spirit. "Much as your father's gift tells me, you and Gordon's djinn-demon spirits have to *destroy* the world. Ain't that a revelation, Miss Forrester? Now you ask me, between your jungle culture's grand wish and mine, which sounds evil and which sounds benevolent?"

The vial was filled, and the needleman stepped back into position behind Stanley. Fey's feral movements tamed, spirit siphoned from her. She considered for a brief moment conjuring Silver for aid, but then thought against putting her tiny, winged companion in danger.

Stanley nodded at Willie, and the overseer opened his grip on the wound up whip in his hand. He gripped the handle, but let the thick lash fall against the snowless, paved path. Stanley dismissed Brice and the needleman inside. "Are you fine here?" he asked his wife.

"Yes," responded Lucretia, keeping her eyes on Fey. "I'll be in shortly, Stanley, as soon as I help Miss Forrester recover her memory a bit."

"Of course," said Stanley. "It's getting cold to me. My trick is wearing off a bit. Don't be long." He kissed his wife on the cheek. He backed away, telling Willie, "Scar her, Willie, but don't take too much time. There are things to do."

"Yes, Master Fallows."

To Fey, Stanley commented, "Poet T.S. Elliot tells us, in his poem *The Waste Land*, that April is the cruelest month. And while I believe that sentiment to be true, I would also contend that there is nothing colder than February. Wouldn't you agree, Miss Forrester?" There was a beat, and then Stanley said, "And now it's time for me to show you fear in a handful of dust. I hope I lived up to your expectations. And thank you for that lovely work of art. Your monsters will be put to good use." Then he walked away, up the path with Brice and the needleman, and back into the house. Lucretia took a position in front of Fey. She signaled Willie to begin, and he raised his whip and smacked Fey hard on the back with a ferocious lash.

Willie inhaled the rush of his violence, which begat more violence.

"I like you," Dajon confessed to her, and it made her smile. She'd never quite heard it said like that, with so much sincerity, and as if there were no strings attached. His words weren't just a stated fact, but an assurance that she knew how he really felt about her. She was happy. Neyeli Kimball held his young hand in hers as they trotted up the sidewalk in the Harlem neighborhood. The charming twelve-year old boy smiled up at her. He asked, *"Well, you like me too?"* It was forceful, but cute.

"Of course I like you, Dajon," Neyeli said to him. *"That's why we hang out."*

"Okay, then. You gotta call me 'baby'," Dajon instructed.

"Excuse me?"

"You gotta say it after my name," he told her. Then he clarified, "Dajon-baby. *That's how we do in my family."*

"Is that how you do?"

"Yeah," spoke the twelve-year-old boy, trying to put gruff in his voice to sound like a man.

"Okay," Neyeli giggled. *"Dajon-baby,"* she teased.

"Right, right," Dajon encouraged. *"And I call you,* Melinda-baby," he said up to Neyeli.

"Yes," Neyeli told him.

They continued on, wading through oncoming pedestrian traffic. Neyeli kept her eyes on the crowd. At the corner, two teenage boys approached them. They wore baggy clothes, but that had little to do with the cold. Both had baseball caps, one had short braids coming from his hat. Neyeli looked at their faces. Their features were blank. No eyes. No nose. No mouth.

The one with braids stepped to Dajon. *"You a wanted little boy,"* he growled.

Dajon looked up at him, no fear in the twelve-year-old's eyes. *"Keep moving, Sean, or this 'little boy' will embarrass you again."*

Neyeli couldn't help but chuckle. It wasn't just a reflex. It was a reenactment. The blank-faced Sean turned to her and said, *"I'll smack that giggle on the pavement, bitch!"*

Neyeli gasped. Fear shivered her person, and the scene around her froze like a video on pause. Her hair blanched a pale white. She exhaled panic's chord, having lived the emotion through vicarious ways, but then she relaxed. Her lips didn't move, but her voice resonated as if coming from the sky.

Melinda, I know you're scared, said Neyeli's voice. *But I need you to come out of this. I'm here. I need you to remember their faces, sweetie. We don't have to relive the shooting. Remember, Dajon's okay. I just need you to give me a description, honey. Come on, now. Let me look at these young men, and you tell me what I should see. What did you see?*

Neyeli turned her head and looked at both young men. Their features appeared. It was slow. Their faces at first went from blank to fuzzy. Then their attributes came into focus. Neyeli described them aloud, but it wasn't in her voice. And she also gave the two older teenagers a name.

"Sean Commons," she identified the teenager with the braids. *"Cole Andrews,"* she identified the second. Her hair turned a dull blue, and tears came to her. *"It was Sean that shot Dajon."*

It's okay, Neyeli's voice came from above. *Dajon is okay, little girl. You're safe too. We're right here, waiting in the hospital.*

In a blink, Neyeli was sitting on a couch in the waiting room of a Harlem branch trauma center. Her arm was around young Melinda Clarke. The girl was weeping after having described and named the two boys that attacked Dajon. The flashes of the gun, the violent force of the first bullet that knocked Dajon to the street, and the second shot at him that clipped the top of his shoulder, Melinda had pushed it all away. But Neyeli recovered it. Her Uncle Martin, Oliver Peters, and Jamie Ryan stood listening in front of her and Melinda. Behind them were Melinda's parents, and four officers and two detectives behind them. Neyeli spoke an incant aloud, acting as if it was a prayer. It relaxed Melinda, but it didn't erase the young girl's emotions, only calmed them.

Neyeli looked up at her uncle as she rubbed Melinda's arm. She concentrated hard to keep her hair from shifting into different colors in front of the regular folk walking about the hospital, including Melinda and her parents. "That should be enough," she said to her uncle. "You and the officers got what you need. There's no need to take this young girl to any police station."

Martin nodded. He turned, walked around Melinda's parents, and spoke to the officers and detectives. "Catch these two kids, here."

"We'll get 'em," assured Detective Kelli Frost.

Her partner backed up the claim and asked if Martin wanted to come along for old times sake. "I'm private now, Vic," Martin declined. "Besides, I'm close to this. I'll kill these two boys. I swear. Macario is waiting for an order. Get him to tag along." Kelli and Vic understood. They left the hospital after giving final condolences. The officers left with them.

Martin turned around. Neyeli and Oliver were there, making Martin flinch and back up. Neyeli relayed, "There was something in her memory, Uncle. The boy named Sean. The first thing he said to Dajon when he walked up to him. It confirms Gordon's suspicions."

"What'd this kid say?" asked Martin, his eyes looking at Melinda's parents as they consoled their daughter.

"He said, '*You a wanted little boy.*'"

"That strike somethin' in you?"

"It did," Neyeli answered. "My instinct felt something. It was a familiar feeling. The last time I felt it was when we were providing protection for…"

"Hey, hey, hey, hey," Martin interrupted her. "The volume in your voice, little girl," he warned.

Neyeli made a face. Exhaling, she completed her statement, whispering, "The museum run."

"Okay. Let's give Maman Anansi and Papa Solomon the update."

Oliver said, "Let me flag down Stella." He walked away and approached the desk, politely requesting Doctor Stella Reed to the front. Stella was a Fable Avenue community member who lived in the Bronx. Her assistant, Manuel Aldama arrived in her stead. He was a Cuban-American man who was also a community member and living in the Bronx. Oliver led him to Martin.

"Detective," Manuel addressed Martin. "Doctor Reed is still tending to Dajon's family in the recovery room…." His voice trailed away as he looked around for the officers and two detectives that were in the waiting room earlier. "Where've the police gone?"

"They're going to find the boys that did this. They got a description and names. How's Dajon doing?"

"He's stable now, but he was going in and out of consciousness." He leaned close to Martin and whispered, "Most likely, the boy's attached to his conjure. This was an attack on us. The boy's blessing saved his life, but it's shaken him."

"That's what we figured," Martin replied. He turned around and saw Neyeli standing near Melinda's parents. "My niece got a feeling about all this when she pulled the information out of Dajon's friend." He said to Manuel, "Go back there and send out Maman Anansi and Papa Solomon so I can update them."

"Will do," said Manuel. He pivoted and walked away.

Martin started pacing. It was an anxious-looking activity, but there was a deep concern as the private investigator made a slow walk back and forth within the area of the waiting room. Maman Anansi and Papa Solomon's appearance halted his strides.

"You want to see us, Martin?" asked Maman Anansi.

"Yes, ma'am," he answered in a humble tone. There was a slight movement of a bow that accompanied his words. "We have some information," he said, straightening his posture. "Neyeli was able to get a description out of the little girl. The police are on it. But she also felt something that confirms Gordon's suspicions."

"Stanley?" Papa Solomon asked.

"Just a feeling," Martin tried clarifying, making a face. "But, it was the same feeling that shut down the blessing on the museum run—and we know how that turned out."

Maman Anansi instructed, "Vencil call your wife. Tell her to use all in her power to alert everyone on the street. Gordon's there. That's protection enough, but just in case."

Papa Solomon decided to make the call outside, away from regular folks' ears. He left the waiting room, exiting the building. Stepping out into the cold, winter evening, and over to the side of the building, he reached into his pocket. He pulled out his phone and then dialed his house number. At the Peters' residence, Papa Solomon's call interrupted Madame Jeliya's nervous pacing in the kitchen. She grabbed the house phone off its receiver and answered, "Vencil-baby! How is everything? Is Dajon okay?"

"Dajon was in and out of consciousness, but he's stable," informed the patriarch. "We have solid identification of the boys who did this. But there's also a feeling they might not've been acting in their right minds."

"Well, of course not, Papa," Madame Jeliya remarked. "Be it a Stanley Fallows hex or these young boys and girls by their own will just running around wild in our neighborhoods."

Papa Solomon added, "Yes, Thelema-baby. I'm aware." He took a breath, and then passed on Maman Anansi's order, "My sister's got a task for you. Focus your thoughts and put the people of the street on high alert. Gordon and Cedron already keeping an instinct out. Get everyone on that too. Has Gordon been able to contact Fey?"

"No. She doesn't answer her phone or instinct," Madame Jeliya relayed. "He called Savannah, and she's worried. Fey's professor said she never arrived for her exhibit. Lena and I have been working with Althea to keep Gordon from flying off. He's staying put, trying to relax. We keep reminding him that Fey has a great power, equal to his. She'll be fine."

"Okay…" It wasn't what Papa Solomon wanted to hear, but it was an update.

"I will alert the street, Vencil-baby," Madame Jeliya assured. "I'll go to Lena's place now and have her assist me. What about our people outside this street?"

"Let's not scream our alert," Papa Solomon guided. "Let's put out an instinct everyone can pick up on."

"We'll make it low so that no haunt or hex will bother it."

"Thank you, Thelema-baby."

"Stay safe, Papa."

"You too."

Madame Jeliya hung up the phone, placing it back on its receiver. The doorbell rang, and Madame Jeliya received no good instinct coming from the door's other side. She stood in the hallway, focusing a conjure.

The doorbell rang again, followed by a succession of knocks. "Come on out, Madame Jeliya," said a voice smothered in a gentlemanly, British accent. "We just want a proper prick of your pretty flesh. It's not what you think, but we wouldn't mind if you gave us a little extra. We just want to take a little of that fine, matured blood and soul you have."

Madame Jeliya stood firm. She addressed the voice beyond the door in an eloquent tone when she stated, "We don't fear intrusion on Fable Avenue. We don't keep our doors locked all the time. You're free to enter, Mister Cadogan."

Brice opened and stepped through the brownstone doors. Three night doctors strode in with him. The needlemen were not dressed in hospital scrubs or surgical masks. They had on expensive, brown suits from the 1950s with matching fedoras. Covering their faces were seventeenth century plague masks with black holes as eyes and long, pointed, hooked beaks. The sight shook Madame Jeliya for a moment, but she gathered her focus. She raised her arms as if in surrender.

From the matriarch's person sprang her conjure. The spirit's construct was a massive-sized, African lioness. Its spectral form roared and attacked the men in Madame Jeliya's hallway. The shimmering, feral beast knocked the full weight of its body into Brice and two of the night doctors around him. The lioness haunt and the Englishman and his cronies tumbled through the door, and down the brownstone stairs. One needleman's downward momentum tossed him into the iron gate, caving his mask and skull. Brice was thrown over the gate, the lioness attached to him. They soared over the sidewalk and smacked against a car, shattering the passenger side's front and back windows. Brice braced himself against the lioness as it recovered from the crash and began attacking him on the ground. He put up his guard, using all the power of the blessed armor piece clasped around his forearm.

The second night doctor landed in the garden, his suit dirtied and ruffled, and the nose of his mask broken. He got up, straightened his mask and suit and ran back into the house to assist the third needleman who was wrestling with Madame Jeliya. She had her hands gripped around his wrist, keeping back the night doctor's attempt to stab her with his syringe. Madame Jeliya sidestepped and dodged the attack. The needleman instead stabbed the wall, breaking the syringe's needlepoint. The night doctor dropped his syringe and used his strength to overpower Madame Jeliya. He grabbed her shoulders and slammed her into the wall. Madame Jeliya bounced off the wall, back into the needleman's hands. He pushed her to the floor, and Madame Jeliya stumbled back into the kitchen.

She recovered and crawled backwards as the night doctor moved closer to her. His cohort was now at his side, syringe at the ready. Madame Jeliya jumped up, landing on one knee. She spread her arms wide, shouting and releasing another conjure. A golden, glimmering African lion, twice the size of the lioness, jumped out of Madame Jeliya's figure. It bowled over the two night doctors, and the haunt's weight snapped both attackers' necks. It charged out of the house with a declarative roar. At the top of the stairs leading to the front door, the lion witnessed Brice hit the conjured lioness with his incanted, armored fist. The punch crossed the ferocious spirit's jaw, backing her up.

Eyes bent on Brice, the lion dived at the armored Englishman, putting all of its might in his attack. It collided with Brice, lifting him high into the air and throwing him across the street and over the iron gate of the brownstone opposite the Peters' residence. The lion hopped onto the car's hood, snarling and baring its teeth. The lioness, having shaken away Brice's attack, scurried up the steps and back into the house to check on Madame Jeliya. The conjured spirit discovered the matriarch out of breath, slumped on the kitchen floor. It ran up to Madame Jeliya and rubbed its nose against her face, licking her cheek. The matriarch reached up, and petted the humble creature, recovering strength with each stroke made upon the lioness. She stood up, renewed of breath and potency, and walked outside with the lioness behind her.

Madame Jeliya's conjured, male lion continued staring Brice down from atop the car's hood. The Englishman goaded the beast. "Keep him still," Madame Jeliya instructed the lion. She looked down the street to her left and then to her right. She saw motion. There was a march of shadows, and a rhythmic clamor of shoes against the pavement on either side of her.

A whip cracked, and Madame Jeliya's lion growled, moving back as Willie made his strike at the beast. He snapped his whip again, and the lion leapt back onto the car's roof. The lioness lunged at Willie, but the cruel overseer turned and attacked the inbound lioness with his whip. The lash sliced through the beast's shimmering frame and dissipated her essence. The lion rushed back to the car's hood and swiped at Willie. The colonial-dressed thug cracked his whip for effect. "C'mon, you savage, jungle monster. Let's see if you all the spirit you made of." He spit in the lion's direction.

Madame Jeliya resurrected her dissolved familiar, and the lioness sprung forth. Willie turned and again cut the large feline spirit down in midair with his whip. Brice jumped the gate and charged at the lion. It charged him, and the two collided in the street. Brice put up his armored forearm and slammed against the conjured construct. The lion hollered, and its voice called Fable Avenue residents to gather. Some peered out of their windows. A few stepped outside, conjures and incants at the ready, and then ablaze in combat as night doctors swarmed them.

Willie moved through the gate, a grin on his face as he stared up at Madame Jeliya. "You got more cats in you, pretty lady? Ain't nothin' I like more than tamin' wild, jungle pussy like the kind you put out." Madame Jeliya was exhausted, untrained in combat with her newfound personal conjure. She made a move to run back into the house, but Willie's whip was quicker than her execution. It ran diagonal across the matriarch's chest, and its hexed potency caused her body to drop and crumple up on the ground.

Willie marched up the stairs with a pleased and triumphant smile on his visage, the image of riot and war at his back. He knelt down and caressed Madame Jeliya's trembling face. He whispered into her ear. "If I had time, Miss Peters, I'd treat you to a rough prick." He turned and snapped his fingers, signaling a passing needleman. "C'mon up here, boy. I got one of our marks subdued. C'mon up here and take her sweet spirit and blood."

The night doctor turned. He walked through the gate and up the stairs. He knelt down and injected his syringe into Madame Jeliya's arm. Her lion disappeared from its fight with Brice. Willie caressed Madame Jeliya's cheek the whole time.

Up the street, minutes before Madame Jeliya's lion screamed its accidental, rallying roar, Gordon and Cedron enjoyed time with their mother's spirit. They were in the dining room on the garden floor, sitting at the table, their mother's specter standing. No other lights in the house were on but in that room. Gordon had listened to Cedron recite the swap of their childhood totems, and the lesson their mother was attempting to bring them as young, sibling rivals. The talk eased his worries about Fey, but she was still on his mind. He reached out with his instinct every-so-often to search for her presence. There was none. He'd hoped she'd gone to the stars to meditate in the heavens. He wanted so much to leave the street, to venture out and find Fey. But he was under orders to remain, give protection with his brother. And it was all because of his personal suspicion, something his instinct culled out of the shooting of young Dajon Brickhouse, and the faint traces of Stanley Fallow's foul haunt over the scene. So Gordon sat still, listening to his brother and enjoying their time together with their mother. They were joking with one another. No words were biting or had a scathing undertone to them.

Cedron was announcing a new custom that he believed his crew of misfits, dubbed the *Court of Gypsy Moon Misfits*, would enjoy. Gordon was invited to partake, but there would be no women allowed, Cedron emphasized much to his mother's chagrin. "It's just about the fellas that night, Mom," Cedron explained. "But I am thinking that we can bring women in on the full moon. Get that feminine energy up in the spot."

Cedron stated he would host a gentlemen's club. It would be a black tie affair. All who attended had to wear their finest suits, or at the very least, the best clothing an attendee could muster. Cedron listed, "Music, games of Majestic and Samedi's Tarot and rum and alcohol-spiced *dragon spit*." Possessed with a wide smile, Cedron leaned over the table, closer to Gordon. "And Frenchie gon' be there. He *got* to be there. He got two Oshun shards." At the revelation of the crystals' names, Althea lifted a single eyebrow. Gordon looked surprised. Cedron closed his eyes, using his imagination as he explained in a slow manner, "They got the spirits of these two exotic dancers inside them." He opened his eyes and saw Gordon's face brighten. "One is this Brazilian sister. Her spirit's from the nineteen-fifties. She preserved herself in it. Second is a sister from Harlem, nineteen-thirties. Frenchie been *tryin'* to find a shard with a way, way, way back spirit inside it. You know, from the days of the Moors or an old African kingdom or tribal nation. But these two women, their spirit can change clothes and put on the illusion of being way, way back when."

"Um, what is all this I'm hearin'?" Althea blurted.

"Aw, Ma," Cedron said, leaning back in his chair. "It's all in fun."

"I'm sure it is," said Althea, making a face and keeping her eyebrow raised. "Having these women's spirit entertain you…"

Cedron protested with a guilty smile on his face, "But they preserved their spirit *for* that purpose. C'mon, Ma." Then Cedron countered, "What about those Ausar stones or Ogun shards women be using? Same thing. Spirit of a man conjured up to entertain."

Althea scoffed at her son, "Those stones are specifically for conjuring heroic men of the past. They are archival like Isis scrolls and stones with the spirit of old conjure women in them."

Cedron rolled his eyes, grin on his face. "Yeah, right. Archival. Well, the spirits in the Oshun shards are the same thing. They cool too. You can just talk to them, learn history. I mean, it's cool that black folks all over were puttin' conjures and incants to use before Fable Avenue popped up. The sister from Brazil talks about it going on down there, how they hid it from public view and stuff."

"You need to be gettin' to know that Peters girl all over again," Althea commented.

Cedron kept his smile, but the wind was taken from him. "I'll reach out to Leah when I reach out to Leah..." he said. Then he told his mother through his sly grin, "I'm sure you could preserve yourself in an Oshun shard."

Althea flapped her lips. "Please, boy. I am on your father's arm, and that's where I intend to stay. Besides, you want the gentlemen at this gatherin' of yours to be watchin' your mamma sway and strut her stuff for them? I am a trained dancer after all."

Cedron's face wriggled. *"Mom!"* he hollered. *"Aww, no!"*

"Oh, it's okay for these two girls but not me? Young as my spirit is still preserved. Uh-huh. That's what I thought."

"I'm talkin' about for the future, though."

"Ain't no other man, or men, will conjure this spirit here. When your father's spirit comes to me, we will walk off into eternity hand-in-hand like the black and cosmic Ixu and the Gira."

"That's sweet, Mom," Cedron teased as he stood and tried to give his mother a kiss on the cheek. His lips passed through her ghostly form. Then he walked into the kitchen.

"Where *is* your father?" Althea questioned. "He was supposed to be here with Wilson by now."

It got quiet. Gordon put his head down. Cedron immersed himself in fetching a cup of orange juice. After a moment, Gordon spoke, "He's probably...at the hospital."

Cedron poured a glass, thinking of Benny and Dajon. "Yeah..." He returned the carton of orange juice to the refrigerator, closed it, and walked back into the dining room.

Althea looked at her sons' faces. She put her hands on her hips and said to them, "Will you two lift your spirits. It's sad what happened to Dajon, but he's okay. His spirit is not meant for my world. He will be fine."

"It's the emotion of it all, Ma," noted Cedron. He sat down, glass of orange juice in hand. His face was still slumped. "All this conjure and incant and knowledge, a bullet can still put us down. And these knuckleheaded fools out here can be responsible."

Althea concentrated, making her spectral form solid. She glided over to Cedron and rubbed his shoulders. "I understand, baby." Her thoughts returned to her husband. She closed her eyes to find him. She saw an image of him driving up Howard Avenue, coming up to Fable Avenue.

Wilson was in the driver's seat. The car moved closer to the block, ready to turn onto the street. But instead of the car pulling onto Fable Avenue, it disappeared, ending up on the other side of the intersection. Maximilian and Wilson's expression exploded with surprise. Maximilian stopped the car. Both he and Wilson turned around and looked through the rear window.

"Is the street outside of time?" Wilson asked.

Maximilian continued staring. *"Seems to be,"* he responded with a question of 'why' in his tone. *"Maybe we on lockdown,"* he guessed. *"Just, uh, concentrate so we can make the turn."*

"I gotchu," said Wilson.

Maximilian turned the car around after waiting for two cars to pass. Wilson closed his eyes and focused. Althea saw her husband pull forward, attempting another turn onto Fable Avenue. But again the car skipped over the street and ended up on the other side of the intersection. Wilson opened his eyes. Maximilian brought the car to an abrupt stop. He cursed, and again he and Wilson looked out the rear window.

"Somethin' ain't right," Wilson said reaching for his phone. *"I'm callin' Papa Solomon."*

Althea pulled away from her vision. She opened her eyes and floated into the front room, gliding toward the window. Gordon called for his mother, asking if she was all right. Althea didn't answer. She looked at the window where the closed curtains displayed faint shadows of movement coming from outside. There was a line of people marching down the street.

"Boys…" Althea's voice called. "I think we're outside of time…"

"Probably on lockdown," Gordon and Cedron guessed simultaneously.

"Pinch! Punch! Knock on wood, nigga," said Cedron, going through the stated motions with Gordon. Instead of knocking on the wooden table, however, Cedron knocked his fist playfully atop Gordon's head.

Gordon cried, *"Hey!"*

"Can't get through all that hair, though," Cedron chuckled.

"Boys…" Althea called again. "There's something happening here."

A lion roared! It sounded like a call, and Gordon and Cedron jumped from their seats. Gordon's cosmic apparel seeped from his flesh as smoke and then wrapped tight around his person. Cedron raised the conjure of his pitched flesh past his neck, covering the remainder of his body. There complete was his tattoo accompanied by ancient gold symbols at intervals along its circuitry.

Althea focused and moved the curtain aside. She saw night doctors wrestling with residents. A few of them bullied their way into people's houses.

"So that's them," pondered Althea. "The men that poisoned and killed me."

Dooley nodded. "Yes, Mom," he said, his voice resonating sadness.

He reached out and surveyed the scene with his instinct. A picture of Top Hat's bedroom appeared. The spiritualist's physical body was fast asleep in its bed. Rising from his physical frame was Top Hat's spirit form. It blinked from the room, and Dooley's vision followed it. Top Hat, in ghost form, appeared in a house down the street, inside the bedroom of some children who were surrounded by night doctors. Top Hat attacked the needlemen, catching them by surprise and knocking them unconscious with lighted fists filled with spirit energy. He warned the children to stay put as he popped away into another house being overrun by needlemen. He assisted a mother and father who were defending their children from capture. But where Top Hat lay, there came a disturbance as needlemen broke through the parlor-floor entrance and swarmed the brownstone. Top Hat woke up, his specter fading from a fight and coming back into his body. He balled his fists, and they blazed with conjured spirit. Two needlemen broke into Top Hat's room. He rose and struck them both.

Dooley's vision came back to the present. He backed up to Cedron and said, "These needlemen got a different look to them. But they can get knocked down just the same, regardless of their threads."

Dooley made a move toward the door. Cedron grabbed his brother by the arm and said, "Hold up, little brother. We need backup. My misfits," he clarified.

"We're outside of time, Cedron," Althea reminded. "And I don't think anybody from our community is doing this. Your father's up the way, and he can't get in."

"Gordon can get out of this," Cedron stated. "Right?" he asked, looking down at Dooley. Dooley nodded. "Okay then," Cedron said. "If Pop is up the street, Mom, see if you can go to him. Stay out of this. Let's not take a risk on them needlemen and what happens when they stick a spirit. Let's be careful." He informed his brother, "Both Ray and Ed should be at the hospital by now, payin' respect. You pop in there and you 'round folk up. Hear? I won't make a move until you get back. They come in here, it's a different story. I hurt them."

"Okay, big brother," Dooley acknowledged his orders. His lilac spirit blazed, and he popped away, forming into spirit among the stars, high above Earth. He focused his sight and dived. Breaking the atmosphere, he appeared to the world as a falling star. He soared toward the Harlem hospital where his Elders and friends were gathered. He slowed his descent, and his fiery-lilac spirit burst away. A display of acrobatics in the air, and Dooley landed gently on the hospital's roof. His cosmic outfit faded, and Gordon's regular clothes appeared. He reached into his pocket, ducking down on the roof. He pulled out his smartphone and called Papa Solomon.

"Gordon?" the Elder asked. "Where are you? We just got a strange call from Wilson and your dad? They said the street is outside of time, and they can't get in."

"It is," Gordon confirmed. "Night doctors have invaded." He heard Papa Solomon curse. The Elder asked about his wife. "Not sure. She's probably leading the defensive with Lady Arachne," Gordon guessed. "I popped out, came here. I'm on the roof of the hospital now. Benny still there?" he asked.

"Benny's here," Papa Solomon answered. "Jamie and Neyeli are here too. Them Shaw boys showed up for support."

"I'll be right inside," said Gordon. He hung up and rushed to the side of the roof. He looked down and spied the front of the building and a nice shaded area he could pop to. He backed away, and with a quick focus, disappeared. He came into existence in the shadows, and walked nonchalantly up to the hospital's front entrance. He used his instinct to guide him, and he walked his way to Papa Solomon and Maman Anansi in the waiting room. Benny and his friends were there too. They crowded Gordon as he walked up to them.

"We got trouble on the street?" asked Benny.

"Yeah," Gordon answered in haste. He looked at Papa Solomon and Maman Anansi, telling his Elders, "I can get everyone back to Fable Avenue. Two at a time, at most."

"I got nothing without that horn," Papa Solomon told Gordon. "No need to waste time for you to bring it to me. Who knows how the house looks." He thought about his wife. He said to his sister, "You go. You got a strong conjure inside you. Just find Thelema for me."

"I will, Vencil," Maman Anansi assured.

Papa Solomon turned to his son and said, "Oliver, you and me will take a drive there. Hopefully, by the time we arrive, this will all be settled."

"Sure thing, Pop."

Maman Anansi shuffled Gordon and the others out of the waiting room. "Come on, now. Outside, where we can make this a private thing," she said.

Gordon trotted past her, Benny at his side. "Fey okay?" asked Benny.

Gordon shook his head. "My instinct can't get a read on her. I hope she's all right."

"She'll be fine," Benny said as a reflex.

Gordon and the others exited the hospital. He took them to the shaded area, and they formed a circle around him. He said to them, "I can take two at a time. But Maman Anansi, I'm taking just you first."

"That's fine, Gordon," she said, reaching for Gordon's hand.

His cosmic suit formed around him, fading his regular clothes. He held Maman Anansi's hand with a tight grip, telling her, "We're going to be on Papa Solomon and Madame Jeliya's front steps, okay?" Maman Anansi nodded. She and Dooley popped away shortly after. In a blink, they were on the top step in front of the open door leading into her brother and sister-in-law's house.

Maman Anansi surveyed the street. It was chaos. There was a fight in every direction, up and down. Night doctors were on the march, and only a few confident residents held them at bay with conjure or incant. Lady Arachne stood at the iron-gate. She projected from her hands, aimed at groping night doctors, a black and purple stream. The mystic missiles effluxed from a black, glowing card-shaped conjuring pressed against the palm of her hands. The effect of the projected stream, on contact, was a black hole opening around her intended target and dragging them inside before closing. It was a blessed sight for both Maman Anansi and Dooley to see a defensive front put up by a few of the street's residents. But the blessing was short lived. At their feet was the unconscious body of Madame Jeliya.

Maman Anansi let go of Dooley and knelt down. *"Thelema!"* she cried, checking her sister-in-law and fellow matriarch's body for life. She held her hand over Madame Jeliya and reached out with her spirit. She could feel that Madame Jeliya was fine, but she was wounded with a hex. She sensed her arm had been punctured by a night doctor's syringe.

"She's okay, Carolyn, despite her wound," Lady Arachne yelled up to Maman Anansi. "She fought well, but she was overwhelmed."

Dooley popped away to retrieve the others.

Maman Anansi put a hand on Madame Jeliya, her palm aglow. The unconscious matriarch stirred. Lady Arachne backed away from the iron gate, noticing the fight dwindling away and moving farther up the street. She gave one last look around making sure no needlemen would sneak an attack. It was clear, and so Lady Arachne turned and climbed the stairs just as Madame Jeliya stood up, noticeably fatigued.

Fight and vigor roused the second matriarch. But it wasn't the presence of Fable Avenue's villains that held her interest or aim. Her eyes, bent with anger, locked onto Lady Arachne. She stepped to the divine card reader and slapped her hard across the face. *"You bitch!"* she snarled. "You stay away from my husband, goddamn you!" She slapped Lady Arachne again. "He ain't yours no more. You stop pining after him!" She charged Lady Arachne, but Maman Anansi held her back. "You hear me, you Fable Avenue street walker!"

Lady Arachne held her cheek, surprise dripping off her and melting into sadness. She moved aside, nearing the brownstone's entrance, and then stepping into the house. Maman Anansi used all her might to hold her sister-in-law back, but there was physical strength building inside Madame Jeliya, a brewing, angry storm that was ready to flood the street and drown indiscriminately attacker and resident alike. But her sight was on Lady Arachne. Maman Anansi knew she couldn't hold Madame Jeliya's hurricane back for long, and so she let her go, charging into the house toward Lady Arachne who was standing in the hall.

Maman Anansi opened the palm of her hand. A cloud of pink dust materialized, and before it condensed and became a solid, throwing dagger, she ran up behind Madame Jeliya and blew the dust into the back of her head. The glittering, pink particles swirled up into Madame Jeliya's nose, and the matriarch collapsed unconscious in the hallway. Lady Arachne, still holding her face and an expression that shifted between sadness and anger fighting off embarrassment, stepped over Madame Jeliya's body and returned to the battle outside. Maman Anansi allowed her to pass and return to the fight outside. She alone examined Madame Jeliya's body, but she already knew what she would find. The scar with the hex. Willie's mark. She inspected her sister-in-law. There it was, beneath the tear on her blouse, the bloody lash running across her chest.

Up the road, Cedron took to the streets with his imported misfits. Conjures and chaos lit up the blocks. The fighting spread in either direction, violent as any gunfight. Benny Brickhouse made himself light as a feather. Becoming nimble permitted him to maneuver around the onslaught of needlemen. Timed correctly, Benny increased the weight of his fists or feet and punched or kicked the needlemen unconscious. He soared from needleman to needleman delivering heavy blows. But a single, hexed punch from Brice Cadogan put the young airmen on the ground. "That's enough of your lot flying about," Brice sneered, standing over Benny.

Cedron crashed into Brice, hurtling the Englishman's body down the road and into another fray, knocking down needlemen and Fable Avenue resident alike. Brice regained his stance. He spied the pitch-skinned and tattooed Cedron and dived forward, leaping into the air with his armored arm cocked back to strike. Cedron charged and jumped, meeting Brice in the air. He caught the Englishman's arm as Brice swung at him. Hexed spirit burned Cedron's fingers as he gripped the armor piece. He and Brice smacked and rolled onto the pavement, and Cedron lost his grip.

Benny got to his knees, looking in the direction of Cedron and Brice's bodies. His gray, cloudy feathers were conjured, but he made his weight heavy, ready to jump into the paused conflict and assist Cedron against Brice. As he motioned to leap forward, there came a crack of a whip, and his neck was wrapped in thick, braided leather. Benny's conjure weakened, and Willie tugged on his whip. Benny dropped to the street, and Willie dragged his body toward him. The cruel overseer tossed the handle to a tree branch where the whip's body shortened, and Benny's body hung, slowly choking. Three night doctors surrounded Benny as he struggled to free himself. They began beating him with their fists. Benny fought back with kicks, still attempting to loosen the hold around his neck.

Brice and Cedron's fisticuffs continued down the road. Both men jumped up, throwing punches at one another. Cedron's reach far extended Brice's, and he landed his fist against the Englishman's jaw. His circuit-like tattoo writhed with spirit that charged the strike against Brice. It was a clean hit, and it moved Brice back, shaking him and causing him to stumble. But the Englishman stayed on his feet.

Cedron stepped with Brice, attacking Brice's body with two, heavy strikes. He cracked two of the Englishman's left ribs, and his second body blow fractured and bruised several ribs on the right. Brice didn't falter even when another solid strike smacked him square in the face. He backed away from the pitch-black colossus. Cedron stepped up to deliver more damaging hits against Brice, but he paused when he saw a green glow bubble from the armor piece clasped around the Englishman's forearm.

Brice placed his forearm against his ribs, and the bruises and fractures sustained reversed and cured. Cedron's instinct sensed what was happening. He stood his ground, ready to start the beating he'd delivered all over again, and more so, if needed to keep Brice down. Brice stood straighter, renewed for combat. Cedron didn't mind. He was ready to hurt the Englishman's confidence. Cedron resumed his stride, returning to fight. He took a swing, but Brice dodged the attack, stepping aside. He countered, throwing a punch at the goliath. He connected, hitting Cedron in the stomach. His hit let loose a hexed spirit into Cedron's mighty frame. The giant's black flesh flickered between pitch and its natural, dark brown hue. His tattooed circuitry and symbols also struggled to stay on his person, and his legs gave way for a moment as his spine regressed to its injured condition. Brice hit Cedron again, this time across the jaw.

"All you jungle spirits have a weakness," Brice commented, his voice fierce. "It's all about finding it." He hit Cedron again in the stomach, shivering Cedron's appearance between conjure and mortal shell. Brice twirled around behind the giant and hit him on the spine. Cedron hollered, and the giant buckled, his conjure and strength faded. He collapsed onto the street, his body crumpled like a discarded sack. Brice stared down at Cedron, a proud smile curled on his face.

Two, glowing projectiles smacked Brice in the chest, backing him away. Brice looked up and spotted Raymundo Shaw projecting spirit at him. The occult archer took a moment to strike incoming night doctors as Brice braced himself against a salvo of arrows, using his blessed armor piece as a shield.

Edmond fell from the sky, landing next to the unconscious Cedron. He gripped his friend's shirt and jumped away, landing atop a brownstone's roof. He checked Cedron. He was still breathing, moaning. Edmond ran to the rooftop's edge and looked down at the street. He saw Benny still struggling, hanging from Willie's whip. The night doctors that had been around him, hitting his body with their fists, were now busy fighting off Jamie's shadow conjures. Something else attacked the needlemen. There were glowing and slithering strands that came up from the ground, wrapping around their limbs and pulling them back. Edmond looked up the street and saw, focused in her conjure, Neyeli. She had absorbed all the emotion around her and made the swirl of sentiments into the writhing constructs keeping the night doctor's at bay.

Edmond jumped down, landing next to Benny. He held the young man's body still, but Willie's whip tightened, continuing to cut off Benny's air. Edmond turned his head and spied the overseer, fist out and tightening. Surrounding him were three night doctors, guarding him as he focused his thoughts and controlled the movement of his whip. Benny choked, small, pained exhales mixed with saliva. His eyelids flapped, struggling to remain open. Edmond cursed. He had no time to let go of Benny and leap at Willie to throw him off focus.

But there came assistance in the form of a small, lilac-colored comet. It smacked against one night doctor's plague mask, shattering his face and dropping the supernatural physician. It ricocheted and smacked against the remaining two like a wild pinball, felling them both. Forming solid in front of Willie, Dooley knocked him across the jaw, loosening his concentration on the whip strangling Benny.

Several of Raymond's conjured arrows severed the hexed, leather chord, setting Benny free. He slumped over Edmond's shoulder, and the section of Willie's whip that had been wrapped around his neck loosened and fell away. Benny remained conscious, and still with fight in him. He lightened his weight, became like a feather, and glided off Edmond, soaring toward Dooley to aid him against Willie.

Night doctors lunged at the lilac spirit, backing Dooley away from their weaponless master. Benny swooped in, using fancy flying maneuvers to stave off the needle-wielding masked men. Willie reached out his hand

and called the severed parts of his whip to him. The whip mended while on its journey back to its master, and when Willie caught the handle of his weapon, he stood tall and cracked it about, keeping Dooley and other Fable Avenue conjurors at bay.

Benny dealt with the night doctors, assisted by Jamie's shadow conjures and Neyeli's snake-like spirits writhing from the ground. Willie attacked the shadow conjures, dissipating their shaded forms with the crack of his whip upon them. He drew closer to Benny as the airman engaged the night doctors, but as he made a motion to strike, Neyeli's snake-like spirits fastened around his arm and neck, holding him back. He whipped them, dissolving their form, and he turned around to address the conjuror responsible.

Willie looked old. He looked out of shape. But he was quick. He lashed Neyeli with his whip, putting her down. Benny swooped down at the overseer, but Brice tackled him. In turn, Cedron, having jumped back into the fray, spirit pitch-black and enlivened, grabbed at the Englishman and tore him off Benny. He picked Brice up by the back of his neck and slammed him face first into the ground. Cedron stomped on Brice's armored forearm, spirit trailing through his circuit tattoo, culminating at his foot and breaking the armor piece's hinges. He snatched the metal covering and tossed it aside. Cedron pulled Brice up by his shirt and hit him in the gut with spirit.

Brice's shriek could've cut the eardrums of any crying banshee, and as it was, his shriek buckled some of the people engaged in battle nearby. The goliath pushed him down, and Brice called, *"Willie! Willie! The giant one will kill me!"* But the overseer was distracted, not by conjure or incant, or even Dooley's lilac spirit. He was lost in thought, looking at his whip and down at the fallen Neyeli. He had an instinct, and it confused him, freezing him in place. There was an empty feeling as he looked at Neyeli's crumpled body. He could not feel her. The young conjuror was hurt by his attack, but she was neither scarred nor hexed. Brice called for help behind him, but Willie was too intrigued. He stepped over to Neyeli, looking down at the fallen conjure woman.

Her hair turned black and gold. Her locks extended, growing rapidly. They reached up and lashed Willie across his chest. He backed away, injured, and with smoke billowing from the seared scars on his flesh and clothes.

Neyeli jumped up. Her hair continued lashing at Willie, and he defended himself with parrying strikes from his whip. The strands of Neyeli's hair merged as one lock, whipping forward. Willie dodged the attack on him, and a night doctor jumped at Neyeli, forcing his needle into her shoulder. He plunged the syringe deep. "Imagine them dying!" the night doctor whispered.

Neyeli screamed! Visions of Benny dying attacked her. He was shot, stabbed, burned. Through different periods of time and lives, he died. Over and over. Her parents and siblings too. They fought each other. They killed one another. They were murdered by strangers. They were hung by Klansmen. They were raped. Their necks were slit. Blood was everywhere, in every time, in every way. Neyeli's hair retracted, its color fading into dull tones. She fell to her knees, crying and screaming.

Benny flew in, punching and kicking the night doctor that attacked her. He was light and heavy. He was ferocious in his attacks, even making a swift move to remove the needle from Neyeli's shoulder and sinking it into the night doctor's chest. And he continued beating the occult physician from there.

But Benny wasn't the one who finished the fight.

A thick, snake-like strand rose from the ground and wrapped around the night doctor's neck. It squeezed and squeezed, all at Neyeli's mental command. "Take it back!" she screamed. *"Take it all back!"* Her conjured strand tightened. The night doctor's windpipe crushed with a loud pop, and the strand unraveled from it.

Neyeli's wound healed. Benny ran to her and put his arms around her.

Neyeli's emotions were in control.

Willie had turned his back on the fight, running up to the one-sided scuffle between Brice and Cedron.

"Willie!" Brice called again, barely forming the name through broken teeth, jaw, and a torn lip. Cedron moved in for another hit, but Brice was spared from the giant's heavy blow.

Dooley's blazing, lilac spirit swooped in, snatching up Brice from the street and soaring up into the sky. The smokeless, fiery spirit popped away, coming into form high above the Brooklyn borough and past the boundary of the hex sealing Fable Avenue outside of time. Brice was still in his grip, and he continued up. As he climbed in height, he shared his lilac flame with the Englishman. At first, Brice hollered by reflex as the flame crept around his skin. But it did not burn, and when he and Dooley penetrated the Earth's atmosphere, his loud holler ceased. He was covered with spirit, unharmed by the properties of the cosmos. He marveled at space around him. His mouth hung open, and his eyes were wide. The fight and its purpose were lost to him as he marveled at the stars, the sun, the bright white moon, the distant planets, and even Earth's blue-green presence. The universe was an ever-expanding gallery of art, and for Brice it was all on display.

Dooley soared higher until the familiar solar system could no longer be seen. Then he let go and pushed away from Brice.

A sting stabbed Brice's heart. He believed the protective lilac flame would wash away, and the invisible hands of the cosmos would tear him apart. But nothing happened. He looked at Dooley, and Dooley looked at him. Or so he believed. Dooley was looking behind him. And Brice became curious, turning his head and peeping over his shoulder.

A black hole was there, widening. No vacuum effect occurred, and Brice remained in place. But that didn't ease him. Black, spirits floated out of the cosmic opening. They surrounded him, and then like police making an arrest, they grappled his limbs. Brice struggled, and his loud screams attempted a return, muted however by space. The black spirits pulled him back, bringing him to the wide-open maw floating in space. Brice reached for Dooley, mouth open but making no sound. He was dragged inside the black hole, and Dooley watched it close. The lilac spirit turned his attention in the direction of Earth, and he dived down to return to the battle in the street.

Minutes upon minutes before Dooley took flight into the heavens, and at the height of the battle, Fey Forrester returned to her family's Fable Avenue residence. Fighting surrounded her, but she waded through skirmishes indifferent to their existence. Inside her home, she walked into her kitchen, turned on the lights and placed her bag on a pulled out chair. She opened the bag and took out her sketchbook, laying it on the table, opened to a page featuring a sketch of all four of her yumboes.

Fey sat down. From the open page swirled a puff of smoke that formed into the yumbo named Silver. The sprite observed her surroundings, but an unseen force pulled her to sit in the chair opposite Fey. Silver looked up at her, eyes filled with concern and sorrow. Fey was careworn, bags under her eyes. She looked at the yumbo and said in a voice not her own, "Don't. Ever. Marry no damn codebreaker. You hear me? Don't marry no codebreaker." She continued talking, reciting word for word from a memory on full display.

Fighting occurred outside the kitchen window. But it didn't hold weight to the yumbo who struggled to move. And it was filled with far more hope as the tide changed from night doctors to conjure folk. Silver was forcibly immobile. She watched Fey talk, ranting with words not her own, in a voice that echoed a different tone from hers.

Silver remembered the memory Fey reenacted. She remembered how it ended. And the only movement permitted was trembling. Fey said, "I saw…" She turned away from the yumbo. "I saw…something…" Fey stood. She went to the window and talked some more, memory still providing her script. Taking a pause in speech, she moved away from the window, walking sluggishly around the table toward Silver. She used the chairs for balance. More speech from the past was reiterated. She knelt down and said to Silver, "You like mamma's drawings, little girl?" Silver gave a slow, affirmative nod against her will. "Then keep them," Fey told the little yumbo. She bent down and kissed Silver on the head, and then she walked away from the kitchen

A tear dripped from Silver's eye, splashing onto the page where the other three yumboes were sketched. Silver turned her head, following Fey's exit from the kitchen. She was able to move, but again her actions were not her own. She jumped off the chair, and instead of flying in Fey's direction, she walked.

Silver wanted to turn her head and see which of the other three yumboes would appear off the page. But her gaze remained locked forward, and she trotted to the stairs, standing still at the base, looking up.

It was Zee that appeared, pulling herself out of the page and twirling around to survey her environment. And it was Zee that used her higher perception to peer into the master bedroom on the floor above her.

The winged creature watched as Fey Forrester opened the top drawer on the dresser in front of her. She reached inside but pulled nothing out. She configured her hand, however, in the shape of a gun and put the tips of her fingers against her head. Fey uttered in a low voice, "Mamma's a mystery…"

Zee's perception of the room faded.

Silver was at the bottom of the stairs.

She waited, knowing what would come next.

There was fighting outside, its noise muted by the quiet and stillness haunting the Forrester residence.

Upstairs, Fey closed her eyes. Fingertips against her temple, her thumb dropped like a gun's hammer. An emerald spirit roared from her fingertips, and Fey Forrester's body collapsed lifeless to the floor.

Silver was free to move, but she didn't. She realized it happened all over again, and she fell to her knees. Zee flew up next to her, landed, and consoled her distressed yumbo sister. She turned her head, and hollered an incant over her shoulder. Em and Jade popped up into existence from their sketch, and they dashed toward their sisters, wings aflutter. Hovering around Silver and Zee, they felt the strong wave of emotion emanating from Silver and it pulled them down. Zee started singing. It was a sympathetic tune in a language known to the yumboes. Em and Jade joined her, and their voices washed over Silver and cleansed the yumbo of the grief holding her in place.

Silver blinked her eyes, coming to. Her wings spread, forcing Zee to back away. Her body became a beam of light that zoomed up the stairs.

Zee and the other yumboes followed, bodies transformed into thin beams of light expressing the color of their flesh. They formed solid behind Silver. All four yumboes hovered in the air, gazing down with the same sad expression on their lighted countenance.

It was at this moment that Dooley returned to Fable Avenue. His reentrance to the fight took witness to night doctors and Willie the Lich fading from the street. Upon their sudden absence, his instinct alerted him. Fable Avenue was now within time. His mask vanished, and Gordon looked around as Benny and the others crowded him. His mother's spirit appeared just as his father's car pulled onto the street and drove down the block.

Gordon asked how everyone was, and they gave their collective 'okays'. He popped away just as his father and Wilson got out of the car. His presence formed solid down the street in front of Madame Jeliya's house. He was on the top step, facing the house's front door, which had been closed. Maman Anansi called him, and Gordon twirled around.

"I just sent Lady Arachne to find you, Gordon," she said up to him while standing just outside the gate, on the sidewalk. "Did Papa Solomon arrive? I can feel we're flowing with time."

Gordon shook his head, no. "I came here. He might've arrived after I popped away."

"Madame Jeliya is hurt," Maman Anansi informed. "She's scarred with a hexed lash from Willie. She needs your chamber."

Gordon nodded. "I'll get her there," he assured. "There are more scarred up the street. We had to put them down, unconscious." Maman Anansi gave an understanding nod. She turned and looked at the street, counting the unconscious bodies lying near her that had also been lashed by Willie. "Are you okay, Maman Anansi?"

"I'm fine, Gordon. I'm fine." She walked through the iron gate and to the garden-floor door. She twiddled her fingers and it unlocked. "I'll be down here. I'm going to take us outside of time again. The last thing we need is for normal folks and they cars coming up and down the road."

Gordon agreed. He popped away from the top step to the hallway. He scooped up Madame Jeliya's body and disappeared to his chamber in the basement. "Spook," he called, popping into existence. "Open up the chamber. This is the first of many that need healing."

The chamber slid open, and Gordon placed Madame Jeliya inside. The chamber closed, and it started rumbling. "Keep her safe, Spook. I'll be back." Dooley disappeared. He materialized where he fought in the street. Lady Arachne was there, talking with Althea and Maximilian Goodspeed and giving orders to Cedron and the others. Wilson was on the phone with Papa Solomon. The patriarch and his son were close by, driving up.

"Everything okay?" asked Gordon.

Cedron shook his head. "No," he said. "It ain't."

"What's going on?" Gordon inquired.

Neyeli stepped up to Gordon. She said with sad eyes, "There are children missing."

"Taken by the night doctors and Willie," Top Hat took up. "I was at rest, using my dream state, protecting people huddled inside they houses. Couple night doctors broke in on me, disturbed my sleep. I fought 'em off, but they kept coming. I never got back into the dreaming. They disappeared once they got the children, we're assuming."

"How many kids?"

"Two kids were stuck with needles and left behind," Lady Arachne answered. "Six were kidnapped."

Gordon turned to Wilson and noticed he was on the phone. He asked him, "Is that Papa Solomon?" Wilson shook his head. "Tell him Madame Jeliya was scarred by Willie, but that she's recovering in my chamber." Wilson nodded and then relayed the message. "Wilson," he called, getting his attention. "Also tell him we're outside of time, but it's through Maman Anansi's influence." Wilson nodded again and repeated Gordon's words to Papa Solomon. Gordon asked of his mother, "Mom, can you go to my chamber and see Madame Jeliya through?"

"Yes, baby," she acknowledged before fading.

Maximilian got back into his car. The driver-side window went down, and Max shouted, "Get as many people up as you can. Get some into the car. I'll drive them to the house."

Gordon watched as everyone shuffled away, tending to the people in the street. His father drove up slowly behind them. Gordon took a step forward, ready to join in, but something tugged at his instinct. He turned to his right. All four of Fey's yumboes hovered in front of him. Gordon expressed surprise, flinching. "Is Fey here?" he asked them. Their melancholy expressions came into focus. Silver glided in front of Gordon and placed her forehead against his. Gordon and Silver closed their eyes, and a cobalt-blue light appeared. Gordon saw Silver's memory. The images came at him with the speed and weight of a derailed train.

He pulled away before he saw through Silver's eyes the lifeless body of his beloved Fey Forrester on the floor.

"No…" he said, losing voice. He gasped, choking on the word. His breath and voice broke, filling his speech with hiccups. But it came to him, crashing into his lungs like the mighty, speeding derailed train of the memory. His holler bellowed with no intelligible word attached to it. It didn't only carry sound up and down Fable Avenue, boring loudly into the residents. It also carried with it the memory, and it played for all to see.

Gordon popped away to Fey's house. Upstairs, in the hallway, he came into form. He was outside the master bedroom, and he saw her lifeless body slumped on the floor at the side of the bed. He couldn't move, save for heavy breathing. He wanted to go forward and be with her, lift her body into his arms, take her to his chamber and revive her. He attempted to move, but his body buckled, trembling in place before falling to his knees. Gordon tried catching his breath. He palmed the doorway, his grip digging into the wood. His vision blurred, and his body went numb. Gordon gritted his teeth, believing he was losing consciousness, and trying to fight back against doing so.

His mask appeared, spherical, lilac eye blazing. He stood, balancing himself against the door. One foot forward. The next foot forward. Progress. Then a vision hit him, and he buckled again. His mystical sight accorded him a glimpse past the bed. There was Fey, slumped and lifeless.

His mask dwindled away, its material seeping back into his flesh.

Gordon collapsed onto the bed.

He cried, gripping the bed's comforter and sheets. He pulled himself up the bed, and then leaned over its side, looking down at his beloved Fey Forrester. The cosmic fabric disappeared around his left hand, and he reached out to caress Fey's face, flesh to flesh.

"You're going to be all right, Fey-baby…you're going to be fine…" He just had to pop away and take her to his chamber, he believed. Behind Gordon, Fey's yumboes flew into the hallway, stopping at the door. They hovered there and watched the scene. Gordon turned and said to them, "She'll be fine. We can revive her."

A cobalt-blue glow distracted Gordon. He turned and watched a sphere of light bloom into existence atop Fey's forehead. It extended, shooting up and into the mirror attached to the dresser drawer. Gordon watched in apprehension as the mirror's face filled with the light discharged into it. A woman's ghostly image appeared in the mirror and emerged from the glowing, glass surface. The haunt was not like his mother's specter. This woman didn't possess a spectral glow. She was very faint, thin to existence. Gordon knelt on the bed, his stance like a lion protecting its domain. His instinct reached out, and it identified the woman as Emma Forrester, Fey's mother. She knelt down near her daughter, moving her head up and down as she looked at Fey.

"No," said Gordon, voice and face burning with anger. "No, you had your chance with your daughter. You failed! She doesn't crossover to you."

Emma looked up at Gordon, eyebrow raised and accompanied by a vexed expression. The anger dissolved, as if realizing the sting of Gordon's words. The feminine spirit cried. Her tears never hit the ground, dissolving as they left her face.

Gordon's anger melted into sympathy. He decided to apologize, but Emma Forrester's faint apparition interrupted him. An unseen force, guided by Fey's mother, lifted Gordon off the bed and tossed him into the hallway. He collided with the wall opposite the door, leaving a dent. He jumped to his feet fully suited and angry. *"No!"* he yelled hurrying back toward the room. Something blocked his entrance. He bounced off the invisible barricade, being thrown back into the wall he'd damaged. He leapt to his feet, deciding to pop his way into the room. He disappeared, but instantly came into existence against the entrance, touching the invisible barricade and again being tossed into the wall. He jumped up again, frustrated. He charged up to the entrance of the master bedroom, but stopped. He watched as Emma Forrester reached down for her daughter.

"No!" Dooley yelled again, tearing up behind his mask.

Emma Forrester didn't scoop up her daughter into a cradle. Fey's physical body remained on the ground, but her mother took up a faint, ghostly image of her instead. Then Miss Forrester turned, and moved back into the glowing mirror.

Dooley put his hands near the entrance, slowly attempting to put them through. They bounced off the invisible barricade.

Another specter emerged from the glowing mirror. It was a man dressed in a sky blue suit. Gordon's instinct identified him as Fey's father, Lewis Banneker. He did the same as Miss Forrester before him, pulling a ghostly image of his daughter from her physical body up into his arms and jumping back into the mirror.

Fey's mother appeared again, doing the same. Her father came after, repeating the action. It occurred thirteen times in total. Her mother emerged from the mirror a total of seven times. And Fey's father manifested from the mirror six times. The process quickened as it continued, like an assembly line getting into its routine, operating at the highest efficiency. Dooley watched on, feeling helpless. He didn't know when his father came into the house and put his arms around him, or when Papa Solomon and Oliver Peters entered too. Cedron, Benny, and Neyeli were in the hallway. He never noticed them.

Dooley saw the mirror lose its cobalt-blue light. He looked at Fey's physical body, still and crumpled on the floor. He wanted answers, and he reached out with his instinct to get them. His transcendental inquiry bore into Fey's head, searching her memories, prying every last moment she'd lived. Her memories were there, but they were sporadic and fading. He saw her take a lash from Willie the night of the museum heist. His instinct culled her motive. *She did this on purpose? She invited the nightmares, allowed them to possess her?* He tried running through her last days, but the loss of her life and the absence of her spirit inside her physical form, dampened her memories.

But he saw something in quick flashes. Water. A beach. There was a house, its image blurry. He saw Fey's arm stuck with a syringe. Her back whipped and lashed. Then it was gone. Dooley's instinct retracted, and he stood there watching as Fey's physical body disappeared like a photograph developed in reverse. His mask dissolved, and tears streamed down Gordon's face.

Maximilian held his son tight. Gordon struggled with his father's embrace. Cedron helped. Both Maximilian and Cedron whispered words into Gordon's ears. He couldn't make them out. He didn't care. Somewhere in his wild flailing he'd forgotten who he was, but as soon as he remembered, he popped away. He didn't form solid inside the room, or near his chamber. Gordon formed solid on the roof of the Forrester residence, clothed in his cosmic attire, mask and all. His lilac spirit burst to life, and he soared away to the stars. He blinked away for a moment, forming into a bright spirit past the boundaries of Fable Avenue residing outside of time by way of Maman Anansi's power.

Up to the stars he went. Earth dropped away. The planet was no longer visible from Dooley's distance. He slowed his ascent and looked in Earth's direction. Nothing was there. A black hole widened into existence behind him. No black spirits came through the cosmic portal. They waited inside for him. Dooley continued peering toward Earth. Something tugged at his instinct, reaching out. His higher, perceptive vision followed. Down it dived, bringing Earth into view. Then Dooley's perception spied New York City, shooting down into Brooklyn, through various neighborhoods and then to Fable Avenue, leading to the backyard of the Forrester residence.

A shimmering, silver cloud appeared high above the ground, raining down sparkles of cobalt-blue light. When the first few hit the courtyard below, they became a foundation for a solid base. More light rained, falling into specific places and becoming solid. Dooley witnessed the raining light turn to stone, forming a two-tier, square mounting. Then more drops of cobalt-blue light rained down, sprinkling into a feminine shape, brightening to a white-hot brilliance and solidifying into a polished silver statue. The cloud of light disappeared, and even in the darkness, Dooley could see a life-size effigy of Fey Forrester. The grand likeness, molded from silver, posed Fey Forrester in her spirit form. Her face was angled toward the heavens. A determined expression etched in lustrous, precious metal. Her lower half was an amalgam of her thighs and a blaze of the power of her spirit expressed as a comet that began at her knees. The silver statue appeared to be launching to the sky with her hands at her side, balled into fists.

Below the silver effigy, at its pedestal, formed from another cloud of light, was an alchemical chamber. Dooley noted the similarities to his chamber, save for one difference. The top was made of glass, and he could see the shimmering specter of Fey Forrester inside. Her eyes were closed, looking beautiful and at peace.

Dooley wanted to follow his instinct and perception. He wanted to dive down and return to Fable Avenue and see the effigy and chamber up close. But his instinct and perception came back to him, rising to his position high, high, high above the Earth and the galactic cluster where the planet resided. He did not move, however, frustration and questions remained holding him in place. But he projected a declaration from his mind.

I promise, he said.

Something called him from inside the black hole.

He thought a thought to himself, curious.

He turned around and floated inside.

The black hole closed.

Sean Commons had a visitor. Stephanie Dumas, daughter to Maman Anansi, had a client of sorts. At this moment, they had one another. She walked into the visiting room, and the sixteen-year-old looked her up and down, face wearing a sneer. He licked his lips and rubbed his cuffed hands together. Stephanie didn't expect much else. Sean Commons had been arrested for the shooting of Dajon Brickhouse. He was guilty, and he was neither connected enough nor was he legally savvy enough to work the system in his favor. His life was over. From here on out it was just protocol and paperwork.

And this is where Stephanie came into Sean's life. A guard accompanied her, posting up at the door as Stephanie Dumas sat down across the table from Sean. She had it all planned out, her talk with this young man. It was going to be simple. She was here to represent Sean Commons, her presence a Trojan horse of a kind, sneaking in as a lawyer to draw out, through incant, this young man's memories, searching for known associates to Stanley Fallows. She was also there to find in Sean Commons any form of hexed scars or bad haunts laid upon him.

But her plans changed the moment she entered the small visiting room. She saw his face, his sneer, and his eyes that ogled her up and down. Even as a corporate lawyer, there was no escaping the horrifying realities of black-on-black violence. Much of Stephanie's experience was vicarious, lived through the heartbreaking tales of lawyer friends that handled this area of law. Stephanie was now face-to-face with it. When her brother was murdered long ago, she was a victim to it as much as her brother was. Now she was planted here to do a job, struggling against her instinct to do so much more for the young man seated across from her.

There were two paths in her decision to do more. And she could easily get away with either, but could only choose one. No one in the building would remember her stay, not even the security cameras. She would remember Sean, however. There would be no forgetting him, especially since he looked no different than her brother's murderer.

Stephanie managed to remain professional, fighting against rolling her eyes or even scolding Sean, demanding respect as the person willing to represent him. She allowed him to behave the way he did in the streets, his nursing grounds. Sitting down, she tried to conjure an escalation of his attitude. He acted up, but his continued misbehavior had nothing to do with her wishes.

"Hello, Mister Commons," greeted Stephanie. She was not polite, but she was not rude. She was professional. "My name is Miss Stephanie Dumas. I'm here as counsel, representing you. Your friend Cole has different representation," Stephanie stated. "I'm here for you." She opened her briefcase and removed his file.

"Okay, then. Whatchu got for me? Get me out this!" he demanded.

Stephanie told him as a matter-of-fact, "I'm here to show you some options, and—I have to say, considering what has transpired—you're lucky you have any options at all."

"Self-defense," pleaded Sean. The statement almost sounded sincere, but there was a telling grin on his face that Stephanie spied. She wondered how many times he'd rehearsed it.

"Is that how you would like to play this?" she inquired. "A self-defense shooting against an unarmed twelve-year-old?" she questioned for clarification.

"Yeah," Sean proclaimed with a wide, confident smile. "That kid's tougher than he look. We had a run in with him a while back. Little boy got rough with me and Cole. He quick. He got good licks in."

"Okay," said Stephanie. "I represent you. I'll be fair to hear your side. Let me lay some ground rules first. There're two types of self-defense claims in the State of New York. The first type is when you take measures to defend yourself or others against harm intended. It's about you, in defense, intervening before harm is done to you or another. You understand so far?"

"Yeah, I got it."

Stephanie nodded. "The second type of self-defense, Mister Commons, is about sustaining additional injury, a defense against harm already inflicted that one believes will be ongoing. Now, you say you had a scuffle with Mister Brickhouse, but that situation concluded prior to the shooting. It can still be relevant to your case. When did the incident occur?"

Sean thought for a moment. "Last year. End of September, early October, like around."

Stephanie nodded again. "Were the attacks from Mister Brickhouse ongoing?"

"Nah. Just the once. But we always kind of got into it with him. Little dude always jumpin' up in our business. It's somethin' between us—"

"*Us*', meaning you and Mister Andrews?" interrupted Stephanie, asking for clarification.

"Yeah, Cole," said Sean. "Yeah, yeah."

"With the two types of self-defense claims I've stated for you, Mister Commons, which does this incident fall under?"

Sean considered the question.

"You can't hesitate on the stand, Mister Commons."

Sean didn't say anything. He grimaced.

"Look, Mister Commons, you're going to prison. I can't stop that, but what we can do is have control over how long you go to prison. I'm not sure a self-defense plea would work, but I can give it a try—I'm certainly willing to do so. But keep in mind, self-defense is for the purpose of escaping danger, not retaliation. And there are limits to the claim. You fired two shots. The first hit Mister Brickhouse in the stomach. He was on the ground when the second shot was fired. That second shot is unnecessary. The prosecution will argue that, attacking your plea of self-defense. I can argue you were in the moment. The shot does appear wild, reflexive, as it only grazed Mister Brickhouse. But it's up to the jury to decide. And that will depend on your demeanor in court, background—criminal history, which you have—and how well you do on the stand."

Sean didn't say anything. His grimace remained.

"You've been identified as the gunman by witnesses, the victim, and the victim's friend. You can't throw your friend Cole under the bus, or use his involvement as leverage. He's probably working out a deal with his attorney right now. He stood next to you as it happened, but his involvement in the shooting, and escalating the situation is miniscule. This is an open and shut case against you, Mister Commons."

Sean shouted, "So why you here?"

Stephanie remained professional even as Sean turned threatening. "Because, Mister Commons, there is something of note in all this. It's about something you said to Mister Brickhouse at the onset of your confrontation. Mister Brickhouse and his friend Melinda Clarke recall a statement you made."

Sean's threatening demeanor washed away. He was now curious. "What's that?" he asked.

"You told him that he was a wanted man," Stephanie answered Sean. "I find this curious because if this confrontation was about you and Mister Brickhouse alone, I feel you would've stated that you'd been looking for him. Your words imply other people were." Sean kept still, managing to smother his reflexive sneer. "Were there other people interested in confronting Mister Brickhouse?" Sean was silent. Stephanie looked at his hands. They began trembling. She rephrased her question, asking, "Did someone order you to hurt Dajon Brickhouse."

Sean didn't say anything, and now Stephanie could tell his legs were trembling too.

She reached for his hand, bringing it into hers. Palm against palm, she felt Sean's emotion, and her eyes swelled with tears. "I know you have a scar, Sean Commons," Stephanie told him while shaking her head. "But I can't bring myself to care right now. And let me tell you something, young man, I see the lash and the pain that brought you to that moment. I know the man that gave it to you. And he's done cruel things to you that you aren't aware of. I know what that man represents. All the damage he's able to do to put us at each other's throats. But I can also feel that it didn't take much influence to move you to the action you took." She held Sean's one hand with both of hers. "I had this all planned," she continued. "I was set to drive here and do my duty, and leave you with something whereby, even in the circumstances you've chosen to put yourself in, you could do some good." A tear hit her cheek and slid down her chin. "I was going to map out for you the history of this system and how it traps young black boys like you." Her voice tripped on tears and frustration, but Stephanie regained her professionalism. "I was going to give you a history lesson detailing all the 'legal' decisions that have been made to make sure your life, and many young black lives before and after you end up here. And these decisions have been made years, years, years, *years* in advance of your birth, young man. But I look at you, and even though I see a life wasted, I also see a young man no different than the one that took my brother's life. And my brother was making something of himself."

Stephanie's grip became harder than what Sean expected. He struggled, but his demeanor was humble. "Ma'am…ma'am…your grip…" Stephanie tightened her hold on Sean's hand. Then he cursed, "Shit! Goddamnit! Ah, lady, my hand!" His anger returned.

"You won't make it to trial, young man, because your life ends when you sleep."

Sean looked up at the guard. "Yo, nigga, you gon' let this lady—*Ah!*"

The guard remained looking forward, eyes on the wall behind Sean.

"I have judged that you, and all you represent, are obsolete," declared Stephanie. Her palm against his, she left a hex inside him. She let go, stood, and gathered her things. "Think about what you've done, Mister Commons, before you sleep tonight."

Sean retracted his hand, rubbing it. He stood too, yelling at Stephanie. But something held him back from attacking her. It wasn't the fear of the guard, or the fear of a longer jail sentence. Stephanie was protected. He screamed, though. And he screamed loud, calling her everything he could think of. *"Bitch lawyer"* seemed to be his favorite phrase to use against her.

Stephanie left, holding her tears in as she walked through the Manhattan jailhouse. Everyone around her was suspended in time. She saw gossamer strands of light connecting everyone in the jailhouse, and she scowled at the cops and lawyers and the perpetrators too. She wanted to hex them all, but she kept walking to the exit. Stephanie got into her car, and movement inside the jail station resumed. She called her mother before starting the car. "It was purposeful," she reported, holding back tears. "I could feel this young man's scar."

"You okay, girl?" asked Maman Anansi to her daughter.

"No," she admitted. Tears poured like a heavy storm.

"Baby, what's wrong?"

"Y-you couldn't feel what happened?"

"Is everything okay, Stephanie? Aunt Thelema and I were concentrating on keeping things still."

"I did something bad, Mamma. And I won't take it back. I can't."

"Baby, just come here. Don't worry about the office for the rest of the day. Talk to us about it."

Stephanie hung up. She dropped her phone. It clanked against the gearshift and fell into the passenger's seat. Stephanie started her car, the tears blurred her vision, but she wiped them aside and drove away.

Inside, Sean Commons had a lot to think about. He was loud, and he behaved erratically toward the guards that brought him back to his room after his real appointed attorney arrived. He screamed about that *"bitch lawyer"* through his second meeting, a person no one but him seemed to remember. He did the same as he was escorted to his holding-cell. He couldn't recall her name. But he had names to call her.

He paced in his cage. He talked to himself, saying, "I don't need sleep."

And, sure enough, he did attempt to remain awake. His mood swung to and fro. He started off angry, pacing and kicking the ground, cursing the *"bitch lawyer"* who'd come to see him. Then he became reflective, something that came as he thought about all the violent ways he would get back at the *"no-good, bitch lawyer."* Then he was remorseful. His mind filled with his deeds and the people he'd hurt throughout his young life. He wanted to scream, and he wanted to cry, but he was too tired to accomplish either. He fell asleep on his bed, back against the wall. Sleep came to him while he blinked his eyes. It was around three o'clock in the morning. He didn't mean to fall asleep as he blinked. He was just tired, and his body conceded to that fact in the slow blink of his eyes.

Stephanie Dumas' hex took young Sean Commons' life soon after, and he was pronounced dead when his body was found at eight-thirty in the morning.

Spring took its time settling in, and even when the weather was consistently warm, winter would sneak back in and cast a chill on the people of the northeast. But a cold, sunny Saturday in mid-April didn't stop the Fable Avenue residents from gathering for their annual Spring Festival. The festival was scheduled for noon, and it required for the street to fade from time where the day's chilly weather wouldn't be a bother.

Today on Fable Avenue was much anticipated. Lady Arachne, with the assistance of her cards, predicted that Gordon Goodspeed would return from his long absence. The specific time was not known. But the day was in place, and Lady Arachne was confident in her prediction. At the moment, the prophesizing Elder sat in her kitchen, smoking a cigarette and having early morning tea with Savannah Forrester. Savannah too enjoyed a smoke and a cup of tea. She'd earlier spied Lady Arachne's cards placed on the kitchen table, and once again her eyes drifted toward the set. Next to the cards was Lady Arachne's cell phone.

"You have a reading for me, Lena?" she asked taking a sip of her tea.

"No, Savannah," Lady Arachne replied, an apology in her tone. She cut the cards, separating them into three piles. She took a random card and flipped it over. It was The Judgment card. "Gordon will be here soon."

"You're sure?"

"I'm sure." She exhaled smoke and pointed to her cell phone. "Papa Solomon will call when it happens, and I'll ask him to come over. And I will give him this card to present to Gordon."

"That's far more specific than your predictions have been, Lena."

"I know," she smoked, a grin shaping her lips. She exhaled. "I haven't been so forthcoming, Savannah. In fact, I know Gordon has been here from time to time, visiting your granddaughter's shrine in the Forrester backyard." She widened her smile, and she called Savannah out. "And you know that. You've seen him, talked to him, at your house."

Savannah shared Lady Arachne's grin, trying to hide her guilt. "Yes, I have, Lena," she confessed. "We've spoken. He's been up there with the spirits. He told me not to say anything."

"And you didn't. Why?" Savannah didn't answer Lady Arachne. Her face contorted for a moment, expressing sorrow. She picked up her cup of tea and hid her face behind taking a sip. Lady Arachne asked, mustering empathy in her voice, "Do you believe we failed you, Savannah? Fable Avenue and all its incants and conjures? More than once, I suppose," she emphasized.

Savannah still didn't answer her question. She put her cup down and composed herself. "The curse of my family…"

"Savannah!" Lady Arachne hissed. "Don't you bring that talk in here, now."

Savannah's cigarette burned. She hadn't taken a puff in a while, and the end grew into a long trail of ashes. "I have never been able to commune with my daughter's spirit, Lena. I can't feel her. And now, my granddaughter is the same." She tapped the long bend of ashes into the ashtray, but she didn't take a puff. "That silver statue of her, and that casing of her, they mock me. She's there as a translucent image. It's a piece of her soul, but just a piece, a small glimmer, and it mocks me. I don't like visiting that memorial of sorts, but I can't help but do so."

Lady Arachne shook her head. "Stanley has taken children from our community," she reminded. "He's hurt us all." Silence lingered after her comment. The two women smoked and drank. "I've made inquiries, Savannah," she admitted after a time. "Your granddaughter is not gone," Lady Arachne revealed, procuring a curious look from Savannah. Lady Arachne sighed while shaking her head and stating, "Fable Avenue has had it wrong for so long." The matriarch paused, looking at her cards and shaking her head. After a time, her eyes moved back up toward Savannah and said, "I don't wish to mock Mamma Indigo or the insight she gave before she passed away at the moment she gave birth them many years ago. Though her insight served us well, it was very much incomplete. Gordon's lilac flame was but the opener, the Grand Architect. Your granddaughter's spirit, the *Cobalt-Blue Flame*, she is the Grand Gateway. It is together they must be; and it's separate Stanley Fallows wishes Gordon and Fey should remain. And to the cobalt-blue flame, other conjure folk in our diaspora did understand that. They had their insights."

"It's a wonder we didn't suddenly all fight over who was right and who was wrong," Savannah commented. "Cobalt-blue flame worship against lilac flame worship," she defined.

"It would've been like them old legendary Pious Wars that time can barely remember."

Savannah huffed with sass, "You preachin' to the choir, sister! I believe them wars took place all them millenniums ago. We all saw the opening to that mythology Fey and Gordon composed. I believe that was what all that Mother Covenant and marchin' army stuff was a reference to. Conjure folk have had disagreements, but I believe it's in our ancestral memory not to fight too hard because of them old, old, old, old-time wars."

Lady Arachne and Savannah nodded their heads at one another.

"Please take no offense when I make promise that, believe you me, your granddaughter will return to us, Savannah," Lady Arachne revealed. "My cards have spoken," she said in a firm manner.

Savannah looked interested, hope in her eyes. She didn't want to appear desperate, and so the expression faded. She was, however, compelled to express, "Oh…"

Lady Arachne asked, "Do you think you could help with the webbing ritual?"

Savannah didn't know how to answer. So she questioned, "But there's Maman Anansi. There's Madame Jeliya."

"Never mind them," said Lady Arachne with swift dismissal.

Savannah was ready to question, a reflex. But she and Lady Arachne had talked before. So, Savannah remained quiet as Lady Arachne swiped a second card from the three piles she'd made. She flipped it over and there in front of her was The Hermit card. She gazed at its picture for a long time, and the ancient script that spelled out "The Hermit" changed before her eyes. Now the ancient characters read: *The Old Goon.*

"Mister Eledas can help with that," she announced in a sly matter-of-fact way.

"Satchel? That old, old, old, *old* fool and his drunken hoodoo?"

Lady Arachne plucked another card, eyes on Savannah. She flipped it over, and there was The Fool. She stared at it, focused. The image of the African jester faded, and the cliff edge where his foot dangled, transformed into two different landscapes. The first was the crossroads. The second was Water Bug Hollow.

"Yes," confirmed Lady Arachne, "that old, old, old, *old* fool and his drunken hoodoo."

Up the street from Lady Arachne's house, a lilac comet streaked down from the sky. The spirit was invisible to regular folks' eyes but a few Fable Avenue residents that meandered on the sidewalk witnessed the phenomenon. Some of them muttered, *"He's arrived!"* Others whispered, *"Now, the children will be saved."* Dooley landed at the garden-floor entrance of the Goodspeed residence. The blaze of lilac spirit burst away, leaving him dressed in his cosmic suit. Dooley's mask retracted, seeping into his flesh. The massive dragon-blessing, Nyami, greeted him with a soft bellow and huff. Gordon was happy to see Nyami's protection rekindled. Her presence said so much, and it made Gordon smile.

Gordon recited an incant. The doors unlocked. He paused for a moment as his instinct made him aware of the people inside. He remained still, considering the option to pop away and form solid inside his room upstairs. He decided against it, but it was after another still minute or two before he opened the door and walked inside the house.

Gordon heard voices engaged in conversation. His family and friends inside sounded happy, enjoying one another's company. Gordon wanted to fly away again, but he didn't. He stepped into the front room, bracing his nerves as if ready for an execution. The talking ceased when his family saw him.

There was his father, and his mother's spirit next to him. Cedron was there too, seated in a chair, and with Leah Kimberly Peters seated on his lap. Benny and Neyeli were also part of the gathering. Neyeli's dreadlocks turned violet, and she beamed a wide smile at Gordon. They were all looking at him, and Gordon was never so much aware of his own existence.

His father made the first move, rising off the couch and making quick strides to him. His mother's spirit disappeared, fading up next to him, beating his father's approach by seconds. She focused and rubbed her fingers through his wild hair. Maximilian hugged him, and Gordon returned the embrace.

"It's not my first trip back," Gordon admitted. "I returned a few times and spoke with Fey's grandmother, and to pay respects at Fey's shrine."

"You're here now, Gordon," said his mother.

Maximilian agreed. "Your mom's right," he said.

Gordon and his father separated, and he told him, "Let me go upstairs. There's a festival today. I'll change." He walked past his father, heading to the stairs. He stopped and looked at Cedron. "The Gypsy Moon Misfits got a gentlemen's gathering tonight? I see you already dressed for the occasion."

"Yeah, bruh," Cedron smiled. "We'll see you there. It'll be in Harlem, at The Hours spot, when the sun goes down. Gon' have a card game or two goin'. But you can save yourself the trip, and just give me your money now." Leah smacked Cedron on the shoulder.

Gordon chuckled at his brother's words. "We shall see," he said in a deep, faux-British accent, quoting a villain from a movie he and his brother loved. He looked at Leah and greeted the dark skinned woman with the long braids and thick figure. "Hello, Miss Leah-Kimberly. I see you lost your taste in men again," he said pointing at his brother.

She laughed.

Cedron remarked, "Yeah, I'mo take your money, bruh."

Gordon gave Neyeli a polite hello. Before he could address Benny, his friend said to him, "When you got time, let's talk."

"Sure, man. Sure," Gordon responded. "Let me get together, then come on up."

Gordon continued upstairs to his room. Inside, he dissolved his cosmic threads and picked out a suit. He was clean, having washed in the heavens, and remaining in spirit form kept him fresh and clean. But even still, Gordon longed for a warm shower, which he took after picking out his clothes. But there was a lack of sensation when the hot, earthly waters covered him. It didn't compare to a cosmic bath, and Gordon had bathed in waters from other realms, covering his physical flesh and cosmic spirit. No regular folk would ever know what that was like. Possibly, with all their incants and conjures, maybe not even a person of the conjure folk.

Gordon considered, *Fey would know.* She was everything that was familiar to him.

Teeth brushed, and with his body primped, Gordon returned to his room and put on his selected attire. Black slacks. White, button-downed collar shirt with a cobalt-blue-colored tie. Finishing his garb, a black jacket.

While he dressed he thought of his father, and the spirit of his mother free to come and go from her spectral realm to the physical plane. He thought about his brother, Cedron, and Leah Kimberly Peters on his arm. His friend Benny-Jah and Neyeli Kimball cuddled up with one another. He thought of this as he gazed out the window, slipping on his black suit jacket, looking down into the backyard and thinking of Fey Forrester. She was preserved in his thoughts, whole there. But she was scattered in so many places. Her mythological doppelganger was preserved in an aged tome mystically inscribed with magic ink. And, just up the street, her ghostly image lay faint, encased in a chamber situated under a silver effigy to her spirit form, blazing and launching into the air.

Gordon's thoughts swung back to their shared mythology, playing the mystically composed legend, *In Thirteen Pieces*, and wondering where things went wrong in composing its poetry into reality.

Someone knocked on his door. Gordon turned around only out of courtesy, his instinct notifying him that it was Papa Solomon. Fable Avenue's sole patriarch sauntered into his room, an envelope in one hand and a glass of red wine mixed with dragon spit in the other. He was dressed much the same as Gordon. The only difference in his outfit was a black vest over his dress shirt, no tie, and a black fedora on his head.

Gordon sat down. Papa Solomon walked over and presented the glass of wine to him. Gordon stared at the drink for a moment. He looked up at Papa Solomon. "Sir…?" he questioned the Elder. "I'm only nineteen," he reminded.

Papa Solomon rolled his eyes and huffed, "Like that's ever stopped you before." He pushed the drink closer to Gordon's face and reminded him, "This is culture here. Push them societal laws aside. After all, you can turn into a beam of light, fly into the cosmos, cross the stars and commune with the spirits above. You've survived lashings from a hexed whip and some heartbreak. A drink with a little kick in it ain't gon' kill you. Besides, you do for one. Now take this."

Gordon did as asked. "Just want to be sure," he said, taking a good gulp.

Papa Solomon pulled up a chair and sat down. "Easy now," he told Gordon. "Don't go swallowin' all that drink in one knock back, there. Its kick is more than the little bit I said before."

"Yessir," acknowledged Gordon, exhaling the drink's burn into a liquor-laced exhale. He sat back, looking out the window, thinking of Fey. She was there to him, looking beautiful and full of life.

"There's been tension here," informed Papa Solomon. "Children ain't been found, and the parents are impatient, as can only be expected. Some of them wanted to go to the police, but they know we can't do that. That's not an option. Never has been for us. And that's not our culture's distrust of the police talkin' either. Besides, most them police probably carry needles as well as guns. Unmask some of them night doctors, and we'll find prominent lawyers, lawmakers, politicians and so forth. We gon' keep this in-house." Papa Solomon went silent. He told Gordon, "We got Martin sniffing around, along with some conjure folk from out-of-state. That's more than enough, but we've been waiting on you, your return."

Gordon looked away. Guilt clouded him, and he wrestled it with his reasons for his self-imposed exile. He'd been holding up the rescue of these children in his absence. "Sorry, Papa Solomon. I needed to…" his words disappeared, losing confidence in his excuse. He took a breath and looked at Papa Solomon. He instead embraced his duty and asked, "You know where they are? The children?"

Papa Solomon looked at Gordon, warning in his glare. "Slow your spirit," he told Gordon. "All we got is a little more insight to what Stanley might be up to."

"Okay…"

Papa Solomon stated, "Your father let myself and Lady Arachne use your black mirror. With her cards and Spook—that whatchu call that thing?—we made an inquiry to it. I listed the names of everyone that was stuck by a needleman, and the kidnapped children." Papa Solomon took a breath, lost in contemplation, eyes out the window. "Madame Jeliya, Cedron, they represented strength. The rituals and conjures used by the families of the teenage boys that were stuck focus on water and earth." He looked at Gordon and concluded, "You can guess from there. The kidnapped children got somethin' to do with the other elements."

"I know Fey was stuck, Papa Solomon. I felt her memory before she…passed…"

Papa Solomon nodded. "You been stuck?" he asked.

"No. I would've said."

Papa Solomon bobbed his head, thinking. "Stanley's tryin' to make somethin' of himself. Lady Arachne did a separate reading on all this."

"And…"

"I was gettin' to that, boy."

"Sorry, Papa Solomon."

Fable Avenue's patriarch reminded Gordon, "Like I said, slow your spirit." He took his time, allowing Gordon to practice patience, and for the young lilac spirit to think about his words. Then he said, "You and Fey supposed to bring about this Grand Conjure and Wish of ours. You *and* Fey. Together." Gordon nodded. A sad expression possessed his visage. Papa Solomon continued, "Stanley has his own wish to make. I'll let Lady Arachne tell the rest. She said the answer is part of a reading she did with you, the one interrupted by that quake."

Gordon's eyes returned to the window. He imagined Fey's memorial chamber and effigy were there. "Papa Solomon, your pops imagine all this when he played that first magical note on his horn all that time ago?"

"I say he knew something was up," the patriarch answered. "It was my grandfather's first note that resonated something. He knew. And he brought us full circle against the Fallows family and all the treachery they represent. I like the fight. We all do. Fable Avenue is conscious of that fight. Our ancient spirits' incants and conjures against his culture's tricks, all their lineage and their wicked allies." He leaned forward. "I've said it many times. I say it like a mantra. Knowing that Stanley Fallows is our enemy is more important than prayer. The problems of the world come down to his trickery. If you don't understand his tricks and their extent, everything else will confuse you."

Gordon considered Papa Solomon's points and responded, "It took all in his power to do what he did to us back in February. He'd been saving up his strength, started when he separated from Fable Avenue."

Papa Solomon agreed. He told Gordon, "We know he concentrated hard—he and his wife, to pull that off." He rubbed his hands together. "I used to date a woman that told me never to curse your enemy when he or she knocks you down. You give your enemy a compliment. You say, *'That was good. You got me.'* Respect your enemy. Respect the moves they make. Then knock 'em on they ass."

Gordon couldn't contain his laughter, though it came out in a weak set of chuckles. He peered down at the floor and imagined that very scenario playing out between him and Stanley Fallows. When Gordon returned his attention to Papa Solomon, the old man was handing him the envelope.

"Lady Arachne said you should have this."

Gordon placed his drink next to his chair. He reached out and accepted the gift. He could feel the stiff body of the age-old tarot card tucked inside. He opened the envelope and pulled out The Judgment card. He examined it. Then he looked at Papa Solomon, his face expressing a question.

Papa Solomon informed Gordon, "Maman Anansi and I are heading down South to go talk to Mister Eledas. Madame Jeliya and Lady Arachne will be in charge of street politics—God help them two to get along."

"And the card?"

"Lady Arachne asked for you to do some scrying. Find the whereabouts of her missing Lovers card. She made an empty flip when inquiring about Fey. Her empty turn of the card covered a reversed Death card. She said take that literally."

Gordon was relieved to hear that, but his expression stayed calm. He understood, but still questioned if finding The Lovers card would return Fey Forrester to him. "I'll get on that," he said, voice calm, but determined.

Papa Solomon stood. "Let me go. Madame Jeliya and I have preparations for the festival."

"Thank you, Papa Solomon."

The street's patriarch nodded, and then he exited the room.

Gordon picked up the wine glass, holding both it and The Judgment card in either hand. He looked out the window again, thinking of Fey. His instinct tingled from the back of his neck to the crown of his head. He voiced, "You coming inside, or you gonna stand there all day." He turned and smiled at his friend Benny who was in the doorway. Benny entered, looking serious. He sat in place of Papa Solomon. His demeanor was contagious, and it reminded Gordon of what transpired months ago, and how it affected him. Gordon offered Benny a sip of his drink. Benny declined.

He said to Gordon, "I just come up to say, that everything is out on the table between your brother and I. He and I, we…we dealt with it." He chuckled slightly, "No fists thrown this time around." His laughter died as quick as it came, as it had no real sincerity behind it. "I still have my debt," he affirmed. "That's self-imposed. But, I'm a Gypsy Moon, so, King is my king. He don't abuse that, though. Things are as normal…as they can be on Fable Avenue."

"Right…"

"But you say your word, Gordon," Benny continued. "You tell me left, when Cedron says to go right, I'm followin' *your* lead. Understand?"

Gordon didn't protest. He acknowledged Benny's remarks with a nod, and then he said to his friend, "I left to be among the spirits. I thought I could find Fey's spirit…somewhere, in the middle of everywhere up there. I came back every-so-often—I don't know if you heard me tell my pops that, or maybe he told you when I came up here. I chose to make a full return this day, specifically, because of the festival." He shook his head. "It was the easiest day to slip in and forget, get lost in all the activities and the happiness outside of time." He held back tears. "It was therapeutic being among the spirits. But Fey wasn't there, as I'd first believed she would be. I was still, immovable, thinking of ways to bring her back. Refusing answers from the spirits, though they didn't have any. They ain't as omniscient as we on Earth would like to believe. They're just waiting for us to get our shit right and join them on a higher level. It is peaceful up there, and they throw more parties." His lilac gaze went to the sky. By reflex, his instinct reached out for Fey, trying to find her among the ether and pry into her memories. But nothing was there, and his instinct retracted. However, the most peculiar thought came to Gordon. He thought of his European Literature professor, James Brede. Then the thought washed away.

"Let's do as you planned, Gordon," Benny announced. "Let's go forget. Let's make a move to get lost in festivities. Let's be somewhere else for a little while." Remaining seated, Benny petitioned, "Let's get outta here, Gordon."

A sting rose from Gordon's stomach. It traveled through his throat, and it rubbed against the back of his eyes where it stirred up tears. He looked away from the sky, a single tear dripping, snaking down his cheek. His eyes first looked at his friend, and he considered the offer to engage in Fable Avenue's Spring Festival, or as he renamed it, *The Festival of Forgetfulness*. But his lilac eyes, by instinct, were drawn to The Judgment card in his hand, tracing its ancient sketch. He took a moment to reflect on his path to now and beyond and understood his errand wasn't his alone. It wasn't only his path to follow. It was his and Fey's. Theirs. How could he bring Fey Forrester back? It was no longer for his sake, and no longer a selfish wish. Fey's return was pivotal to completing their grand errand.

But Benny's suggestion reminded him why he'd returned to Fable Avenue. Gordon considered he'd earned the right to forget for a little while and relearn to smile. Then he could fly away or remain still to obsess over his errand and the destiny of Fable Avenue and Fey Forrester's resurrection.

So, Gordon agreed with Benny, telling his friend, "Yeah, Benny, you're right. Let's be out."

High above Fable Avenue's story, the celestial bodies watched on, anxiously waiting for Benny Brickhouse to stand first and lead his friend Gordon Goodspeed into the grand procession of the Spring Festival.

"And yet," said Gordon to Benny, "we do not move."

End Act II

References

"Sweeping" card used by Maman Anansi in Gordon Goodspeed's Second Gateway Rites inspired by the High Priestess card in the Afro-Brazilian Tarot deck by Alice Santana and published by Llewellyn Publications; Cards edition (October 8, 2006)

"...there's water in the basement and the pilot light is out." Dialogue "borrowed" from the movie Ocean's Twelve, Steven Soderbergh, Warner Bros. Pictures Roadshow Entertainment, 2004.

"A once faithful world has become a prostitute! She once was full of justice; righteousness used to dwell in her—but now murderers!" Isaiah 1:21

"He put on righteousness like a breastplate, and a helmet of salvation on His head; and He put on garments of vengeance for clothing and wrapped Himself with zeal as a mantle." Isaiah 59:17

"So justice is driven back, and righteousness stands at a distance; truth has stumbled in the streets, and honesty cannot enter...Truth is nowhere to be found, and whoever shuns my presence becomes a prey." Isaiah 59:14-15

"I saw among the captives a beautiful woman, and hast a desire unto her, that thou wouldest have her to my *wife." Deuteronomy 21:11*

"They that sow the wind shall reap the whirlwind." Hosea 8:7

"I have three chains of gold and they will shine forever." Referencing lyrics by ***Prince. Three Chains 'O' Gold. Prince. Rec. 1992. CD.*** " "

Izenth-Elai; skin shinning like dew – a reference to the character *Hyzenthlay, fur shinning like dew* from ***Adams, Richard "Watership Down." 1972. Rex Collings.***

"Bury me in Africa!" – Line taken from a verse by Raekwon of the Wu Tang Clan, ***Raekwon "House of Flying Daggers" Rec. Aug 26, 2009 CD Only Built for Cuban Linx 2.***

"Don't hesitate…I will spill on you and kill you on the battlefield true!" Line inspired from a verse by Raekwon of the Wu Tang Clan, ***Raekwon "House of Flying Daggers" Rec. Aug 26, 2009 CD Only Built for Cuban Linx 2.***

Donavan Cross initiation ceremony inspired by lyrics by GZA of the Wu Tang Clan, ***GZA "Pencils" Rec. Aug 19, 2008 CD Pro Tools.***

Joseph Pepper's recount of The Waterberry Massacre lifted from the Wu Tang Clan leader RZA's monologue beginning the song ***House of Flying Daggers", RZA "House of Flying Daggers" Rec. Aug 26, 2009 CD Only Built for Cuban Linx 2.***

"I will show you fear in a handful of dust" ***Elliot, T.S. "The Waste Land." 1922.***

"Gordon considered he'd earned the right to forget for a little while and relearn to smile. Then he could fly away or remain still to obsess over his errand and the destiny of Fable Avenue and Fey Forrester's resurrection." Inspired by lyrics Prince, ***Prince. "Anna Stesia" Prince. Rec. May 10, 1988. CD. Lovesexy.***

Final dialogue inspired by ***Bryan Thomas. "Yet" Bryan Thomas. Rec. 2013***, referencing ***Beckett, Samuel. "Waiting for Godot." 1949.***

Please visit the website http://fuckyeahafricanmythology.tumblr.com/ for an enormous amount of African mythology. From "yumboes" to "night doctors."

Twin Griffin Books
PRESENTS